BATTLEFIELDS
AND
PLAYGROUNDS

BY JANOS NYIRI

Streets
Battlefields and Playgrounds

BATTLEFIELDS
AND
PLAYGROUNDS

JANOS NYIRI

TRANSLATED FROM THE HUNGARIAN

BY WILLIAM BRANDON

AND THE AUTHOR

FARRAR, STRAUS AND GIROUX

NEW YORK

LIBRARY OF CONGRESS CATALOGING-IN-PUBLICATION DATA
Nyiri, János.
Battlefields and playgrounds / Janos Nyiri ; translated from the
Hungarian by William Brandon and the author.
p.   cm.
I. Brandon, William. II. Title.
PH3291.N828B38 1995   894'.51133—dc20   95-5389 CIP

To Danny and Polly

BATTLEFIELDS
AND
PLAYGROUNDS

1: The Menace

The mountain rolls in from the west, a slow, lazy slope of vineyards that turns gently south, cradling the village of Oszu.

I was little then, and I found it impossible to believe that the world was any older than I was. Yet the grown-ups all claimed that it had been created in six days, before even they were born. They also said that only one God was responsible, which was obviously untrue, but the grown-ups couldn't see facts that were staring them in the face. In our village alone there were three Gods, all of whom had houses; the Catholic One had the biggest, then came the Calvinist One, and then the Jewish One. Not to mention the One who owned the little chapel on the hill above the High Street. He had a Son, so there were really two Gods living in the same tiny building, which was even more puzzling.

I thought that God might own several houses, like the Count, who was also invisible and had palaces in Vienna and Budapest as well as the Castle at the edge of the village. But it wasn't the same, because people ganged up together and each gang only ever went to one of God's houses, quarrelling with anybody who didn't go to the same one; and they all spent their time insulting each other's God.

But I was above all that because I was only passing through the village. On this particular occasion I had stayed for two years, but I was just passing through all the same. There was certainly no question of my staying once I was old enough to go to a proper school. Until then, I had to learn Hebrew at the *heder* in our Jewish temple, our *shul*. Grandfather grumbled that if I didn't play truant so much I'd find out more about God and not ask so many questions.

At midday, the Christian kids would wait outside the *heder* for a stone-throwing fight. The stones were small and didn't hurt much,

1

and afterwards I'd play football with the enemy until it was time for lunch. It was this that caused the trouble.

We were in the middle of a stone fight one afternoon when Laci Fried, one of the strongest boys in the whole *heder*, turned on me. 'Why are you fighting for the Jews?' he demanded. 'You never come to *heder*!'

'I'm from Budapest!' I replied, making it clear that I wasn't going to let myself be pushed around by country bumpkins like him.

'Then what are you doing here?' he asked with cold superiority.

'My parents are getting divorced,' I explained, 'but my father doesn't give my mother any money, so she can't afford to keep me and my big brother, who's nearly eight. My grandfather wants Mother to come home but she doesn't want to so she sent me to live with him and sent my brother to live with my father's father.'

'To your other grandfather, you mean,' said Laci Fried officiously.

'If you like, except he isn't my grandfather.'

'Why not? I thought you said he was your father's father.'

'Because I don't like him.'

'You ought to like your grandfather.'

'Well, I don't really know him very well,' I admitted. 'But he says nasty things about my father.'

'So? Your father's a pig.'

'How do you know? You haven't even met him! I'm not going to be your friend!'

'If he doesn't give your mother any money then he's a pig,' he repeated firmly. 'Or doesn't he have any?'

'My mother says he's got lots, but he won't give it to her unless she divorces him. And she doesn't want to.'

He nodded. After a while he asked, 'Where does your father work?'

'I don't know where he works nowadays. My mother begged him not to throw his job away, but he said that if he didn't they'd make him write antimesitic things.'

'Antisemitic,' he corrected.

'But he's writing a film and if Mother divorces him he'll give her lots of money and then I'll be able to go home.'

'All right,' he said. 'But until then you must come to *heder* if you want to be friends with me and my friends!' And to prove his point, he walked away.

I watched him, wondering how far he would dare to walk. We were outside the Jewish baker's, and although the High Street went on for another fifty houses, the Jewish village stopped there. If we didn't stop too, they set dogs on us. Sometimes they did that on our side of the village as well, but if they did, you always knew that someone would rescue you. It was a game of hide and seek, and the Jewish houses were our shelters.

On our side of the baker's, hidden behind a vine-covered trellis, stood a house whose roof sloped down over the courtyard to form a kind of verandah which supported the canopy of rush matting at *Succoth*. It was one of the biggest, most talked-about canopies in the whole village.

'I've come to play with Kica,' I said when I called there one morning. Her parents gave me funny looks because they knew I was meant to be in *heder*, but I managed to fool them.

'We fixed it up at *shul*,' I explained, and Kica and I ran off together to play. She was six. We rubbed noses. I kissed her.

'Now it's your turn,' I said. She frowned, and for a second she was scared of me, as if I had been a grown-up who was going to tease her.

'Do you still love Ágnes?' she demanded.

'Yes,' I sighed. 'But I'm not allowed to see her because I keep bunking off *heder*.'

Kica nodded gravely. And then she kissed me.

Later, she used to insist I choose between her and Ágnes, but I couldn't see why. She must have heard something silly from her parents.

'I will choose soon,' I promised, fingers crossed, my worries as sweet as the *kiddush* wine that we drank in front of the *Torah* on Friday evenings. We were only allowed one sip.

Next door to Kica lived old Mr Grossman, with his white hair and his frozen, benevolent smile. He gave me the creeps.

And then there was Mr Zafir, who owned several houses. He actually lived opposite my grandfather at the northern end of the High Street, in an enormous house with eight windows overlooking the street. It had two front doors: one led into the biggest eating house in the whole village and the other led into his skittle alley. The game sometimes spilled out into the street and I often used to watch the players and the drunkards. He was an imposing figure, puffing and panting as he walked along in one of his ten *shabbes* suits even when it wasn't the *shabbes*. Maybe he didn't have everyday clothes.

Zafir had a great deal to answer for.

3

Our mountain was part of the Eperjes-Tokaj range, which wouldn't have mattered if Oszu hadn't produced the best wine in the whole world. The most southerly slopes of the mountain, where the sun stays the longest, are directly above the village. Yet we had to watch while our wine was poured into bottles labelled 'Tokaj'. All the Christians said it was because of the Jews. All the Jews. But we knew it was because of the Zafirs. Zafir had a brother who lived in the neighbouring village of Tokaj, and between them they did most of the buying. Tokaj was bigger than Oszu and produced more wine, so they called our wine 'Tokaj' even though the Tokaj stuff was pure vinegar. So we had to sell our wonderful wine to the Zafirs for much less than it was worth, and they used our Oszu wine to push up the price of the inferior Tokaj wine. Grandfather was as cross as anyone about his wine being insulted with 'Tokaj' labels, and about having to sell it cheap, but he only cursed fate and the Zafirs, not the Jews.

The Town Hall stood directly in front of the Market Square. The villagers called it the Town Hall because there were over eight thousand of them, but I came from Budapest, so I called it the Village Hall. The road that led down to the station started there; a group of peasants had declared it a Jew-free zone. I became so scared that one evening I had to walk all the way along it just to see if they would throw stones like everyone said they did. No one even noticed me, but I'd faced my fears, and never went back. I boasted about it, though, and all the *heder* kids dared me to do it again. When I wouldn't, they said I was lying.

Beside the Village Hall, but on our side of the village, was the Co-op. I hardly ever went in there, but when I did, I used to buy four fillérs worth of sweets so I'd be allowed to gaze at all the bicycles and boots and tools. Of course, I'd seen bigger shops in Budapest, but they only sold clothes. The manager was called Virgula, and if he hadn't hated Jews I would have spent all day with my nose against the window.

I often used to hang around outside, and whenever I couldn't be bothered with *heder*, I'd come and listen to the news blaring out of the radio. It sat on a small table in front of the shop, surrounded by the groups of men who always congregated there after going to the market or the Village Hall. I felt almost as important as they did as they sighed loudly and argued about whether or not the English would 'come to an agreement' with the Germans. I never dared say anything, but I joined in the calls for silence at the end, when the news stopped and the Voice came on.

4

'Give us back Transylvania!' it would cry. 'Give us back Kassa and Pozsony!' and the men would cheer. But I kept quiet, because my grandfather had told me that Pozsony and the rest weren't worth it. I knew that he was right. I had carved up countries myself.

Carving up Countries was a game. Each player was the king of half a big circle scratched on the dusty ground, and you took it in turns to throw a knife into the other player's country. If the knife stuck in the ground, you drew a line from the enemy boundary to the edge of the circle following the line of the knife. The smaller segment became part of the attacker's empire. When you didn't have enough territory left to stand up in, you had to surrender. I used to play with Jancsi Kovács, the blacksmith's son. Once, when I had won, Jancsi begged me to give back Pozsony and I wouldn't. We had a fight. Jancsi went mad, kicking and biting because he was fighting for the Fatherland.

That's why I never cheered when the radio was shouting for Transylvania and Pozsony, even when they all started looking at me.

The man with the crutch sat in a small workshop. During the harvest parade – which no Jews ever went to except for me and Adler the drunk – the children used to break ranks for the sweets that people held out to them from the doorways, and the village idiot and the man with the crutch used to chase them. The idiot, dressed in rags, waved a stick and wouldn't have hurt a fly, but the cripple, even though he couldn't have overtaken a snail, brandished a leather cosh in his free hand. He wore an officer's jacket without epaulettes, black trousers on his worm-ridden legs, and shiny black boots. His charges made everyone laugh – the onlookers in the doorways, the people in the procession, the children, even the village idiot. So the man with the crutch would curse and swear, making us laugh even more.

I often had to pass his shop, and one day he called me inside. He was carving a shoe support, sitting on a three-legged stool in a khaki shirt and knee breeches. His officer's jacket was hanging on a nail in the wall, and from time to time he took a swig from a white bottle.

'They say you're Hungarian, József,' he said. 'You've got a Hungarian father, a Hungarian name. Lucky boy, eh?' I was glad that he said I was lucky, but I didn't know why.

'Did your father tell you how they laughed at Hungary, József? How they scoffed at us? Well, soon it'll be our turn to laugh at them! We'll deal with the scoffers, just like the Germans are dealing with theirs. Won't we! Do you know what Hitler's doing with the Jews, József?'

5

'Who's Hitler?' I asked. I didn't know about politics.

'The German leader. He was an ordinary corporal like me, and now he's their leader. He has a moustache like mine, too. He locks all the Jews in a cage and gives them nothing but dead rats to eat. Anyone who refuses to go into the cages is strung up on the nearest lamp-post. And the Germans pick out the best-looking women and screw them whenever they want.'

'What do they screw them to?' I asked.

He laughed so much he started hitting his workbench with the shoe he was mending.

'And do you know what they're going to do with the Jewish children? What they're already doing to them? They're training them to be dogs. Can you bark?'

As I didn't answer, he winked at me.

'Can you neigh, then?' And he neighed. 'Can you miaow, at least? If you do it properly, I'll give you a sweet.'

'They're bad for my teeth,' I said hypocritically.

'Well, I won't force you. But the Jewish dogs don't get sweets, József. They get bones. Tell me this, then. Who'll be leader of our town?'

'I don't know.'

'Can you read?'

'A bit.'

'Have you read what's on my sign, then?'

'Cobbler!' I announced triumphantly. But he was furious.

'My name!' he barked at me. 'My name isn't "cobbler", it's "Ungár"! Even my name is "Ungár", and I'm telling you the new leader of this town will be a Hungarian. So go and fetch me a box of Balkans. Hurry! *Schnell!*'

I didn't dare disobey. Coming back, I put the cigar box on his workbench, took a deep breath and said as fast as I could, 'There isn't any Hitler!' and ran out of the shop.

In the evening, when I told my grandfather, he said in a slow, quiet voice that even a little child could understand: 'He lost his mind when his wife hanged herself.'

'So there really isn't a Hitler?' I cried happily.

Grandfather looked down shamefacedly at the dough he was kneading, his fingers moving faster than usual.

'Yes,' he replied. 'There is.' He turned to my two uncles. 'The child needs new boots. Get them done at Ungár's.'

6

Uncle Elek didn't agree with Grandfather, but Grandfather was stubborn.

Uncle Elek was very strong. He was the strongest man in the whole village, perhaps in the whole world, so for a long time no harm came either to us or to the Zafirs. Grandfather's house was on a triangular piece of land that he had bought from Mr Zafir, but for some reason Zafir hadn't sold him the tip of the triangle where the High Street meets Valley Street. This was a smithy, and had been for as long as anyone could remember. It was close to the little stream which ran in a ditch along Valley Street, so it was ideal for a blacksmith. After several years, Grandfather finally decided to pay the outrageous price that Mr Zafir was asking for this little corner, yet when Grandfather made an offer, the big man wouldn't sell because it would put the smith out of business. Nowadays, he said, a Jew shouldn't anger a Christian, even for a whole sack of gold.

The blacksmith, Kovács, knew about all this, but it didn't stop him dropping in every morning for a 'little neighbourly chat over a spot of brandy'. Grandfather always supplied the brandy.

But his son Jancsi, who had wanted Pozsony back, called me a yid one day. Frightened and confused, I told my grandfather, and Jancsi only took it back after his father had slapped him so hard he nearly knocked his head off right in front of me.

'If it weren't for the Jews,' he roared, 'I wouldn't be able to stuff your filthy mouth with dry bread.'

There was a low bridge where the High Street crossed the blacksmith's stream; the village boys used to gather there. They would balance on the parapet like sparrows and tease the girls going to the well on the far side. At night, the men would stand around on the bridge after Zafir's had closed, carrying on conversations that had started in the bar. One evening Kovács invited some of his drinking companions into his workshop and started complaining that my grandfather wanted to take the bread out of his mouth. The drunken men wanted to smash our windows and Kovács was having trouble dissuading them, when suddenly in walked Uncle Elek. He had been standing behind the mulberry tree in our courtyard and had heard what was going on. He walked straight up to the manager of the Co-op, Virgula, who was as strong as an ox.

'I can hear that you're the hard man here,' said Elek.

Virgula stuck out his chest. 'That's right.'

'Then I'm glad you're rolling your sleeves up,' answered Elek. 'We'll be able to see if your muscles match your mouth.'

'One Jew isn't enough for me,' sneered Virgula, facing Elek nervously with his feet apart.

'Don't worry,' smiled Elek, 'I don't want to beat you up. I won't even ask you to lift a stone – we all know you find it easier the more you drink. But what about that anvil? Can you lift that?'

Virgula crouched down to take a good look at it, then heaved at it and tipped it over.

'Two hands?' said Elek in amazement. He righted the anvil and sat down on it. 'Perhaps you'd like a couple of horses to help you?' he suggested. With that, my uncle stood up, passed two fingers through the ring on the top of the anvil and lifted it right up.

While it was dangling in mid-air he said to Kovács, 'If you must wake us up, bash this anvil instead of smashing our windows.'

They weighed the anvil the next day. One hundred and twenty kilos. But we still had Ungár make my boots. I decided that when I grew up, I would be like Uncle Elek, not like my grandfather.

Nevertheless, from then on I always crossed the road if I had to go past Ungár's shop. He often propped himself up in his doorway, staggering occasionally, trying to attract the attention of the people going in and out of the Co-op by making speeches and shouting 'My Hungarian brothers!' every time he forgot what he was going to say. He hurled insults at the British, the Czechs, the Rumanians, the Bolsheviks, the Jews. He would shout 'Long live Hitler!', and sing, with tears rolling down his cheeks: 'Awaken, Hungarians, the land of your fathers is threatened!' He implored the men to stand to attention so that they wouldn't be ashamed when the song became the national anthem. And while he sang and wept, everyone listened and laughed at him. Sometimes he would be so surrounded by people I couldn't see him. But when he sat behind the bench in his shop, I used to see him out of the corner of my eye and think it was because he was so far away that he looked so small.

I passed there every day. My cousin Ágnes lived in the next house but one, and the parents of the kids at *heder* said I was in love with her. So did the kids too. They used to tease me on the way, chanting:

> *'József pays his nightly calls*
> *Kisses Ágnes, when night falls,*
> *Twirls his whiskers, climbs the walls,*
> *Up to her window, when night falls.'*

It was perfectly obvious I wasn't in love with her and didn't have whiskers, and anyway it wasn't safe for Jews to be out at nightfall. But that didn't make any difference, they carried on with their stupid teasing. It made me sick. I couldn't even marry Ágnes when I grew up, like these idiots said I would. She was my cousin.

Anyway, why did they always have to go on about marriage? I knew from my mother and father that marriage was a disaster, but most children aren't told. As for that song about kissing Ágnes and climbing through the window, it simply wasn't true. It all happened later, in a different way. I don't quite understand how myself, so how could anyone else?

I went to Ágnes's to bunk off *heder*, but I liked going to *shul*. It was just coincidence that they happened in the same building.

The smell of sweat filled the hours before Sabbath. Everyone would wash at the same time, furiously, which drove my Uncle Elek out into the courtyard to shave. I'd go there too, to escape the bundles of dirty and clean washing that flew around the rooms like the flags of two embattled armies. My other uncle and my grandfather wandered about, half-dressed, searching for the various bits of clothing which had disappeared because Mariska, the vintner's wife who looked after the house, always left the Friday cleaning till the last minute. The house had to be immaculate for the appearance of the first star. The Sabbath.

Elek never used a razor, because touching the skin with a knife was forbidden under Jewish law. Instead, he used a thin strip of wood with a powder called 'rasol'. The result was that he had to shave three times, wiping the bristle and rasol off the bit of wood after each stroke so as not to make it even blunter. It was disgusting to watch, but there was nothing else to look at, and if I had gone back into the house my grandfather would have sentenced me to several hours' hard labour, polishing my shoes. He said that I could show my respect for religion by my shoes if by nothing else. So I watched Uncle Elek shaving instead.

This led to a serious theological debate.

'Last year my mother was operated on for appendicitis,' I said to Elek. 'With a knife!'

'It doesn't seem to worry her,' he replied.

'Of course it doesn't. But what would you do if you had to have your appendix out?'

'I wouldn't let it worry me either.'

I put the same question to Grandfather.

'Your mother's a *shikse*,' he said simply. 'And a lancet isn't the same as a knife.'

'Why isn't it?'

'Because the Law that forbids us to touch our skin with knives is intended to save life. It's different if the knife is used for healing.'

'Then it's nothing to do with the knife,' I objected, but I couldn't express myself clearly. Still, I was sure I was right, and carried on asking questions until my grandfather called me a '*shaygets bocher*'.

'Why does your wife stick all the knives in the ground on Friday afternoon?' I demanded.

'You mean your grandmother. Because—'

'My grandmother's dead. She's your wife.'

'And you are a wicked child to keep bringing that up when she is so good to you.'

'She isn't anything. I don't speak to her.'

'You mean she doesn't speak to you. The reason she sticks the knives in the ground is to purify them, make them *kosher* for the Sabbath.'

'Then why doesn't Mariska do it? She does everything else.'

'Because then the knives wouldn't be *kosher*.'

This puzzled me. 'So it isn't the earth that makes them *kosher*? Well what's the point of sticking them in the ground, then? I thought the ground was *kosher*.'

'Only the earth of Judea is *kosher*, Józska. But the earth in other places absorbs impurities, takes away the *treyf*.'

'But why are the knives *trayf* when everything we eat is *kosher*?'

'Because Mariska uses them, and she's a *goy*.'

'That means we eat *treyf* all week!' I said, and burst out laughing. Grandfather was shocked.

The Friday night service was short. The assistant rabbi, who ran the *heder* and when necessary replaced the Rabbi, used to race through it. The Rabbi was very old and ill, and had trouble standing up. Even on Saturdays, all he could do was officiate in a faint voice from underneath the stone tablets and let the assistant rabbi and the cantor do the rest.

On their way to the Friday service to which only men could go, the Jews who lived near the *shul* would wait in their doorways for those men who had further to come. Afterwards, the dogs barked at us while we all walked back together, and the group would slowly thin out as one by one we reached our own houses.

During the prayers before the evening meal, candlelight shimmered on the white damask tablecloth and swayed in the bottles beside the plaited loaves, the bright wine darkening towards the base. The black prayer book on the corner of the table lay by Grandfather's hand, while the fine features of his face, framed by his white hair and beard, were transformed by his prayers like a smooth rock that is washed by the rising tide.

This ceremony held the promise of Friday night, a promise only fulfilled much later, when I was alone.

Everybody ate quickly and avidly, and from the first spoonful of the traditional chicken soup I prayed for supper to be over as soon as possible. I stared at the candles so as not to see all those greedy mouths; I was silent, not wanting my voice to blur the sharp magic of waiting; I tried to shut out every sound.

The front rooms with their barred windows overlooking the street were all occupied, and I wasn't considered worthy of the empty room that had once belonged to my grandmother, except when I had chicken pox. So I slept in the main room, surrounded and protected by other sleepers. This meant that even during the week I witnessed all major events, while on a Friday night it was an indispensable part of my starry happiness.

The candles on the table would be left burning after everyone had gone to bed. The rhythmic patter of the falling wax reminded me of the murmur of the prayers, and I could watch the light reflecting off the three glass doors into the shadows.

Sometimes I saw two little eyes opening wider and wider on the ceiling above me as a car drove up towards the main road. As it came closer, an untouchable foliage of shadows formed on the wall, bringing with them the hardly remembered echoes of Budapest. And when the car arrived on the bridge the entire wall would become a conflagration of shadows where I could see pictures no film could show me; they glided past in a frame of darkness, and when the car

11

reached the bend in the bridge, the slow edge of the frame closed in, snuffing out the flame. I used to reassure myself by looking back at the dull red dots of candlelight reflected in the glass doors, and by glancing at the stars that sat like baubles among the branches of the mulberry tree outside. I pictured my mother's two different faces, the one which changed every time I saw her, and the one on the photograph I kept of her. And I waited for another car to open its eyes above my head.

That was why I had to have the shutters open. Grandfather always closed them before going to bed, but as soon as he had left the room I used to open them again. So our traditional Saturday started with me being told off. It wasn't until Elek took my side that I found out why the shutters had to be closed and why I couldn't have the spare room.

One night, the gate that led into the courtyard was taken off its hinges and stolen. My grandfather ran frantically up and down the house, lamenting the fact that this kind of thing had finally happened to us and wanting to call the constabulary. Elek tried to calm him, pointing out that they hadn't even dared to smash the windows because they knew he'd do the same to their heads, but Grandfather wouldn't stop trembling until someone suggested that the gate had been stolen for timber. That seemed to calm him down, but some time later we found it lying in a ditch at the foot of a crucifix that stood opposite the path up to the church. Grandfather thought this meant that our Jewish gate had been sacrificed to Jesus, and for him it was the most terrifying declaration of war.

Elek remarked that if I became their target I'd squeak a lot more loudly than the gate had done; but Grandfather refused to listen. All Elek could do was to reopen the shutters for me after the others had gone to sleep and then be first up in order to close them again. Whenever Grandfather caught us my uncle took the blame, and their quarrel always ended in irritable silence.

On Saturdays, I enjoyed going to the service, walking up the badly cobbled street that started opposite Ágnes's and led to Mountain Street. The sun shone more brightly there than anywhere else in the village; you could hear the singing and the music from the *shul*. My grandfather was always early, so I would arrive with my two uncles just as the organist was playing the music composed by our teacher, Mr Dévai.

József Dévai wore a soft, elegant hat that matched his suit. He shaved every day, and when he asked how you were, he listened

12

attentively to the reply. From the moment I entered the roughly cobbled street I would be looking forward to seeing him, more even than to seeing Ágnes, because she had to go up to the women's gallery. I would only be able to see her when she went in and when she came out, and then only for a second. It made me happy to know that the beautiful music I could hear in the street was written by Mr Dévai, and I even learnt the words, though you could scarcely hear them above the noise of the organ and the chant.

> *'Let my right hand forget her cunning,*
> *Let my tongue be stilled for ever,*
> *If I forget thee, O Jerusalem.'*

I decided I would never forget Jerusalem if Mr. Dévai didn't want me to, and was sad, because I knew that he couldn't come with me when I went back to Budapest.

The old men would already be chanting when I arrived. There was a big man whose black beard was the longest in the whole *shul*, and whose voice was so loud you could hear it above a hundred singers. There was talk of finding a new Rabbi because the present one was too old and his assistant too mediocre, but I couldn't see why they didn't choose the man with the black beard. His prayers rang out like orders. He was a born leader.

Sometimes my grandfather would turn my head towards the front so that I couldn't keep looking round all the time. The interminable prayers made me fidget. The prayer my mother had taught me to say before bed was quite long enough for me; anything else I wanted to ask or tell God could be said in a couple of sentences. Going to *heder* had made no difference to my non-existent Hebrew, so I went on looking around.

A tall, skinny man with a white beard used to bow so low that I started to giggle, waiting for him to fall flat on his face. Fat Mr Schlesinger would moan quietly with his prayer book in one hand and a handkerchief in the other. When he became really fervent he used to open his mouth as if he were screaming for help. I longed to give him a good kick up the bum. He was flanked by his sons, one of whom was my age and had the longest plaits in the village. They had to be curled up to make them shorter.

I often glanced over my shoulder at old Schozberger's hands shaking over his prayer book. I used to wait until we came to the bottom of the page, when Schozberger, who was slightly deaf as well, would glance at his neighbour's book and panic, making a terrible mess of his pages. Once I burst out laughing and was slapped in the face.

Without turning round, Ignác Schwartz's father used to slap his son's hand to stop him picking his nose. Ignác watched his father out of the corner of his eye, but always took his finger out at the wrong moment. His father never missed. The hapless Gyurka Sternberg was always stuck between his gigantic, grey, crew-cut father and the lectern. Sometimes his father would absent-mindedly rest the prayer book on his son's head, and Gyurka would lean forward, looking miserable. Laci Fried, standing between his father and his elder brother, stared straight ahead like a statue. The men, bending like reeds in the wind, were a painful spectacle, and the stupid, spluttering *bochers*, the apprentice rabbis, were a repellent one. How could a religion which forbade kneeling, even before God, tolerate this?

József Dévai never bowed or rocked during the chanting like all the other scrubbed and trimmed Saturday men. He just lowered his head.

Suddenly, after a beautiful song, there would be silence. The windows shone. The grown-ups started looking for the page with 'The *Kaddish* for the Dead', and the children had to leave the *shul*. I wanted to stay and listen in on the grown-ups' secrets, to learn the magic they used against death. Perhaps if I knew it I might find a way to use it better than they did. I used to turn round when I reached the doors and walk the last few steps backwards to see if my uncle's *talith*, his prayer shawl, would suddenly float into the air as a sign from God. I went through the entrance hall that was used for *heder* during the week, and past the grease-stained table where the Rabbi ate his tea. I walked across the water marks left on the floors by the sprinklers, and breathed in the smell of sweat and dust. The fear I had felt a moment earlier at 'The *Kaddish* for the Dead' was now a fear of dirt. I wanted to scratch myself all over, and would run outside to be blinded by the sunlight, whose thick beams seemed to link the earth to the sky like ropes of gold.

As time went by, I realised that my mother's letters and the rare parcels of toys she sent me always arrived on Saturdays. The few clouds slipping by above me came from Budapest. Perhaps she had seen them too.

Most of the children used to tumble down the steps of the *shul* and rush up the little hill on the far side of the road. They pushed and shoved – the hill belonged to whoever reached the top first. Laci Fried, the stocky eight-year-old who had told me off for missing *heder*, was in charge. He shouted orders and tried to push everyone off the top, including his allies. The boy-girl with the long plaits shouted 'I'm the king of the castle', over and over again, even when he was losing. I hated him out here even more than I did in *shul*, but one day it struck me that he might be slightly mad and the thought made my skin creep.

I played marbles with Gyurka Sternberg in the *shul* courtyard. Ignác Schwartz was our age, but all he could do was watch, as his father would have beaten him for playing in such a place. The father sold mineral water at fairs, and didn't want any gossip because he was always meeting people. Gyurka's huge father, by contrast, beat him for just about everything except playing marbles in the *shul* courtyard. Mr Sternberg was a horse-dealer and, dealing with horses all day, didn't know his own strength. I don't think he even knew he was slapping his son sometimes, because he would carry on talking affectionately to Gyurka as if nothing was happening. Béla Engelhardt was the other spectator of our games of marbles. His family was so poor he didn't know how to play – we'd have won his marbles in the first few minutes, if he'd had any.

After we had played for a while, someone would come out to shoo us away, usually the zealous *bocher* in curl-papers whose main occupation this was. He would declare that we were not allowed to play marbles in the *shul* courtyard. We would then reply that we played here every day during *heder*, whereupon he would tell us that this was the *shabbes*, which was different: marbles were forbidden on the *shabbes*. And then he'd tell us that we were playing for gain, and that this was also forbidden on the *shabbes*. We would have to collect up our marbles and go and play at the far end of the grounds where it wasn't sunny. But marbles weren't allowed there either, so after a while the *bocher* or someone else would come out and the four of us would shuffle back into the sun. We would watch the other boys assaulting the hill, talk, play a bit more, and wonder what to do next.

'Why don't we go and spy on the women?' I exclaimed one day. It wasn't a game but at least it wasn't allowed. Men and boys were forbidden to set foot in the women's gallery.

'We could throw sand and pebbles at them!' suggested Gyurka Sternberg, improving on my idea.

Béla and Ignác opposed our plan with trembling admiration, which of course added to its appeal. Then Béla plucked up his courage and offered to join us in exchange for one glass marble or fifteen clay ones. We refused at first, but Gyurka made a generous concession by declaring that if Béla was prepared to pour a bucket of water from the top of the gallery on to the red head of the *heder* teacher, we could do business. Béla giggled but chickened out. So while we were creeping up the stairs, the other two hid behind the open doors waiting to see what happened, ready to flee. I was against the throwing of sand, and particularly pebbles, but Gyurka said it would be childish if we didn't. Unfortunately he won the argument, and we were caught. His father beat him senseless. My grandfather covered his face with his hands and bowed several times to the wall as if he were at *shul*. I thought he had gone mad. I was hoping his tears would be my only punishment, but Elek's beating soon cured me of that.

On my way to *heder* I used to step and jump from one stone to another in the street that led to the *shul*, trying to reach the doors without touching the ground. Eventually, I changed the rules of this game and decided that if I touched the ground I wouldn't go to *heder* at all. I missed the stones more and more often, and finally gave up leaving it to fate to decide whether I should attend *heder* or not. I went there very rarely.

My mother had asked my grandfather not to send me to *heder* at all, and I knew it. Grandfather had needed a great deal of persuading to agree to this, but I ruined it all on my first day at the village.

'Give your grandmother a kiss,' he said when I arrived, showing me an old, dwarfish lady who was smiling at me. I was frightened she'd bite me with her two buck teeth.

'She's not my grandmother, she's your second wife,' I objected. Later he decided I should call her 'ma'am'.

'She's your step-grandmother,' he explained, but the 'step-' part made matters worse.

'Give her a kiss.'

'She's ugly!'

The old girl burst into tears, stood up, and ran to lock herself in her room. I soon began to blame her for all my ills, but nevertheless she used to promise me the earth if I would only call her 'granny'.

I decided that she was 'the Iron-Nosed Witch', and I called her that in front of my friends. Occasionally I made sure that she could hear me. I accused her of separating my parents and turning my mother into a beggar to keep us apart. Uncle Samuel acted as a buffer between us,

16

and more or less became my nanny. Grandfather spent most of his time at *shul*, and the vineyards and the wine were almost exclusively Uncle Elek's province, so sometimes Samuel would tell me stories all day long. He taught me to read to give himself a break, and to write a little, but one day he had to go and do his military service.

He returned on leave a few weeks later. He came in, took one look round, and slumped down at the big table in the dining room, cursing the army and his own bad luck. Then he burst into tears. Grandfather sent a barrel of wine to the captain in command of his company, and Samuel became battalion chef. I think he even learned to cook eventually.

I used to go with Elek when he recruited his day labourers from around the village, and when he supervised their work. I wore my winter coat in the middle of summer to watch the wine being filtered in the cold cellar. I helped bind the vines alongside the day labourers, and with the picking at harvest time. When I wasn't out on the mountain, I joined the two kids who lived each side of us. They were both called János, and we ran riot in all our three houses. The Iron-Nosed Witch used to follow us everywhere, telling us to play 'like good boys', and complained to my grandfather that I was 'wrecking the house with the little *goys*' while he was out at *shul*.

I suppose our games were different from the ones my elder brother played at my other grandfather's house, where boys wearing ties would tinkle on the piano and imitate the grown-ups.

Piroska Roba, the daughter of one of our more distant neighbours, was two years older than me. We met just before I was sent to *heder*, when I wasn't even six.

'Have you got a lover?' she asked.

I thought of Kica and Ágnes. 'No,' I replied, embarrassed.

'Neither have I. Will you be mine?'

'All right. What do we have to do?'

'Go up to the attic and take all our clothes off,' she explained.

'All of them?'

'All of them.'

'Well, I won't be your lover, then,' I decided.

'You only have to take some of them off.'

We went up to the attic, but didn't pull up the ladder because it looked too suspicious. We romped around for a while, but we made too much noise, and her father came up the ladder. He grabbed Piroska and slapped her.

'You're still too young to be a slut,' he told her, and threw me out, even though we hadn't taken all our clothes off.

Grandfather thought I lacked sophistication.

'You're turning the boy into a peasant,' he complained to Elek.

'What do you want me to turn him into?' retorted Elek. 'A bishop?'

Grandfather turned to me. 'Are the Asztaloses good to you?'

'Yes.'

'What about the Hajdus?'

'They always talk very grown-up to me, and if I come at the wrong time they make me read aloud for half an hour with János. The Asztaloses make us grind corn for the pigs, and won't let Ilonka play with the boys even though she's pretty.'

'You're just like your father. Don't these little *goys* call you a Jew?'

'They haven't for ages. Why does it matter when one person's a Jew and the other isn't?'

'When they eat, do they offer you anything? Like an apple or a sweet?'

Elek was looking up at the ceiling with one eye while the other gazed at the floor, but I didn't understand.

'What about pork?' Grandfather demanded. 'Have you eaten bacon?'

Elek, standing behind his father, shook his head, but I ignored him. If I'd had a bar of chocolate for every time I'd seen Uncle Elek eat bacon I'd have looked like Schlesinger.

'What's bacon?' I asked Grandfather. It was then that he sent me to the *heder*.

I stopped in the doorway. The Rabbi was sitting at the head of the table facing the few rays of muddy sunlight that seeped through the grubby little window. He had his back to me. In the semi-darkness I could see children sitting round the table and along the walls. Adolescent *bochers* with long, girlish plaits sat behind lecterns like the ones in the *shul*. They had books open in front of them.

The children told the Rabbi I was there. He turned round.

'Come in,' he said. Then he turned back to the other children and carried on with what he was saying. I went up behind him, and suddenly the room went quiet. Embarrassed, I pulled off my cap.

'Good morning, sir,' I said.

The class started to giggle.

'*Guten Tag, Josef Sholem,*' he replied, and as he turned round, I saw that he was laughing too.

'Your cap,' he sniggered.

Terrified, I put it back on my head and held it there with both hands.

'Can you pray?' asked the thin-faced Rabbi, fingering his red, goaty beard.

'Of course I can,' I replied.

He sighed and placed the prayer book in front of me. 'Excellent. Then, read this.'

'I can't read that!'

'Well, what can you read?'

'Proper letters.'

'Not these?'

'No.'

He didn't believe me. 'What's this?' he asked, pointing to a letter. He waited until the children stopped laughing, then told me what it was. '*Kumetz Bais*, which makes the sound "Booo". And this one is *Kumetz Alef*, which makes the sound "Ooo".'

'Booo ooo?' I asked suspiciously.

The Rabbi smiled but waved the children quiet. I didn't like it. He seemed not to want me to understand. I thought he was making fun of me.

'Show me how you pray,' he said.

'Now?'

'Now.'

'But it's not bedtime.'

They all burst out laughing again. One of the big girlish-boys in pigtails stood up behind his lectern. He was laughing too.

'Pray as if it was bedtime,' the Rabbi encouraged me.

'Dear God,' I began, 'my eyes are closing, but yours . . .' I stopped. The children were shrieking with laughter and jumping up from their places, and the Rabbi had doubled up in hysterics, his beard between his knees.

'I'm going home,' I said firmly, but my legs wouldn't work. 'I'm not going to let you laugh at me!'

The children giggled even more, but I saw the Rabbi was trying to pull himself together. His lips were moving, although nothing came out until finally he said, 'Anyone who laughs will be beaten.'

But the idiots kept on sniggering and he did nothing about it.

'Don't you know any Jewish prayers?' he asked me after a while. 'I mean, you go to *shul*, don't you?'

'*Borei pri hagofen*,' I quoted confidently, at which the Rabbi began to slap his thighs. The words were from the blessing of the wine, they came just before the moment when the children were allowed to run to the *Torah* to have a sip.

'You do know the *Sh'ma Yisroel*?' he asked when he had recovered.

'Yes. *Sh'ma Yisroel Adonoy Elohanu Adonoy Echod!*'

The smile left his face. 'Who's the neologian?'

'What's a neologian?'

'Who says *"elohanu"* instead of *"elohaynu"* in your family?'

'My other grandfather, but only sometimes.'

'Well,' he paused. 'When you come to *"Adonoy elohaynu"* you must close your eyes.' And he shut his so tightly his eyelids became all wrinkled.

'Why?'

'Because you are speaking of God, who is invisible. You mustn't spy on him. To see him is to die.'

I leant against the Rabbi's chair.

'Start again,' he coaxed. 'And when you get to *"Adonoy"*, shut your eyes. Better still, put your hand over them.'

'I never shut my eyes before and I'm not dead. I didn't see God either, so maybe there isn't one.'

'What did you say?' he exploded, almost falling off his chair in the process.

I tried to explain. 'Well, if you shut your eyes so you won't see Him, and I keep mine open, and don't see Him, then perhaps He isn't there.'

The Rabbi jumped out of his chair, raised his arms to heaven, twisted up his face, and shouted as loudly as he could, *'Laï lüni!'*

I was suddenly very frightened.

'What does that mean?' I whispered.

'What does it mean?' He eyed me from head to foot and lowered his arms. 'Perhaps you'll understand if I say it in *goy*: *Get thee behind me, Satan!*'

I looked round fearfully.

'Where is he? Is he invisible too?'

'He's within you!' shouted the Rabbi.

He tried to tear the collar off his jacket like someone in mourning but then changed his mind. I burst into tears. The Rabbi placed his hands on my head and murmured something in Hebrew. I sat down at the table, put my head on it, and cried, and when I had finished crying I stood up and said, 'I'm going home.' I headed for the doors, but Gyurka Sternberg came up to me and put his hand on my shoulder.

'Don't worry,' he said. 'We play here too.'

'When?' I asked, sniffing.

'Now!' interrupted the Rabbi. *'Yozunt!'* he shouted. I looked blank. *'Yozunt* means elevenses,' he explained. 'Did you bring any?' And he took out a bar of chocolate from the drawer and gave it to me.

Some days I went to the *heder*, some days I didn't. When I didn't I usually went to Ágnes's. I used to go past her gate as far as Ungár's, and then stop outside his door to listen until my courage ran out. Then I'd turn round and run as fast as I could back to Ágnes's house.

We pushed each other on the swing until we reached the tops of the trees. We played hide and seek with Jutka, her little sister, and when it was Jutka's turn to find us we pretended to be frightened so we could huddle together like sheep in a storm. We wouldn't come out until Jutka started crying because she couldn't find us.

We sat in the flower beds and read fairy tales.

'A prince can't ask for the hand of two princesses at once, can he?' demanded Jutka.

'Yes, he can,' I said angrily so that they wouldn't start making comments about Kica. Ágnes disagreed, although she pretended she was talking about people in stories.

'Anyway,' suggested Jutka, 'he'd be cleverer to ask two princesses because then he'd be sure to get one of them.' Her father wasn't a shopkeeper for nothing.

And so, more and more, I'd only meet my other friends when they came out of *heder*.

One Friday at midday, I went with Ignác Schwartz to buy mineral water. We walked for ages.

'Why can't we get it in the village?' I asked.

'We're going to the brickworks,' he replied. 'The water there is a bit cheaper, and I've got two sisters to marry off.' He frowned, and said worriedly, 'They haven't got dowries and, what's more, they're ugly. I told my dad I could help him sell water at the fair, even though there's not much money in it, but he wouldn't let me.'

'Why not?'

'Because I wouldn't be able to go to school. What about you?' he asked sadly. We would both be school age the following year.

'Me? Things may get better before then. My father's father would go mad if I didn't go to school. All his children did, but my youngest uncle wasn't allowed to go to University because of the *numerus clausus*,' I boasted.

21

'What's the numerous whatsit?'

'It's a way of stopping Jews from going to University.'

'Then you'll go to secondary school!' he said in amazement.

When we got to his door he took a huge swig from both bottles.

For months nobody seemed to mind me only going to *heder* to play. But one day Grandfather decided to cross-examine me.

'Why is it so difficult to learn the Hebrew letters?'

'Because even if I learnt them they wouldn't mean anything.'

'In that case you ought to work harder. Learning nothing won't help.'

He saw to it that Ágnes's parents and Kica's parents sent me gently off to *heder* whenever I came round. Even my Christian friends' parents stopped welcoming me. None of them wanted trouble because of me. I mooched around all day long, and missed *heder* less and less often although I didn't work any harder. People said I was stupid as well as stubborn, but I didn't care. The endless rows were much more fun than the Hebrew alphabet.

Laci Fried was the gang leader at the *heder*. He was already in the second year at school, but his parents thought *heder* was more important. He didn't just come two afternoons a week like the other schoolchildren: he actually missed school so as to come to *heder* more often. He always decided what we were going to play, and whether we were cops or robbers.

One day, I won all his marbles.

He stood up. 'Give them back!' he demanded. 'You cheated!'

The others watched us, glad that he'd lost, but they kept quiet. We glared at each other, but he didn't hit me.

'Wait here,' he announced. 'I have to decide what we're going to play next.'

We waited. He went in to the Rabbi and had a long consultation. Then he came back and stuck out his chest.

'We're going to collect scrap metal. For the *shul*. Mr Grossman pays two fillérs a kilo. I get half the money because it was my idea, and I'll beat up anyone who cheats. Let's go.'

'You can count me out!' I exclaimed.

'You'd better come or else,' he threatened.

'Get lost.'

'But everyone has to give money to the *shul*.'

'My grandfather does give money. He even pays for this stupid *heder*.'

22

'You know what you are? You're a *Shabbes goy*!'

'And you're a *Shabbes* pig.'

'You're a *goy* every day,' he added, leaving himself wide open.

'And you're a pig every day, even when you're asleep.'

After that he had to defend his honour, and he went for me. He was stronger than me, but I had the knack of getting so angry I couldn't feel anything. He must have had it too, because while we were fighting he was shouting, 'Filthy *goy*!'

'Filthy yid!' I yelled back at him.

The Rabbi, alerted by the others, came and separated us.

'Did I hear you say "Filthy yid"?' he choked.

'He said it,' I lied. The others booed but I didn't give in. 'We were rolling on the ground; no one could tell who said what.'

'But before,' said Laci, calling on himself as witness, 'I called you a *goy* in front of everyone, and you called me a pig.'

'Yes, but then it was the other way round.'

The Rabbi stood for a few minutes nodding his head slowly, then pronounced his verdict.

'Prove to me that you didn't say it. Go and collect scrap metal for our *shul*.'

'No way,' I said angrily, strengthening the alliance between the Rabbi and Laci Fried.

'So you did say it,' said the Rabbi menacingly.

'But why should Laci Fried have half the money?'

'Because it was his idea to get the children to contribute to the *shul*. It's very beautiful. And it deserves a reward.'

That was when I thought of it. I'd trick the lot of them.

When they all set off in a big group I went the other way. I was going to collect scrap metal too.

'Don't worry,' said Laci as I walked away. 'I'll be waiting for you at Grossman's – even if you take till midnight!'

I went to see Fat Schlesinger, whose son had such long plaits.

'We're collecting scrap metal – all the *heder* kids. The Rabbi sent me.'

Schlesinger's eyes shone, and he congratulated me. I just shrugged and smiled, and he left me for a few minutes. He reappeared staggering under the weight of an enormous and very rusty old stove.

'Have you got a barrow?' he asked, looking at me rather doubtfully.

'I'll come back for it,' I promised.

I visited every Jewish house in Mountain Street. All I had to say was that the Rabbi had sent me, so I didn't even have to lie. Scrap metal fell like manna from the sky.

I went to look for the others when I had finished. They were all wandering around in a herd, looking for lost horseshoes in the dust and begging from the shopkeepers. They hadn't had the nerve to turn up on people's doorsteps. They probably hadn't even thought of it. Their pockets bulged sharply, and their hands were full of bits of old iron. I grabbed Gyurka Sternberg by the arm.

'Come with me.'

'I can't carry more than this,' said Gyurka, showing me how heavily loaded he was already.

'Give it to Laci.'

'What? To keep?'

'Go on,' I urged.

After a moment's hesitation he handed the metal to Laci Fried, who hesitated even longer before taking it.

'Thank you,' he said, looking at me suspiciously and wondering if I was surrendering.

'My pleasure,' I said magnanimously.

'I must have had six kilos,' complained Gyurka as soon as we were alone. 'Grossman would have paid twelve fillérs for that much, and I bet Laci would have let me keep two.'

'You serf!' I reproached him.

Gyurka stared at the ground. I couldn't make out whether he was ashamed or just looking for another horseshoe.

'Cheer up, we're going to your house first,' I said cockily. 'Is your father in? If this works, you'll be richer than your wildest dreams.'

His father was at home. He nodded emotionally as I explained myself, but Gyurka was dancing for joy and I had to scowl at him to make him shut up. When I had finished, Mr Sternberg brought out his cart and drove us all the way along Mountain Street to collect my scrap metal.

The whole *heder* was waiting for us under Grossman's 'Hardware Bazaar' sign, and there were cheers as we arrived.

'Why didn't you let me come too?' cried Ignác Schwartz.

Then Laci Fried came up to me. 'Give me half of half,' he said. 'And half my marbles. We'll be friends.' He was offering me half the leadership, but obviously the smaller half, so I ignored him.

When he saw the size of the load, Grossman came over and put his arms round me. He was a tiny old man, a toy old man, and I didn't

24

even have to tell him about the Rabbi because he already knew all that. He took off his glasses and started rubbing them with his handkerchief although he wasn't crying. He was smiling. Benevolently.

Instead of the four pengős he owed us he gave us five. I immediately promised two to Gyurka. Laci Fried turned pale. He was swaying slightly, like a drunkard, and staring at me, and he looked so weak I nearly picked a fight with him right there. Then, with him behind me and all the others following at my heels, I marched off like a victorious general towards the coming battle.

'Half of half,' hissed Laci. But he didn't try to overtake me till we reached the *shul* courtyard, where, suddenly, he grabbed me by the arm and made me face him. The others formed a circle around us.

'Give it to him or he'll beat you up.'

'I'll beat him up!'

'Don't let us down!' said Gyurka Sternberg.

'Give it to me,' demanded Laci Fried, holding out his hand.

'No.'

He hit me in the face. I didn't fall, but I staggered. Seeing a stone, I grasped it in my fist and smashed it into his nose, but lost my nerve and pulled the punch just as I hit him. Even so, blood started pouring from his mouth. I couldn't believe it! Laci Fried bleeding! I threw the stone away and carried on punching him with my bare fists.

The Rabbi separated us again.

'Who started it?' he demanded, but for a long time Laci and I were so dazed we couldn't hear what was going on around us. I could see his blood on my hand and feel his warm breath on my skin. I stood on tiptoe and put my elbow on his shoulder, so I wouldn't dirty him any more with my hands. Then I turned my anger on the Rabbi.

'We both started it.'

'Give it to me,' said the Rabbi, holding out his hand.

'No.'

'Five pengős. What do you want five pengős for?'

'I don't know yet. Anyway, two of them are Gyurka Sternberg's.'

'So give them to him.'

'No, because you'll take them away from him.'

'And I won't from you?'

'No.'

'I don't want to have to take them. I want you to give them to me. Nicely.'

'One pengő if you leave me alone,' I grinned.

He grabbed me by the collar and dragged me into the *heder*, where he picked up his cane and swished it about, catching me on the shoulder.

'Ginger goat!' I screamed.

The afternoon worshippers poured out of the temple, their prayer shawls crooked and their *tzitzits*, their holy vests, showing under their shirts. Grandfather wasn't there. The cane stopped in mid-air and was slowly lowered down to the ground.

'Have you eaten pork?' asked the Rabbi so that everyone could hear.

'Yes.'

'And was it good?'

'You bet!'

I felt a sharp pain in my thigh. The cane flew back into the air, but I grabbed the Rabbi by the beard and kicked him in the shin. He lifted me up with one hand and tried to put me across his knee. I bit him on the thigh and scrambled to my feet, then kicked his other shin and ran out through the doors.

'*Laï lüni!*' he yelled, and raced after me. Glancing round, I saw him slow down to a more dignified pace as he reached the steps of the *shul*, but I kept on running.

The Rabbi reached our house a quarter of an hour after I did. I rushed into Grandfather's room and bolted the door. Through it I could hear his wife wailing, 'I knew it, I knew it, the child will end up in a gaol or a church! His father's an atheist too! Don't say I didn't warn you . . .'

She went on and on, moaning as if it were she who had been beaten. I couldn't care less. They weren't going to break the bolts just to give me another hiding.

'Witch!' I yelled. 'Scrap-Iron-Nose! You're an idiot! So are you, Goat-face!' That was meant for the Rabbi.

But then came Elek's voice: 'Come out.'

'I'm not that stupid!' I remarked.

But I had been wrong about the bolts. Not only did Elek eat pork: he could also break doors down.

'Give them the money,' he said, standing in the wreckage.

'No.' He was breathing so heavily that for a moment he couldn't speak.

'What do you need five pengös for?'

'For running away if you hit me.'

'Give me the money and I won't.'

26

'Not even for calling her a witch?'

Elek looked at the old woman. 'Not even for that,' he said quietly. I saw a little smile cross his face, but she didn't notice.

'Witch!' I shouted at her triumphantly. Elek slapped me.

'You see, you lied,' I said.

'Come on, give me the money.'

'I won't. I'm going to run away now.'

'You stole that money.'

'I didn't. Grossman gave it to me for the scrap metal.'

'You told everyone you were collecting for the *shul*.'

'No, I didn't. All I said was that the Rabbi sent me.'

'It comes to the same thing. You tricked everybody.'

'It doesn't. They all tricked themselves.'

'Give me the five pengős. It's as if you'd stolen them.'

'But I *didn't* steal them. And if you hadn't hit me I would have given you half my three.'

'You've got five.'

'Yes, but I owe Gyurka two for the cart.'

We agreed on one pengő fifty. The price included a promise from Elek that Grandfather wouldn't punish me when he came home.

'Kiss your grandmother's hand,' said Grandfather gently, standing in the centre of the room with a vine-branch in his hand. Just as gently, I pretended not to hear him. Uncle Elek, as agreed, came to my rescue.

'He's already had a slap for that. And she did say the kid would end up a Christian.'

'Or worse,' sighed Grandfather. 'Like his father.' He looked deeply into my eyes, and with tight, trembling lips said to me, 'It has never been easy to be a Jew.'

I lowered my eyes, not understanding what Grandfather was trying to say. But he thought I was ashamed, and became calmer. 'Come on. Say you're sorry.'

The old woman straightened up her tiny frame and stood motionless.

'I paid so I wouldn't have to say sorry,' I remarked coolly.

'Hang on,' interrupted Elek. 'We only agreed that you wouldn't be punished.'

'All right, then, punish me. But give me back my one and a half pengős.'

Grandfather was staggered to hear that that was all I had given back. He had met the red-haired rabbi outside and had given him ten pengös for the *Torah*, as compensation for all the trouble I had caused.

'He's a crafty child,' Grandfather remarked, shaking his head. 'Say you're sorry.' He was almost begging me, but the unintentional compliment made me lose my head.

'To that witch? No, never!'

Grandfather lifted his vine-shoot and began to beat me. I ran into the kitchen, but he caught up with me and carried on. The old woman quickly pushed a chair underneath him, so that he could put me across his knee and beat me more comfortably. Then she stood up again and continued to look hurt.

I had a great idea. I waited patiently for the blows to slow down, then jumped to my feet and ran to the bench where we kept the water. One of the four buckets was still half-full, so I grabbed it and drenched the old woman with the contents.

I got a real thrashing this time, from Elek because Grandfather was exhausted.

'I can't do any more,' he had murmured. Elek's beatings weren't funny, and afterwards they locked me up in the kitchen because I was screaming that I would run away in the night. I smashed the glass with my fist, and felt incredibly brave. Then I stood on a stool, leaned out of the window, and opened the door. Finally, feeling very proud of myself, I went off to bed.

Next day, Grandfather took me by the hand and led me all the way to the *heder*. Elek came with us in case I tried to escape. The Rabbi was wonderfully understanding as Grandfather lied through his teeth about how sorry I was for yesterday's events.

Gyurka had been ordered by his father to give all the money I had promised him straight to the Rabbi. Grandfather handed over one pengö fifty on my behalf.

'I shall announce it at the *Torah* on Saturday,' promised the Rabbi, beaming with the pleasure he thought he was giving us. Gyurka and I exchanged looks, and swallowed hard.

'I managed to hang on to one pengö fifty – the fifty's yours,' I whispered to cheer him up.

When the others went off during elevenses, I stayed in my place and looked as sad as I could.

'What's wrong, *Josef*?' asked the Rabbi softly.

'I left my elevenses at home,' I replied in a voice that would have broken his heart if it hadn't made him suspicious.

'If I let you go and fetch it you won't come back.'

'I'll leave my jacket here!'

'All right. I'll trust you.'

With that I left, and went straight to Ágnes's. She ran up to me, her little sister following.

'Is it true you beat up the Rabbi?'

'Yes.'

'Did he cry?'

'Neither of us cried.'

'I prayed all night for the Rabbi to drop down dead. Don't tell my father,' she added. 'Did you really call him a goat?'

'A ginger goat.'

'A ginger goat,' sighed Ágnes deeply, her eyes sparkling.

Judit was jumping up and down with glee. She grabbed our arms. 'Don't you two ever kiss?'

Ágnes and I looked at each other, horrified. We had kissed each other several times, but never on purpose. I coughed a little and then kissed her. I was dizzy. With embarrassment.

Grandfather decided to supervise my religious education himself. He bought me a brand-new prayer book printed in big letters, and shook his head in disbelief when even that failed to arouse my interest. I slept through his lessons with my eyes open, a trick I had learnt in *heder*. I wasn't allowed to leave the house until I could read fluently whatever passage was set for that day, so I spent more and more time in the attic with the ladder pulled up behind me. My experience with Piroska had taught me that much.

I sat at the door of the attic, just far enough back not to be seen from the courtyard. I read *Grimm's Tales*, and *A Thousand and One Nights*, and the story of the Trapped Giant, which I hated. The giant was very big, and he bullied a village full of children until they got the better of him and lived happily ever after. Grown-ups make up a lot of nonsense about the happiness of childhood. They forget.

We had two kittens in the house for a few weeks. One afternoon, Mariska's husband, Borsodi, took them away. I thought he was stealing them, so I followed without him seeing me. He took them to the vintner's house where he lived and tied them to a tree. Then he picked up a stick and beat one to death. Before I could make a sound, he'd brained the other one.

I dragged myself home. I hid in an empty barrel in the wine-cellar, surrounded by darkness, until I heard Elek's voice calling me.

'Borsodi's murdered my kittens,' I told him.

He seemed shocked. 'Didn't he leave you one?' he asked.

So it had happened with his consent. I went up into the attic and stared at the sky, as I had stared into the darkness earlier. It seemed to be made of stone. Where a bird dived across it, a momentary crack appeared.

I wanted something that no one could take away from me. The birds? They could be mine. They would fly for me, carrying my messages to whoever I wanted. First of all, I sent a message to the King of England to tell him he was an idiot because it suddenly seemed childish to want to be a fireman or an engine driver when I grew up: I'd much prefer to be King of England. Then Hitler would really get what for. I'd lock him up in a cage and give him nothing but bones to eat. Then I declared war on the King because he called himself George like my friend Gyurka Sternberg. He had usurped my friend's name as well as my throne and, what's more, he had given the Jews to Hitler at Munich. Soon a kestrel descended on the courtyard with the King's reply, screeching that I was an idiot too. I ordered the eagles to attack the British pilots. A stork arrived with dispatches: the British pilots had fled before my invincible eagles. Generous in victory, I told the King that his planes were to join my eagles and attack Hitler under my command or I wouldn't wait until I grew up to take my throne: I'd banish him there and then.

Kica was at Ágnes's house one evening, and I was filled with happiness at being able to play with both girls at once, while the flowers formed a rainbow in the dusky greenness of the courtyard. But they wouldn't stop whispering to each other.

'Which of us do you love?' demanded Ágnes at last, so brazenly that Kica lowered her eyes.

'Both of you.'

'But who do you love best?' she insisted.

'I love you best when I'm with you and Kica best when I'm with Kica. And at the moment I love both of you best.'

They carried on whispering and waving their arms around, until Ágnes suggested we play hide and seek. They'd look for me first.

I hid in the toolshed and watched them through the cracks in the planks. But they weren't looking for me. Ágnes had folded her arms and was looking at Kica, who was standing still. Ágnes stamped her foot, but Kica took no notice of her. Suddenly, Ágnes pulled down

30

her knickers, bent over, lifted up her skirt, and pointed her bottom in my direction.

I was terrified that someone was going to come into the courtyard. Kica was clapping her hands. In the dusk, Ágnes's bottom glowed amongst the flowers like a strange white flame.

'You can come out now,' she shouted. 'We're not playing hide and seek any more. Did you see anything?' she asked, hurrying, poppy-red, towards me.

'No, nothing,' I said innocently.

'You did!' She studied my face and went beetroot.

'I wasn't looking.'

'Couldn't you see between the planks?'

'No,' I replied, a bit too decisively.

'But . . . but you can!' she stammered.

We went to check. Of course you could see out of the gaps if you pressed your nose against the planks, but from where I said I'd been standing, all you could see were bright streaks of air.

'Don't be angry,' she said, putting her head on my shoulder.

'I'm not.'

'Yes you are!'

'What about?' I asked, still pretending to have seen nothing; but I wasn't angry at all. I ran home.

The dusk sky and the grass curled into flame, a blue and yellow and green rainbow. The evening trailed like smoke out of the falling sun, and the neat hedges on the side of the road reached out to prick my hands as I ran past them. The miller's horse shied away from me at the last moment, and the cobbled street echoed behind me with the sound of hooves. My breath was burning.

For days, when I closed my eyes in bed, I could see Ágnes, phosphorescent in the darkness. On my shoulders, my cheeks, my hands, it was her skin I sensed, not my own. I chased galloping horses, and woke slippery with sweat, my lips chapped and everything in my room melting as the light poured through the windows like white-hot metal. I had to hammer on my chest to stop myself suffocating.

While Grandfather was showing me his Hebrew letters, I sighed out loud. He was surprised.

'Are you ill?' he asked, feeling my forehead.

'Can I go and read?'

'If that's all it is we'll carry on. Fairy tales are a pack of lies.'

'So's God,' I said, and told him about keeping my eyes open

31

during the *Sh'ma Yisroel*. 'Try it yourself – you won't see Him!'

'*Sh'ma Yisroel*,' he stuttered, beaten.

From then on he spent our lessons walking up and down the room like a sleepwalker, pointing silently at the passages for study. I fell asleep without him noticing.

In the mornings I used to cover my head with my pillow so as to wake up slowly, because I felt stronger in my dreams.

Grandfather decided to buy me a Bible in Hungarian.

'You'll find plenty of fairy tales in here if that's all you believe in,' he told me. In return, he said, I had to work much harder on my Hebrew, although I only had to do one hour a day. But it was already too late, because I had decided that the religious stories were all made up by Grandfather, and the others belonged to me. I ordered a swallow to carry a message to the oldest parrot in the world. He had only just dived below the horizon when I saw a sparrow fly towards me. I made him the bearer of the parrot's reply, and he told me that his master was so old he could hardly speak, let alone fly. It was a bit boring because I knew what was going to happen. I had asked the parrot if it was true that once upon a time there had been a Jewish country where they set dogs and lions on the Christians. He said yes, there had been such a country, but the stories about it were all mixed up.

With this in mind, I went to see Grandfather.

'The story about Samson wasn't bad,' I conceded, 'but I don't believe a word about him being stronger than Elek.'

Grandfather smiled and pinched my cheek. It made me want to bite him.

The sun blazed in through the attic door for hours on end, making me drunk with heat and stories. I could feel like that whenever I wanted. All I had to do was think of Ágnes, naked.

I wanted to put a stop to the Hebrew lessons for good, even if it meant a beating. I switched my line of attack.

'Grandfather, is it true what it says in the Bible about Jesus healing people by talking to them?'

Grandfather didn't answer: he seemed to have been struck by lightning.

'Why did we crucify him?' I carried on, dropping some of my pretended innocence.

'Because he was a traitor!' shouted Grandfather. 'He said, "Render unto Caesar the things that are Caesar's." Nothing in Judaea belonged

to Caesar, nothing! He was a usurper. Everything was God's and ours.'
I could see that he was too angry to hit me.

'And was he the Son of God?' I asked.

Grandfather tottered, and I thought he was going to drop down
dead. 'No,' I said, beginning to feel sorry for him. 'I don't think so
either.'

'Israel is the Son of God,' mumbled Grandfather, 'and Jesus was
a bad son of Israel.' He stared at me, his eyes screwed up into slits.
Then he turned his head away, and so did I. I was frightened.

'You're going back to *heder*,' he said at last. I realised it was
no use arguing. 'And I want that Hungarian Bible back.'

I sat in the attic. I could smell the mouse-eaten pages of *heder*,
and the image of that huge, badly lit room floated before my eyes
like an approaching blindness. My eyes no longer followed the birds
who hurtled across the sky like stones thrown with murderous force.
My sight was blurred with tears. The earth was dirty and far away.

'They say the birds fly south in winter,' I thought. 'But no
one knows for sure. Perhaps they go somewhere else, to a country
between the earth and the sun, a country which flies. It's a cloud,
pushed along by the wind, flying high above the aeroplanes. That's
why no one has ever seen it, and even if they did they'd just think
it was another cloud. Maybe it doesn't exist, but I'm going to look
for it. I'll walk until I find it. I've still got one pengö left.'

I ran to the Sternbergs and took Gyurka to one side.

'I'm running away. Do you want to come too?'

'What? Now?' he asked, terrified. 'All right. Where are we going?'

'Away. Have you still got those fifty fillérs?'

'Only twenty. Why? Are we going by train?'

He pretended we were going to play at my house, and stole
a big round loaf of bread from their larder. When we had passed
Grandfather's house and the Zafirs', Gyurka stopped.

'They'll set the dogs on us!' he frowned.

'Not if we're together,' I assured him. 'They know me round here.'

And so we left the village behind us, and then the brickworks.
Gyurka walked very fast, with his shoulders up and his jaw clenched
and the big loaf squashed tightly under his arm. His feet stirred the dust
up around his knees, and it trailed behind him like a little cloud.

'My aunt lives in Kisvarda,' he said. 'She'll put us up.'

'Is she your mother's sister?'

'My father's.'

33

'That means she'll send us back.'

'Why wouldn't my mother's sister?'

'She'd be less scared,' I explained.

'We won't stay, then,' Gyurka said. 'We'll just spend the night there before going round the world. But you'll want to go and see your mother in Pest, won't you?' He studied me suspiciously.

'No way. She hasn't any money to look after me.'

'What about your other grandfather?'

'No.'

'Where will you go, then?'

'I'll tell you later,' I promised.

Gyurka took big, stubborn strides, but the anger in his eyes wasn't meant for me. It was the kind which darkened his face after he had been slapped, but this time his gaze flashed through it, like lightning through fog. The heat was pouring down from the sky as a large white cloud glided towards us very low, planning to pass to the left of us.

'Let's leave the road and turn left,' I suggested.

'You can't be tired yet.'

'I'm thirsty,' I lied. There was a well about a hundred yards away.

'You're right,' said Gyurka. 'Who knows when we'll find another well?'

We drank from the bucket and sat down at the foot of the well on a large stone.

'Ágnes showed me her bottom,' I said dreamily as I watched the big white cloud approaching.

'Did you jump on her? Is that why you ran away, because you think she's going to have a baby?' I looked at him in amazement. 'Don't you know how babies are made?' he asked.

'Of course I do, but children can't have babies.'

'Exactly,' replied Gyurka. 'It would've been silly to have run away because of that. Do you really know where babies come from?'

'From their mothers' tummies,' I answered with great precision.

'Yes,' he said, 'but how do they get in there?'

I shrugged my shoulders.

'You don't know!' he accused triumphantly. 'Haven't you seen the dogs jumping on the bitches in the streets?'

'Of course I have. Why?'

'What about horses?' he asked, a little disappointed that I knew as much as he did.

34

'No, I haven't seen horses. But I've seen cocks and hens.'

Gyurka burst out laughing. 'Cocks and hens!' he scoffed. 'So what? I've seen that thousands of times! Next you'll be telling me that children start off as eggs! People are made the same way horses and dogs are made.'

'You're crazy,' I remarked.

'Don't you believe me?' he asked, squaring up for a fight.

'No.'

'You're just shy!' he declared, lowering his fists.

I looked at the cloud. It was just above our heads.

'I'm not, because it's not true. If it was, we'd be like dogs and horses.'

'You're right,' admitted Gyurka with a sigh of relief. 'So how do you think people are made?'

'By lovemaking.'

'That's true too,' he agreed. 'Who told you?'

'My mother. Isn't that cloud beautiful?' I said, pointing to it, although he had noticed me gazing at it.

He shrugged.

'So how do people make love?' he insisted, but I made signs that I was more interested in the cloud. I still didn't dare admit to him that I thought it was going to land. A peasant walked slowly past with a white sheepdog at his heels. I didn't know him but I thought I'd better greet him because of the dog.

'Good day, sir,' I said. He returned my greeting politely but he didn't look at me, which made him even more mysterious. Without knowing why, I thought it was a good omen that his dog was white like my cloud. I thought of Mr Dévai, who always wore a white shirt even when it wasn't Saturday.

'Of course,' I thought, 'it won't land on our heads. It's going to land at our feet.' Birds scythed through the air round it, and each time one of them disappeared behind my cloud, I turned my head away so as not to see it come out the other side.

'I'm going to ask Dévai to let me start school a year early,' I said, standing up.

'You're not going home?'

'No, I'm going to Dévai's.'

'Are you chickening out?'

'No,' I answered calmly. 'Dévai is sure to give me a place, and then I won't have to go to *heder* any more.' Bunking off two afternoons a week would be child's play.

35

'Well if you're chickening out,' Gyurka said disdainfully, 'I'm going home. If I'm not back for supper I'll be beaten.'

I went straight to Dévai's house.

'I don't want to go to *heder* any more,' I told him.

He nodded gently. 'You'll still have to go twice a week,' he warned. I nodded gently back.

He said I couldn't register at his school until the autumn, when I would be the right age: but I could attend if I liked. He'd reserve a place in the elementary class from tomorrow.

And from that day on I went to Mr Dévai's Jewish school. All six classes were held in the same room, the boys on one side and the girls on the other. There were seventy-three of us in all, so I learnt whatever caught my attention. Most of the time when we made mistakes or worded something wrongly Mr Dévai didn't correct us. He simply asked us to rephrase the sentence.

For more than a year I went to his school, and to the vineyards with Elek, and to *shul* on Friday and Saturday. I never went to the *heder*. My life ran smoothly but I still missed my mother and my brother.

And then luckily the war broke out. I could go home.

2: Boots

Elek and Samuel had asked a man from our village to look after me on the journey, but he was half asleep; or rather he was pretending to be in order to stop me asking him every five minutes how long it would be before we reached Budapest.

The train tore up the ground like an earthquake: the rails fled backwards, criss-crossing tracks leaping out of the train's way in terror; telegraph poles flung themselves at the windows to have their heads chopped off, and green and gold fields slipped down from the horizon to be ploughed into brutal furrows that the train devoured and discarded. Under my gaze the future was evaporating into the past.

Sometimes, in Grandfather's courtyard, I had seen my mother peeping out at me from behind the clouds. She would disappear whenever I opened my eyes wide, but now I could only see her faint shadow against the sky because I knew she was waiting for me at the station.

Dim, distant scribbles were · turning into houses; thin shadows into vast green trees; yellow cornfields were rising out of the cloudy earth and being swept away like waves from the bow of a boat. The train smashed through a bridge that was trying to stop it like I wanted English tanks to smash through Germany, chopping it into a hundred flying bars.

Father! It was him. He popped up suddenly out of nowhere, a smoky statue cast in iron. Words were flashing up around him, words spoken by Grandfather and by Samuel.

'Good for nothing!' they said. 'Scoundrel! The Devil himself!'

Grandfather would always curse my father in the same feeble voice he used for praying, and his wrinkled face would turn into parchment as dry as the pages of the *Torah*. Samuel's cheerful expression would turn dour and his big eyes would bulge from their sockets as he muttered in a tearful voice, 'What a beautiful girl she was . . .'

'. . . and proud, too proud!' Grandfather would add, though Elek always kept quiet.

'Who is stronger, you or my father?' I had asked Elek one day, worried that he might just smile. He took some time to reply.

'Me,' he said finally, and moved away. But the way he had had to think about his answer gave me courage.

'My father is very strong, don't you think?'

This time he did smile.

'. . . Strong,' he said, and I laughed. It was a silly question to have asked Elek. I decided that only the village idiot or Ungár, the cobbler-corporal, could have dared to steal our courtyard gate.

'Is father a devil?' I wondered. Grandfather was easily scared: at the slightest trouble he would start moaning and run off to *shul*.

I had a vague picture in my mind from before I could remember things properly, from when I was in Budapest. Mother had been waiting hours for my father; I was dashing up and down on the fourth-floor landing – or was it the eighth? It was very very high up, and my head didn't yet reach the top of the railing. I was reporting to my mother through the open kitchen door.

'Father's not here yet!' I shouted as I rode back to the staircase on my imaginary motor-bike, hooting loudly.

Twilight reddened the back wall of the house, and the staircase darkened downwards like a well. Perhaps it led under the earth, to where dead people live.

Suddenly he appeared under my feet at the turning of the stairs.

I had never seen a man like him. People come and go in the streets. They raise their hats and straighten their backs; they run sideways to slip through the crowd; they step aside for the mayor like peasants, with their hats in their hands. But my father was not like them: he didn't hear or see anything. He wore a dark suit, and as he came up the stairs his features crisped around the still-burning cigarette stub that hung from his mouth. His small eyes burned like embers; strength pulsed like a sleeping tiger in his automatic movements. He almost tripped over me, greeted me with an exclamation, swung his hand towards his bristly chin and creased shirt-collar and threw his cigarette away in the same movement. He stamped it out as if he were dancing, then tousled my hair and wrapped himself in an invisible black coat, a dark cave of dreams. He moved on, and the fire that was burning him up scorched me. I wasn't frightened of him in the least.

But I also had another image of him.

One morning I had woken up alone in a lavish, unknown room, among heavy curtains, ornate carpets and dark paintings. The evening before, my mother had dragged me along as she hunted through the town for my father. When I had burst into tears we had taken the tram. She had looked for him at a boarding house where we were received by a wobbly old couple: a grey man who was going bald and a thin, tired, weepy-eyed woman. They made us sit down, and gave us coffee while my mother complained and the old woman sniffed. They talked in low voices.

'Poor things,' said my mother when we left. 'Your father seduced their lovely daughter.'

I couldn't remember how I'd got into that rich room.

The door opened and my father walked in. Behind him I could see a tall young woman dressed up in shop-window clothes; she was pretty, and smiled as if she had chocolate in her mouth. My father was wearing a pigeon-grey suit from another shop-window, and a slightly darker coat was hanging from one shoulder: not a winter coat or a raincoat, but the sort of coat rich men wear when they don't really need a coat at all.

'Get dressed,' he told me. My mother was leaning in the doorway, breathing as fast as if she had just run a mile.

The beautiful young woman put her hand on my father's shoulder and looked dreamily towards me. I could tell she didn't see me.

My mother suddenly sprang in front of them and started screaming at them with all her strength.

'You're frightening the kid,' said my father nonchalantly.

'You're worried about him? It's not me he's scared of!' my mother yelled. She was right, it was my father who frightened me then. I feared for my mother. I could hear she was screaming with pain.

'Forget it, Judit, I haven't got any more money.' My mother's hands were full of banknotes. She threw them on the floor.

'What about the money from the famous play? Is this all I get? All you can spare for your children? All that's left of the thousands?'

My father's laugh was brittle. 'All that's left and more,' he said.

My mother picked up the notes in a rage. 'I have to grovel to him

39

for money. And to his mistress – in her ten-star hotel! Just so I can pay the rent on his children's room!'

My father sighed and moved away, bored, but the pretty lady stayed where she was.

'The child needs clothes,' she murmured.

'Judit can buy him some now,' shrugged my father.

'This is for bread! And rent!' shouted my mother. I was scared she might bite my father.

'I've got clothes!' I whispered indignantly and pointed to the chair they were lying on. Father mentioned a street-name and a time to meet us.

Later in the day we waited for ages in front of a clothes shop. Father arrived with the tall elegant woman, walking fast, and almost without stopping pushed a few notes into my mother's hand.

'Buy some clothes for him.' He was gone before my mother had drawn breath to scream. Her shoulders drooped; she took me by the hand as we walked away from the shop.

I asked whether the pretty woman was the daughter of the old couple we had visited the night before.

'This is another one,' muttered Mother.

'Did he seduce her too?' I looked around furtively to see if policemen were following my father.

'Beautiful young girl . . . hardly a year since she got married,' said Mother in a sad, dreamy voice, but she woke up as soon as she had spoken. 'Her sort know how to look after themselves,' she remarked with sudden hostility.

When Grandfather talked in his biblical tone, laying into 'that worthless man', I didn't know if he meant the dark, unshaven, hell-travelled man who came to our flat, because for me the 'nobody' was this cashmere dandy. My real father was the shadow who rose from the blackness of the staircase. I believed that he could see some wonderful and terrifying secret while people like Grandfather didn't even dare look into his eyes.

The locomotive shrieked. It was like my mother screaming in the hotel room. But now she had a job and a flat. Was she getting money from Father as well? She couldn't be, because she would have told me about it in one of her letters. My father had never written to me. Not once, not a single line. But when people gossiped about him they used to deepen their voices and raise their heads and turn into rock, because they were lying. Those he had actually harmed used to

40

complain, like Grandfather and Samuel; but they always tensed up as if they expected to be hit. Elek's voice was quiet and calm, and he had never said a bad word about my father. Perhaps he didn't want to hurt me, although I didn't understand why I felt so hurt when people called my father names. I knew he was a bad man because he never gave my mother any money, and because he never wrote to me. But I did wonder why he wouldn't do these things.

I shivered. I had suddenly remembered another train journey, years before. I leaned out of the window to make sure that this time the train was taking me in the right direction, and not towards my brother Dávid's grandfather – who everyone tried to pretend was mine too . . .

Samuel had been with me on that trip, but he had hardly uttered a word. I asked him how long I would have to stay at my grandfather's, whether it would be a week or a month, but he wouldn't tell me. Instead he tried to paint rosy pictures of how well I'd get on with my brother, and he smiled, and blinked to see if I was smiling too. And then his mouth closed abruptly, as if he had swallowed something.

We found Dávid's grandfather's house closed. Samuel banged on the door and on the dark windows.

'I told them well in advance that we were coming,' he moaned bitterly. He went on rattling the window and repeating that he had written a letter. If he had been swearing like a man I would have felt better.

'Why did we come?' I asked for the hundredth time.

'To visit,' Samuel lied for the thousandth. 'So you can be with your brother.' He took me by the hand and we started walking.

I burst into howling sobs.

'You're tired,' Samuel said reproachfully. He took me on his back. I went on howling. He threatened to put me down if I didn't stop.

He walked all the way along the street and then back again. He asked two late-night passers-by if they knew where some people called the Grüns lived, but they didn't. I had no idea who the Grüns were, but I refused to go to their place anyway. I started kicking and Samuel put me down. I stamped my feet instead.

We returned to Dávid's grandfather's house. It was still dark. Samuel knocked on all the windows. Then we set off again in search of the Grüns. I fell asleep on his back.

I was awakened by the noise of Samuel knocking on another door, a bigger one. Half asleep, I was still hanging on to his back when a peasant girl opened the door and shut it in our faces immediately. A

41

few minutes later a bad-tempered old man in a nightshirt opened it just a fraction. He listened to Samuel, who told him that he had brought me to stay with my grandmother. The old man pointed to a bench in the garden and shuffled into the house.

We waited a long time. Eventually a light came on in one of the windows. The peasant girl pushed a fat, silver-haired woman in a wheelchair towards the lace-curtained window, which she half opened.

I started howling. I thought they wanted to give me away to the old woman. This seemed to frighten her because she shouted at me, telling me that I was a wicked child. I didn't need any further encouragement.

'What's got into you, waking us up in the middle of the night?' the old witch shouted at Samuel.

Samuel stuttered his excuse. Polio had broken out in our village and he had written to Aunty Eszter to say that he was bringing me to her place for the duration of the epidemic. Aunty Eszter was my grandmother; the fat silver-haired witch turned out to be her sister.

We were told that my grandfather was away on business and that my grandmother had gone to their wooden house by the lake with my brother; they often stayed there overnight.

The old witch lied to us, pretending that she didn't know exactly where Eszter's wooden house was as she couldn't go to the beach with her paralysed leg, and had to suffer and pray between these four walls, and the doctors were only good at stealing money, the good money which her blessed husband earned by the sweat of his brow . . .

They wouldn't let us into the house. We sat down on the bench again. Behind us they lit a round glass lamp, and above it the full moon cast its paler light.

Samuel sniffled and snuffled. He would have liked to cry but didn't dare because he was a grown-up. The light of the lamp grew brighter as the night darkened; the shadows grew enormous and an open-mouthed giant peeped out at us from between two branches. Samuel moved along the bench to let me lie down. I closed my eyes and the shadows immediately grew even bigger. Samuel took off his jacket and covered me up with it, though after a while he started rubbing his arms. I realised that the old woman had lied about being lame and unable to walk. When we fell asleep she would come out of the house and . . . there seemed to be two moons . . . witches' moons . . .

42

I woke up on another train. Samuel was asleep on the seat beside me. I shook him and asked him where he was taking me. Back to his father, he told me, to my real grandfather. So everything was all right.

The train's happy whistle reminded me that this time I was going home, to Budapest; Dávid had already been there for several weeks. I couldn't picture him. For years I had kept a photo of him when he was a toddler. I had treasured it the way girls treasure their china dolls. Before I had last seen him, a good year ago, I hadn't known who to expect either, but when I had heard that he was coming to visit our village I had raced joyfully up and down the High Street telling everybody the good news. At one point I came across a crowd called together by the town crier beating his drum. Before he could say anything apart from 'It is to be brought to the notice of the public that . . .', I cut in and shouted to all and sundry, 'My brother is coming! My brother is coming!'

He did come. He was enormous. He was pleased to see me too. His eyes shone, but he was a quiet, well-behaved boy. He looked shocked at my bare feet and asked me if he could ask me something. I laughed at him.

'Haven't you got any sandals?' he said, amazed.

'What for? When it's cold they're not warm, and when it's hot you don't need them. Only girls wear sandals here – if they have them that is – and then only on Saturdays – or Sundays if they're Christians, I suppose.'

Dávid laughed, happy that I wasn't missing what I didn't have.

'Are you learning the piano?' he asked.

I told him I wasn't even learning bell-ringing, and proudly showed him my mouth-organ. He was impressed until I told him that I couldn't actually play any songs on it yet.

Dávid was learning English. He mentioned it to me in a rather off-hand way, probably to get one up on me, but perhaps he was being tactful. I nearly pushed him off his feet in my excitement.

'How do you say "king" in English?' I demanded. He told me, but he didn't know the English for 'Hitler can rot' and so I had to make do with 'Hitler is a dog'. On the train, I wondered if he had found out what 'rot' was by now. When people spoke Yiddish at Grandfather's their faces went all soft and the furniture looked wobblier than when they spoke Hungarian. English makes you strong because the English are such tough soldiers.

43

Now Dávid is already in Budapest! So I'll always have somebody to play with, and if the Christian kids happen to be stronger than us or older than us or there are more of them, he won't run away without me. I'll teach him how to throw stones . . .

The wheels were cracking like whips and the train was flying . . . The English King was arriving in Budapest by aeroplane. His Serene Highness, Governor Vitéz Nagybányai Miklós Horthy receives him on his knees; the King takes pity on him and doesn't throw him into gaol; he allows him to keep his uniform, without the golden stripes of course, and lets him become a railwayman till the end of his days. The King flies away . . .

The passengers gathered their luggage together. Instead of the sky, a vast and grimy glass roof covered the station, breaking the rays of sunshine into yellow patches. The air was as grey as the stone floor. The platform was covered with people, suitcases, bundles. There were several trains – how could my mother know which one I was on? My guardian on the journey, only a vague acquaintance, was already collecting his luggage from the rack above my head. Was he going to leave me before making sure someone met me?

She appeared in the crowd and then vanished. A second later she emerged. I had imagined her as small, waiting for me at the end of the rails, but as she stopped in front of the next carriage she seemed even smaller than I had expected and her blue eyes fired anxious darts into window after window. I quickly shouted to her in case she started crying. She looked much more fragile than I remembered.

Her face, framed by her chestnut hair, lit up. She turned towards my voice, caught sight of me and ran to my window. I quickly passed her my canvas bag and then jumped out of the window. Standing beside her, she looked much bigger. She laughed as she kissed me, first hugging me, then pushing me away to have a better look at me, then hugging me again and laughing and talking at the same time . . .

'Jumping out of the window! Little menace! You travelled alone? How you've grown! You should have used the door, it's lucky you weren't caught by the guard!' At first I laughed with her, and then I suddenly grew afraid that she wouldn't stop. Her smile was as stiff as a narrow cart-track in the snow, and her eyes glittered like sun on ice. She pulled and pushed me while words poured out; she talked about everything at once, asking me questions but not giving me time to open my mouth, petting me like a baby. Finally she exclaimed, 'But you're bald! They've cut off your beautiful hair!'

44

That made me laugh. I told her I liked being bald.

'But why, silly?'

'Because it's the summer. Everybody's bald.'

'And they allowed it?' There was such anger in her voice that I didn't know what to say. 'Stupid village people!' she shouted at last. That calmed her down. I didn't understand why Grandfather and Elek and Samuel were stupid village people. I had never asked their opinion about my hairstyle.

She forgot the disaster straight away and went gurgling on like a brook; but from time to time her soft voice grew tense and high-pitched, piercing my head like a needle. I guessed, since she had sent for me, that she must be managing without my scoundrel of a father; but she told me she had to go back to her office very soon.

An enormous square opened up in front of me as we left the station. It was big enough for fifty marketplaces, and coming down the steps I felt as if I was falling; heat beat at us in waves. Three trams crossed the square without crashing into each other.

'Why didn't Dávid come to meet me?' I asked. 'He is back, isn't he?'

'Of course he is. He can't wait to see you.'

'Then why didn't he come?'

'I had to come straight from work . . . not from home.'

'Couldn't he have found the station on his own?' I asked.

Mother blushed. 'It would have been one extra tram-ticket. Two with the return.'

'My father doesn't give you money, does he?' I said, but there was no reply. 'Nothing at all?' I went on hesitantly.

'I haven't seen him for two years. He didn't even turn up to see Dávid.'

I felt dizzy. 'Is he living in Pest?' I asked. Maybe I was going to have to take the same train back again: the fare had been a waste of money.

'The last time he wrote was from Paris when he went there a year ago.' Mother sighed, almost in tears. 'He had the cheek to send a picture postcard! Now he's back, and carrying on with his debauchery here.'

'Debauchery' meant my father standing in his pigeon-grey shop-window suit in the middle of some pub for gentlemen. It's much bigger than Zafir's, but Father is tired of dancing and the gypsy violinists are dozing off. A plate lies broken on the floor, and an overturned golden goblet rests on the table . . .

45

'Is the tram very expensive?' I enquired.

'It all adds up.'

'My bag isn't heavy, let's walk home,' I suggested.

'The tram isn't that expensive,' laughed my mother, but she added that the journey would take over an hour on foot and she had to go back to work.

'Tell me,' I began. I must have sounded grave because Mother slowed down.

'What do you want me to tell you?' she asked warily.

I put my question very fast: if it was going to offend her I didn't want her to hear. 'Are we very poor?'

'No. We'll have enough to eat. We have a flat to ourselves, we're the official tenants. I've got a job! That's tremendous luck these days, and if they don't tighten up the Jewish laws it'll be confirmed next year.'

'Isn't your job confirmed yet?' I saw the train again. But Mother laughed.

'It's just a formality. I'm a good worker: the head of my office said so just the other day. I like working.'

We boarded a tram. I calmed down enough to wonder at the passers-by. I had forgotten that in Pest people don't look at each other, not even when they collide or take the seat next to each other on the tram. They pass each other like horses. Budapest people wear invisible blinkers.

'Do you have to work very hard?' I asked.

'Hard enough. And in the evenings I work for a fortune-teller.'

'For a gypsy woman?' I panicked. 'So that's why you're wearing that skirt!'

Mother looked down at her colourful gypsy skirt and began to shake with laughter. The tram was moving; she had to spread her arms out like wings so as not to lose her balance. Some of the other passengers laughed too, but Mother turned pale. People frightened her.

'I'm her secretary,' she whispered.

'In the street?' I was stupefied: I was thinking of the gypsy women who catch people's hands in the street.

'N-o-o-o,' Mother whispered, 'at her . . . flat. I answer the phone and write letters for her.'

'Can't gypsies read and write?'

'She's not a gypsy, don't you understand? She's well brought up, she's even done her matriculation. It's just that she has this special gift!'

46

While reassuring me, Mother was blushing in front of all the strangers. She asked me to speak quietly.

The houses scared me. A normal house, in a village, looks on to the street with two, or at most four or five eyes, but the great long rows of buildings in Budapest are built shoulder to shoulder with no spaces between them, like thousand-eyed monsters. In the country, one forgets that there are no houses in Pest: only streets.

We got off the tram. On one side of the wide road stood a church with a round green roof; the Catholic church at Oszu would have looked like a hut beside it.

'It must be too big even for God!' I commented. Mother laughed out loud as no one was watching us.

'Here we are,' she said, and pointed down the street. We turned in through a huge archway, a kind of tunnel where three grown-ups could have stood on each other's shoulders. It led down towards a large courtyard; on the far side a high brick wall faced us, growing taller with every step we took. At the end of the tunnel lemon-coloured walls appeared on either side of us, with balconies running along, one on top of the other, as if all the houses in a village had been stacked up like crates.

We came to a staircase of brown stone that went up as high as a tower, cool and dark in the middle of that burning summer. On the third floor we stepped out into the sun on to a dazzling, semi-circular balcony. To the left were a series of double doors, but we turned to the right where a number of single ones huddled together more closely. I felt as if I was walking in mid-air.

'Do many people crash over the side at night?'

'After a few days you won't be frightened,' Mother assured me.

'Yes I will!' I shouted. The height was making me drunk.

We went through one of the doors. A shaft of sunlight as wide as three sheaves of wheat poured through the window on to the floorboards, which were freshly sprinkled with cooling water. The room was swaying in the light like a boat in heavy seas, and only the floor, a three-door cupboard, and a few shadows kept the whole place from tipping over. While my eyes were still dazzled, Mother hurried back to work.

'You won't need boots here,' my brother said. He was unpacking my canvas bag. With his black hair and his yellowy brown skin, Dávid could have passed for a Japanese boy. His eyes sparkled with mischief, but his speech was thoughtful and slow, his gestures measured.

47

'Why not? No mud in Budapest? Nowhere? Never?'

'Never.' He laughed at my surprise.

'So every street's the High Street,' I laughed back.

'Budapest doesn't have one main street, it has hundreds.'

'Ours is one of them,' I said approvingly. 'We've got the biggest church in the whole world!'

'Saint Stephen's Basilica.'

'Church!' I said.

'A basilica is a big church!' he explained.

'Smart-arse! Just because you arrived here two weeks before me.'

'Also because I'm two years older.'

'I've seen dummies who were five years older.'

'I don't want to beat you up on the first day,' he said kindly.

'Same here, but I will if you say things like that. I suppose it never snows in Pest?'

'It does but they clean it away.'

'Do they? When it comes up to people's knees? Where do they put it? Into the lofts like wheat after the harvest?'

'They clear it into heaps,' answered Dávid hesitantly.

'Heaps? Don't you mean hills? And I suppose people just jump over them, do they?' I said triumphantly.

'I haven't been in Budapest in the winter for years,' he admitted, 'but if I remember rightly, they push the snow off to the side of the road and leave passages between the piles. Work it out! If ten centimetres of snow falls on a street ten metres wide, two heaps on each side of the road, each heap measuring one square metre at the base, will only need to be . . . half a metre high. There would be passages between them.'

'And what if it snows again next day? Do they come and make one-metre snowmen on top of your half-metre heaps?'

Dávid waved his hand, admitting he couldn't blind me with science, but I advanced through the gaps in his snow-heaps.

'When it snows, do you wait by the roadside in your shoes until they shovel it up? So your feet won't get wet?'

Dávid argued that ten centimetres of snow doesn't fall in one second flat as if it were a brick. But I had tasted blood and pushed on.

'And you need boots for other things too! Even in the summer if it isn't too hot!'

Dávid laughed at me. I had gone too far. 'And in winter one could walk barefoot if only it weren't too cold,' he scoffed.

48

'Don't be funny! Boots make your legs stronger!'

He looked at me as if I were an idiot and made me forget what I was going to say.

'Much stronger!' I shouted threateningly, ready to defend my reasoning with my fists. He gaped at me, but before attacking him I remembered my argument: 'For example, if they set a dog on you it can't bite your leg so well if you're wearing boots!'

He laughed, relieved that I was not as stupid as he had thought, and assured me that there were very few dogs in Pest. That just annoyed me even more. Then he added that the few people who did have dogs didn't set them on anyone, or even use them to guard their houses. And they weren't houses anyway, but flats. Only very rich people lived in houses, but that was in Buda, never in Pest, and the houses were called 'villas', and only people who had no children had dogs, except sometimes very rich children. And, and, and . . .

Dávid knew everything. I was just waiting for the right moment to hit him. He had a dog at his grandfather's, though he couldn't bring 'Chew' home because Mother's flat was too small. All the same, Dávid had had to come home because his grandfather had told him that he would have to go to Mother whenever she sent for him.

'You mean,' I remarked, interrupting his boasting, 'they don't set dogs on Jewish kids in Pest?'

'They don't set dogs on anyone. They only do that in the country.'

'So what do they get to attack us? Canaries?'

'Nothing,' answered Dávid with great superiority.

'Don't Christian boys throw stones at us?'

'There aren't any stones in town, silly! You can't break bits off the pavements!' Dávid was starting to lose patience with me.

'I see! You have to carry the stones in your pockets.' At last I understood.

Dávid huffed and puffed angrily without even answering me. I cross-examined him: 'What do they smash our windows with here? Chocolates?'

'They don't do that sort of thing here,' he said, lying like mad just to prove he was older and wiser. He was asking for trouble, there was no way the matter could be settled without a fight.

'So they don't persecute the Jews here?' I was giving him a last chance before hitting him on the chin. He started to back down, not surprisingly; the cissy was wearing a silk shirt and sandals like the doctor's son on Sunday.

'Of course they persecute us,' he said, sighing like a grown-up.

'How? What with?'

'With laws,' Dávid said. 'Grandpa says they're stopping us doing anything. A Jew can't be the director of a bank, or the manager of a factory or a big shop—'

'That's nothing,' I interrupted. 'I've heard that Jewish footballers aren't allowed to play in the First Division. Is that true?'

'That's another law, you see. Persecuting us with laws is worse than it sounds. Uncle Józska wasn't allowed to go to University because of the *numerus clausus*. They said they had too many Jews already.'

'I know that,' I nodded. 'But what do they do to us kids?'

He shook his head, worried.

'I don't know. We'll have to see.'

We agreed on this and made peace. After the discussion about boots he scrutinised the rest of my belongings less severely, but he was uncertain where to put them, and piled everything on to a large divan.

'Have you only got three books?' he asked gently.

'Four, including my prayer book,' I said vaguely, not knowing whether it counted as a book. After all, it was sacred, so I never read it unless I was forced to. It turned out that I had forgotten to pack it.

'Grandfather will be furious when he finds it,' I laughed. 'How many books have you got?'

'About thirty,' he sighed. 'And we'll have to share everything.' He shook his head at the unfairness of it. 'I get first choice.'

I was so delighted by this prospect of sharing everything that I forgot to protest. Dávid had bigger worries than where to put my things. Like where to put me.

'The chair-bed is yours. Almost new.' He pointed at it proudly. 'Mother said you were going to have it.' He opened it out. 'Funny, isn't it?'

Apart from the big divan and the chair-bed, there was nothing in the room to lie on. I smelt a rat. 'Where are you sleeping?'

'In the little room. Which we let. But I'm living in it.'

I didn't follow. 'Whose room is it, then?'

'Gyula's, but he doesn't live here,' he explained impatiently, as if he had already said it ten times.

'Who's Gyula?'

'The lodger!' Dávid shouted, irritated.

50

'Who doesn't live here?'

'Who doesn't live here! You've got it, finally!'

'Who *is* Gyula?' I insisted, confused by Dávid's reluctance to talk about him.

'You'll see,' said Dávid curtly. 'He'll be coming this evening.'

'So he does live here!' I cried.

Dávid took a deep breath. 'He comes for supper. Then he goes away again. Aunty Felice is coming to supper too; she's Mother's friend.' He took another big breath. 'She's very beautiful and very rich. She always brings chocolates.'

'Does she come every evening?' I asked, amazed.

'No. Maybe once a fortnight. But she always brings chocolates. Now they'll have to do for both of us. I hope she brings an even bigger box,' he brooded. 'Maybe two boxes . . .'

'Is she a lodger too?' I asked.

Dávid looked up at the ceiling. 'I just told you: she comes once every two weeks. She is not a lodger. You're a moron.'

'And the lodger doesn't live here. You see? You're the moron. Or does the lodger come every day?'

Dávid's anger suddenly left him. He became worried, hunting for words.

'Gyula is our friend,' he stammered, then blushed and looked defenceless. I guessed I had stumbled on a secret. This time I took a big breath to ask him a question but he looked at me in such a panic that I didn't dare. We stood there, feeling awkward.

'Who's the fortune-teller?'

'Big fat woman,' Dávid shrugged. 'Very dirty. Her clothes, her neck, her room. She lives in a lodging house. They clean up after her but she stays dirty all the same.'

'Mother says she passed her matriculation.'

'Maybe she did.' Again, Dávid shrugged his shoulders. 'It doesn't stop her being dirty. Don't tell Mother, but she – she stinks too. You can't go near her.'

'And Mother still works for her,' I said, shuddering. 'Dávid, tell me the truth: we're very poor, aren't we?'

'No,' he answered truthfully. 'I asked Mother. She said that if I'd seen the people she works for, I wouldn't ask that. They're really poor. We always have something to eat. Not like at my grandpa's, but something. Yesterday evening when I was asleep Mother baked cakes for tonight's supper. She hid them.'

'Then how do you know you didn't dream it?'

'Because I found them!' Dávid laughed. 'But I didn't tell Mother. And I didn't touch them either.'

'Neither will I! Where are they?'

'In the kitchen cupboard, covered with newspaper. You can look at them if you want, but don't forget: they're a surprise. Mother would be sad if we ate them. We need them for supper.'

'What for? Not if that woman brings chocolates.'

'She's called Aunt Felice. It's bad manners to eat the chocolates in front of her. Even to open the box.'

'Don't worry. I'll open it,' I assured him.

We went to the kitchen. Dávid showed me the two covered-up cakes, one walnut and one poppy-seed. Dávid preferred the walnut one, but I loved poppy-seeds so we were in luck.

'Pity you're such a goody-goody. We could have a nibble.' I clicked my tongue.

'I'm not a goody-goody! But it'd show.' Dávid swallowed, then added, 'Don't forget to be surprised when we see them at suppertime. I shouldn't have shown them to you, you won't be able to look surprised.'

'Me?' I laughed. 'When my grandfather told me off because he heard that I'd eaten bacon, I asked him what bacon was!'

I was still fiddling around the cakes, looking at an old newspaper.

' "The victorious Germans have stormed the fortress city of Dunkirchen." Tell me, Dávid, since you speak English . . .'

'I'm only learning,' he warned, then added sheepishly, 'I was only learning.'

'Tell me all the same, why do the English put up with it? Why didn't they march straight into Berlin and hang Hitler at the beginning?'

'The French betrayed them.'

'Yes,' I agreed. 'The French are cowards. Have you learned how to say "Hitler can rot" yet?'

Suddenly he remembered me asking him that the year before. He clenched his teeth and closed his eyes. He was trying to think. I watched him, mesmerised; great magical things might depend on his answer.

'I know how to say . . . "Die"!'

' "Rot!" '

'I only know . . . "Die",' he stammered.

'That's chickenfeed.' I sat down, disappointed. I also forgot about the cakes, which Dávid hurriedly put back in their hiding place.

'I only had two lessons a week and none in the holidays, so I kept forgetting everything,' he confessed.

'How long's the war going to last?' I asked.

This time he didn't have to think. 'Might last a whole year,' he said. 'But we'll win in the end.'

'I know *that*,' I said contemptuously. I wasn't going to let him get away with not knowing the most important words in English. Of course, I couldn't even ask for a glass of water in Hebrew, but on the other hand I could say 'The *Torah* is great because it gives life to its followers'; I even knew that it was Esther who had said it. To Achashverus.

Dávid looked so downcast that I decided to cheer him up. 'And then she'll be able to drop the fortune-teller!' I told him.

'When?'

'When we win the war! How much is Mother's pay?'

'Eighty pengős a month. She's a "temporary white-collar relief worker" at the Town Hall,' he quoted. 'That's the lowest pay-scale, but it's very difficult for a Jew to find a job at all when they're being sacked all over the place. Specially at the Town Hall!'

'After the war they'll promote all the Jews,' I assured him. 'They'll double their wages at least.'

'Who will?' Dávid asked, once again challenging everything I said. I had to think fast.

'The people whose job it'll be to put everything right again.'

I was sure that once upon a time everything had been fair; just as all the fairy stories had really happened. On another planet.

This time Dávid basically agreed with me. 'What's for certain is that Grandpa will be able to kick out his *goy* puppet and trade under his own name again. Puppets are only interested in lining their own pockets,' he said, quoting his grandfather.

Meanwhile I was measuring up the flat. I didn't give a damn about his grandpa's business.

'Eighty pengős?' I asked, not wanting to be side-tracked. 'A labourer's pay for working in a vineyard is one pengő fifty a day. I know that because Grandfather always complains it's too much. A woman gets paid one pengő, and children get seventy fillérs – which is how much the grower charges for one litre of wine. The labourers are all dressed in rags, even on Sundays, so they don't go to church because people would see they didn't have any Sunday clothes. The stupid old priest says they're Godless. How much does being tenants cost?'

'You mean how much is the rent, silly. Sixty pengös a month.'

'How much?' I gasped. 'Out of eighty?'

'Yes,' he nodded gravely. 'That's why we need the lodger.' His face tightened. We both fell silent, avoiding each other's eyes.

'We'll manage for one year,' Dávid sighed. I understood: he meant until the end of the war.

Our big room was six metres by six; Dávid's 'lodger's' room was half that, and so was the kitchen. The big room had a set of polished wooden furniture and a coal-burning stove, which was obviously too small for the room.

'Town furniture is beautiful,' I said admiringly. 'Is it ours or does it come with the flat?'

'It's ours,' Dávid said heavily. 'It was in the flat and they made Mother buy it. On credit. A thousand pengös.'

I was staggered. I had to sit down. The flat vanished and I saw myself sitting on the train on my way back to Grandfather. Dávid walked up to me and put his hand on my shoulder for a second, then without a word he sat down too. Minutes passed; eventually he muttered something about having ten years to pay for the furniture if necessary.

'Doesn't Father give anything to Mother?' I asked finally, feeling like somebody turning out his pockets for the third time to look for a lost marble.

Dávid, almost bored, shook his head. But I must have looked miserable because he made an effort to cheer me up: 'Mother earns about an extra forty pengös at the fortune-teller's; and when we can we write addresses on envelopes to make a bit of extra cash.'

We sat at the table, breathing deeply. From time to time Dávid cleared his throat as if he had thought of something worth saying, but then kept quiet as though he was checking his idea over. I spoke first, slowly and carefully so that I could see from his face whether or not my idea was any good.

'If we sold this beautiful town furniture . . .' I started. He seemed taken aback by something but said nothing, so I went on: '. . . and bought village furniture instead . . . get the idea? We'd make a lot of money.'

'Town? Village? "Modern" and "antique" is what you're trying to say,' said Dávid irritably.

54

'No, it's not. How do you know what I'm trying to say? I don't even know what "modern" means . . . "Modern weapons, modern tanks . . ." I think it means "new". But I haven't got a clue what "antique" means.'

' "Old," ' he explained more patiently, swallowing his irritation. 'You're trying to say that we could keep the difference. But it doesn't work, because old furniture costs much more than new, see?'

'You're a cretin. I suppose worn shoes are more expensive than new ones, are they?'

'No, but worn furniture is!' Dávid didn't only raise his voice; his fist came up: he was obviously planning to hammer his words into my head. 'Grandpa has four antique armchairs that are worth more than a small house!'

'Stuff your grandpa. If he's so rich why doesn't he help us out! Why doesn't he give us a couple of chairs? He used to have seven houses!' I fumed.

'He did, but he lost six of them.'

'At cards!' I shouted. 'It's his fault Father is such a bad man!'

I was waving my arms and jumping about, but Dávid sat still and talked quietly; he was almost ten.

'Grandpa is a good man,' he declared firmly. 'He has a lot of expenses. Aunt Luci has come to live in Budapest. She's taken it into her head to become a concert pianist instead of "a little provincial piano teacher". Now, of all times, when all the Jewish lawyers and journalists and actors are being thrown out. And Grandfather's puppet manager . . .'

'What's that?'

'I already told you: a man who rents his name out to a Jew so the Jew can do business. He steals like a magpie. Anyway, why doesn't your grandfather help us out? Mother's his daughter after all, and his vineyards are still in his name.'

I had been thinking about this. There were four hundred and thirty hectolitres of wine sitting in that cellar. Famous old wines, the best 'Tokaj': Oszu. Yet, without thinking, I gave the same answer Grandfather always gave when Elek and Samuel were trying to get him to spend money: '1927 didn't produce enough to fill a bottle. The hailstones ruined it.'

'This is 1940!' cried Dávid, swooping down on my hidden thoughts. 'How much wine has he got in his cellar?'

55

'Four hundred and thirty hectos,' I admitted. 'That's what I've heard, anyway,' I added.

'How much is a litre worth?' he demanded, keeping up the siege. 'You just said it cost seventy fillérs at the grower's. But that's for the new wine. The old stuff is more expensive. You see: it's not just antique furniture that's dearer, it's the same with antique wine!'

'Old wine isn't antique, it's vintage,' I said with great superiority.

But Dávid shut his eyes and made signs for me to keep quiet. I saw that he was counting: he was frowning, and fidgeting with his fingers. Then he announced his verdict: 'Thirty-two thousand two hundred and fifty pengős! That's at seventy fillérs a litre. But there are some old wines that sell for five pengős a bottle.'

'My grandfather is a good man too!' I shouted, thinking to myself that Dávid's wasn't.

He decided to make peace. 'Your grandfather wants Mother to go back to him,' he said, adding apologetically, 'That's what my grandpa wants too. He thinks she should go back to her father.'

'But why?' I demanded.

Dávid shook his head. 'That I don't know.'

Tired of the discussion, I calmed down and left the room so as to stop Dávid carrying on. I also wanted to investigate the smaller room and the kitchen.

At first glance there was nothing worth looking at. Yet the rooms were like two magic boxes where tomorrow lay sleeping. The kitchen led out on to the balcony. There was a table with square stools round it, a stove for cooking, and in one corner a shower, separated from the rest of the room by a curtain. All the flimsier pieces of furniture had been assembled in the little room, and its window overlooked the balcony like the two in the main room. When I went back and sat down on the divan, Dávid didn't even look up from his book. The whole flat was floating weightlessly in the afternoon sunlight; the freshly scrubbed floor smelt like trees in the rain; and the air was sparkling. Even with my eyes closed, I saw light.

'He's woken up,' I heard some man say. Dávid was sitting sleepily at the end of the table, near my head. On his right a black-haired woman sat with her back to me: she must be Aunty Felice of the chocolates. On her right, beside my mother, was a red-haired man. He stood up very straight with his hand resting on his belt and his shirt-sleeves rolled up, although he was wearing a tie. The four of them seemed to vibrate in the lamplight reflected

56

from the polished wooden furniture as if they were about to float up to the ceiling.

'. . . because, ma'am,' the man was saying, 'I bet Józska Herz, a Jewish friend of mine, two hundred pengös that we would lose the war.' This remark would have set bells ringing in my head if I'd been properly awake . . . The man with the red hair and the stubborn chin – he's backing the English when his Jewish friend is betting on the Germans! This Christian's OK – everybody who isn't a complete moron knows Germany and Hungary are going to lose the war hands down, but his Jewish friend? 'No one's thicker than a thick Jew,' that's what they say . . .

'We're not at war with anybody, surely!' said Aunty Felice.

I vaguely remembered that when they wanted their prayers answered, Christians offered candles to a saint called Anthony. I wondered why this Jew hadn't given his two hundred pengös to the *Torah*.

'We haven't stayed out of a lost war since King Mátyás. In the newspapers they're already advertising bomb-proof air-raid shelters,' the man went on.

'We might still avoid it,' said Aunty Felice.

'Up you get, Józska! Come and introduce yourself!' said the man.

I stumbled off the bed and faltered towards the light.

'Not so fast! Put your shorts on!' the man laughed at me.

I had fallen asleep in my clothes. Mother must have undressed me, leaving me in just my shirt and pants, and covered me with a blanket.

He knows my name and yet he wants me to introduce myself! To him, when he's the lodger who's not living here anyway, and to this strange rich woman just because she brings chocolate! Where did Mother put my shorts? Why doesn't she give them to me? She's sitting all pale and still, as if she's scared of them . . .

Finally I found my shorts; I turned away and put them on.

'Introduce yourself!' The lodger sounded friendly.

Shining eyes as black as beetles were suddenly turned towards me. Her gaze spilled like a shadow out of her eyes, veiling her pale face.

'You're beautiful, Aunty Felice!' I announced.

The man hooted with laughter: ' "Drunks and children tell the truth." '

My mother laughed briefly; it sounded like the tinkle of broken glass.

Aunty Felice seemed not to hear any of this.

'Did you arrive today?' she asked quietly, re-establishing some order. 'Did you have a good journey?' I didn't understand how I could have had a bad journey. The train had stayed on the rails, hadn't it?

'Of course you did, you were coming home,' she said, answering for me.

'Aunty Felice, why do you talk so quietly? Is it because you're sad?' I asked. My mother's head jerked. Dávid winced.

'Aunty Felice doesn't look sad!' rumbled the man like a drum. But Aunty Felice didn't seem to hear.

'Do I look sad?' she asked me with a slight smile.

'No . . .' I stammered.

'Do I make you feel sad?' she asked.

I shook my head.

'Then how could I be sad?' she went on. 'If someone laughs, you laugh with him, and if he cries, you feel like crying, don't you?'

'I'll have to think about it,' I said.

'Aunty Felice is not sad!' the man butted in again. 'I told you so, and she told you so too.'

She was waiting. I knew she would wait for hours. I shut my eyes tight, searching for what I wanted to say.

'Wood gets burnt up keeping people warm,' I said, opening my eyes.

Her gaze lit up for a second, like a match in the dark. In a light voice she said, 'We'll be great friends, if you like.'

The following morning, after Mother had gone to work, there was a tap on the kitchen door. It opened a little and a lanky boy of twelve or thirteen put his head round: 'Are you busy?'

The door opened wider and a platoon of kids sneaked in. The long thin one waited until the movement had settled, then he came in too and perched on the kitchen dresser. He was the eldest, and the leader of the group. Before I knew where I was they had all sat down, and like a polite host I was left with a low stool.

'This is my little brother,' Dávid introduced me.

'I know. I know your name too. I am sure you've heard of me. My father is the caretaker. I am a goalkeeper.'

'Me too.' My answer came back at him like a gunshot.

'Who do you keep goal for?' he asked.

'Who? Whoever. Why, who do you play for?'

'Me? The Ferencváros.' With that he pulled a cigarette out of

58

his shirt pocket. It seemed he only kept one cigarette there at a time. But he had to ask for a match.

'For the Ferencváros? You?' I asked disbelievingly.

'Not in the big team, dummy. Pálinkás is their goalie.'

'I suppose there's a little team too, is there?' I asked, sarcastic and surprised at the same time.

'Of course there is! Two junior teams and two cub teams with two players for each position.'

'So are you the goalie for the Ferencváros Cubs?' I asked admiringly. A few years before, Ferencváros had beaten the world champions, Uruguay, three-nil. My respect for the boy's greatness made him even more friendly.

'I am. There are two old bunglers as well as me. They play in the matches, but one's going up to the junior team this year, and next year the other one goes up too. Then the world will see who Laci Mester is! I'm twice as good as them already! You'll see. When they've finished beating carpets in the courtyard we'll go down and play. We use the carpet-beating frame for a goal, but I hate it when the women are hopping about the place doing the carpets while I'm trying to play football! Where have you played up to now?'

'Wherever they were playing football,' I answered wisely.

'Where are you from?'

'From the country,' Dávid pleaded on my behalf.

'There are some excellent provincial teams,' Laci conceded magnanimously. 'Have you ever played on a real football pitch?'

'Of course. Behind the station, when the village team or the bigger boys didn't want it.'

Laci nodded. 'But have you ever stood in a real goal? Seven metres wide, and two metres ten high?'

'Yes, but then we used to make it into an ordinary goal by marking out posts with our shirts and shoes . . .'

'Shoes?' Laci Mester stared. 'You actually had football boots?'

'Football boots?' I laughed out loud. 'Mostly we just took our shoes off for football. Don't you do that here?'

'We all play in football boots,' he said and, seeing the effect of his words, added, 'even for training.'

Also present were Pöci and his toddler brother, Kaci. Pöci reported that he was no football player, but nobody in the world could piss as high as he could. He offered to lay a bet that he could piss over my head, and when I turned it down, he shrugged his shoulders,

59

saying his little brother was no good. Anyone could piss over him . . .

Géza Gyak from the first floor was the son of an amateur weight-lifter. The assistant caretaker's son from the ground floor, Pista Rácz, was my age. He kept his mouth permanently shut, and looked like a dumb statue, but his saving grace was Laci's guarantee that when Rácz did open his mouth it would be to swear, and no trooper could compete with him.

Laci fed us with gossip about all the other tenants, most of which was very boring, like who came home late, and how sober they were at the time, and who they were with, and how mean or generous they were when they gave Laci's father a tip for opening the gate. Laci also told us about the people who wanted to ban football from the courtyard. Our chief enemy was a snobby lady from the posh side of our floor who never came out on to the balcony without her jewels and who even dyed her hair silver! She was the proud mother of a famous soprano. When we bothered to greet her, she merely sniffed. While she quite appreciated that children who were growing up in the gutter and possessed relatively few toys had a certain right to amuse themselves, it was her considered opinion that it would be more advantageous to all concerned if the said children played football for a definite and regular half hour a day, reserving the rest of their time for their homework, and thus opening a wider gateway to life than that provided by two goalposts.

The manager of the building, who had two big flats knocked into one on the second floor, was against football. Luckily, as we all knew, he had a strictly guarded secret known only to Laci's mother, which was that he actually owned the whole building. He was afraid that if the tenants knew this they'd pester him mercilessly about their rent arrears. So the manager had to keep in with Laci's mother, and it was she who tackled him for us, in her permanently hoarse voice which regular doses of apricot brandy seemed unable to cure.

'I'm always after them with my broomstick,' she declared, 'but these days the little brats have no respect . . .' She also explained to him that it was impossible to ban football because it had already been banned for years.

The owner's daughter, Marika, was a little angel, the perfect schoolgirl. The silver-haired lady told the rest of us to model ourselves on her. When Laci Mester became goalkeeper for Hungary he was going to marry Marika. I couldn't understand why. I saw her one day looking out of her window, and she was fat and ugly even for an angel. Laci, a goalie, deserved better.

We went down to the courtyard to play one-goal football, and Laci let me be the goalie. We played with a tennis ball – which is harder to stop than a flea – but I was doing all right.

'You jump well, very well,' Laci commented. 'But you've got no technique.' He took my place in front of the carpet-beating frame and we threw balls at him. He was very good, although he showed off non-stop. He showed me how to wait for the ball with fingers spread wide, and how to biff it away with my fist, something I'd never seen before.

All the kids who played football in the courtyard lived on the single-door side of the balcony. Laci was from the ground floor, as was Pista Rácz, the swearing champion. Apart from being thick as two short planks, Pista might as well have been blind too, because he missed the ball all the time and we had to watch out for his foot instead. We had been playing together for several days when he asked me, 'Why are you a Jew?' He lifted up his chin as he said this, while his face went rigid and he looked straight ahead like a soldier.

Laci prodded him on the nose with his finger, saying to me: 'Don't answer him. The poor kid can't help it, he's daft.'

I nodded.

Laci sat on the lower bar of the carpet-beating frame. 'I've got nothing against good, hard-working, poor Jews,' he said generously. 'They're like us even if they are Jewish.' Laci was thick too, but good-natured.

'Who are you against, then?' I asked.

'The blood-sucking bankers and the plutocrats.'

'What are plutocrats?'

'Jews who suck the blood of the people.'

'What's their job?'

'They're plutocrats!' Faced with my obtuseness, Laci was getting jumpy.

'But what do they do for a living?' I insisted.

'I keep telling you! They suck blood!' he yelled.

In short, he didn't know either.

'How many of them have you met?' I asked.

'I haven't. They don't meet ordinary people, let alone children . . .'

'Who met them, then?'

'My father.' He looked at me severely.

His father was a little shrimp of a man, run off his feet by his fat wife. She only spoke to him in words of one syllable: 'Come here! Out of my way!' as if he were a dog. When I came round, the father would scrutinise me silently, but the mother used to smile at me because I was her son's friend. Sometimes, to show her friendship, she'd send me on errands.

'They say you're a fast runner, Józska. I don't know where my rascal of a son has got to – will you throw this letter in the box for me? And if you must kick your shoes to death, then at least give them a clean! Your mother works hard for you!'

I just shrugged. As I kept telling my mother, she was lucky she had a goalie for a son and not a centre-forward.

Pöci, our next-door-neighbour-but-one, had a tailor for a father, but he was always badly dressed. His mother spent half the day screaming at her children outside, and the other half yelling at her husband inside. He seemed to have few customers, and shabby-looking men at that. I found out that he was something called a 'patching tailor'. His wife often went out at night and came home late and drunk.

The rest of the team was made up of other kids from the area, but only on a temporary basis. We had one spectator (not counting the grown-ups, who used to rush out on to the surrounding balconies at the slightest noise and raise a far louder rumpus than we ever did). This loyal spectator was a little boy of six, who apart from the angelically ugly Marika was the only child living on the double-door side of the building. During the day he was looked after by his grandparents. He wasn't allowed to go out on the street alone, and had to be taken out by a maid. He used to turn his head away from us as he went past, either because his family was better off than ours or perhaps because he was frightened we'd start pushing him around the way we pushed each other. When he was confined to barracks he used to hang over the balcony railings gawping at us. From time to time we'd do exaggerated imitations of his grandparents: 'Pali! Don't hang over the balcony, your nose might drop off!' we'd squawk. 'Go indoors, Pali, before the sun strikes you dead!'

He didn't dare answer us back, but he showed great courage in defying his grandparents: 'The Captain is sitting outside,' he used to say, 'so why can't I?'

He was referring to a retired army captain, who sat in his uniform outside his double door for hours on end, an officer's hat on his head and medals on his chest. Beside him on a stool were his newspapers, his bottle, and his glass; and leaning against the wall was his silver-handled walking-stick. He was lame. We decided that he had been wounded heroically in the First World War and was forced to retire and take fresh air sitting down.

Laci Mester occasionally played with me alone. He was the coach and I was the player.

'You could turn into a great goalie too,' he stated after a few of these sessions. 'You chuck yourself down on the cobbles as if they were grass! Doesn't it hurt?'

'Not at all!' I lied, and laughed.

'Pity you're a Jew! What a waste!'

'Jew-baiting again?' I refrained from raising my fists, as I didn't want to get myself beaten up.

'I said it's a pity! Are you deaf?'

'That's Jew-baiting too. Why is it a pity?'

'Because Jews can't play in the First Division, and anything else isn't worth the bother.'

I laughed. 'You're silly! By the time we're old enough to play for Hungary, there'll be six Jews and five Christians in the team!'

'Józska in Wonderland! You know there aren't many good Jewish players. They're soft! They sit all day behind their counters—'

'Am I soft?' I crossed my arms.

'No,' he shrugged, 'you're not. You're just unlucky.'

One evening, Mother took me with her to the fortune-teller, who rented two adjoining rooms in a boarding house. The smaller of the two served as a waiting room. When we arrived, Mother sat down straight away on a rickety chair behind a rickety table and put a block of paper and a pen in front of her. A cumbersome sideboard hid a third of the window, probably to stop anyone opening it. It hadn't been opened for a hundred years judging by the air, which was as stale as the inside of a long-emptied barrel.

'Where's the cat?' I asked, taking it for granted that the fortune-teller had one.

'There isn't a cat,' Mother answered. 'It's witches who have cats, not fortune-tellers.'

The fortune-teller rolled out through the open door of the big room. Her uncombed hair seemed to have been cut out of an oily rag. It hung down to her dirty, crumpled dress. She was like an old fat cat herself.

'They've given me cold toast with my tea!' she whined. 'Julia, call in Schönfeld, I'm going to sort him out!'

'You'll only make him furious,' said my mother calmly, 'asking for breakfast at seven o'clock in the evening again—'

'Let him be furious! I'd like to see that! All my precious money goes on renting this stable! I only stay because I used to live here with my darling! Schönfeld can say what he likes! If I curse him his beastly dump will be burned to the ground!'

I was less clear than ever about the difference between fortune-tellers and witches.

Suddenly she crossed herself. Mother tried to calm her: 'If it gets burnt down, where are you going to live? Your mother's spirit likes coming here.'

'My darling will follow me anywhere,' the fortune-teller mewed in a trembling, trance-like voice; but a second later she had got back into her stride: 'I'll have breakfast when I feel like it! I suppose he's been telling you that I live like an owl again?'

'He hasn't said that in the last few days . . .' Mother stammered, as if it were she who had been accused.

'The owl is a sacred animal!' The fortune-teller opened her eyes wide. 'Julia! Make them send me fresh toast from the kitchen!'

The owner of the boarding house was dead right. The fortune-teller was an owl, not a cat.

'Let me see you.' She turned towards me. 'The child is very pretty,' she told my mother, full of kindness.

'I'm not pretty!' I snapped at her angrily.

'You're right, Julia, he's a menace! What will you be when you grow up, child?'

'How should I know? I'm not a fortune-teller!' I yelped. Of course I knew perfectly well that I was going to be a goalie.

To my surprise the woman wasn't offended. She laughed: 'All right, all right! I was expecting you. Aunty Felice told me you were a nice boy, so I bought some special chocolates for you.'

'I don't like chocolates,' I declared bravely, but luckily the fortune-teller didn't take me seriously.

'Where did I put them?' She couldn't find them. 'Schönfeld's cleaning woman must have stolen them. She doesn't clean, she just leaves the place filthy and eats my chocolates!'

She gave me a pengö to buy chocolates, but for a pengö I could buy a rubber ball three times the size of a tennis ball – and it would be so

64

much easier to catch! It would push my value up a hundred pengös in Laci Mester's eyes.

The fortune-hunters began to arrive. An old man turned up; I thought he must want to find out when he was going to die, but while he was in the fortune-teller's room Mother told me that he was trying to find a cure for his son, who wanted to marry a poor girl. Later a dyed blonde came to ask whether her boyfriend would marry her. I was bored stiff, and dozed off.

When I came to, the fortune-teller was quarrelling with my mother: 'Why don't you get married to your policeman?' she demanded, referring to Gyula, who had been in the military police until he was pensioned off because of his varicose veins.

'It'd break my father's heart. He'd rend his clothes as if I were dead,' my mother answered quietly, sniffing.

'Then throw him out and marry a decent, well-off Jew!'

'Where can I find one?' Mother laughed nervously.

'Where? Wasn't the chemist from Csaba good enough for you?'

'No, and neither was Csaba! Who wants to live out in the sticks?'

'I shall find someone suitable,' the fortune-teller assured my mother in a voice loud with irritation.

'Someone who will love my children?' Mother was tearful. 'Even their beast of a father doesn't care about them.'

'You're an idiot, Julia.' The fortune-teller's voice softened. 'Why do I bother with you? You're still waiting for that beast to come back to you!'

Then they started talking about boring things and I fell asleep again. When I woke up, the fortune-teller was standing beside the sofa looking down at me, and she told me that I should join the scouts. She said she knew the scoutmaster of the best pack. She would tell him about Dávid and me, but in the meantime I must be good, and I mustn't play football with working-class oiks and grubby street urchins. The scouts went on adventures in the forests, and camped beside Lake Balaton, and were woken every morning by the sound of trumpets as if they were real soldiers . . .

But I had other ideas. I turned to my mother. 'So will you throw Gyula out?' I asked.

3: Dark Doors

Sombre double doors opened into the school like the covers of a giant's prayer book. Above them, a black wooden arch made me feel I was walking between the Tablets of the Law.

The archway led into a vast hall, most of which was taken up by a flight of stairs. Daylight filtered through dirty windows, and the shadows cast by the neighbouring houses fell in a heap with the shadows of the clouds onto the brown stone floor. Long passages started at the top of the thirty steps, lined with the heavy doors that opened into the classrooms. This was the neologian primary school of the Budapest Synagogue: the orthodox school must surely have been built in iron, its windows glowing with embers.

I pulled down a door handle that was level with my nose. Shouts were breaking through a general din, and screams could be heard above the shouts; five boys were jumping on the benches, two pairs of kids were thumping each other; about ten had plaits, and almost all of them were wearing dark jackets. There was no doubt about it: this was a *heder*.

The middle benches were empty, with enough room for two on each. The front row was full, and so was the back where all the dummies were hiding. I could have faced a pack of wolves, but the few glances thrown in my direction passed over me indifferently.

A pin-headed child was screaming the same words over and over again, his features blurred with the pain of trying to attract the attention of the other noisy kids: 'Bilicsi was the funniest! Bilicsi was the funniest!' The kid was clearly a half-wit.

Another was spinning round on the top of a bench, beating the air with his arms and making an impossible noise with his nose. I guessed he must be imitating someone. 'Have you seen my hat?' he kept snorting.

Four boys were sitting on the teacher's desk like some kind of jury sitting in judgment over the others' games, but their dignity was being undermined by a fifth boy jumping madly about on the desk behind them.

They were all showing off which films they had seen during the holidays.

'Did you see— ? Have you seen— ?' they yelled, competing for the glittering prize of having seen the newest film in the most expensive cinema.

Bravely, I sat down in the middle of the empty benches. At once, without even asking who I was, several boys shouted, 'That's Aaron Kohn's place!'

I knew that if I accepted the rule of 'first come first served', I'd always be the new boy, licking their boots until the leather wore out . . .

'I've got to stand up for myself,' I thought. 'If I beat up a couple of them, or pull off a few plaits, I'll be respected . . .'

'Aaron Kohn can jump in the Tisza.' The words were on my tongue but I swallowed them just in time. 'The Tisza flows through Tokaj,' I thought. 'They'll laugh at me for being a country boy. "He can jump into the Danube" must be what they say here but it sounds silly, and in any case it's not nearly rude enough . . .'

'It's Aaron Kohn's place!' They're trying to get me to move, and if I put on a friendly face they'll think I'm a cissy and I won't just have to lick their boots; they'll start asking me what films I've seen, and I haven't seen any. I know there's a famous actor called Latabár, even country boys know that, but I've only seen him on posters and if he passed me in the street I wouldn't recognise him, not without his straw hat anyway. I once saw *The Frozen Child* but it made me cry because I was little then, and if I say I've seen that they're bound to think I'm wet. But I have seen *The Heroic Defenders of Alcazar*! That's nothing to be ashamed of – it was about a lot of wild Spaniards fighting . . . but all the same, if they cross-examine me about new films they'll have a field-day . . .

I slid sideways along the bench, yawning casually.

'That's my place!' yelled a kid as long and thin as an unrolled tape-measure, interrupting his clowning. The others were arguing, everyone wanted to sit next to this Aaron Kohn. I stood up. I laughed loudly.

'You can eat your Aaron Kohn. With ketchup!' I announced, and sat down on an empty bench at the side of the room. I looked at the grey sad day outside the window.

There was a general move towards the door. The crowd hid whoever was coming in, so it couldn't be the teacher. They opened ranks for him to pass through, and I saw a curly, golden-haired boy who slipped his satchel off his back and listened to the others with a smile. They besieged him: 'Have you seen Latabár?'

The boy nodded.

'What about Bilicsi?'

He nodded again. Making his way towards the benches through the double line of boys, he sat down where I had been sitting. So this was Aaron Kohn. The other kids scrambled for the place beside him, almost pushing the golden boy off his seat.

What did they see in this boy? He certainly wasn't the strongest – he was the same size as me, but quiet, and smiling. Gentle. I could've beaten him up with one hand.

The teacher was called Ödön Berger. Ödön was a round, silly-sounding name; he ought to have been a small, fattish, friendly man; but the man coming through the door was big, with a large rectangular body and a heavy square stuck on top for a head. The doorway must have been built to fit him. With each step he tilted dangerously as if he were going to break in half. He was carrying two big parcels tied up with string and a huge briefcase.

Some creeps were shouting 'Hurrah' so that they wouldn't have to shut up and stop fooling about. The Tape-Measure, who had managed to keep his place next to Aaron Kohn, tried to include the teacher in the fun and games.

'Sir, have you seen Latabár's new film?' He started snorting: 'Where have I put my hat?'

'Silence!' bellowed the teacher.

He went to the platform, took a blue coat out of his briefcase and put it on. His shoulders were broad, but his back was slightly bent and you could see that he was weak. Even speaking was an effort for him. His face matched his blue coat. He fumbled with his papers and then started the roll-call, making marks with his pencil and giving each boy a glance. But when he came to Aaron Kohn he asked him if he'd had a pleasant holiday.

'Yes,' said Kohn.

The teacher nodded. 'Very glad to hear it.' He smiled. 'How are your parents?'

'Fine,' said Kohn shortly. Perhaps he was ashamed of being singled out.

'Delighted to hear it,' said the teacher. He was genuinely glad, delighted even. What was going on? Who was this Aaron Kohn?

'Schwartz?'

'Here.'

'Weiner?'

'Here.'

He had left me out.

He was looking at me. 'What's your name?'

Couldn't he figure that out from the register?

'József Sondor.'

'József Sondor?' he asked.

I didn't answer. He repeated the question.

'Sondor, that's right, sir. Not Sándor.'

'Sondor, not Sándor,' he repeated, amused. 'Not Jakobovics either?'

My heart thumped. 'No,' I answered coldly. 'That's what they used to call my grandfather.'

The teacher thought this funny. 'They don't call him that any more?'

'No. He changed his name.'

'Why?' asked the teacher brightly, and the whole class flattered him with laughter. Almost everybody had a Jewish name.

I'd put the ginger Rabbi in his place. I'll sort this one out too . . .

'So he could join the club. They told him that Kohns and Jakobovicses weren't allowed.'

'Why was the club so important to your grandfather?' the teacher asked, stupefied.

I answered him straight: 'For gambling.' My heart was like a hammer, but I was going to talk tough to this man. Till the day he died.

'Why didn't he change his name to Jákob . . .?' he wondered. 'That's both Hungarian and Jewish.'

'My father talked him into calling himself Sondor. It's a better pen name.'

'Is your father Ádám Sondor?'

'He is,' I answered proudly. The teacher knew my father's name! He calmed down.

'I didn't know Ádám Sondor was Jewish,' he remarked. 'Could

69

you ask your father to see the Headmaster?' he went on politely. 'Your papers are incomplete.'

'I can't,' I replied.

He looked at me enquiringly and I spat it out, 'I don't know where he lives.'

The whole class was in fits of giggles. The walls shook. Berger, the teacher, was looking at me with worried eyes. Could he see that mine were burning with shame? My teeth were chattering, but I felt like sinking them into his throat . . .

'What's your mother's name?' he asked carefully, almost backing away. 'Her maiden name?'

'Julia Salamon,' I answered. 'Is that Jewish enough for you?'

The teacher nodded benevolently, but then closed his eyes to think. 'Salamon . . .' He savoured the name. 'Was her father always called Salamon?' he asked carefully, almost apologetically. I understood: it's easier to turn Salamon into Sondor than Jakobovics. The greasy little *heder* kids smelt something nasty, and a snigger went round the room. Julia sounded too Hungarian to go with Salamon. Hannah, my grandmother's name, would have been more natural. But Julia was her name. It was a beautiful name. Even if her real name was Judith it was none of the teacher's business. But the teacher must have been suspicious, he was still talking in his sarcastic voice for the greater glory of the synagogue: 'Is your Salamon grandfather a member of the club too, by any chance?'

The class hooted with laughter. The fun and games were continuing after all, with a vengeance in fact, masterminded by the teacher! My knees trembled. I knew that I ought to walk out. But I wouldn't be able to tell Mother why . . .

I pulled myself together.

'No, he isn't.' My voice was steady, though the laughter swelled around me like a red and yellow wave, and a dark shadow covered everything, the boys, the benches, the blackboard, the walls. My neck and chin tightened but, luckily, words came out of my mouth, and my voice surprised me, stronger, more grown-up than usual: 'Six wild horses couldn't drag him out of *shul*. That's where he spends his whole life, bowing and scraping till the cows come home.'

The laughter stopped. The teacher took such a deep breath he nearly fell over. I collapsed on to the bench, empty. For a while I saw only the grey air swaying around me.

I came to in a great silence. The teacher was standing in front of me, and everyone was staring at me.

'Sixty-four!' sang out Tape-Measure from Aaron Kohn's bench.

'Didn't you know that?' the teacher asks. 'How many did you learn to count up to at your last school? Where was it?'

'In the country,' I answered.

The teacher sighed. 'That's why you don't know. It's not your fault.'

'What don't I know? What makes sixty-four?'

'Tell us if you know,' the teacher urged.

I shrugged. 'Lots of things make sixty-four.'

The idiots started giggling again.

'What things?' the teacher insisted.

'Sixty plus four, for a start.'

The class applauded.

I had hardly set foot in the classroom and they had already appointed me Form Fool. I decided to beat someone up in the first break. Probably the Tape-Measure. He was tall but weedy.

'What else?' the teacher asked.

'I'm going to beat up Aaron Kohn,' I announced.

The teacher was horrified. 'Why do you want to beat up Aaron Kohn?'

I must have been thinking out loud! Still, there was no going back . . .

'Because everybody licks his boots. "I am glad. I am delighted," ' I smiled greasily, mimicking Berger.

His eyes went muddy. 'I promise you, Sondor: in my class you are going to behave,' he said.

'The others must behave too.'

'I think we can agree on that.' He acknowledged my restraint. 'So what else is sixty-four?' he asked.

I sighed with boredom, figures flashing through my head. 'Twice thirty-two, half one hundred and twenty-eight, three times twenty-one with one over . . .'

'And eight times eight,' shouted the creepy Tape-Measure.

'Any idiot knows that,' I said with pretended calm.

'Well, at least you can count,' the teacher nodded, but he didn't look too happy with me. I wondered whether I should ask him what I was doing wrong, but it might have been cheeky; that would have been bad, but if I sounded humble he'd think I wanted to make peace, which would have been even worse . . .

71

I shrugged and sat down.

Quite a few boys could count as well as me. The teacher didn't ask anyone to do long multiplication except Aaron Kohn. He always asked him questions with a treacly smile, confident of success, and although Kohn answered fairly fast he didn't show off. I was debating whether or not to loathe him. The teacher asked me a few more questions and his voice became more tolerant every time. He seemed reconciled to the fact that I didn't make mistakes. When the bell went Berger stopped the arithmetic, but he didn't give us a break so I didn't need to summon up my fighting spirit straight away.

He unwrapped one of the two big parcels and told us that we would be reading the *Torah* this year. We needn't pay for the books until tomorrow. They were two pengös each.

Three days before, Mother had put all her money on the table and counted it down to the last two-fillér piece. She had written out all her expenses on a piece of paper, and when she had added them up she had sighed, saying that if she were to go on spending at her present rate she wouldn't have enough money left by the end of the month to take the tram to work.

She only took two pengös fifty with her when she went shopping so that she couldn't spend any more. She came back with dripping, milk, eggs, bread, malt coffee and some cauliflower for our supper. That was a lot of shopping by our standards. Often she sent me and my brother to buy a kilo of sugar or a bottle of milk, giving us the exact change so she wouldn't have to tell us not to buy sweets. My brother didn't dare to come into the shops with me because Mother occasionally made mistakes and didn't give us quite enough money and then we had to sneak out of the shop empty-handed.

'I dare you to go in alone!' Dávid said.

'I'm not scared!' I swaggered. 'The shop-keeper can't bite me! Anyway, I can always ask for ninety-five decagrams of sugar.'

Two pengös is a lot of money. She's only paid four an evening by the fortune-teller, and that's only twice a week, and out of that she has to pay for a taxi because it's so late when she comes home that the poor people are already asleep in the streets and there are criminals hiding round every corner . . .

'I don't want one!' I came to with a jerk at the sound of a defiant voice. It was a small, wiry, gypsy-faced boy who had said it; he hadn't even got up from his bench.

'You don't want it?' The teacher was flabbergasted. 'You don't want the *Torah*?'

'We've no money for God.'

'How dare you speak of God in that way!' cried the teacher, lifting his arms towards the ceiling. My ginger Rabbi couldn't have done it better.

'Only people God gives to can give to God,' said the boy.

'And how will you ask God for help if you don't know your prayers?' argued the teacher.

'We've asked Him often enough. It's about time He did some giving,' the boy explained. Then the teacher suddenly remembered something.

'But you're entitled to it free! Why didn't you remind me?' The teacher came over and put the book on the boy's desk.

I shivered. I knew I ought to do the same as that boy, we were just as poor. But I had told them that my grandfather gambled at the Club, though maybe he didn't do it any more. Anyway, even when he had lots of money Mother never saw any of it. He only took Dávid to live with him, not me . . .

We went up for the book, bench by bench. I took one off the pile without saying a word, and we started reading immediately. They were all good at it, even the gypsy-faced boy, whose name was Lang. I had counted on him. I remembered how I had been laughed at by the *heder* kids for pronouncing the only two Hebrew words I knew like a neologian. But this is supposed to be a neologian school! No way were this lot neologians, with their plaits and their dark clothes and their sickly, sing-song Hungarian . . .

When I arrived home Mother sent Dávid to the shop for two turnips. She gave him fifteen fillérs.

'That's not enough,' I said firmly.

'Yes, it is.' Mother waved me away. 'You can always get two small ones.' But then, hesitantly, she gave him another five fillérs. Dávid squinted at me, so I went with him.

'Grandmother has a larder,' he sighed. 'The maid does the shopping, and Grandma goes with her to see she doesn't cheat. At Grandma's we had stacks of carrots and turnips . . . we had so many we had to throw them out sometimes because they'd gone bad, and Grandpa didn't even tell her off!'

'Have you got the Five Books of Moses?' I said, changing the subject.

73

'No,' he said, and slowed down.

'Don't tell Mother,' I started, but Dávid stopped short.

'You bought it on credit!' he accused.

I nodded. 'I was forced to.'

'I was forced to too,' Dávid muttered. He sat down on a step and I sat down beside him. We eyed each other warily.

'Are you good at reading Hebrew?' I asked him.

'Not brilliant,' he answered cautiously.

'Is there anyone in your class who reads as badly as you?'

'Of course there is!'

'Then you'll have to tell Mother. Because in mine there isn't.'

'That's got nothing to do with it!' he argued. He thought I was stupid. I thought he was.

'Why should I tell her?' I asked.

'Because otherwise I'll beat you up!'

'If you can!'

Suddenly he thought of a better argument. 'Why should I tell Mother when it's you who's worse at reading?' he demanded.

I said nothing, waiting for him to answer his own question so I could contradict him.

'If your reading is so lousy it's you who needs the book most so you can learn. That's obvious.'

'Rubbish!' I snapped back. 'What do I want a book for if I can't read it? You'll have to tell anyway, because you're older.'

'You're stupid!'

'You're stupider!'

Dávid wasn't listening. He was gazing thoughtfully in front of him.

'What time did you buy the book?' he asked.

'Any time. How should I know? In our class there's a boy called Aaron Kohn who's got a wristwatch.'

Dávid sighed slowly, threateningly. 'What time did you buy the book?'

'In any case, you're older,' I said.

He saw he wasn't getting anywhere with me. He bit his upper lip. He looked sad. He bit his lower lip.

'Neither of us will tell,' he decided, and we went off to buy the turnips.

Next day at school I sat very still and tried to avoid Berger's attention. I wondered whether to be brave like Lang and tell him that we sometimes couldn't even pay the rent, or whether I should just mention casually that I'd clean forgotten about the whole thing. But then I'd have to think up some other excuse tomorrow. On the other hand, at least it would give me time to explain everything at home. When I gave Berger quieter, more thoughtful answers than the day before, he looked at me suspiciously.

He made us open the Five Books of Moses. Some boys jingled their money, but he waved them away. 'Later,' he said.

The Hebrew letters looked like forged iron, hammered and squashed somehow on to the thin white pages. While the others were reading, my ears switched on and off. I hardly heard each second word. Berger could see that I was frightened. He was looking at me while he got the other boys to read. He was enjoying my confusion, delighting in my ignorance.

I shall tell him that we weren't taught to read Hebrew in the country. That's silly, he won't believe me. Got it! I'll say Mother only let me go and live with Grandfather on condition he wouldn't send me to the *heder*. Mother? Who hardly dares look up when she speaks to Grandfather? I feel like I'm made of glass. Everybody can see into me.

Pale pictures swirled out of the meaningless, threatening letters. In a remote country I walked out of the desert and wandered into a market. Merchants in tents were bargaining with customers, but I was a thief, sneaking among them, terrified of being recognised. The turbaned men in their long, thin white shirts were examining silks, plunging their hands into bags of flour and jingling gold pieces in their pockets.

Suddenly the Caliph shouted, 'Silence!' and I expected him to declare the price of some precious merchandise, but instead he spoke in a Sabbath voice and the tents and the noise dissolved and the light faded. It was night. The Caliph broke into Hungarian: '. . . and the Spirit of God floated above the depths . . .'

In the darkness, a new market was coming to life. Jews with curled plaits were bargaining for *taliths*, for sunlight and stars, and I was afraid that the shadowy river of voices would be turned against me in a mocking rush of laughter. The Hebrew words clattered out of the night like the wheels of a train. Bits of translation flared up like fireworks, dispersing in seconds into nothingness, 'The abyss under the feet of God . . .'

Through my deafness I sensed the silence. It was my turn.

My first two words raised the expected snigger. The teacher made hissing noises and so did a couple of the boys. I started to hiss too. Laughter exploded all around me. Even the teacher, who didn't know how to laugh, was panting.

'I don't understand a word of this,' I snorted angrily.

'Go on, go on,' nodded the teacher happily. I was clearly serving as a shining example of a terrifying condition. I sealed my lips and glared at him. Then he expressed his amazement that anybody with my orthodox pronunciation could read so badly. He asked me about Grandfather.

'Didn't he send you to *heder*?'

'He did; but I didn't go.'

'Why not?'

'Because I hated it. Specially the Rabbi.'

'Still, you speak Yiddish, don't you?'

'Not a word!' I answered proudly.

He looked puzzled. 'Don't they speak Yiddish at your grandfather's?'

'Sometimes. But I don't listen.'

Berger's square head dropped forward and froze. Few children are that stupid. But in his eyes a dark flame lit up, just as it used to do in the Rabbi's, only this flame didn't flicker. Berger wasn't frightened of me.

Mother organised her work so she could see us to school for the first few days until we became used to the journey. The Basilica beside our flats was a darker grey than any of the houses round it; its dome was a mossy green. Buildings turn grey, like people. The houses pressed together, only breaking ranks for the narrow side streets, but the Basilica was surrounded by a square, and didn't let any other buildings come near it. It was a bald king among houses, looking down on the others as if it were left over from an old world where everything was big and had its own space like in villages, where even the smallest house has its piece of sky. Or had the Basilica been brought there from another world – or was it maybe the entrance to one?

Priests were always bustling about in the square, giving the passers-by filthy looks as they all headed off in different directions; but these black-skirted men, with their black looks and their black steps, who seemed to hide a lameness under the dignity of slow movement, were only strange, sad civil servants, domestics of death. Every now and then the purple of their chief glowed in their midst: a pale, ancient skeleton, his face a mask on which the skin was stretched like parchment, his clothes painted with the blood of his victims.

76

Less than a hundred metres further on began the pride of the city: the Andrássy Avenue, which went on as far as the eye could see. On the other side of the square the town broke up into little short streets where we had to push our way along crowded, narrow pavements. A few minutes further on, street vendors' tables and piles of merchandise blocked the pavement and we had to step down into the road.

In Kazar Street *taliths* hung like frayed curtains in several shop-windows. The plaits of the passers-by grew longer with every step we took, and in Dob Street small children were trotting to *heder* with plaits curled under their ears. Instead of caps they wore gold-embroidered, sky-blue *capels*, while boys of my age with books or ragged canvas bags under their arms were going in the opposite direction to us, their *tzitzits* hanging out under their jackets. My Hebrew-crazy school wasn't even the orthodox one!

Men stood in the doorways of their shops and called to the passers-by in Yiddish. If the clean-shaven men and the women whose hair was their own were Christians, then Christians were rare round here. Many of the signs were in Hebrew only. *Taliths* hung like scarfs from the men's necks as they popped into *shul* for a quick prayer, or rushed from their prayers to their work. One street vendor's *tzitzits* hung down to his knees to lure the faithful to his stall. Even this early in the morning the smell of stale clothes and greasy food filled the air.

Dob Street opened out on to Klauzál Square. On the far side stood a glass-roofed market with a hundred or so stalls, whose stink of raw meat and rotting vegetables was mixed with the Dob Street smell by the wind. With its two see-saws, its three swings, its rusty slide, Klauzál Square was a forlorn playground. Dirty windows peeped down on them from walls of cracked plaster.

Mother's office was near here, just a few minutes from our school, and during those first few days she often managed to meet us for lunch at her friend's shop.

Fifty steps beyond Klauzál Square, where plaits became shorter and jackets replaced kaftans and *tzitzits* tassles didn't show below men's waists like frayed, yellowing shirt-tails, two steps led up to a tiny shop. The outside doors were open, chewed red by rust, and it was easier to guess than to see that the worn-out inscription read: 'BOOKSHOP'. Inside, five people couldn't stand between the door and the counter without touching each other. Hanging from a beam above the counter a piece of cardboard advertised 'BOOKS TO LEND' in black printed letters. The walls seemed to have been built out of books and the small counter was overloaded with them. In an alcove behind the counter a large cooking pot balanced precariously on a small round stove.

The owner, a small, fat, ugly Jewish woman, complained loudly about fascism and the cost of living and the war we'd lost before it had begun and the poverty of people who had no money for bread, let alone books; but she spoke quietly about books, as if she were saying her prayers, only raising her voice again to defend her prices against stray customers. She let Mother make us soup or an omelette on the stove, and we ate around a small table. Sometimes the owner joined us, contributing a couple of eggs more than her fair share, and she often gave us dripping or peas or salt even when she wasn't eating with us, because she was trying to lose weight. The musty smell of paper mingled with that of food. We didn't have to pay for the books we borrowed. Their pages were crumpled, and the covers of many of them were torn. Maybe she'd bought them second-hand herself.

Lunch was often cheese and milk, which Mother bought at wholesale prices from an old acquaintance of hers, 'Gisella Milky', who owned a dairy near the market. She was a dry, wrinkled, lifeless-looking spinster, so sunk in solitude that even when you were talking to her she would continue gazing into nothingness through her great thick-framed spectacles and instead of answering would just hum and nod at her own tired thoughts. When we went to her shop, she used to point at the milk can we had to roll into place for her. If we made a mistake, she didn't tell us off. Instead, as if speaking were painful, she would manoeuvre the can into the right place herself. The squeaking noise as she pushed and pulled it seemed to come from the depths of her soul.

On the top shelf stood huge round cheeses as big as cartwheels, wrapped in silver paper. She'd be rich if she sold them, and must have lived in the hope that one sunny morning the owner of a big restaurant would come in and ask for ten cartwheels for each day of the year. But nobody bought a single slice for weeks on end, and one day I found her standing on a chair, dusting them.

Mother only bought small slices cut from little cheeses. The giant cartwheels never seemed to get sold. They must have been going off by now: Gisella Milky would probably have to starve herself to pay for them, selling food hungrily to other people, and maybe she'd soon be forced to close down her shop . . .

'Do you only sell those whole?' I asked her.

At first she didn't understand me, so I explained. 'They're there week after week. How come they don't go off?'

Gisella Milky cackled happily behind the counter. She reached towards me with her dry, bony hand, and would have touched me if I hadn't jumped backwards. She didn't care, she just went on laughing the first and last laugh of her life.

'Go off! . . . Oh dear! . . . Oh dear! . . . Children! . . . Children! . . . ' she hooted, saying finally: 'They won't go off in a hundred years! They're made of cardboard, they're just advertisements!'

That cheered me up. Even rich people weren't that rich after all! They ate the same kind of cheese as we did!

Four mornings after buying the Moses book on credit and three mornings after buying a 'reader' as well so that the teacher wouldn't think it was lack of money that was stopping me paying for the first, Mother turned to leave us at the school door.

'You should see the Head,' I remarked to her back. 'My papers aren't complete.' Mother thought for a second and decided that she could be half an hour late for the office if she caught up with her work during the afternoon. She came into school with us.

'Everybody had to buy two books on credit,' I said quickly, adding knowledgeably: 'It'll be all right if you promise to pay for them on the first of next month.'

Dávid had been looking unconcernedly into the middle distance. 'I only owe three pengös twenty to the school,' he announced virtuously.

I hit him in the stomach. Feeling brave for a change, he replied with a whole barrage of blows.

'Don't fight! Not here in front of everyone!' my poor mother shouted in a panic. I hoped it was our fight that had panicked her and not our debts.

Something I had seen a few days ago came into my mind: a bald man standing in an archway with a pile of furniture behind him. His wife was sitting on a chair and his two children on the stone floor, and Mother had told me they were there because they had been evicted. They couldn't pay their rent . . .

I cried out, and Dávid's hand stopped in mid-air, so I hit him on the chin to stop him imagining that his blows had made me cry.

And then Mother spoke, so quietly that we both froze: 'Tell your teacher I shall come in after the first of the month. I don't have time until then . . .' She paused. 'No, I'd better go in as I'm here,' and started off towards the Head's office, slowing down with every step.

Dávid was looking pleased with himself. He'd disposed of his debts for the price of a sore nose and had the added pleasure of knowing that my nose hurt even more than his. I was wondering whether Mother would be able to cough up seven pengös on the spot. How was I going to know during the long school day whether she had managed to pay or had had to ask for a postponement?

I couldn't tell from Berger's face what had happened in the Head's office. What if the Head refuses to wait for the money and we can't pay up? Maybe I won't have to come to this school any more . . .

The air was grey and leaden in the sleepy light. Only the blackboard was steady, watching its offspring, the thirty black Books of Moses, appearing before us on our desks. Berger was pacing up and down in his dark blue coat, his swelling voice cutting through the obscurity like a train through the night. When he translated some of the more difficult Hebrew phrases for us the shadows of the room seemed to lighten a little. His square head tilted forward again and again as if his neck couldn't support its weight any longer. When he told us to close our books without asking for the money, I almost felt sorry for him, condemned to carry such a weight.

I decided the square head with its great ears looked like an enormous jar with two handles. I immediately shared my discovery with my neighbour, Tamás:

> *'Ödön Berger's got no head,*
> *It's a jar of fat instead.'*

Tamás looked at me scornfully to show that for him, a boy in his second year at the school, my invention was old hat. He bent over his exercise book and drew a fat woman with a steaming saucepan in front of her. Two seconds later, lines were spiralling upwards from her bottom, and he had provided a caption:

> *'Aunty Sári's cooking beans,*
> *Her bottom like a chimney steams.'*

As art, I felt that this compared rather feebly with my poem, but I had to admit that where my poem had evaporated into thin air, his work was exposed to public view. Pulling a face, I casually flipped

80

the exercise book shut and dismissed his drawing with the contempt it deserved.

A few minutes after we had started writing our compositions I heard the teacher's steady puffing behind my back. Then the puffing stopped.

'That's all we needed!' he remarked.

For a good half minute he just stood there silently, leaving me wondering what it was he disliked. If it was my handwriting, he was welcome, because even Dévai used to mark me down for that.

'Village life will remain, it seems, for ever stuck in the mud of ignorance,' Berger finally declared wisely. Piecing together his fragmentary remarks during the next few minutes, I discovered that for a number of years a new type of handwriting had been taught in Budapest. It was known as 'lacing', and some time ago the government had made it compulsory in all schools. Berger repeated the bit about the government several times to make it quite clear that I had offended against great things. Before my eyes the teacher's severe face became a whole cabinet of frowning ministers, and every one of these dignitaries proposed and then seconded a motion condemning me to a hundred strokes of the cane . . .

Suddenly, I don't know why, I became quite calm. My ignorance of Hebrew, the way they had mocked my name, even my debts weighed like feathers. I decided that I would never learn Hebrew, and that if Berger asked for the four pengös thirty I would give him back the Five Books of Moses – with a sixth for good measure.

He stuck his square head forward like some old-fashioned camera. I felt unable to smooth the sneer off my face, so for the further benefit of the camera I crossed my eyes.

Berger must have understood vaguely, because he turned away from me and addressed the class.

'Will somebody show this blockhead how to write?' he asked, to which I retorted – in view of the distinctive shape of his head – 'Anybody can see who the blockhead is round here.'

The abyss, the one God's Spirit is supposed to hover above, threatened to engulf me.

'Who?' thundered Berger.

For a moment, darkness swallowed me completely, but suddenly a vague memory swam into my head and popped out of my mouth: 'Thou sayest . . .'

With these words all my strength suddenly drained away, and a

81

great weakness paralysed my arms, my neck and my legs. Berger's eyes flared like dark torches with the bliss of victory, and I was sure that he was about to ask for his four pengős thirty and that any moment I would have to confess in tears that we hadn't got it. Instead, though, he drew a red pen from his pocket; he unsheathed it with a triumphant flourish, and on the left-hand page of my exercise book – which had to be kept clear for corrections – he wrote: 'Your son's behaviour is unqualifiable.'

I gazed at the red ink, debating whether it was his blood or mine.

Berger took a step backwards and, retrieving his dignity, announced, 'You must show that to your parent, who must sign it.'

In the break my deskmate Tamás turned to me, looking confused. 'You're an idiot,' he said.

'And you're a fat bum,' I responded wittily.

The others were looking through me as though I were made of glass. It was like when I had chicken pox as a toddler and a plague notice had been stuck in my grandfather's street window, warning people off. Naturally the sign had attracted Jancsi Kovács, the blacksmith's son, who couldn't read yet. He was very excited when I yelled what it meant through the window. Terrified of catching my dreaded illness through the windowpane, he started leaping about as if his feet were being scorched, and he did his best to hold his nose and block his ears at the same time . . .

Still, Lang went past me, saying cheerfully, 'Don't worry. When we grow up, we'll bash his head in. Together.'

Aaron Kohn came up to me, looking shy. He lifted his head and said, 'You shouldn't have said that, you know . . .'

I shrugged my shoulders, quite pleased he'd bothered to come over.

'I'll show you how to do the letters, and how to join them up too,' he offered.

'What with? Shoelaces? What for anyway?' I grinned nastily. 'Sucking up to teacher again?'

'Not at all,' he said calmly. 'I won't tell him.'

'You think you're so clever!' I said.

'I don't,' he answered. 'You count well, you read well in Hungarian, you speak well, even if you do say stupid things. I think you're clever . . . only . . .' He hesitated.

'Only you're cleverer! But you don't dare say so because I'm stronger!'

'Only . . . it's difficult for you. That's what I was going to say.'

'Don't cry for me, or I'll beat you up. And you don't have to show me anything. My brother can write like you.'

I had meant to stroll off casually, leaving him planted there, but my legs wouldn't work. We stared at each other, me threateningly, him calmly, until I sneaked away.

At the end of the school day, Berger announced that gym classes would recommence shortly. Every boy must have his equipment . . .

'. . . Four pengös thirty . . . ' I thought.

'Gym shirt and shorts . . .' he said. I'm sure he's looking at me. '. . . and gym shoes . . .' I don't have any . . .

'For children in indigence . . . ' He's not looking at me, there's no need . . . '. . . it will be sufficient if they come equipped with gym slippers.' He's playing soldiers again . . . 'Anybody's mother can make them with little effort. I shall not accept excuses.'

You will. Mother addresses envelopes every evening. She works in the daytime and then she goes to the fortune-teller and she's not going to address four pengös' worth of extra envelopes just for you . . .

He looked directly at me.

'You will have your reprimand signed and bring it to me tomorrow. You could do with a good hiding.'

The class giggled. We were obviously out for each other's blood. He hadn't used red ink for nothing. I decided not to have anything signed.

At home I learned that the Head had let us both off all our debts and that we would be getting all our schoolbooks free. At the end of the year, we would have to hand them back. Mother looked relieved. My grandfather had gambled away my Moses books and my gym shoes, and all the plaits in the class would shake with laughter at me; but the worst thing of all was that Mother had arranged with the Head for us to go to the play-centre every day after school until five o'clock. Only the poorest kids went there, the ones who'd be alone if they went home. It was only the poorest whose mothers worked.

I didn't bother to mention the reprimand. Next morning Berger didn't ask me anything during arithmetic, or reading, or Hebrew, but from time to time he gave me meaningful looks. While we were reading the *Torah* his glances were like the knives they throw at people in circuses. Hours went by, and it became more and more difficult to chase away the hope that the reprimand had by some miracle been forgotten. Then, towards the end of the lesson, he gave me a look of reckoning.

'Now then, let's see it.'

'See what?' I asked curiously and, on being told, lied that I had shown my mother the reprimand while she was busy cooking, so that she was unable to sign it and had subsequently forgotten.

'Of course, and no doubt you forgot about it too,' the teacher joked, straight-faced. The class laughed.

'You wait!' I thought, but aloud I responded coolly: 'Yes, me too.'

He cross-examined me. 'Were you spanked for it?'

'No.' Calmly, I looked him straight in the eye.

'Was your mother very upset? Very angry?'

'No,' I said, then added reasonably, 'she was busy cooking.'

Such impudence choked him rather effectively. When he'd recovered he said, 'You will ask her to come and see me tomorrow without fail.'

'She can't come here every day. She has to work,' I explained apologetically. 'Perhaps you could give me a message for her? She was here only yesterday to see the Head.'

'The Headmaster!' he shouted at me in frustration.

'The Headmaster, sir,' I repeated. I conceded the point. Not having met him, I had no quarrel with the Head yet.

'Mother has arranged about the books with him,' I added. That was a mistake.

'I know,' he nodded. 'You will not have to pay for the books, but at the end of the year you must hand them back in impeccable condition.' He piled it on. 'You are also entitled to attend the after-school play-centre. You will start today.'

'I might,' I answered, as though I had been asked a question. But Berger wouldn't leave me alone.

'The play-centre is not a café. You may not come and go as you please. The kitchen caters for every boy, every day, and any absences will be reported first thing the following morning. The Synagogue cannot afford to waste money.'

At the end of the school day, at noon, all five boys going to the play-centre from my class assembled in front of the teacher's desk, closed ranks, and 'proceeded to the lunch room in a disciplined manner'. Until then I'd been saved from this distinction, and on that first day we had to meet Mother at the bookshop for lunch, so in the end Dávid and I turned up at the play-centre late, as visitors.

Apart from the lunch room the play-centre consisted of two classrooms, one for the older children and one for the younger lot. Both groups were supervised by the same person, so there was no danger of too much discipline. Instead of benches there were chairs and small tables, but a big blackboard stood on a platform at the end of the room like in class. A round, pig-faced woman was sitting at the desk dressed in a white overall. I felt more certain with each passing minute that I'd seen her before. She wouldn't let me be in the same room as my brother so Dávid had to join the oldies.

'The greater the friends, the worse the noise,' she explained, and I gathered from this wise proverb that the purpose of the day-centre was to achieve complete silence. But Little Lang was in my group, so I didn't despair.

First we had to do our homework. I finished my sums fast and my written composition even faster, using the old-style letters. My brother had shown me how to do the letter 'a' in the new writing and, to be safe, I did a whole line of new 'a's. I wondered if I should read some Hebrew, or would that be really giving in to Berger? I took my black book and glared at the Hebrew letters. They were black teeth, crawling around on the page and turning themselves into new letters.

'W-O-L-F,' they spelt, Gyula's surname, and the black-and-white page became a blur. Years and years ago, before I could even read Hungarian, before my long stay at Oszu, my mother had had something to do on her own one morning. She had taken me to some place where a pig-faced woman in a white overall sat on a platform, and Mother told me she would fetch me as soon as possible. That day had grown longer by the hour.

There had been picture books in that place, so I picked one up and found the story of the three little pigs. One of them built a very strong house that the wolf couldn't destroy, but Mother still hadn't come back to fetch me, and the wolf had left the page, and I could feel it breathing behind my chair . . . I shut my eyes, terrified . . .

The memory of it leapt out of the shadows like the wolf itself. Looking up at the platform, I recognised the pig-woman.

But the next day brought a whole army to my rescue. Only six of us lined up in front of the teacher's desk, but after we had proceeded to the lunch room in our disciplined and orderly manner the others arrived in groups until everybody was assembled. Although the pig-woman was reinforced at lunch by two teachers, and although there was an iron rule against touching your knife and fork before the food arrived, somebody always did, and following his lead half a hundred children grabbed their own weapons and started clinking and clattering and banging them together in a chaotically wonderful symphony of rebellion, each child sheltered by the rest of the orchestra. Soon they broke into a chant:

> *'Fill our tummies*
> *Big fat dummies!*
> *GRU-U-UB!'*

The battle cry rang out, leaving the enemy in a state of silent shock. The pig-woman was always on duty, but the other two worked on a rota, and only did lunch duty once or twice a week. Soon we were veterans, while they remained armchair generals who had no experience of the trenches. The pig-woman was the least hopeless. Cunningly, she started from a position of surrender.

'Children, children, for God's sake . . .' she would plead, taking it for granted that God was on the grown-ups' side. 'Be a little more patient, you're not that hungry . . .' Hardly a military secret, this wasn't enough to convince us; but because she was a woman she was protected from our more obscene chants, a fact completely unappreciated by her male colleagues. They always thought she'd managed to impose some degree of order and would begin scolding us again, pouring oil on the fire.

These were the only occasions when they resorted to corporal punishment in our school. Being hit was the high point of the day, acknowledgment of individual bravery and distinguished service in the underworld of our play-centre. Then the soup would arrive, and the party would be over.

The pig-woman's grand passion was origami. Whenever we asked her for ordinary drawing paper she would haggle to her last breath, rabbiting on about rubbers and using both sides, but she handed out origami paper by the stack. She taught us enthusiastically how to make salt cellars and pepper pots, sailing boats and steam ships and aeroplanes. I was bored enough once to make a whole fleet of German steam boats, soon reduced to pancakes on the English Channel by a few British aeroplanes. The pig-woman came to the defence of the German navy because the British bombs were my fists, which made bombing Germans a noisy and disruptive activity.

Our favourite occupation was folding the paper to look like pointed devils' ears and then flicking it cunningly to make a small bang. This relatively peaceful activity was encouraged by the pig-woman, who tolerated the bangs and called it 'childish fun'; but what she didn't know was that the devils' ears made perfect waterbombs. They were mass-produced and filled with water, which they could hold for a minute or two, and when thrown they exploded beautifully on impact. The fields of action were the corridors around the school lavatories.

These corridors were also the scene of many a memorable game of marbles. We would ask to 'be excused', and then happily settle down to marbles. Sometimes the majority of the kids were queuing up for the lavatory, so eventually they had to make playing marbles – in an orderly manner – a legitimate activity, provided of course that we had finished our homework first. The pig-woman was surprised to find that after the first few days of play-centre, we all had very little homework to do . . .

One big glass marble cost as much as fifty clay ones, and was exactly the same price as an egg. For some odd reason all our mothers seemed to count in eggs. At the play-centre, owning a glass marble gave you the same kind of status as owning a racehorse would in the world outside. To the boys who didn't attend the play-centre, it would have been unthinkable to go without exercise books and rulers and coloured pencils; but things like that didn't matter to us, nor did torn shoes or patched trousers. Anyone who didn't possess a glass marble, however, was soon blackballed from our best circles. Before the start of a game, each player had to show a glass marble, like a ticket at the cinema.

The older boys had an even more prestigious pastime called 'The Line Game', for which you needed hard cash. It consisted of throwing coins towards a line drawn on the floor in chalk; but if there was no chalk, a coin called the 'leader pengö' was thrown first and became the target. The aim of the game was to throw your coin closest to the target: the owner of the nearest coin took the lot.

This game was strictly forbidden, so it was only played inside the washrooms, which were guarded by lookouts. In theory any boy could play – or, according to the school rules, nobody. But the bigger boys did not on the whole trust the discretion of the smaller ones, who were inevitably the losers. Little Lang, my gypsy-faced classmate, was the exception. Although he was known to his friends as Mik, he acquired a new nickname from playing the line game with the older boys, who trusted him so much that they even tried to cheat him. Mik soon emerged from the resulting dogfights as 'Spitfire'.

Mik never fought in class. He probably didn't consider anybody there a worthy opponent. I wanted to be the best fighter in the class, but I doubted the effectiveness of my mindless rages against Mik's street-wise fighting technique. I promised myself solemnly that I would pick a fight with Mik on the first plausible pretext. But, unfortunately for my ambitions, we became great friends.

4: Membership Fee

I no longer knew whether I had heard or dreamt the fortune-teller's promise to get us into the best Boy Scout troop. The troop was named after an English outlaw: Robin Hood, who used to rob the rich and give their money to the poor. I thought it must be a wonderful scout troop to have kept its English name after the outbreak of war! They only took Jewish boys, so they could trust everyone to side with the English.

In the half-light of this hope I saw boys helping old widows to collect dry wood and welcoming the hungry to share their bonfire feasts of game hunted in royal forests. Aunty Felice had given me a book with big pictures showing the adventures of Robin Hood and his men. I had read it three times in one week.

The scouts would play football in their free time of course, and when they weren't saving people from the snow with the help of their St Bernards they'd ski and have snowball fights. I couldn't ski, but they'd teach me. Perhaps they'd even teach me English.

I gazed at groups of scouts in the streets, and if a nasty-faced boy caught me staring I just shrugged, knowing that he was from some second-rate team, probably Christian. Some of the *goy* scouts might even support the Germans.

I couldn't figure out what a scoutmaster could possibly have to do with a fortune-teller. Perhaps she was showing off, or perhaps her crystal ball had told her that I'd soon become a scout. It would happen in the street one day: I'd get into a fight with three huge yobboes, and I'd stand my ground without even noticing a scoutmaster who'd be watching the fight. Afterwards, he'd come up to me and say, 'We need lads like you.' And then I'd persuade him to take Dávid too.

At school, when Berger and his bootlickers were getting up my nose, I used to rest my chin on my fist and look out of the window, making plans. Robin Hood's merry men would form an alliance with the play-centre boys. Led by Mik, we'd charge into the school through doors and windows, smashing benches to smithereens and pulling the boys' plaits off. We'd shut all the teachers in the lavatories.

One morning, Mother was quite unlike her usual tired and sleepy self. Jauntily, she put the mugs and plates and bread on the kitchen table, and then she couldn't keep her secret any longer. The coffee pot steamed in her hand as she made her announcement: 'Dávid, Józska: you're going to be Boy Scouts!' She looked at us triumphantly, then glanced up as if she expected angels to appear.

She told us that the scoutmaster had been to see the fortune-teller the previous evening. This scoutmaster, who called himself 'Akela', went to see the fortune-teller because – and I couldn't believe my ears – he wanted to know whether, as the world became bleaker for the Jews every day, he could continue to trust his *goy* puppet, the Christian under whose name he traded and who was taking an ever-increasing interest in his silk-stocking business.

Until then I had imagined my initiation into the troop taking place in a great square field surrounded by hundreds of scouts in broad-brimmed hats. They would suddenly look up flabbergasted as I jumped into the air and caught a ball flying twenty metres above their heads.

Silk stockings. I had to rethink my ideas about the initiation.

The troop's headquarters were in a little street branching off from the Danube into the area where the rich Jews lived. We glimpsed a wide staircase covered with thick blue carpet, and thought we must be going to some palace, before we realised just in time that our destination was in fact a flight of dark and narrow steps to the side of the palace which led down to a cellar. There was a metal door, without a handle, set into the cellar wall, but we had never seen that sort of door before. An iron bar half a metre long curved out from it, and though we examined the door we couldn't find any bolts or secret push-buttons. There had to be a magic word, like 'Open Sesame'.

'This is a scout door,' Dávid explained loftily. 'Bang on it! You're smaller, so they won't tell you off.'

I pounded on the door. The metal bar moved downwards as if by magic, the door opened, and a uniformed boy three or four years older than me stood in front of us:

'Are the Tartars after you? I'm not deaf, you know!'

'We've never seen a scout door before,' Dávid apologised. 'We've come to be wolf-cubs. As from today.'

'Scout door?' The boy laughed. 'It's an air-raid shelter door. The whole cellar is reinforced against bombs!' I remembered having read something about this in the papers. As well as the original stone pillars there were wooden beams propping up the ceiling. By one wall lay a heap of sand with two shovels stuck in it.

'The war hasn't got here yet,' I said, apologising for my ignorance of air-raid shelters.

'It will!' laughed the scout. He directed us into the wolf den. About thirty kids were standing around a red light placed on the floor. They were singing. The light wasn't a real camp fire, but a pretend one made out of an ordinary bulb covered with crumpled red tissue paper. A command was given and the kids all sat down.

A small young man turned towards us. He introduced himself as 'Bandi-Ba' and then ordered the 'Tiger Family' to stand up. Seven or eight boys assembled and went over to the red bulb in single file. On Bandi-Ba's orders the first tied a string into knots of different kinds, and then gave the string to the boy behind him, who repeated the exercise. The whole pack were wearing green jerseys, but I brushed my worries away: after all, soldiers don't have to buy their own uniforms. Then I realised that every single Tiger was wearing a wristwatch. On the other hand, there wasn't one plait in the whole room . . .

'Quick Wit!' called Bandi-Ba. A curly-haired, skinny kid wearing gold-framed specs stepped forward and recited the laws of the pack. He couldn't pronounce his 'r's, and I wanted to laugh as I listened to this weed talk about the toughness of the wolf-cub pack.

All the laws were brand-new to me, they sounded a bit like preaching. Still, God wasn't mentioned more than twice, which cheered me up.

Rows of fashionable raincoats hung on hooks round the walls.

Bandi-Ba didn't speak any louder than the children, and although he called them by silly names like 'Quick Wit' and 'Fast Messenger' and 'Brave Heart', he sounded more like an uncle than like a teacher. Dávid and I were to join the 'White Family'. Bandi-Ba explained that he had to get to know us a little bit before he could think up 'totem names' for us; until then we could be Dávid and Józska.

He took out two typewritten pages, but he didn't give them both to Dávid just because he was the older: I got one too. He made the camp fire darker by covering it with a wolf-cub scarf and started

91

to tell a story about a sailor who was robbed while he was asleep by a wicked shipmate. The thief stole the sailor's wooden leg as well as his money so as not to get caught.

I found a ray of light and deciphered the sheet of paper letter by letter. It was a questionnaire asking for name, address, father's name, father's religion, his academic qualifications and income . . . It didn't ask anything about mothers . . .

At the bottom of the page it said: 'Membership Fee'. Membership fee? What is this? A private school? A club? I pushed Dávid's elbow and swapped sheets of paper with him. The page rustled in his hand.

The other sheet was a list of necessary equipment: scarf, khaki shorts, belt with fleur-de-lis buckle, penknife, boots, storm jacket, knapsack, water-bottle . . . A footnote read: 'NB: All items available from Gutmann's at twenty per cent discount on presentation of this leaflet.'

Poor Mother. We'd had it. We'd finished scouting before we'd even started.

On my right sat a tall, soft-mouthed boy who looked as if he'd come straight from the barber. I pulled the sleeve of his green jersey. He hissed at me.

Bandi-Ba's story had progressed a long way since my new worries had made me deaf. It must have been a sad and terrifying story because the sailor had died and his ghost was visiting the thief. Bandi-Ba's ghost imitation was perfect: 'Whe-e-ere is my wo-o-oden leg?'

The terror in the room almost got me. The poor sailor had died because he hadn't any money for a new wooden leg. It reminded me of my own worries.

I pulled the tall boy's sleeve again, and he reluctantly turned his ear in my direction.

'How much do you pay for membership?' I whispered. I had to repeat the question.

He turned towards me, offended, but answered politely, a metal tooth glinting in his mouth. Gold.

'Mummy sends it in evwy month. By post.'

'How much?'

Gold-tooth looked at me, confused. 'One doesn't ask about money,' he whispered.

Somebody with a gold tooth daring to tell people what they should and shouldn't do! I thought of the rich peasant women who have their healthy teeth pulled out to be replaced with gold.

'Whe-e-ere is my wo-o-oden leg?' wailed Bandi-Ba.

'I'm asking all the same,' I hissed at the tall boy.

'Twenty-five pengös,' he hissed back. I felt as if a serpent had bitten me. He must take me for an imbecile.

'You're a berk!' I answered loudly. I thought he must be joking. 'Every month?' I asked indignantly.

Gold-tooth nodded, offended.

I turned into a pillar of salt, and stared at him as if his whole head were made of gold.

We had just been reading about Lot's wife in school, in the Hungarian reading lessons, which were much more lively than the Hebrew ones. When we read Hebrew, the black letters would melt and surge around me like a great river. I would be trying to make out the words when the torrent would suddenly roar my name, and then my throat would go tight as if I was drowning. I would be submerged in fear for minutes on end, and only the odd phrase would reach me: ' . . . A God-fearing man . . .' I didn't know whether this meant Abraham or Berger but I knew that the man must have feared God as I feared Hebrew. I decided that since God spoke perfect Hungarian, reading Hebrew must be a punishment for something I'd done.

Abraham said unto someone: 'If thou wilt take the left hand, then I will go to the right; or if thou depart to the right hand, then I will go to the left.' I decided to say the same to Berger at the first opportunity.

God was definitely friends with Berger, but I had begun to realise that Berger only called on me for the second reading of passages, and my fear eased. Then one day, when my name hit out at me unexpectedly and the world turned black, I heard my own voice. I was stupefied as I listened to myself speaking staccato Hebrew without drying up. Words, sometimes whole passages, flared from me like flames from smoking embers. Without realising it, I had learnt whole lines by heart, and when I missed out a word, Berger's correction would remind me of another whole line. I forgot to pretend that I was reading, and I quoted five or six words in one breath without looking at the book. My eyes met Berger's bewildered gaze and fell back to the page.

We didn't show the membership form or the cub shopping list to Mother, and we didn't go to the wolf-cubs' Sunday excursion nor to the following mid-week pack meeting, as we didn't know what excuse to make for having been absent the last time. A week later we had two absences to explain, and I hid both sheets of paper in the Moses book, where Mother wouldn't find them. I was ready to give up scouting. The weed's golden fang made me laugh, but if he had so much as caught a glimpse of our poverty I'd have knocked his beautiful tooth down his throat.

One day Dávid sighed and asked me whether we were going to the next meeting, as if I were his big brother. So I took pity on him and got the form out of its hiding place. With a rubber, I scraped away the word 'father' and made Dávid put 'mother' in its place in almost identical printed letters. We gave it to Mother to complete. Where she had to put her own academic qualifications, she put 'four years at secondary school'. My mouth went dry and I would have liked to ask her to lie and put 'matriculation' but I didn't dare. She was proud of what she had achieved, because there wasn't a secondary school in Oszu, and secretly, aided and abetted by my real grandmother, Mother had enrolled at the secondary school in Tokaj. Grandfather had caught them at the station on the first day. It was the only time he ever slapped my mother, for trying to be 'Little Miss *Goy*'. Grandmother pointed out that she was herself a qualified teacher without being Madam *Goy* or any other sort of *goy*, and put her foot down. Grandfather told her what he thought of that too and wanted to drag them both from the station until Grandmother told him that she'd already paid the first year's fees. He started moaning that his own wife was robbing him. She reminded him that two out of his three vineyards had originally been hers, and the larger ones at that, but Grandfather raged at them until the train arrived, by which time he was almost at his last gasp and in need of a doctor. But with the fees already paid most of the damage had been done, so eventually he let them take the train to school.

And now this beautiful story was being threatened by the silk-nappied wolf-cubs, who would mock at the 'four years at secondary school' as if Mother were illiterate . . .

'Don't put "temporary white-collar relief worker", Mother. Put "civil servant",' I advised.

Mother pondered for a minute, because after all she was a civil servant even though the anti-Jewish laws meant that they could sack her at a moment's notice.

'Civil servant . . . ' she mused, then she laughed nervously, without smiling. 'If I make them think I'm a Cabinet minister they'll push the fees sky-high!'

'White-collar relief worker holding temporary employment under the Jewish laws,' she wrote. I thought of Mik, who wouldn't be ashamed, and cooled down.

We arrived at the meeting on time. The camp fire had already been switched on, and I watched the boys arriving. As they came in they nodded politely at Bandi-Ba with well-bred smiles on their in-bred faces. There was a disciplined reserve about them that was something quite new to me. It was obvious that they had all come straight from the tailor or from Gutmann's.

Bandi-Ba had appeared until now to be a kind and modest man and, because he spoke plainly, even a bit roughly, a poor one. But at exactly half past six he made me jump out of my skin. 'Stand for PRA . . . YER!' he barked, sounding like a drunken corporal.

The wolves lifted their left hands, separating their index fingers from their middle fingers, and looked as foolish as the eternally swaying orthodox Jews. Then they started reciting:

> '*I believe in one God.*
> *I believe in One Fatherland.*
> *I believe in One Eternal and Divine Truth.*
> *I believe in the Resurrection of Hungary.*'

My foot!

Bandi-Ba barked once more: 'End of PRA . . . YER!' All the left hands fell smartly and slapped left thighs.

Could this wolf-pack really be on the side of the English? I wondered. Surely every Jewish child knew the second verse of the fascist credo:

> '*I believe in Szálasi, I believe in Hitler,*
> *I believe in beating yids with blackjacks.*'

Once Dávid was travelling with his grandpa in a train. At one station four or five drunken fascists got on to the train wearing Arrow Crosses – Hungarian swastikas. Shouting and vomiting, they sang patriotic and antisemitic songs, until one of them suddenly called for silence. He turned towards Dávid's grandpa and shouted, 'Look, boys! This Jewish sod doesn't like our songs!'

'Of course I do,' he answered. Grandpa had got cold feet.

'Then prove you're not a dirty yid,' the fascist mocked. Grandpa got to his feet and sang with them: 'I believe . . .'

Elek would have thrown the lot of them out of the window. From then on Dávid's grandpa travelled first class.

The coddled little first-class children stood up and sang 'The Song of the Wolves':

'The storm is blowing
We're cold and hungry
We're bruised and bleeding
But we are free . . .'

In the books of Petőfi's poems, 'The Song of the Wolves' is followed by 'The Song of the Dogs':

'Our Master beats us,
Then calls us to him;
Supremely happy
His boots we lick.'

If Elek were a kid or if Mik were here they wouldn't be impressed or ashamed among these rich children. They wouldn't even hate them. Especially if they hardly knew them. They are people too, they are children . . .

Gold-tooth stepped forward. It was his turn to recite the scout laws. It was difficult not to laugh as he was a good head taller and two years older than me but still spoke in that whiny, kittenish voice, with a baby lisp. He told us all how fine and brave and honest a boy scout is.

Then we played silly games. Many of the kids were giggling like women. They all must have been taught to laugh by their mothers. Do rich ladies often lisp? I wondered. Aunty Felice spoke as simply and beautifully as my mother. What was the matter with this Budapest world? I blamed my schoolmates for their plaits and these snotty rich kids for singing songs about the glory of the Fatherland.

Then Bandi-Ba went on with another episode of his spooky story, during which I forgot my troubles and was scared to my heart's content.

At the end of the meeting, when the pack was dispersing, I loitered near Bandi-Ba, waiting for him to be alone, but quite a few wolf-puppies were sucking up to him and asking flattering questions like: 'Will the aptitude test be very difficult?' I didn't dare ask to speak to him alone because then he would have known that I was trying to hide our poverty, and 'Poverty is no crime'. So I was doubly ashamed. In the end, I crept up to him and slipped the form into his hand. The curly-haired boy with the gold-framed spectacles managed to peep at it and I prayed God to strike him blind.

'Twenty-five pengös is too much for us,' I said with bravado, because of the audience.

'How much isn't too much?' asked Bandi-Ba, glancing at the form. 'One has to pay something.'

To my relief, he bent down close to me. 'Is twenty fillérs too much?' he asked. My teeth chattered as I shook my head dumbly.

'Mother! It's twenty fillérs!' I shouted triumphantly when we arrived home. Gyula was there again, and he hissed at me from behind his newspaper to shut me up. Gyula's hissing was a warning, like a train whistle, of approaching trouble. It was also an obscure rebuke for bragging that I had passed the poverty test like Mik Lang.

Gyula the lodger didn't lodge. Dávid slept in the lodger's room and I had joined him there two weeks previously from the big room, where Mother and I had slept at first. Yet Gyula continued to pay us rent, and I suspected him of paying more than the agreed amount. He spent four or five evenings a week with us, and never went into the lodger's room even by mistake. But in the big room he made himself completely at home.

I knew that he would willingly have given three or four pengös for our membership fee, but I was against that at all costs. He would probably have come round seven evenings a week in exchange. Dávid had become used to his presence and found it natural. He would tell Gyula about all the little events of the day, and occasionally even asked him for help with his homework. I never spoke to him unless he spoke to me first. When he came in I stood up as if he were a teacher, and I didn't sit down until he did. I answered his questions politely and briefly, putting on my best manners. He did his best to feel as comfortable as he had before my arrival.

He took us to the cinema. At last I could see how funny Bilicsi really was, although Latabár turned out to be an imbecile who made his living by imitating other imbeciles. Gyula bought cakes and gave them to Mother to give to us, but while he was there we only nibbled at them politely. As soon as he'd left of course, Dávid and I used to gobble them up.

He was a principled, military sort of man, who spoke firmly, but not loudly, and underlined the important bits of his speeches by slowing down and falling silent for a few seconds, nodding to himself thoughtfully. Maybe he spoke faster than he thought and had to stop to give his brain time to catch up. He had a great respect for commonplaces, and regularly came out with such gems as 'His bark is worse than his bite' and 'A Hungarian doesn't speak with his mouth full', producing them with all the conviction of a prophet.

I had another piece of business to settle that evening. Berger asked to see Mother's acknowledgment of his written rebuke about once a week. He didn't demand it, just mentioned it from time to time. I wasn't sure whether he was trying to use my own fear of a confrontation to keep me quiet, or whether he was worried that a battle would undermine his authority as the first one had. It wasn't of him that I was afraid and as far as I was concerned he could shout himself sick; but the slightest trouble would make Mother launch off into one of her heartbreaking lamentations about children's ingratitude. Trembling with anger and sorrow, she would look at me with empty eyes and murmur half-finished sentences like: 'How can I . . . all alone . . . Did I deserve such . . .?' It wasn't her indignation that I really feared, or even her anger; it was her sadness, her wretched mumblings that left me not knowing whether I was miserable on my account or on hers.

'Such good-looking, lovely children . . . Why should it be my children who are deprived of a father . . .?' When Mother got into this sort of mood it would always be Dávid who pulled himself together first, telling her that a mother like her was enough for us . . .

Our plan was for Dávid to discredit Berger to Mother at an appropriate moment by telling her that 'The whole school knows that . . .' and with the ground well prepared I would then bring up the subject of the rebuke. Dávid and I had been mulling over what it was that the whole school knew.

'He shouts at us and canes us like a Turkish Pasha . . .'

'But a Turkish Pasha has to have a big round tummy. Berger has a big square head, it's not the same, the story won't ring true . . .'

'What about "He's known as 'Sergeant Major' because he shouts and yells all the time, even during the breaks and in the corridors. He bellows at children he doesn't even know in the street . . ."?'

'But Gyula used to be a sergeant major . . .'

I imagined Berger at dead of night, in dark clothes, tiptoeing along close to a wall on his way to commit some horrible crime . . . What crime? Burglary? Too boring. Murder? Out of the question. He couldn't possibly kill anybody, or even hit anyone. He barks but he doesn't bite . . .

It had annoyed me that we seemed quite unable to think of a good way of discrediting the monster.

'How much do the other cubs pay?' asked Gyula, interrupting my train of thought.

'Some a little more, some a lot more,' I replied carefully.

Gyula coughed, but didn't dwell on the subject. A few minutes later he read about some irritating aspect of the Church in his newspaper, and took his bad mood out on the priests – a traditional Hungarian pastime.

'I'm in trouble with religion too,' I said, sadly.

'Are you?' Gyula laughed. I had all his sympathy.

'My teacher told me off because he says my Hebrew letters are ugly.' I gasped at my own ingenuity. Gyula laughed again. We were clearly on the same wavelength, so I went on. 'I told him that I'm only learning them because I have to. What's the point of my knowing Hebrew perfectly? God speaks Hungarian, doesn't he?'

'Of course he does!' Gyula agreed with great pleasure.

'But it's a Jewish school!' Mother was scared, frightened that they would take back the free books.

'The teacher told me I was cheeky, and I told him that I was quite serious and asked him if it was true that God knows everything, and then the teacher wrote in my exercise book that I was badly behaved – "Unqualifiability" or something.'

'It's a Jewish school!' my mother repeated anxiously. Gyula and Mother started arguing about how much religious dogma ought to be taught.

'What's important is that the boy is sincere and stands up for his beliefs,' said Gyula. They agreed on that, and Mother hardly glanced at the page when she signed the rebuke.

Gyula remained in a good mood throughout the evening, and rewarded me for my cunning. Addressing me for once instead of Dávid, he announced that he would take us both to the funfair the following Sunday.

My miraculous lie had opened a magic door for me. I couldn't have sat on the English throne more proudly than I sat on my school bench the next day. A thousand forged gold pieces chinked in my pockets, but I didn't intend to give Berger my mother's signature. On the contrary.

During Moses I put a few clay marbles on my desk and concentrated all my attention on stopping them rolling off, rearranging them again and again in different colour patterns until Berger paid attention. He swept them together and put them in his pocket.

'I didn't know you played marbles, sir! I'll win them back in break . . .' I said, getting a satisfying laugh.

But Berger controlled his anger. 'You won't be winning these ones back,' he remarked before going on with the lesson. After a couple of minutes he called on me to read.

'Where are we?' I asked with interest. He showed me the place, a new and unfamiliar passage which I had to read syllable by syllable so as not to get confused.

'You'd better pay attention!' needled Berger. That was enough for him. But not for me.

I fixed an elastic band on to the thumb and index fingers of my left hand, and tried to see if I could make a catapult.

Berger had been a teacher long enough to see what I was doing, and this time he didn't let me off. 'Don't you think you've caused enough trouble already, Sondor?'

'It's the Hebrew letters that cause the trouble,' I explained.

Berger took out his red pen, bent forward, and turned my exercise book towards him. Then suddenly he straightened up. 'Have you had it signed by your mother?'

'What?' I asked, puzzled. Then with an annoyed sigh I added: 'I forgot.'

'You won't forget this one.' He bent forward again and wrote exactly the same words as he had before. I was flattered that he had remembered them so clearly: 'Your son behaves in an unqualifiable manner at school.'

'What are you looking so pleased about?' he asked, glancing suspiciously at my sneer.

'Should I cry?' I asked politely. Behind Berger's back, Mik Lang nodded vehemently, but as I mistook this for simple admiration, Mik opened his mouth wide and started wiping his eyes with the backs of his hands. This made me laugh, so Mik started to sob. Berger turned towards him.

'What's wrong?' he asked sceptically.

'I left my elevenses at home,' Mik howled. 'I'm hungry!'

He never brought any elevenses to school, as he could always confiscate half of everyone else's instead. The whole class hooted

100

with laughter, and at last Berger bellowed, more like a kicked dog than a corporal: 'It's impossible to teach here!'

As usual he didn't write anything in Mik's book, which set me thinking.

An hour later, when we were reading in Hungarian and I felt more secure, I apologised humbly for interrupting the lesson.

'What do you want?' Berger asked cautiously.

'Please sir, did you give me this rebuke because I hadn't had the first one signed by my mother?' I asked sheepishly, so that the teacher would say 'yes'. He did.

'For that among other things.'

'Then could you cross it out please, sir? I've had the old one signed.'

Berger was non-plussed. 'You have told me at least ten times that you had forgotten to get it signed.'

As nonchalantly as I could I shrugged my shoulders. 'I forgot that I hadn't forgotten.'

The classroom echoed with laughter. Mik applauded. Berger shouted for a while, then examined my mother's signature at length. Finally, he said, 'You will now ask your mother to sign today's rebuke. It is well deserved.'

'That won't surprise her,' I yawned. 'My mother knows that sir picks on me . . .'

'Doesn't she know what a rascal her son is?'

'No, she doesn't,' I replied. 'I don't have to be a rascal at home.'

Berger lifted his head and looked at me with an air of curiosity. I was worried that he might cross out his rebuke.

'Have it signed,' he concluded finally.

'Once or twice?' I asked, setting the class laughing again.

Berger didn't bellow this time; his head just drooped, and he shook it slowly and sadly from side to side.

Gyula was almost pleased to be able to take my side against my teacher, although having the first rebuke signed turned out to have been a mistake. Berger had tasted blood. For a while, however, Gyula's complicity helped, and the endless stream of Berger's complaints seemed to be nothing more than an inconvenience to Mother. She signed them all quietly, preoccupied by greater worries.

I continued to play the ill-treated orphan at home and Robin Hood at school. Berger and I now had a daily ritual. Before the first lesson, I would take my exercise book up to the teacher's desk, present

Mother's signature and ask, 'Will you be writing today's rebuke in now or later, sir?'

Berger shouted at me more and more, but I might as well have been deaf. All he managed to do by yelling was to raise my standing among the other kids. He gave me several messages for Mother, asking her to come and see him, but of course she never received them. I would find excuses or make bored promises that Berger wasn't even meant to believe.

'She'll come some day . . . Maybe next week . . .'

I was walking a tightrope between school and home, and my growing arrogance became the balancing pole I needed. I dreaded Berger showing up at our place one fine evening and seeing our poverty at first hand. He would probably find Gyula there too, and realise that as well as hardly having a father I was also faced with a stranger who was trying to take his place, a Christian, living in sin or whatever it's called with my mother. Whenever I imagined the scene I would be gripped by panic, and had to mutter the spell that used to protect me from lightning when I was a little boy: 'Don't strike me down, don't . . .'

In the meantime everything was fine. I kept everyone under control with a system of lies that spread like a safety-net under my delicate tightrope.

One morning, while getting ready for school even more slowly than usual and being hurried along by Mother and by Dávid, I surprised myself by blurting out: 'My tummy hurts.'

Mother touched my forehead and immediately decided that I had a slight temperature which could become more serious during the day. I had a bit of trouble persuading her not to call Aunty Sarolta, our doctor friend. I was made to swallow half an aspirin with some lemon tea, and was forbidden to spit it out. Finally, before Mother would leave for work, I had to give my word of honour that I would take the other half later.

I was pleased to be alone. So pleased in fact that I took the other half of the aspirin straight away to get it over with. I hadn't had a moment to myself since my return from Oszu, and had a vague feeling that I had faked illness to get a break from the tightrope. Even that had been achieved by lying.

'It is wearisome to be human,' I murmured in irritation, having discovered Japanese poetry a few days before. The fat lady in the bookshop had made a politely anguished remark about how thin

Mother was, and Mother had replied out of the blue with a Japanese poem:

> *'It is wearisome to be human,*
> *It is wearisome to be Japanese;*
> *No wonder I am so thin.'*

She had been quite serious, although I thought she was showing off, and after she had said it they both went into raptures about Japanese poetry.

I was thin too, but until then it had never occurred to me to write verses about it. For me, poetry had always been stuff like 'Let the Song of *Purim* Rise' and Petőfi's 'Hang All the Kings'.

Alone in the flat, I lined up my football team of coloured buttons against Dávid's, and played both sides. Mine won 26:1. I read a story by Hoffmann which frightened me so much that I ate twenty-five lumps of sugar, a double blunder since sugar was expensive and I was supposed to have a tummy-ache anyway. I was desperately trying to remember whether it was possible to feel hungry on top of a tummy-ache when I suddenly had a burst of inspiration. Mother thought pretty highly of that Japanese poet.

I took out a piece of paper. At the top, I wrote: 'The Sick Boy'. It looked pretty good. As Japanese poems didn't seem to have to rhyme, the rest was child's play.

> *'Fever eats his body.*
> *The sun shines outside.*
> *But he lies like a log turned to ash.'*

Mother was over the moon. The twenty-five sugar-lumps were dismissed as poetic licence, although Gyula was as dubious as I was about a poem that didn't rhyme.

My tummy-ache persisted into the next day – the sugar of course! Dávid was green with envy. He didn't see why poets were exempted from going to school. The only problem was that because of my illness all I'd had for supper was a bowl of caraway-seed soup. I was starving. Luckily Mother asked me whether I could manage to make it down to the shop for some ham and biscuits, and I bravely declared that I could just about stagger that far. The real treat was the biscuits because the packet had English words on it and I could get an idea of how England tasted.

I was grateful to Mother, so I tried to write another verse to my poem and tore it up immediately because it was such whining that even Mother would have guessed there was nothing wrong with me. Next day I went to school.

The other war was going well. The entire Luftwaffe had been shot down in flames by the Royal Air Force, and the newspapers seemed to have forgotten their predictions of the summer, when they had joined the French in saying that England would have its neck wrung like a chicken by the autumn. We still couldn't afford to have our radio mended, so I only heard the English figures second-hand. Apparently the BBC's figure for German casualties was ten times higher than the one quoted by Hungarian radio, and everyone knew that the BBC never told lies and that the Hungarian news never did anything else.

It was still a bit early to be sure exactly when the English would be reconquering France, Poland, Belgium, Holland and Norway; but Horthy would have had to be even stupider than he was to bring Hungary into the war now that the main German weapon, the Luftwaffe, had been defeated. It was true that their other main weapons, the Panzers, were still around; but without air support they weren't much better than bicycles, and the English tanks and planes were made by America so they were much better than the German ones, which might as well be scrapped and, anyway, how were the Germans going to land all these hundreds of thousands of stormtroopers in England when their boats were too scared of the Royal Navy even to go out fishing?

All the same, the Germans were gradually luring Hungary into the war. They had made the Rumanians give most of Transylvania back to us, which would have been fair enough if the Germans hadn't been involved. On the platform beside the playground in Erzsébet Square, a military band broke into the 'Transylvania March' every half hour, and spent the rest of its time bashing out Hungarian and German marching songs. A few weeks before it had been playing nothing but waltzes. The Boy Scouts had already taken refuge in an air-raid shelter, and while I was prepared to admit that most of the Jews – apart from me and Mik – were a pretty faint-hearted lot, I noticed that even the fascist newspapers, who didn't give a damn about us Jews, were advertising bomb-proof shelters complete with beds. Unlike Petöfi, who had wanted a hero's death, most Hungarians preferred to die in bed. If only the English would start bombing . . .

Since the heroic reconquest of Transylvania, officers had been swaggering in the streets, behaving like lords and treating civilians as if they were serfs. A news-vendor whom I knew well by sight passed our home shouting about the 'Transylvanian Triumph', as if the army had fought a series of bloody battles for it instead of licking Hitler's boots until he threw us a bone. The news-vendor appeared to believe that he and Horthy had led the charge.

The classroom door opened one morning to reveal Mrs Pig from the play-centre instead of Berger. Nervously, she announced the approach of the beautiful festival of *Chanukah*, and told us that the Head-master had asked her to teach us some Jewish songs, although she was sure that coming from good God-fearing Jewish families and having lived through eight *Chanukahs* already we must know lots of songs – which would facilitate our learning and deepen our enjoy-ment of the singing . . .

Her nervousness surprised me. At the play-centre she was a tough woman and didn't look particularly small. Here she seemed to have shrunk. She didn't know how to handle good children. In a faint voice, she asked us if we knew the song '*Maoz Tzur*', 'Rock of Ages'. But her shyness didn't frighten all the goody-goodies like Benjamin Steiner, who was poor enough always to be dressed in his five brothers' cast-off clothes but didn't quite make the grade for the play-centre. He was terrified of Berger, but faced with the unexpectedly mild Mrs Pig his confidence rose alarmingly. He started thumping his desk and shouting, 'Transylvania is ours! Long live Mount Hargita! Teach us the "Transylvania March"!'

Then Bolgár the Tape-Measure burst into the last verse of the song and about ten children joined in:

> '*Sweet Transylvania hear our cry*
> *For you your sons will live and die!*'

Meanwhile, another group launched into the first verse, and after a few bars the others took it up as well:

> '*From woods and valleys, mountain peaks,*
> *A single word our nation speaks,*
> *A song arises from that word,*
> *And naught but "Transylvania" heard!*'

'Silence, silence, please,' snuffled Mrs Pig delicately, although I knew from the play-centre that she could shout loudly enough to bust our eardrums, and was quite capable of throwing a sponge or even a flowerpot at the wilder ones. The class took no notice of her, and I

105

half expected her to burst into tears. I nearly burst into tears of rage myself. Only a few days previously the cubs had sworn their oaths on the Only Fatherland and the Resurrection of Hungary, and now this bunch of wimps in plaits were singing a fascist hymn. If this had been the play-centre I would have been breaking noses.

And then something extraordinary happened. Aaron Kohn jumped on to the teacher's platform, turned to face the class, and raised his clenched fists towards the ceiling.

'SHUT UP!' he shouted, and like Moses during the battle against the Amalekites, he held his thin arms in the air until the song died out and a breathless silence fell upon the class.

'Don't you see?' asked Aaron Kohn, scarcely raising his trembling voice. 'We Jews will pay for this in the end. Maybe with our blood.' His arms dropped, and he looked at us.

'I read an article called "The Transylvanian Problem" in yesterday's paper. Shall I tell you what it said? Or can you guess? It said that with the reannexation of Transylvania, Hungary is lumbered with even more Jews. That they occupy even higher positions there, hold even more of the country's wealth, and that an urgent solution must be found to this Hebrew plague . . . Shall I go on?'

There was a stunned silence. Kohn walked sadly back to his desk, and quietly began to sing a *Chanukah* song. Everyone joined in.

I had never felt anything like that. It reminded me of when I heard about Elek lifting Kovács's anvil up to the trembling Virgula's nose, but Elek was a grown-up. This boy was no older than the rest of us, but he had become a high priest and our true teacher, Aaron Cohenite. From that moment on, he was a prince, a prince of Judaea.

Of course the miracle didn't last for ever. At the end of the song Mrs Pig remarked, 'We don't engage in politics.'

Still, when she decided that we needed air to sing and couldn't open the window, Bolgár the patriotic Tape-Measure, who was a head taller than any of us, went to help her.

'Let me do it, Miss,' he said. 'I'm bigger than you.'

I heard the 'Transylvania March' at every street corner.

The 'English Park', as the funfair was called, was already closing down for the winter by the time Gyula kept his promise to take us there, and there were only a few stalls and arcades still open. Soldiers were flying along in swing-boats with screaming girls, while other lonelier soldiers stood by, looking up and whooping as the wind caught the girls' skirts. The House of Lilliput stood nearby, where you

106

could see fire-eating, weight-lifting, somersaulting dwarfs for a quarter of the price of going to the circus. The way they recruited their audience was an event in itself, and happened free of charge between each of their twenty-five-minute shows, on a platform in front of the entrance. A robust twenty-stone woman stood surrounded by a group of dwarfs, all of them shouting and interrupting each other. It was hardly how I imagined Snow White and the Seven Dwarfs.

'Roll up! Roll up! See the amazing battle of Cyclops the Dwarf and the Giant Serpent! The most gigantic snake in the known universe pitted against the smallest man of all time, a dwarf among dwarfs! The brains of the Serpent against the cunning of Man! The Mightiest Midget in the world! Tickets only thirty fillérs, soldiers twenty-five, sergeants twenty . . .'

When a large enough crowd had gathered, about ten dwarfs marched out of the House of Lilliput and lined up in front of a flagpole as if on parade. One of the dwarfs from the platform stood up on a stool that made him slightly taller than Snow White, and launched into a short oration for the benefit of the soldiers and the crowd.

'Our mutilated Hungary,' he declaimed, 'its body crippled, its soul unbowed, weeping for its past, yet confident in its present and trusting in a brave and joyful future, this Fatherland of ours is asking us a single question . . .'

He paused. A long pause. Then, in a voice the size of the woman, the dwarf roared: 'Will the Sons of Hungary live to be happy again?' and the tiny troops yelled, 'YES! YES! YES!' with about half the crowd echoing the cry.

'Hoist – the – FLAG!' ordered the dwarf, jumping down from his stool and running over to the flagpole to hoist the flag himself with a piece of string. As it rose, the dwarf army broke into song; the familiar strains of the 'Transylvania March' rang out as two more dwarfs emerged on the platform, one blowing a trumpet and the other beating a drum. Another flag was produced and given to the chief dwarf, who barked another order. The miniature army began marching on the spot and then, with a smart about-face, trooped off towards the House of Lilliput to the stirring sound of the two-bit band and the 'Transylvania March'.

As they disappeared inside, the woman's voice tore through the closing lines of the song to shout, 'Cyclops the Dwarf against the Giant Serpent! Tarzanito – the strongest half-man in the world! The performance begins in two minutes . . .'

107

'The English will surrender tomorrow if their spies report this!' laughed Gyula. He had brought along his camera to immortalise the occasion, and paid generously for Dávid and me to go on the merry-go-rounds and to do target practice with wooden balls and catch clay fish. But on the following Tuesday, when I brought back what was only Berger's second rebuke of the week, Gyula muttered, 'They must mean something . . .' And when the third arrived he actually raised his voice: 'Behave yourself in school!'

'Here we go,' I thought, realising that he had only sided with me to gain authority at Berger's expense. He hadn't been in the military police for nothing. Still, it was a relief to be out of his good books . . .

5: Sheep in Wolves' Clothing

The cubs had a secret language. Bandi-Ba was always in the middle of a story, and everyone knew what was going on and what was about to happen except me and Dávid.

'And then Mowgli fell off the tree,' interrupted a tiny but enthusiastic wolf called Calm Smile.

'That comes later,' said the priggish Sharp Flair, who was wearing a tie under his cub's scarf.

A creature called Bagheera, who might have been a bear although I couldn't tell because all the animals were like people, was carrying Mowgli towards a river. It was clearly some kind of Tarzan story, although I couldn't work out whether Mowgli was a child or a monkey. Whether they were bears or snakes, all the animals talked like the rich kids' mothers, and each one was nicer and kinder than the last. The story wasn't a fairy tale, but it wasn't true either; apparently Baden-Powell used to like it.

This Baden-Powell was a shady sort of fellow, and he soon got me into trouble with Bandi-Ba. He had died a couple of years previously, and a black-framed photo of him was hanging on the wall. It showed a lean, severe, dense-looking old soldier with a scout hat on his head. He had invented scouting. What made me suspicious was that newspaper cutting underneath the photo, which read: 'Compassion and love suffuse his noble face. His Serenity the Governor had the highest regard for his achievement.' Above the photo, in big coloured letters, the cubs had written: 'His memory will live for ever in our hearts.'

At first I couldn't understand how an Englishman could be loved both by Miklós Horthy and by Jewish Boy Scouts, but it didn't take me long to decide that he was a German spy and had been found out and shot by the English. They were only pretending that he'd died of a stroke because they were too ashamed to admit that an Englishman had been a traitor.

We were supposed to buy caps, scarfs and jerseys, but first we had to wait for Mother's November money. Then we discovered that even her December wages wouldn't go far enough, and in the end I got a cap, Dávid got a scarf, and neither of us got a jersey since we already had warm blue ones and it was silly to buy new green ones just for the colour. We had to take turns wearing the cap and tie, which meant that Dávid went one week and I went the next, both lying left, right and centre about why the other was absent. So I never heard the end of the ghost story about the sailor and his stolen leg. When we finally realised that I wouldn't be getting a tie and that Dávid would always be short of a cap, we went together wearing what we had. The others looked at us as if we'd come from Mars, and an ugly Jewish-faced Jewboy with big ears called Csaba Krausz-Keszi started whispering to his neighbour. They giggled.

Our first excursion started at the Margit Bridge, on the Buda side of the river. We all met up in the middle of a square beside a huge statue of a lion lying down. Carved into the pedestal was a word which God Himself couldn't have pronounced: 'Przemysl'. We had enough trouble recognising the wolf-pack, who were gathered together on the far side of the statue in storm jackets, with big daggers on their wide belts. Dávid and I were wearing our ordinary winter coats, and as soon as he saw them Dávid grabbed my arm and said, 'Let's go home,' but I pulled him with me and joined the others.

I learned from Bandi-Ba that the unpronounceable word was the name of a Polish fortress in the First World War. It had been defended heroically by the Hungarians until they had lost the battle to the Russians.

'If they lost the battle, why isn't the lion lying on its back?' I asked Bandi-Ba. His mouth fell open, and stayed like that for about half a minute, so remembering the nationalistic 'prayers' of the normal meetings, I went on to point out that supporting Ferencváros made sense, because they won the cup more often than any other team; but supporting the Hungarian Army was silly: they hadn't won a war since King Mátyás, and that included this one, which they'd lost before the kick-off.

'No scout should talk like that about the Fatherland!' declared Bandi-Ba when he finally managed to say anything.

'What about an English scout?' I asked. 'What would Baden-Powell say?'

It eventually emerged that both English and Hungarian scouts had to love their Fatherlands, and I asked if that made them enemies. What Bandi-Ba hadn't grasped, perhaps because I was only vaguely aware of it myself, was that the reason I was being so awkward had less to do with wolves and lions than with the fact that everyone except me and Dávid was wearing a dagger.

We got on to a tram as far as Zugliget, and then headed towards the hills on foot. Dávid was carrying our knapsack, which was half the size of everyone else's. They'd all brought the kitchen sink. A fat kid with black, curly hair was panting beside me. Being used to walking to my grandfather's vineyards, I was just beginning to wonder when the excursion would begin, when Bandi-Ba ordered a rest. The fat kid fell on his bottom and set upon his knapsack, but Bandi-Ba stopped him, saying that it wasn't lunchtime yet.

'I hate scouting,' whispered Fatty bitterly. 'But Mummy says I must eat less or do some sport. What does she want me to be, a wrestler?'

'What do you want to be?' I asked him. He was called Calm Bear, although his real name was András Fodor.

'All I got for breakfast was two eggs and a bite of sausage,' he went on sadly. 'Even a mouse would die of starvation on helpings like that . . .'

It turned out that he wanted to be a pianist. He had his own piano and sat playing it all the time he wasn't at school or at scouts or doing his homework. The trouble was, his Mummy chased him away to walk their dog five times a day because that was healthy, like scouting.

We ambled along for about an hour until we reached a big clearing, where Bandi-Ba gave the order to have lunch. András the pianist opened his knapsack like a shot, but was stopped yet again by the command: 'Let us . . . PRAY!'

What next? Please, sir, shall we turn towards the Wailing Wall or do you want us to kneel down like the *goys*? Everybody stood to attention and raised his arm in the wolf-cub salute. Luckily, we didn't have to goose-step in front of the Almighty, but we had to pray for everything and everybody, including our parents, the Pack, His Serenity the Governor and Our Beloved Fatherland, while András

111

Fodor's mouth moved greedily, chewing his words for want of food. We had to throw in an 'I believe' or two, and only just stopped short of *'Sieg Heil'*.

Tin boxes emerged from all the knapsacks, and smaller tin boxes from the bigger ones. From these, the wolf-cubs extracted several tons of roast meat and cakes; from their pockets came ivory-handled penknives; our fat friend the pianist had brought along two thermoses the size of cooking pots – apparently his mother didn't want him to die of starvation after all. They were food thermoses, which I'd never heard of before, and when he lifted the lid of one of his tin boxes and gazed with satisfaction on its cargo of cakes, I couldn't help laughing. His lunch would have been enough for a peasant family at harvest time.

'Won't you starve?' I asked sympathetically. He measured up the cakes again with a frightened glance, and then looked at me. The box was as big as a tray, and wordlessly he pushed it towards me.

I nodded bravely, and offered some of our food wrapped up in paper napkins. He understood straight away that he'd got the worst of the bargain, but his smile didn't waver. Without fuss, he tore one of our sausages in half and took such a bite out of it that even two of his church mice wouldn't have complained. I was quite careful about eating too much of his cake, but Dávid ate back our sausage with interest when he got going on the chicken. In the end, though, our host-guest didn't seem to mind much about sharing, and I realised that his heart was in the right place.

We strolled for a while to walk off our lunch, and then lined up in a field to do some jousting. This involved splitting up into pairs: one person became a horse and the other was his rider, who had to pull all the other riders off their horses.

'Why do I always have to be a horse?' moaned Fatty. 'Pity you're so thin.' At least he had a light rider, I pointed out. But he was a rotten horse, they'd hardly touched my arm when he dropped me. In the second game he couldn't even find a rider, and had to become a spectator, walking sadly up and down the battlefield. I rode Dávid, and we survived quite a while. He made quite a strong little pony, but I made him swap to show him what a real war-horse was like. I kicked about a bit, and we came through the early stages without much trouble. Dávid hauled at the rider's arm while I tripped the horse up, and then as they went over we'd take off and do the same again. We were heading for total victory when who should appear but Bandi-Ba, just when I happened to be punching an enemy horse in the stomach.

On top of disqualifying us, he told me off for being a badly broken and unchivalrous horse.

One evening, Aunty Felice came to visit us. Beforehand, Mother washed the kitchen tiles and polished the floor in the big room, and made me and Dávid put on clean shirts. She couldn't understand why I wouldn't wear my best suit, but I didn't want to show anyone, least of all Aunty Felice, how much I was looking forward to the visit.

She was even more beautiful than I remembered her, and just as unreal. She was wearing a short, sleeveless fur jacket, and a dress that almost swept the ground; she came in slowly so as not to trip over it. And it wasn't just her eyes that sparkled, her ears did too: with long, glittering pendants.

'Diamonds?' I guessed aloud. 'They must be worth a hundred pengös!'

'Józska!' my mother gasped indignantly.

'Nasty little brat!' muttered Gyula, stupefied. Then he tried to defend me. 'Take no offence, he's just a country boy.'

'I have to go on from here to a place where jewellery is *de rigueur*,' explained Aunty Felice. 'But it was more important to come here and I wouldn't have had time to change . . .'

'I see,' I nodded. 'Better to come dressed up. Anyway, I've never seen diamonds before.'

Gyula winced. 'He'll be seeing what six of the best are like if he isn't quiet.'

'What for?' asked Aunty Felice, sticking up for me. Then she took out two parcels wrapped in coloured paper and put them on the table. The first was a big square box that was obviously full of chocolate. She handed it to Mother, which meant that the other one must be for us.

Gyula brought a chair for Aunty Felice, although not for Mother. He didn't quite brush the dust off the seat like a peasant woman, but only just stopped himself. He was practically standing to attention, hanging on Aunty Felice's words as everyone chatted and pretended to ignore the parcels on the table.

Aunty Felice asked me how I enjoyed school, but Mother answered for me before I could open my mouth.

'He loves it!' she exclaimed. Aunty Felice looked at me to show that she expected me to answer for myself, but Mother butted in again. 'Józska, tell Aunty Felice what you said about her after the last time she came.'

I didn't have a clue what she was talking about. I must have looked an idiot because Mother tried to remind me.

'About chocolates . . . ' she said encouragingly. I was still in the dark, but I had to say something polite . . . I must have said something like 'thank you for the chocolates' but it'd be silly to say it all over again when I'd just thanked her for the new box. Why didn't Dávid open it? He was standing just beside the table and he'd already thanked her too . . .

'Did I say that the chocolates were great?' I guessed, and everyone laughed.

'Yes, but you said something else, do you remember?'

'About the chocolates? What else? I can't have said they were nasty.' Everyone laughed at me again, but Mother wouldn't give up.

'Something about Aunty Felice . . .'

I felt like sinking into the floor. I must have said something incredibly soppy. I hated the grown-ups, endlessly chirping and chattering and kissing. I was grateful to Aunty Felice for not even shaking hands with me. I was dizzy with embarrassment.

'He said, "I would like Aunty Felice even if she didn't bring us chocolates," ' I heard Mother say proudly. I went deaf for about a minute; then I tried to get my own back by being cocky without even noticing that they were already talking about something else.

'I never said I didn't want Aunty Felice to bring chocolates,' I said, pointing to the oddly shaped parcel on the table. 'What's in there? It doesn't look like chocolate.'

Mother hissed, but Aunty Felice burst out laughing. 'Open it and see!'

Together, Dávid and I slowly opened the parcel, trying hard not to seem greedy. Inside was a big box, with two separately wrapped objects in it. The grown-ups went on talking, but they were watching us out of the corners of their eyes and I was listening to what they were saying about the war. Gyula was talking about the Battle of Britain, but he didn't seem to know anything I didn't. Still, he was quite sure he knew everything about it, and wouldn't let Aunty Felice get a word in edgeways.

'Do you listen to the English radio?' I asked Aunty Felice. Gyula made one of his train noises to tell me that I had interrupted him, but Aunty Felice ignored it.

'Every day,' she replied. 'In English,' she added, unable to resist showing off.

'Aunty Felice!' I cried. 'Will you teach me English?'

She looked startled, but Gyula flew to her rescue. 'You'll have to learn to write your Hungarian alphabet properly first, young man.'

'Problems with writing?' asked Aunty Felice, surprised.

I answered as quickly as I could so she wouldn't think I was a dummy. 'I had to learn the new letters, the city ones. The ones we learnt in the country are beautiful but they're old-fashioned.'

'That must be difficult,' she said, taking my side. 'You'd just learnt to write and now they want you to forget it again for another sort of writing that isn't even beautiful. Silly.'

'The writing's not the difficult bit,' I replied, trying to cheer her up. 'It's my teacher. He's a moron.'

'Józska!' shouted Gyula, but I didn't hear him. Neither did Aunty Felice.

'Doesn't Dávid help you?'

'He tries, but I mustn't learn too fast or the teacher will be too pleased with himself.'

'You don't like him, do you?' said Aunty Felice. I could tell that she agreed with me already.

'Here we are!' interrupted Gyula. 'It's all coming out now. We'll have to have a word about this, you little imp.'

'Why is it good if the teacher thinks he's failed with you?' asked Aunty Felice sympathetically.

'Because this child has no respect! That's why!' Gyula was having trouble keeping his voice down. Aunty Felice remained curious.

'Doesn't your teacher deserve your respect?'

'Of course not,' I answered. 'If you get a question right, he just nods as if he's bored.' I started imitating Berger's nod. 'But he loves it if you get it wrong, he blossoms with rage . . .'

'That's silly, Józska,' interrupted Gyula. He was trying to sound jolly.

'Blossoms with rage?' Aunty Felice shook her head, smiling.

'He's only happy when he's shouting,' I went on, 'and he's always trying to find some reason for blowing his top unless it's Aaron Kohn. If Aaron Kohn said three threes were a hundred, Berger would still be over the moon . . .'

'Is Aaron Kohn a bootlicker?'

'No! Aaron Kohn's going to be a great man; it's Berger who licks Kohn's boots.'

Aunty Felice frowned and lifted her head.

'A teacher, licking a child's boots? Is that likely, Józska?'

115

'It's Mr Kohn's boots he's licking really. "Give my regards to your eminent father . . . Wonderful, Kohn, wonderful! Three threes are nine, yes, exactly, exactly nine, yes, always exactly nine, very good, very, very, nine, very, very nine, indeed . . ." ' I may have been exaggerating a little, but it was a good imitation. Aunty Felice burst out laughing again.

'Does Kohn work out the answer on paper before he replies?' demanded Gyula irritably. God knows why he was so annoyed. I had only used three threes as an example, but there wasn't time to explain.

'For three times three?' I asked scornfully. 'Of course not. Aaron Kohn's the brightest kid in the whole school.'

'Now then, slowly does it,' said Gyula, raising his index finger to show how wise he was. 'Your Aaron Kohn may be bright, but he's only a child.' He started telling an anecdote.

Meanwhile, Dávid had unwrapped the parcel. A china cat and dog were standing on the table, and it was lucky I'd thanked Aunty Felice in advance because she could tell by my face that I had no use whatever for china livestock. These things were meant to sit on a mantelpiece; she'd bought them for Mother and then given her the chocolates by mistake. I wanted to point this out, but Gyula was talking again.

'It was during the Slump, around '33 or '34. Several hundred men turned up for an assistant accountant's job. Each man spent less than a minute in the interview room, and they were all asked the same question: "What's two and two?" Everyone outside was getting angry about the bosses making fools of the poor, but even the men who'd already been thrown out hung around to find out what they should have answered. They were furious; they thought that they'd been tricked into a charade and the job had already gone to some nephew. One little shrimp in glasses went in laughing his head off, and told them that two and two was three. He got no points for originality: he got slung out faster than the rest of them. Well, after a bit, this bony, clumsy-looking bloke goes in. He looked more like a peasant than an accountant – he had one of those short coats on, and he stamped his feet on the mat like he'd just walked in from his fields – anyway, they asked him what two and two was, and he said: "If you give me a pencil and paper I'll tell you." They gave him the job.'

Meaningfully, Gyula stopped talking. I couldn't see the point of the story. All it seemed to prove was that Gyula wasn't alone in being completely off his head.

116

'Why?' I asked.

'Don't you see?' Gyula smiled wisely. 'They wanted a man who was reliable, someone who didn't take any chances. The man showed that he was solid, dependable . . .'

'And thick,' I added. Gyula went redder than usual and Aunty Felice, who had been smiling until then, bit her lip.

'Thick?' Gyula snapped. 'Why thick? Perhaps you'd like to explain.'

'If you like,' I replied cheekily to show Aunt Felice how brave I was. 'He must have been thick or he'd have realised that you either know what two and two is or you don't. Pencil and paper can't help you. The boss must have been thick as well if he didn't realise that. The others were probably right about him just making them turn up so he could enjoy throwing them out. I bet the peasant ended up sweeping the floor.'

'It wasn't how much two and two is that the boss wanted to know,' Gyula said heavily.

'So why didn't they ask him what twenty-two twenty-twos are instead? It's worth using paper then, you just might make a mistake.'

'Just might,' Gyula mocked. 'Quick, what's twenty-two times twenty-two?' He must have imagined that I wasn't expecting him to ask, but I'd already started working it out. Dávid tried to help me, but I got the answer out first.

'At least he can count,' Gyula commented, 'even if he can't write.' He turned to me again. 'But Józska, you didn't use a pencil!' he pointed out triumphantly.

'I would have done if I hadn't been sure, though!' I replied in even greater triumph, checking the figure just in case.

'So, what were we talking about before the kid interrupted us?' said Gyula, searching his memory.

'England?' I suggested politely. Gyula swallowed furiously. I knew that while Aunty Felice was there I could say whatever I liked, but I shut up. The subject interested me.

We were all pretty much in agreement about the war situation. But, in general, even grown-ups who supported the English spent too much time sighing and moaning about 'what we'll have to suffer'. It wasn't enough for them to know that we were going to win in the end.

Aunty Felice had heard a lot of things on the English radio that I only half knew, but she had a few ideas that surprised me. I almost got cross with her when she told us that some people reckoned that Hitler never intended to land in England.

117

'Well why did he send all those thousands of planes over?' Aunty Felice thought – or rather the people she'd heard thought – that Hitler had been making a show of strength to force England into signing a peace treaty recognising his conquests. And she couldn't understand why the British wouldn't sign; after all, they hadn't lifted a finger for Poland. One theory was that if a single German platoon had set foot in England the United States would have come into the war, which would have been a whole lot worse for the Germans than losing a few thousand aeroplanes. Apparently Hitler hadn't used a quarter of his planes in the Battle of Britain, he'd only wanted to show that he could have invaded if he'd wanted to. In the end all he'd proved was that he couldn't have invaded even if he *had* wanted to. The conclusion Aunty Felice drew from all this was that the war was going to last much longer than anyone had thought a few months ago.

While listening avidly to the conversation, I had been playing with the china dog to attract attention to it and clear up the misunderstanding over the presents. This happened. Rather suddenly. I was just trying to be polite and tactful when the room went quiet for a moment.

'What's this stuff good for, anyway?' I blurted out, forgetting all the cunning questions I had prepared so carefully. Mother looked horrified, but Aunty Felice just smiled.

'They're for eating,' she replied.

At first I thought she was being sarcastic to get her own back after my brutal question, but I must have looked silly, because she giggled.

'They're meant to be eaten,' she repeated, and for a second I realised how stupid it would be to be a rich, gold-toothed kid. It turned out that the china was just a thin layer of sugar that peeled off as easily as paper, but I couldn't see the point.

'Why's it a dog, then?' I asked.

Aunty Felice shrugged cheerfully. 'So it can serve some sort of purpose before it's eaten.'

I still didn't understand. 'Why is chocolate better if you have to eat a puppy for it?'

Pain flared in Aunty Felice's eyes like blank grey steel. She shook her head gently and only her earrings flashed with a dead light.

'It's only a pretend dog,' she said. She had to leave.

The puppy and the kitten looked sadly at me from the table. They had overheard that they were only made of chocolate.

6: Heading for Trouble

After Aunty Felice had left, Mother and Gyula both started telling me off for talking about the diamonds in such a badly brought up way and being so ungrateful for the presents. They told me that I was greedy, that I had made it quite clear that I wanted a real puppy instead of a chocolate one – what were we going to do if Aunty Felice listened to me? She's so generous she might give me a dog. It'd cost a fortune to feed and there'd be no one to look after it during the day; it'd chew up all the furniture that hasn't even been paid for and in any case we weren't allowed a dog on our side of the building, we could only have a cat . . .

I pointed out that we'd received a chocolate cat as well, and keeping a real one wouldn't be that expensive, but my arguments were dismissed as yet another example of my impertinence and I knew quite well why. I had interrupted Gyula several times, scoffed at his anecdote and treated him as if he had been a stranger. But what was I to do? I really did resent him as an intruder when Aunty Felice was there, a nosy, uninvited guest who went rambling on and on instead of letting me talk to Aunty Felice. In the few minutes since she'd left, the room had become shadowy and cold, and now they were trying to make me believe that it was my fault that the warmth and the light had gone. But I told myself that this sombre room with its tired light wasn't the real one, and that it should always be the way it had been half an hour before, and that if Gyula weren't there it would be.

The next day, at school, I was still half asleep when Berger came round handing back the special exercise books that we only wrote in when we did our monthly compositions in class. He announced that everyone, no matter what mark he had received, was to take his book home to be signed. No excuses.

119

I opened mine. The page was raw and bruised with red slashes and scrawled comments. Underneath my composition burned three 'E's – for spelling, style and presentation. Beneath them Berger had engraved a warning in letters of blood: 'You are heading for trouble.'

Three 'E's?

'How dare you?' I roared.

Berger must have been very pleased with me.

'Who is daring what?' he asked calmly, faking indignation.

'You!' I shouted. I didn't give a damn about trying to look cool. This time we weren't playing a friendly.

'You!' I shouted again, my voice tearing into the stunned air. I was through with border incidents; this meant war and I wanted Berger to know who he was up against. 'You can give me what you like for presentation and style. You can give me a "Z" if it gives you a kick. I don't give a damn about what pleases you – that's your business . . .'

Berger was enjoying the situation. He must have foreseen it. 'You can't behave like this in my class, Sondor. I'm going to have you kicked out.'

'Do! Feel free. But why do I get an "E" for spelling? There isn't a single spelling mistake in the whole bloody thing. You just painted the page red. And what did you scribble on it? "I cannot read this, illegible, unreadable" twenty-five times . . . How can you give me an "E" for spelling if you can't even read my writing? Give me an "A"! Or learn to read before you go around teaching other people! Aaron Kohn!' I called on Kohn as if he were the teacher, and in his stupefaction, Berger forgot to shut me up.

'What were you given?' I asked.

'Three "A"s,' replied Kohn. 'And I made three spelling mistakes,' he added, supplying me with ammunition without my having to ask.

'So I have to have my three "E"s signed while Kohn shows his father his three "A"s. What did you write underneath his composition? "Send my regards to your eminent boots. Your affectionate jar of fat, Ödön Berger?" '

The class didn't laugh. The silence was ominous. I decided to break it.

'Our teacher can't read. Kohn, you know how to read, you tell me if there are any mistakes in it!'

I got up, walked over to Kohn's desk and threw the book down in front of him. Berger stared into the air, blind and deaf. Invisible lightning had hit his classroom, and he didn't dare move for fear of burning. He was as unprepared for this as I was.

'You're going to have me kicked out, are you? I'm going to show my composition to the Head, he'll realise what sort of teachers he's got in his school! A bunch of sadists! Nazi thugs!'

For a moment, Berger stood there like a pillar. Then he jerked into motion, and came down to Aaron Kohn's desk like a falling cliff. He snatched my exercise book from Kohn's hand, and lifting it into the air, he ran at me.

I was sure he was going to hit me, and I lifted my fist ready to hit him back, not caring that this was the one thing that could really get me thrown out, not caring about anything. He could have had thirty witnesses, but in his berserk rage he didn't even notice. He drew his red pen from his pocket and gripped it like a knife. His other fist crashed down on to the desk, crumpling my exercise book as my neighbour ducked away to avoid the blow. Berger bent over the book, but he couldn't think of anything to write that would fit my crime. He drew himself upright, almost bending backwards, and shook his pen, grinding his teeth as he lurched back and forward. But suddenly sanity began to return to his eyes; a dark, gloomy sanity that slowed his breathing and gradually brought it back to normal. He threw back his head to think of some final, fatal punishment, and as if I could hear his thoughts, I suddenly remembered that I had raised my hand against him. I saw him recover his composure and knew he had reached his verdict. He drew a deep breath, slowly and calmly this time, not like a drowning man, rather like a soldier taking aim at a hated enemy.

But it was Aaron Kohn who spoke. Incredibly calm and objective, full of the confidence of the star pupil, he sounded nonchalant, almost indifferent.

'In the four lines I read, I didn't find a single spelling mistake,' he remarked.

Berger's breath died in his throat. It was as if his windpipe had been slit. After a few seconds, he began to howl like a wounded animal.

'I cannot teach here!' he wailed. 'Traitors! Conspirators! Two-faced brats!' He was striding up and down between the desks, but nobody dared laugh. The children in the front benches were bending aside like reeds in the face of the gale.

Berger rushed to my desk and, moving the pen from his fist so as to be able to write with it, he scrawled giant, drunken letters all across the page, more shapeless than mine, as if they were new to him too. His pen dug into the paper and then almost skidded off the page.

'VErY bIG tROUBle!!!' he wrote.

During break, while the others stood around looking confused and stayed away from me as if I had some contagious disease, Mik came up to me and made a low bow.

'In the next world,' he declared, 'I shall be your slave.' He was paying me the tribute due to a pagan hero from an old tale.

At the play-centre, I was the hero of the day. Everyone wanted to play marbles with me, even the line game. I was offered two cigarettes, and Mik clowned around like a showman, lifting up my arm as if I were a prize-fighter and announcing me to the others as: 'Joker Jo, Terror of the Teachers!'

I forgot all my anguish, the panic that had triggered my blind explosion, my indignation at the trampling of my rights, the injustice that had brought about my duel with Berger and without which I might have gone crying to Kohn instead of commanding him as witness and judge. There I was, smoking my first cigarette in a concealing bend of the corridor, chewing a toffee, surrounded by friends who admired me through the smoke. I was sampling the pride of a Chicago movie-gangster or a crime-baron from the papers, a pride as bitter as toffee and as sweet as smoke. Though I was the Terror of the Teachers, I couldn't boast too much at home about my deeds, or even explain the strange meaning of the red warning in my exercise book. I would have to present it to be signed a minute before bedtime, yawning sleepily and muttering about forgetfulness.

Gyula would have to be by-passed, as he was obviously still nettled by my cheekiness towards him in front of Aunty Felice. I didn't know whether this meant that I had broken our alliance, or whether it just meant that the alliance hadn't been worth anything anyway; but it didn't matter as Gyula had been faking his friendship all along. On the way home I explained to Dávid that, as far as I was concerned, Gyula was only a lodger, even if he didn't live with us. Dávid made wise remarks about Gyula being 'a nice man' and 'caring for us', to which I replied that I didn't care for him and I wished he didn't care for us and it's none of his bloody business who writes what in my exercise book. Dávid promised that he wouldn't rat on me and I switched to more important topics such as playing button-football on the table before supper, and informing him that if he wanted to be worthy of his younger brother he'd better stop being such a good little boy, always diving into his books the moment we got home.

It was no accident that I started talking about button-football at the height of my glory. We named all our buttons after real-life players, and my team, naturally enough, was the Ferencváros, the greatest team in the history of Hungary, and probably the world. Dávid's team was Szolnoki MÁV. The trouble was that the button that I had playing G. Sárosi was too light and tended to skid over the ball – usually a shirt button. I had been watching Dávid's team, and had my eye on the talented Kollát who, despite having holes rather than a loop, was a first-rate right-wing. Vainly, I made an appreciative remark about it, but Dávid didn't offer it to me as tribute and I had to change the subject fast so as not to compromise any subsequent transfer negotiations.

Mother and Gyula were sitting around the table in the main room. Gyula was holding his paper stiffly, and didn't even look up as he curtly returned our greeting. Mother was staring straight in front of her, her face flushed. She didn't seem to notice our arrival, which had obviously interrupted a quarrel. I realised that it would be minutes before we could get to the table.

Hinting gently, I started the ball rolling by asking a neutral question about what we were having for supper. If Mother would wake up and head for the kitchen, I could start lining up the buttons and force Gyula to give up the end of the table.

'Don't you have any bigger worries?' Gyula asked in a deep voice. He still didn't look up.

'Not really,' I replied absent-mindedly, knowing that too much self-confidence might stir up Gyula's smouldering temper.

'Didn't you get a reprimand today?' he asked, sounding bored. Suspicion must have got into his blood, working for the military police.

'My teacher forgot to give me one today. He must have had a headache,' I laughed.

'Today? Just today of all days?' Gyula nodded meaningfully, but he couldn't know anything.

'He's forgotten five times in the last month,' I said, labouring the joke. 'Maybe he's getting senile.'

'Show me your exercise book,' ordered Gyula. I couldn't understand why he was pushing so hard towards his goal, or even why he had one. I had been lying faultlessly, and Dávid's worried face couldn't have given me away because Gyula still hadn't looked up from his paper. I concluded that Gyula was looking for a fight, and trudged over to my satchel.

I took out the book we used for every day, and put it in front of
Gyula with an air of obedient boredom, just far enough away to make
him stretch. I reckoned that by the time he reached the last page and
saw Mother's signature, his suspicions would have faded, so I pulled a
cheeky face to obstruct the enquiry.

Gyula put down his newspaper but, like a true policeman, the
good fellow looked at me instead of at the book. He could stare at
me until his eyes ached, I wasn't even going to push the book in his
direction in case he thought I was trying to escape having to blink. I
gazed into his eyes, intensely sincere and bored, and stifled a yawn.

Gyula's face softened, and his gaze dropped to the exercise book.
He searched through it, glancing at my face every time he turned
a page. After a few pages, I moved respectfully and slowly to the
other end of the table, and began to set out my team with modest
self-confidence. I told Dávid to get his team out, but he moved too
slowly, his eyes on Gyula. He nearly gave me away. Frowning, Gyula
examined the last signature, and I grinned at him openly. I'd made a
fool of him again.

He turned the page and fixed his eyes on the emptiness that
followed the last rebuke. He could stare at it until moss grew on the
paper, for all I cared. His mouth hung open, his face growing longer
and longer by the minute, and the more he gazed at it the stupider he
looked. Mother came back into the room, her face burning.

'It must be there,' she said.

She must have met someone who told her about my duel with
Berger! But she didn't know anyone in my class – how could the news
travel so fast? While I was celebrating being the Terror of the Teachers
in the play-centre my fame seemed to have reached the Town Hall! It
must be guess work, the only people who had seen the rebuke itself
were Berger and Aaron Kohn, and Aaron Kohn wouldn't have told.
How could Gyula be so sure?

Mother stood in front of me, looking ashamed. Gyula had given
himself away – they must have been quarrelling about me before we'd
come home. I decided it was my turn to be underhand.

'Why don't you come in and have a chat with Berger some time
in the next few weeks if you're so worried?' I asked.

Brilliant – 'the next few weeks'. No hurry, just if she's nothing
better to do, there's no problem . . .

Mother didn't answer. She was trembling. Gyula seemed to be
waiting for her reply as well, and I guessed he must have promised to

hide the fact that she had betrayed me to him. He jumped to his feet, knocking the chair over, his face even redder than his hair. Dávid jumped into the corner for cover, and Mother took half a step forward.

'Jesus bloody Christ!' shouted Gyula. He'd flipped. ' "Why doesn't she come in and have a chat?" As if his teacher hasn't asked every bloody day to see his mother! This hell-spawned plague has got to be stopped! He almost made me believe you'd dreamt your conversation with his teacher! The Devil himself couldn't lie better!'

His fury inspired him. With a policeman's unerring instinct, he snatched up my satchel and tipped everything on to the table. He seized the newest-looking book and opened it. At the right place. Not the stuff to calm him down. I put one hand in front of my stomach to defend myself and had the other ready to attack. Transferring my weight to my left leg, I tensed my right thigh in preparation for an almighty kick.

'What's that?' he yelled. Not surprisingly, he was pointing at Berger's most threatening reprimand to date, sprawled drunkenly under the three 'E's. This time Gyula really lost control. He shouted so much he nearly lost his voice as well. The fight was about to start, and there wasn't much point in delaying any longer, with him already howling that I'd remember this day for the rest of my life . . . He doesn't realise that he's going to remember it too . . . What am I waiting for? The first blow often decides the battle . . . Hitler overran Holland and Poland and Belgium without a declaration of war . . . but Gyula is stronger than me and I'll be lucky to poke an eye out, Jo the Joker, Terror of the Teachers, Terror of the Police, Terror of the Hitlerites . . .

Gyula was still thundering out a storm of curses more like hail than rain. He was saying that he'd never come across such an inveterate cunning lying dissembling dyed-in-the-wool rogue among grown gangsters who'd all ended up swinging on a rope or rotting in gaol. He didn't realise that this was music to my ears and that I took the coming beating for granted. I didn't give a damn about the blows I was about to receive; my only concern was the blows I was going to deliver. Gyula ran out of breath just at the point of saying: '. . . and his father's son!'

'Thank God!' I said with deadly calm and superiority. 'Take that down in your little notebook,' I added.

His next line stuck in his throat. His eyes shifted above my head and locked on the wall behind me, his face petrified in disbelief, as if

125

he didn't know whether or not he was hallucinating and feared for his sanity. He started to breathe slowly, and his eyes sank back into their sockets as if he were thinking very deeply. For a second, he seemed to have calmed down, but I knew that my shaft had hit a more sensitive target than the one at which I had aimed.

'Take it down? I'll give you "take it down".'

Carefully, as if he were carrying out a definite, religious ceremony, he took off his jacket and laid it over the back of a chair. I couldn't escape him except by running around the table; Mother couldn't stop me getting out of the door – but who wants to run away? Gyula's undressing mesmerised me, and I guessed from his self-satisfied glance that that was exactly what he intended. Still, it didn't prevent me from showing my curiosity at this strange ritual of his. He rolled back his right shirt-sleeve.

I regarded myself as already beaten to a pulp, and looked round the room. While lining up the buttons, I hadn't noticed a cup on the far side of the table. Too small. Beside it was a teapot. The right size, and it would fit the hand perfectly . . . Mind you, the best thing would be for Dávid to get behind him without him noticing, which he could do easily, he's such a good quiet child, and while I'm attacking from the front he could hit Gyula on the head with the teapot, or why not a chair?

But Dávid, paralysed with fear, was looking at me imploringly from the divan; he wasn't even looking at Gyula . . . What the hell did he expect me to do?

Gyula pulled up his sweater and unfastened his belt. Slowly, he pulled the belt from the loops in his trousers, took it in his right hand, checked his grip, lifted it, slipped his right foot forward and quietly and calmly, without any anger, he gave the order: 'Come here. Twelve.'

I waited for a second, then with tiny steps that could have been mistaken for fear, I walked towards Gyula. He didn't move a muscle, but the distance was closing fast. It would have been difficult for me to grab the teapot without giving away my plan, but I wasn't bothered. I didn't feel entitled to a weapon: the danger didn't merit a breach of the Commandment. Mother stared at me from behind Gyula, her shoulders hunched, her eyes wide with fear, though whether it was fear for me or of me I didn't know. I kept approaching, drifting slightly to the side, and stopped sideways on to Gyula, a good step away from him. I could now feel the rhythm of the ceremony, and waited attentively for the next command.

'Bend over.'

Gathering every ounce of my strength, I kicked at his balls. Bull's eye!

Gyula gave a short scream and doubled up. He stayed like that for a few seconds, and I could have walked out of the flat with ease; but I folded my arms and waited for Gyula to stop bowing to me. Mother was screaming and running up and down the room, and Dávid was sobbing.

Gyula straightened up and threw himself at me. He began to thrash me, thumping me with his fists. The first few blows numbed me against the rest, and the world became a simple red cloud outside and inside my head, even in my stomach. I didn't know any more what was outside and what was inside, I only knew that Gyula was standing in front of me, my enemy. I hit him, kicked him, tried to bite him but only scratched his hand, my nose was wet and only hatred kept me conscious enough to catch the inside of his wrist between my teeth . . .

'. . . and he bites like a rabid dog,' I heard Gyula's voice saying, and went on biting on his veins until he tore his arm from my teeth. I felt disappointed that a chunk of it didn't remain in my mouth.

Suddenly Gyula stiffened, and I was able to straighten up. To my surprise, the blows had stopped. I punched Gyula's reddish nose; he didn't punch me back.

'You can see what it's like,' I heard Gyula's voice remark, and I looked around to see whom he was talking to. I could make out the shapes of several grown-ups standing in the doorway beside my mother, and I heard our neighbour, Mr Csolnoki, saying: 'But for pity's sake, how can you beat a child like this?'

'It's not a child,' replied Gyula. 'It's a devil's whelp.'

'All the same . . . ' reproached plump Mrs Kovács.

'I'll send him to a remand home,' Mother assured the neighbours.

'Rotten whore!' I yelled at her. The neighbours winced. Gyula slapped me lightly to keep up appearances and I didn't hit him back. It wasn't necessary.

My outburst must have reassured the audience. Having seen Gyula's brutality justified, they shuffled out of the flat. We stood immobile. In Gyula's glass eyes the lamplight didn't even flicker and I could hear the dumbness in his head; he couldn't talk, even to himself; he couldn't remember his name. I knew that I had wounded him far more jaggedly than I could ever have hoped. Worse than the shame he had felt in front of the neighbours was the gash in his pride as

127

a policeman. The angels were smiling. The Devil winked at me.

Dávid was sitting on the divan where he had been knocked down, looking at me with dry, fevered eyes as if he were hallucinating. I laughed at him comfortingly, but it did no good.

Mother was standing unsteadily in one place.

'His grandfather couldn't cope with him either,' she sighed. 'I'll have to send him to a remand home,' she repeated, sadly this time.

'And I'll have to send you to a brothel,' I answered quietly, but Gyula was already deaf. Mother too. And Dávid. Couldn't they see that I was the strongest in the room, stronger than all three of them put together?

Dávid was the first to move. He came over to me like a sleepwalker and put his hand on my shoulder, leaning on me for support. The movement seemed to wake Gyula up a bit, but he didn't do up the shirt-sleeve which was hanging uselessly from his arm. He lifted his jacket off the back of the chair and put it on, and later, from the kitchen, came the sound of him getting into his raincoat and shutting the door.

'And don't come back!' I shouted after him.

7: War on Two Fronts

Next morning, we tottered to the kitchen table and sat gazing vacantly into space, like castaways wondering where on earth they'd been washed up. No one said a word. Dávid made coffee and put the toast and dripping on the table, then sat down too. Mother cried silently, focusing on nothingness to stop the tears that filled her eyes whenever she looked at me.

Breaking the paralysis, I poured myself coffee and milk and started to eat. Having laid the foundations of the new order, I thought I'd better set an example. The immediate advantage of this was that I had avoided having to brush my teeth or wash. Sadly, Dávid's perfect manners hadn't changed.

'Go and wash your face!' he ordered.

Look who's playing big brother! And after taking such a small part in yesterday's performance . . . I shan't bother to answer him, I'm not going to let him use cowardly little rows about everyday things to rebuild that old superstition about the first-born being best. So, little brother's already recovering, is he? Still, it's too early in the morning to fight . . .

'Wash your face! It's all bloody.'

Bloody what? It might be worth taking a look at anyway. Blood? Mustn't wash it, they'll carry me round the play-centre on their shoulders. I'll go and have a look, admire it, it's my face after all . . .

It was even more beautiful than I had hoped. Blue, green and swollen. But as I stood delightedly in front of the mirror, a thunderbolt split my head: Berger! I couldn't allow him to see this, it would make him happier than seeing the Messiah.

'I'm not going to school,' I announced carelessly.

129

'You are,' said Mother in a weepy sort of voice.

'You go,' I answered, 'like yesterday. No point in both of us going.'

I'll have to tell Berger something feeble, so that he'll immediately decide that I've been playing truant. I mustn't look as if I'm desperate to hide it; I'll ham it up: 'Terrible tummy-ache, sir,' hand on stomach as if its still aching, any moron would guess it's not, never was. But that's not going to work either: how many days will it take to get rid of the bruises? And if I'm absent the day after Mother showed up, he'll guess the truth no matter what I tell him. He'll be delighted, no doubt about it! Worse still, the kids at the play-centre will pity me for being beaten up at home, and I won't be able to explain to them about it being a triumph. They get beatings every couple of days at home, they won't see the difference. They don't hit back, it doesn't occur to them, the same way that I take no notice of the occasional smacks Mother's given me since my happy home-coming. I was beaten up worse than they've ever been in their lives, but so what? They're tough kids, they're not going to cry over my black eyes. If I tell them it wasn't my father who beat me up they'll pity me for being a weedy orphan and they'll realise my mother's got some bloke into the bargain. Mind you, they'll be impressed with the way I kicked the sod in the balls. If they believe me . . .

'I didn't cry!' I boasted, making sure that Mother and Dávid wouldn't forget the truth about my heroic deeds. I wasn't going to let the details get buried in the dust of history. My words made Mother cry.

They're not going to believe it at the play-centre. My mother's got a bloke . . . It's none of their business what I think of my mother, but if they find out I'll have to be ashamed in front of them and all those big tough yobs are right little mummy's boys. I'll think up a good story on the way . . .

'Maybe I will pop into school,' I remarked casually. My timid obedience made Mother's eyes light up for a moment, but a second later she panicked.

'What are you planning to do to your teacher? You haven't got a knife on you, have you, Józska?'

If only Spitfire and the rest could hear this . . .

'No,' I answered with deliberate vagueness. I didn't want her to be too sure.

Mother stared at me wide-eyed. 'You can't go in with your face like that! They'll think we're barbarians, child-beaters . . .'

'You are, but don't worry, so is Berger,' I replied. Mother started sobbing and I had to look away so as not to be moved by the sadness of my world.

'Mother isn't a child-beater!' Dávid declared threateningly in the comfortable knowledge that he was stronger than me in an everyday fight. He was careful never to provoke me into a real one; I'd take him apart. But I hadn't the time to sit around worrying about Mother's villainy or Dávid's chivalry. I hardly wanted to draw even more attention to myself by making a late entrance. Dávid was trying to trip me up, but I side-stepped him.

'It's the only face I've got, so I'm going to school in it,' I told them. I quickly rinsed my face – which made no difference whatever – grabbed my coat and satchel, and off we went.

The second we reached the street, I had a brainwave. It must have been the fresh air. I grabbed Dávid's arm.

'Punch me on the nose!' I ordered.

Dávid stopped walking.

'Punch me on the nose!' I repeated.

'For being cheeky to Mother?' he asked angrily.

'You're such a creep,' I sighed.

'Watch it!' He raised his fist. 'Here? In the street?'

'Stop arguing; just hit me.'

'Why?' he demanded obstinately. 'For what you said to Mother?'

'Never mind. Hit me. Come on! Moron! Moron! Moron!'

Dávid lowered his fist. 'No. I'm not having you ordering me about.'

'What if I say please? Pretty please . . .'

'I'm not hitting you if you won't say why.'

'Why are you being so awkward all of a sudden? There's no time to explain. You're my brother, aren't you? So hit me!'

'No.'

'Weed! You're just frightened I might hit you back.'

'Me? Frightened of you? You need your head examined.'

'Cowardly little rabbit,' I taunted with my nose two inches from his.

'Me?' he repeated, raising his fist again. But straight away he lowered it.

'Coward! Weed! Frenchman!' I yelled, but Dávid gave a dismissive wave of his hand and walked on. He didn't understand. How could he? Suddenly he stopped and looked thoughtful.

'If you don't tell me why you want me to hit you, I'm going to beat you up.'

131

'Go on, then!'

He looked at me for a while, unable to decide what to do.

'Forget it,' I said. An irritating thought had just struck me. 'It wouldn't help, I'm a moron.'

'That's true,' Dávid answered automatically. 'Wouldn't help what?'

'Anything. I can pretend we've had a fight without us having to have a real one. Mind you, a few fresh bruises would look more realistic.'

'Good idea!' Dávid's eyes sparkled. 'That wouldn't shame the family – brothers are always having fights.'

'Sod your family!'

'What did you say?' Dávid yelled. He grabbed my arm. 'What did you say? Repeat it – if you dare!'

'Except you,' I conceded, without withdrawing the insult from Mother. This left Dávid torn between his personal satisfaction and his sense of duty. 'We must rush,' I added, increasing my stride. 'I've got a better idea.'

'You're not rushing anywhere till you take it back. From the whole family.'

'OK, I take it back. Numskull.' I started running.

I could hear Dávid shouting behind me: 'Even from our father! Take it back!'

'Not from him I won't.'

'Yes, you will!' he shouted, but he was a few steps further behind by now; I could hop faster than Dávid could run. 'You will!' he yelled again, trying to defend an authority that was declining with the distance. A few seconds later he gave in. 'All right, not from him, then . . . Wait for me!'

'I can't,' I shouted, but slowed down. He carried on nagging but I really was in a hurry. 'See you at the play-centre,' I said, speeding up again.

'I've got to look after you,' I heard from behind me. 'I must, you idiot!'

'Look after yourself!'

'You too! Don't fall in front of a car!'

'Don't you either,' I shouted over my shoulder as I galloped away.

I knew which side Mik came to school from. The street was still swarming with kids, and he didn't hurry when it wasn't too cold. He could never arrive late enough. By the time Mik appeared swinging his books in a string shopping bag, I'd got my breath back. I ran up to him.

'Don't hurry!' I urged him.

He gave me an odd look. 'Do I look as if I'm in a hurry?' he enquired.

'We must have a talk! Now. Right here.' We stopped. I sounded silly, like a grown-up. I'd never told someone that I wanted to talk to them before; I'd just talked. But luckily I didn't have to. Mik leaned towards me, studying my face, his mouth hanging open in admiration.

'Who did the decorations?' he asked in a respectful whisper. That respect was something I didn't want to lose.

'It's for yesterday. My mother came round after school and had a little chat with Berger.'

'Shit!' exclaimed Mik. Then his eyes clouded with incomprehension. 'Your mother beat you up like this?' He answered his question straight-away: 'Impossible. Who was it? Your dad?' he mumbled, knowing I hadn't seen him for four years.

What could I say? I could lie and say 'my uncle', but what would Elek have to say about that?

'My . . . step-father,' I stammered. It was plausible anyway, and I could face that sort of lie. But even Mik didn't have to know about Gyula being a *goy* and them not being married.

'You've got a step-father?' Lang looked suspicious. 'Didn't you take his name? Or didn't you want it? Tell me!'

'I can't! You keep asking questions. Listen, Mik, will you keep a secret?'

'Under torture,' he assured me. I gave him a hug, which surprised him although he put up with it.

'They're not married,' I said. Mik just nodded; he'd heard of things like that before. I sighed with relief: this wiry little kid was almost my brother.

'And he's *goy*,' I added. This he hadn't heard of before.

'*Goy?* You're joking!'

'I'm not . . .'

'Son of a Christian bitch!' he shouted. 'Did he do this to you? And your mother let him? Did he beat her up too? Was he drunk or what?' He had obviously heard of kids being beaten up, but not of a mother who allowed it to happen. My silence told him what he wanted to know. Mine had.

'Why did your mother . . .?' he asked, panic-stricken. Then he tried to help. 'Is the *goy* supporting you?' he asked. I shook my head, but having got this far I wanted to get things straight.

133

'Mother works. But the *goy* helps out.'

'How nice of him,' Mik replied. 'But you're not dependent on him. You come to my place and I'll show you to my dad; my dad'll go round to your place and your *goy* step-bloke will forget he ever heard of Jesus Christ! Let's go!' I realised that he meant to his father, not to school, but that wasn't what I wanted, not yet anyway.

'Later,' I said. 'We've got to sort Berger out first.' Mik thought I wanted his dad to beat Berger up too, and wasn't very keen. But when I reminded him about the reprimand, he understood what I meant. We couldn't let Berger dance on my grave. Mik also acknowledged that even Berger would put two and two together if he saw my face, and we couldn't allow that either. I told Mik my plan: we'd have to pretend that he and I had had a punch-up.

'Us?' Mik was indignant. 'But everyone knows we're best mates!'

'So what?' I argued. 'Even friends have fights. Me and my brother fight every other day.'

'Same here, but never like that. Even enemies don't fight like that, at least not every day.'

'Don't worry, we just fell out, we'll make it up,' I laughed. He laughed too.

'We'll manage. But what were we fighting about? In case they ask.'

'Marbles?' I suggested. 'Ten glass ones?'

Mik waved his hand contemptuously.

'A hundred?' I haggled.

'There aren't that many marbles in the whole play-centre,' he replied.

I made a final offer: 'I was rude about your mum.'

Mik's eyes froze, but he dismissed the idea. 'You wouldn't dare.'

'That's the whole point!' I yelled triumphantly. 'If I did!'

'I'd smash your face in,' sighed Mik, adding politely, 'and you'd smash mine in. And I'd be rude about your mum . . .'

We agreed. That was exactly what had happened. I suggested that we start fighting in the street so as to end up in front of the classroom, and then, as we were already late, Berger would come out to see what the noise was and never know the real reason why my face looked the way it did. Mik liked the plan.

'So hit me,' I ordered.

'What for?' he asked. I thought he was being stupid.

'Go on, hit me!'

'You? Never! What for?'

'To show we've been fighting, silly!' I shouted.

134

He burst out laughing, and that set me off too. Tears of laughter were running down my cheeks; we were in stitches. Passers-by stopped and stared at us.

'Do you think it doesn't show already?' he asked when he got his breath back. We couldn't speak for another minute or so.

'To make it look fresh,' I finally managed to explain.

'It does,' he laughed, and I suddenly recognised my mistake.

'I'm a complete moron,' I declared. 'Two Jews fall down a chimney, one gets covered in soot, the other doesn't: which one goes and has a wash?' Little Lang knew the puzzle – the clean one heads for the basin because, seeing his friend, he thinks he must be dirty too but the sooty one realises that he's all sooty because the clean one thinks he needs to wash but the clean one . . .

'*My* face!' said Mik, hitting himself on the forehead, and once again, we fell about laughing. No one was going to believe that Little Lang had finished me off without a scratch. We paid each other various compliments about whose face would be uglier if we'd had a real fight, and wondered what to do, grinning at the obvious solution.

Mik put his bag down on the pavement.

'Hit me,' he commanded. I looked away. It was cold. I rubbed my hands, stamped my feet. I shook my head. 'Don't be such a weed,' he exclaimed. I laughed. 'You're just yellow!' he went on. I swung my arms. 'I'm not standing here all day,' he said with sudden annoyance. 'I'm the weed; one more second and three of my teeth'll go flying!' I nodded agreement. 'I'm frightened, stupid, so get on with it, hit me, don't stand around torturing me like this.'

I sighed, and struck him on the jaw.

'What was that?' he asked mockingly, looking around. 'I thought it was too cold for flies, but one just landed on my chin.'

'I'll think of something else,' I said, waving him away.

'No, you won't. If my mug doesn't look just as bad as yours it won't make the slightest difference what you tell Berger. He speaks to your mum and the next day you come to school with a face like a pancake. Even Berger's not that thick!

'Hit me!' he ordered, and the next second hit me on the nose. I almost fell over: I hadn't been expecting the blow at all. I rushed at him, flailing at his face, but as he didn't fight back I came to my senses and stopped.

'At last,' he grinned. 'Does it show?'

I nodded uncertainly.

Mik looked up at the sky. 'Please God,' he said. 'Multiply this by a hundred for Berger and a million for Hitler.' Then he gave himself a tremendous punch on the nose. It made me dizzy. Mik came over and embraced me, and I hugged him too; then I took a step backwards and bowed low, just as he had done the day before.

'I shall be your slave in the next world,' I promised.

We assaulted the stairs, skipping and jumping, but the silence of the building quietened us down. We were only a few steps from our classroom when we started raising a din again, swearing furiously and punching each other. To be on the safe side, Mik rubbed the blood from his nose all over his face; I fought with almost all my strength and I wasn't sure that he didn't too. We might have finished each other off for good if the classroom door hadn't opened. Berger appeared.

'Fuck your Aunty!' screamed Little Lang, secretly addressing Berger while punching me in the stomach.

'Same to you!' I answered prudishly, although my fists were less polite. All the other kids had come swarming out of the classroom, while Berger, shouting at the top of his voice, tried to haul us apart by our shoulders.

Legs firmly apart to wrestle me, Mik grabbed my arms. But instead of trying to pull me down, he used me for support and delivered a goal-kick to Berger's ankle. Berger screeched and let go, and in my joy I almost forgot to carry on fighting.

'Who was that? Which of you kicked me?' Berger bawled, but we didn't hear. After all, we were fighting. Then we each delivered one good parting blow and obediently allowed Berger to separate us.

Back in the classroom he ordered everyone back to their desks except us. We had to stand on the platform and were meant to look ashamed of ourselves. Berger cleared his throat, but then changed his mind and rolled his sock down anxiously to examine his ankle. He looked up from his injury, trying to catch one of us smirking so that he'd know who the culprit was, but neither of us was born yesterday. All the same, laughter was tugging at the corners of our mouths as we watched him, knowing that the main entertainment, the big speech, was still to come. Two such prime examples of depravity were 'an opportunity not to be missed', as the street-vendors say. I knew the script: 'Fighting . . . swearing . . . late . . . lazy . . . players of marbles . . . smokers in toilets . . .' When Berger eventually began his oration, it was as if I had been prompting him, and although I tried to keep a straight face, Mik kept pointing at himself behind Berger's back after each accusation, so in the end I burst out laughing. That made Mik explode into fits of giggles, which triggered the class off, and when they started laughing, it was Berger's turn to explode. The pain in his ankle and soul merged as he interrupted his speech with a howl. He collapsed into his chair to rest, mumbling breathlessly, 'This will end badly, very badly indeed.' These fine words seemed to give him strength, because he immediately wrote them down in my everyday exercise book. Secretly, though, I was enjoying the thought of my composition book lying unsigned in my satchel: everyone at home had forgotten about it after the fight – clear proof that my face hadn't been redecorated on that score.

Berger decided to concentrate on Little Lang's background.

'Ask your father to come and see me,' he ordered, but Mik answered him dead straight, managing to sound just a little tired: 'He hasn't got time, sir. He has to work. Isn't it a shame that one has to work to stay poor?'

'And that's how you show your gratitude, is it?' interrupted Berger, halting Mik's meditations and calling the class to witness. 'Lang's father earns a modest living for his family by the sweat of his brow, carrying wood for other men's hearths from dawn till dusk . . .'

'Coal. Not wood,' interrupted Mik. He was poker-faced. 'But maybe next year they'll promote him.'

Berger's head drooped as he started to shake it. He was so sad he was almost pitiable, but by the time I got around to feeling sorry for him he was bellowing again.

'So you won't ask your father to come and see me, eh?'

'Of course I shall ask him, sir. He just won't come. We can have a bet if you like . . .' The class laughed.

'Are you laughing too now,' roared Berger, 'like these two rogues? You? Respectful, hard-working children encouraging the two whose laughter . . .' He got stuck for a second, then went on. '. . . whose laughter deafens them to the words of those older and wiser than themselves. A cynical child is an abomination! But has Nature ever created anything more monstrous than *two* cynical children?'

'Three cynical children!' I whispered, egging Mik on as he was undoubtedly braver than me. Sure enough, he passed it on to the class in a louder whisper, shamelessly pretending that my witty remark was his own.

'Three cynical children!' he suggested.

The helpless giggles confused Berger. He seemed unable to relate the remark back to his own rhetorical question, and did a double take, looking first at the class and then at us.

'Who's the third?' he asked, and then suddenly understood. He just shook his head. 'No hope . . . no hope at all,' he muttered, but the now continuous giggling seemed to sober him up, or perhaps he was just worn out. In any case, his sadness was not followed by another bout of rage. 'The whole world is turning bad around us,' he sorrowed. 'Must we be bad as well?'

But Berger judged this line of thought too difficult for children, and started talking about the school and family order instead.

'These foolish boys don't honour their educators or their parents. They respond neither to kind words nor to punishment. What am I to do with them? They bring their problems to school with them – do they think that grown-ups have no worries? Do they imagine that the teacher was born in the classroom and will die there too? Take Józska Sondor, for example . . .'

He was speaking seriously, not threateningly. I had never been so afraid of him.

'. . . His poor divorced mother has to work her fingers to the bone providing bread for her two children . . . ' he went on. How come Mik felt no pain when Berger held his poverty up to public view? I was trembling as he spoke of ours, and could only feel relief when he returned to my moral failings. He might as well have been preaching to a tree.

'One child, Józska's brother, is good, grateful, quiet, an exemplary pupil. The other you know. Ungrateful, lazy, a disruptive pest. And now this fight: look at their faces, there's a lesson to be learned from them! Two healthy children! God didn't afflict them with blindness or deafness or physical deformity. And in reality they're not much stupider than the rest of you . . .'

At this point, Mik and I shook hands behind Berger's back, congratulating each other on our intelligence. Although Berger had almost managed to get the class's attention, they sensed the opportunity for more fun and started laughing again. But this time Berger didn't try to swim against the current. He just waited until the laughter had died down, and then carried on.

'But God has punished them nonetheless, and with an affliction worse than blindness, or deafness, or physical deformity. Their faces show all too plainly that a malicious character is as fearsome a punishment as any physical defect. I'm not just talking of their sly expressions and shifty eyes . . .'

138

Right on cue, Mik went cross-eyed and I started to roll mine.

'. . . but of their blood-stained faces, grinning and smirking without understanding that every bad man or wicked child is the punishment of the next.' At this, Mik and I nodded sagely, and Berger yelled, 'Get back to your desks!'

Even some of the kids who had been given high marks had not had their books signed, so Berger put off checking up on us until the following day.

Mother came home tired, her eyes still as clouded as they had been that morning, still fixed upon some horrible pictures in her mind. She wandered about silently, sighing from time to time, and didn't look at me openly until she started preparing some cabbage for supper.

'Józska, Józska, do you want the stalk-a?' Mother sang as she always did when we ate cabbage; I preferred cabbage stalks to apples and Mother enjoyed being able to give me a treat that cost so little. But this time Mother was clinging to the words, trying desperately to squeeze some happiness from our peculiar little song.

'No,' I answered morosely. I couldn't just ignore yesterday's betrayal. I held my composition book in front of her. 'Don't you dare sign it,' I warned her. 'Just read it and mark my spelling.'

She dropped everything and started reading. One day too late. I watched her as she read; afterwards, as she stared into space with frozen eyes, I carried on watching her, not understanding why she wouldn't speak. She served supper in a half-dream, and when supper was finished she forgot to send us to bed. Sitting at the table, Mother took a pen and began to write; she wrote page after page, and it was past ten o'clock when finally she called me over. Solemnly, she read out what she had written.

12th December 1940

Dear Sir,

You have sent my son Józska home with three 'E's in his composition book and request that I sign it. I refuse to do so. I regret having to begin this letter in this manner, but I do not agree with you.

Please read this letter patiently and attentively, as I hope it will cause you to revise your position. It is your view that my son 'behaves in an unqualifiable manner at school'. You said so at our meeting yesterday, and have written the same words in his exercise book almost daily for the last three months. Hitherto I have respected your judgment, but in sending me this composition for signature, you force me to question it. You have awarded the said composition three 'E's, one of which is for spelling, and you are asking me to acknowledge your judgment by signing. Personally, I should like to see what standard of spelling would merit an 'A' in your eyes, or even a 'B' or a 'C'. Unless I am myself mistaken, there are no more than two spelling mistakes in my son Józska's composition. Do you regard two spelling mistakes in a thirty-line composition by a child of eight as a sign of such wilful ignorance that you mark it 'sub-standard'? My other son, who is two years older, also goes to your school. He regularly receives 'A's in spite of two or three spelling mistakes.

Furthermore, I find the explanation you gave my son, to the effect that his handwriting is so illegible as to render every word a mistake, frankly absurd. If you are unable to read the composition, it follows that you can judge neither style nor spelling. Could you not at least reserve judgment on these matters and give an 'E' for presentation if that is what you feel is right – in spite of the fact that the boy has been learning the old handwriting until this year. In the meantime, I would stress that an unreadable composition is neither good nor bad, its spelling neither correct nor incorrect, merely unreadable.

I can only guess that you did as you did as a matter of educational principle. If so, I am stupefied. Children of your acquaintance must have been bred behind bars. Did you really believe that my Józska would despair? That in his despair he would learn to write perfectly? You have offended against a child's sense of right and wrong; how can you now complain about the child's 'unqualifiable behaviour'? In asking for my signature you ask me to condone your attitude, and I will not. Do you wish our children to respond to injustice by behaving like angels? Submit like cowards? I cannot believe that you do.

I am at least partially aware of the tragedy that blights your life. I can imagine that teaching children who are fortunate enough to be both physically and mentally healthy must demand a tremendous sense of vocation, real heroism. I sympathise with you, but you must fulfil the requirements of justice if you are to assume the title of a teacher.

Yesterday you said that József is 'sharp enough when it comes to naughtiness'. I repeat what I said then: if a child is

140

bright in one respect, he is bright in others. You are puzzled by his numeracy, yet you took my assertion that he is no less intelligent than his brother as being mere motherly pride. The two boys are completely different characters and have until now lived in very different surroundings. József has returned only recently after spending several years with his grandfather, and finds his new environment strange.

Moreover, this is not the kind of home I would like to give my children, as in addition to working hard for eight hours a day at the Town Hall, I also have a part-time secretarial post. Furthermore, I take on casual labour, addressing envelopes for four pengős a thousand to pay for my sons' physical support. My working day usually lasts from six in the morning until midnight; I dream all week of Sunday and the chance to catch up on some sleep. As a result, I am impatient and irritable. My nerves have never been good, and I try not to think of the image my children must have of me. Dávid, my eldest, is more understanding and more accommodating, perhaps by virtue of his calmer nature. Józska, however, is basically well-meaning; and kind to those who take the trouble to get close to him. He is both sensitive and tough, wild and gentle at the same time. And, as you know, he can be disrespectful and even – when driven by circumstances – fearlessly aggressive towards authority. On a number of occasions I have known him face violence without the slightest hesitation and attempt to fight back against insurmountable odds. I hope that you will never find yourself in that position, and consider it a great achievement that our religion regards any teacher who strikes a child as unfit to teach.

József respected the teacher at his village school, who treated him considerately and taught him to spell and count exceptionally well for his age. I mention this in an attempt to convince you that József is not simply obstinate or vicious.

Finally, Mr Berger, I should like to state here and now that if there is not a complete change during the forthcoming months, I shall be forced to send my son to another school.

Trusting in your understanding, yours sincerely,

Mrs Ádám Sondor

Mother looked at me wordlessly. She expected me to say something. Taking an envelope, she addressed it and wrote 'By hand' in the corner. She asked me to give it to Berger, but I looked dubious.

'What do you think?' she asked.

'Lots of things,' I replied. 'But they don't matter.'

Mother watched my face, disappointed. 'Well, what does matter?' she demanded.

I was watching her too. I knew she expected her letter to please me more than it did, but I couldn't help myself. It told Berger too much; our poverty was none of Berger's business and in any case the only things he worried about were money and power. Praising me wasn't going to convince Berger either – mothers are always singing their kids' praises to teacher. The only good bit in the whole letter was the stuff about not signing the composition, and she could have done that without all the fuss. Why couldn't she just write: 'You can't give an "E" for two mistakes. Give him an "A" or else. You smell'? Maybe something ruder.

'What's Berger's tragedy?' I asked.

'It's none of your business. He's got problems of his own.'

'Does that give him the right to know all about ours?' I burst out. It was unthinkable that Berger might have a child of his own. 'What are his problems?'

'I told you, I don't know exactly.' I realised Mother wouldn't tell me even if she did know. 'Tell me what you think matters,' she went on.

'Tough,' I remarked, feeling better. 'The more problems he's got the better. I hope he rots. What I want to know is whether Gyula's coming back.'

Mother was taken aback. 'What's that got to do with it?'

'Is he coming back?' I demanded.

Mother hesitated. 'I don't know,' she said eventually.

'Well, who does know?'

'Who knows . . .?' mused Mother, echoing me sadly.

'Is it up to him, then?'

'Not entirely . . . no . . .' Mother replied uncertainly.

'It can't be left up to him! No way! Promise me if he comes back you won't let him in!'

'Gyula has a key,' remarked Dávid. I had forgotten he was there. 'He's our lodger even if he doesn't live here,' he added.

I dashed over to the door and bolted it.

'Promise me!' I shouted at Mother.

142

'I can't promise . . . I don't know what to do . . .'

'Promise all the same!'

'Do you want me to make a promise I might not keep?'

'Keep it!'

'The letter's great!' exclaimed Dávid, trying to make peace. Good old Dávid: big brother, quiet, understanding, regularly receives 'A's . . .

'Gyula is not coming back!' I insisted. The matter was closed.

Mother went into a long speech about 'children don't understand this, that and the other but when they grow up . . .' She might as well have packed it in straight away. Anyone who tells me 'you're a child, you don't understand', is wasting his breath. I go deaf anyway . . .

The next morning, Berger waited for everyone to arrive before starting business. He looked amazingly cheerful, greeting the late-comers with sarcastic little remarks like 'Better late than never' and 'Did you have a nice breakfast?' When at last it looked as if the remaining absentees were going to remain absent, Berger started to collect up the composition books. He took his time, enjoying it hugely, making more little remarks as he went along and expressing compassion for the parents of the thicker kids. Nobody, least of all me, had any doubt that I was to be the star of the show.

I let him stretch out his hand towards the exercise book on my desk, and watched his self-assurance cloud over as he debated whether to pick it up or wait for me to give it to him like everyone else. I didn't move an inch. He withdrew his hand, then stretched it out again meaningfully. I folded my arms and leaned comfortably against the bench. Berger decided that he could be obstinate too, and clasped his hands behind his back, a sign that he was trying to exercise self-control. His chest was heaving. Slowly, he lifted my exercise book from my desk like a threat. The class waited. He opened it.

Berger's eyes blurred as he stared at the unsigned page. And then, like a centre-forward rolling the ball into the net behind an already beaten goalkeeper, I yawned lazily: 'I forgot.'

The class exploded, but it wasn't laughter. It was like the noise the crowd makes at Üllöi Avenue when Ferencváros score the cup-winning goal. Baying, hooting, shouting – an unstoppable, unquenchable hurricane of sound. It annihilated Berger. He knew it. He was standing in front of me like a boxer knocked out on his feet. I could have counted up to fifteen.

I never gave that letter to Berger. I lied to my mother that I had.

8: Retreat

Hell doesn't exist. They just made it up so that they could chase Christian children to school with flame-throwers at their heels. And who was the idiot who dreamt up the flames?

Cold is the real punishment. Cold exists, but invisibly, like the air and God. Snow and ice are only its clothes . . .

In the battle between Rich and Poor, mysterious powers were fighting for the Rich. God didn't intervene, He had better things to do. God knows what they were, but by doing them He was helping the Rich. After a heavy snowfall, even football matches were cancelled and the only happiness left for the poor was squatting in front of the fire. Meanwhile, the Rich put skis over their shoulders and went outside, or paid hundreds and hundreds of pengös to be taken to the mountains where it was even colder.

It was unthinkable that the King of the Cold or his Viceroy would even talk to Berger; but was it pure chance that going to school in the cold was a worse punishment than anything Berger could hand out?

There was a stationery shop on the corner of Király Street. It had KOHINOR written above it in great curvy wooden letters, so the owner was probably called Kohn; he just didn't want to frighten all the Christian customers away. The window was full of fountain pens and crayons in huge boxes. While the weather had been good, Dávid and I hadn't dared to go in. But the cold started to bite, and the day we went in it was minus fifteen and my nose was burning.

If I hadn't seen it, I wouldn't have believed that a shop like that existed. It was spacious; the whole floor was covered by coloured rush mats. All around us were notebooks and sketchpads of all shapes and sizes, rulers and protractors, drawing boards, sets of compasses with twenty different pieces. The shop was heated by an enormous, white-tiled, wood-burning stove that almost reached the ceiling.

The shopkeeper was a hunchback. Stolidly, Dávid asked for a rubber. The little shopkeeper patiently showed him twenty different sorts, and while they were doing business, I looked around.

We went in more and more often while the cold weather lasted, just to get warm. Nine and a half times out of ten we didn't buy anything, but the hunchback always returned our greeting politely before walking back to the crowded end of the shop to fiddle with the things on his desk, which was crammed into a space between all the shelves. When we bought something, he would praise our taste in stationery, but otherwise he left us in peace. We soon baptised his shop 'The Oasis'.

I gradually worked out that the reason he kept the shop was that he had nobody in the world. He'd never found a wife, but he liked children, so he had opened a shop mainly for kids. Not a toyshop, because only rich kids go to toyshops, usually with their rich parents – the kids mightn't even notice him and even if they did they'd probably try to buy him as a pet. I'd never met a grown-up who was scared of children before, but he was. He spoke very quietly, even shyly, and like a good shopkeeper should he always thanked us for our custom. When we didn't buy anything, he asked us how we were. After a while he began asking us how our 'studies' were getting along and where we went to school.

'Excellent school, you'll both become good Jews,' he nodded. But he only spoke to us for ten seconds at a time before rushing away and pretending to be busy. I wondered if maybe he was a magician, whether by pushing a button on his desk he could open the huge cave underneath the shop where he brewed his secret potions over magical fires that gave birth to strange spirits who leaped from the flames to do his bidding, invisible, disguised as smoke . . .

Next, we discovered that he stocked marbles. Even the cheapest sort, the clay ones. So when I lost any at the play-centre and had three or four fillérs to spend, I could enter this palace as a proper customer, and soon he started offering his marbles at a reduced price. By re-selling them at the play-centre I could make a profit of fifteen to twenty per cent!

But there was another man there, almost as small as Uncle Hunchback. I had seen him shuffling along several times without really noticing him until the day I saw him sitting at the cash till. He was gazing in the direction of the window, not deigning to give the children or his busy brother a glance. Sometimes he stood beside the till and stared smugly at the notebooks and ink bottles in the window, the little notices saying 'Oil Paints' and 'Waterman' and the bright patterns made by coloured squares of paint blinking in the morning mist. He looked out at the street as if he owned it, and stared at the children like Mussolini watching a parade.

Uncle Hunchback had been cheated out of their father's blessing – like Esau. He had had to become his brother's slave and wasn't given enough to eat and the brother only came to the shop occasionally to check up on him and gloat.

When I asked my own brother whose side he was on, he told me that he supported Able Body. I thought Dávid must be wicked too, siding with the strong against the weak. Later I understood. Dávid was frightened of the hunchback. The truth was, I felt sorry for him, looking sadly at children hardly smaller than himself and thinking all the time: 'They'll grow . . .'

Gyula came back. Filtered back. Scarcely ten days after our fight, I came home from the play-centre and found him there. Mother had got in before us, which never happened, so they must have planned it to stop me bolting the door. They couldn't have been there long: Gyula was still in his overcoat. The stove hadn't really got going yet, and the big room was the only one we heated – Dávid and I had moved into it for the winter – but that wasn't the reason for the overcoat. They were trying to prove that he'd only just arrived. The brown furniture turned black, and the lamplight filled the air with needles. He only said a few words. Polite, controlled, he was soon gone.

He came a few days later for a short while. But this time he took off his coat.

Next time, he sat down in his old place at the table, and read his paper as if nothing had happened.

Slowly, almost unnoticeably, his camouflaged soldiers infiltrated my position. Soon he started to honour me with humorous enquiries like 'had I burnt the school down yet'? When I told him that I'd rather set the flat on fire he didn't seem to understand. He took it as a joke and made witticisms about the fire brigade.

When Gyula was there, I spoke slightingly to Mother. When he wasn't, I was really rude to her. I treated her like an idiot. It no longer mattered how many times she told me off, it made no difference. I stopped making my bed in the mornings, and when she shouted angrily at me I just clapped and laughed. Anger froze inside me; I didn't share her worries. When she railed at me, I joined in and beat her at her own game.

'Ungrateful children . . . is this what I deserve? I slave all day and night, but do I ever get so much as a thank you? I'm bringing up my children all alone,' she'd start off, and I'd come in: '. . . with only my pimp to help me beat them up.' This kind of thing was worth a few tender motherly smacks.

Dávid kept telling me off and lecturing me, promising to be a father to me and offering to beat me up. But we didn't fight except over really important issues like button-football, and eventually Dávid followed my lead, speaking irritably to Mother and treating her in as off-hand a manner as he could manage; and although he wouldn't use words unworthy of a well brought up child and future gentleman, he tried not to let me outdo him.

I started making demands: 'Why do I have to carry a satchel like a junior? And why haven't you made me any gym shoes?'

'Be thankful you've got shoes. And boots.'

'They laugh at my boots. And they're too tight.'

Gym had practically been struck off the curriculum. At the beginning of the year, Berger had dutifully instructed us to acquire our kit without fail, but as there weren't any lessons he hadn't pushed it. During the autumn they'd been painting the gym-hall, and although it must have been finished ages ago, there were still no lessons.

Hebrew took their place, needless to say, and I would have demanded to do gym if I had only had the shoes. It was Mik who stood up for our rights, and his argument with Berger revealed that there would be no gym until the spring: the school had to economise and couldn't heat the hall.

'The shoulders of the Synagogue ache with the weight of its many burdens,' Berger declared.

'The Synagogue should do some gym,' advised Mik. 'It's good for the shoulders.' He looked at me, inviting me to join the battle, but I was thinking about people who live in glass houses . . . People with no gym shoes shouldn't demand gym. Berger urged us to have our equipment ready: 'The Synagogue itself regards physical education as a necessary part of the educative process,' he told us, meaning that they might suddenly decide to heat the hall. But quite a few other things were revealed in the course of the discussion.

When our nation had spoken its single word, and Hitler had

147

said it was all right, the brave Hungarian army had marched into the woods, valleys and mountain peaks of Transylvania, Upper Northern Hungary and Lower Carpathia. In the process of re-annexation, they had also re-annexed one hundred and fifty thousand Jews. The glorious Fatherland had taken away all their trading permits on the spot, and as a result the Synagogue was supporting tens of thousands of people on one thin bean soup a day. Compared to these soup-kitchens, the lunch room at the play-centre was a classy restaurant. I imagined the endless queues of old people, women and children, waiting in the snow for soup.

I was ashamed that I hadn't stood up for Mik when he had demanded the gym lessons. But the cold that was biting at the Transylvanian Jews made me numb, and the more numb I became, the more I longed for a pair of gym shoes. I decided to fight for them at home, and as soon as I had some I would descend on Berger to make it up to Mik.

What I really wanted was a pair of football boots, but I knew that was silly, and not worth thinking about for years. In any case, the cold and the snow had interrupted the football season in our courtyard. As we couldn't practise, Laci Mester had lent me a copy of József Hada's book *The Goalkeeper*. The book was full of pictures, and I spent a lot of time miming the different positions and ways of holding the ball. But while I practised with an invisible ball, my imagination wore the cherry-red shirt of Hungary.

Late in the afternoon, after Mik's battle with Berger, I faced my mother.

'You've had loads of time between now and last September to sew me a pair of gym slippers! Why don't you buy me some gym shoes?'

'Why bring it up now?' asked Mother, suspecting me of making trouble.

'Because there were no gym lessons until now! You've been lucky. But now they might start any day.' My nagging voice upset me too, so I went into a long explanation. The delay was because the Transylvanian Jews had no bread, I told her, but she cut me short.

'How long will we have bread?' She sighed like an orphan, and told us that under the Jewish laws she should have lost her post as a civil servant by the first of January; fortunately, some rule concerning 'relief workers' had allowed certain kind city fathers to keep her on for a few weeks, but the news that she would soon be sacked had hit her like a blow to the skull.

148

I didn't dare ask what would become of us. Instead, I tried to cheer her up. Grandfather would give us money, I told her, he wouldn't let us starve; but she just shrugged. Grandfather's answer would be the same as always: she ought to go home to Oszu and become a normal Jewish woman.

Suddenly, Mother cheered up so much I thought she'd gone off her nut. She had decided that soon the Synagogue would be needing experienced welfare helpers like her to cope with all the poor Jews. They would employ her like a shot, she declared, and then a second later her face fell. She was chilled by the thought that the general misery would drive more learned Jewish women than her away from their mirrors and out to work.

She forgot about my gym shoes, and so did I. When I remembered them again after an hour or so, I didn't dare say anything.

Gyula turned up, but not as a guest any more. He made himself completely at home, and then, as if that wasn't enough, he launched a preliminary bombardment of my in-depth positions.

'How are your sums these days?' he asked, knowing as well as I did that I never had any trouble with maths. It was a transparent diversionary tactic.

'Cheer up,' I thought. 'You won't have to keep up the good mood for much longer.'

'Badly,' I replied indifferently.

Gyula looked shocked. Mother too. My counter-attack proceeded according to plan towards the enemy's main forces.

'I'm told I don't write my figures neatly either,' I remarked, which was a total fib. Berger had never said anything against my sums or my figures.

Dávid's jaw dropped, and he looked up from his book. He read grown-up books called novels, while I only read fairy tales and newspapers and *The Goalkeeper*. I could see that he had fallen for my feint, but I could also see that Mother hadn't. She tried to neutralise my armoured spearhead by opening up a second front.

'Can you believe it? They don't heat the gym. The Synagogue says they can't spare the money!'

'What do they spend it on?' asked Gyula, successfully distracted. 'Pigs?'

Mother recounted how, the year before, there had been a fundraising drive among the Jewish community in aid of the needy. It had raised one million pengös. That worked out – if you only counted half of the Transylvanians – at twelve to fifteen pengös per person per year. In fact, the soup kitchens of Lower Carpathia and Upper Northern Hungary were funded by American Jews. JOINT had given half a million dollars for that purpose – they weren't going out of their way to help either. This was because about twelve years ago a Jewish member of the Upper House had announced that we were Jewish Hungarians and not Hungarian Jews. Whether this was a ruse or a sincere gesture, Mother didn't know, but the result was that the Hungarians went on calling us Jews while the Americans decided we were Hungarians. Of course, if you are a member of the Upper House, it doesn't much matter to you how many bowls of soup are distributed each day.

'If we don't help each other, who will?' Mother asked. Her breath hardly lasted to the end of the sentence. She must have been wondering who would give her work.

Gyula had read in the fascist press that the Jews possessed a quarter of the nation's wealth: twelve billion pengös. So, like the accountant in his story, he took out pencil and paper.

'Assuming at least half of what the fascists say is true, that means that the rich Jews offered one six-thousandth of their wealth to help their destitute brothers.'

So that was how the figures stood on that early-winter evening. Not just for me, but for all the Jews in the country. They didn't improve much the following Sunday.

The ground disappeared under the snow and merged into the whiteness of the sky. The world moved one floor up. We were going on an excursion that morning, and when I took out my laughed-at boots Dávid stared at them so gloomily that I didn't have the heart to ask him whether 'they' had cleared away the snow yet. I eventually managed to get the boots on over two pairs of socks, and we went to meet the rest of the Robin Hood pack at the feet of the poor old Polish lion. The last few weeks had turned him white. The cubs had given up their posh uniforms; they were wearing padded ski clothes, warm ski boots, fur-lined mittens and hats with earflaps. My cap and Dávid's tie were the only bits of uniform left. Several of the cubs had brought beautiful sledges.

Csaba Krausz-Keszi watched us arrive, and his Jewish monkey's eyes lit up at the sight of us. He started whispering, and then came swaggering over to us, followed by two of his pals. They were all wrapped up to their ears. If my feet hadn't hurt so much I would have kicked him.

'Marnin' to 'ee, young marster, 'ow bee the 'arvest?' he asked, showing off to his giggling cronies. I couldn't tell any longer whether my boots were part of my feet or my feet part of my boots. Shame burnt my face while I tried to think of an answer, but my voice came out cold and humourless.

'The snow-crop's great, I'll give you a taste in a moment,' I said, only realising that I'd made a joke because the others laughed. I envied Krausz his warm clothes that allowed him to joke, and I was ashamed of my peasant boots. 'Rich kids are born in clothes,' I thought, as if their clothes made them stronger.

We started off towards Gugger Hill. I was wearing shorts under my coat. The grown-ups were always saying 'Wait until you've got long trousers' whenever I said anything about the war or wanted to stay up late or go to a proper film. Why couldn't the cold be reserved for people in long trousers? Dávid complained in a whisper that his shoes were soaked; he asked me if I thought we should go home, but that would have been a major defeat: the softies would have thought themselves terribly tough if we had given up. Each step drove a red-hot nail through my foot.

We reached Gugger Hill in the opening gusts of a blizzard. This was the true, fabulous snow; the dream door that leads to white blindness; the whirlpool that hunts its victims on the wings of the wind . . .

Bandi-Ba shouted 'Stop' several times, and after tightening the pack into one group, he and Brave Heart took the lead. We went to shelter in Brave Heart's house.

They lived in a big house with a garden. Inside, it was spring; there were flowers and plants everywhere. Brave Heart's mother was a robust woman who kept running up and down, chirping about the 'delightful surprise' in a tiny voice that didn't match her build. She invited us all for a cup of cocoa, although at that time cocoa reserves of more than a certain number of kilos had to be declared. The thought of anyone owning that much cocoa was ridiculous. Rich people keep their fortune in diamonds – not cocoa!

The Brave Hearts were clearly in the china trade. We settled down in various different rooms: the dining room, the 'drawing room' – a kind of living room full of flimsy furniture – and Brave Heart's room, which was as big as our big room. Bandi-Ba stood on one leg like a butler and stammered to Mrs Brave Heart until she let him go, whereupon he rushed happily round all the rooms making speeches about her kind hospitality. He was very careful to stress the pricelessness of the cups

151

we were holding, which were made of Herend porcelain and precious foreign china. When he mixed up the names of all the different makes, the rich kids fell over themselves to help him out. It seemed that whole towns – Limoges, Dresden, Derby – were named after their porcelain. With Budapest made of snow, I wondered whether all these porcelain towns were built out of china. Despite my anger, I smiled at the thought that these well-off brats were made of china too.

The secret language grew. The kids in the withdrawing room spoke of every rarity they could think of, just to prove that they felt at home in this huge house and show that they weren't impressed. They talked about restaurants and grown-up theatres and the opera, where the actors sing! I hadn't even been to a children's theatre; all I had seen was the circus. Suddenly I knew that these children didn't live in Budapest. They were from some other town with the same name.

Maybe it was a German town, because I also discovered that these kids were traitors. They praised the English, certainly, and said that Hitler couldn't beat them; but they also argued that he'd soon admit it and make peace, which would be good for everyone because the English would stop him persecuting the Jews; and then their daddies could go back to running their 'modest' factories, legal practices, clinics and wholesalers under their own names. So much for Robin Hood!

Quick Wit, the curly-headed boy in specs who would have been called 'Half Wit' if Bandi-Ba's names had meant anything at all, said that Horthy was only persecuting the Jews to please Hitler; Horthy was a wise statesman who only desired the Resurrection of Hungary and would rescue the Fatherland from the slavering jaws of the approaching war. I soon realised that Half Wit's dad was a quarter-wit. In any case, the kid went on, some of the Regent's best friends were Jewish: Baron This and Baron That for example; and his son's girlfriend was a nice Jewish girl . . .

I couldn't let them get away with this rubbish. You can't tell a mad dog like Horthy how long he can go on biting you.

'In the country,' I remarked, 'they shoot mad dogs before anyone gets hurt.'

'Let them,' quipped Krausz-Keszi. 'That's all they know about in the country.' His monkey face danced before my eyes.

'You are a Dresden lap-dog,' I grated. 'Barking about chocolate drops.' They laughed more at his joke that at mine, but András the Pianist took my side and agreed with me that Hitler was a mad dog.

Encouraged by this, I started to do my Hitler impression. Screaming, flailing my arms like a windmill, I threatened the Jews. The porcelain wolf-cubs backed away from me, terrified that I might break one of them and spoil the set. Bandi-Ba had to clap his hands to get us to be quiet. He told us that we were a pack of cubs, not the Cabinet, and we should be good Jewish children and trust in the humanity of our Fatherland.

'Like Hell!' I said.

Bandi-Ba declared this an unpatriotic remark, so I asked him whether he had ever had stones thrown at him or dogs set on him.

'There are more good people in Hungary than bad people,' he replied. I asked him whether he had counted them up, and he asked me, quietly, to stop being cheeky.

After that, András the Pianist and I went on talking quietly. He noticed how little of my information came from the BBC, and so I told him that I hadn't even listened to Hungarian Radio, as our wireless was bust. I made it sound as if it had once worked. Not only did András agree with me about everything, he assured me that Churchill agreed with us too. He would never make peace with Hitler, he would 'fight them on the beaches and the streets and the roofs'. András the Pianist was fat, like Churchill, and I pretended that it was really Churchill speaking.

In Brave Heart's room, the kids were trying to win a race on a rocking horse the size of a pony. Those who were waiting for their turn on the horse chatted about their toys, actors, famous pâtisseries and fathers. I felt as András the Pianist must have done when he couldn't join the jousting. I was outside each little conversation whether I joined it or not.

Sunday supper was waiting for us at home. On Sundays we always ate in the big room, and Mother put a cloth on the table. That evening, however, she took it off again after supper and laid out several hundred envelopes together with a good ten pages of addresses. It must have been the first time she had ever done extra work on a Sunday. Usually she only did the washing, ironing, cooking and housework, and then rested. We were no poorer than usual, so I didn't understand the point of doing the addresses, but then I remembered that the restoration of the school gym was practically finished. I had already boasted to everyone about what a fast runner I was, and it would be better to line up in proper gym shoes rather than in slippers. The price of a pair was four hundred envelopes – two and a half hours fast work. So I settled down to help my mother.

Since our fight, Gyula had come round less often and hadn't stayed as long when he did. But on this occasion he happened to be present, sitting behind a newspaper in his usual statesmanlike pose. He made several remarks to Mother in an effort to start a conversation, but received only one-word answers. After a while, for the first time since our fight, Gyula lost his temper.

'You're not reduced to that!' he exclaimed.

'I prefer to be independent,' answered Mother objectively, without whining or sounding defiant.

I had only been scribbling for about ten minutes when Gyula took up position behind my back. I was laughing to myself, as I hadn't brought an 'E' home for weeks and Gyula must have been getting furious. Yet at the same time I was pressing my pen hard against the paper to stop it shaking. Gyula picked up a pile of the envelopes I had already done and began examining them under the glass lampshade that hung over the table. Then he laughed.

'So how's the postman going to find the address?' He was only joking, but I knew his jokes.

'Postmen can read,' I replied. 'That's how they get the job.' After a moment I realised that I had hit a sensitive spot. Gyula had been retired early from the police force on account of his varicose veins. His status as an ex-policeman had opened a number of doors for him and he had ended up in charge of a large Jewish-owned bookshop. As the *goy* manager, he was well paid and had almost nothing to do: the Jew went on running the business.

'Teach your offspring how to write,' grunted Gyula. 'And stop his impudence!' He took his hat and left.

Mother stopped work the moment the door was closed, and made me stop too. I didn't understand.

'Is my writing that bad?' I asked.

'It's not that. This kind of work's too badly paid.'

No worse than any other job, I thought, and then realised that the whole thing was just a charade for Gyula's benefit. Mother was asserting her independence.

'But I need the money!' I said. 'I need gym shoes within a week.'

'Gym shoes?' Mother started to panic. 'What for?'

'Gym! They've put the hall right.'

'Lucky it's not the music room they've put right!' exclaimed Mother. 'We'd have to buy a piano.'

I stood my ground: 'I'm writing as many envelopes as it takes.'

'That's not the point. You should be nicer to Gyula – he'd willingly buy you gym shoes. And a proper scout uniform. He'd buy one for Dávid, but he doesn't want to upset you.'

I laughed heartily, showing off the worldly wisdom recently acquired in the play-centre.

'Not me. I'm not a whore,' I said. I got quite a slap but I went on laughing. Mother removed the envelopes from the table.

'There go my gym shoes!' I almost cried. Mother took pity on me and put a hundred envelopes back on the table.

'That's not enough,' I sulked.

'It's enough for today. It's almost bedtime. Gyula is trying to be a father to you.'

'It doesn't work. Why can't he try and be someone else's father?' I complained.

Dávid decided to intervene. He put down his book.

'Gyula is a good man,' he assured me.

'Well, he can go and be good somewhere else. Not here.'

'You ought to love him. He deserves it.' Treason again.

'The main thing is that you love him,' I replied. 'Why not put your price up to two pairs of gym shoes?'

Dávid stood up. So did I.

'You won't get any gym shoes,' Mother told me, trying to make peace.

'Just because I don't like your pimp!' I screamed.

She started to cry, but I didn't have time to feel sorry for her because Dávid fell on me. It wasn't out of anger, it was just for form's sake; so we didn't fight for long.

Mother went on snivelling, but she stuck to her guns. 'Is it your beast of a father you love?'

'When I haven't seen him for God-knows-how-many years?' I laughed. 'Still, I won't love a stranger.'

'But I'm your mother!' she exclaimed.

'True. So what?' I asked coldly. 'What's that got to do with anything?'

'I'm bringing you up alone, without a father,' she began. It was the same old song. 'I walk miles every day to save money on trams . . . I deserve some recognition . . .'

155

If I closed my eyes, I could still see her as she was when I lived in Oszu. But when I opened them again, a bad copy of her floated in front of me: an exhausted, sharp-chinned, sad-eyed woman whose whole strength was concentrated into her faltering, shrill voice. I could see that her nervousness was hurting her too, but then why was she like that?

'You promised me you'd throw Gyula out!' I shouted.

'I didn't promise,' she answered, but she was looking at the floor.

'Yes, you did!' I was so angry I didn't know whether I was lying or not. But it was Sunday, and Mother regained her calm faster than on other days.

'You asked me to promise; but I didn't.'

'Why not?'

'My life is hard . . . ' Mother sighed, but I took that for an answer and continued my attack.

'And mine is hard too because of that bully of a sergeant major! So what if he helps? You still like Grandfather even though he doesn't help! Does Grandfather know about your *goy*?'

Mother stared at my face, trying to see whether she had understood me correctly. She turned to stone.

'I didn't know you could be so evil,' she breathed. She didn't scream or stamp. She wasn't nervous. I had hit her heart. I knew that if I shut up now, she'd think I had got cold feet, and although I didn't want her to think me evil I couldn't afford to let her out of the corner.

'So Grandfather doesn't know,' I concluded. Too gently, because my mother's eyes lit up, and she out-manoeuvred me.

'But Elek does,' she said.

'And what does he say?' I went on like a judge.

'Nothing,' replied my accused mother.

'And what would Grandfather say if he knew?' I only asked this for the record.

'He would die.'

So I didn't succeed in forcing a tank battle. My hatred might have been fading, because the skirmishes that followed were more like hide and seek than all-out war. They were fought across heavily wooded, boggy terrain, and Gyula pushed imperceptibly and inexorably forward. In the same breath he would invite me to the cinema and belittle the way I had laid the fire.

One afternoon when the winter sun was as white as the moon,

156

Gyula asked to see my composition book. I had only just arrived home. Mother was standing motionless, so I knew that everything had been decided in advance.

'Show it to me!' pressed Gyula.

I turned to Mother. 'Shall I?' I asked her. She looked sad, already resigned to my being beaten up.

Dávid, who was standing beside me, answered for her: 'I think you'll find it'll be better if you do.'

'Too many cooks spoil the broth,' I reminded him, although it was obvious that I wasn't referring to Dávid alone.

After his last humiliation, Berger had given up scribbling rebukes in my composition book. I was only defending my right not to let Gyula see it.

He waited patiently. Mother trembled but didn't budge.

'What if Berger hasn't written anything?' I laughed. 'Will it make you both cry?'

'We'll see who'll cry,' said Gyula. It wasn't difficult to get the poor man to betray his intentions. He wanted to punish me for the way I treated Mother when he wasn't there, so all I wanted was to show that the composition book was just an excuse. That would prove that Gyula was in the wrong.

He leafed through the pages. Twice. The second time was a little hasty. He swallowed. Then he sighed. Finally he had an idea.

'It's still full of "E"s!'

'Those are old "E"s,' I pointed out.

'They're still "E"s,' he insisted, colouring slightly.

'Really? I thought a couple of them were "D"s,' I remarked with faked surprise, determined to undermine enemy morale. It worked: Gyula jerked out of his calm.

'I'll teach you to joke!' He undid his belt. 'Come here!'

Mother stood her ground without flinching, snivelling a little but wearing a virtuous 'I'm-bringing-you-up-all-alone' expression. I didn't feel sorry at all.

'Go to him,' begged Dávid, knowing perfectly well that I could have walked straight out of the flat. He also knew what was at stake. Mother was going to lose her job in a matter of weeks. Grandfather wouldn't help us. We would need Gyula. Mother was still standing there with a noble expression on her face, watching the verdict like some statue of Justice. I felt like spitting on her. I moved. Slowly. Curious.

157

'Bend over,' ordered Gyula tonelessly. The matter was a formality for him too: he was just asserting his right to hit me. My mother looked away. I bent forward.

I heard the belt flick through the air. Twice. I scarcely felt a thing. Mother flopped into a chair and Dávid gave me a jolly slap on the back. Gyula praised my manly behaviour as he threaded his belt back through its loops.

Suddenly I started howling like a dropped baby. I threw myself on the divan and cried myself into a stupor.

'Don't be silly,' frowned Dávid. Mother ran over to me as if I was dying and tried to cheer me up. She almost cried herself. I pushed her away.

'Go to Hell!' I cried. The tactic was sound. Gyula didn't hit me again, he just told me off.

After that, I stopped turning down Dávid's offers to help me with the new letters. He had really beautiful handwriting that joined up very cleanly; he was also very good at drawing. Within days, the old letters had disappeared from my home compositions and from the ones I did at the play-centre. I dreaded Gyula's check-ups. But at school, my writing remained artistically messy; half the letters were still from the old alphabet and the joining-up was a joke.

Berger smelt a rat. He stood in front of me with a slight stoop, and I knew that he had just asked me a question. His face was still shouting, but it was already filling up with the stupidity that flooded it whenever he shut his mouth. Dévai walked through my mind in his *shabbes* suit; stood in his shirt-sleeves by the sunflowers in the school garden. I remembered how he seemed to be listening even when he was speaking. Berger shouted even when he was silent.

'It's nothing to smile about!' said Berger. He spoke severely to be on the safe side. 'Why don't you try a bit harder?'

'Because the old letters are so beautiful,' I replied at last.

'Rubbish! What makes them so beautiful?' he scoffed. I thought for a moment.

'The old "B" has wings,' I told him. 'The new one is like a dead fly. You write "bee" but all you see is a dead fly.'

I thought of town flies, buzzing angrily and dirtily in the cramped streets. I compared them with the humming bees going from flower to flower in the bright fields.

'A letter isn't a picture,' snapped Berger. The class laughed

158

on his side, hoping for a town–country duel, but I could feel their disappointment when the bee didn't sting back.

That day, Berger gave me an 'E' without even having to be angry. And Gyula wasn't angry either when he gave me three cuts of his belt. It didn't occur to me to cry, or even to laugh.

'Why three?' I asked. 'Why not five for an "E" and one for an "A"?'

'Do you want a couple more?' asked Gyula in defence of his system. After some reflection he decided that the principle behind giving me three instead of five was that he was feeling indulgent. Gyula taught me a lot about principles.

I started a new composition book, and saw it blossom with an 'E' on the very first day. Back at the play-centre, I began to feel ashamed of myself. If I couldn't outsmart two thickies like Gyula and Berger there was something wrong with me. That set me thinking, and Mrs Pig told me off several times for being idle. She offered me a few stacks of origami paper, but I lied to her that my homework was very difficult. Then I asked her whether I could go out for a few minutes to buy a new exercise book. She let me. I also bought a bottle of red ink. Carefully, I copied my 'E'-graded composition into the new book; I made it fairly pretty so that Gyula could see the progress I was making.

Towards the end of the afternoon when discipline had become fairly slack, I called Dávid in. Furtively, I put my notebook and red ink in front of him.

'Don't you think this deserves a "D"?' I whispered.

Dávid got the message straight away. His eyes streamed with laughter.

'I'll give you a "B"!' he spluttered. He hugged me happily, knowing that he wouldn't have to watch the process of Justice that evening. Dávid had a bad conscience about that as Gyula hadn't hit him once, and even Mother didn't give him half the slaps she gave me.

' "D" will do,' I answered. 'They don't deserve a "B".'

Dávid traced one of the 'D's from my old composition book a few times to get the hang of it, haggling for a 'C' all the time. But he eventually copied the 'D' so beautifully that Berger would have believed he'd put it there himself.

Weeks passed before Gyula and Mother even got a 'C'-minus from me.

9: The King Wants Soldiers!

Mother wasn't actually dismissed until the first of March, although the letter was dated the first of January to comply with the Jewish laws. That was when she should have been sacked, but there had been an administrative error. The error was that the 'benevolent town fathers' had delayed her dismissal so that she could receive her pay for March as well as her copper handshake, which was three months' wages. The grand total, three hundred and twenty pengös, would have to last us until Mother found work or the English won the war. Our rent was sixty a month.

Mother wandered around in a frozen dream; she didn't snap at us; she spoke quietly as if she needed all her strength for breathing. The two symbolic pieces of crackling disappeared from the fried bulgar wheat we ate for supper, and then reappeared as Mother tried to give us courage. What would the Rabbi at the *heder* have said? Probably that God was punishing us for eating crackling.

Mother brooded, wondering to whom she could sell our meat ration cards as she didn't want to sell them to anyone she knew. Gyula took them away from her and had them honoured in the shop. She must have sent some desperate letter to Grandfather because a parcel arrived from him with a large loaf of bread and a roast duck inside. There was also a letter asking Mother to come home. Mother cried. She wanted to send the duck back – but not the bread, as that was a sin – so while she was crying, Dávid and I ate the duck's legs. She couldn't very well send it back without them.

The air around me became thin. I grew lighter and slower, wrapped up in a mild sleepiness. When I was small I used to spin round and round until I had to sit down; and now I regularly felt as I did then, except for the way the ground and the trees and the houses all stayed still. I argued feverishly about the war and about football and I found fierce pleasure in quarrelling over the rules of marbles.

I knew that when I came to, the sunshine would be thick as honey; the winter nights would be warm; English trumpets would be echoing through the town . . .

The spring was rainy, foggy, so dank that it could have passed for autumn. All the same, Dávid and I moved back into our own room. One morning we woke up to find the air outside the window as grey as dusk, and heard Gyula's voice coming from the big room. It was the first time he had ever come round in the morning: he was standing with his greatcoat on, pointing at a newspaper lying on the table.

'PÁL TELEKI TRAGIC DEATH RIDDLE,' said the headline. Teleki had been the Prime Minister, the man who had introduced the second set of Jewish laws; but Mother was standing mesmerised as if a relative had died.

'Will the Jewish laws stop?' I asked, not very hopefully. I could see the gloom in everyone's face. Nobody even answered.

'The war has just started,' said Gyula calmly after a while. 'We'll be in it within a week. Teleki was probably murdered by the Germans.'

I didn't understand.

'But Teleki was sitting on Hitler's right at some supper where they signed some treaty or other,' I protested, remembering an old newspaper article.

Gyula sighed: 'We're going to war. Teleki wanted to stay out of it.'

I still didn't understand: it seemed that Teleki hadn't liked the Jews or the Germans. He went to supper with Hitler and ganged up with him, but if he didn't want war what was the point? It didn't make any sense.

Patiently, Gyula explained: 'The Germans pressurised Teleki into making a Friendship Treaty with Yugoslavia. But now the Germans have attacked Yugoslavia, so the Hungarian army is on its way to re-annexe the "Southlands" – the part of Yugoslavia that used to be in Hungary – and Horthy and his officers are dancing over their prey.'

'The main thing is that Teleki's been bumped off,' I remarked in an effort to cheer them up.

'You're an idiot!' said Dávid.

They were the idiots. What was so 'tragic' about an antisemite dying, especially the one who had put Mother out of a job?

'The only bad thing is that it wasn't Hitler who got bumped off. Is it really true that the Germans killed him?' I laughed.

'What'll happen to the Jews?' asked Dávid. 'Are things going to get better or worse?'

'Worse,' said Gyula. 'For everyone. Particularly when Hungary starts losing.'

There was a tremendous din at school, with all of us arguing, as if we were pleased that some great event had taken place no matter what it meant.

Berger tried straight away to make some capital out of the news with a solemn speech: 'These tidings are very grave. Very grave indeed. We must turn our hearts to God and pray for His help with greater piety. The storm clouds are gathering over our beloved Fatherland . . .'

'Actually, it's raining already,' remarked Mik Lang.

The evicted families and the uniformed children from the orphanage represented a special degree of misery that lay roughly mid-way between our own decent poverty and that of beggars who sleep rough in boxes and sacks. Less than a hundred metres from our school stood the 'Hannah Orthodox Children's *Mensa*', which was apparently Latin for 'soup kitchen'. At midday there were a hundred and fifty children queueing in the street outside, most of them in orphanage uniforms like little convicts of hunger. When I finally dared to peep at them I was surprised at how different each face was. I had imagined them all looking like me, like paler, hungrier, wider-eyed, disinherited brothers. Looking away didn't help; my feet dragged me that way and I knew that if I crossed the road or even stepped off the pavement, Fate would shuffle me into the line. Vainly I turned away and tried to bind God with simple spells.

'Don't send me there,' I prayed as the Hannah *Mensa* spread its net to catch me. The putrid stench of burnt food blew across the street and mingled with the taste of my rising nausea.

That day there was no cutlery waiting for us in the play-centre eating hall. We recognised this as the latest tactic to stop us yelling 'Gru-u-ub', the idea being that if we couldn't clatter we wouldn't shout. So we thumped the tables with our fists instead. Mrs Pig dashed in and out several times and eventually announced that we were going out for lunch. We lined up and trooped out of the school door in the direction of the *Mensa*.

162

Mik's thoughts weren't much different from mine.

'The Devil's farted,' he declared. 'Fart soup followed by fried shit.' Without any more indignation or discussion, we sloped off. Dávid went home; Mik and I loafed around. But the rain started again; at Klauzál Square the street kids were playing football with one goal and a rag ball. It wasn't worth joining in. Another lot were playing marbles, but we knew they'd beat us up if we won. In the market hall Mik scrounged two carrots off a stallkeeper, but when we asked to borrow a knife to peel them with, the woman got irritated. Mik threw the carrots back in the box.

'I'm not hungry anyway,' he decided.

'Me neither,' I said, following his example. I had ten fillérs for a new exercise book so I spent them on some sugar-beet. Sugar-beet is hard, and it takes two minutes to chew one bite and your appetite is gone within five minutes even if you're dying of starvation.

'What about selling a couple of glass marbles?' suggested Mik. He was dreaming of salami and cake. But he wanted to win some marbles to sell, and that was only possible at the play-centre.

'They can't hang us for missing lunch,' we decided, and trailed back to school. The porter gleefully informed us that the whole play-centre had gone off to the cinema. It must have been a reward for the heroes who had managed to eat their lunch. Mik got cross.

'Movies are for weeds!'

'I bet they took them to something educational,' I said.

'They can eat their movie!'

But we were walking in the direction of the cinema, and our former good mood soon caught up with us.

'If it's a Western, we sneak in,' decided Mik. By that time he was singing:

> 'I came to Pest from Tennessee,
> My name is Big Bill Hennessey,
> Whoever dares to menace me
> Will get a bloody nose!'

During the song he somehow acquired a horse, so we arrived at the cinema at a gallop.

We told the usherette that we belonged to the group who were already inside. She was short, with the face of a beggar, but her power over us added twenty centimetres to her height.

163

'You're just trying to sneak in!' she accused. 'Bloody little oiks! Sod off!'

'Don't shout today, Miss! The country is in mourning,' sighed Mik patriotically.

The usherette shrank again in order not to look unpatriotic. 'A count goes and kills himself! I've seen it all before. Gambling debts, I tell you. It's always gambling debts . . .' She called Mrs Pig, who came outside.

'Where have you popped up from?' asked Mrs Pig. 'Where were you at lunchtime?'

'The pong was enough for us,' I told her bluntly.

Mik made up for my subtlety. 'That's a lavatory, not a soup kitchen!' he declared, and I waited for the inevitable telling-off.

Mrs Pig must have gone crazy, because she opened her handbag and gave me fifty fillérs.

'Buy some rolls and cheese,' she said. 'And some milk. Then come back and eat them in the movie.'

According to the calendar it was now spring, and as a result irregular gym lessons began to take place. Our turn could come up any day now, since the school had announced that there was no need to heat the gym: the exercise would keep us warm. I needed gym shoes more than ever. I was a very fast runner and good at jumping both heights and distances. My handwriting had improved greatly since the winter; Berger himself was giving me 'C's, which saved me having to copy everything out for Dávid to re-mark. Gyula hadn't hit me for weeks; Berger hardly bothered to tell me off for my Hebrew any more. My popularity at the play-centre declined without the support of any worthwhile new scandals. I even distanced myself from the brawls between the play-centre boys and the others, although these rows were becoming a more frequent and important part of the life of the class. The only two who never fought were the chiefs of staff, Mik Lang and Aaron Kohn, despite the fact that many of the skirmishes were actually started by Mik. There were a thousand and one pretexts for these engagements: marbles, buttons, disappearing rubbers, nibbled elevenses, vanished sweets, drawing pins on chairs . . . In any case, the non-play-centre boys had it in for Mik Lang – although no one dared stand up to him alone. They didn't dare attack him as a group either: that would have been obvious cowardice; it would also have been fairly dangerous, since Mik would have knocked four or five sets of teeth out without any help but mine. Meanwhile, the non-play-centre boys murmured against King Mik and lived in the hope that they would one day be able to teach him manners. They would certainly have liked to put an end to the Food Tax, which was Mik's way of redressing minor social injustices.

Someone like Bolgár the Tape-Measure would be peacefully leaving the classroom at break when Mik would order him back inside, on the grounds that Bolgár had forgotten to kiss Mik's hand. Poor Bolgár would start whining that he didn't even kiss his grandmother's hand, and very soon Bolgár would gain a crowd of supporters. Mik never dirtied his hands with weeds, and only started these scenes out of boredom, to tease the Bolgárs and maintain their respect for his authority; but once things had gone this far Mik couldn't drop them. He was only playing, but Bolgár was serious. If Bolgár could have laughed it would have been all right: Mik would have laughed too. But because Bolgár took it all too seriously he ended up being fined two days' elevenses. After pronouncing his verdict Judge Lang gave leave to appeal to the more lenient Judge Mik, who then commuted the sentence to five days of half-rations. While all this was going on, some of the defence lawyers started a scuffle, but I remained a police reserve who was never actually deployed. I was even too shy to accept my share of the booty. Yet my credit with Mik lasted, and he remembered what I was capable of without needing everyday reminders.

One morning when Mother came in to wake us up I remembered that there was to be a gym lesson that day. I made a decision.

'I'm not going to school!' I announced, still half asleep.

'Are you ill?' asked Mother suspiciously.

'Even Mik Lang has got gym shoes!' I burst out. He had nothing else. His ordinary shoes had 'gone out of fashion' – as he put it – in February. I dragged myself out of bed.

'Mik Lang has also got a father,' replied my mother.

'Too right!' I shouted, shaken out of my half-dream by real anger. 'His mother isn't a *goy*'s whore!' Mother slapped me in the face, but she still seemed to be dreaming. I went on swearing in a daze.

My father walked into the room.

He looked as if he hadn't slept. He was unshaven and his shirt was creased.

'Shut up,' he said calmly, and equally calmly gave me a smack. A real one.

I turned and looked at him. He met my gaze. I hadn't seen him for a good four years.

'Buy me a pair of gym shoes,' I said slowly, scrutinising his face. 'This morning.'

'Is that how you speak to your mother?' he said in a quiet deep voice. It was as if he had already forgotten smacking me.

'None of your business!' By asking for the gym shoes I had almost recognised his right to smack me. I withdrew it. 'What gives you the right to come here and smack people?'

'Guess,' he replied. He moved towards me, looking at me sidelong with eyes that held mine.

'You've come to help Mother bring me up!' I accused. He just laughed.

His eyes were smoky. A cigarette smoked in his hand, too. He brought it to his lips with a slow ritual movement, and drew on it. The stillness of his body suggested great strength. He seemed to be gazing across a huge distance. I didn't like him. Yet in spite of the smack, I wasn't afraid of him. I watched him distrustfully.

Mother tried to hurry us off to school but our father waved her down. She went off to look for a job. He started chatting to Dávid. It was as if they had seen each other every day for years. They belonged together. Dávid had lived at his grandfather's for years: he had adopted our father by knowing his father.

'What are you living off?' Dávid asked him.

'I often wonder,' our father smiled.

'Whereabouts do you live?'

'It depends. If I manage to pay my hotel bill today I'll live there. I couldn't borrow money from your mother.' He grinned. 'If I don't give her a few hundred pengös – maybe today – my conscience will make me ill.'

'You? A few hundred? Today?' I nearly spat the words out. Our father frowned, nodded almost imperceptibly, and didn't answer.

Tired, thin smoke trailed about him. When he drew on his cigarette, his eyes glowed more brightly too. Unemotional, hard, cruel sadness was engraved into his face. He watched me without any good will, with the same suspicious gaze that I was levelling at him. His pupils flickered quickly, gathering my movements into the mirrors of his eyes, unhappy with what they saw.

'What sort of a man is Gyula?' he asked Dávid.

'Nice.' Dávid sounded apologetic.

166

'A peasant,' I interrupted. My father turned his head towards me, expecting an explanation. He got one. 'Gyula's not as cruel as you, but he's more brutal,' I told him. 'I think he's stupid; but he does support the English.'

My father nodded, dissatisfied. 'It's time you went to school,' he told me.

His impudence amazed me. I could see why he'd smacked me, but what gave him the right to behave like a real father?

'And what am I supposed to say about being half an hour late? That my father came round to hit me?'

He didn't just sigh. He emptied his lungs with anger. Then he added quietly, 'You'll be glad of that smack one day.'

I laughed. 'When?' I asked, but he just nodded again. He demanded my exercise book, and in it wrote: 'For family reasons, my son was unable to attend school today. Ádám Sondor.' His style impressed me.

'But it's good for the whole day!' I said in surprise.

'Be my guest,' he smiled, spreading his palms in a gesture of huge generosity.

'Do you really think I need your permission to bunk off school?' I asked scornfully. 'I've got to go today anyway.'

'All you want out of me is a pair of gym shoes,' he stated sarcastically.

'The hell I do! I don't want anything from you.' To give more weight to this I added, 'I don't even want to see you,' although this was a lie. He intrigued me.

He stood up.

'You can't complain you see me too often.' He started to leave. 'What's your size? I'll bring you a pair of gym shoes this evening.'

'I won't need them by then.'

'All right. I'll get some money and we'll go and buy them now. Let's go.'

We headed towards the school. Our father made us wait in the street while he went into a house for money. He came out empty-handed.

'It's always difficult to scrounge money off people in the morning,' he said, half to himself. He re-promised the gym shoes for the evening.

'I don't want them!'

'You waited to say that until you knew you couldn't have them,' he observed.

'I didn't wait. I'd already told you. You're the one who was so keen to bribe me with them.'

He trudged along behind us without another word. In front of the school he said goodbye to us politely, without shaking hands, but then changed his mind and ruffled Dávid's hair as he went off.

I heard from Mother later that our father had turned up at our place in the middle of the night with a fair amount of booze inside him, either because his conscience had suddenly grabbed him or because he had nowhere to sleep. He couldn't publish under his own name any longer because of the Jewish laws. He was thirty-five, with quite a few successes behind him; these gave him enough literary credit to make a living by making other people's scribblings vaguely readable – mainly dilettante noblemen. He had lived it up for six months in some baronet's castle on the pretext that they were writing a play together; but Father had seduced the baronet's favourite mistress before the end of Act One, and the baronet had renounced the glories of authorship.

In the changing rooms, Berger shook his head back and forth and side to side over my lack of gym shoes. I didn't even have slippers. I had to keep my socks on, as bare feet left marks on the rubber floor. My big toe was sticking out of one sock and my heel showed through the other, and I was afraid that I'd be too ashamed to walk, let alone run.

Mik Lang was fully equipped: gym shoes, satin shorts, a gym vest that was also part of his everyday wardrobe. He started laying into the Synagogue, which had done very little to the gymnasium considering that they'd had several months to do it in: all that was new was the paint and the rubber carpet. But a moment later Mik was throwing cartwheels, walking on his hands, and swinging through the air on the rings. Pirate fashion, he took over the gym.

As for me: I'd never seen a gym in my life. Along one wall stood a giant abacus with eight poles across it instead of ten and not a single ball on it anywhere. It must have been for mental arithmetic. Ropes hung from a beam. Half the class got halfway up them. At Grandfather's I used to sit up in the branches of the mulberry tree for hours on end. It was a good place from which to insult the Iron-Nosed Witch and when Elek came up after me I used to make a fool out of him. I was only ready to come down on condition that the encircling forces withdrew, but they wouldn't. So Elek and Samuel used to stand there with their mouths open until they got bored and went away, whereupon

I disappeared for a while. By the time I returned home they didn't think it was worth punishing me. Occasionally Elek threw stones at me; but that just made me laugh because he always took such care not to hit me by mistake.

Mik turned into a monkey. He climbed a rope using only his hands, swung over to another, and then lowered himself down, forcing the blockhead below him – who was gripping with hands and feet – to skid down the rope.

When my turn came I darted up the rope using only my hands. But I'd hardly reached the middle when my body suddenly stretched out like a weak spring and I found myself dangling in the air like a hanged man. I resigned myself to using my feet as well, but they kept slipping on the rope. Then Mik came and tickled the sole of my foot from the next rope along, and I fell rather than skidded right down to the floor. It wasn't just my hands that were burning: my face was on fire too.

Mik patted me on the shoulder. 'Glad to see you landed safely.'

'You too! You're laughing at me just because I haven't got gym shoes?' I asked furiously. I was wrong. He showed me how to climb properly. With great difficulty I got all the way up to the beam, and for five minutes there was a sacred truce between us.

The 'abacus' was for doing 'bridges', but when Mik enlisted as my helper I found myself hanging upside-down watching tears of laughter pouring up Mik's cheeks. This attracted the other kids' attention and soon they were all hooting with laughter. I made up my mind that the day I came down from the abacus alive would be a bad one for Mik Lang.

But in the end it was Mik who helped me down. Drunk with laughter, he asked for my word of honour that I wasn't just taking the piss out of everyone. When I promised him that I really was a complete fool, he showed me the basics of how to do bridges on the abacus, which turned out to be called the wallbars. I hated him for watching me and helping instead of letting me slink off among the Bolgárs and crib the exercises by looking at the others.

The next exercise was running races. We ran in heats of six and the first in each heat went on to the final. Aaron Kohn came last in his heat despite his snow-white gym kit.

'Bunch of snails,' Mik remarked scornfully. 'Don't you agree?' He looked at me suspiciously as though he'd never seen me playing football.

'Who's the fastest in the class?' I asked.

'Me. By miles.' He was stating a fact. 'Are you fast?'

'Yes, I am!' I answered furiously. My speed alone couldn't make up for all my clumsiness. I longed for some jumping exercises.

'Are you faster than me?' asked Mik – to see whether I was just a big-mouth or whether I'd actually bet a few glass marbles on myself . . .

But that wasn't the reason.

'Nobody's ever beaten me who wasn't older than me. Never. Not once,' I told him. 'You won't either. Want a bet? How many glass marbles?'

'No fear. I'll just slope off and change heats. I don't want to go out in the first round. But calm down, no one's beaten me yet either.' He walked off and joined another group.

In the final we had to run three lengths of the gym instead of two. At the first turn I could feel Mik's breath on the back of my neck, but I finished a good two steps ahead of him.

I looked at him in triumph. I got a shock: he was looking back at me in triumph too.

'A hare wouldn't stand a chance against you!' he smiled.

'You mean you let me win?' I studied his smile threateningly.

He laughed. 'Why? Were you just jogging? Was that why I nearly beat you?'

I laughed too then; but the running race remained a private matter between the two of us. The others were used to being beaten and they didn't much care by whom.

'What kind of a class is this?' I exclaimed to Mik while we were changing. 'It doesn't matter who the fastest is, all they care about is whether you've got gym shoes!'

'You've got wings,' laughed Mik, and then made a solemn declaration: 'Whoever beats Józska at running will receive five glass marbles. From me.' But the challenge was never taken up because he added: 'Entry fee, one glass marble.'

I checked him over, looking for wings.

That evening there was a knock on our door. A boy hardly three years older than me wearing long trousers and a new suit was standing on the doorstep. He had a hard round hat on his head and his jacket had 'Hotel Bristol' embroidered on it in gold letters. He looked surprised when I opened the door, and glanced past me into the kitchen as if he was scarcely able to believe that he'd come

170

to the right place. He handed me a box with a message on it and an envelope addressed to Mother.

The message read: 'I told you you'd get them this evening.' Inside the box were a pair of gym shoes and a refillable pencil. The pencil was for Dávid. When my mother opened the envelope she almost dropped it: there were three hundred pengős inside it with a note telling her not to spend the money all at once: there would be more coming in a couple of weeks. Mother stood and stared at the notes she was holding, not knowing whether to laugh or cry. In the end she said bitterly, 'Your father must have got at least three thousand pengős to have sent us three hundred.'

The promised bonus never came, and we lost all trace of Father. A few days later, Hungary invaded Yugoslavia.

'Forward to the Thousand Year Frontiers!' yelled the headlines. Hungarian troops had crossed the border and were advancing irresistibly. That morning Gyula was standing in the big room again with his raincoat on.

'When will the English arrive?' I asked. I didn't even get an answer.

'Will the government call you up for the military police?' my mother asked Gyula.

'Don't be silly, Julia. Only the military police can recall me to their ranks.'

'And you've got varicose veins,' said Mother, trying to reassure both of them.

It was a pity about the veins, because if they'd been all right he might have been called up and then at least I'd have got something useful out of Hitler. But it wouldn't have been fair to make an England supporter fight for the Germans. He could shoot backwards of course, but that would have made him into a hero and I'd have had to admire him . . .

The sun was up and it was quiet outside. Why weren't there a thousand English planes zooming through the sky? Why weren't there any bombs dropping? On the table, a few cups were scattered among the newspapers like a boring still-life. Was war going to be like an away football match? They could at least drop a bomb or two on the school – at night of course, when even Berger wouldn't be there . . .

Pöci and Kaci, who lived two flats away, came charging along the balcony. Kaci was shouting, 'Boom Boom Boom!' He was four. If they were charging Jews I hoped they'd fall over the railings. But they were probably charging the English. I wasn't sure whether I wanted them to fall if they were only charging the English. Maybe they were just stupid. I'd better beat them up anyway . . .

The news-vendors didn't have to run after the passers-by that day. They stood at street corners and tram stops with people pushing and shoving to get at the remaining papers. The hunchbacked vendor was shouting triumphantly, 'Great Hungary's gates open to our Army! We have broken through on all fronts! The Serbs are running! Forward to the Thousand Year Frontiers!'

He could have been the wicked twin brother of my Uncle Hunchback, who ran the stationery shop. One might have taken him for a beggar in his dirty, weather-beaten clothes; yet when I looked away and only listened to his voice, I could imagine him sitting on a bench in the street with Saint Stephen's crown on his head and a pile of newspapers beside him, but no one was paying for them because everyone was kneeling and kissing his hands . . .

At school we closed our eyes in shame as we mumbled the slogan that had become a prayer:

> *'Hungary crippled is but rocks and sand,*
> *Great Hungary shall ever be the Promised Land.'*

Berger stammered an apology for having to make us recite this when we knew perfectly well that the invasion of Yugoslavia was only carrying whips and hunger to the Jews.

'But we must hope that all this is simply the work of a few misguided officers taking advantage of the temporary disorder, and that His Serene Highness Miklós Horthy will soon ensure fairer treatment for the Jews.'

Apart from a few officers who had distinguished themselves in the Great War, Jews were now forbidden to carry arms. Those who were called up for military service were formed into 'labour companies'. At parades they had to obey the command, 'Present . . . spades!'

The military band in Erzsébet Square didn't play waltzes at all any more, and even children could hardly hear themselves shout. The best football pitch lay just behind the bandstand, and the noise we made tended to diminish the patriotic glory of the square. After repeated warnings the park-keeper chased all of us – including Laci Mester, son of the pro-German caretaker – off to the far corner of the square.

172

Our Jewish wolf-pack went rabid. We learnt a new song at the next meeting:

> 'The Southland joins us as of old
> Returned to us by Horthy bold,
> Who like a shepherd guards the fold
> Protecting us from heat and cold . . .'

On the Sunday excursions a new game became popular. We would split up into two teams and line up opposite one another, holding hands as firmly as we could to make a chain. Then one of the enemy team would step forward and shout: 'The King wants soldiers!' and the reply would be: 'The King can't have them!'

The attacker would then yell: 'I'm going to break you!'

'If you can!' would come the answer, and the attacker would charge. If he broke through, he captured a prisoner; if not, he became one himself.

When it came to my turn I shouted, 'The King wants labourers!' and ordered my prisoner to 'Pres-ent . . . spades!'

Bandi-Ba told me off, warning me that if a passing hiker had heard me I might have got the whole pack into trouble.

At the news of the war and of Mother's unemployment, Dávid's grandpa turned up. He came several times during the three weeks that followed, arriving by the Árpád rail-car, which cost him half of what Mother's monthly salary had been before she was sacked. His luggage consisted of one briefcase, and he only ever spent one night in Budapest. He had a reputation in the family for being extraordinarily clever, which he must have been, since most of what he said was totally mystifying.

'The pengö will go down . . . It's time to move out of potatoes and put everything into wheat . . .' He made silly jokes like 'You can't buy gold with gold', and smiled at them happily. He gave Mother fifty pengös on a couple of occasions, and once he gave her a hundred. He also brought us a fifth of a kilo of 'real' coffee, which Mother put aside for a special occasion.

We walked over to his hotel with him once. I knew that he only wanted to spend a little longer with Dávid, and had invited me as a formality, hoping that I wouldn't want to come. I didn't, of course, but I went anyway because he hadn't wanted me to. In the hotel room he took out a bar of real 'foreign' chocolate and broke it into two halves to give to us. I had finished mine before Dávid had eaten one square.

173

'You gave Dávid the biggest bit!' I said, looking accusingly into his eyes.

But being a smart sort of fellow he answered my words instead of my eyes: 'I gave you each the same. You are just greedy.'

'I'm not greedy. I'm hungry. The hungriest should get the most.'

'You can't fill your belly with chocolate . . .'

'What else can I fill it with when the bread ration is only a quarter of a kilo a day?'

'A quarter of a kilo is quite sufficient if you eat plenty of other things,' he assured me, and then thought for a moment as he remembered that meat was rationed too – he didn't want to fall into my trap. 'One should eat plenty of vegetables,' he declared finally. 'They are both nutritious and cheap.'

'Potatoes, in other words!' I said furiously, knowing that he was still selling these by the wagon-load under the name of his puppet manager.

'Lots of potatoes,' he agreed, smiling.

Later, I was horrified to hear that my father's brother Józska was still in the army. He hadn't been accepted at University and had stayed on after military service as a re-enlisted acting second lieutenant. They hadn't transferred him to the Jewish labour companies, they hadn't even demobilised him. I remembered how Grandfather had got Samuel promoted to battalion chef by sending the colonel a barrel of wine.

'Wow! That must have cost you a few wagon-loads of potatoes!' I exclaimed.

Dávid's grandpa looked at me severely. 'No. His superiors like him.' This was obviously aimed at the fact that some people didn't like me. I was non-plussed. The screws were being tightened on the Jews; those in the re-annexed territories were living on one soup a day; and meanwhile my own uncle was clicking his heels to Christian officers, was an officer himself – if only a second-class one!

A few days after that, the first bomb of the war scored a direct hit: Mik's father was called up for labour service. Poor Jews had no choice. The class gathered around Spitfire, who sat hunched over his desk close to tears.

'Leave me alone!' he grated, and chased us away. 'If you need any wood chopped at home, tell them I'll do it for half-price.' But it was spring, and no one needed a wood-chopper.

Mik's brother was helping out by working for some relation who kept a second-hand clothes stall at the flea-market in Teleki Square.

His mother did cleaning jobs, and Mik decided that he wasn't going to live off their backs, so he brought a stool to school one day. When Berger asked for an explanation, Mik told him that his grandmother had asked for it back and he was taking it round to her, but that wasn't true. After lunch we escaped from the play-centre and I learned that Mik had decided to become a shoe-shine boy. All the American millionaires had started off that way, so why shouldn't he?

In front of the Hotel Royal, in a courtyard that lay slightly back from the Erzsébet Avenue, a professional invalid was cleaning shoes. He had been wounded in the Great War. Behind him, a colourful placard listed all the battles he had fought in. The ones where he had been wounded were marked with stars. We couldn't compete with him. We tried the corner of Dob Street, but the traffic swept us away; so, learning from the veteran's example, we pitched our headquarters in a recess of the ring-road. It wasn't as good as our master's but it would have to do. Mik sat on his stool and opened his string shopping bag; in it were two brushes, two tins of polish and half a dozen rags. Armed with these, we waited for customers, but apart from a few puzzled glances we failed to arouse any interest. Not having a placard, we tried advertising our services aloud: 'True gentlemen have clean shoes! Don't visit your fiancée with muddy footwear!' More puzzled glances. No customers.

We remembered our master the war-veteran and tried another tack: 'True Hungarians have clean shoes!' we shouted. This lured a young army officer over, although his toecaps were already like mirrors. While Mik threw himself at the boots, the officer questioned us. Mik lied brilliantly. His father was serving the Fatherland in the south, liberating Hungary from the Yugoslav yoke. The officer was scandalised that the children of a Hungarian soldier should have been reduced to such menial labour. He tipped us two pengös.

But for the next half hour business was non-existent. So I turned tout. I would select a well-dressed man whose shoes weren't quite as clean as they might have been, and accompany him for a few steps offering a cut-price shoe-shine service. This brought in a few customers, but they only paid us twenty fillérs a time. We were standing around idly when suddenly a policeman appeared in front of us.

'What are you two up to?' he demanded.

'Trying to earn some money,' countered Mik. 'No luck. Officers and policemen only twenty fillérs . . .'

'Leave my boots alone! You come with me!' Apparently we needed a licence to clean shoes.

'Don't lie! Of course you knew! Come on!'

'It was only me,' said Mik. 'Józska only came along to cheer me up.' In my fright I didn't contradict him. My mother would faint if she discovered that I had stooped so low.

'Are you going to charge me?' Mik protested sadly. 'If you were a soldier serving in the Southland and your kid was arrested for trying to earn his daily bread, would you be happy?'

The story worked again. The policeman let us off 'just this once'. But we had to stop trading. Aaron Kohn had a word with his father and the Synagogue intervened on behalf of the Langs. After a few weeks Mik's dad was declared a 'bread-winner' and released from labour service.

It was soon rumoured that the reason for our valiant army's irresistible advance in the Southland was the lack of any resistance – the Serbs had been too busy concentrating on the Germans. But the fall of Yugoslavia brought English troops to Greece.

I was delighted. The papers only showed small-scale maps of North Africa, so I had no more than a vague idea of where it was. It didn't matter to me how far Rommel pushed forward, he was fighting a second- or third-rate war, fourth-division stuff. But I knew exactly where Greece was. The English could be in Budapest within two or three days. Mother would get her job back. She'd probably be promoted. I didn't mention my hopes to anyone: you have to wish silently if you want a wish to come true. But there were encouraging signs: the benevolent city fathers were already scared enough to grant Mother permanent assistance of fifty pengős a month. Mother didn't understand; she thought it was the work of the few decent souls left at the Town Hall, who did what they could because they detested Teleki and the new Prime Minister Bárdossy and all the other Hitlerite scum.

The newspapers were too frightened to spout anything but hot air about the zillions of tons of English shipping being sunk by German U-boats every month. The whole English navy went down at least once a week. When Gyula sent me out to buy a paper one afternoon, I decided not to get worked up if the front page had the usual close-up picture of an English ship sinking. How had they got close enough to an enemy ship to take a photo like that? The ship must have been one of their own.

I squinted at the paper: 'GERMANS TO TAKE ATHENS IN HOURS'. It was a golden spring afternoon, and from the dark of the staircase I could see the clean blue of the sky. Either the paper or the sky was lying. I bargained with God offering to let him relegate Ferencváros in exchange for the immediate liberation of Athens. But that Sunday Ferencváros won again.

Uncle Hunchback told me that his real name was Mr Klein. It was his pencils that were called Kohinor. He also told me, as did Gyula and the kids at school, about the behaviour of our triumphant armies in the Southland. Jewish homes had been pillaged; dozens of Jews had been murdered. There were pogroms going on in Bucharest and various other Rumanian towns, but the Jews of Upper Northern Hungary had suffered the worst. A new Slovak state had been set up there with a Catholic priest for a Führer. I was talking to Aaron Kohn about it when he unexpectedly rebuffed me.

'Stop going on about the English. My father says that a lot of this blood is on their souls, even if their hands are clean.'

I felt dizzy.

'How can your father say something like that?' I demanded. 'What kind of a man is he?'

Kohn looked at me as though I had hit him. 'My father?' he whispered.

I was suddenly scared that I had hurt him irreparably, and reached towards him apologetically. But he started to smile, then shook his head and shrugged.

'My father,' he said as if he were explaining the word to me, 'my father is a good and wise man.'

'How can he be wise and say things like that?' I asked.

Kohn replied hesitantly, as if he had at last stumbled on a question he was unable to answer. 'It's true that the English are our only hope,' he nodded, 'but they aren't much of one.' He stopped, and for a second I thought he had lost his mind; but a second later he was calm again. He spoke evenly, as if he had suddenly remembered what he had heard from his father. 'You see, they shut us out of Palestine so as to stay friendly with the Arabs. Because of the oil.'

I was shocked. 'You mean to say the English can be bought?' I scoffed. I couldn't believe it. I had occasionally read a few boring lines about British oil in the papers, but it was obvious to me that the important things in a war were steel and gunpowder; anyone could buy oil if they had the money, and the English were rich in spite of being good. Like Aaron Kohn's father.

I became confused and tried to help Kohn out of his momentary loss of sanity. Remembering the candles at *Chanukah*, I threw him a

177

lifeline: 'They'd be cleverer if they made friends with us. Jews can make one day's oil last eight.' Yet although he laughed, Kohn didn't take the opportunity of saving himself.

'So why don't they let us into Palestine?' he demanded. I couldn't answer this – not immediately at least – but Kohn didn't take advantage of my silence. 'It could be too late already,' he went on. 'Not for Hungarian Jews – and how long will that last? But it's too late for the rest. On the first of January Hitler announced his plan for the complete extermination of the Jews. He said that by the end of the war there wouldn't be a single Jew left in all Europe.'

In a dream, I heard him tell me of atrocity after atrocity. In Poland the German and Polish Christians had led Jews outside the towns and then shot them all. I tried to argue, saying that whatever else Horthy had done, he had at least jailed Szálasi, the leader of the green-shirted Arrow Crosses. I said that Hitler did as he liked in Poland because it was a defeated enemy, that Hungary was different. But Aaron Kohn's father had spoken to Poles who had escaped, and they said that the Polish Christians were as bad as the Germans. Jews were only allowed out of their houses at certain times of day and only within designated Jewish areas. Many towns had created closed Jewish ghettos. Papers were confiscated or simply stamped 'Jewish', and the holders of such papers weren't allowed to cross a Christian street, let alone a frontier. Pogroms were a national tradition. The Poles had been beaten by the Germans and by the Russians: they were taking it out on the Jews.

But it wasn't confined to Poland. The Hungarist Green Shirts wore crossed double-pointed arrows in imitation of the swastika. They had beaten Jews half-dead in village squares, with the constabulary looking on and laughing. In one village – Csikszereda – thirty Jewish families had been dragged from their homes into the fields, forbidden to return. In another, Putnok, the district sheriff had imposed a nine o'clock curfew on Jews. Yet another village banned them from buying bread. In Rimaszombat they weren't allowed to be in the street before midday.

'Jews can only trust other Jews,' Kohn concluded. 'No one else is going to help us.'

'We don't help each other,' I retorted. 'The rich won't help the poor.' I told him that the wealthy Hungarian Jews had only given one six-thousandth of their riches to help people who were living on one soup a day. But he knew about all that. It made him gloomy.

I reported the whole conversation at home in detail. Mother

just stared straight ahead of her all the time I was speaking, and I had to ask her several times whether she was listening. Did what I was saying frighten her so much that she couldn't listen? Or had she heard it all before? Gradually I began to suspect that it was not the reports themselves that shook her, but the fact that Dávid and I now knew about them.

'You mustn't believe everything you hear,' she said, but I could see that she did. I mentioned Palestine, though with great reservation as I was convinced that it must be one enormous *heder* where everyone had to speak perfect Hebrew and grow plaits, and if they ate anything that wasn't *kosher* only the English soldiers would be able to save them from stoning . . .

'Elek wanted to emigrate,' said Mother. 'But my father said he wouldn't sell three good vineyards just to buy a patch of desert sand.'

'Maybe now he'll change his mind!' I exclaimed hopefully. After a moment's deliberation I had decided that plaits and Hebrew were better than being shot like the Polish Jews.

'It's too late,' Mother sighed. 'There's a war on. Elek and Sam might be called up any day now.'

'For labour service,' I muttered. And then I remembered that despite the invasion of Yugoslavia, war with England had not yet been officially declared. I stammered like a coward: 'We could still get out.'

Mother didn't even answer. It was a stupid suggestion in any case. Grandfather would have to sell at least his best vineyard to provide for our escape, leaving him and his sons at Hitler's mercy. I had revealed my cowardice in vain; all I had discovered was my readiness to betray Elek.

It was Gyula who solved the problem for me.

'The Germans might occupy Palestine any day now. They want to get their hands on the British oil supply.' I was still mystified, so Gyula finally explained the importance of oil.

When I next went to buy a paper, my prayers failed again. Half of the front page was taken up by a giant photo. A grey sky was filled with thousands of white circles. Beneath them hung shadow figures as thin as thread. German parachutists. I could have knocked them out of the sky with a pea-shooter, but they had succeeded in taking Crete. I could only imagine that the English were too sporting to shoot them in the air, and had waited for them to land to fight on equal terms.

Still, the good news was that Hitler didn't dare attack England any longer! The real war would only begin when the English swung into the attack, everything until then was just a warm-up. It was similar to Ferencváros's off-side tactics, which tired out the enemy forwards before their own side took the initiative. The problem was that it might take months . . .

A week later, the rumour reached us that the Germans had lost thirty-five thousand paratroopers over Crete. I suddenly saw the situation in a different light, and was glad that the English hadn't pushed sportsmanship to the point of suicide. It was now impossible for the Germans to support an invasion of England with any useful number of airborne troops.

Coming back from the play-centre one afternoon, we found Mother standing in the kitchen in the dark blue suit and white lace blouse that she usually wore only for celebrations. She was cooking in them – she hadn't even put on an apron. The stove was already lit; there were poppy seeds and walnuts on the table, cauliflower in the colander, and the almost forgotten smell of roasting poultry filled the warm air. When we came in, Mother hugged us both so hard that I thought my neck would be dislocated. Her face was red from the heat, but she went to the stove and pulled out a baking tray with a whole chicken on it!

She had found a job! At the Synagogue, as a 'welfare helper'. She hadn't dared to mention that she was applying, because better-educated and -connected Jewish women were now looking for work and Mother hadn't expected to stand a chance. She wouldn't start work until July, but she would be paid from May onwards – one hundred and eighty pengös a month! Two and a quarter times her old salary! It was a pity to have to lose the assistance from the Town Hall, but at least Mother wouldn't have to take on extra work any more. Her new employers had been delighted to find someone with experience in welfare. They needed her badly – Jewry was suffering the worst persecution for years, and they expected it to get steadily worse while the war lasted. Mother had a job for the duration.

I was fairly sure that one hundred and eighty pengös a month were enough to give Gyula the sack. We certainly wouldn't have to eat bulgar wheat with crackling and carrots any more. Dávid and I began discussing what toys we wanted first – I decided on a football like the one Half Wit had. Mother panicked. She told us not to be greedy or we'd soon be on the street.

180

When I told Aaron Kohn that my mother had found a job he was very pleased and said that his father would be very pleased too. I asked him why his father would be so pleased when he didn't even know us, but Aaron Kohn replied that his father was always pleased when something like that happened to a Jew.

'Do you know where my mother will be working?' I asked suspiciously.

Aaron shrugged; he didn't know.

'At the Synagogue!' I said, staring into his eyes.

'Naturally,' he smiled.

I went for him. 'How did you know?' I demanded.

'I didn't,' he replied. 'But who else would give a Jewish lady a job today except for other Jews?'

The conversation hadn't left me any the wiser. Mother went on speaking gratefully of her possible benefactors, the most important of whom seemed to be God, who always helped her in the end. After a while even that didn't seem impossible.

The school year ended suddenly. It was like waking up from an infinite winter's night to find oneself in an aeroplane bound straight for the Australian summer. One bright morning, chairs lined the classroom walls. Dávid's speech day went on longer than ours, as his class were leaving primary school for good. His small teacher said goodbye to each boy in turn. His desk was covered with flowers.

To Dávid he said, 'I shall miss your warmth and calm intelligence. Stay serious and wise. We have recommended you for a bursary at the Jewish Grammar School. Safe journey, Dávid.'

Out in the street, Gyula was waiting for us. He wore a grey suit, and had an unnecessary raincoat over his arm. We wandered towards home. Dávid was wearing a pair of snow-white shorts and a brown silk shirt; he was silent, thinking serious and wise thoughts about secondary school.

'You're lucky,' I said, disturbing his daydreams. 'You don't have to go back.'

'Neither do you,' said Mother. 'It's too far for you to walk on your own.'

My joy flung me a metre into the air. Maybe two metres. I hardly touched down as I raced off back to the school to ask Mik Lang and Aaron Kohn for their addresses. But they'd already left: the building was almost empty. Still, I galloped back to Mother and Dávid in high spirits, soaking up the light like a sponge. I ran faster than ever, my eyes half closed against the glare of my happiness, seeing the dark doors closing behind me as Berger thumped on them in desperation . . .

With the beginning of the holidays in June, the pack's activities really took off. I gave up sharing the tie and cap with Dávid and let him have them both, and that Sunday I looked like an ordinary civilian with a knapsack. We took the tram to meet up with the rest of the pack under the old lion. Half the seats on the tram were empty; apart from us the passengers were all grown-ups. Nearly everybody had a newspaper, yet they were all glancing at each other's paper as if it might contain something theirs didn't. Some made short remarks to the rest of the tram.

'Its going to be pretty hot,' said one.

'This'll make a few people sweat,' remarked another.

I concluded that there was going to be a heatwave. It was a cold, drizzly morning and, although I didn't have a raincoat and was used to getting wet, the news cheered me up. The man sitting beside me was still reading the front page, and I waited for him to turn over so that I could confirm the forecast. He didn't. Bored with waiting, I glanced at the headlines to see if England had been sunk by a U-boat.

'GERMANY INVADES RUSSIA.'

'The Panzers are advancing irresistibly . . . ' I read.

The skinny man whose newspaper it was noticed me reading, but he didn't seem to mind. 'We'll cut the Bolsheviks' throats,' he remarked proudly.

'Who are the Bolsheviks?' I asked, slightly ashamed as I had heard the word hundreds of times but only knew that it meant Communist, which meant 'mother-murderer' or something like that. Some deadly insult.

'The Russians! The filthy Russians!' said the man with controlled, triumphant excitement.

'Russia's very big,' I pointed out, bringing to bear all my geographical and strategic knowledge.

'Big?' snorted the man with uncontrolled, contemptuous laughter. 'Big? Is a pig's throat too thick for the slaughter? Poland took two weeks, France took six. This Bolshevik pig's throat might take a couple of months for the Panzer to saw through. But don't worry, your Christmas tree will come from Siberia all right!'

'But I'm Jewish!' I stammered in my fright.

The skinny man whooped. 'Then you'll have to go and get the Christmas tree, mate!' He looked at me angrily. 'You don't look like a Jew!'

My brain unhinged.

'You don't look like a moron until you open your mouth,' I told him.

The mouth opened. 'Conductor!' he shouted, jumping to his feet. 'Throw this little Jew off the tram!'

'He has a ticket,' the conductor replied. He turned away.

'I'll call the police if you don't get off,' threatened Skinny. His blue eyes sharpened as he joined the war effort.

'Get off yourself!' I laughed bravely.

We were approaching a stop. He grabbed my collar. 'Off! Filthy little yid!'

'You haven't the right!' shouted Dávid.

The conductor stepped between me and Skinny.

'Off!' he ordered. I thought he was talking to me. 'Get off!' I didn't move. He gripped my shoulder. Skinny didn't move, but the conductor was bigger than him. Suddenly the conductor grabbed Skinny by the coat and pushed him towards the exit.

The weed writhed. 'Budapest Public Transport won't put up with Bolshevik traitors like you much longer!' he yelled. 'Don't worry, I've got your number, you Jew-lover! Yid's pimp!' he shouted proudly. Still swearing, he got off the tram.

The excursion was very political. Gold-tooth, Half Wit, Cowardly Sheep and the rest of them all thought that Hitler had at last done a great deed for Mankind and that England could now make an alliance with him. Apparently Bolsheviks didn't allow Jewish daddies to hire *goy* managers for their clinics, wholesalers and 'modest' factories.

'Nobody's ever conquered Russia, not even Napoleon,' declared András the Pianist. He was very learned. He told me that Napoleon was a great general, despite being a Frenchman. At the battle of Győr the Hungarian nobility had run away from him after half an hour. But the one-eyed Russian General, Kutuzov, beat him. It sounded like beating someone with one hand tied behind your back. 'Churchill will make an alliance with Stalin,' András predicted. He looked too much like Churchill to be mistaken.

That evening, Gyula confirmed the news about Napoleon.

'Does this housepainter corporal really think he can do better than the greatest general in history?' he said scornfully.

'They're pushing forward irresistibly,' I said, quoting the newspaper.

'Kutuzov didn't resist either,' Gyula replied grimly. 'Wait until the winter, Józska. When he takes Moscow Hitler will catch a cold that won't go away in hell.'

183

The Panzers raced forward; the newspapers spoke of hundreds of thousands of Russians killed, thousands of planes and tanks destroyed; they seemed to be publishing Hitler's dreams. After a while, even those who supported the English began to shrug their shoulders: maybe the Russians really were very weak.

A few days later the papers carried photos of aeroplanes and twisted metal, claiming that the Russians had bombed the town of Kassa. Neither we nor the Hitlerites believed this; only a few very stupid children swallowed the idea that the Russians had nothing better to do than to provoke neutral Hungary into a real war.

On our communal balcony, I met up with Pöci, Kaci, Laci Mester and Pista, the son of the vice-caretaker. We studied the pictures and the maps showing the German advance, read out the lustful reports of endless German victories. Pöci was keen to play hide and seek, but we politicians made him shut up.

'If we enter the war,' said Laci Mester, summing up his views, 'we'll be able to re-annexe the rest of Transylvania on our way to Moscow. With any luck we'll be able to occupy Bucharest as well.'

The real politicians must have come to the same conclusion. The next day, Hungary declared war on the Soviet Union – which was what Russia was now called. Pista, the vice-caretaker's son, greeted all the tenants with a 'Heil Hitler' until the old doctor from the first floor slapped him in the face.

'You'll pay for this, you dirty yid!' screamed Pista. It led to a huge row; Pista's father beat his son until the whole building echoed with his howls. He had to beg the old doctor's forgiveness.

'Don't be cross with me, Uncle Doctor,' he pleaded. 'I didn't know you weren't a Jew . . .'

Laci Mester enrolled as an unpaid batman to the retired army captain on the second floor. He cleaned the lame officer's shoes and walked his dog for hours on end. He vowed to become an officer cadet even though he was only the son of a caretaker. At the same time, he grieved over the fact that the war would be over before he'd be commissioned, and he wouldn't be able to join the army when it paraded through the streets of Moscow.

10: Saint Stephen's Square

My new school was just across the road, in the same square as Saint Stephen's Basilica. The building was new; the classroom light. Large pictures of Petöfi and Kossuth hung opposite one another on the walls. Each corner of the room had a triangular shelf on which geraniums grew in pots. I knew a few of the kids, although many of them only by sight. Some were Jewish, some Christian. Ferdi Schuster was a real street urchin: I'd played football with him when they'd let me join their game in Erzsébet Square. Pista Rácz, the little Hitlerite from our building, went to my new school too. My deskmate was Sándor Katala, who wore a grey suit and spoke with the disciplined dignity of a government minister.

'Which leader have you got two of?' Katala asked me incomprehensibly as we settled down for the first lesson.

'Two what?'

'Pictures of course!'

'I don't collect Hitler or Mussolini,' I whispered back. 'I don't even collect Horthy and they don't sell any of Churchill.' Katala burst out laughing. The teacher asked him what was funny, and Katala repeated our entire conversation out loud. The stocky teacher laughed too.

'All right, Józska Sondor, name the seven leaders,' he said.

I stood up. 'Hmm . . . Churchill is the first and the greatest, then Roosevelt, then Stalin . . .' I paused before the names of the Führer and the Duce to gather strength for the ensuing battle.

'Not those leaders!' said the teacher, moderating his laughter into a smile. 'We hear enough about that lot in the papers. The leaders of the seven tribes!'

'Which tribes?' I asked warily. 'Don't you mean the *twelve* tribes, sir? Jacob's sons? Reuben the eldest, Joseph my namesake, the best and the cleverest, Simeon, Levi . . .' I stopped. The class was in fits. The teacher's head fell back, but his laughter was light and so I didn't mind too much about being Form Fool yet again.

'It's not the filthy yid leaders we want to hear about!' shouted Pista Rácz from the back of the class. The teacher's laughter broke like a shattered vase. A second later, he was calm. With a controlled voice he told Pista Rácz to take out his exercise book.

'You, my boy, will write out one hundred times: "Baiting Jews is blasphemy against Jesus Christ. Exclamation mark." You can start now, and if that doesn't cure you, next time it'll be a thousand lines. OK?' He turned back to me. 'And now let's hear the names of the seven Hungarian chieftains, Józska Sondor.'

'Álmos the sleepy,' I said, remembering suddenly, but as my memory then failed me, the usual laughter began to rise around me like the echo of all my other first days at school. The teacher laughed too, but in order not to embarrass me he went through the names of the other chieftains himself:

'Elöd, Hont, Kont, Tass, Huba, Töhötöm. Which one is missing from your collection, Sanyi Katala?'

'Kont and Huba. But I've got three Töhötöms.' The class laughed again, and I could sit down without anyone noticing. The teacher told us to do our picture-swapping during break.

He was called Imre Torma, was not yet thirty, and was short and stocky. His head was big, his face wide, his eyes lively, voice deep and calm.

I got a shock when the class split up for Religious Studies: out of the eleven Jewish kids in the class, I was the best at reading Hebrew! I was told that everyone had been given an 'A' in Hebrew the year before, as a matter of course. They were all well-dressed children. Tomi Fried's face was so fat that his eyes were always half closed and he looked like a baby. Peti Hoffmann was small but tough, and never tired of pointing this out: 'Peppercorns are small but strong . . . ' he kept saying.

Karcsi Drack was thin, with an aristocratic lack of expression that made him look like a dry stalk. Gosztonyi's tired eyes peered wisely out of his milk-white face but one never heard his voice. There was no sign of an Aaron Kohn or a Mik Lang among them; no High Priest, no Robin Hood. Who was going to be my friend?

There were quite a few thick oafs among the Christian children: stubborn, stupid-looking Hungarians. Lorentz was a slim, pretty boy, with easy movements and a delicate line in clothes. I almost expected to see a diamond ring on his finger.

During break, a curly-haired, bright-eyed boy came up to me. He was called Karcsi Konrád.

'I'm an anglophile too,' he told me. 'Did you hear vot Torma said? Don't vorry, he'll defend you against the antisemites. Vot do you think about the vor? Vhy do you think Hungary's joining in?'

'So as to occupy Bucharest,' I laughed. Karcsi Konrád laughed too.

'But vhy else?' he asked, and then answered his own question: 'Because a military victory is the only vay this vobbly half-feudal régime can hope to survive.'

'Your father told you that,' I stated. 'But what does "feudal" mean? Do you know?'

'It vosn't my father, it vos my brother. He's very intelligent.'

'How old is he?'

'Thirteen. He's in the third year at grammar school.'

'Thirteen. . .?' I repeated respectfully. 'So what does "feudal" mean?'

'Run by landowners and army officers. Landless peasants are vorse off than the serfs used to be.'

'Why do you say "vorse" instead of "worse"? Your "w"s sound like "v"s. Is there something wrong with your mouth?' I asked sympathetically.

Konrád blushed, then laughed. 'That's the Germans' fault too. I started learning German from our *Fraülein* a bit too early.'

'What's a "froyline"?'

'An *au pair*.'

'Tell me, are you by any chance an idiot?' I asked. I wasn't being unfriendly: it's always better to know that sort of thing in advance because otherwise you don't know what to expect.

'I'm learning English too,' he explained apologetically. 'If the vor goes on long enough I shall escape and join the British army. My brother vill join them too. Vot are you laughing at? You're Jewish, aren't you going to join up?'

'I don't speak English,' I apologised. 'We haven't enough money for me to learn. Still, you can't really believe that the war's going to last until we're grown-up! You're a funny sort of "angle file" if you do, at any rate.'

But Konrád didn't take offence, he laughed. 'If ve escape to

187

England ve can lie about our age. I hope I grow fast.' He sounded keen, but his "v"s spoiled the effect.

The Christian kids I sounded out over the next few days all hoped for a 'Hungarian' victory, and were sure it was bound to happen. My football chum, Ferdi Schuster, was the only one who predicted an outright 'German' victory.

The beginning of the school year added a new item to our supply of patriotic gibberish. At exactly midday, all activity at every school in the country had to stop. We then had to recite something that wasn't a prayer, although it referred to God and the like in an effort to be solemn. It was some sort of patriotic declaration of faith, full of lies such as the claim that Hungary had entered the war in self-defence when the truth was that no one had so much as said boo to us.

'The midday bells are ringing all over Hungary. They remind us of the heroes of Nádorfehérvár. Let us also remember our living heroes, for Hungary has once more taken up arms in self-defence. Our Fatherland has bravely accepted the challenge, and noble Hungarian soldiers are risking their lives for our frontiers. On the infinite Russian steppes . . .'

Torma, our teacher, was visibly confused when he had to teach us this rubbish, and never spoke of the existing war. Instead, he told us stories about János Hunyadi and his battles with the Turks. We learned how the Pope had dedicated the midday chimes to the eternal memory of Nádorfehérvár, because the Hungarians had saved Christian civilisation from the Turks.

'Hitler is saving Christian civilisation too!' exclaimed the elegant Lorentz, interrupting our glorious past.

Torma gulped: 'We are talking about the Hunyadis, not Hitler.'

'Who's Hitler saving Christian civilisation from, the British?' asked Konrád.

'We're not at war with England,' said Torma defensively. Technically he was right. 'And the Russians don't believe in God.'

'And the Nazis do, do they?' Konrád probed.

'I have already told you that we are praying for the *Hungarian* soldiers,' answered Torma. His voice was like lead.

When lessons were over, Lorentz walked elegantly over to Konrád.

'How dare you call the Germans Nazis? They're our allies. Are you a converted Jew by any chance?'

'I might be,' said Konrád, pursing his lips. 'It so happens I'm

188

not. I'll call them Nazis if I feel like it. I'll call them imbeciles too.'

Torma never shouted at us. Even the Hitlerites weren't afraid of him. They were only afraid of losing his good will.

At home we had enough to eat, went to the cinema once a week, and saw less of Gyula. He and I maintained an armed truce. But despite all this, I could see grotesque figures moving almost imperceptibly on the horizon; and I knew that if they moved one step closer, they would become real. The front was brought home in newsreels, but the sound of the guns was drowned out by the cheering. Our soldiers were risking their lives for the frontiers of the Fatherland – at Kiev, a distance of three Hungarys away.

There was no play-centre at my new school. Mother left us a cold lunch, or if Dávid arrived home early he'd cook a few eggs for both of us. One afternoon I dropped into the Kohinor stationery shop to buy an exercise book. Uncle Hunchback was alone, and when I came in he stopped his bustling about and asked me why he hadn't seen me for a while and about my new school. He was pleased to hear that Imre Torma was prepared to defend the Jews. But suddenly he asked me an incomprehensible question: 'Is your citizenship in order?'

'What's that?'

'Are you Hungarian?'

When I told him that my parents, grandparents and even great-grandparents were born in Hungary, he nodded approvingly.

'But my mother's mum was born in Transylvania!' I suddenly remembered. 'Is that bad?'

'Where in Transylvania?'

'At Bánffyhunyad – in the lands of the Hunyadis,' I boasted, frightened.

'That's all right.' Mr Klein calmed down. But the sense of menace still hung about him, and I began to worry that he might be a wicked elf and that I had made a mistake about him liking children and opening a shop for them. He just wanted to frighten them. That's why he couldn't find a wife even though he had a shop and a fortune to go with it. He was evil. And then he began to speak quietly and frightened me even more. He had the educated voice of a bookseller, not of a stationer.

It had started at Marmarossziget in Transylvania and then spread to Upper Northern Hungary. The provincial governors and high sheriffs had made it known that any Jew who left Hungarian territory of his own free will would be resettled in Galicia on highly favourable terms. Free will? The police set on people daily, demanding proof of Hungarian citizenship. When it wasn't forthcoming, shops were robbed and houses ransacked. Some people were arrested; those who emerged from the police stations had been beaten half to death. Many had died. In the end, thousands and thousands of Jews reported ready to leave. After all, the posters and newspapers promised them new homes and trading permits in Galicia. They would be allowed to open shops. Apparently Galicia needed people. Whole towns and villages had been depopulated: most of the Galician Ukrainians had fled from the German and Hungarian troops or had died in the bombing. People volunteered by the thousand. Even in Budapest. Most of the provincial Jews were rounded up into camps in the county of Zemplén; the rest were interned in temporary jails in Budapest. By then they knew that they'd been duped, but it was too late. They were all detained. And then . . .

'I heard it from eye-witnesses,' Mr Klein went on. 'First they were freighted east over the frontier, and then transported further in lorries. They were told that they were being taken to nearby villages where they were to settle; but the lorries stopped at a brick factory and the prisoners were lined up alongside a giant ditch. The SS were waiting for them with machine guns. The main centre for the extermination was a place called Kamenec-Podolsk. There alone, people were murdered in their tens of thousands – local Jews as well as the volunteers from Hungary.'

He spoke more and more quietly, glancing at the door. Suddenly he went pale. 'Don't tell anyone what I've just told you!' he warned.

'Why not? Isn't it true?'

For a second he seemed confused; he hesitated, muttering. I expected him to tell me that it was all a lie, but he didn't. His hesitation proved it was the truth. He sighed and his eyes froze over with fear. 'Because they'll put me in jail for scaremongering. And they'll take me off to Kamenec-Podolsk . . .'

'But Mr Kohinor . . .'

'My name is Klein. My pencils are called Kohinor – call me Uncle Miska . . .'

'But Uncle Miska, if you really don't want me to say anything why did you tell me? Do you just want to scare me?'

His eyes were wide with panic. 'I couldn't hold it back. I sit here alone with these terrible thoughts going round and round my head. Laughing children come into my shop and I see them lying in ditches with their throats cut. My puppet manager is an antisemite; he's looking for an excuse to get rid of me. One word could destroy me. You're an old customer. Just remember what I've told you, and tell them at home not to believe any, but *any*, promises. However good they sound. They all hate us here. They want to bundle us into their hunger camps and surround us with barbed wire and bayonets. They want to send us all off to the scaffold, line us up in front of their machine guns like cattle in a slaughterhouse. Look after yourselves, my beloved Jewish children – tell your parents to look after you, trust no one . . .'

He gulped. His mind went. His clenched teeth chattered and his bunched fists trembled as he exploded: 'Tell them at home . . . tell everyone . . . shout what you've heard in the streets, tell them who told you! Everyone must know! That's all that matters. Why should I care what happens to me? Who needs me? Who wants me? Even I don't . . .' He picked up a stack of notebooks and a big box of coloured pencils and pushed them into my hands. Panting and snuffling, he hustled me out of the shop.

Out in the street, it took me a minute to walk two metres. I hardly noticed as I walked into a sweetshop and bought a packet of tutti-frutti with the money I had saved on the exercise books. By the time I had finished chewing the last one, it felt as if I had only dreamt my encounter with Mr Klein-Kohinor. Amazed, I clutched the stack of notebooks under my arm, and tightened my grip on the big tin box in my hand.

Arriving home, I glanced round the courtyard to see if there was any chance of a game of football. It was empty but, looking up at the third-floor balcony, I saw my brother Dávid standing in front of our door with a cap on his head. From the way he was standing I knew it had to be his new grammar-school cap. I dashed up the stairs.

He hardly glanced at me; he didn't allow my cheers to distract him from standing there like a statue of Dávid. The cap had a hard peak and carried the insignia of the Jewish grammar school. Naturally I wasn't permitted to hold it in my hand, but he had to do something about my presence.

'I am now a student,' he announced. His forehead wrinkled after he had said this, which showed he was thinking. Very hard. Eventually he filled his lungs, pursed his lips, stuck his nose in the air and made a second announcement: 'I shall now beat you up.'

Then, seeing my total incomprehension, he added an explanation.

191

'It's traditional. Second-year grammar-school boys are allowed to beat the toddlers up.'

'Why?' I asked. 'And who are the toddlers?'

'The first year, stupid. But only the senior boys are allowed to call us that – you can't. And for that I'm definitely going to beat you up. Come inside.'

We went into the big room, where Dávid placed his cap on the table as carefully as if the peak were made of glass. Then he turned to me.

'You aren't allowed to defend yourself because if you do the beater-up gets angry,' he informed me. And with that Dávid began to hit me.

I had always rather suspected that being a model child wasn't easy for Dávid. He must have had to work at it. I let him hit me quite a few times: one ear had begun to ache, breathing was a little difficult on account of a blow to the stomach and my brain had gone grey. Although he was stronger than me, he usually only won on points; when we wrestled he could never keep me on the floor for more than a few seconds. But this was different. He wasn't angry, he was just doing his homework.

When my nose began to bleed, my fist went off like a hand grenade. The blow surprised him; he stopped dead and started rubbing his mouth.

'You back-stabber!' he accused. 'You'll pay for that!'

'You're mad,' I told him. 'Not a normal madman either. You're a Hitlerite.' I kicked him as hard as I could. This seemed to bring him to his senses; he raised his hand like a policeman directing traffic and said: 'That's enough. The initiation is over. But in future you must remember that you're not allowed to hit me back.'

I laughed despite the pain, so Dávid added a further explanation: 'It's because I'm a grammar-school boy. When you're a student you can hit me back – after the second year, at any rate. This time I'll let you off, but remember . . .'

He was convinced he was in the right. His rules were like the Nazis' Jewish laws: the more unfair they were, the more convincing they seemed. The world was still grey to me; it was see-sawing slightly as he went over to the table and lifted up his cap with both hands. Slowly, he placed it on his head like a crown.

Before supper, Gyula listened with nods of pride while Dávid told him all about his new school. There was no mention of toddlers being

192

beaten up, and Mother acknowledged the bruises on my face with a disapproving shake of her head.

'One shouldn't stoop to playing football with street-urchins,' she told me. 'Especially in the street.'

'To whom should one stoop?' I mimicked.

Mother had turned pale. She was listening to Dávid's equipment list, much of which was not provided free by the school. Set square, compasses, gym kit . . .

During supper, despite Gyula's insistence that Hungarians don't speak with their mouth full, I asked innocently, 'Whereabouts is Kamenec-Podolsk?'

Mother and Gyula exchanged glances, confirming my suspicions.

'What have you heard?' Gyula demanded. He sounded almost threatening, as if I had used bad language.

'I've only heard that . . .'

'Who from?' Gyula interrupted, but this time indifferently. He didn't want to scare me into lying. I wasn't sure whether Mother's continuing pallor was caused by my question or by Dávid's shopping list.

'How many thousand Jews did they kill?' I asked, fixing my eyes on Gyula. He watched my face, not wanting to tell me anything I didn't already know.

'Something must have happened, of course,' he conceded. 'But there's a lot of gossip going round. Who've you been talking to?'

'No one says that kind of thing to children . . .' whined Mother. 'How do we know it wasn't an Arrow Cross? They'll come round here . . . That's what comes of hanging about in the streets . . .'

'He can't have been a Green Shirt – he had plaits,' I lied. 'He didn't tell me: I overheard him talking to some grown-ups in a shop.'

'Which shop?' The policeman in Gyula got the better of him.

'The one I bought some tutti-frutti in.' My box of pencils was safely hidden.

'So you breeze into this shop,' Gyula mocked, 'and they take no notice of you. And despite the fact that they'll be jailed if you repeat one word, they go on chatting without a care in the world . . .'

'I won't repeat anything.'

'How did they know that?'

'OK.' I proposed a compromise. 'If you tell me the truth, I'll tell you who told me. Fair?'

193

'No deal.' Gyula straightened up. 'I caught you lying. You're lucky not to be punished.'

'I'm not lucky!' I looked Gyula in the eye. He moved towards me. 'So who told you?'

'Somebody who made me promise not to tell anyone who he was,' I said firmly.

'Why not tell me instead?' suggested Dávid with all the assurance of a non-toddler; he wanted to save me a beating.

'You? You're the last person I'd talk to!'

'Well, what did the mystery man tell you?' asked Gyula. He tried to laugh, as he now owed me a beating but was too embarrassed to do anything about it.

'The truth. It must have been true because you don't dare answer my questions. All you can do is ask who told me.'

'Now now,' murmured Gyula threateningly. He adjusted his trouser belt but didn't pull it out of its loops.

'If you don't dare talk about this, let's have a chat about football instead,' I remarked brightly. It worked: Gyula turned red. I thought he was going to attack, but then he sighed like a steam engine and threw up his arms in insulted fury. Confused, he fell into a chair.

Mother was the first to come to her senses.

'You know, if we talk about this sort of thing in front of other people we could all be interned.'

'For scaremongering,' I grinned.

Mother misunderstood the grin. 'Children may go to remand homes for ordinary crimes,' she said. 'But they get jailed for propaganda offences.'

'Or shot,' I grinned. 'At Kamenec-Podolsk.'

After that, Mother gave up trying to be mysterious and tried to get away with telling me as little as possible. 'No one knows what the figures are. But we do know that none of the people who died were full Hungarian citizens.'

I turned to Gyula. 'It's against the law for you to come here any more. It says so in the newspapers.' Gyula rose to his feet, strangled with fury. He knew that I was referring to the law that forbade marriage and sexual relations between Jews and non-Jews. He slapped me twice across the face and left.

Mother sighed tearfully.

'Gyula's sticking up for us. He's defying the law to be with us – and that's how you thank him!'

194

'The only good thing about the law is that it gets rid of Gyula,' I told her.

She gave me a slap in the face – quite soothing after Gyula's. 'You're mean,' Mother snivelled as if she were the one who'd been slapped. 'You didn't even let Gyula give Dávid his grammar-school present. I don't know if I can now that he isn't here.'

'What is it?' Dávid demanded, leaping into action. Mother sighed again and took a parcel out of the cupboard. It turned out to contain an enormous, shiny brown briefcase. Dávid admired it, hypnotised. He put it on the table, picked it up again, walked round the room with it and put it back on the table; then he put his cap on and started again.

'All this Kamenec thing is just scaremongering, isn't it?' he said. The question alone was reassuring.

'Hungarian Jews have nothing to fear,' said Mother quietly.

Dávid's satchel was handed down to me immediately, but it didn't interest me much.

'Why aren't Jews from Upper Hungary and Transylvania Hungarian?' I asked. 'Wasn't Grandmother Hungarian?'

'Of course she was,' Mother assured me.

Bit by bit, she told me what had happened after the Great War. During the census that followed the original annexation, many Jews had decided that being Jewish was enough of a curse without being Hungarian as well. Hoping to obtain Czech or Rumanian citizenship in exchange, they had declared themselves to be Jews rather than Hungarians; and had also hoped that this would help protect them from future persecution. But now, with the return of the Hungarians, they were out of the frying pan and back in the fire.

'Where is the tutti-frutti shop?' she asked.

'Somewhere in Dob Street,' I replied vaguely.

'Where in Dob Street? What were you doing in Dob Street anyway?'

'I was going to Klauzál Square to see if anyone was playing football.' I was making it all up but it seemed to work. 'I was looking for Mik Lang.'

'You went to Klauzál Square to play football?' Mother protested.

'They weren't playing at Erzsébet Square,' I went on innocently. It was like some crazy dream: Mother gaping at me for trying to find playmates in the streets while kids at Kamenec-Podolsk were getting the full grown-up treatment. I took pity on her. 'There was no one playing at Klauzál Square either . . . ' I told her.

195

Eventually Mother tried to calm my fears by complaining about the minor forms of persecution that were even being reported in the newspapers – confiscation of trading permits, robberies, Green Shirts wrecking Jewish market stalls and the like. It was like a football player with a broken leg complaining about a cold.

Pale as he was, Dávid passed the time by packing and repacking his shiny new briefcase.

Torma was in love with the Hunyadis. He told us stories about their battles against the Turks, their nobility, their kindness to the poor, their fairness and greatness. He told us how János Hunyadi's son László was beheaded, an exceptionally blood-curdling story. A Jew couldn't have been more unfairly treated than this Christian prince, who was condemned to death out of sheer spite. When his long hair blocked the executioner's sword – which was a manifestation of divine judgment – the wicked Hitlerite Czech king, Ulászló, signalled the executioner to strike a second blow. This time, divine justice failed to manifest itself. Torma's favourite poem was 'The Black Raven'; when we recited it, he used to wince if we missed out a single 'and'. It told the story of how Erzsébet Szilágyi, János Hunyadi's wife, wrote a letter to her son Mátyás when he was in Ulászló's dungeon. Miraculously, a raven seized the letter from her hand and delivered it to Mátyás, and then flew back straight away with the reply. Mátyás later became the greatest king Hungary has ever known, and invited the Jews into Hungary.

All the Christian children thought that Torma was using the Hunyadis as a historical parallel, yet although János Hunyadi was a regent, like Horthy, that was the end of the similarity. The Turks and the Russians could hardly have been more different, and the Turks had been the aggressors. It was Vienna that King Mátyás had occupied; so, had he been alive in Hitler's time, would he have sent his army against Berlin or Moscow? This question was put to Torma by Lorentz; Torma thought for a moment before replying and then said, 'King Mátyás is dead.' He was referring to the saying that 'Justice died with King Mátyás', which was a clear statement and a clever one as there was no answer to it.

Torma warmed to me. He praised me, saying that one could tell that I had been brought up in the country because the way I talked was so colourful. He underlined words in my compositions and wrote 'Well put!' in the margin. I warmed to him too.

After a while I began to wonder whether it was right that I

should pray the way I did: 'Please God, hit the Hungarian army and its Commander in Chief with the biggest thunderbolt you've got and help our enemies.' After all, the soldiers were as Hungarian as Torma and the Hunyadis. Instead, I asked God to make Hungarian soldiers worthy of the Hunyadis by turning their guns on the Germans.

My new-found and rather selective patriotism was soon rewarded in a big way. Torma made me recite 'The Black Raven' from beginning to end. Standing up on the teacher's platform!

> *'Erzsébet Szilágyi*
> *Finished her letter;*
> *The words of her loving*
> *Were written in tears.*
> *– Deliver this letter*
> *To Mátyás Hunyadi,*
> *His hand must receive it,*
> *Trust nobody else . . .'*

Torma told me that I had recited the poem very well, which must have decided some great argument that had been raging behind my back. After school, a small, skinny, bespectacled boy called Petes drifted up to me and asked me if I liked playing football.

'Who doesn't?' I laughed.

'Then come with me,' he said, 'but don't tell anyone.'

I was amazed. 'Since when has football been a military secret?' I asked.

He just told me there was no point in watering the team down with bad players, and went off without giving me time to ask him how he knew I was good. A hundred yards away we caught up with a group of kids from our class, and I realised at a glance that I was honoured: they were all Christians. They had sent their weakest player to deliver their kind invitation, and I hadn't even asked for the privilege.

'Is this an Aryan football team?' I asked.

'No, no,' replied Lorentz delicately. 'We just don't want to water down the team.' He used the same expression as Petes, so it had to be a plot. I gave in to temptation and went with them 'just this once'. They could hardly have thought of a better present.

We walked in silence. I tried to chat about football, but everyone was thinking about the one subject we didn't want to discuss.

'You're a Ferencváros supporter, I believe,' said Haraszti, who was a head taller than Katala and talked down to everyone. I would have to watch his headers.

'Yes, but not because it's a fascist team,' I laughed angrily.

'That's not my reason for supporting them either,' he agreed. 'But it's not the team that's fascist – it's the fans on Terrace B.'

'Why talk politics?' interrupted Lorentz.

I didn't bother to look up at him but went on. 'Our caretaker's son, Laci Mester, keeps goal there for the cub team. He's a fascist.' I laughed. 'Well, a half-fascist anyway.'

'You're an England supporter of course,' stated Lorentz.

'Of course,' I replied briefly, not wanting the game to be spoilt by quarrelling. Lorentz took a deep breath and took an elegant step away. Apparently he didn't want a row either.

But why had they invited me to play at all? Because of King Mátyás? Because Torma had liked my recitation? Or because I was good at gym? The last was the most likely explanation. I was by far the fastest runner in the class, no one even came a close second. Mik would have left them miles behind. How come a Jew could beat them on one leg when they were supposed to be the Aryan Master-Race? Once I was in my goal I'd leave them gasping. They'd see who the Master-Race was . . .

Eventually we came to a wall running parallel with the Danube. The top of the wall was level with my head. We all swung ourselves over. On the other side lay a grassy field that sloped down from the walls which surrounded it on three sides. The field sloped gently down to a great tunnel, over which rumbled the traffic on the embankment road. Disused iron tramway rails, partially covered by grass and rust, shimmered in the ground. Rain gathered in pools inside the tunnel.

We played six-a-side; the captains chose the teams and the thirteenth player joined the weaker group. The graceful Lorentz picked me on his second go, out of politeness. He didn't lose by it. The surprise was Petes, the skinny kid in specs. His passes found their men as if by magic. He paid me a compliment after the game too, telling me I jumped 'like a panther'.

Yet as Petes went up in my estimation, I began to doubt my original belief that I had been invited to join the game on racial grounds – Torma having made me an honorary Aryan. But if that wasn't the reason, what was? Surely they didn't want me just because I was good at football . . .?

11: Moscow

That autumn, my main subject was neither Hebrew nor Handwriting nor Hungarian nor the Hunyadis. It wasn't even football. Slowly and painfully, I was learning Geography from the newspapers. I followed the beaten English troops across North Africa, and in the wake of the triumphant German armies learnt the names of town after Russian town. One by one, they were besieged and captured: Smolensk, Kiev, Bryansk, Orel . . . Only Leningrad withstood the German siege.

The newspapers were delirious: '*Budyonnie's defeated armies are routed by our warriors . . . All meaningful resistance is at an end . . .*' The page burned gleeful echoes of Hitler into my eyes ('Militarily, Russia has been annihilated . . .') and I had to breathe deeply and stare at the marching black letters until they froze and died.

At school I fought my own stubborn battles. Most of the Jewish kids shrugged off the Russian defeats, saying that the real battle would only begin in Europe, with the English. The Germanites just laughed; Rommel's job in North Africa didn't seem any harder than Guderian's or Bock's or Rundstedt's in Russia.

'The Russians are luring Hitler into a trap,' I announced in the courtyard at home during a break in the football. 'Wait till the winter: when Hitler takes Moscow he'll catch a cold that won't go away in hell!'

Pista Rácz choked with fury. 'The Jews will dance when Moscow falls,' he spat. 'Hanging from lamp-posts!'

'The English,' I replied with quiet dignity, 'will re-cobble Andrássy Avenue with Christian heads . . .'

Winter came at last. Hard early frost began the attack, yet I sometimes found myself slowing down in the street so as to feel the cold better, sure that my shivering was a prayer more powerful than words, a sacrifice to winter. The cold would be multiplied by a thousand, freezing German and Hungarian hands to the metal of their guns . . .

The journalists' hands didn't freeze: '*Moscow lies at the German army's feet . . . Russian resistance is broken . . . Moscow's suburbs have been penetrated by German units . . . from our present positions we can see the Kremlin with the naked eye . . . the Russians continue their hopeless struggle . . .*'

And then, for several days, there was nothing but 'local skirmishing' . . .

War broke out between America and Japan. Allied to the Germans, the Japanese had attacked Pearl Harbor treacherously without declaring war.

For a few days the papers were filled with far-away happenings, and mentioned only in passing that the '*Russian counter-attacks have been courageously repelled*'. It was only after several courageously repelled counter-attacks that we were finally allowed to read of a '*Russian offensive at Moscow*'.

I laughed happily when I heard the news. Everyone now knew the truth. A few days earlier, a hitherto unknown general called Zhukov had launched attacks from Kalinin to Yeletz and had thrown the Germans back all along the six-hundred-kilometre front. Guderian was on the run, he had been forced to retreat one hundred and fifty kilometres, leaving most of his heavy artillery and frozen-up tanks behind him to escape encirclement. Everywhere, German soldiers were dying by their tens of thousands as airborne troops cut off their retreat to leave them trapped in armoured pincers. The Great Russian Storm rolled forward, spitting fire and snow and steel, sweeping yesterday's triumphant horde further and further away from Moscow.

I dug my hands into the snow, lifted it up, tasted it. I paraded through the streets, through the corridors of the school and along the balconies of home, feeling like Zhukov's chief colonel – at least! I didn't need to hear the BBC to know that '*the myth of the German army's invincibility is gone for ever*'. It was written in the sky and on the buildings, the faces of the officers and the faces of the Jews.

Forgetting all modesty, I celebrated openly. It was our turn to be delirious. At school, Konrád congratulated me on the hundreds and hundreds of Germans killed in the last week; I returned the compliment, congratulating him on a retreat of one hundred and fifty kilometres when the real running hadn't even started. We began a victory dance in front of the whole class; the Jewish kids watched us with happy smiles and a few cheers while the Christian kids sat pale and immobile, unable to believe their eyes. Only Lorentz mustered enough dignity to get up and walk out, slamming the door behind him.

Pista Rácz was the next one to find his wits.

'Ten yid shops lost their windows in Dob Street,' he reminded me.

'Hitler must have thrown in his reserves,' I replied.

One morning when Mother had already left to go to work, Dávid unrolled a poster. It was a picture of Hitler a metre high. I was puzzled. It turned out to be part of a ceremony that had become the latest craze in Dávid's class. The high point of the ritual involved burning a portrait of Hitler, and the flames of fashion swept quickly over the whole school. Frightened teachers tried to scare the kids into stopping; cleverer teachers argued.

'Bright Jewish kids filling the pockets of Hitlerite printers?' they asked.

I was dumbfounded by God. His wisdom didn't always seem to make Him good, but at least He didn't always use the cold against me.

The newspapers stammered; the politicians stammered; the military experts stammered. The papers did their best to make people believe that our troops were *'retreating in good order'* to *'cold-weather positions prepared well in advance'*. Where exactly these positions were remained a military secret.

'Blitzkrieg!' shouted Konrád, pointing at the swirling snow beyond the windowpane. 'Talk about lightning warfare – the Germans have retreated a hundred and thirty years in thirteen days and caught up with Napoleon!'

Lorentz stiffened. 'You're a Hungarian! You ought to be ashamed of yourself!' Lorentz was confused by Konrád; but his hatred for me was pale and controlled. At first we simply forgot to say hello to one another, then it became a habit. During the autumn a shadow had been wearing my clothes and using my voice; the celebration of the battle of Moscow had rubbed salt in the Christian's wounds, breaking the unspoken rule existing among the more moderate kids on both sides. For the time being, however, my love for the Hunyadis assured a temporary truce with the class. Home was less peaceful: Gyula and I tolerated each other's presence, but that was only a truce too.

I saw my real self wandering on the mountain with Elek. My memory of this became my true home, and my real mother was the mother I had remembered then.

Because at home she found something wrong with everything, every minute. I hadn't washed up a cup; Dávid and I were too noisy;

we weren't doing our homework; if we were, it took up too much room at the table. Even while she was reading she had to jump up every five minutes or so to adjust the position of some object in the room or send me out to the shop. It was always me she sent, as Dávid was shy and his grammar-school studies were sacred. Sometimes she would send me out three times for three different things, not deliberately, but with a sudden urgency. Perhaps she had trouble making up her mind whether we really needed the things she sent me out to buy.

Eventually, Lorentz had had enough of the Battle of Moscow. It was during a 'discussion class'; all the Christian boys were talking about the war and all the Jewish boys, including me, were keeping their mouths shut; Torma was skating delicately around various delicate questions. Solemnly, Lorentz rose to his feet.

'József Sondor is a traitor,' he announced.

Torma frowned. 'Nonsense,' he said coldly.

'Sondor wants the Hungarian army to be defeated,' Lorentz stated, almost dispassionately. I had the feeling that his attack had been prepared in advance; he might have talked it over with his father.

'Only if it fights on the wrong side,' I explained cleverly. 'It's the German army I want defeated.'

'It's the same thing,' he replied calmly, dismissing my defence.

'The *same*?' I shouted angrily. 'The Hungarian army is the same thing as the *Wehrmacht*? Look at the great patriot! *Heil Hitler!*'

'Boys! Boys!' protested Torma, waving his arms around.

'Hungary took them in, and this is their gratitude!' ranted Lorentz grandly, remembering his script. This was too much, Torma had to show his colours.

'Lorentz,' he began, 'isn't your name the tiniest bit Italian? Who took you in?'

'But I—' Lorentz stammered, and then bit his lip. He was about to say 'I'm not Jewish'.

'But you?' asked Torma. He was calm by now. 'You were born here? Is that what you were going to say? Quite right! Take Petöfi, whose original name was Serb: Petrovics!'

This was my cue:

> '*Croatians, Germans, Wallacks, Slovaks, Serbs,*
> *Has Hungary deserved to be so scratched and clawed?*
> *That shielded you from Tartar and from Turk?*
> *Hungarian hands did wield the flashing sword . . .*'

202

I shouted the lines joyfully; I had been waiting ages for the chance to quote Petőfi at the Germanites.

'Hear that?' Torma asked them, pointing to me. 'No one can take away your right to the land of your birth. Where were you born, Józska?'

'In Budapest,' I replied with a show of modesty.

The teacher nodded. 'That makes you as Hungarian as I am, or Lorentz or anyone else in this classroom. But stay Hungarian even if other Hungarians hurt you,' he told me. Without pausing, he changed the subject. 'Our soldiers are freezing to death. They need warm clothes: boots, waterproof coats, blankets. Talk to your parents. Bring in all the warm garments you can spare from your homes.'

'I don't want to take anything to the clothes-collection,' I told my mother. 'If our soldiers are freezing to death in Russia they should come home!'

'If they don't have warm clothes the soldiers will just take the Jewish labour force's clothes instead,' Mother argued. I had to put a pair of cheap wrist-warmers on the altar of the Fatherland.

Lorentz must have been moved by what Torma had said; he had come up to me during break.

'Let's make peace,' he said, offering me his hand. I had to push mine hard to make it move, and we shook hands with our eyes fixed firmly on each other's ears. We were really only making peace with Torma, but even this false peace interfered with my rightful joy at the Russian victories. Victory – defeat of the Germans and Hungarians – meant everything to me. It meant my mother sitting on a lawn surrounded by blue sky, reading a book, smiling.

The front seemed more distant, although it was actually moving nearer every day. The slaughter of the Germans continued steadily, but my grandfather had fallen ill and his sons put him into a hospital in Pest. They had wanted him to have a single room, but he refused.

'What am I, a king?' he asked. He stayed in a public ward.

All that summer and autumn, Elek had been doing labour service. The hoeing and spraying and even the harvest had fallen on Grandfather's shoulders. Samuel had done his best to help, but Samuel had always been a sleepy, dreamy man and didn't speak the day-labourers' language or understand the vineyard properly. By the time Elek was released, Grandfather was exhausted. Thin all his life, he now seemed parched. He lay white and calm in his hospital bed, spending most of the time – even during visiting hours – buried in his prayer books.

'I'm not praying for myself,' he apologised once when I was there. 'I don't have much time left in any case . . .'

He prayed without visible fervour; he just looked at the book and surprised me whenever he turned a page. When the nurses adjusted his pillow or his blanket, or gave him medicine, he just nodded slowly, thanking them for their care.

He asked for the newspaper every day, but only glanced at it for half a minute before folding it up and putting it aside with a sceptical smile. Yet despite being wrapped up in lies, the news was good. The German High Command was still unable to register the force of the blow it had received.

Grandfather gave a long sigh. 'I'm leaving soon. But what will become of you?' he asked.

He never uttered one syllable of complaint. He kept himself clean, and smoothed away the creases in his blankets; when he sat up on the edge of his bed, he would tidy the bedclothes with slow, precise gestures. He piled up his books in regular stacks, the small ones sitting on the big ones like the layers of a pyramid. Beside them lay his neatly folded prayer shawl, and the *twillem* that he wore at his forehead to pray. Perhaps it was because of the black books that the room was dominated by shadows; Grandfather himself looked like a white shadow in his nightshirt, moving slowly so as not to disturb the ancient order of the books. Yet none of this frightened me for a second; the shadows were too indistinct, like the soft uniformity of mist.

Coming home from the hospital we had to walk under the railway bridge to reach the tram stop on Arena Avenue. I used to wait underneath for a train to cross, although Mother always scolded me and tried to pull me away. The Western Station was nearby, and we never had to wait more than a couple of minutes. There would be a rhythmic knocking, louder and louder, and then suddenly an ear-splitting clatter would possess the air under the thundering creaking iron of a bridge that couldn't possibly hold. I used to shut my eyes, with the din almost tearing my hands from my ears, and wait until the monotonous clatter finally echoed itself away into a deep, numb silence. I was half-aware of testing out whether or not we would survive the war. Once my mother left me to wait for the train alone, perhaps hoping that I wouldn't dare stay, but on every other occasion she stood beside me with her hands on mine. Maybe the bridge would collapse, after all.

204

Elek and Samuel were staying at the flat. They slept in the little room which we heated in their honour. Samuel took the kitchen over, and despite having trained in the army, he turned out to be an excellent cook. He had an impressive intelligence network through which he received frequent reports of black-market poultry and veal. My uncles didn't economise; Samuel was a great gourmet. He also helped Mother with the housework. He seemed to be taking advantage of Grandfather's illness to explore Budapest, and was always visiting remote relations, vague acquaintances and 'people from home', most of whom were really cinemas. Samuel denied this, but nobody minded. Even I wasn't jealous, because Samuel would go into full mourning if Grandfather died. He wouldn't be able to go to the pictures for at least a year, and he might be called up for another stint of labour service. Suppertime became erratic. Samuel always went straight to see his 'acquaintances' after leaving the hospital and, as my smiling Uncle Elek suspected, his brother was simply incapable of passing a cinema if there happened to be one on his way home. From time to time he took me and Dávid with him, but this involved advance planning. The films he went to with us were the only ones he admitted seeing, but again and again he would make me sit down in a quiet corner and listen as he dreamily told the story of 'a beautiful film' he had seen 'long, long ago'. He had an extraordinary memory . . .

Mother was as quiet as a dream during the weeks that followed their arrival. She was ashamed to quarrel in front of her brothers.

'Judit,' said Elek quietly one evening. He hesitated for a few seconds before continuing. 'You must come home.'

'You're not serious,' said Mother, taken aback. Elek explained that even if Grandfather were to get better he would be too old and too weak to organise the workmen. While Elek had been away, everyone had cheated Grandfather, especially Borsodi, the vintner, the one who'd killed my cats. Elek had thought it over and had decided that if he and Samuel were called up again the vineyard would go completely to the dogs. There was only one way out.

Mother refused. She sounded meek, but she meant it. Elek promised in vain that Grandfather wouldn't be tightfisted if Mother came home, but Mother shrugged.

'What's the point of having money if you're stuck out in the country? Dávid goes to grammar school now and I don't want him to board. Józska's new school has quietened him down; in another eighteen months he'll be going up to . . .'

'Another eighteen months?' smiled Elek. 'I'd be happy to know what's going to happen over the next eighteen days.'

'I'm not letting them out of my sight,' said Mother.

Elek sighed, but his sigh changed into laughter. 'In that case I've got to get married!' he said. 'How many women know anything about vineyards? To be precise, how many pretty women? You grew up there, you understand hard work. Everybody will respect you.'

'I won't do it,' pleaded Mother firmly.

Just before Christmas, Samuel went out visiting his acquaintances and left the three of us at home with Elek. Unexpectedly, Aunty Felice knocked on the door. Her chauffeur had come up too, and was standing on the doorstep with several parcels in his arms – including two big ones. We helped Aunty Felice bring them inside; seeing how keen we were, she calmed us down by telling us that the parcels weren't to be opened before Christmas. She was wearing an astrakhan coat and a short veil, and long pendants made of blue stones. I noticed Elek sizing her up distrustfully, but I wasn't worried on her account. No one could possibly find anything wrong with Felice. It wasn't her fault she was rich. I was more worried about Elek, although there was no need to be. He was polite, but without changing his voice or falling over his feet to offer her a chair the way Gyula did. Elek remained completely himself, regarding Aunty Felice's beauty and wealth as one of the sights of Budapest, without gaping at her.

'I see the labour service let you go after all,' said Aunty Felice, showing that she knew who he was.

'The same way a cat lets go of a mouse!' laughed Elek.

'Was the service that cruel?' asked Felice.

'I wouldn't have volunteered for it, but no, it wasn't cruel. We were lucky though: we had a decent Hungarian for our company commander.'

'My company commander's decent too!' I remarked, using Torma to try to push my way into the conversation. But this time Aunty Felice seemed more interested in Dávid. She definitely overdid her respect for grammar schools.

'I hope my Christmas present isn't too childish,' she blushed.

'What is it?' I demanded instantly.

She shook her head unhappily. 'I think it'll be better if I tell you even if it spoils the surprise,' she said. 'I'll whisper it to you, Dávid, and if you're too grown-up it can go to Józska and I'll find you something else.'

It hardly took much brains to work out that Dávid could double the number of presents by saying he was too big for the one we'd already got. But grammar school obviously didn't involve brains.

'No, I can still play with it!' he protested violently, flattered by the whispering. Very generous of him.

'So much for the surprise. I hope knowing won't spoil your Christmas.' Poor old Dávid. The surprise wasn't spoiled for me though, as Dávid decided that knowing in advance wouldn't do a primary-school pupil any good at all.

'Sad woman,' said Elek when Aunty Felice had left. The remark surprised me. I remembered saying the same thing long ago, but since then I had only thought of her as being beautiful and quiet. Yet it was true that her eyes were too deep, more like mirrors than flames.

Her visit provided little in the way of military intelligence, despite the fact that she listened to the BBC in English. Like Elek and Gyula, she felt that the legend of German invincibility had been shattered at Moscow; but she didn't think they were finished yet.

'They'll go on winning battles, but they're sure to lose the war,' she said. Typical grown-up hair-splitting.

On the subject of Christmas, Elek took the view that, however 'freethinking' Mother might be, it was going too far not to have a candelabrum *menorah* in the house. So on Christmas Eve – so as not to 'spoil Christmas for the kids' – Elek put our two candlesticks on the table. Although it was Thursday, he made Mother light the *shabbes* candles and repeat the Hebrew prayer that he'd modified for the occasion. Gyula sniffed throughout the ceremony, and when Samuel slipped his hat into Gyula's hand I hoped he wouldn't put it on, so that Elek would throw him out. But Gyula did.

Our secret present from Aunty Felice turned out to be a fantastic train set with huge carriages and a clockwork locomotive that made a real noise and whistled as it went along. There was plenty of track and a big yellow metal house with 'Station' written on it in red letters. Not surprisingly, I had trouble reminding Dávid that he was at grammar school now. He claimed to be interested in the mechanism . . .

Our building was shaped like a horseshoe, with the single doors facing the double doors across the empty space of the courtyard. The main staircase was at the centre of the curve where the tunnel led into the street, but elsewhere the balconies were straight, ending in a blank wall. The double-door flats were bigger, and overlooked the street, but for some reason the entire army of kids who lived in the building lived on the side with the single doors. There were only two exceptions to this rule: the first being the landlord's daughter, Laci's fiancée, and the second being Palika, the puny, delicate, sad little boy who used to stare at us over the balcony. He was eight, only a year younger than I was, but he was still a little boy. He had plenty of toys, but no one to play with as he wasn't allowed to mix with 'proles' or '*goys*'. Dávid and I were only disqualified on the first count, but it was hard to play with him even out of pity; whenever you picked up a toy he'd snatch it out of your hand and shout 'That's mine!' If you pushed him by mistake he'd be smeared all over the wall before you knew what had happened, and his grandparents would shuffle into the room to check that the wicked little beggars hadn't unscrewed the dollies' arms and noses. When we played in the courtyard, Palika used to watch us for hours on end; but he wouldn't have lasted five minutes in our wild, rough games.

Everyone in the building knew everything about everybody else.

'Poor Palika,' they said. 'He'd have been better off as an illegitimate *goy*, living with his mother.' Palika's father owned a couple of shops. He had legitimised his son, which made Palika Jewish.

He also gave Palika a bicycle for Christmas. Palika informed me that we could come in and look at it for five minutes at a time. The entrance fee was ten fillérs. When he said that Dávid and I would have to pay like everyone else, I laughed in his face and demanded half the receipts for acting as tout.

The other kids took up the offer, although they beat Palika down to five fillérs. Panic-stricken, Palika's grandmother opened the door about an inch before banging it shut so hard that the frosted-glass window almost broke. Then we heard Palika's piercing shrieks, and saw the door open again. Grandma and Grandpa were standing there, stooped with age and fear, and their faces filled with fright as they watched us march into the flat.

It was a slow march, as the kids were at least as interested in the flat as they were in the bike and the toys. To reach Pali's room we had to walk through the living room, where a gilt-framed picture of a melon hung on the wall as if the fruit were being served on a vertical tray.

'Crikey, what a big melon!' exclaimed Laci Mester, impressed. Géza Gyak, son of the weight-lifter from the first floor, stretched himself out on the purple velvet sofa without showing any intention of ever getting up again. He wanted a good rest for his five fillérs. In the end nobody paid.

The idea of an entrance fee inspired me. For several weeks I had owed myself – and the others – another of my one-man theatre shows. I had done two of these already, but I hadn't charged for them. The early darkness of January was very good for business, a full house was gathering outside as I took Laci Mester's money at the entrance. Tickets were ten fillérs, the price of an ice-cream or, in winter reckoning, six tutti-fruttis. Pista Rácz came, bringing further inspiration although I was well prepared and already had some vague ideas for the script of the show. Elek and Samuel were present; I charged them twenty fillérs each, just to show the kids that they were getting in for half price.

I had never been to the theatre, but had guessed long ago that it was simply a mixture of the cinema and the circus. The 'Bloke' whom I impersonated could have been anyone from a king to a beggar. To warm up, I started with some Chaplinesque scenes, getting stuck in the revolving doors of an expensive restaurant. My audience laughed all the more for having seen this in the real cinema. I occupied an imaginary table and ordered plate after plate loaded with bigger and bigger helpings. I ate with silly gestures, starting with a knife and fork before moving on to eating with my hands. This increased my popularity with the audience, and meanwhile, out of sight of the imaginary waiter, I turned out my pockets several times to show that they were empty.

I never knew in advance where the scene would take me, but I liked the game, and my fear of drying up grew less with every laugh. I beckoned the head waiter. I had only been to a restaurant three times in my whole life; the movies were my sole source of information on this sort of restaurant, the kind that has a head waiter who shows people to their tables and takes their money. When he tried to take mine, I checked the bill over ten times, complaining that the chicken-paprika had too much chicken in it before dropping the bill in my wine and asking for a new one while I invented the rest of the scene, stole the head waiter's wallet, paid the bill with his money, and was chased out of the restaurant. The scene ended with both of us stuck in the revolving doors.

After a few more scenes from civilian life, I presented the highlight of the performance: the newsreel. In the cinema they did it the other way round, but this was Theatre, with the proud German general watching the Battle of Moscow through binoculars. He dives on to the floor a few times as the Russian planes zoom overhead, machine-gun noises emerging from his terrified face. He stands up, but starts

209

to freeze, so he goes into his bunker. Now he can't see what's going on, so he picks up a field telephone. Bad news. Another phone rings. Even worse news . . .

On the divan, Pista Rácz clenches his teeth and sticks out his chin like the German general. Elek smiles. Samuel, Pöci and the Dara kids are watching with their mouths wide open, but not in admiration. They look bored.

Two field telephones are ringing now, the general rushes from one to the other and stops halfway because a third starts up. He sticks his fingers in his ears and gets a laugh from the smaller members of the audience. He runs frantically round the room saying 'hello' into each receiver in turn. Pista Rácz laughs. The general does another lap and asks each phone for the news without waiting for a reply. Laci Mester laughs, so the general runs round the room to hear the news, and as each receiver knocks him on the head he staggers on to the next with wobbly legs, hearing worse and worse reports from each one. The audience can't hear the news, but they can see my legs getting wobblier and wobblier and I can say what I like because they're all laughing now.

'Zere vill be no retreat! I forbid it!' I yell. The news becomes ominous; Palika is applauding every pained cry and grotesque gesture of the stricken general. Finally, someone starts hammering on the bunker door.

'Who's there?' asks the general with his hand on his heart.

'The Russians,' comes the reply, and the general dives under the table whimpering: 'Don't hurt me, please don't hurt me . . .'

The applause didn't last long. Everyone was still a bit drugged. Pista Rácz was the first to come round.

'Isn't little Moses clever?' he shouts furiously. 'How does he imagine it all?'

'What a shame it didn't happen the way Adolf imagined it,' I retorted, giving my clowning the status of an objective historical reconstruction.

'It's only theatre,' Laci Mester explained in an effort to pacify Pista. As an aspiring first lieutenant Laci was a professional patriot, but he was also the self-appointed leader of the gang, so he had to keep in with everyone. Despite being a staunch supporter of the German cause, he was quite pleased about the defeat of the *Wehrmacht*. The delay offered him unexpected hope of taking part in the march down Moscow High Street. I encouraged this hope, telling him that by the time the Hungarians paraded in Moscow he'd be a retired general . . .

Pista wasn't pacified. He jumped over the chairs and table and on to the 'stage' shouting, 'I'm going to play the Russians!'

'You go and play in the sand,' I told him calmly. 'Go home and do your own show and we'll see who pays ten fillérs to come and see it.'

I could have finished the performance there and then, as I'd already given the public their money's worth. But my power over them fascinated me: while acting, I could say anything and people would listen to me; more than to themselves, more than to the teacher, more even than to proper newsreels . . .

But Pista wasn't listening. He started acting, throwing his arms around and shouting his head off. Seeing he was going to be a flop, I let him carry on.

'I am a Russian soldier! I want to surrender!' he announced at the top of his voice.

'Bad luck,' I laughed. 'You can't. All the Germans have run away.'

That shut him up, but a second later he began bellowing again – this time as Pista Rácz: 'The German army is invincible! Germany will win!'

Laci had to calm him down. 'This isn't theatre, Pista. Stop it!'

By public demand, I continued my performance. I decided to take my revenge. The beginning of the new scene was almost a follow-up to the one before, but this time it wasn't a general who was standing at the field telephone. It was easier to go down a few ranks and play a corporal.

'*Ja?* Adolf Hitler here. Ze Führer speaking. *Heil* me!'

We all knew Hitler's hysterical voice pretty well, his way of standing to attention while foaming at the mouth. It was common knowledge that his favourite dish was the corner of a carpet. When he spoke on radio or in the cinema, it became clear that he was an insane screaming buffoon who astonished people in much the same way as someone pissing on the tram. What frightened me was the fear I saw on the faces of the England supporters. If he'd come into Zafir's pub they'd have thrown Hitler out without even thinking about it. He was dangerous, noisy and stupid, like a bomb. Churchill didn't bother to insult him, he merely provided accurate descriptions like 'bloodthirsty guttersnipe'. What mad people loved in Hitler was the mirror of their own insanity . . .

Worse and worse news reached him. He started chewing the wooden spoon that symbolised the receiver. He decided to commit suicide and lifted the wooden spoon – now a revolver – to his head. Then he began to cry and threw the gun away, but it went off on its own and frightened him so much that he had to go and hide in the cupboard. Every time he came out the wooden spoon went off again . . .

Mother's return ended the performance abruptly. I tried hard to convince the audience that the show was already over, as several of them asked for their money back. They didn't get it. After all the kids had left, Mother told me off, warning me that one day I'd cause real trouble. She banned the newsreels, and Elek agreed with her. I didn't.

Grandfather's inflammation of the middle ear turned into pneumonia. His ears were bandaged with gauze that merged into his beard. His eyes looked out at us from a deep snowdrift.

'Let me see you,' he said, calling Dávid over to him. 'Are you really as good a child as everyone says?' He didn't look at him long, though. He raised himself from his bed, put his hand on Dávid's head and muttered something. Then he called me over and put his hand on my head too; but it wasn't until later that I realised he had blessed us then. He told Mother not to bring us to visit him again until he had recovered.

'It's difficult for children to sit in silence,' he said.

A few days later, he died. His three children were prepared for this. They said prayers together. Elek and Samuel travelled back to Oszu together to organise the burial; Mother followed them two days later. When she returned home, she covered up the mirrors, placed our little stool in a corner with a prayer book beside it, and put on an old dress. She tore it, put on a scarf, and sat in *shivah*, mourning.

Several times, she repeated the words I had heard from Grandfather.

'I am leaving you soon. I have lived. But what will become of you?'

12: Echoes of the Guns

Weather permitting, we carried on with our football where we had left off at the onset of the autumn rains. I was still the only Jew in the group.

The Russian offensive petered out, the Germans taking up firm defensive positions, much as the grown-ups had predicted. But the winter campaign was still carrying me forward. On the second day that was fit for playing football, I stood up on Torma's platform after lessons were over, and instead of my planned declarations of equality and defiance shouted good-humouredly, 'Who's for football, boys? We've got a ball!'

Half the Jewish kids wanted to play, and a minute later we didn't have a ball.

'I'm not coming,' announced Lorentz. 'Are you?' he asked his friends. But they didn't consider it a great political issue. 'Play with a rag-ball!' he said with sneering contempt for his friends' political principles. Then he picked up his ball, put it under his arm, and went home.

Luckily one of the Jewish kids lived nearby and owned a ball, though it was only Size Two. Nevertheless, the price of my political victory was a severe drop in the standard of the football. Most of the Jews were better off than the Christians, so they were softer and slower. The increase in the number of players to eight- or nine-a-side meant that the pitch became overcrowded. But from that day on, the Jews and Christians mixed much more in class.

Everyone simply avoided Rácz, but Lorentz withdrew into himself. He had always considered himself to be honouring the people he bothered to address; now he scarcely spoke at all. There was something military about his reserve, despite his fragile slimness.

'Are there many career officers in your family?' I asked him searchingly.

'A few,' he answered with a certain restraint, and immediately found a way of moving on without insulting me. I didn't mind, yet I couldn't get it into my head that this well-mannered, well-off, basically agreeable kid was pro-German and an antisemite.

I realised that it was simple need that inflamed the hungry anger of the poor, in the same way Mother's nagging was a product of her worries. The fascist press poured oil on the fire, preaching continually that the Jews were robbing the poor – as if most of the Jews weren't poor themselves. The papers never mentioned the fact that when all Jewish-owned land in excess of fifty hectares was confiscated, the thousands upon thousands of hectares belonging to Christian landowners remained untouched, as did the hundreds of thousands of hectares owned by the Catholic Church. I remembered the labourers who signed up to work at the castle in Oszu. They wore rags, and lived ten or twelve to a room in tiny hovels built of mud bricks. Pista Rácz's antisemitism was a bottomless hatred, like mine for him. Lorentz's moderation filled me with hope sometimes. And sometimes it filled me with fear, a far worse than that inspired by the white-hot Hitlerite madness of the exceptionally stupid Rácz.

I experienced the brutality of the poor at every street corner. It wasn't just the kids in our building who got hit: Nagy from the second floor beat his wife up every night after closing time. Rácz's father was less punctual. I saw this kind of thing in other places too. There was an angular kid with a big head who looked as if he'd been cobbled together from spare bits of machinery; he came to the Tunnel now and then to play football, and one day invited me round to his place to see his button-team. We had hardly entered the small dark flat when his father, who was a tailor, came out of the larger room that he used as a workshop. When he found out that his son was two hours late home from school because he'd gone to play football, he belted him so hard that the wind from the blow made me dizzy.

'Do you want to end up uneducated too?' he roared. 'Working from dawn to dusk, hungry as a dog? You won't get a bite to eat till you've finished your homework. And you, you'd better go home!' He threw me out.

I also realised that no one at home ever hit well-off kids like Aaron Kohn or Lorentz or the Chocolate Wolves.

Karcsi Konrád invited me to his birthday party. I went. One of

214

my main occupations during the festivities was trying to count up the number of rooms they had in their house. The entrance hall was a huge room in itself.

'Not that way – that's my father's study.' We went through a big room into an even bigger one, the living room. They called it a *salon*, so I asked Konrád whether this was where they ate *szalonna* bacon. He immediately relayed the question to all the children and grown-ups in the room, putting everyone in a good mood. The grown-ups didn't realise that I thought very rich people ate each dish in a different room. They decided I was a 'witty child'. I was under the impression that *salon* was a yiddish word, and that they had chosen it because they were pro-English and wanted to show solidarity with the Jews. When I hinted at this they laughed even louder, but this time I wasn't so sure that it was my wit that had made them laugh. Next I discovered that Karcsi and his brother each had their own rooms. So did the 'Froyline'. Their father had a butler, and he had his own room too. I went on with my innocent investigations at full volume out of sheer curiosity. I couldn't understand why their answers became more and more inhibited.

The grown-ups all sat on one side of the *salon* with the children on the other. An ugly woman of thirty-five was sitting beside Konrád's grandmother. I thought she must be his mother, but she turned out to be the Froyline. I was glad that Karcsi's mother wasn't ugly. Beside them sat a row of women – the other kids' mammas.

A long, low table divided the row of children from the row of grown-ups. It was smothered in presents: books, boxes of chocolates, toys. Konrád stood in front of them, grinning. Beside him stood a poker-faced boy, his thirteen-year-old brother, Edward. I'd never heard the name before, but discovered during the course of the afternoon that he was called after no less than eight English kings. Karcsi was short for Károly; two English kings had been called that, too. I thought that ten kings in one family was a bit much, even if they were rich . . .

All the kids had been dolled up for the occasion, I was the only one who had come as he was, although I was glad I hadn't put on my old suit from Oszu. It was very traditional and pretty and Hungarian and far too tight – I would have looked as if I'd made an effort but had failed hopelessly.

Karcsi started opening his presents. He picked up a parcel that was lying on the table, but his mother caught his eye and looked meaningfully towards the row of children. I couldn't take my own eyes off a real Size-Five football; Karcsi never played football . . .

He looked at us with a well-bred, blasé smile. All the other kids were holding coloured parcels behind their backs or under their chairs. Inside one was a big car, another turned out to be a clockwork locomotive and a third contained a box of chocolates. Edward watched his little brother good-naturedly, showing no sign of jealousy, but their mother stood up and handed him a five-kilo book – clearly a consolation prize.

I hadn't brought anything of course. If I had known I was supposed to, I wouldn't have come. I had shared Uncle Hunchback's twenty-four coloured pencils with Dávid long ago, and in any case it would have been absurd for me to give Karcsi Konrád presents.

There were only two other kids from our class at the party. Péter Erdei, a convert, was shunned by the Jews for being Christian and by the Christians for being Jewish. Drack was the other, a boy so thin that it was a miracle the wind didn't blow him away. The other five children were all older than us: relations, or friends of Edward's.

A tall, straight-backed man walked into the room. His hair was greying slightly at the temples, his forehead was broad. He was smiling, but it wasn't a happy smile; it seemed instead to express some hidden irritation at being dragged out among women and children. The row of mammas greeted him noisily and smiled as hard as they could.

I had a good look at him. What could a man who had a butler be like? I'd seen such people in the cinemas of course, but they were only actors and so were their butlers. I was surprised to notice that the butler wasn't with him to shine the parquet floor in front of his master's feet and brush imaginary fluff off his jacket. Mr Konrád was alone, wearing a grey suit that had almost lost its creases, and no tie. Torma dressed more impressively, yet you could tell that Konrád was an important man from his calm, dominating way of looking at you. He knew his own importance. After a while he took all the grown-ups off to the small *salon* and the maid came and served tea.

Yet there was nothing showy about all this wealth. When the blizzard had driven us into Mrs Brave Heart's villa, we had to admire each piece of china. Here, everything was natural, even the fact that I hadn't brought a present. While the others were handing over theirs, I gritted my teeth and looked fixedly at Karcsi's mother, and yet she simply gave me a smile. I wasn't sure she didn't wink. All the same, when the

216

cakes, sandwiches, chocolates and other 'elevenses' were cleared away,
I stepped aside and didn't join in as the others started to play with
Karcsi's new toys. How could I when I hadn't brought a present?

The only other kid who wasn't playing was Karcsi's brother,
the boy with the boastful foreign name. He wasn't really a show-off
though; he was standing around looking slightly embarrassed.

'Are you pro-English?' I asked.

'Why? Do I look like a Hitlerite?' he laughed. I laughed too.

Edward spoke like a grown-up, explaining all the things I already
understood and not explaining the ones I didn't. Occasionally he'd
make a point as if it were the punchline of a joke, throwing it at me
in triumph as if he had just invented the wheel. It wasn't just the fact
that he was too clever by half that made him difficult to follow; he was
talking more to himself than to me.

'Over and above the material fact of the conflict – in which they take
a great part – the English incarnate the transnationalistic abstraction of
an essentially local, albeit continental struggle. Their significance as a
nation is in fact supra-national and pan-global. One doesn't call oneself
"pro-Russian", despite the greater sacrifices the Russians are currently
making, precisely because we cannot assess their values and may even
suspect them. We fear the possibility that the Russians are themselves
barbarians and are only fighting the Germans because "one town ain't
big enough for both of them".'

Edward was very proud of this expression and repeated it straight
away although it didn't suit him at all.

'Truth be told,' he went on, 'the English don't risk one tenth
of the men the Russians do – even in proportional terms – and
they don't suffer one hundredth of the casualties.'

He was thirteen, and very bright. Brighter than anyone I had ever
met. I had discovered the source of Karcsi's intelligent remarks. But
Edward used endless foreign words, and I soon became too shy to ask
him what they meant. I was worried that he wouldn't want to go on
talking to me if he realised how stupid I was.

He pointed out a lot of things that I should have worked out for
myself, like the fact that the 'Horthy mob' hadn't actually had much
choice about joining the war. If they'd refused to do so, Hungary
would have been overrun like Czechoslovakia, Yugoslavia, Greece
and everyone else. On the other hand, they were loving every minute
of it; they'd spent their whole lives wanting the annexed territories

217

back, and now they were looking for a slice of Russia as well.

Edward also told me various stupefying, unbelievable things about the English. They had encouraged Hitler's expansionism; thrown him Czechoslovakia in the belief that he was only sharpening his teeth against the Bolsheviks. At that time the Czechs could have beaten the Germans if they'd had a little help, they certainly could have weakened them enough to blunt Hitler's appetite for a while. The English had sold the Czechs down the river to buy time, but they had fallen into their own trap. Churchill was the only one who saw through the Nazis. Not surprisingly, the English sabotaged all Russian offers of alliance until the summer of 1939. They sent third-rate officials to negotiate with Litvinov, Molotov and Vorosilov, so no wonder the Russians became suspicious. Not being much better than the Germans, the Soviets had a non-aggression pact with the Nazis and the two of them carved up Poland between them while they knew that war was coming; the pact just delayed it for a while.

I began to wonder whether bright people see a darker world.

'Don't you believe that the war is a fight between good and evil?' I asked him.

'Of course I do,' he said, but he was laughing at me.

I asked him what he wanted to be. His first choice was to become a soldier in the British army, but he wasn't sure he'd get the chance; this reassured me – it meant that he didn't expect the war to last that long. Otherwise, politician or astronomer, he didn't know. His father had been a politician for a while when he was younger – junior minister for external trade – but his main job was dealing in shares and finance. Finance meant having so much money that you don't have to show off. Edward didn't play football or tennis, didn't swim, did no sport whatever, although his parents nagged at him. Sport was 'a game for children', 'the cult of the body, a precursor of Hitlerite militarism'. I couldn't understand how such a bright kid could talk such rubbish. The Konráds showed off their intelligence instead of their money – and Edward was trying to be the brightest of the lot.

One tenth of what I saw and heard at the Konráds would have been enough to make me envious, secretly at least. Yet this sense of jealousy, scraping at the back of my mind, sharpened my admiration instead of blunting it. I couldn't take in all the details of the splendid old furniture, carpets, toys and bookshelves that filled the endless rooms; the calm, modest, self-contained affluence of the place; the centuries assembled in the paintings and furniture; the Konráds' knowledge of

218

where they were and where they were heading. I imagined myself inside an English castle wrapped in mist, a citadel made impregnable not by its walls, but by magic, a deep and hidden fire, of which material wealth was just the surface.

After the Konráds, the flashy, glitzy, whining and lisping pack, with their wristwatches strapped over the sleeves of their jerseys, seemed like a bunch of performing poodles. I didn't even bother to shrug when Half Wit won the recitation prize for squawking his way through Petőfi's thunderous 'To the Hungarians'. For a while, everything went on in the usual idiotic fashion. Bandi-Ba spent several weeks telling us – in instalments – the story of an officer who had been ordered to hold a mountain pass against the Russians during the Great War. He was faced by overwhelming numbers and commanded his forces to retreat, whereupon he was promptly court-martialled and sentenced to death.

'First Lieutenant Gábor Kalocsai faced the firing-squad. As they raised their rifles, he barked out the final order: "Fire!" '

The story moved the junior Jewish Boy Scouts to tears.

They soon found ways to get at me. The new fashion on Sunday excursions was a game called 'Number War'. You tied a big number to your head, front and back, and ran around. If anyone read your number and called it out, you died. The other way to die was being hit by a ball of screwed-up newspaper called a 'grenade'; remembering the religious stone-throwing fights of Oszu, I spent hours tearing up old newspapers at home, wetting the balls of grey pulp and then drying them out by the stove until they were as hard as rocks and would fly twenty metres. Between us, Dávid and I had about sixty hand-grenades.

The Number Wars involved the bigger boys as well; we represented the light infantry. As well as civil wars among the two hundred scouts and cubs of our own group there were foreign wars against other packs.

I was gunned down ten minutes into the first war when someone called out my number. This was fairly irritating until, in the 'cemetery' where all the dead soldiers were assembled, we found a football which kept us going until the armistice.

Next time, I saw Bandi-Ba – who was one of the referees – writing our numbers down in a little book. I decided to investigate, and deserted my squad to hide in a thick bush. I took off my numbers, sat on them, and waited.

The voice came from far away. Someone, somewhere, could read

219

the number I was sitting on. I stayed put, and then towards the end of the war moved up to the front line. By now there were only fifteen or twenty soldiers left on each side, so I put my number plates back on and infiltrated enemy lines. I had just taken out a binocular nest with a barrage of hand-grenades – the scout with the 'machine gun' was looking the wrong way – when Bandi-Ba emerged from a bush.

'How did you get here?' he asked in surprise. 'Your number's already been called.'

'My number? No, it hasn't!' I lied. Bandi-Ba went on repeating himself. 'I didn't hear it,' I told him. He showed me his notebook: my number had been crossed out. 'OK,' I said. 'Then how come I was sitting on my number when it was called out?'

That did the trick. Bandi-Ba realised that his honour was at stake; he had a brainwave and put his hands up.

'You've caught me: I'm a spy!'

'How can a referee be a spy?' I demanded, stupefied.

'Anyone can be a spy. Even a Prime Minister. One of the other referees is a spy too.' How did he know?

This was funny; but there was some logic to it. With a hundred or more kids on each side the wars could have lasted days, so the grown-ups became referees and exchanged most of the numbers before the fighting started. By passing them on to the generals, they accelerated the battle without affecting the outcome too much. More often than not the war ended without victory going to either side, as our superiors were into honourable draws.

I gave up being a cub, and started going to football matches instead. For more than a year I followed the league as closely as the war. Famous players ranked higher than generals, which confused me because their insignificant, stupid faces in sports magazines hardly reflected the almost supernatural qualities I expected of them.

At Kálvin Square I had to push my way on to the tram that took me to the football ground. Ferencváros were known as the Fradis, and their fans' home territory was Terrace B, where there was standing room only and you had to fight for a place. Hearing my battle-cry someone shouted, 'Let the kid see!' and they allowed me a few steps nearer the pitch.

I recognised the players from posters and photos; Laci Mester had told me all about them. They didn't look at all like heroes; I wondered why the Fradis were rumoured to be a fascist team. I soon found out.

It was the third time I had been on my own. The Fradis were down to fourth place in the league and badly needed a win. Terrace B was a storm of voices, a hurricane of shouting that threatened to blow both teams away. I had to shout too to stop myself being deafened.

A Fradi player was brought down by a foul. The referee awarded a free kick, but one of the green-shirted men grouped around the team's green and white flag shouted, 'Kick his Bolshevik mother to death!' His thin face was blood-red.

I wondered whether it was just a coincidence that the team colours matched the Arrow Crosses' green shirts. I was sure it was – after all, even leaves are green!

'Send him off!' shouted a Fradi-supporter.

'Send him to the front!' shouted another, but you could see from his face that he wasn't joking.

There was another dubious tackle.

'Kick the Jew to death!' yelled the skinny red-faced man. I assured him that the fellow couldn't be a Jew because Jews weren't allowed in the First Division, but he snorted and waved me down. 'They're all Jewish!' he told me, looking hard at my face. He didn't seem to come to any conclusion though, because half a minute later he was still harping on the same theme: 'The dirty yids! Break their necks! Manfred Weisz's bloody factory will win the league if we don't watch out!'

'Who's the Jew?' asked a balding man with a paunch.

'This kid says that that thug of a right-back isn't a yid,' explained Skinny as the whistle went for half time.

'Who said he was?'

'I did,' laughed Skinny, but Baldy seemed to take this seriously.

'This kid's no yid anyway!' He thumped me on the shoulder. 'You wouldn't have the gall to turn up here if you were a yid, would you? Eh?' He grinned at me, then asked sympathetically: 'Are there many kids with plaits in your school?'

'Not one!' I assured him a little too firmly.

'Not one?' frowned Baldy suspiciously.

'Well,' I explained, 'I don't know about the other classes, but there aren't any in mine.'

'It shows!' said Skinny approvingly.

'No plaits in my class,' I repeated, 'not one.'

They asked me where I went to school. I told them, knowing that the name 'Saint Stephen' would protect me.

221

'They creep in everywhere, the cheeky buggers,' mused Baldy. Skinny went one better and, leading each other on, they eventually decided to turn up outside my school and 'winnow out the chaff'. I knew they were bluffing; they'd be working at midday.

'The nation has been nourishing a viper in its bosom throughout the centuries!' said Baldy, as proudly as if he had thought of the beautiful phrase for himself. In fact the newspapers vomited buckets of this kind of thing every day. The two of them decided that the war was a good time to 'eliminate the enemy within'. They weren't worried about the defeat at Moscow: 'One swallow doesn't make a summer . . .'

Skinny turned round and tried to trap me with a trick question: 'Who do you think will win the war?' he demanded.

I didn't want to deny the fact that I was Jewish, but wasn't mad enough to announce it either. I had suspected for several long minutes that I'd seen Skinny before.

'Us!' I answered quickly and firmly so that they wouldn't ask who I meant. They didn't, but Skinny wasn't going to let me off that easily.

'Haven't we met somewhere?' he asked.

Wasn't he the man who had wanted me thrown off the tram on the day war broke out? There was no time for fear or thought: I had to answer.

'Here, I should think,' I replied casually.

The second half started and they left me in peace. I didn't give in to my fear by slipping away, but I watched the next match from the stands on the far side.

13: Waiting to Be Asked

Dávid's grandfather had promised us that his daughter Luci would give us piano lessons, and a few months after we had forgotten all about it a postcard arrived from Luci. I was to come on Tuesday, Dávid on Wednesday; she couldn't spare us two hours of her valuable time on the same day.

She rented two rooms in a flat, sleeping in the small room and keeping the big one for her piano. She was a tall, bony woman, twenty-eight for the second year running and still single, because she'd had a 'liaison' with a married man for years and nobody was good enough for her.

Luci didn't make much of an effort to be friendly. Neither did I. She asked me whether I'd like some tea and I told her 'No.'

'But it's real Russian tea,' she said, shaking her head incredulously. We left it at that.

She sighed expressively to let me know we were living in difficult times. One couldn't afford to be entirely straightforward with people: things might get worse. Jews were definitely handicapped and she was very glad I hadn't passed anyone on the way upstairs. She was very lucky; her brother had come home on leave from the Russian front in uniform – his *ensign's* uniform. He had visited her, and she had been forced, quite by chance, to introduce her officer brother to a few of the neighbours. So everyone thought she was a Christian, even the caretaker, and if they rounded up the Jews one day like they had in Poland and Slovakia and Croatia, the caretaker wouldn't send the hunters to her. I was to behave accordingly. I didn't have to deny being her nephew, but had to remember without fail that I was a Roman Catholic in her house. I was even allowed to use my own name (which was particularly generous of Luci, as she had only changed her name

223

to Sondor after my father had had a few successes). Furthermore, it would be useful if I could learn the names of a few saints and possibly the stories of their lives, together with some prayers. I should at least know the '*Pater Noster*' and the 'Hail Mary' – they might get me out of some sticky situations in the future. I asked her whether her father had to deny being Jewish when he came round, but Luci just told me that I was an awkward child who shouldn't be so cheeky.

She was still in a bad mood when she pushed a score into my hand and asked me to sing. She was mortified by my total ignorance of the notes: I could read 'A', 'B' and 'C' all right, but I couldn't sing them. She summoned me to the piano and told me to sing the notes to 'la'. She hit the keys and I croaked a bit, and then before I'd really grasped what on earth she wanted me to do, she jumped up from the piano.

'It would represent too much effort for both of us,' she said. 'The time and energy invested just wouldn't be worth it. Unfortunately, you have a very bad ear. My father will be so sad.'

I saw straight through her. Grandpa had ordered her to give us piano lessons, she had put it off as long as she could and now she was trying to get out of it. I wasn't too subtle myself.

'I won't have to come here any more, then, will I?' I remarked, but my sincerity was too much for her.

'Despite your abominable performance, József, I would still be *quite* prepared to spend many precious hours teaching you, if I felt that depriving you of music would cause you unbearable pain. But as your impudence is to be my only reward for this considerable sacrifice, I am forced to conclude that my culture and refinement would be wasted on you. You are almost tone-deaf and abysmally arrogant . . .'

I knew from my own faking and acting that whipping oneself into a frenzy isn't that difficult, but my aunt's indignation was so transparently phoney that I felt amused rather than worried. I watched her comfortably, like a spectator at a film or a toddler at a puppet show, until I finally gave in to the temptation to pull the strings.

'That's OK, you can stop now,' I laughed. 'I won't tell your daddy that you didn't even try me and that you just wanted to get rid of me!'

I was taking a big risk here. I might have stung her into torturing herself with me and me with her, but I had to see what kind of face she'd make when she had a real cause for indignation.

I must have hit the jackpot. The indignation stuck in her throat.

Her broad, ugly face went rigid and the skin tightened under her chin as if she were trying to swallow and couldn't.

'How . . . ' she moaned at last with a certain admiration. She was visibly collecting her strength to give voice to a deeper and more sincere anger, but I beat her to it by a split second.

'How is Józska the Ensign?' I asked. The question was a lifeline for Luci.

'Well,' she said, hesitantly. 'He's on good form.' Her confidence grew as she proceeded: 'Luckily they were only in battle for a few days and now his unit has been assigned to occupation duties.'

Even Luci found this terrain a little boggy. After all, it wasn't terribly nice for a Jew disguised as an officer to be executing occupational duties in the service of his enemies. But a second later her voice recovered its music, and if it wasn't virtuoso stuff, it was at least a passable social tinkling.

'He's *such* a wonderful man. Everyone *always* loved him. He was good-natured even as a child; quiet and *so* well mannered. Just think how much his superiors must love him! And respect him!'

Several months previously, a ministerial decree had ordered all Jews – including those decorated with the Silver Medal for Gallantry during the Great War – to resign their commissions in the Warrior Army, take off their uniforms and report for transfer to the appropriate Jewish labour units.

'You, Józska, maybe don't realise how incredibly brave one had to be to get the Gallantry Medal,' gushed Luci. 'Especially if you were Jewish! But your Uncle Józska was never a Hungarian Jew; he was always a Jewish Hungarian, like me. My brother embodies the noblest features of the Hungarian officer, he is a law-abiding . . .'

It sounded as if she were addressing a concert hall full of imaginary admirers.

'. . . he got into civilian clothes and put on a yellow armband, just as the decree demanded. That was how he reported to his commanding officer – a captain. But the captain took one look at him and said, "Józska! What's wrong with you?" and Józska replied: "In accordance with Ministerial Decree number such-and-such 1941 . . ." The captain interrupted him and told him to wait until he got back. He returned half an hour later with the Colonel of the Regiment.

' "I shall not tolerate officers of mine parading in civilian garments on active service!" bawled the Colonel. Józska tried to interrupt but the Colonel wouldn't let him. "Rubbish! Imbecile! Shut up! You are of Aryan-Christian stock to the third generation! Do you understand? Dis . . . MISS!" He tore Józska's armband off and marched out.'

Anger rose in me, mixed with laughter; a strange, sick feeling. I wasn't altogether sure that I was awake.

Luci tinkled on triumphantly.

'Isn't it beautiful!' she sighed joyfully, licking her lips. 'What a pity they can't promote him. His superiors must think it such a waste! A magnificent man! Who knows! Maybe in the end . . . in one go . . . Captain . . .'

The upshot of all this was fairly predictable. Dávid received piano lessons once in a blue moon and I didn't. Not that I missed them.

Dávid's grandfather invited us both to spend three days over Easter with him. I couldn't understand it. Why had they bothered inviting me when everyone knew I wasn't welcome there? I needed them like a sock on the jaw. We were supposed to leave within a week, so I wasn't too worried: a week was long enough for them to invent some reason to exclude me from the invitation. On the morning of the day we were due to leave, I expected Luci to burst in and tell us that the smaller guest bed was broken. But she didn't.

Mother accompanied us as far as the station. Grandpa had sent her money to buy us tickets on the express – for a stay of only three days! For the same money I could have seen every film in Budapest and gone to all the football matches till the end of the season. Someone, presumably Dávid's grandfather, must have gone crazy.

Mother told us – ten times – not to give away the fact that we were Jewish when we were on the train. As we said goodbye she whispered, 'If you don't betray yourselves to anyone you'll come to no harm. It doesn't show. Not a bit.'

We arrived at dusk. It was *Seder*, the evening before Passover, and as the youngest male I said the '*ma nishtana*'. Dávid's grandmother was an excellent cook; but the supper was served by the *goy* maid, *Seder* or no *Seder*. Grandpa was a neologian. Then we sang 'Next year in Jerusalem', and left the front door of the flat open for the Messiah. He was supposed to come on a *Seder*.

I had been thinking all day of the time when Samuel had brought me here to escape the polio epidemic in Oszu and we had spent the night in Dávid's wicked great-aunt's garden. As Dávid's grandmother was famous for her meanness as well as for her cooking, I waited until the table had been cleared before asking for one more cake. I knew I could force one down somehow.

226

'You can't still be hungry!' said Dávid's grandmother, taken aback. 'Your poor mother!'

'A little bit,' I answered cautiously.

Grandpa was sitting in a rocking chair, humming a tune and sipping his wine. Still rocking, he said to his wife, 'He's not hungry, he just wants to show you don't want to give him any more. So give him some.'

I was stunned. How had he known? To avoid blushing I decided that I really was hungry.

'We've already cleared the table. There's no question of his having any more,' declared Dávid's grandmother, pointing at the table. Nothing was left except a glass of wine for the Messiah and a bottle for Grandpa.

Dávid's grandfather didn't want to interrupt his humming with a quarrel.

'Have a baked apple,' he suggested by way of compromise.

'Damn your baked apple!' I said. The humming stopped.

'You can't speak like that here,' said Dávid's grandfather. 'I think you meant to say: "No, thank you, I'm not that hungry." ' He laughed. 'Listen, Józska! It's not we who don't like you, it's you who don't like us. Don't answer now. Think it over.' With that he went on humming.

I hadn't been to their flat before. There were six or seven rooms, and Dávid went to bed in the room which used to be his. Uncle Józska and Aunt Luci both had big rooms of their own, neither of which was being used, but I was put into a much smaller one that must have been built in the last half hour especially for me . . .

In the morning we went to *shul*. We sat on either side of Grandpa, who thought of something else while he muttered his prayers and followed the ceremony with dignified boredom. The ceiling of the *shul* was made of frosted glass. It reminded me of the covered market in Budapest. Choosing a moment when Grandpa wasn't thinking or praying too hard, I asked him whether they'd made the ceiling out of glass so that God could see whether people were praying or not. I said it fairly loudly so that everyone could hear what a bad Jew Mr Sondor's grandson was.

'Shut up!' he said severely, and prayed with extra piety for about a minute before whispering, 'It's so that we can see. The Synagogue is surrounded on three sides by tall buildings, and we're neologians. If we can't see our books, we can't pray.'

227

Even in a neologian *shul* the women had to sit separately. Dávid's grandmother joined us on the way home. Mother said she'd turned beautiful in her old age. A few years ago she had been a plump-faced woman with greying black hair, but now it was white. Her expression was full of kindness, and however wicked her words were, her voice was warm. It was her husband's gambling that had made her so stingy. She had learnt to sew as a girl; at times she had had to go back to her machine to be able to feed her children. I was surprised to see her give money to every single beggar – only one or two fillérs each, but she gave something to all of them.

'You're not carrying money on a religious holiday, are you?' I asked Grandpa in a horrified voice. I was being awkward again.

'Don't worry,' he smiled. 'God won't report us to the Rabbi.' As we approached the next beggar, Grandpa took a one-pengö piece out of his pocket and gave it to the beggar.

Grandmother gasped. She never raised her voice when she quarrelled – she whispered instead.

'A pengö!' she breathed. 'I saw it! If you're going to throw money around in the street like that, don't be surprised if we get burgled!'

'They won't find much treasure at our place,' laughed Grandpa, but Grandmother didn't give in.

'One pengö is a lot of money these days.'

'All your one-fillér pieces will come to at least a pengö,' replied Grandpa. 'I bet you my tip wins! I'm not a gambler for nothing, you know. He's the one – I'll break the bank yet!'

I knew that this was gamblers' slang, so when we arrived home I asked Grandpa what he'd meant. He transferred me to Grandmother.

Grandmother sat down. She made Dávid and me sit beside her and closed her eyes. Then she waited for a long time, quietly, while her face unwrinkled and her forehead began to shine. Gently, she started to speak in a low voice; an incredibly beautiful, silvery voice. It didn't sound like Grandmother.

'Long, long ago, before you were born or I was born; before my father or my grandfather was born; when my great-grandmother, who lived to a hundred and five and rocked your father's cradle, was still a little girl, my great-grandfather, her future husband, finished studying at the *Yeshivah* and became assistant rabbi to the famous wonder-working Rabbi of Nagykálló who could cure people with his prayers from a hundred miles away and to whom scholars came from far-away lands to learn the *kabbalah*.

'One rainy, muddy April day, Eizik Taub and my great-grandfather set out for Várad in a cart. The Rabbi of Várad had just died, and he had expressed a wish to be buried by his friend and disciple the Rabbi of Nagykálló. There was none of today's Passover sunshine; the weather was so bad that they were forced to spend the night in a seedy, shabby inn. Of course there was no *kosher* food, and they realised to their surprise that they had brought very little with them: they had expected to reach the good Jewish inns of Debrecen that day. All they had to eat was half a roast chicken – and a small roast chicken at that – while their driver at the next table was sitting down to a veritable feast. They were very hungry.

'They had brought their own plates, forks and knives, but hardly had they laid the table when the door opened and a strange man walked in out of the rain. His clothes were grey and worn; a broad-brimmed hat shaded his white face and his big eyes. He walked straight over to them and took off his hat. Underneath it was a black skullcap, a *kapel*.

' "I haven't had a bite for two days," he said. "I'm travelling on foot. I can see you have very little yourselves, Would you share it with me?"

'My great-grandfather reached for a knife as soon as the words were spoken, ready to cut the half chicken into three. But the Rabbi stopped his hand.

' "No, my friend. We have eaten. At midday and at breakfast and at supper last night." He handed the half-chicken to the stranger, who accepted it and put it in his shoulder bag.

' "Thank you, Eizik," he said. "And thank you, Dan. I see that the tales of your kindness and justice are more than the fables they seem. And maybe tomorrow I'll show you how grateful I am," he added with a smile. With that the traveller left the inn.

'My great-grandfather ran after him to ask him how he had recognised them, but by the time he reached the door the traveller had vanished without trace.

'A terrible storm rose during the night. Thunder and lightning shook the inn and the wind howled in the eaves. By morning, the road was awash with water and thick with mud; and the storm's fury wasn't yet spent. They had no choice but to go on: they had to reach Várad for the funeral. Beaten by rain, torn by the wind, they struggled onward. The horses were stumbling, but they carried on, deciding not to stop for the night until they reached Várad.

'Finally the cart ground to a halt, its wheels embedded in mud. The driver cracked his whip, my great-grandfather Dániel – not yet twenty and strong as an ox – pushed and shoved; even the wonder-working Rabbi lent a hand. But the cart wouldn't budge.

'Through the thick rain they saw a dark shadow approaching them from the direction of Várad. It was the traveller of the evening before, though how he had overtaken them they couldn't guess; he must have been walking all night.

' "Climb aboard!" said the traveller. Without knowing why, they boarded the cart with the driver.

'With one frail hand, the traveller pulled on the shaft. The wheels lifted out of the mud, the horses lifted their heads. Interrupting his prayers, the Rabbi asked the traveller to come with them, but he declined the offer.

' "I'm helping you on your way, because you're helping me on mine," he told them, adding quietly, "and if you're wondering when you'll be arriving, then maybe tomorrow I'll tell you . . ."

'The horses started off at a trot. They couldn't have gone faster on the best-paved road through the clearest summer morning. But when the passengers turned to look back, the traveller was gone.

'When they had buried the Rabbi at Várad and said the last prayers over his grave, a deep voice rang out over the congregation. It was a deeper voice than any man's, deeper than the sea; yet it somehow resembled the traveller's voice.

' "In one hundred and thirty-one years," said the voice, "if you don't lose your way, you will reach Jerusalem." '

Grandmother fell silent. She was waiting for us to ask questions. But when Dávid and I couldn't find the words, she answered of her own accord.

'On one night of every year we await the Messiah. Yesterday night. Why not tonight? Elishah has been walking among us every blessed day for thousands of years. A migrant, a day labourer, a poor man, he always asks before he gives. The man who refuses to grant the favour asked of him will never discover the truth.'

Dávid and I started calculating. Yet although we knew that the prediction had been made in April, we didn't know what year it was; so we couldn't come to a precise date for the arrival in Jerusalem. We set about interrogating our grandparents.

'A hundred and twenty years ago they didn't keep proper death registers,' laughed Grandpa. 'I tried to work it out too. By my reckoning we've still got another eight or ten years to go.'

230

'There'll hardly be any Jews left by that time,' I said.

The remark made Grandpa angry. 'Are you calling God a liar?' he roared with sudden fury. I thought he was going to jump up and kill me. And then, just as suddenly, he calmed down.

'God promised us that Israel would last as long as the Creation,' he explained. 'We may not know how many Jews will survive but Israel will live for ever.'

'Aren't we Hungarian and Jewish at the same time?' I asked.

'We were,' he replied. 'But now, after hundreds of years, the Hungarians have outlawed us. The Polish and Croatian and Slovak Jews are already being murdered. In Újvidék last January a thousand Jews were thrown into the frozen Danube. They were all Hungarian citizens. But Hitler cannot exterminate us. Israel only perishes if we deny ourselves.'

I didn't give in.

'Isn't that what Uncle Józska's doing? He's an ensign in the army.'

'That's no more than a cloak,' shrugged Dávid's grandfather. 'A uniform. Why shouldn't he wear it if it saves his life?'

I told him about Aunt Luci praying for her little brother Józska's promotion, and Grandpa's eyes became clouded again. It took him a while to reply.

'Why don't you like me?' he sighed, more to himself than to me.

I answered him all the same: 'Because you won't help Mother. When she was out of work you just gave her a few fillérs. It was like Grandmother with the beggars this morning.'

Grandfather's head sagged and he nodded. Grandmother came to his rescue.

'We've very little ourselves, József,' she told me. 'At least your mother is earning now. Luci can't earn, she's a concert artist, not a teacher: teaching would ruin her touch. Or so she says.'

'Your father is talented but shallow . . .' muttered Grandpa. 'Luci . . . Only Józska, only Józska . . .' He nodded slowly and continuously; a broken, orphaned old man. In the end Dávid told me not to nag at Grandpa: he'd explain everything to me himself.

At home, Dávid's expression was always serious, but here he looked cheerful all the time, even when we were arguing. In the afternoon we visited Judit, who was ten and, as far as I could tell, Dávid's fiancée. I thought it was all a game until we actually went there. The parents greeted Dávid like a long-lost son, and even extended some of their love to me – even though it was the first time we had ever met. Judit

231

was a lively, bright-eyed girl. When we arrived she kissed me on both cheeks and embarrassed me horribly. I hated kissing. I didn't kiss her back; I just smiled as much as I could.

She dragged Dávid everywhere, showing him her latest toys and introducing him to her new dollies. She took out her sheets of music and played him a freshly learnt piece on her piano. Then they withdrew into a corner and sat there whispering with their arms round each other's shoulders like lovers.

After three days, Grandpa took us back to the station in a taxi. While we were waiting for the train he counted out five hundred pengös and gave them to me, not Dávid, to give to Mother. He also told us not to breathe a word of this to Luci or to Grandmother. I hesitated, wondering whether to refuse the money, but decided that I hadn't the right to deprive Mother of eight months and ten days' rent.

I didn't understand why he gave the money to me rather than Dávid, nor how he could trust me to keep a secret. I usually used every opportunity I could find to irritate either him or Dávid's grandmother. For that matter, I still didn't understand why he had invited me in the first place. I felt as if I had dreamt the last three days.

A month later, Dávid's grandfather followed us to Budapest. He stayed there for three weeks. Mother said he was suffering from bladder trouble. He never asked for me but Dávid visited him several times, leaving his bedside for the last time only half an hour before Grandpa died. Because it wasn't bladder trouble he had, it was cancer and they hadn't told us because we were children and they were hoping he might live for a while. If I had known, I would have behaved differently.

Grandmother, Luci, and Uncle Józska were around his bed when he died. Uncle Józska was on compassionate leave. They couldn't find my father.

Grandpa's last words were: 'Dávid, light of my eyes. Don't abandon him, ever.'

14: Black and Gold

They buried Grandpa without inviting Dávid to the funeral, let alone me. My Aunt Luci said that funerals weren't suitable occasions for children. I reckoned that they just wanted to save on train fares, although we hadn't gone to my grandfather's funeral either.

Why do they hide death from children? Do they think we believe that we'll live for ever? When I was living in Oszu, the funeral procession used to follow the hearse and its black-feathered horses down the High Street. I often joined the march, forcing my steps into its slow rhythm, hanging my head like the others while peering up into their faces to read their secret. I would go to the cemetery and try to unravel the secret of death from the funeral speeches, but not even the priest's words revealed it to me. People cried or at least tried to cry; some tried not to. But the priest just stood there in his long vestments and his solemn face, speaking in his grave voice of the 'life of the world to come'. Grown-ups try to believe in 'eternal life' and they suppose children believe in it anyway. They bury people in the name of this 'eternal life', but they imitate the dead: standing immobile with rigid faces, speaking in deep voices as if their words were coming from underground. Nobody knew anything about death; the priest least of all. They'd made him priest to help them believe what they wanted to believe . . .

But there was peace in the cemetery where the watchful trees stood about the graves. I thought dead people probably grow into trees.

Elek had talked the Rabbi into letting him off the full year of mourning for his father so that he could get married. Sooner or later he'd be called up again. Samuel had already been summoned for another spell of labour service and Elek didn't want to have to leave everything to the thieving vintner. It would take time to train his wife in the art of wine-growing, so the Rabbi eventually gave in and Elek got married. Dóra was the sister of a labour service friend. She had always worked hard on her father's farm, but had never lived in a wine-growing area. She had a lot to learn.

The sudden marriage nearly spoilt my summer holidays, as Mother said that Elek wouldn't want me around during his honeymoon. But Elek solved the problem by arranging for me to stay with his wife's family in Adna for two weeks before coming on to Oszu. I had to travel alone – and about time too, as I was nearly ten. I remembered thinking when I was five that in five more years I'd be as big as Elek. I now realised that it was going to take another ten years – at least – and I wasn't waiting ten years to travel on my own. So I promised not to tell anyone I was Jewish and boarded the train.

Dóra's family were well-to-do peasants. Her father didn't just order his day-labourers around like some farmers did, he worked hard alongside them all day. His wife was a real peasant woman in a headscarf, who wore twenty skirts at once. Their other daughter, Kata, was beautiful, quiet, well spoken, prettily dressed, and worked just as hard as her parents.

During the week, God Himself wouldn't have known that they were Jewish. It was only on Friday when they all gathered around the candle that He knew. They couldn't go to *shul*; Adna was in Upper Northern Hungary, re-annexed territory. Most of the Jews in the village had already been taken to Kamenec-Podolsk. There weren't ten men left to form a *minyan*, the smallest number of men who could gather to hold a service. The nearest *minyan* was twelve kilometres away, which was too far to go on foot and they were too orthodox to travel by cart on the *shabbes*.

'Soon it'll be our turn,' Dóra's huge father said calmly. I couldn't understand how he could be dispassionate, why he didn't do something about it, why he worked so hard if he knew there was no point.

They were all busy, all the time. Kata looked after the cows and the vegetable garden at the back of the house; she was the only person who could find time during the day to exchange a few words with me. She stopped me from turning into an orphan, chatting to me a little and pressing an apple or a piece of chocolate into my hand from time to time.

She was lovely. It occurred to me that if her sister was good enough for Elek, I could marry Kata when I grew up. If only she weren't so terribly old. She was eighteen.

It was the first time I had ever been away from my family, but I didn't really feel like an orphan. The horizon was softened by green hills; there were furrowed fields and scattered houses; the bright air was full of breezes that brought back my childhood at Grandfather's. Across the hills, unseen, I could imagine the mountains of Tokaj. The landscape was mine.

When I thought of my mother, she was the mother of the old days before I left Oszu. I loved her more when I wasn't with her all the time. I also remembered her undelivered letter to Berger and understood how much her nerves hurt her because she couldn't control them. The distance helped me realise that Gyula was a decent man, and his prowling presence seemed less of a disaster.

I had left the North African and Russian fronts behind me, although they were both in a dreadful state. Dóra's family had a wireless of sorts, but I could only just raise Kassa and Budapest and it was a very crackly old thing anyway. The peace of the landscape around me made me forget the wars elsewhere, and I tried to chase away the suspicion that Torma's calm and good spirits had placed a rosy screen between my life and the lives of other Jews, a screen that muffled their cries for help, turned them into rumours and shadows. My school was an oasis; glancing through the trees I glimpsed the corpses in the desert.

But I walked happily through the countryside, like Dóra's father as he carefully harrowed the fields with his horse Kesely. When the beautiful Kata wasn't looking after the cows or milking them or being kept busy in the house, she worked in the vegetable garden, her face slightly flushed, her eyes full of the strong sunlight. Occasionally, when she was working near me and bending forward, her thighs would flash white from the dark of her wind-blown skirt and I would turn my head quickly away.

Until then, the thought of girls and women without their clothes used to turn my vision into a narrow tunnel of grey-white cloud. I would have to wait until it dissipated before I could think of anything else. My mother often wandered round the flat in her underwear because it was 'natural', 'nothing to be ashamed of'; but I was ashamed. Women's bottoms might be 'natural' but their bosoms certainly weren't – they looked to me like odd double humps. Imagining women's nakedness or peeping at my mother blinded me. Yet when the wind caught Kata's skirt and I didn't have time to turn away I felt a sharp moment of joy before coming to my senses and telling myself off.

Kata was a grown-up; her breasts were rounded. Luckily they weren't too big.

The vegetable garden and the trees, the ploughed fields and the tiny triangle of the vineyard, even the orchard gave off a scent that blended with the colours that I saw around me. Yet the yellow quinces smelt, incomprehensibly, of stiff mauve smoke and the green apples smelt white.

The tomatoes in the vegetable garden were more beautiful than flowers; I bent back their leaves and admired them like so many tiny sunsets, stars of the earth in their green twilight. Sometimes I'd walk up to them from a hundred yards away to check that they were really that beautiful. Once I tore one off its stalk and kept it tenderly in my palm for half an hour until I stumbled unexpectedly upon Kata, bending forward among the bushes.

'Can I pick one?' I asked. She looked over her shoulder at me, and I slipped my hand furtively behind my back to hide the already-picked tomato.

'One what?' she said, surprised.

'Tomato!' I answered fervently. Her teeth flashed; she laughed happily and straightened up. Taking me by the shoulders she kissed me all over my face.

'You can take two, you donkey! A hundred! But look at them first to see if they're ripe – don't upset your tummy.'

Two? I was sure she was going to see the one behind my back, but luckily Kata returned to her work. I picked another tomato and wandered off with one in each hand. Half an hour later we met again on the verandah.

Kata looked at the tomatoes that were still in my hands.

'Why don't you eat them?' she demanded, almost frowning because she didn't understand. 'We've got masses of them.' I opened my hands and showed her the tomatoes. Looking at them, I became calm and clear-headed.

'They are too beautiful,' I explained.

Kata sat on the knee-high wall and looked at me as if I were a picture. Her face lit up, her eyes grew brighter, but I stood her regard like a rock being burnt by the sun. And suddenly Kata burst out laughing and clapped her hands. 'Józska, why aren't you ten years older?'

I had to tense all my muscles, but I stood my ground and waited until Kata had left the verandah. Then I ran, faster than ever before,

236

faster than I thought possible. In the middle of a field my strength left me; I sat down, and within a minute fever overtook me. I had never been so sick. I spent the rest of the day loitering, wondering. When Dóra's father came home from the fields I drifted towards the house to be near it when they called me for supper. I hid in the stables where no one could see me or ask me what was wrong.

Kesely was there too, a giant of a horse. I'd never seen a horse like him. His beautiful firm brown flank shone, filling me with a hunger that I didn't understand. I couldn't take my burning eyes off his hindquarters, and hissed at myself, ashamed.

Dóra's father walked into the stables.

'Here you are!' he smiled. 'Beautiful horse, isn't he? Not a riding horse though, I'm afraid.'

'He's a big horse,' I said, trying to sound like an expert.

'He frightens you, doesn't he, town lad?' Dóra's father laughed good-naturedly and patted the horse's rump. I gave him a hard look. Was he only pretending not to understand me?

I travelled on alone in a huge semi-circle, heading towards Oszu by bus and train. I was proud to change onto the Kassa Express: I was travelling on a train that had had a song written about it. I leant out of the window to make the wind blow in my face and, fixing my eyes on the ground near the track, willed the train to go faster.

> *'There it goes, the Kassa train,*
> *Bears my sweetheart off again,*
> *Train's so fast, burns the track,*
> *When will my beautiful one come back?'*

I sang myself drunk. Kata was so beautiful. I couldn't even begin to imagine how beautiful Dóra must be.

She wasn't. She wasn't ugly either. Small and trim, she might have been as old as twenty-four. Her hair wasn't exactly chestnut, it was reddish, and her eyes were small but bright. Her nose had a few freckles on it, her smile was narrow. I decided that since she wasn't beautiful she must be very kind or Elek wouldn't have married her. All the same, I felt a bit sorry for Elek; he had fallen victim to the old habit of marrying off the eldest daughter first. The silly thing was that I was too young to marry Kata.

The Iron-Nosed Witch came out of her room when I arrived. I had made a resolution to be kind to my grandfather's widow, but just as I was steeling myself to kiss her, my mouth turned to vinegar. I did what well brought up children did in the cinema: I clicked my heels and bowed my head. Then I went over to Dóra and gave her a big kiss. The old lady hurried back to her room; but she started sobbing in the doorway.

Elek grimaced and looked up at the ceiling. Then he slapped me on the back and gave me a hug.

'I see that wickedness is making you grow!' he laughed.

'You're no dwarf either!' I retorted.

Dóra laughed too, raising her eyebrows. 'You're right, he has got the gift of the gab,' she told Elek. And I was at home.

'Do you want some soup or will you make do with cakes?' asked Dóra.

'You're spoiling him,' scolded Elek.

'I thought you just said he was bad already. It makes him grow.'

'I'll have a little soup too,' I said to make peace between them. They laughed again. Together.

It soon became clear that Dóra understood money. Elek had to leave, to go to work. It was a job he'd never done before, surveying the wheat harvest on a section of the Count's estate.

'Why are you working for other people?' I asked. 'Didn't Grandfather leave you any money?'

Elek looked taken aback but he didn't tell me off. He answered me seriously. 'We're short of cash. Overheads are high this year.'

'How many hectolitres of wine have we got in the cellar?' I demanded.

For half a second, Elek looked irritated. Then he laughed. 'Here's twenty fillérs. Go and buy yourself some chocolate at Frenkel's and make yourself ill!' I refused the bait.

'Be serious!'

Elek came over to me and put his hand on my shoulder.

'Last year's harvest was bad. There weren't enough grapes and the sugar content was low so the wine was weak. Listen, after the harvest I have to join up again; don't cry or I'll beat you up. I didn't want to spoil your first day with the bad news, but there it is. We need the money; God alone knows how much there'll be left over for your lot to live off while I'm away. This harvest could go wrong as well – have you thought of that? And next year's.'

'You'll be home by then,' I said falteringly.

'God willing.'

'The Germans won't last a year,' I said, confidently summing up the military situation. I accompanied Elek to the end of the village and then turned back.

In front of me a bony figure staggered along under the weight of two buckets suspended from a pole across his shoulders. His white shirtsleeves were rolled up because of the heat, but he was still wearing a black waistcoat. It was my old friend the ginger-bearded Rabbi. I caught up with him just in front of his house. I could see over the fence into the courtyard. His eight children were all there; they were all younger than me, screaming and running around half naked. The few clothes they were wearing were dirty.

I greeted him. The Rabbi tried to smile but he returned my greeting as loudly as he could to keep me at a distance.

'*Guten Tag, Josef Sholem. Gemacht?*' The idiot had forgotten that I didn't speak Yiddish. Or did he think I might have learned it in Budapest? He turned his back on me and walked towards his gate. He was ashamed to be seen working, ashamed of his miserable family and his weak, bony frame without the black coat down to his heels and the cane carved with Hebrew letters in his hand.

I dashed in the direction of the marketplace towards my old school. At the corner of the cobbled street that led up to the *shul* I passed Virgula, the big storekeeper who hadn't been able to lift the anvil. In spite of the heat he was wearing a long-sleeved coat, walking slowly and haughtily like a proud bull. He ignored my greeting.

I went to my old teacher Mr Dévai's house, but only his wife was at home. She was very pleased to see me; she was just writing a letter to her husband who was away on labour service. Old Mr Atlasz had taken over at the school. Mrs Dévai urged me to write a few lines to Mr Dévai; he'd be so pleased. She handed me the pen but it was a difficult business. I'd expected to be able to chat to him all afternoon. In the end I wrote: 'I'm OK. I had a bad teacher called Berger but the new one is good even though he's Christian. Nobody is as good as you. With affectionate regards . . .' Mrs Dévai smiled but then looked unhappy about something.

'Don't tell him you're going to a Christian school,' she said sadly, handing me the pen again. I didn't take it.

'It's mixed denominational,' I told her, remembering the right word.

'That's almost Christian,' objected Mrs Dévai.

'Possibly, but Mr Dévai knows I'm Jewish anyway.'

239

I found Ágnes in their haberdashery shop where her skinny mother was standing behind the counter. Ágnes had grown a lot; her head seemed too big for her body. Her little sister Judit flew in to the shop; she had become much prettier.

'Are you happy living in Budapest?' asked Ágnes.

'Yes,' I lied.

'You're lucky all round,' she chattered. 'Your Uncle Elek doesn't have to join up until the autumn.' Her father had been called up with Samuel in the spring.

'You're lucky too,' I told them to try to cheer them up. 'Your shop wasn't big enough for them to take away your trading permit.'

'Well, they did and they didn't . . . ' answered Mrs Salamon.

Apparently the permit had been withdrawn, but without immediate effect. I learnt more about these half-measures at the Sternbergs'. My stone-throwing friend Gyurka was away on holiday, staying with some aunt in a nearby village. His father had gone to market. There was only Mrs Sternberg left to congratulate.

'Great luck that they didn't take your permit away!' I said.

'They did,' she replied. Her plump white face sharpened for a second and her voice trembled the way Mother's did when she was getting ready to shout. Until then I had thought of Mrs Sternberg as a quiet woman. 'The only luck we've had is that they haven't called my husband up for labour service. He's over forty,' she added apologetically.

I discovered that fewer than one-third of the Jewish men were still at home, including those like Elek whose labour service had been postponed. Mr Sternberg's horse-trading permit had been 'suspended' but not 'confiscated', a difference of one thousand pengős to someone at the Town Hall. But they could 'confiscate' it or ask for another thousand pengős whenever they liked. Mrs Sternberg protested vehemently that if they tried to blackmail her again she wouldn't give in. They'd live off their savings for a year or two and once the war was over she'd sue them for the first thousand pengős, which had been forced out of them. I tried to cheer her up too, telling her that the Russians would finish the Germans off come the winter and the English and Americans would land in Greece in the spring.

Mrs Sternberg smiled at me happily, but her smile wavered. She gave me a cake and let me go on my way.

I was surprised to find myself heading in the direction of the station. Without asking me, my feet were carrying me away from my old chums Ignác Schwartz and Béla Engelhardt, and towards the house of my arch-enemy: Laci Fried. An even bigger surprise awaited me there, because when he saw me outside their gate Laci ran to me from the other end of the courtyard shouting, 'Have you come home?' as if I'd been his long-lost brother.

Privately, I was congratulating myself on having left Oszu in the first place. Laci had grown tremendously in the last two years, and if we'd had to fight for the leadership of the gang I wouldn't have bet one rusty horseshoe on little Józska Sondor.

We talked at each other for about half an hour, neither of us listening to what the other was saying. I noticed a cradle in a corner though, which turned out to be Laci's little brother.

'We need Benjamin for father to qualify as a bread-winner,' Laci explained. 'Isaac doesn't count as a child any longer, and you have to have at least three children if you don't want to be called up. Now we need another one so that Ben won't grow up all alone, but it'll have to be a girl because we're four boys already and we've run out of names. Mind you, Mother's already expecting so we now count as a family of three and a half children . . .'

'I see your dad doesn't believe in dying for the Fatherland!' I laughed. Laci went purple. I had to explain – at speed – that all I meant was that Laci's father wasn't a fascist. I eventually got him to sit down, reassuring him that in any case the war would be over before the new baby was born.

'Then it'll have to be a girl, or it won't be any use!' he sighed, a touch desperately.

We started talking about the military situation. It seemed that while I had been wandering and philandering in Adna, the Germans had broken through on the Russian front. Laci knew very little apart from the fact that the German offensive was 'very very big' and that they were 'advancing irresistibly'. I sighed heavily, full of remorse at not having prayed for nearly two weeks. The effect had been catastrophic. At the same time I had to back up my optimistic forecasts, so I put on my general's voice and started pumping Laci for facts. I interrogated him vainly for names of towns and assault areas; all he knew was that 'the Don' and 'something called Tobruk' had fallen. His geography wasn't much better than his business sense had been two years before.

'Upper or Lower Don?' I demanded, jumping up.

'The Don,' he replied carefully.

'Have you heard the Donetz Basin mentioned in the last few

241

weeks?' I asked. He nodded, frowning like a schoolkid who hasn't done his homework. 'Give me the names of some towns.'

'London, Paris, Berlin . . . ' he said promptly, looking pleased at being able to answer a question.

'Between the Donetz and the Don!' I screamed. Laci looked as frightened as if I'd been twice his size.

'Rostov . . . ' he stammered, but it didn't help much. There might have been a battle at Rostov, but on the other hand Laci might have just stumbled on the name by accident. 'I think it fell . . . ' he said shamefacedly, adding apologetically: 'Sevastopol.' Things looked grim. The muscles of Laci's forehead were strained with the effort of trying to remember. 'And the Volga . . . I think.' I realised that I had to shut him up. In another five minutes he'd have lost me the war.

'Don't be silly!' I told him, mainly to give myself courage. 'How broad a front are the Germans attacking on?'

'Let's listen to London,' gulped Laci, pointing towards the radio. He switched it on, and for a while we could hear nothing but faint crackling noises and a voice that didn't sound Hungarian or anything else for that matter. The noise woke Benjamin, who howled steadily while Laci took no notice and fiddled with the knobs. It wasn't until the voice had cleared a bit and become recognisable words that he deigned to pay attention to his little brother.

'Mum! The baby's turning German! He's trying to drown out London!'

Mrs Fried dashed in from the courtyard and picked up the baby, but as soon as she had calmed it down she started it off again by shouting at Laci: 'Don't yell like that! Do you want them to take your father off to jail for listening to enemy propaganda?'

In between the crackles, wheezes and strange whistling noises, the drift of the news became clear. Rostov had fallen and the Germans had crossed the Don. They were now pushing south and east.

'Hamburg is in ruins . . . ' we heard. The numbers of dead and wounded ran into the thousands. Laci and I jumped for joy.

Suddenly he turned pale. 'Do you still reckon the English will be here by February?'

'March at the latest,' I assured him, not very convincingly. I had to voice my doubts if only to myself: 'The Caucasus oil fields . . . ' I muttered gloomily.

'What are the "cork soil fields" ?' asked Laci, in the humble tone he reserved for speaking to English field marshals.

242

'The Germans are pushing towards the Caucasian and Middle Eastern oil fields,' I explained.

'Oil fields? Who wants oil fields?' he scoffed.

'Hitler,' I replied darkly.

'Listen,' said Laci, obviously deciding it was his turn to cheer me up. 'Have you any idea how rich America is? It's a land of milk and honey, a real Canaan. My uncle lives there!'

'I'm not talking about cooking oil, stupid!'

'Any old oil!' said Laci, waving my objections aside. 'They don't just have fields full of the stuff, they've got whole lakes of oil. They've got so much bicycle oil that they could fill an ocean with it!' He paused, racking his brains for some scraps of geography: 'The ATLANTIS Ocean!' he exclaimed triumphantly . . .

After Grandfather had been buried there was a service at the *shul*. Mother told us that the old Rabbi – the proper one – had wiped his eyes during the service.

'Asher ben Moishe, Izidor Salamon,' he had said, 'you have been coming here every day for sixty years, ever since your *bar-mitzvah*. The greater part of your life was spent in prayer. This *shul*, the holy place of our little community, rests as surely on your pious soul as on its own foundation stone . . .'

So there was nobody to chase me off to *shul* any more. Elek wouldn't have been too happy if I hadn't gone at all, but he wasn't going to nag me. After thinking about it, I decided to opt for the shorter service on Friday evening rather than yawn my way through Saturday. I wanted to go at least once.

Under the carvings on the walls, the men's long prayer shawls fluttered over their sombre suits like yellow veils. The upraised prayer books patched the golden candlelight and carvings with bricks of darkness. Blackest of all were the abandoned benches of the men who were working as Hitler's slaves, quarrying, building, digging defences to shelter their hangmen in all the drill-grounds of torture. Elek had taken Grandfather's place, I took his and Samuel's was empty. Mr Dévai's bench was empty too, and Béla Engelhardt, Gyuri Friedmann, Sanyi Altmann and fifty other kids were standing in for their fathers. The old Rabbi must have been over eighty; he stood unsteadily in front of the half-empty benches, wearing his black and gold mantle, stooped with age under the arch of the *Torah*. The service was actually conducted by the ginger-bearded *heder* teacher. He had acquired a velvet robe

243

and a rabbi's hard-brimmed hat in the last two years, and when the kids stormed the pulpit for the *kiddush* wine he offered it to me first over the others' shoulders, nodding to me.

The old Rabbi shuffled towards the pulpit. He couldn't climb the steps; he stood on the lowest. He uttered a few words to the congregation, asking them to pray for strength in these cruel times. His voice was dying too.

'Let us say together King David's Prayer.

'O Lord, deliver mine enemies into my hand, and turn Thy anger against the Murderous Nation and against its Leader, Chief among Murderers. Loose Thy fury upon his willing servants, be they peoples or kings, and annihilate them. Let the weapons of our liberators triumph, and lead to victory the enemies of Death and Hatred.'

This was suicide on about five counts. 'Blaspheming against the Nation', 'Outraging the Regent', 'Praise of the Enemy', 'Incitement to Hatred against our Allies', not to mention 'High Treason'. The minimum penalty was ten years' hard labour.

Elek's eyes glittered as he listened to the Rabbi's weak voice. His face was tense, and at the end of the prayer his deep lovely voice rang out like a reborn echo of the old man, resounding all over the *shul*: 'Amen!' A second later the rest of the congregation followed his lead.

The old Rabbi sighed.

'Until now we have offered up a prayer for the Regent at this point,' he continued. 'O Lord, Thou who knowest how limited and foolish our minds have been, how craven our hearts, believing that we could appease his pride through humility, turn Thou Thy grace upon us and hear our prayer. Efface, O Lord, every prayer we have offered for the Regent, and turn them to curses casting down the tyrant. Amen.'

'Amen,' the congregation repeated.

Did the old Rabbi somehow think they'd let him off because of his age? Did he trust toddlers and shuffling ancients not to talk? Or didn't it matter to him any more?

We sang the '*lecha dodi*'. Every note filled the air with gold and diamonds. At the end of the service, when we all shook hands and wished each other *gutshabbes*, everyone seemed happy. This luminous gaiety astonished me every time I went to the Friday service, and on this occasion I was very surprised to think that I ever played truant.

People going in the same direction always gathered in groups. We walked slowly for shaky Mr Schlossberger and old Berkovics, a friend of Grandfather's, whose sons were away on labour service.

We didn't want them to have to walk home alone. Samuel was one of many people missing from our group, but his friend Arthur Glück joined us and chatted to me.

'Tremendous luck – Samuel not having to leave Hungary,' he nodded.

'You can't complain either,' I snapped back. This was unfair as Arthur was lame but I was irritated. Samuel's luck was very relative.

'I know,' said Arthur. 'I'm the luckiest. My name isn't Glück for nothing. I wish God had made all Jews as lame as me!'

'That wouldn't help you much,' laughed Elek. 'They'd just call up the lame!' I felt embarrassed at having brought up the subject.

From behind us there came a strange caterwauling. It was a child's voice; a seven- or eight-year-old boy was hurrying towards us. He was barefoot, wearing nothing but a pair of shorts, and as I watched, he broke into a run. He was on the far side of the ditch and we were on the road. He was singing.

> 'A hundred Jew-boys, all in a row,
> Going to the temple, plaits hang low,
> Hunchbacked Moses,
> Two big noses,
> Leading the Jew-boys, all in a row!'

The grown-ups pretended not to hear him. The child suddenly grew braver and crossed the ditch; two years previously he wouldn't have dared. He was now running sideways three steps away from me, and started a new song:

> 'One Rabbi, two Rabbis,
> Here rots the Chief Rabbi,
> Szálasi for ever, boys!
> Hitler and Szálasi!'

I started to move but Elek's hand was on my shoulder. 'Don't – they'll burn the house down. With us in it,' he warned.

The kid ran forward and barred old Berkovics's way. Berkovics was seventy at least, and the most bigoted Jew in Oszu – which was saying something. He wore a fur hat and a velvet caftan that almost reached the ground – in high summer! He looked like the pictures of the Galician Jews in Hitlerite magazines. Even my grandfather used to laugh at him: 'You don't have to wear a skirt to be a good Jew, Moishe!'

The kid was standing about a metre in front of him. They faced each other, and I moved but Elek stopped me again. The whole group came to a halt. And then the kid spat at Mr Berkovics. 'Dirty yid, dirty yid, dirty yid . . .' he chanted.

Mr Berkovics just bent forward slightly, with a slow, tired movement. He lifted his caftan over his knee like a peasant woman wading through mud, and then, with an expression of utter revulsion on his face, he stepped round the child with elaborate care, as if he were afraid of treading on a dead rat.

My eyes filled with tears. A smile warmed my face and the blood returned to my arms. But Berkovics's actions were lost on the little boy. He started again.

'Dirty yids, dirty yids, when are you going to lick my arse?'

Elek snatched him up with both hands. I could already see the kid flying over the roof of a house and was hoping he wouldn't land on his head and die. He was too scared and too astonished to scream; Elek spoke to him very slowly.

'You do know that every Easter the Jews soak their *matzos* in the blood of a Christian child? I see you do. Well, next Easter it's going to be you. Tell your father.' He put the kid down and we walked on. A few seconds later we heard a wailing scream behind us.

'What happens when he tells his father?' I asked Elek.

'I break the father's neck.'

That Sunday I dragged Laci Fried down to the grass pitch by the railway. He regarded playing football with *goys* as outright treason, and in any case they wouldn't play with Jews.

'I suppose you're going to deny that you're Jewish!' he accused me.

'The whole village knows me, silly.'

'But you've grown!'

'That'll just make it easier for them to see my face.'

'Will you deny it if they don't recognise you?'

'No.'

'In that case I'll come with you,' he conceded. 'They'll find it harder if they have to beat two of us up.'

I laughed a little, thinking how nonchalantly I had swapped camps a couple of years before. In the stone-throwing fights I'd be on the Jewish side naturally, but an hour later I'd be playing football with the enemy.

We went down to the railway. Boys from ten to fifteen were running after the ball in packs, most of them with bare feet. The goalie at one end was having a friendly wrestling match with the full-back. Definitely amateur football. We stopped on the touchline. A girl of fifteen or sixteen walked slowly along the edge of the pitch, and the centre-forward – if you could call him that – left the ball and ran towards her. Another boy came along with him and they caught up with her near us.

'On heat today, Bözsi?' whooped the centre-forward. His hair was a dirty straw colour.

'Stiff as a poker!' said the other. I didn't know what he was talking about. The girl walked on slowly, giggling.

'Is it true you're asking a whole bar of chocolate for it these days?' laughed the straw-haired kid. 'Is demand that high?' Suddenly he had a bright idea. 'I can pay cash if that's what you want!' He started off in our direction, and his friend Galambos got the joke immediately. The girl stopped and waited to see what happened, smiling.

The centre-forward stood in front of us.

'Do you expect to watch the match for nothing?' he demanded.

'We haven't got any money,' replied Laci wisely and calmly. But I wasn't calm or wise.

'Call this football? I wouldn't watch this if you paid me a pengö a minute!' Galambos's eyes went wide. He recognised me.

'If it isn't that little jerk of a yid!' he said. Slowly, everyone stopped playing and gathered around us.

'They're insulting the Hungarians!' Galambos informed his mates. 'They're insulting the honour of the *Levente*.' The *Levente* were the Young Knights – a Hungarian version of the Hitler Youth.

'Without provocation!' added Straw Head indignantly. 'One pengö and I'll forgive you. Come on, pay up!' He looked over at the girl. 'Is that enough?' he asked. The girl laughed flirtatiously but didn't answer. Straw Head corrected himself: 'One pengö per Jew,' he said. By this time the goalies were coming towards us too.

'It's unfair the way they live in our village for free!' said Béla Sarkadi. He had never washed in his life, he lived in a mud hut with his ten brothers and sisters; they were the poorest family in the village. 'My dad's mate guards Jews in Russia. He's only been doing it six months and he's already bought himself a house at Mezözombor.'

By now the centre-forward was pushing Laci Fried. 'Are you going to pay up or shall I kick you in the balls?'

Laci hit first. Blood came pouring out of Straw Head's nose. After that I couldn't see who was hitting what, I was kicking out and

247

being kicked. They pulled me down to the ground from behind. The Galambos kid was punching my face, the rest were kicking my head like a football. Luckily they were barefoot. As the world turned grey I saw the girl clapping excitedly.

I thought I must be seeing things. The Galambos kid began to rise off my chest as if he were levitating. For a while he pulled me with him, but then he let go and I fell back to the ground. Galambos was swimming in mid-air, and I was amazed by his ability to hold his body at an angle of forty-five degrees with only his feet touching the grass.

The face of Pista Kenyheczi emerged from behind Galambos. Pista was the son of a vintner, but I hadn't noticed him among all the other players. He was holding Galambos up by his hair. His intervention had clearly surprised his mates as much as it had me. In a few seconds the fight had frozen into confused immobility. I staggered to my feet. So did Laci Fried, his face covered in blood. Our shirts were torn.

'A hundred against one!' spat Pista with calm, military contempt. The others mumbled and made noises.

'A joke . . . they're only yids . . . yids' flunky . . .'

'Who said that?' demanded Pista, looking round and grabbing Galambos again. 'Take it back!' Galambos's lips tightened. Pista smacked him hard in the mouth, the kind of smack a grown-up gives when he doesn't dream of being hit back. He was a broad-shouldered, wiry, tough-looking lad of fifteen. He handed out another smack.

'Do you take it back?' he enquired.

Galambos sighed bitterly and muttered, 'OK, I do. But all the same . . .' *Smack!*

'No buts!'

Pista Kenyheczi turned to me.

'You OK, Józska?'

'I am now,' I laughed. 'Cheers.' We used to eat bacon together at their house. The others listened with their mouths wide open. He must have been the strongest of the lot.

I went home to Budapest, just to say hello to my school at the start of the new academic year. It had been decided that I should return to Oszu after a few weeks to help with the grape harvest. I was glad about that. Within three days of arriving home the triumphant cries of the hunchbacked news-vendor in front of our building had almost deafened me. People in shops and on trams spent all their time celebrating the great German victories. Worst of all was the modest smile that never disappeared from Lorentz's face.

One evening Mrs Csolnoki walked into our kitchen without knocking. She was our pretty, dark-haired, next-door neighbour, and had never entered our flat before, even when there was a telephone call for Mother, although she had often dragged us into endless conversations on the balcony. This contrasted sharply with the behaviour of the Kovácses, who lived on our other side and never said a word to us if they could possibly help it. They were Arrow Cross supporters.

'Pack up your most important things . . .' panted Mrs Csolnoki. 'Quick! The radio has appealed to the population of the capital to switch off all lights . . .'

Although she was gabbling and talking nonsense, she didn't seem to have gone completely crazy.

'Huge formation of enemy aircraft approaching Budapest!' she quoted. My heart jumped.

'A thousand planes?' I exclaimed. The bombardment of Cologne on the thirtieth of May came rushing into my head. Hamburg and Düsseldorf in July. 'Two thousand?'

Mrs Csolnoki went pale. 'Maybe not that many, please God. But it's a "huge formation". From tomorrow they're going to enforce the blackout. The alarms will start up in a few seconds; radio listeners have been asked to remind everyone what the sirens mean and tell people to take at least two days' supplies with them to the air-raid shelters. In a gas attack you're supposed to hold a wet handkerchief over your nose. I do apologise for the intrusion.'

And off she went. But she left their radio on the windowsill facing the balcony – despite the light from the tuning dial.

'Little crocodile . . . big crocodile . . .' the radio crackled. 'Miskolc, remain on station . . . Miskolc, remain on station . . . Kecskemét, stand ready! Cegléd, stand ready . . .'

Mother dashed around mindlessly, packing randomly and shouting at us, but it was no use. Dávid and I had rushed to the balcony to put our ears to the bellowing wireless set. Kaci and Pöci were standing nearby too. We didn't have to wait long.

'Little crocodile . . . big crocodile . . . little crocodile . . . big crocodile . . . Budapest! Budapest! Air defence red alert! Air defence red alert! Air alarm Budapest! Air alarm Budapest! Activate sirens!'

Dávid and I cheered. Kaci and Pöci looked at us in amazement for a few seconds and then cheered too, which was pretty stupid of them as they were pro-German. Their mother called them and they dashed into their flat.

The sirens began to wail. Dávid and I threw our arms up towards the sky and broke into a war dance. We started singing too, and although we were each singing different songs it didn't matter. The sirens were too loud.

People were pouring out on to the balconies. They were carrying suitcases and baskets, pushing and shoving. All three staircases were jammed. Some were shouting for lights, others shouted, 'Switch them off! You're guiding the bombers!'

Mother dashed out of our flat with a suitcase then put it down and shouted at us: 'Are you going to leave me to pack all on my own? The only suitcase we've got is the one your gangster of a father brought back from Paris!' She was beside herself.

'We're not going down to the cellar,' I told her in an effort to calm her down. 'We're going to stay up here and watch the Allies pulverise—'

I didn't get the chance to finish. Mother belted me. If I hadn't actually felt it, I would never have thought Mother capable of delivering such a smack.

'You are coming! Now get a move on!'

'NO!' I howled. 'I won't!' I wasn't crying because of the smack. I was crying because she wanted to deprive me of the fun of watching real Allied planes in action. And above our building too! How many years had I been waiting for this? How could Mother possibly think that an English or Russian bomb would even dream of landing on a Jew?

But Mother could only think in terms of smacks that evening. I had to walk down the stairs in front of both her and Dávid to prevent my doubling back. Temporarily at least, it seemed that I had to go down to the cellar.

It was worth it though. Most of the hundred or so inhabitants of the building were sitting in cramped positions looking as if they'd been there for hours on end. Others were pacing up and down, slightly stooped because the cellar hadn't yet been fully converted into an air-raid shelter on account of the glorious German victories. Everyone seemed to be waiting for the Last Judgment and their well-deserved punishment. Kovács, the young Arrow Cross hairdresser from next door, had his ear to the wall. Those pacing up and down were allowed to continue, but everyone kept giving them sharp looks, and whenever a shoe squeaked the silver-haired woman winced indignantly. She was sitting in an armchair brought down for her by her maid, sweltering in several fur coats.

'If only they are English!' she remarked. 'We must recognise that the English are a thoroughly civilised nation. A Christian people. No English pilot would ever drop a bomb on Saint Stephen's Basilica.'

Kovács the hairdresser lurched away from the wall. 'What about the German churches, then? Eh, ma'am? What about them? The English don't respect nothing, ma'am. England's all Americanised and America's all niggerised and yiddified!'

'The English are niggers,' said Dávid, concluding the conversation. 'Yid niggers.'

Several people laughed at this but the barber grew even wilder. 'Nothing! Not nothing! The opposite! The contrary! They've got direct orders to bomb Faith, Hope and Love!'

But we couldn't hear a single bomb. I began to lose patience with the Allies: what was the point of coming all this way if they weren't going to drop any bombs? I could only suppose that they wanted to prove that they could.

The silence outside loosened Pali's father's tongue. He was Jewish – why didn't he like being bombed by the English? I sidled over to hear what he was saying. Others were listening too; he was a respectable man, co-owner of two shops.

'The only people who benefit from air-raids are thieves! Burglars! They can walk in anywhere, any flat they like!'

'Sweet Jesus!' exclaimed the silver-haired woman. 'Tercsi! Did you bring the green box?' The maid kept quiet. Laci Mester's corpulent mother shot up out of her chair and scuttled away. I was prepared to bet she'd forgotten to lock the main gate. Swallowing tears, Tercsi crept after her. I started calculating how long it would take for Silver Hair to recover the price of the diamonds from Tercsi's salary if the green box were gone. I put it at about eighty-three years.

'Would you like me to go and see if you've been burgled, sir?' I asked Pali's father. Unfortunately my mother was on her way towards me and I had to shut up. She grabbed me by the ear and pulled me back to my appointed place beside her.

At last a few explosions broke the silence. They weren't very loud; the bombs were either small or far away. A few more exploded, but they didn't make much more noise than a decent drum. I joined the other kids and we formed a small group. Then Mother dozed off and I sneaked up the stairs to the courtyard to listen, happy to know that the Allies were there and that any second they might emerge above my head.

251

I was wondering how much worse the beating would be if I were to go up to the third floor, where the view was better, when Dávid called up to me from the cellar: 'Come down! Mother's woken up!' But he came and joined me. 'How many planes have you seen?' he asked.

I was silent for a moment, furious with him for seeing as much sky by being good and keeping an eye on me as I could see by being naughty. Cunning, hypocritical model child, everybody's pet . . . I nearly said 'Fifty!', but he was gazing up at the night with sparkling eyes, watching for bombers, and my anger evaporated. I looked back up at the sky. My brother was standing beside me, and up there our elder brothers were sitting in their aeroplanes. The deep blue night breeze blew on my face, stirred by the powerful engines of the bombers. Warmth poured from the sky like the midday sun. We stood there together for minutes on end until Mother appeared suddenly beside us. I jumped away, but she didn't shout, she whispered softly so that the planes wouldn't be attracted by her voice.

'You must have enjoyed it enough now.' She said it almost tenderly, but when she caught my arm her fingers dug into my flesh. Like a prisoner walking into a jail, I cast a last glance up at the sky.

Slowly, summer gave way to autumn. Mother and I went back to Oszu for the harvest.

Virgula was holding parades in the High Street. All day. Alone. He would walk up and down ten times, slowly and haughtily. He had an army cap on his head and wore a woodcutter's jacket buttoned up like a soldier's tunic. It had a couple of medals attached to the pocket – he'd got them on some training exercise. Elek told me that every second man who'd done his national service had at least a couple of medals, even Elek, although he was too lazy to look for them among all the other bits of old junk. Virgula had risen to the rank of sergeant before being demobilised, and had now been called up again. He was going to be in the same unit as Elek, and had whispered, confidentially, that he would be guarding him. Elek laughed when I told him how Virgula never returned my hellos.

'He never greets anyone. He expects the whole village from the district sheriff down to raise their hats to him. He only deigns to notice a few of the prettier girls – he salutes them! Don't expect him to acknowledge you: he was hoping I'd give him a big barrel of wine as a bribe and he didn't even get a glass!'

It was an open secret that they'd all be going to the Russian front, probably near the Don. Hungary had sent the Second Army there a couple of months previously – two hundred thousand newly mobilised soldiers. In spite of all the brilliant victories, they had been decimated and needed bringing up to strength.

I was proud of the way Elek stood up to Virgula the stone-thrower and didn't cringe or try to bribe him, even when Virgula was about to become Elek's slave-driver. My uncle threw himself into the harvesting as if he had no other care in the world – as if he wouldn't have to report to Szerencs in twelve days' time.

Dóra went over every seam of Elek's newly acquired winter clothing. Two pairs of fur-lined boots, woollen jerseys and a short leather coat lined with sheepskin. Dóra poured several buckets of water over the coat to check that it was waterproof.

'Sergeant Virgula will take it off you if you don't give him a barrel of wine,' Dóra told him. The thought almost made her cry although she was a good economical housewife.

'I wouldn't even let him help me put it on,' joked Elek.

Dóra conspired with Mother to help Elek. Dóra was only a new arrival in the village, and Jewish at that, but our documents were in Hungarian rather than Hebrew because someone called Count Károly had rented a house to a Salamon in 1730 so that the Salamon could start a butcher's shop. We were also a part of village history. My mother's great-great-great-great-great-great-great-great-great-great-great-great-grandmother was a Jewish girl from Italy called Esther Luria-Ashkenazi, and Esther had married a naturalised Hungarian Turk who had converted to Judaism during the late 1580s and changed his name to Salamon. We knew all this because their tombstone had been deciphered a few years before the war by some people from the Debrecen synagogue who had wanted to establish some remote relationship to a great medieval miracle-Rabbi, known as Ari Kadosh. The Virgulas had lived in the village for ages too. The Stone-Thrower's great-grandfather had been our vintner for a time.

So one afternoon, while the Stone-Thrower was on parade in the High Street and Elek was out on the mountain, Mother went to visit the Virgulas. She took me along to show off my little *goy* face. Only the oldies were at home. Mother sprinkled her conversation with 'quotes' from Jesus Christ, setting various saints spinning in their graves and making my little *goy* face burn with shame, until I was finally sent out 'to play' in the courtyard while they came to an agreement. They decided that we would provide the Virgulas with five hectolitres of wine per year 'in the boys' absence'. If Elek came home safe and sound this would be increased to twenty hectolitres, and Elek would testify to the English that the Stone-Thrower was a decent slave-driver. The Virgulas quibbled a bit over the last point, as they firmly believed in Our Ultimate Victory, but with a little encouragement from Mother they decided to accept the deal. Mother made me swear to keep the visit a strict military secret, even from Elek. Especially from Elek.

The harvest was at its height. When Elek came home from the mountain with the last cart, there was a loaded barrel in the courtyard waiting to be taken into the wine-house. We gathered round it. Dóra and I were a step behind Elek and Mother. Mother promised to come home as often as possible while Elek was away, so as to help organise the work, especially at harvest time. Dóra still knew very little about wine-growing. For the first time, they talked about the property they had inherited from Grandfather. After his funeral the three of them had shared out the small amount of money that had not been tied up in the business and had left the rest alone.

Mother proposed selling the vineyards, the house, the wine and everything so as to bribe our way out to Palestine. Elek was stunned. He didn't say a word for two or three minutes.

'With a call-up order for next week in my pocket? And what about Sam? Who do you think we are? The Manfred Weiszes or the Rothschilds?'

'We can get good money for everything,' argued Mother. 'The price of wine is rising steadily.'

'Right,' smiled Elek. 'When the blood starts flowing, so does the wine.'

'Money buys everything! Black-market butter, military service exemptions, you name it. The whole country stinks of corruption from cellar to ceiling. This new Prime Minister is so two-faced he's counting on no one winning and the war ending in a draw!'

'If Kállay thinks that, then he'll be the loser. This war isn't going to be drawn.' Elek laughed. 'All these victories in Russia and North Africa must have addled the few brains Kállay has. But anyway, let's suppose that by some miracle we get out of Hungary; and let's suppose there's another one and the English allow us into Palestine – what the hell would we do there?'

'In Palestine?' Mother was dumbfounded.

'With Rommel about to march in?'

'He won't!' I interrupted feverishly.

Elek didn't get annoyed with me though, he answered me quietly: 'Even if he's only there for a week there'll be a bloodbath as bad as Poland.'

'Turkey . . . ' muttered Mother, 'we had a Turkish ancestor.' The idea surprised her visibly and she fell silent. After a minute's thought she spoke again: 'Then give me my share,' she said quickly. Elek kept quiet. Dóra watched him closely; she was standing on tiptoe.

'If you wish.' That was all he said. Mother didn't speak; she didn't really want her share. She didn't know what she wanted any more.

'What will you do with it?' Elek asked gently. Mother mumbled something about money never hurting, particularly when times were bad. Elek explained that times couldn't be worse for selling vineyards. Most of the men were already away, and soon all the able-bodied Christians would be gone too. Only the wine itself could still command a good price: that could be sold as and when it was needed.

'It'll keep on going up!' remarked Dóra. It was the first time she had spoken. Mother lifted her head and looked at Dóra. Then she laughed cheerfully in her face.

'Shall we wait for a bit more blood to flow, then?' she asked. Elek gave his sister a disapproving glance, but only one. He knew she didn't mean to insult Dóra: there was no malice in her laughter. It was just that she didn't value money very highly. Neither did Elek.

'Sell some if you need to,' he told her. Then he turned to his wife. 'One-third of the wine belongs to Judit; let her have whatever she wants out of her share.'

'One-third?' queried Dóra. She tried to make it sound as if she were merely checking the figure, but the unspoken questions could be heard in her voice: Who made the wine? Who has done everything round here, year in, year out? Who went to work on the Count's estates to save us from selling wine on a rising market? Yet Elek left her tone unanswered.

'One-third,' he repeated calmly. 'After the war we'll take more precise account of things. There's no need to be stingy, we've got enough in reserve to keep the business going for years. It's just that we do have to allow for bad harvests – like last year's for instance.'

His tone changed. He went to the core of the matter.

'Look, Judit, ever since your husband left you you've been working for strangers who have paid you dry bread and water. Who'd have thought you'd have made such a good pauper? But do you want to go on like this for ever? After the war you could buy a small shop in Budapest with your share, a pâtisserie or something . . .'

'After the war . . .?' Mother's lips were trembling. With me she never stopped grumbling, but if she disagreed with her father or her brother about anything important she just went pale and stammered in a monotone like a little girl caught stealing a cake. 'Do you believe . . . that I'd . . .? Do you really think I would go on living in Hungary with my children? Among these . . . these savages who have outlawed us after four hundred years . . . thrown us to the wolves when we needed them most?' She spoke blankly, without any emotion in her voice. It was only the difficulty she had in speaking at all that betrayed her feelings.

Elek tried to calm her. 'This is heaven compared to Poland.'

Mother's eyes went wide as she gazed at him. 'For how long, Elek? How long have we got? They beat us up and torture us but they don't quite murder us. Not yet. Not on Hungarian territory—' She stopped. Frightened, she looked up at Elek. He smiled at her.

'Don't worry. You don't have to tell me that in Russia the Hungarians and Germans get Jews to dig their own graves and then make them stand on the edge to be shot. The minute I cross the frontier I might as well be a Pole.'

'Well, if you know all that, then why don't you just fall over and break your leg?' screamed Mother.

'I'd hate having to limp,' joked Elek. I couldn't begin to guess what made him so confident.

The barrel we were standing around was the next one to be emptied. Three of the day-labourers came out to pour the grapes into the wine-vat to be trampled. Elek helped them carry it in.

'Come on, Józska, off with your shoes and wash your feet. You can help me trample some *kosher* wine.' A Jewish man left the next-door vat – which was used for Christian wine – and joined us in the *kosher* one. For the next hour the three of us danced on the grapes.

The next day, the one before my departure, Elek and I strolled up the mountain together. It was his second trip that day, a perfect summer's noon in early October. The rust that would cover the leaves in a couple of weeks could just be seen in the sunlight. We talked of the war, of the terrible German victories that summer. The summer was theirs; the sun was shining for them.

'How are Virgula's old mum and dad?' asked Elek laughing. He

256

must have heard about Mother's visit. I had to drag my foot forward to stop it being rooted to the mountain, but I kept my word to Mother and acted stupid. It didn't do any good. The evening before, Virgula had been boasting in the pub about how 'the Jew will lick my feet'. The news had been reported to Elek in the wine-house.

'Too bad.' Elek clapped me on the shoulder. 'If it makes the girls feel happy it's worth it. Still, a few drops of Valerian would have been cheaper than all that wine.'

I didn't understand why Elek was telling me, a child, not to be fooled or quieted by the bribe.

'Virgula must be making it up to show off,' I assured him. 'He'd handle you with kid gloves if you were really bringing in that much wine!' I didn't sound too good. It was difficult to invent a story at the same time as telling it.

Elek just stopped and looked at me very seriously as if I weren't a child, or as if I were his own, from whom he expected no lies and to whom he would tell nothing but the truth. 'The day Virgula treats me well will be the worst in all my life.'

'Winter is far away,' I sighed. Elek waited to catch my train of thought. He could see that I was carrying a heavy load.

'It will come,' he replied gravely. 'And a Russian offensive with it.'

'This'll be the last one!' I was trying to warm my heart with the thought of winter.

'Let's hope it will.'

'Hope?' I demanded. 'Don't you think it will be?'

'Yes. I do,' Elek nodded. I wondered whether he was only agreeing in order to reassure me as he had wanted to reassure the women.

'Wouldn't it be better to bribe Virgula just in case?' I asked hesitantly. It was silly to go on pretending but I was bound by my promise. 'In Russia the guards make the Jews climb frozen trees and crow at sunrise.'

'I've heard those jokes too.' He still sounded jolly.

'Wouldn't it be worth a few litres of wine to make sure that Virgula won't chase you up trees and nick your good coat? He is a sergeant.' Elek's jolliness evaporated.

'He'll be able to get drunk on the wine for a few days, maybe a few weeks. But out there, he'll be even more drunk. On blood. He's been thirsting for it for as long as he can remember. Jewish blood.'

'All the same,' I persisted, trying to convince myself that all

257

the good wine wouldn't go to waste. 'Wouldn't it be worth giving his parents a pig or two if it makes him slip you a scrap of bacon when you're starving?' I decided not to mention wine any more.

'Their thirst for blood is worse than their thirst for money. I don't trust their good will. I don't even trust their greed.'

'What do you trust, then?'

'Myself,' he replied meditatively. I could hardly hear him.

'It won't be like it was at the blacksmith's when you lifted the anvil up to his nose. He'll have a gun.'

'He'll need it on the Russian front.' Elek smiled again.

'So what can you do against a gun?' By now I knew I couldn't frighten Elek.

'What can I . . .?' he sighed heavily. Then he looked at me very seriously to see if he could trust me with a big secret, and must have decided that he couldn't because he started joking again. 'The Russian front is very big. Maybe I'll find a gun too.'

The air glittered. The brown and green vine-leaves that sparkled from the spraying, the orchards that were lit with grey and yellow, the mountains around us and all the landscape of Oszu floated in the unreal air like images in clear water. I knew, but could not believe, that all this heat and golden light served Germany and Death.

15: Messages

Back at my desk I lazed around drawing English bombers soaring over mountains of crashed German fighters. Yet the noise that went round and round my head was not the drone of aeroplanes; it was the clatter of a train. I couldn't tell whether the train in my head was the one that had brought me back from Oszu or the one taking Elek into slavery.

I now refused to be 'the Enemy' when we played soldiers in the breaks, despite the opportunities it gave me to annoy the Germanites. I still found it funny just watching Rácz and Schuster fighting each other for the rank of general. Laci Mester's hopes of going to cadet school floated off into Cloud-cuckoo-land. He had failed several subjects at the end of the last school year and his parents didn't want to waste money feeding him if he wasn't getting anywhere, so they took him away and apprenticed him to a locksmith.

'I won't be parading through Moscow at Christmas,' he said bitterly, 'I won't even manage it by next Christmas.' I tried to cheer him up by telling him that he wouldn't be the only one, but he refused to believe me because the newspapers said that the only thing slowing down the Germans was the autumn mud.

The wine brought in a small trickle of money but, however much I begged and persuaded her, Mother refused to buy a wireless set capable of receiving London.

'Bad news finds its own way,' she said firmly. In the meantime she bought us new shoes – in a shop! Our clothes continued to come from the Synagogue – rich kids' cast-offs. Dávid talked about his 'new' overcoat and scolded me when I threw my 'new' coat – his old one – on the floor.

While I had been strolling through the fields of Adna and mountains of Oszu, peace had broken out at home. Dávid, Gyula and Mother had strengthened their unspoken alliance against me. Gyula had been taking Dávid off to cinemas and pâtisseries, and the Devil alone knew what horrors he had whispered into my mother's ears . . .

He started off by speaking to me in a jolly tone of voice and tried to treat me as he did Dávid. I listened rigidly and politely, so he became more martial when he sent me out for a paper. Soon he was snapping at me for occupying the middle of the table and not washing my face.

I felt like Russia must have felt. They had stolen part of me. My two grandfathers had died within a year; Elek had been carried off into slavery; and my mother was a prisoner of the icy, cruel need to make a living.

Not even Aunty Felice could help me. The first time I saw her that autumn was when she dropped by in a hurry because she had heard I was back from my holidays. She only stayed ten minutes, but the next time she came round we chatted together for a while. I did most of the talking; I told her all about my summer adventures, some of which amused her.

Dávid had to compete, of course. Aunty Felice was too fair-minded to interrupt him, so we heard about the boat that capsized when he was rowing and how he swam to the shore and panicked because it was so far away and tried to stand up and found that the water only came up to his chest. We were also treated to a list of the books he'd read and the tunes he'd played on the piano. I was bored stiff and so was Aunty Felice.

When Felice realised that Luci gave Dávid piano lessons but not me, she looked astonished.

'Do you want me to give you piano lessons, Józska?' My jaw dropped.

'Can you play the piano too?' I asked, amazed. Felice found this funny.

'It's my profession. Well, it used to be anyway.'

'But you paint . . .'

'Badly.'

'And you take photos!' Dávid had three of Felice's photos hanging on the walls.

'They're all right, I suppose,' smiled Aunty Felice. 'At least you don't have to be able to draw to take a photo. So what do you think about the piano?'

'What do I think?' I felt as if I'd been offered the Royal Castle.

At that moment, Dávid leapt up from his chair. 'It's not fair! Why do I have to have lessons from stupid old Luci with her horrid moustache while Józska gets taught by Aunty Felice? And anyway, how many lessons has Luci given me? About two before the summer, two when she visited Grandma, and one since then! ONE! Because her head aches all the time and she's always got a cold and she has to teach for money. The only reason she ever teaches me is because she's scared stiff of Grandpa's ghost!'

No one had ever heard such an eruption of words from Dávid. But the treasonable bit was yet to come: 'Józska's just got a lousy ear. That's why Luci doesn't give him lessons.'

'Maybe your Aunt Luci likes Józska even less than you like her,' suggested Felice.

For once, Dávid didn't answer like a grown-up. 'I loathe Luci!' he shuddered. All the same, he went on having lessons with her, although his remarks about my ear put an end to any chance of my being taught by Felice.

Dóra received a coded letter from Elek that had the number three in it. This meant he was on the Don.

As I walked into the classroom one morning Konrád came running up to me chattering excitedly, which wasn't like him at all; he usually tried to be terribly English.

'What about that, then, eh?' he shouted, clapping me on the shoulder.

'What about what?'

'Haven't you heard? They've beaten Rommel! To a pulp!' Konrád looked drunk; at first I thought that Rommel must have been to one of Hitler's beer-drinking sessions in Munich and got himself beaten up in some pub.

'Who has?'

'Montgomery!'

'Montwhatery?'

'Montgomery, stupid! The new English general! Where have you been? Rommel's fleeing across the desert with a quarter of his army. The rest have all been killed or captured!'

Schuster and the rest shuffled into the class so slowly that they seemed like Rommel's soldiers crawling into captivity.

Rácz went straight for me: 'Stinking, filthy Jew!' He made me feel very proud. I burst out laughing and Rácz dropped his fists in confusion. 'You'll pay for this!' he threatened in an effort to recover his fury; but his breathing slowed down as I grinned at him happily.

Lorentz arrived like a sleepwalker. A few minutes later I heard the sound of someone crying. Looking round, I saw Lorentz with his head bent over his desk. He was snivelling quietly. Little Fonó, the class baby, went over to him and offered him some of the stuff they called 'War Chocolate'. Fonó had apple cheeks and big brown eyes and was friendly to everyone. Lorentz looked up at him and then buried his face in his hands again. Then he had second thoughts and, as Fonó had not withdrawn the chocolate, Lorentz looked up and broke a piece off. Then he sank back onto his desk.

Konrád lost all his inhibitions that day. Even his good manners were just a nicely carved handle for the knife he twisted in the Hitlerites' wounds. It was easy for him; he wasn't Jewish. He took advantage of a break in the lesson to put a riddle to the teacher: 'Sir, why is Rommel so like Moses?'

Torma's eyes sparkled for a second, then went blank. 'This isn't the time or place for that kind of thing. Where were we . . .?'

'Because Rommel has to lead his people out of Egypt!'

We laughed. Lorentz's fist thumped his desk. Rácz jumped up.

'I did say that this wasn't the time or the place!' snapped Torma. But he could only delay the explosion. He forgot to be careful during the geography lesson and moved into dangerous terrain by crossing the borders of Hungary to test some of the weaker geographers.

'Fonó. What's the capital of Russia?'

'The Volga,' answered Fonó without the slightest hesitation.

'That's a river,' the teacher explained patiently. 'What's the capital?'

Fonó frowned and thought for a while. 'Kiev?'

'No, not quite. That's the capital of the Ukraine.' Torma must have sensed the danger; he switched to neutral countries but received no replies. Finally, he offered Fonó a lifeline: 'What's the capital of Germany?'

'Hitler!' exclaimed Fonó with renewed confidence. There was a general roaring noise, and then Konrád flew mercilessly to Fonó's rescue.

'The capital of Germany is El Alamein,' he announced with a poker-face.

Lorentz jumped up and hit him. Konrád reciprocated with a rapid sequence of punches.

Torma dashed down and separated them. 'This behaviour is quite unheard-of!' he blustered.

262

Lorentz flipped. 'It's also unheard-of for Sir to tolerate people laughing at our allies' defeats!'

'What I will not tolerate is people fighting in my class. Especially over a silly joke.' Torma sounded defensive, but Lorentz couldn't see or hear. His voice changed, and he became a mouthpiece for a speech he knew by heart.

'Well, I've been told to tell Sir that my father views Sir's tolerant approach towards subversive elements and their opinions with some considerable concern.'

'Whom does your father call "subversive"?'

'Sir knows perfectly well!'

'Surely your father can't be referring to your non-Christian classmates,' Torma remarked drily.

Lorentz threw his head back confidently. 'That's right. The Jews!' he snapped. Rácz, Schuster and a few of the others muttered their approval. Torma looked down at the floorboards for a few seconds to recover his equanimity, then turned back to Lorentz.

'What would your father do if Jesus Christ were alive today?'

'Sir always brings Jesus Christ into it. My father sees through that kind of nonsense.'

'Sees through?' Torma enquired calmly. 'Sees through what? What is this smokescreen through which your esteemed father claims to see? Does he regard Jesus Christ as a "kind of nonsense"? Listen. Your father sent me a message through you, so you can take my message to him.' He paused.

'If certain Italian immigrants, Lorenzo, wish to uphold the military honour of Germany, then they must allow me to uphold the humanitarian honour of Hungary. I refuse to encourage my pupils in the commission of crimes that will stigmatise my country for centuries. This is a Christian country, the land of Saint Stephen; and I reserve the right, regardless of the law, to accept everyone in this country as my equal, invested with the same human and social rights as any other citizen. And I shall uphold those rights, in the hope that our great-grandchildren will be able to travel the roads of Europe without being spat upon for being Hungarian.'

This time the battle was between grown-ups. We couldn't intervene; even Lorentz was no more than a messenger.

One didn't need to be a genius to read between the lines in the newspapers that day. On the way to play football with the others I stopped in front of the news-vendor on the corner of Erzsébet Square.

263

The papers were arranged vertically in a wire stand; I could read half a page of each one free of charge.

'Bitter Battles Rage between El Alamein and Fuka.' A couple of days before, the headlines had been 'British Attacks Repulsed at El Alamein', so that particular paper had conceded around thirty or forty kilometres. Another, lower down, was more generous: 'Rommel Disengages Successfully'. I didn't read on.

Nearly all the Christian kids stayed away from the pitch that day, so we had no ball. The following day I took a tennis ball to school just in case and recruited Jewish children to fill the gaps left by the mourning Hitlerites. I also asked Konrád to play. He realised immediately what was at stake, although I knew he despised football. He said there was a new ball in their 'junk room' that had been given to him by some 'idiotic aunt', and he offered to run home and fetch it. He also agreed to play, but only as 'cannon-fodder', and in exchange we were forbidden to laugh at him. When I asked if he knew the rules he merely shrugged disdainfully.

Konrád would have made a good clown. He didn't just play badly like most of the rest of us, he played as if playing badly were an art form in itself. He sauntered around the pitch as if he were waiting for a train, occasionally stopping to watch the other players fighting for possession and moving away politely if they came too close. When by some strange chance the ball came near him, he demonstrated his participation in the game by touching it with his toe as though testing his bathwater.

One day after school, Lorentz's head appeared above the wall that separated the Tunnel from the street. He waited for a while without saying a word, and we all swarmed over to where he was. The whole Christian team was massed behind Lorentz.

'Who's your captain?' he asked politely, holding his football under his arm.

'Everybody,' replied Konrád, who thought faster than us.

'We can't negotiate with all of you at once.'

'You'll have to,' stated Konrád.

'It's going to be more difficult this way,' sighed Lorentz. 'We didn't want to fight, but there are more of us than there are of you. That's why we didn't run to get here before you. Go away, we were here first – before we allowed Józska Sondor to play with us. That's gratitude for you: take a Jew in and he'll push you out. This is our pitch.'

'Yours?' Konrád laughed. 'Who's "we"?' Lorentz wasn't prepared for this; it was an awkward question. There were three Christians in our group. Konrád moved into the breach. 'Maybe Árpád the Conqueror used to play football here and named you his heir? So good of an Italian like you to stand up for the House of Árpád. But I hope you realise that the English invented football. Aren't you worried that the God of the Hungarians will twist your ankle for playing His enemy's game?'

Schuster and Rácz were getting noisy, but Lorentz waved them down, despite not knowing what to say. I knew we'd lose if it came to a fight; Rácz and a couple of others were right little thugs and hard as nails. I could take one of them on at a pinch, but Haraszti wouldn't fight Christians for Jews; Petes might, but he wouldn't want to get his specs broken. The Jews couldn't fight for toffees. Luckily, Konrád had an idea worthy of a great leader; it was the sort of idea I might have had, but didn't.

'We won't go away, Lorentz. But I'll tell you what: why don't you come and join us?'

The offer surprised Lorentz as much as it did me. His army was beginning to mutiny and his authority was at stake.

'We won't play with you!' he announced vigorously, then turned to his men with the same decisive air. 'For the time being, we'll go back to Erzsébet Square.'

They left. Three days later the weather brought the football season to a close.

At home we continued to heat both rooms for two hours a day, but when the weather got colder we only heated the main room and I was condemned to Gyula's company. He came every day. In his presence my steps grew shorter, my voice quieter. He watched me out of the corner of his eye, and I felt that if he could, he would reproach me for the colour of my hair.

I began to wander the streets, and went out on any pretext I could think of. 'We agreed to do our maths together . . . I'm helping him . . . I've got an important button-football match, an away fixture . . .' I walked the rainy, windy streets, and occasionally backed up my excuses by dropping in on my classmates, uninvited. Sometimes I was received kindly, sometimes politely or reluctantly. Sometimes I stuck to the street. I had been going to my new school for over a year but I hadn't made any real friends there.

Mother couldn't understand why I was always going out to play

265

button-football with people who never came to visit us. I had to invent professional reasons: our table was oval and 'only good for training', the offered kitchen table was too rough; the chest of drawers was too high and the 'players' might be 'injured' if they fell off it on to the stone floor.

My main reason for not inviting my mates over wasn't my desire to keep away from home. I knew the misery of the other kids in our building as well as they knew mine. Mik Lang had known about our poverty, and about Gyula, but his knowing had never bothered me. Mik had seen it all before. My present classmates were different. None of the Jewish kids was as rich as Half Wit or Gold-tooth, but they still lived in three- or even four-room flats with real bathrooms, and would have choked if they'd seen the shower-handle above the wash-tub in the corner of our kitchen.

I sighed to Mother that it was impossible to organise button-football matches at our flat because we would disturb everybody and they'd disturb us. I considered this a particularly ingenious excuse and a very tactful introduction to my next proposal.

'We ought to move into a bigger flat,' I told her. Mother looked at me as if she were about to call the doctor. I mumbled something about wine, and Elek letting us sell some of it, but afterwards I wasn't sure whether I had actually mentioned this or merely thought of it. The next day she bought a rush-mat to protect my button-players from injury.

I could more or less grasp the two separate sources of my shame – poverty and Gyula – but I could not connect the two. Above all, I was ashamed of being ashamed.

Torma made us write a composition entitled 'The Cleaning Lady'. As if they had made an agreement several boys began their essays with the words 'There is no shame in being poor'. None of them was. Lorentz's opening line was 'The man who sweeps the streets is human too'.

'Who on earth said he wasn't human?' asked Torma. Lorentz mumbled incoherently. Péter Erdei, the convert, included both clichés, and only just stopped short of saying that Jews were human. I wrote that the school cleaning lady always growled at us when we said hello; she wasn't a guest in the classrooms, she was there to sweep the rubbish, so she preferred to pretend that she wasn't there at all; she never shook hands with anyone because her hands were rough from her work. I had the bad luck to be complimented by Torma on writing down exactly what I saw. If the well-off Jewish kids ever dropped in on me they'd

266

see why I knew so much about poverty. They'd end up believing that my mother was a cleaning lady herself.

And what about Gyula? He wasn't my father, he wasn't even married to my mother, and he was a *goy* to boot. What would they think of my mother? If my father, whose address I didn't know, had been dead, their eyes would have filled with tears. 'Poor widow . . . two children . . . all alone . . .' The first thing they'd ask if they did come round would be, 'Where's your father?' I wouldn't even be able to say that he was away on labour service. 'Aha,' they'd think, 'and the mother's got herself hitched up with some *goy* as soon as her husband's back is turned . . .'

For some time after the end of the football season we remained in the habit of leaving school as a group. We would chat together as we went along, and one day I waved goodbye to four of the other kids right in front of our building.

'Which floor do you live on?' asked the baby-faced son of a leather merchant.

'The third.' I didn't tell them which flat number it was; I couldn't afford to give away the fact that the building contained fifty flats. Theirs only had six.

'Aren't you going to shout up to say you're coming?' asked a convert.

'Who to? My mother's out.'

'Who does the cooking, then? The maid?' demanded a doctor's son.

'My mother, of course.'

'When she's out?' the convert smelt poverty. His parents owned a restaurant.

'It doesn't take much skill to heat it up and eat it!' I declared, trying to sound superior. But they weren't satisfied with my answers. They must have been holding an independent inquiry, probably with my enemy Rácz as the star witness. They didn't like me being boss when we played football.

'Do your windows overlook the street?' said the doctor's son. I turned and faced him.

'Yes,' I told them, but either they saw through me or they already knew the truth, because Baby Face immediately ordered me to shout up. He had to be pretty sure of himself; he was a wimp.

'I already told you: Mother isn't in. Nor's my brother; lessons at the grammar school go on till two on Tuesdays.' The mention of grammar school seemed to impress them a little. They stood silently for a moment, but then the convert found a solution to the problem.

267

'We'll wait until you get to the top, and then you can open the window and wave.'

My muscles were tense but I could still think fast. If I sent them round the corner I could wave from Pali's flat. It only overlooked a narrow side street but it'd have to do. What if Pali was out? Could I break in?

'I won't wave. You're not on a bloody train.'

'We'll come up with you,' said the convert confidently. The four of them started off towards the main gate.

'You can't – the flat's in a mess – my mother has to leave early to go to her office—'

'We won't look at the messy bits,' suggested Baby Face.

'Too right you won't! You're not coming up.'

'Your windows don't overlook the street!' the doctor's son declared triumphantly. The others agreed.

'They do!' With that I left them. As I reached the second floor I turned and started running down to tell them, while my anger lasted, that our windows didn't overlook the . . .

But they were gone. I nearly went after them, but the thought of that little Hitlerite Rácz telling them about Gyula stopped me cold. My shame made me panic, and I started running in the opposite direction to the one they had taken. I couldn't work out whether I had been right or wrong to lie and to show off, but if I had admitted . . . 'confessed' . . . 'the criminal confessed' . . . 'the repentant thief' . . .

I slowed down. It was far more likely from now on that they would visit me, and catch me red-handed. That would be even worse than a confession. Instead of the judge 'taking the defendant's confession into account' he would sentence me heavily for being 'caught in the act of theft'! I had attempted to steal their four- and five-room flats for myself, tried to appropriate a maid, and fine china, and rows of uniformly bound books. Why did they want to humiliate me? Before they'd asked me I had never even tried to pretend that our windows overlooked the street, or that we had a maid or an antique silver teapot. I hadn't even acted as if we had. Not once. OK, so I'd admired Konrád's brand-new ball and cast an occasional glance at their fountain pens; but only out of curiosity, not envy.

The truth was that Torma had told them off for their snotty compositions about the cleaning lady. Konrád and I had been their leaders in the face of the enemy, that was what they couldn't bear. And because they were no good at playing football or leading gangs, they were taking it out on me this way. They didn't dare provoke Karcsi Konrád, they almost licked his boots just because he wasn't a Nazi. The Konráds were rich and Christian. Karcsi had punched Lorentz three times after being hit once, and Karcsi wasn't even a toughie. These little softies had never fought in their lives, Daddy had never smacked them, the worst they'd ever had was a pat on the bum from Mummy.

The only way out was to say, 'Look here, you snotty little creeps! We're poor. So bloody what? Our flat's got two rooms and a kitchen. The windows overlook the courtyard – in fact they don't even do that – they overlook the balcony!' And I'll smash one of them in the teeth as I say it, I'll beat up the lot of them, I'll kick them too . . .

'Mik Lang would never understand this!' I thought, suddenly realising that I was heading straight towards my old school.

I was prepared to be told off. Mik's face would darken when I told him about my lies.

'You've disgraced the poor,' he would say. 'You've betrayed me to the rich. I won't be your slave in the next world now . . .' I was determined to explain it to him, confident that I could think up some excuse for my betrayal, yet I knew that Mik would laugh at me, just as the rich kids had laughed . . .

Mik wasn't at the play-centre; he had taken the day off. He was cleaning shoes, or helping his aunt on the stall in Teleki Square, or chopping wood at cut-price rates. It was Friday; the Jewish primary would be shut until Monday and there was no way of seeing Mik before then.

Dávid went on the Sunday excursion with Robin Hood and his Chocolate Wolves. I played football in the courtyard with Laci Mester and the other kids. Pista Rácz joined in without saying a word; I thought the only reason he was there was so he could kick me, but in fact he played fairly cleanly so I didn't kick him either. I couldn't understand why our enmity became neutrality within the walls of the building. Maybe he was scared of being excluded from the game.

I had lunch with Mother and Gyula, glad that Hungarians didn't speak with their mouths full. Afterwards I headed for the Üllői Avenue stadium, but changed my mind halfway and got off the tram. I wanted to save the money for a more interesting match. The tram ticket wasn't wasted, as it gave you unlimited travel for an hour on Sundays as long as you didn't use the same route twice. I went round in a big circle.

Arriving back at the flat, I had to knock on the door for ages. I had begun to think that Mother and Gyula must have gone out, but finally Gyula opened the door. He had no shoes on and was doing up his belt. I felt dizzy. The thought of Gyula beating my mother with his belt shot across my mind. Stammering, I explained that I had changed my mind about going to the football match. He looked at me suspiciously.

'Then go to the cinema,' he said eventually.

'I don't feel like it.'

'Go to the cinema!' He wanted to shut the door in my face but I stepped inside just in time.

'You go to the cinema!' I told him. He smacked me.

Mother rushed out of the big room. She was wearing nothing but her slip. The look on my face sent her running back through the doorway.

I turned round too and dragged myself out on to the balcony. Gyula shut the door behind me. I leant over the railings and watched my vomit fall three storeys into the courtyard below.

On Monday I found Mik at the play-centre, but by then my heart was wrapped in darkness, and I felt that if I opened my mouth I would break the dam that held everything in, and the dark would rush out like a river and drown me. I only wanted to see Mik to chat about nothing and listen to his voice.

When he saw me his mouth fell open and he forgot to shut it again. The pat he gave my shoulder left the marks of a small fight.

'At last!' he shouted. 'I knew you'd come back!' Of course Mrs Pig started hissing at us to be quiet, but she let us go out into the corridor to chat.

'Life'll be great now!' rejoiced Mik. 'Milk and honey! I'm afraid we've lost Berger and the new teacher's a good bloke, worse luck, but never mind, we won't get bored!'

When I told him I'd only come back to visit him, a shadow came over his face.

'Then go away! Now!' he said bitterly. I didn't understand. His eyes burned me. 'You went off and joined the Christians!' he went on. 'I never expected you to do a thing like that. And now you're not even coming back.'

I tried to explain that nearly a third of the kids in my class were Jewish but Mik hardly listened.

'So you've only come home on leave?'

'Home? I don't have a home. My uncle was taken off to the front, my mother . . . her bloke . . . they're still . . .'

'Her bloke? Why didn't he get called up?'

He eased up after that and before I knew it I had told him all about my problems with the snotty little Jewish kids and the way I had lied to them about our windows. He started laughing, and although I didn't know why, I laughed even louder and went on laughing after Mik had stopped.

'So what if you lied to them? Do you think I never lie?'

He was only trying to reassure me. When Mik told lies he went all the way, like the time he told the policeman at the shoeshine stand that his dad was off butchering Jews in the south. Mik's lies were even funnier than telling grown-ups the truth.

'And if they find out, so what?' he went on. 'Tell them to stop showing off!' But as I followed him slowly, Mik turned to me with frightened eyes. 'You're not scared about them finding out, are you?'

'No way!' I decided.

'Then the little snots can piss off. They can jump out of their posh windows and land on the bloody street.'

I walked out on to a different street from the one that had brought me to the play-centre. The rain was still falling and the sky was darker, but now the steely twilight was gone and the streetlamps were big, close stars.

I had been walking for about ten minutes when Mik's accusations began to sink in. Was I really trying to leave my Jewishness behind me? Mik had dropped the charge because he'd seen that I was in trouble, but that didn't mean I wasn't guilty. After all, I had stopped going to *shul*.

Crossing Klauzál Square I saw a couple of news-vendors selling the same paper on the edge of Dob Street. One was walking along quietly with a huge stack of newspapers under his arm; the other, a few paces behind, had only ten or so papers. He had plaits as well. He danced up to each passer-by, but when he told them the news he spoke in a bored, almost neutral voice.

'The offensive has begun,' he said. 'The Russians have broken through in the Rumanian-held sector.'

Rummaging through my pockets for my last ten fillérs, I ran after the two news-vendors. Panting, I stepped into a lit doorway to read the paper, but there was nothing in it about offensives or Rumanians, just a lot of 'heavy fighting' and similar waffle. Jews weren't allowed to sell newspapers. Perhaps it was a sales ploy. Any Jew would be glad

271

to read of a Russian breakthrough, and any Hungarian would be glad to hear that the Rumanians were the ones who had run away. It was everyone's patriotic duty to hate the cowardly Rumanians; the fact that they were our allies was a constant source of surprise to most of Hungary.

As it turned out, the man was telling the truth. Konrád confirmed the news the next day. The Russians really had launched an offensive on the Don, and the first wave had broken the German front at a point that the Rumanians were meant to be defending. The Russians had attacked simultaneously from the north and from the south, and within a few days they had encircled twenty or twenty-five German divisions near Stalingrad. A German counter-offensive followed; and even the newspapers couldn't hide the fact that the two sides were now engaged in the greatest battle of all time.

At Christmas, Aunty Felice dropped in for five minutes, just long enough to put down our Christmas presents and say hello. It was as if Dávid's whining demands had scared her. I didn't dare ask her about the piano lessons.

On Christmas Eve I arrived home from my wanderings to find a little Christmas tree sitting on a small table in front of one of the windows. The shutters were open. Four or five candles stood around it.

'What the hell is that?' I shouted angrily. 'You only lit *Chanukah* candles on Elek's orders and now this!' My indignation was a private answer to Mik Lang's accusations.

'It's just a habit!' replied my mother, confused.

'Of course you expect the presents,' remarked Gyula, but he left it at that and went off to spend 'the holy evening' with some Christian friends. The battle came a few days later.

That Sunday I strolled through the streets with my football team in my pocket. I couldn't make up my mind whether to call on a friend or not; perhaps I was frightened of a return visit. My shoes grew wetter and wetter in the snow, and eventually I went home. Gyula opened the door wearing nothing but a pair of trousers. He took a deep breath:

'Go and look at what's written in Latin on the side of the Basilica.'

'I'm cold. Let me in,' I said. He didn't seem to hear me.

'If you can remember what it says when you come back I'll give you two pengös to go to the pictures.'

Two pengös were enough for four films. My teeth were chattering but I burst out laughing. '*Ego sum via veritas et vita*,' I quoted. 'And I claim my two pengös. I won't go to the movies because I'm freezing.'

Gyula turned white.

'How do you know what it says?' he demanded. His teeth were chattering too. He was sure that I was lying.

'I've been going to school in that square for nearly two years.'

'But you don't know what it means, do you?' taunted Gyula. 'You can't understand Latin. Go and find out, and when—'

' "I am the way, the truth and the life," ' I interrupted. 'Dávid's top in Latin, remember? And can I have my two—?'

I received two huge smacks on the face, right there in the doorway. Yet despite the blows I broke through enemy lines and staggered into the kitchen.

'To your room!' bawled Gyula, slashing the air in the general direction of the small, unheated room. Then he turned and stalked off into the large, heated one.

'How dare you hit the boy!' my mother screamed. I sat dizzily on a stool while the battle raged, caught in the cross-fire of imaginary cannon, hearing vague shouts and screams and finally a great explosion. It was Gyula, slamming the kitchen door behind him.

All the same, he showed up a couple of days later, sniggering good-humouredly and talking about the war like a scratched record. He always talked about the war when he wanted to make peace with me.

We weren't ten days into the new year, but any idiot could see that the German front in Russia was about to disintegrate. The newspapers were running out of lies. *'The Russians are making huge efforts to dislodge General Paulus's units from their positions between the Don and the Volga, positions that they held heroically until today's tactical withdrawal . . .'*

The German front was two thousand kilometres long, and they couldn't hold any of it. It wasn't long before Gyula realised that I was perfectly well informed without him, and he left in a bad mood.

I woke up in the middle of the night to hear Mother shouting Elek's name in her sleep. Her shouts woke her up too, and she sat up in bed, white as the walls. As soon as she could speak she started to pray. In Hebrew. I joined in and so did Dávid.

'Something important has just happened to Elek,' said Mother. 'This very minute.'

'He's alive. I can feel it,' I reassured her. She looked at me as if I were her nanny.

273

'Is he wounded?' she asked. I closed my eyes and, half praying, looked into the darkness. Maybe I was playing Rabbi.

'He's fine,' I said.

Mother sighed. 'Then he must have been captured.'

The chances were that this was true. One of the newspapers had mentioned a few days earlier that *'Our armies are beating off massive counter-attacks and are, as a consequence, suffering graver losses than they have in the past. We do not at this present moment in time wish to misinform the public with ill-researched numerical data . . .'*

I was terrified that by reassuring Mother I was tempting God. I had assumed visionary powers, yet all I really wanted was a spell that could release me from my own panic. Mother talked very little during the days that followed, as if she were suspicious and ashamed of being duped by a child's play-acting. But the signs were that God was feeling indulgent towards me. The proud German army was being devastated by snow and shrapnel; the Hungarian Second Army, once two hundred thousand strong, was estimated by Radio Moscow to have lost one hundred and forty thousand men, killed, wounded or captured. As for the level of casualties among the fifty thousand Jewish labourers attached to the Second Army for trench digging and mine-clearance, no one even hazarded a guess.

'The enemy troops encircled at Stalingrad have reduced their rate of fire,' said Radio Moscow, broadcasting to our school via Karcsi Konrád. The two opposing classroom factions had long since given up arguing. We viewed each other with open hatred.

I was at Pali's when the news finally arrived. We heard it on his grandparents' wireless.

'Stalingrad has fallen,' it announced. The voice sounded so distressed that Pali's hand froze on the Meccano crane he was pushing round the room. His grandparents were sitting on the sofa; they said nothing; they just held hands. The furniture in the room came alive. The chairs and tables put on leaves and shed a warm light, while beyond the windows the blinding white roofs sparkled and announced a greater holiday than Christmas.

'This afternoon, men all over Germany took their hats off in the street to listen solemnly to the announcement on the loudspeakers. They raised their right arms in the German salute, then sang the National Anthem.'

The wireless played the first few bars of *'Deutschland Deutschland unter alles.'* Pali's doddery old grandad smiled and nodded.

274

'*Gott erhalte*,' he said to his wife, reminding her of the old National Anthem from the days of the Austro-Hungarian monarchy. The tune was the same as the one on the wireless, but the words were different.

'*The Sixth Army*,' the wireless went on, '*under the command of Field Marshal von Paulus, fought to the last gasp against overwhelming enemy forces and highly unfavourable conditions. The Army's fate . . .* '

Different-coloured lights drew flowers in the air. The voice on the wireless set evaporated into the distance like the puffing of a train going to unknown destinations. In that room, each object, each pair of eyes, each breath tried to utter the word on the tip of my tongue, the word I couldn't find because I no longer knew what it meant. Was it . . . peace?

There were prouder words than that, and easier ones to remember. Two weeks ago, the newspapers had laughed and mocked at the demands of the Casablanca Conference. Even the best of the papers had seemed puzzled at the Allies' decision to accept nothing from Hitlerite Germany and its satellites except Unconditional Surrender.

Now, suddenly, a few days later, fifty million mad drunken murderers and their sick accomplices were staring with skull-white faces into the bloody mirror of their hopes. And the smirk froze on their faces.

One hundred thousand German soldiers were captured in the town of Stalingrad alone, more than Rommel's whole army at the height of the North African campaign. Thousands upon thousands of Soviet tanks had rolled across the axle of the war's see-saw, restoring the balance of the madly rocking world. Hitler was gnawing the edge of his carpet, and in the subjugated states of Europe decent men raised their heads.

16: Aunty Felice

Spring came, and I thought Aunty Felice must have forgotten me. Mother seemed frozen; she spoke to me quietly, almost suspiciously, as if she were afraid that I might read her thoughts. Gyula appeared no more than twice a week, and only stayed five or ten minutes at a time. He looked gloomy, as though he had turned up at a police parade to check that everything was in its proper place and had found that nothing was.

One Sunday afternoon, Mother put on her best clothes: the black suit with the astrakhan collar that Aunty Felice had given her. Then she sat down and waited. I asked her where she was planning to go, and she told me that we were both going to Aunty Felice's place. Felice wanted to take some photos of me, like the ones she had taken of Dávid while I was in Oszu.

Dávid was out with the wolves again, and we were alone. Weak sunlight on the wall coloured our silence.

'I haven't been bad to you, have I?' my mother asked me quietly. 'My life is hard, you know.'

'No, you haven't,' I replied. 'But Gyula has.'

Mother sighed. 'I know. But I've always put my children first . . .'

The old, sick trance smouldered in her words, the stifled everyday reproaches: 'Your scoundrel of a father . . . I'm sacrificing my life for you . . .'

I opened the door. Aunty Felice stood on the threshold and looked at me for ages, then walked into the room like someone waking from a dream.

'Don't be angry with me, Józska, for not keeping my promise sooner,' she said before she'd even sat down. 'You did know I'd keep it in the end, didn't you?'

276

What's she talking about? She never promised to take my photo. Never said anything of the sort. The only promise she made to me once was that she'd give me piano lessons and I'd be able to see her once a week. That'd make the silly old piano lessons worth while. She looks pale. When she speaks to me she stares at me silently first. Something's very wrong.

A black car twice the size of the old Mercedes taxis was waiting for us in front of the main gates. The chauffeur, a big balding broad-shouldered man of forty, opened the door for us, and I sat between my mother and Aunty Felice on the back seat. Felice was still breathing slowly and heavily, staring rigidly ahead with wide eyes. Mother was looking down at her hands, speechless and immobile. They knew something I didn't.

We drove across Margit Bridge and up to the top of Rózsa Hill, where we stopped in front of a wrought-iron gate, twice the height of a grown man. A young, thin woman in a black dress and white apron ran down the steps from the front door and opened the gate. The house was two storeys high, the upper floor alone had eight windows overlooking the street. An old man in a frock-coat held the door open for us, and at first I thought he must be Aunty Felice's husband but the way he nodded and stood to attention made me realise that I'd seen him before in the movies. He was the butler.

My feet got stuck, so Aunty Felice took my hand and led me into an enormous room. It was bigger than our whole flat. Mother followed us, but she was a good five steps behind and she stopped in the doorway. A few seconds later someone closed the door on her heels.

My legs had gone wobbly again because my feet had sunk into a carpet. My mother stood white-faced in front of the double doors. Aunty Felice pointed through the window.

'How do you like the garden, Józska?' I followed her gaze. The garden was half as big as a football pitch.

'Too many flowers,' I answered sullenly.

Aunty Felice looked back at me. She tried to laugh. 'Why too many?'

'You can't play football: they'd get in the way.'

'Yes, you can.'

'How come? Isn't there a gardener?'

This time Aunty Felice really laughed. 'There is, yes, but we can always tell him that the garden's a football pitch from now on.'

'Football pitch?' I asked suspiciously. My mother still hadn't moved away from the door.

Felice came over to me. 'Józska. Would you like to come and stay here . . . for a couple of weeks, let's say . . . or as long as you like . . .?'

I looked at my mother. She looked at me. Her face was as blank as the doors. As if she hadn't heard the invitation. Her eyes were empty.

There was a black piano in the middle of the room. It was as big as my Aunt Luci's piano but here it looked as small as my chair-bed did when we moved it into our big room for the winter. There were low tables at the far end of the room, a black one and a red one; beside the black table sat two blood-coloured armchairs. All around the room, enormous plants towered above us as if the garden had overgrown the house.

'My school's too far away,' I replied at last, without paying attention to what I was saying.

'Béla – Uncle Béla – will drive you there.'

Uncle Béla must be the huge, balding chauffeur. So much for you, Baby Face! I'd love to see your expression when Mister József Sondor steps out of his T34 while you watch from your windows. You'll be lucky not to fall out on to the street . . .

'My friends will be cross with me,' I said, forgetting that Mik Lang didn't go to my school. Aunty Felice smiled. Her pallor had gone.

'That's all right. You can go by bus, that won't take too long either. And in any case, you'll be going to grammar school in the autumn.'

'Isn't there a tram?' I asked. Yet I knew that the nearest tramline stopped at Margit Avenue, twenty minutes' walk away.

'You can take a bus to the tram stop,' said Aunty Felice. 'It doesn't cost any extra to change from bus to tram.' She looked up at Mother. 'Or does it, Julia?' Mother was still pale. She took a step forward and pretended to laugh.

'I don't know, Felice, I never go by bus.' Aunty Felice turned to me again.

'I don't know either,' she told me. 'I'm going to go across to the studio now, to set up the camera and the lamps. Have a look around the house. I'll be back here in about ten minutes. Julia, could you come and give me a hand?'

They left. My eyes were drawn to the shining piano, a black

278

mirror that cast its light on everything around it. It showed me the room as far as the window, but not the trees beyond. I was enclosed in luminous shadow.

A plump man in shirtsleeves walked into the room.

'I just popped in to say hello,' he said. 'Don't let me disturb you. I'm Albert, Felice's husband. Make yourself at home.' He gave me a slight pat on the shoulder. 'No rest for the wicked. Even on a Sunday. I must go and pay my debt to the Devil. We'll meet properly soon, I hope.'

He was gone. I had imagined Aunty Felice's husband as being older and fatter and uglier. This Mr Albert was jolly and friendly and well-meaning. He didn't call himself 'Uncle' either; and Aunty Felice was just 'Felice'.

The ceiling was about twice as high as the one at our flat. 'How can they heat such a huge room?' I wondered. There was a vast tiled stove in the corner, two metres tall and two metres wide. At the other end of the room was a fireplace as tall as me. It wasn't lit, but it was loaded with logs.

Mother re-entered the room alone, like a sleepwalker. She sank immediately into a big armchair.

'Is the studio ready?' I asked her. She didn't seem to hear me. Then, perhaps in answer to my question, she said, 'One minute. Tell me . . .'

She faltered. I thought she was ill. I started towards her but she signalled to me that she was all right and I stopped.

'Do you want . . .?' She didn't say what, so I asked the question for her.

'Can I stay for two weeks?' Mother didn't reply. 'I'll get up earlier to go to school – I'm sure Aunty Felice will give me money for the bus.' Mother nodded, but she shivered. 'Or even earlier and I'll come and have breakfast at home.'

She bent her neck forward like someone trying to stop a nose-bleed. A minute passed. Then, heavily, she lifted her head and cast her eyes on me. They were blank as snow, but little sparks flickered across them. She stood up calmly.

'Do you want to be Felice's child?' she asked me quietly. Her voice was like cold glass. I thought she had gone mad.

'You'll have a nice life,' she went on quickly. 'She likes you very much. She wants to adopt you. Do you want that to happen?'

But I'm far away, standing in the middle of the desert, all alone as

279

far as I can see. I know only one thing. My mother is trying to trick me. I'm spoiling her relationship with Gyula and this is her revenge. She's set me a test; the subject is love, and if I say 'Yes, yes, I want to be a rich kid and have a full-size football and a room of my own with a window that overlooks the street', then I'll have failed and my mother will send me off to some remand home for being heartless and wicked and I'll have to live in a cell on dry bread and water . . .

The rest of me was running on automatic.

'Can't I stay here for a couple of weeks? The bus . . .'

Mother shook her head. No. It was for ever, or not at all.

'You're my mother,' I told her. 'Aunty Felice . . . I just like her a lot. Let's go and do the photos.'

'We're going home,' said Mother. Her cold hand grasped mine and we left the room.

'The photos!' I protested. 'Aren't we going to say goodbye to Aunty Felice?' Mother was almost dragging me along.

'No. She said that if the answer was "no", we shouldn't say goodbye. She isn't well . . . she's feeling . . .'

The butler let us out. Uncle Béla was waiting for us in the car and the gate was already open. I didn't see who closed it behind us.

When we reached the tram stop on Margit Avenue, Mother asked Uncle Béla to let us out.

'Thank you. Here's fine. Very kind of you.' While we waited for the tram, Béla turned the car round and drove off.

Four days later, Aunty Felice was admitted to hospital. Mother said she had tonsillitis. The day after that, Mother was summoned to our neighbour's telephone. The call was from the hospital: Aunty Felice had died. Blood-poisoning, they said.

She had given me a book called *The Jokes of King Mátyás* for Christmas the year before. She knew I liked King Mátyás. The author, Ernö Szép, wrote a poem about Aunty Felice which was engraved on her tombstone. I read it there when I went to visit her.

> *'Fly here in the winter*
> *You sparrows who shiver,*
> *The love lives for ever*
> *That God sowed within her,*
> *Sending sunlight and spring*
> *Where the cold shall not cling.'*

17: The Cat's Ninth Life

Aunty Felice had hardly been buried a week when our father walked in while we were having breakfast. Mother wasn't even surprised, despite the fact that he hadn't showed up for over two years; not since the morning when he'd smacked me round the face and then sent money and gym shoes by a bellboy in the evening. I now had the pleasure of seeing him for the second time in six and a half years. I was ten and a half.

He looked fit, self-assured, elegant. His spring coat hung from one shoulder. He was thirty-six.

'No time to be amazed,' he laughed. 'We're in a hurry!'

'Father!' shouted Dávid, jumping up and throwing his arms round his neck. I didn't budge.

'Thanks for the warm welcome,' he laughed, 'but "Father" is too generous a title for me. Ask your brother.' His eyes challenged mine. 'Józska will testify that I don't deserve such a noble form of address. Call me Ádám: everyone's father is called that, so Józska can't take it as a personal insult.'

'I don't care if Dávid calls you Grandpa,' I replied, not getting up.

'This scoundrel wants me dead,' he remarked, looking at Mother for support. 'But we've no time for psychologising, we're late.'

I didn't know what he was on about. Cycleawhat? Why did he think I wanted him dead just because I mentioned Grandpa and Grandpa happened to be dead? And it wasn't late anyway . . .

'It's early,' I objected.

'It isn't late at all,' confirmed Dávid, slowing down a bit.

'Isn't it?' asked our father. 'Why, where are you off to?'

'Grammar school,' replied Dávid.

'Ahh, yes, of course!' our father drawled, bending low in a mock bow. 'The young gentlemen are making their way to school. Not an urgent appointment, I agree. It can certainly wait till tomorrow. In fact I suggest it does.'

Mother put the pot of *ersatz* coffee on the table, but our father shook his head.

'I should like to propose an alternative entertainment. The indoor swimming pool. And we must have breakfast first at the Pâtisserie Gerbeaud.'

Dávid was off. Gerbeaud was a name to reverence. Even the Chocolate Wolves pronounced it with a certain piety.

Mother had stood up. It was only my obstinacy that kept me on my chair.

'Why have you come round here?' I asked.

Father's eyes darted over me as he took a couple of steps in my direction. 'Why should I stay away?' he said lightly.

'Out of habit,' I snapped angrily.

'Out of habit . . . ' he mused. 'How old is this kid? Don't tell me – I'll tell you in a second. Out of habit, he says.'

'Ten and a half,' I prompted.

'He doesn't take prisoners either,' he laughed. 'I've met my match here.'

Mother winced. 'He's your child,' she protested.

'Certainly he's my child! A chip off the old block.'

He was trying to flatter me, but when he saw that I hadn't fallen for it his voice became severe.

'So, not coming round was a good habit, was it?'

'It was better than the time you came two years ago. The first thing you did was smack me.'

'I'm glad you remember.' He sounded tough. 'It seems you deserved it.'

'Maybe. But not from you. You had no right to hit me.'

His face clouded over but his tone remained bright. 'Maybe I didn't have the right. But there wasn't anyone else around who did. Hang on a second.' He signalled that I should wait, and I did, not knowing why. He didn't seem to know either; he held his half-closed fist in front of his face, shut his eyes and thought. Everything moved away from him, he turned inwards, searching for something tiny. He found it. He straightened up. Smiled.

'Get up.' I looked at him. What for? Not getting up was the core of my resistance effort. 'Get up,' he repeated. 'Please.'

I shrugged and stood up. He sat down in my place.

'Your turn,' he said. He stuck out his chin. 'Hit me.'

'Why should I?' I asked stiffly.

'Hit me! You'll feel why. Use all your anger, all your strength.'

I stood there, hesitant. I didn't feel like hitting him at all. Dávid came closer.

'What about me?' he asked.

'What about you?' replied our father with a friendly gesture. 'You don't hate me. Come on, hit me!' he urged again. 'Don't leave me here gibbering with fright!' It was all theatre. He was smiling. 'Don't worry, you won't smash my nose.' He flattened it against his face. 'They took the bone out in the days when I used to box.'

'What are you hoping to pay for with one blow?' I asked, thinking aloud.

He nodded approvingly. 'Good question.'

'Why do you want me to hit you when I don't want to?'

'I'd like you to want to,' he admitted.

'Why?'

'So that we don't have to waste any more time discussing a two-year-old smack.'

'What a clever man you are,' I remarked coldly.

'I agree,' he laughed. 'And you're quite a clever kid, come to that.'

Mother marched up to him and whacked him in the face. I took a step backwards, feeling as if I'd been hit myself. Dávid's face froze with fright. Our father laughed good-naturedly and patted Mother on the shoulder.

'You're not getting any older, Judit,' he told her. I had almost forgotten my mother's real name. I had always told people that she was called Julia.

'You're trying to take my sons away from me!' she shouted.

'Did you just ask me round here so you could hit me?' he enquired.

So Mother had asked him round, had she?

'Why have you come?' I demanded, repeating my first question.

Father's face became serious, almost solemn. 'Do you want me to tell you the truth?'

I could see he would if I wanted him to. 'The whole truth,' I replied.

'Because I can't allow you to be subjected to a step-father whom you dislike.'

'I like Gyula!' shouted Dávid.

283

'You shut up a minute,' Father told his favourite son. 'Is that a good enough reason?' he asked me.

'Is it the real reason?'

'Yes.'

'Fair enough, then.'

Father turned away and rubbed his forearm across his face, but by the time his arm had finished its arc he was laughing.

'Thank you. We can't live under the same roof, but from today onwards, if you will permit me' – his glance took in Dávid as well – 'I shall provide for you.'

'You're seducing my children,' snivelled Mother.

Father smiled and shook his head. 'You slap me in the face and then it's you who starts to cry. If I remember rightly, the next item on the programme is "Jutka asks for damages". So here they are.' He reached into his pocket, pulled out a wad of notes and counted three hundred pengős on to the table. 'Next month I'll give you another three hundred. I'd rather send it, if you don't mind. Now, may I have your permission to take your sons out to breakfast? Don't worry, they'll be back by suppertime. And no need to cook either: they'll have tummy-aches.'

Father's joviality was like the spectacular gesture of a conjuror whose other hand is up his sleeve. He was a tightrope walker, hurrying to safety before he could fall. Mother's smack had woken a real gaiety in him; he laughed at the blow, but not on principle as I always did. He thought it was funny.

The Pâtisserie Gerbeaud had two eating halls and a terrace. The walls were covered in dark panelling. Stupid idea Number One: the place was gloomier than our Headmaster's study. The waiters and waitresses marched majestically about, dressed in green para-military uniforms. Stupid idea Number Two: you expected them to shoot you if you held your fork wrong. Any fool could have seen that the pâtisserie should have been staffed by women in pretty dresses and the walls should have been covered in red and green blobs with a Mickey Mouse or two for the toddlers. It might have been disrespectful to paint Robin Hood on a wall, but Friar Tuck would have been just the job, he was a greedy-guts. I had imagined Gerbeaud's would be fun. When I got there, I realised that the only thing that the management wanted people to know was that Gerbeaud's was a Very Important Pâtisserie for Very Important Persons. Very Rich Important Persons. It certainly wasn't built for kids. The bigger of the two halls had at least three huge mirrors on the wall; the smaller one had two. What for? So that rich kids could make sure their hair was properly brushed? Surely their mummies would tell them if it weren't? The whole pâtisserie was specially designed so that mummies could take their kiddies somewhere posh. Maybe the mummies went there on their own. Maybe even non-mummies went there . . .

Father ordered a black coffee and a cognac. The waiter brought them immediately, which proved that the place catered for grown-ups.

Did people take on the flavour of their favourite foods? There was something sour about Father. Not bitter; sour. Sugarless black coffee and cognac must taste sour. He didn't want cake; he said it tickled his throat . . .

He asked why I'd only eaten two cakes. He told me that I was only prepared to accept as much from him as would allow me to believe that I'd accepted nothing. I couldn't answer that, but I told him what I thought of his famous pâtisserie. He was irritated by my determination to find fault with everything, but admitted in the end that I was right. Well-off women came here on dates. The men drank cognac. It wasn't really much fun for kids.

Outside, Father put two fingers in his mouth and whistled like a steam engine. A taxi screeched to a halt. Dávid and I tried to imitate Father but could only hiss. The taxi took us all to Margit Bridge; and on Margit Island we caught a glimpse of the polo pitch where gentlemen on horseback were hitting a ball with long sticks. In the middle of the morning, too. When did they work? Or were they army officers on leave?

I had never been to the indoor swimming pool before. Actually there were two pools, one outside and one inside, each of them fifty metres long. I didn't have any swimming trunks. We had to hire a pair that were far too big for me. All the attendants wore white trousers and gym shirts and sailor's hats. Instead of a gold ribbon like Miklós Horthy's, they had blue ones. Uniforms again, just like the waiters and waitresses at the Gerbeaud earlier. On the banks of the Don, the Second Army had failed to hold the Red Army for more than half a day, and back in Hungary the entire capital was playing soldiers.

The sun was shining but it was cold outside. Father suggested that I should jump into the pool and swim a length, but I told him I couldn't swim. He looked horrified, as if I had already drowned.

'Unbelievable. This'll have to be dealt with as well.' He then told me to jump about and keep warm – as if I needed telling. We then headed for the indoor pool, but all of a sudden there was a blonde woman of about twenty-five waving at Father.

'Damn. I'd forgotten about her,' he laughed. He waved affably and went towards her.

'Do forgive me, please,' he apologised. 'I had to save these kids from school. My sons: mischievous-faced Dávid and angelic-looking Józska. The cold blue eyes are what give him away: he's a menace. In another ten years he'll have the face of a devil.'

'This lady,' he continued, pointing to her ceremoniously, 'likes to be called Daisy, as she is a tremendous anglophile. Besides that, all you need know is that she is a lady of leisure from the Lipót district. Come on, boys, Daisy's been waiting for you for two hours! Don't let me down – compliment her on her beautiful legs!'

'I kiss your hand,' said Dávid, using the old form of greeting reserved for ladies.

'Morning,' I said, having decided that pretty legs didn't need to be greeted like grand duchesses.

'Józska grew up in the country,' grinned our father. I was sure he knew what I was thinking.

'I really am called Daisy, you know.' Gently, she shook Dávid's hand and then turned to me. 'Your eyes aren't cold,' she smiled. 'They're rather dreamy.'

'And God help us all if he has a bad dream,' added our father, banging me on the back. 'Now stay here and chat her ladyship up, please, while I have my swim.' With that he dived into the pool. He swam very fast, but after about thirty metres he changed stroke and started doing butterfly. I reckoned he was just showing off his broad shoulders and strong muscles. Later he invited the blonde woman to supper, but she could only manage to fit him in in two days' time.

Outside the building our father whistled another taxi to a halt. We still couldn't imitate him. We drove to the bank of the Danube and sat down at a flower-laden table among the golden pillars of a big hotel restaurant.

'We must buy some clothes for you after lunch,' said Father, after glancing round at the elegantly dressed clientèle. Yet he was quite unembarrassed as he called the head waiter over. While looking at the menu, he announced casually that he had no meat-ration cards with him. The waiter shrugged politely. Among the rich, ration cards were obviously no more than a vulgar formality. Father ordered caviar for three.

'How dare you?' I croaked, choking with fury. I didn't know whether caviar was something you ate or drank. All I knew was that it was Russian.

Father straightened up and took a deep breath. 'Do you want me to beat you up right here?' he asked. 'How dare *you* speak like that?'

'You ordered caviar! The spoils of war!'

Father eased up. 'You're quite right. Forgive me. It was stupid of me to order it. I just wanted you to know what it tastes like. We can't cancel it now, I'm afraid; it'd look suspicious. But I give you my word that I shan't eat caviar again until after the war is over.' We shook hands on it.

'There won't be much of it in Budapest for a while,' I laughed. 'Not after Stalingrad.' Father hissed at me to be quiet, but he laughed too.

The waiters were wearing white jackets covered in gold braid and had epaulettes to make the rich believe they were being waited on by generals. I told my father what I'd noticed; he listened appreciatively with one eye half-closed.

'Waiters in uniform at the pâtisserie, sailor-suits at the swimming pool, and now generals standing to attention! Meanwhile, at Voronezh, our army—'

'Speak more quietly,' interrupted Father. 'I agree with you, our army isn't worth shit; but our police force is the best in the world after the Gestapo.'

The caviar arrived. I had decided not to touch it, but I loved poppy-seeds and the biggest poppy-seeds I had ever seen were being piled on to my plate. I couldn't understand why they'd served them with lemon instead of with sugar, but it took a lot of self-control to keep my hand off my fork. Father understood how I felt.

'You may as well eat it now that it's here,' he said, so I put a few of the black bits on the edge of my fork and nibbled at them cautiously.

'What *is* this stuff?' I grimaced, practically biting my tongue off. Father roared with laughter.

'What were you expecting?'

'Poppy-seeds.'

He explained what caviar was; treason clearly didn't pay.

'What would you like most in all the world?' asked Father solemnly as he drank another black coffee and smoked his fiftieth cigarette of the day. He only stopped smoking when he was swimming.

'A nice brown velvet suit with long trousers,' said Dávid. He had obviously come prepared. 'I chose it long before I ever thought we could buy it, and you said that after lunch . . .'

Father nodded. 'Apart from that?'

'Apart from that?' This time Dávid was surprised. 'Exercise books, and . . . because it's difficult for Mother . . . we were poor until today . . .'

I blushed, ashamed. But I remembered how I had lied about our windows, and suddenly I wasn't sure whether my cheeks were burning for Dávid or for me.

'. . . and a really good fountain pen,' I heard Dávid say. Father reached inside his jacket and drew out a pen.

'Here you go, then,' he said. Dávid gaped, then reached slowly over to the pen. Half in a dream, he took the top off and admired it. He held it so close to his face I thought he was going to stick it in his mouth like a dummy.

'Real gold?' he asked wonderingly.

'Real gold,' confirmed Father, leaning over the table, filled with joy at Dávid's rapture. Then, leaving my brother completely mesmerised by the nib, he turned to me.

'What about you?' he asked, but I was mesmerised by Dávid. He had been poor 'until today'.

'Nothing,' I said at length.

Father could scarcely hide his annoyance. 'You're mean,' he told me. 'You won't let me give you anything. Let's go and buy some clothes.'

'I've got clothes,' I told him, but he raised his eyebrows as if to ask whether such rags deserved to be called clothes. I felt mean and envied Dávid his pen. 'I could use a pair of shoes though. For football,' I added, holding on to my pride.

'Football boots?' asked our father, stressing both words. He had cheered up.

'No way,' I laughed. I thought of Half Wit kicking holes in the air with his brand-new football boots. 'Ordinary shoes. Mother keeps complaining that I kick mine to bits.'

Father just nodded. No point in wasting words on a boring little present like that.

'Let's go to the shops and see what we can find,' he sighed and started to move.

'I already told you: I don't need any clothes. I was given some by the *Omzsa* Welfare Centre just the other day. They were almost new.'

'Almost what?' Father's eyes went wide. And then, as if he'd heard some terrible news, his head fell forward on his hand. 'God . . . why do you have to humiliate me like this?'

Despite my astonishment, I laughed.

'What's the matter?'

'Please don't torment me,' he said. Then he shook himself like a dog coming out of a lake. 'Let's go.'

He left the bill for the head waiter to pay.

Two urgent telephone calls – from another hotel lobby – took Father away on some important business that couldn't wait. He was about to leave us when he suddenly remembered the clothes and gave us each a hundred pengös: enough for two expensive suits each.

'What about a sick-note for missing school?' said Dávid before Father rushed off.

'Get one off your mother. Have a headache or a toothache, you don't need a doctor's certificate!'

'Mother doesn't give false sick-notes,' objected Dávid.

Father walked over to the reception desk and asked for two pieces of paper. He borrowed Dávid's new pen.

I laughed so hard I nearly cried.

'Sick-notes? On hotel paper? I suppose we came here to cure our tummy-aches? Sick-notes have to be written in exercise books!'

'Not if you're at a grammar school,' corrected Dávid. 'We have to have our sick-notes on special cards.'

Father smiled. 'Ask your mother, just this once. We'll carry our satchels with us on our next pub-crawl. I'll visit you again within a week. No, I won't. I'd forgotten about my smack.' He wrote his address down on the crested notepaper. I was sure I wouldn't see him again for at least another two years. I certainly wouldn't be making a big effort to keep in touch.

He stepped into one of the taxis waiting in front of the hotel. It drove off, leaving Dávid and me alone. Dávid immediately pulled out his pen and gazed at it happily.

'Never seen a fountain pen before?' I asked him.

'Not one like this,' he replied. 'Shall we go and buy some suits?'

'You can if you like. I don't want anything from our father.' Dávid looked at me severely.

289

'Don't you like him?' he enquired in an oily voice. Berger would have been proud of him.

'No.'

'Then why did you accept the hundred pengös? And the cakes? And the caviar and the . . .' His face was becoming progressively stupider with every word.

'Because,' I explained, 'he promised to chase Gyula away.'

'All he said was that he wouldn't allow . . .'

'Does it matter how he said it?'

'He didn't say it! He doesn't have the right! He and Mother are divorced!'

'Dávid. Tell me something. How come you're not bright red in the face?' I wasn't even trying to insult him, I was genuinely curious, almost meditative.

'I'm going to beat you up right here!' he threatened, rather half-heartedly. 'What am I supposed to be ashamed of?'

'What kind of a person are you?' I asked admiringly. 'You get on with our con-man father; in fact you get on with everyone from Gyula to the next-door neighbour's kitten.'

'I love my father!' Dávid declared with the dignity and clear conscience of a model child, good pupil and God-fearing apprentice Rabbi. No wonder Cain got rid of Abel.

'What a nice little first-born you are!'

'And you're just a nasty jealous little brother! You accepted the hundred pengös – naturally. But thanking anyone for anything makes you choke.'

Somehow I picked up his self-righteous tone.

'A hundred pengös will be a big help to Mother,' I told him. 'It's hers, and she doesn't have to thank anyone for it. Father owes her far more than a hundred pengös. The court order said he had to pay back her dowry, and maintenance, and . . .'

'No!' yelled Dávid, not listening to a word. 'You can't give Mother your hundred pengös! She's already been given three hundred!'

'So?'

'But what am I supposed to do?' he demanded, turning to face me. He hadn't yet made up his mind whether to cry or to fight. 'I'll have to give her my hundred pengös, too!'

'No, you won't,' I laughed. 'You love our father.'

'But . . . don't you . . . don't you want a full-size football of your own?' He had finally stumbled on a rather convincing line of reasoning. A football wasn't going to cost much more than ten pengös. I could still give her ninety . . .

'No!' I declared.

We wandered along side by side, speechless. At the beginning of Andrássy Avenue Dávid stopped in front of the ten-metre-long window of the Minerva stationery store.

'Either way I'll need exercise books and drawing-pads and rubbers and pencils and ink for my new pen,' he explained to his conscience. It seemed convinced. We went in. Dávid showed his pen to one of the shop-assistants, a skinny woman in a white blouse.

'Doesn't it take special ink? It's gold.'

'No,' replied the woman, looking us up and down. 'Where did you get it from?'

'My father gave it to me,' Dávid answered with great dignity.

'Beautiful pen. Would the young gentlemen prefer blue or black ink?'

I hid my hundred pengös in a safe place for a few days while I decided whether to spend fourteen eighty on a football. I could have given the whole lot to Mother and then asked for fifteen of it back, but there was an element of blackmail there; and I wasn't sure it would work.

So, leaving the decision to fate, I felt my football ripen in the sun like an apple. The weather grew warmer every day, and every day more of us headed for the Tunnel after school. Occasionally Konrád lent us his ball as a bribe to stop us press-ganging him into playing; from time to time he came along as a sort of reserve in case another Anglo-German war flared up, but the chances of that happening became more and more remote. We had plenty of footballs, and some of the Christians rejoined us as if nothing had happened in November after El Alamein. One could only guess at the reasons for this gradual cooling of the hatred between the two camps.

Goebbels's propaganda belittled the disaster of Stalingrad: it was the exception that proved the rule of German invincibility. But the thunder of the Russian guns at Kharkov, Kursk, Rostov and Krasnodar reduced Goebbels's ranting voice to a grotesque, almost pitiable squeak. Bone-chilling Siberian winds had frozen the fascist delirium. Of the one hundred and twenty thousand Hungarian Christians on the casualty list, four were the fathers of boys in our class, and God knows how many uncles and cousins were dead. As for the Jews, there was still no word of several boys' fathers. There

291

was no news of Elek either. Two and a half months after the Voronezh breakthrough the newspapers were still black with the frames of death notices. Sometimes there would be three different announcements with the same name on one page.

Corporal István Szabó – killed in action near the Don.
Sergeant István Szabó – awarded Bravery Medal (Second Class), killed in action near the Don.
Colonel Árpád Szabó – awarded Silver Bravery Medal (posthumous), killed in action near the Don.

The Germans had gone on to the offensive near Kharkov and Kursk, and were doing quite well. But while Hitler might easily believe that Stalingrad could be undone, it surprised me that Lorentz, with his misplaced nobility, seemed to think so too. He stayed away from the Tunnel, as did the football-mad Hitler-maniac, Schuster. They no longer even demanded the use of the pitch; they just stayed away. This was odd, and the German offensive didn't provide much of an explanation.

We arrived one morning to find Torma already in the classroom. This was unprecedented: the bell hadn't yet been rung for the start of lessons, yet there he was, standing by the window and looking out across Saint Stephen's Square. He turned as each boy came in, greeting us with a silent nod.

'Let's wait a while in case anyone's late,' he said when the bell rang. 'I want to speak to all of you.'

When everyone had finally turned up, Torma came away from the window. He didn't go up onto the teacher's platform, he just stood in front of his desk.

'Boys: I must say goodbye to you. I am going away. Not because I want to; but because I must. It's nearly four years since most of you first arrived at this school, and in that time I have come to like you. Four years is a long time. Many of you are very bright. I am not referring to you, Konrád.'

'I didn't imagine that you were, sir,' interrupted Konrád, not understanding the solemnity of the moment.

'Well, that's all right, then,' Torma laughed. 'If you keep your brain under wraps, less of it will evaporate; although you may find it difficult to think in silence today, with Stupidity crowing from every rooftop. But I don't just want to talk to your brains . . . Basically you are all good – like all children. All of you. Lorentz!'

'Yes, sir?' said Lorentz, standing up.

Torma waved him down. 'Don't you need glasses?'

'The doctor didn't . . .' stammered Lorentz.

'What can you see from your desk if you look out of the window?'

'A swallow flying past . . . trees . . . leaves . . .' Lorentz, embarrassed, was forcing himself to speak fluently.

'So you can see as far as the church named after the founder of our nation, Saint Stephen. But you have become so used to the sight over the last four years that you don't see it any longer. It's just a grey wall. You can't see the cross from where you're sitting. If you wanted to do that you'd have to go over to the window and look up at the sky. I don't blame a child for what he says at home; I blame the home for what it chooses to hear when the child speaks. I make no accusations, I am merely warning you that we live in an age where all relation between intent and effect has vanished. The sober word fans hatred into madness. You were children; but I was always honest with you, even if I didn't tell you everything I thought. Who can I tell now? I'm still unmarried, and I thank God that I have no fiancée. Besides my parents, you are closest to me. You may learn something from what I tell you in this last hour.

'Yesterday morning I was summoned by the Regional Education Authority – that's why I had to leave you at eleven o'clock. The Inspector then told me that a complaint had been lodged against me at high level. I was said to be "educating the young in an unpatriotic spirit". My call-up documents were waiting for me at home.'

Torma was a short, stocky Hungarian. His blue eyes were bright, his face calm. His arms hung immobile by his sides and his feet didn't move an inch, but he turned his eyes away from the window and looked straight at us. Tense with feeling, neither his expression nor his voice wavered as he went on.

'I have tried to shut politics out of the classroom. Not history. I shall not speak of politics now, either. I shall speak of history. Listen to me, carefully, and if there is anything you don't grasp at once, think about it. Ask each other, or your parents, and if you still don't understand, remember nonetheless. I must speak now because I am going away tomorrow and because I will cease to be a civilian the day after. As a civilian I shall be punished less severely for what I am about to say. Now listen.

'Germany has lost the war. Past tense.'

'We're winning at Kharkov!' shouted Pista Rácz.

293

'My poor boy,' continued Torma. 'We are like a man who has lost a hundred gold pieces and finds a brass button. The outcome of the war has been decided. The roof of the Third Reich has caved in; the stones are already falling. The only question is when they will reach the ground.

"The heavy stone flies through the air, who knows where it will land? Who knows where it will land, or whom it will crush, or how?"

At the same time, Hungary has also lost the war. The war she should never have begun. The Russians didn't harm us, meant us no ill. They had no business with Hungary, nor we with them. Hungary has lost a lot of wars – every war since King Mátyás in fact – but never a war like this one. In the wars of the past we were more or less in the right or in the wrong, but we only risked our well-being, our growth, our Hungarian pride. Never before have we gambled our existence as a state, our identity as Hungarians. Most important of all, we have never staked our honour on the dice. Our attack on Russia might be explained away by arguing that we didn't want to be overrun by the Germans as Czechoslovakia, Yugoslavia and Poland were overrun. We could cite our territorial claims, our *folie des grandeurs*, our hunger for prey, and we could have atoned for all these things. But that will be impossible; over the next thousand years, dogs in the street will bite the man who calls them German or Hungarian. We have deprived our own citizens of bread, of human dignity; we have sent our Jewish compatriots unarmed to the front line, made them dig trenches, fortifications, tank-traps, forced them to clear mines with their bare hands, dig the graves into which we have shot them. Genghis Khan and his tartars didn't treat us the way we are treating the Russian population in the occupied territories. The only thing worse than losing this war would be to win it. God has saved us from that. Our existence as a state and as a nation is in the hands of the victorious Great Powers. But our honour can still be ours, and that's what matters most. We must find a way to remain both Hungarian and Christian. Ibolya Hartó will be taking my place, an intelligent and kind lady. I shall introduce you to her after the break. Good luck. God bless you all.'

He shook hands with each of us in turn, treating Lorentz no differently from anyone else. Then, with his usual firm, slightly hurried steps, he walked out of the classroom.

Three days later, when we were picking teams for football, mixing

294

the Jews and the Christians, Lorentz's head and shoulders appeared above the wall of the Tunnel. I went up to him.

'Can I join in?' he asked.

'Go to hell!' I replied. He turned round and shambled away.

We received a two-line postcard from Father inviting me and Dávid to Sunday lunch. Dávid had some vital homework to finish. I was bored, so I set off for lunch at ten o'clock in the morning. Father lived very close to our flat; we'd have bumped into him in the street if he hadn't gone everywhere by taxi.

He lived in a posh boarding house. I was stopped by a maid, who told me that my father had specially requested not to be woken until half past eleven, and she ushered me into the drawing room. It was full of beautiful old furniture and Persian rugs. I asked which my father's room was, and as soon as the maid left me alone I went to his door and knocked. There was no reply. I opened the door, but there was no one in the room. A pair of red boxing gloves lay on a chair, and there was another door in the far wall. I knocked on it in vain and then pushed it open.

My father woke up.

'Who is it?' he asked, opening his eyes for a second and then shutting them again as if he hadn't seen me. He reached blindly for his cigarettes, then for matches. Lighting up, he started smoking with his eyes closed and muttered to me to sit down. Then, half asleep, he picked up the receiver of his bedside telephone and ordered one coffee, one coffee with milk, and some cakes.

'Walnut, poppy-seed or cream?' he yawned into the phone. It took me a moment to realise that he was talking to me.

'Poppy-seed!' I said, amazed. I thought I must be dreaming. Poppy-seed cakes for breakfast! That was what I imagined Rothschild eating every morning.

'And make sure the seeds aren't caviar,' he laughed sleepily down the phone. With that he rang off. He stubbed out his half-smoked cigarette, shook his head, nodded. 'I came home late. You'd probably call it early.' He yawned again.

'Where were you?'

'Working,' he laughed.

'Writing? Where?'

Father opened his eyes and looked at me.

'Writing? Don't be silly. I haven't been allowed to publish anything for five years, why the hell would I be writing? What do you think I am? A dilettante? A medieval monk? Write for nothing! I've never heard of anything so stupid in all my life!'

'What were you doing, then?'

'I was taking part in a spot of debauchery with some officers,' he yawned cheerfully. This time he wasn't playing round. Irony pulled his face into furrows, his eyes sparkled.

'Debauchery? Is that work?' I stammered. I thought he was making a fool of me.

'Not half!' He stretched luxuriously until his bones cracked. 'Each day the lieutenant general sits behind his vast mahogany desk, sticking out his chest to show off his rank and with a solemn face deals out law and order. But later at nightclubs he employs the services of waiters and actresses and other ladies of the *demi-monde* and undoes by night what he does in his office during the day.'

'Do you really know lieutenant generals?' I asked admiringly. 'I once saw a full general at the station: he must have been about eighty-five.'

'You're confusing age and rank. Don't worry, it's an easy trap to fall into; grown-ups do it all the time. But the answer's yes, I know about a dozen generals. I live off them.'

'How?' I demanded, pouncing on this revelation like a bird of prey. Dávid and I had spent a long time wondering where all Father's cash was coming from. 'Conning people,' was Mother's simple answer.

'That's a military secret,' he smiled, and suddenly woke up. 'Forget what I just said. It was stupid. I was half joking anyway. I'm still a bit tipsy.' He wasn't.

The maid came in with a tray. Breakfast.

'Does knowing these generals get you off labour service?' I asked as I attacked the poppy-cakes.

He smiled ambiguously. 'Let's just say that I can't be called up because I have a hollow kidney. And kidney stones into the bargain. I have several medical certificates on the subject. The hollowness cannot be reliably refuted other than by a post-mortem dissection, while an operation to remove the stone would require a six-month convalescence. If I postpone the operation for another six or eight months plus six months' recovery time, that makes twelve to fourteen months. I don't think I'm being unreasonable in expecting Messrs Zhukov and Montgomery to win the war in that time.'

I thought of the general in the picture he had just painted, sitting

296

in his office in a uniform that he wore all the time. And here was my father, this strong, devil-faced man who predicted a devil's face for me. Sitting beside him, I half felt that I was in the cinema.

'Whose are the boxing gloves in the other room?'

'Mine.'

'Do you box?' I asked, amazed. 'Still?'

'The gloves aren't there to keep my hands warm.'

'But . . . you've got a bad kidney,' I said hesitantly, wanting to catch him lying and afraid of succeeding.

'Being overweight makes it worse,' he said, making up for the absent audience by laughing at his own joke. 'I have to keep my eye in. My coach comes round three times a week, but that's just because I'm lazy. I ought to train every day.'

It was the generals that interested me most.

'So you must know a lot about the war,' I said.

'I know a lot about a lot of things,' he answered, suddenly sad. 'I was once a Hungarian writer, and one day I shall be again. In the meantime, I have to collect experience as a con-man, a difficult and respectable profession which also involves trying to save a few people's skins, particularly mine.'

'How?' I asked.

Father gestured meaninglessly. 'I do what I can.'

I wasn't satisfied but I knew that he wouldn't be drawn any further on this subject.

'How many soldiers were lost at Voronezh?'

'Military secret,' he said, sitting up on the edge of his bed. 'In fact it's such a big secret that the High Command probably has to rely on enemy radio for the figures.'

'A hundred and twenty – a hundred and thirty thousand?' I prompted.

'Listen!' he said, standing up to underline his words, or perhaps to put an end to the conversation. 'I wouldn't tell you even if I knew. It would be very dangerous for you, for me, and for whoever I had got my information from. Those are the kind of figures they talk about, but no one knows for certain, at least I don't.'

I brought the conversation round to the Jewish labourers, as I would have liked to hear something about Elek's probable fate, even if indirectly. My father could only confirm that the current figure for the number of labourers serving on the Don was around fifty thousand, and that the level of casualties among them was far higher

297

than that among the soldiers. They were being shot at by both sides.

One thought kept going round and round in my head. Father could intervene with the generals. He 'worked' on them at nightclubs, he was a con-man. He was loaded. Did the generals pay him? Unlikely. Then who did?

'You know that we haven't had any news from Elek since the Russian breakthrough? You know all these generals . . . well, if he turns up . . .'

'Let's wait until he does.'

'Why didn't you do something when they called him up?' I demanded.

Father became angry. 'At the time I didn't know anything about it. And what makes you think I can order these generals around?'

'Why didn't you know?' I wasn't going to let him off the ropes. He slammed his fist into the palm of his hand and stalked off into the bathroom that led off from the bedroom, where he started to shave. Although he left the door open, he was concentrating so hard on the mirror that I began to think that he'd forgotten all about me. After he'd finished shaving he took a shower, and eventually came back into the bedroom in a jolly mood, rubbing his back with a towel.

'I seem to have woken up at last. My body has, at any rate. Now for my head.' He picked up the phone and ordered another coffee, and it wasn't until he had drunk it down that he looked me over thoroughly. 'You've lost weight while I was in the bathroom,' he laughed.

His words, his bursts of emotion, his movements were all like blows. He leant heavily on my shoulder.

'What makes you look so sour?' he asked.

'You said to wait until Elek turns up! OK then, but you said you helped other people save their skins! So why don't you help Samuel? They haven't carted him off to Russia yet! He hasn't had a single day's leave in the last eighteen months!'

My father bore with my anger. He stood and listened to the sense of what I was saying, and when I had finished he answered me quietly, calmly, clearly: 'Do you know his service number?'

'Not off-hand.'

'Bring it to me. I'll do what I can for him. And don't think I don't trust you. Your anger proves that I can. I know you hold me responsible for the past – Oszu, Gyula and the play-centre. But it's not just that: you hold me answerable for the future as well, and what can I promise you? Truth's a beggar. So is God. The Jews in Poland, Slovakia and Croatia have almost been exterminated.'

'What's almost?' I asked, and he fixed his eyes on my face again. His own face became almost naked with the effort. I couldn't understand what it was that he was trying to see. I looked away. It was then that he trusted me with a big secret.

'The Jewish ghetto in Warsaw has risen against the Germans.'

Risen . . .? I had heard of the Polish ghettos, but hadn't dared imagine anything worse than the area around Dob Street. I had just thought of a ghetto as a place where very few Christians lived. I had heard the word 'exterminate' before, too, but I had been sure it was an exaggeration made out of fear or hatred. I had pictured the good Poles having a few drinks in the pub after Mass and then going down to the ghetto for a quick pogrom before lunch, just as they had done for the last few hundred years, only this time it'd be a bit worse because the Germans would be lending them a hand. Now I tried to imagine Dob Street in revolt. They'd throw eggs at policemen and passing soldiers, shout insults and refuse to serve Christian customers. Not that there'd be any.

'Don't be afraid of fear. Use it,' Father said slowly. 'It can be a good warning signal instead of just a chunk of the enemy inside you.'

Then he told about the ghettos in Warsaw and other Polish towns. How they were surrounded by walls and guarded by German soldiers. Jews weren't allowed out, Christians weren't allowed in. People were dying of starvation. Being murdered. They were treated like the Hungarians were treating Jewish labour men in Russia, but women and children too. No one knew how many of them were left alive behind the ghetto walls.

It was as if my father were speaking to me from the far side of a river, his voice soothed into a murmur by the rushing water. I felt that I was only imagining his vivid words. I couldn't hear half of what he was saying.

'At this very moment the Germans are blasting the ghetto into rubble. The Jews are fighting back: men and women, old people and children. With guns, petrol bombs, knives, bricks . . .'

18: Statute 4, Article 3b

Dóra received a letter notifying her that Elek was missing. It could have meant anything; they often pronounced Jews missing even if their bodies had been identified, as this reduced the very high level of Jewish dead compared to Christian units. The object of the exercise was to conceal the nature of the labourers' duties and cover up the thousands of shootings carried out by their Christian 'guards'. Even so, many Jews still received official confirmation of the death of their relatives. The phrase used was 'died in the execution of his duty', rather than the *'pro patria mori'* reserved for Christians.

'Missing'. Mother was on the verge of fainting when she read Dóra's letter. For days she staggered about, pale and trembling. At times she would suddenly stop whatever she was doing and begin to pray. I tried to explain that this was the best news we could possibly have had; Elek was free of Sergeant Virgula and Corporal Hitler: for the time being he was safe in the hands of his Russian captors. I reminded her of Elek's remark about finding a gun. Maybe he was already in a Red Army training camp.

To cheer her up, I gave her the hundred pengős that I had been hiding for the last few weeks. I regretted it the moment I had done it. Dávid was forced to give up the eighty-two pengős left over from his spending sprees in stationery shops and pâtisseries, but Mother didn't even look at the money, so she didn't ask about the missing eighteen pengős. I could have bought a football and said that Father had given it to me. He'd already given Mother six hundred pengős to cover April and May and she had accepted it with the meekness of a martyr and not a word of thanks. Since we had plenty of money to live on, giving all mine away left me with at least as bad a conscience as keeping it would have done. Mother continued to count every

300

last fillér, saving up for a rainy day while the rain poured down outside.

Father's help came in handy. Mother didn't ask Dóra for money, not even her own, and wouldn't have received any even if she had: Dóra was within a few days of childbirth and had written an anxious letter complaining that with Elek missing she only had enough in reserve to last three or four years.

By May, summer had arrived. Since Torma's departure school had become a deadly bore. After it was over I'd go and play football or beg fifty fillérs back from Mother to go and see a film. I became so bored, I even read books; the newspapers had lost their fascination now that the war was won. Occasionally I'd pick one up just to check that everything was progressing as it should.

I couldn't think what to do with myself. Laci Mester never came home from work until late in the afternoon; Pöci and Kaci's father went 'missing' on the Don and was rapidly replaced by his wife's lover, who must have decided to turn his new kids into scientists. He forced them to spend all their time gazing at their books – no great loss as they were totally useless at football. I usually demolished my homework in twenty minutes flat, and as Dávid seemed to think that masses of homework were one of the benefits of grammar-school status, I was left without companions. I had no friends. And then one day I remembered that I had, so I decided to surprise him. Straight away.

There was a twenty-pengö note from Father in my pocket. It had been rustling hesitantly for some time. Mother accepted money too indifferently to make me want to give it to her.

After school I went straight to the play-centre. Mik's crowd were just coming back from lunch. He was pleased to see me.

'Come on!' I told him. 'We're going on a binge!'

'What? Where?' he asked as if he were hard of hearing.

The next stop was Mrs Pig.

'Please, Miss, can I go out? I've got a job for the afternoon and I can earn a pengö. You know we need money at home, my father's away on labour service . . .'

My presence there didn't make his case very convincing.

'What's the job? Is Józska going with you?' asked Mrs Pig, looking at me as she spoke.

'He was the one who got the order. We'll be chopping wood.'

This was too much for Mrs Pig. 'Who wants wood chopped in this heat? Little Lang!'

But catching Mik out wasn't that easy.

'People who cook,' he explained. 'Lunch and supper: they were talking about them on the radio, so they must exist . . .'

Mrs Pig didn't want to risk robbing Little Lang's starving family of a pengö. She let him go.

'After you,' I declared, holding the door of a big pâtisserie open for him while motioning him inside with my father's grand gesture. Gazing at me, he almost walked in backwards. We sat down and I ordered two raspberry juices and four cakes each. He wolfed three down in a single glance, watching me with his other eye.

'What are you grinning at?' he asked as he bit into the fourth cake. 'Promise you won't run off without me.'

We went on to the cinema from there, and after the movie we sampled another pâtisserie. It was there that Mik began the interrogation.

'Who did you nick the bread off? If it was your mother I'm not eating another bite.' I shook my head and indicated that he could carry on eating. He started to laugh.

'I know! It was her bloke!'

'No. He's on his way out.'

'We'll eat to that,' said Mik, and squashed his cake against mine. 'So, who did you nick it from?'

'I didn't.'

He stared at me. When he'd established that I hadn't nicked the money he seemed to bite into his cake rather disappointedly. I told him about the abundance of manna falling all around me, but he didn't touch his last two cakes.

'Do you mind if I take them home with me? My father was called up again and we hardly have anything to eat at home. Sometimes we don't have anything at all. On Sundays I find myself looking forward to Mondays, to school and the play-centre. School! Me!' I took this as an accusation.

'I feel bad,' I said, upset.

'You what? Don't be a fool, I'm glad for you! At least you've got enough to eat. On Tuesdays and Thursdays I get up before dawn to do deliveries for a Jewish greengrocer. His customers are too lazy to carry their own shopping, thank God, so I do it for them on a tricycle. He pays me a pengö a day, not that a pengö's worth much these days, it only buys a couple of litres of milk. Problem is, a Jewish woman is trying to undercut me: she's promised the greengrocer that she'll do the deliveries for just eighty fillérs. And now he's decided that he might be done for exploiting child labour! I'll have to go down to seventy fillérs.'

'Kids of our age in Oszu do the hoeing for half the normal wages. No one ever got done for it. The authorities aren't that tender-hearted.'

'By saving himself twenty fillérs a day, my shopkeeper can stop having to worry about the law . . .'

'But the authorities don't—'

'They won't be doing him for child labour, idiot. They'll do him for being Jewish. The result is that we lose nine pengös a month.'

I had heard somewhere that Jewish labourers' families, like soldiers', could receive assistance from the state if they needed it. I asked Mik why his family didn't claim.

'You think we haven't?' he laughed. It turned out that he was a complete legal expert on the subject. He told me that the wife of a mobilised officer in the reserve was automatically awarded three hundred pengös a month. A private's wife got eighty, a Jewish labourer's wife twelve. Mik threw his head back and began rattling off the regulations:

' "*Auxiliary Jewish service (Labour Service) effectives under regulation 55055/1939 Statute 4 paragraph (i) confirmed under Article 45101/1943 no. 3b are entitled to twelve pengös pcm, additionally eight pengös per child per month . . .*" '

That meant that the Langs received a grand total of twenty-eight pengös a month. My mother earned two hundred, and we weren't exactly rolling in it.

' ' *. . . In cases concerning family benefit claimed by families of auxiliary Jewish servicemen I hereby direct the aldermen, magistrates and mayors of all municipal and county districts not only to refuse appeals against their ruling . . .*" ' At this point Mik straightened up to show that the best was still to come: ' "*but also to refuse such allowances to those families*

(a) *to whose circumstances the chief bread-winner's mobilisation has made no significant difference*

(b) *whose circumstances would be improved by such allowance as compared with their circumstances prior to the mobilisation of the said chief bread-winner.*

In such cases no allowance should be granted." '

Pain must have scratched these words into Mik's memory. It wasn't often that he bothered to learn poems by heart for homework.

'What does all that mean in Hungarian?' I asked. He told me that every month they received the twenty-eight pengős 'for the last time', together with a copy of these regulations. The Town Hall argued that Little Lang's father had earned nothing; without him, therefore, there'd be more nothing to go round. The family was already far better off as a result of the father's call-up: there was one mouth fewer to feed – and a good-for-nothing mouth at that.

This was because they had no written proof of the father's earnings. Delivering coal was seasonal work, and he had found other odd jobs in the spring and summer. He had been working for a Jewish wood and coal merchant who had made him moonlight in order to avoid paying tax and health insurance. The merchant had been called up too, and when Little Lang's mother went along to beg for a certificate of her husband's earnings, the merchant's wife engaged her in a sobbing competition, saying that the heartless brutes wanted her to pay arrears of tax, poor, fragile, grey-haired old lady that she was, not even knowing whether or not she was a widow . . . Instead of providing a certificate, she offered to pay Mrs Lang twenty-eight pengős out of her own pocket in case the Town Hall stopped the payments. Mrs Lang took the cash. Meanwhile, Mik's aunt's stall in the Teleki Square flea-market had been closed under the Jewish laws. Mrs Lang was working as a cleaning lady and eating lunch at the Synagogue soup kitchen. The Synagogue paid the rent, but wouldn't pay the electricity bill so the Langs ate supper in the dark. If they ate supper at all. Heating was more of a problem. Mrs Merchant – the trainee widow – had given them a couple of bags of coal as a present the summer before. From December on, Mik and his brother had had to steal coal from freight trains in railway sidings.

'We're still incredibly lucky to be living in Hungary,' I said, quoting my father.

'If I'd heard anyone else say that I wouldn't have believed them!' laughed Mik.

'They've put down the rising in the Warsaw ghetto. They're murdering Jews by the thousand; by tens of thousands.'

'The ghetto rose? How many thousands of Germans did they take out?' shouted Mik, hitting the table with both hands.

Everyone was looking at us. A fat man of fifty came out from behind the till and waddled towards us. A first lieutenant at one of the other tables stood up. Mik came quickly to his senses.

304

'They'll pay for this, the dirty yids! Don't you worry!'

The lieutenant, who must have been around thirty, sat down, but the fat owner of the pâtisserie wasn't fooled.

'Get out of here, you shitty little yids!' He grabbed Mik by his shirt collar.

'Yid my arse!' protested Mik, but Fatso was trying to pull him off his seat. Suddenly he cast a suspicious glance at my angelic *goy*'s face.

'What are you doing making friends with yids? Does your father know about this?' I almost said 'no', but at the last moment I pulled myself together.

'He isn't a yid!'

'Don't lie.' For a moment, he let Little Lang go and aimed a colossal smack at me, but I bent backwards and only his pudgy fingers touched my face.

'Just filling in for Dad,' he said good-humouredly. By then the lieutenant had come over.

'His dad?' he asked, and then turned to me. 'What rank's your dad?'

'Captain,' I boasted. 'He's at the front.'

'Then please allow me to take your father's place for a moment.' He gave the owner two terrific smacks in the face. 'Beating officers' children! You scum!'

My father was horrified when I told him the story. He gave me an envelope for Mrs Lang with 'some Jewish money' in it, and a note asking her to excuse his not being able to milk any more money out of the rich at that time. He smiled politely at the funny bits of the story; usually mischief impressed him.

'Statue 4, Article 3b . . . ' he muttered. 'One day we'll put it in one of our holy books as a footnote.' I couldn't tell whether he was joking.

'What's so holy about it?'

'Suffering for God,' he said, and then, almost as if correcting himself, he added, 'suffering for our faith.'

'The Langs don't want to suffer,' I stammered, puzzled.

'But they take suffering upon themselves. It's a bit late now to do anything else, but they suffer from generation to generation, as our ancestors did, simply by remaining Jewish.'

'What is a Jew?' I asked suddenly, and then I laughed because it seemed such a stupid question; everyone knew what a Jew was. But Father took me seriously.

'Ask me something easier,' he said to my surprise.

'What's so difficult about that?' I said, gaping. Then I realised why it might be difficult for Father. 'Of course!' I went on. 'You never go to *shul*.'

'Rarely,' he smiled slightly.

'My grandfather hardly considered you to be a Jew,' I told him.

'And I'm very tempted not to consider him and his kind Jewish either. Just bigoted and stupid. No, that's not true – but I am tempted to say it! After all, they know all those hundreds and hundreds of prayers and laws by heart, and I don't know how much they understand and how much they just chant mindlessly. It's no easier for me to have patience with them than for them to have patience with me. What would . . . what would they say? How would the Rabbi answer your question? Would he say that a Jew was someone who lived according to the *Torah*? That all you have to do to wash is spill three drops of water on each hand? Better than nothing, I suppose. They can't get it into their thick skulls that nine-tenths of their dietary laws spring from the fact that Moses didn't have an ice-box. To swallow the story of the Creation, even as a symbol, demands a fairly serious degree of religious prejudice. Some people have nothing else, psychologically or spiritually, and I wouldn't want to take away the only prop they have; but they shouldn't try and dump their accumulation of laws and habits on to my back. Even the Ten Commandments are one or two too many for me. I do covet my neighbour's house, not having one myself, and as for his lady-wife . . .' He stopped, realising suddenly that he was talking to me.

'Don't you even accept the Ten Commandments?' I asked, frozen.

'Yes, I do. After all, Moses killed, but even he accepted them in the end.'

'So, a Jew is someone who accepts the Ten Commandments?' I concluded.

Father nodded. 'We're getting closer.'

'But the Christians accept them too!' I objected. It was Father's turn to freeze.

'The hell they do! Didn't those Jews teach you anything apart from chanting? Where shall we begin? In the beginning, at the First? No, the First is a bit hard . . . It's the source of all the others. Let's begin with . . . hmm . . . Christians . . .? Then let's start with the Second: "Thou shalt not make unto thee a graven image; nor the form of anything that is in heaven above, or that is in the earth beneath . . ." '

To show him that I'd understood I quoted the few words of Hebrew that Berger had succeeded in drumming into my head.

'Then why don't you pay attention to what the words mean?' demanded Father. 'Is that a Christian Commandment? They kneel in front of a graven image, the model of all the other graven images of their society – from the medieval kings anointed in the name of Jesus's Church to – less directly – the dictators, the Hitlers. They took their model from the god-emperor of Roman slave-society. The god-emperor became the god-king. Of course, they say, their graven image is only a reminder . . . Wasn't the statue of Apollo the same for the Greeks, and Moloch for the Egyptians?'

'Why is it so important that one cannot see God?' I asked, as this had always intrigued me.

'One cannot,' stated Father with a smile. 'For the time being let's just content ourselves with the fact that one can't. It's always possible to construct theories and hypotheses around it. The Jew who said that God was part of the Creation was excommunicated like a shot. Let's just say that one can sort of see Him in His laws. "See" isn't quite the right word for it, but man likes to see everything he thinks and feels, like Moses with the burning bush, when apparition, hallucination, thought and fire must have been pretty mixed.'

'Then, how . . .?' I began, fishing the question out of the thoughts pouring into my head. 'Which law can we "see" Him in?'

Father bent his head back as if trying to remember something, then asked, 'Which is the most important Commandment?'

'Thou shalt not eat pig,' I laughed.

'Stop playing the fool. The most important of the Ten Commandments.'

I thought. Then said that I didn't know. But Father wanted an answer at all costs and in the end I said, 'Thou shalt not kill?'

Father nodded, and then seemed to change his mind. 'Wouldn't you kill Hitler?' he asked.

'Of course I would. That couldn't be a crime.'

'Quite, how could it be anything but a blessing, the greatest *mitzvah* of all time. So: which Commandment?'

I started guessing and then asked him to tell me. Instead of answering, he told me how an expert on the law had gone to Jesus and asked him what the greatest commandment in the law was.

'What did he say?'

'I'll tell you in a moment. First, you tell me how the First Commandment goes.'

'*Anochi Adonoy Elohecho asher hotzeisicho m'eretz Mitzrayim mibeis arodym,*' I quoted, managing to remember the Hebrew.

'And in Hungarian?'

'I am the Lord your God, who brought you out of the land of Egypt, out of the house of bondage.'

Father nodded.

'That's not what Jesus said. He quoted Moses's injunction to the people after he had repeated the Ten Commandments and was warning them to keep the laws: "Love the Lord your God with all your heart, with all your soul, with all your mind." Many other tough Rabbis would have said the same. But without the First Commandment that injunction is just the squeaking obedience of an idolatrous slave, or the crack of the slave-driver's whip. Jesus says, "That is the greatest Commandment. It comes first," but it's not a Commandment at all, and certainly not the First. It's unconditional surrender before God instead of alliance with Him.'

'Is that wrong?' I asked hesitantly.

'Well, take the frightening example of a Polish Jew who is being starved behind barbed wire until they kill him. Why should he love God?'

'But is that God's fault?' I said, defending Jesus in my confusion.

'Arguable. In my opinion it is, yes. In any case, what Jesus said was not the First Commandment. You recited the real one to me just now. Think it over. Don't rush it. What does the First Commandment command?' The question was almost an attack. I thought and thought.

'Nothing,' I stammered at last.

'Of course it does,' Father smiled. 'It commands you to listen, and think over what you have heard. God says: "You are free, and your freedom is from and through Me. That's how and why I am your God. You may be capable of not loving Me despite this, but whether you want to love Me or not is up to you." In other words: "If you are not free, then I am not your God. If you accept this, then here are nine Commandments which will enable you to use and to defend your freedom." I can think of a good Jew who had trouble with all the Commandments – not just one of them – and yet God continued to love and respect him.'

'Who?' I asked.

'Moses,' laughed my father. 'He broke both of the stone tablets
. . . *cherus* and *chorus*,' he said after a moment's dreaming. 'It looks
better on paper,' he added, and, taking a pen, wrote two identical
sets of Hebrew letters on a piece of notepaper. 'The two words are
spelt exactly the same way; no one whose Hebrew is any good ever
puts in the dots for the vowels. "*Chorus*" means "engraved"; "*cherus*"
means "freedom". Exodus says: "And the tables were the work of God,
and the writing was the writing of God, graven upon the tables." *Chorus
al ha-luchot*. An old rabbi told me that the Talmud misunderstands it
on purpose – as it often does – in order to bring out a deeper meaning:
Altikro chorus elo cherus. Do not read "graven upon the tables" but
"the tables of freedom". *Cherus al ha-luchot*. Tradition tells us that the
tablets broken by Moses and the unbroken ones were kept together in
the Holy of Holies. Whether or not you break them is up to you. God
punished Moses for it, and yet He loved him. By the time Moses came
along God had become used to the idea that the Jews were hard-headed,
free-souled men with minds of their own. Maybe that's why He chose
us. I say "Jews" – "Juda" – which isn't a bad name for us, but we have
a more accurate one . . .' Father smiled sourly. 'When German Jews
were still allowed to travel – more or less – Hitler made them add the
name "Israel" to the names on their passports.

'Ádám Sondor Israel,' Father said, introducing himself with apparent
pride. 'The miserable fool didn't know what he was doing. Do you
know who "Israel" was, Josef Sholem Jakobovits Sondor Israel?'

'Of course,' I grunted. 'Jacob.'

'And do you know what he was? Was he a big strong bloke – like
Elek?' Father asked the question as if it were some cunning riddle, but
at the same time his face wore a helpfully mischievous expression.

'No way!' I laughed dismissively. 'He was a skinny little smart-arse
Jew. Lame too – only that was later. He never stopped haggling with
everyone – his brother, his father, his uncle Laban – and he ripped
them all off as well. He ran away like a frightened rabbit when he
realised that Esau had had enough of his little brother's dirty tricks.
He wouldn't have done that if he'd been stronger than Esau, now
would he? Hey! He haggled with God too – even if he didn't dare
rip Him off!'

'This kid's Jewish all right,' Father remarked to his invisible
audience.

Then he turned back to me. 'You don't say?' he asked teasingly.
'Did he really bargain with God? How?'

'The ladder. God promised him everything in his dream, but when he woke up Jacob said, "If God will be with me, if He will protect me on my journey and give me food to eat and clothes to wear, and I come back safely to my father's house, then the LORD shall be my God." Only then.'

'You see,' said Father. 'You know the answer, you just don't know that you know. Do you understand the First Commandment yet? Jacob sees God and His angels in a dream! God promises him the ground he's lying on, says that *All the families of the earth shall pray to be blessed as you and your descendants are blessed.*" Any self-respecting saint would give his right arm for a brief vision of one small angel, but what does a Jew – I mean Israel – or, rather, Jacob – do? He bargains. He says, "If you are with me and keep me in peace, wealth, health . . ." He says, "Money on the table." If God had told Jacob "Be a good Christian and I'll reward you in the next world," Jacob would obviously have answered, "Fine, I'll start worshipping you when I get there. If you're selling a religion of despair and death, you can find yourself another customer." God found this a bit much and in the end they had a show-down. Do you know what I'm talking about?'

I had to think. Berger had made us read the whole story of Jacob and Joseph in Hebrew, but Father seemed to be talking about something completely different. Suddenly I remembered.

'Of course! When he's rich, he goes back to Bethel – the place where he had the dream – with all his wives and family . . .'

Father took over.

'To raise an altar. But he didn't do it of his own accord: God had to nag at him. He'd given Jacob what he'd asked for, but Jacob's household was still keeping foreign gods. It was Jacob's turn to keep his side of the bargain. He knew he needed God, but he knew that God needed a people even more. But before that Jacob had a fight with a "Man" – they wrestled until dawn . . .' Father winked: 'Big strong Esau would have put that man on his shoulders in the first round, wouldn't he? No? I don't think so either. The match ended in a draw. But the "Man" seemed to recover form after the fight was over, because he dislocated Jacob's hip with one hand by hitting him in the hollow of the thigh. He obviously didn't want Jacob to get too cocky. Then he said: "Your name shall no longer be Jacob, but Israel, because you strove with God and with men, and prevailed." God learnt something from this struggle, that's why He gave Moses the First Commandment before the other nine. The First is a pledge,

310

and without it the rest are just hot air. Freedom is the pawn of God. Without it, the foundation of our faith is quicksand. Do we have any other name for God? And where there is only one God, how can there be any other guarantor of our freedom?'

Father bowed his head and remained silent for a long time. Then he murmured, 'Nothing like this has ever happened to us before. People blame us and accuse us of sin – but what sin can possibly deserve one thousandth of this punishment? Whoever among us does not accuse God for tolerating this is a slave and doesn't deserve the name of Israel: God has broken the tablets.'

My voice stuck in my throat.

'What can we do?' I asked at last.

He didn't answer for a while. Then he said, 'We are wrestling with the Man.'

19: Hard Labour

The summer term gradually came to an end, and with it my time at primary school. I was given a 'B' rather than an 'A' in three subjects, and Mother despaired of getting me into a grammar school. The Christian ones only took two Jews per year – including converts – and at the Jewish grammar there weren't enough places even for the straight 'A' pupils.

'I'll have to send you to a secondary modern,' Mother sighed during one of her moods. 'Such a bright child too . . . And it's only because he's so lazy . . . It'll affect his whole life . . .'

I couldn't understand why she was going on about me being so bright, but then again, I was her kid. And she hadn't met Aaron Kohn so she probably didn't know any better . . .

'I'll take the bridging exam after the war,' I told her to cheer her up. You could sometimes get into the grammar from the secondary modern, even if you were Jewish. I wasn't worried: the Hungarian football team only had one O-level between them.

Father couldn't see the problem. 'I'll find you twenty places at the Jewish grammar,' he assured me.

During the last few days of term I had gone to see Little Lang at the play-centre. He told me that the envelope of 'Jewish money' that my father had sent them had contained five hundred pengös.

'One hundred would have been plenty,' said Mik, not knowing what else to say. I was embarrassed too; we didn't spend much time together. The Synagogue was sending him away to the country to spend the summer with some rich Jewish family. I didn't know when we would be seeing each other again.

I couldn't really imagine Father beating Gyula up in some dark alley, but he seemed in some strange way to have kept his word.

Gyula only turned up once in a blue moon, and when he did he was as polite and formal as a stranger. I only caught him quarrelling with Mother once.

'Don't worry! I know who that whore is!' she was shouting. Gyula didn't worry and didn't come round, and that was fine by me.

Towards the end of term the Germans launched a huge offensive. One million men tried to fight their way towards Kursk. The offensive began with triumphant battlecries that gradually diminished in direct proportion to the level of German success. The Russians were ready for them. They took the assault on multiple lines of defence, and withstood it. I dug feverishly through the newspapers and listened avidly to the radio. Who was commanding the Russian armies? I had to know whether *he* was there, Zhukov the Liberator, the man who had defended Moscow, lifted the siege of Leningrad, commanded at Stalingrad . . . He was there. I knew it. I could see Zhukov's hand in the way the campaign developed.

In the middle of July the Russians launched the first stage of their three-pronged counter-offensive. The attack broke through German lines on the first day. During the fifty-day battle the Germans lost half a million men and the best part of their tanks and aeroplanes.

On the orders of the Duce, the Italians evacuated North Africa. Rommel succeeded in a 'strategic withdrawal'. The British and the Americans landed in Sicily and the Italian king threw Mussolini into jail. The Axis sky was falling in; the earth had opened under the fascists' feet.

Every house in Hamburg had collapsed. Its one million inhabitants were wandering shell-shocked through the ruins. Kovács, the young Arrow Cross barber who lived next door, stopped me on the balcony one sunny afternoon. He was carrying a copy of the *Hungarian Messenger*, the filthiest of all the filthy fascist rags, and he shoved it under my nose to show me a picture of Cologne Cathedral after some bright Englishman had hit it with a bomb.

'What do you say to that? Your friends bomb churches!' he spat. Not surprisingly, I felt rather proud to be considered an accessory to the bombing.

'Was Hitler in there, praying for the Final Victory?' I asked sympathetically. I thought Kovács was going to hit me, but instead he just looked threatening.

'You'll pay for this!' he said.

Samuel arrived for a few days' leave. He had lost weight. His face

313

was rigid, his eyes had grown even bigger and stared unblinkingly ahead of him as if fixed upon some invisible monster. He was lucky: his labour unit hadn't been sent outside the country. They had gone hungry for over a year, they had been made to work very hard, they had been beaten up regularly, but only five out of one hundred and sixty men had actually died. During the last year and a half Samuel hadn't had one hour's leave. He had received a total of two letters, having found the one informing him of Elek's disappearance on the rubbish heap where all letters to the labour men were thrown. He had been taken off kitchen duties at his moment of greatest need: a textile wholesaler from Budapest had bribed one of the officers to get himself the job. By that time there was nothing much to cook anyway.

Then, suddenly, their lot had improved. The most sadistic of the guards were removed, the food got better, the labourers started receiving fifty or even eighty grams of meat a day instead of none, with a quarter of a kilo of bread and a handful of beans in their soup instead of the three pieces they had been given before. And now Samuel had been given three days' leave, together with half the company, so it couldn't have been my father's doing.

The sadists on the High Command had clearly suffered an irreparable loss of confidence following the battle of Kursk. Even before the battle was over, some ghost had appeared to tell them that the impossible could happen and that one day they might even be called to account for the worthless lives of Jews.

Samuel's clothes hung in rags from his shoulders. The sole of one boot was held on by string. His three days weren't enough to travel to Oszu for clothes; it was us he wanted to see. Watching him, I thought of what Christians meant when they talked about 'sacrificial lambs'.

Samuel objected when Mother wanted to buy him some clothes. He thought we couldn't afford it; and in any case he could ask Dóra to send him some now that parcels were being delivered properly again. Mother assured him that we were getting lots of money from Father.

'Then at least the war is doing someone good,' Samuel remarked. 'If it can make Ádám's heart . . .' But he still wouldn't let Mother buy him clothes. 'Waste of money when I've got some at home,' he said.

'Surely you don't want to ruin your Sabbath suit building roads?' protested Mother. 'You'll need it after the war.' Samuel smiled as if she had made a joke. Mother eventually succeeded in convincing him that he needed strong boots and clothes that wouldn't tear, but Samuel found a new objection.

'You can't go out on to the street with me looking like this! What'll the neighbours say?'

'They can blush till the skin burns off their faces,' said Mother, and they set off.

After leaving the shops, Samuel went straight to the cinema in his new clothes. He was late home for supper, and already full of *ersatz* chocolate. He went to bed immediately and woke up at midday. After lunch he headed for the cinema again, although he only stayed for one film.

On the second morning, the monster in Samuel's eyes became visible to all of us.

The sudden thaw had brought greater concessions to soldiers and even labour men than a fistful of beans and a mouthful of meat. Anyone who won such and such a medal, or received a wound that kept him in hospital for six or more months, was exempted from further services. This also applied to anyone – Jews included – whose father, son or brother had fallen at the front.

'Elek is only missing,' said Samuel, the sweat breaking out on his forehead as he spoke. He hoped his brother was still alive, of course, but there could be a way to make the authorities believe the opposite. The very probable opposite.

'There's no shame in lying these days,' Samuel went on. His face was scarlet. Mother sat listening to him, dead pale, deaf. Expecting her to fall off her chair at any moment, I brought her a glass of water.

'I didn't say a word,' Samuel murmured. I could scarcely hear him.

'Yes, you are right,' said Mother, sitting up straight. 'We can't afford to be superstitious. God doesn't listen to the lies we tell to save our lives; he listens to our prayers. Elek is safe.'

The task facing us seemed impossible. We had to find two of Elek's former comrades on the Don and persuade them to testify to having stumbled on Elek's corpse. But we didn't know where to start looking. How could any of Elek's unit have got back from Russia? Only one in ten Jews ever returned. Mother's only hope was to bribe Sergeant Virgula's parents with another barrel of wine or, if necessary, with half an acre of vineyard, and get them to use their influence over their son when he next came home on leave. While Mother thought about all this, her eyes became opaque. Samuel watched her, breathing heavily and wiping his face.

I brought the newspaper to the table and showed them the map on the front page. They looked at me, surprised but glad of the interruption. Only Dávid looked at me a little mockingly, as if to say: 'Here you go again, you little idiot . . .'

I pointed to Kharkov.

'There,' I announced. 'Elek isn't far from there.'

'That's the front, stupid,' Dávid said.

'I know, stupid,' I replied proudly.

'You think that Elek's fighting . . .?' Mother stammered. 'Against his country . . .?'

'His country?' I asked angrily.

'It's his country all the same . . .' She shook her head. 'Elek is a prisoner of war.'

So Mother had thought I was only trying to reassure her when she had woken up in the middle of the night screaming Elek's name and I had told her about his strange remark before he left. 'I shall find a gun too,' he had said. She thought I'd made it up.

'What we do know is that he wanted to fight,' I said. I suddenly understood why Elek had entrusted me with his secret. It was this sort of situation that he had had in mind.

'Where did you get this idea from?' said Mother. 'Please, please don't make anything up.'

'I'm not,' I said, and reported in detail how Elek had known about our visit to the Virgulas and how he had said nothing so that Mother and Dóra wouldn't worry.

They could see that I was telling the truth. I also told them how I had tried to make Elek have the sense to be frightened of Virgula, who would have a gun out on the front, and quoted Elek's reply a second time, the reply that I had taken as a joke in the mountains of Oszu.

Mother cast a furtive glance at the map.

'Elek wouldn't risk being captured by the Germans. He'd be shot on the spot.' I laughed cheerfully at this new worry of Mother's. She called me a stupid child and calmed down a bit. Samuel looked at the wall as if it were the screen in the cinema. He was admiring his brother.

But on the third day, saying goodbye, they stared at each other, frightened, looking for signs of betrayal. Samuel's eyes were glazed with ice when he left us.

316

One morning I went to see my father alone. Dávid had gone off on holiday with a classmate of his who had a house in the country. I found Father speaking into the telephone in an unusually pleasant voice.

'Please stress to the Colonel that my call is of the utmost importance. I am not exaggerating.' He put down the receiver, and as he did so the pleasant expression faded from his face to be replaced by a pulsing anxiety. His breathing was fast and jerky, and although there was a cigarette still burning in the ashtray, he lit up a new one. He gestured to me to be quiet, and paced up and down the room with the expression of someone who is lifting a heavy weight. He stopped. Then started walking again and lifted up the receiver. The rest of the telephone jumped into the air; he caught it and dialled a number. This time the worry in his voice was naked.

'I wish to speak to his honour the Brigadier General Kapossy. It's vital.' He waited. I could see that he meant it. 'No, it's rather . . . personal. When could I ring again?' He asked the person on the other end to stress the urgency of the call to General Kapossy. Then he put down the receiver and turned to me.

'It's my turn. With interest.'

He had learned from a well-wisher that he was due to receive his call-up within hours. It was to be an 'Eagle' call-up, which meant that he would have to report to Nagykáta within twenty-four hours of receiving it.

'But you were exempted because of your kidney,' I objected, surprised.

'Only temporarily. It's an exercise in personal harassment: the lieutenant general who used to be my protector has turned against me.' Father paused. 'Punishment unit,' he said blankly.

He started pacing the room again. Then he stopped and barked an order at me to calm his anxiety. 'I need to gain time and money. Lots. Go home!' A second later he changed his mind. 'No. Stay with me. You might throw them off the scent. Let's go!'

'Where?'

Father looked irritated but he laughed. 'To gain time. And money.'

'At roulette?' I asked in a panic.

'That'd be easier than what I'm thinking of. Let's go.'

I tried to calm him down by telling him that the labour service had got better recently.

'Not in Russia, not in punishment units, and not for me.'

317

From his clipped half-sentences I gradually pieced together what had happened. His former protector was spreading the rumour that Father had failed to pay a gambling debt of some fifty thousand pengös. No senior officer would be likely to help a man who had defaulted on a debt of honour.

'Fifty thousand!' he said, pronouncing the verdict as he walked down the stairs. He intended to obtain that sum during the course of the morning, the equivalent of my mother's pay for the next twenty years. I could already see my father on the edge of a ditch, facing gun barrels.

'What are you snivelling about?' he demanded.

'Fifty thousand . . . ' I mumbled. He laughed.

'Look at that chap over there!' he remarked, pointing to a man reading a newspaper in the street. We jumped into a taxi. My father looked out of the back.

'He wasn't the one,' he said evenly. 'He didn't even look up from his paper.' Suddenly he laughed angrily. 'There we are!'

A car was following us. Father told the taxi-driver to turn into a side street as fast as he could. The driver gave Father a hard look, then looked less severely at me. He must have concluded that he was dealing with a couple of criminals on the run, but he nodded. Father pushed a twenty-pengö note into his palm.

'My creditors,' he explained. 'They've set a tail on me.'

The driver, who had the face of an ex-boxer, grinned. He was enjoying the fun. 'Don't worry, guv, we'll lose 'em.'

'I'll pay any fines twice over,' Father assured him.

The accelerator hit the floor. We turned sharply into a side street and two seconds later I heard the screeching of brakes behind us. We were being followed all right.

Father began to debate the wisdom of showing that he was aware of the tail by giving them the slip. After all, they hadn't gone up to his rooms. In the end he decided that the escape was a good move as he had to delay receiving the 'document' for as long as possible. He told the driver that the 'document' was a 'registered letter' posted by a 'charming and extremely beautiful maid' who had warned him on the telephone. He described the maid's beauty light-heartedly; she had posted the 'letter' on her boss's orders but she was a 'good, true Hungarian girl, whose heart was with the poor'.

The driver smiled happily. He liked the pretty maid. He shot through a red light and left our pursuers stranded by the traffic crossing the junction, then zig-zagged for a while, turning several times to make sure that we had shaken off the other car. Father stopped the taxi at a phone booth, but he didn't have any tokens for the telephone. He sent the driver off to get twenty.

I asked him why the lieutenant general had turned against him. Without beating about the bush, Father told me that there had been a dispute over the fees he was receiving for delays and exemptions from labour service. He didn't spell it out, but he had clearly been acting as a middle man for rich Jews who wanted to bribe senior staff officers.

'How much does he want?'

'Only he knows that. But I'll bowl him over with a tiny little sum like fifty thousand.'

I was almost bowled over myself. I had seen in the papers that a four-bedroom flat in Buda cost thirty-five thousand. I also realised that Father must have donated a substantial amount of the loot to himself – at least fifty thousand pengös more than his protector considered reasonable.

'Where are you going to find fifty thousand pengös in twenty-four hours?'

'Twenty-four?' he laughed. 'More like two or three. We need a miracle. Or a woman who thinks I'm a miracle. There are quite a few of those.'

'A woman?' I asked in fright. 'What sort of woman?'

Father laughed happily at my horrified expression; his ability to laugh when he was in such a tight corner definitely made things worse.

'The rich sort,' he said. 'Love won't help us here.'

More to himself than to me, he explained that the general didn't have to hate him to send him to a punishment unit. After all, if he was dispensing with Father's services he had to make sure that Father wouldn't talk too much. Or too long.

'I can't really complain if he likes me less than he likes money. If only he was slightly less repulsive . . .' Father mused for a moment, 'I could sweep him off his feet with a mere twenty-five thousand.'

He seemed to have recovered his confidence. Motioning me to be quiet, he walked round the phone box making the occasional gesture – like an actor rehearsing alone. Then he entered the booth and picked up the receiver with the romantic flourish of a cinematic lover picking up his violin to serenade his lady. The conversation began

319

with a terrifying expression and hand movements that plucked daggers from the air. But gradually these gestures became more rounded and genial, and he stepped out of the telephone box ten centimetres taller than when he went in.

'We're winning,' he said.

But he was only halfway there. We met up with Daisy, my swimming-pool acquaintance; first in a pâtisserie in Old Buda and then a second time, half an hour later, in another cake-shop somewhere in Pest. There, Daisy handed Father a box covered in blue velvet, assuring him that no one would miss it as she had an exact replica. She would have this replica copied immediately; it would be indistinguishable from the original. It seemed that the jewel – whatever it was – didn't even need to be sold: it was worth fifty thousand at a pawnbroker's. I would have liked to have a look at a jewel that could buy a house, but they didn't show it to me.

The next day Father was in a festive mood. He had spoken to the lieutenant general and the call-up had been cancelled. The fifty thousand pengös had sorted out any misunderstandings.

A day later, I went looking for Father in vain. Early that morning, soldiers had come for him with his call-up papers. They wouldn't allow him to say goodbye to anyone, not even on the phone. He was guarded all the way to his destination.

After a few weeks a soldier arrived at our kitchen door. He was a private, one of the guards assigned to my father's unit. He was in Budapest on leave and had brought us a letter.

My dear sons, Dávid and Józska. It was good to be a father for a few weeks. They passed too quickly, and won't make up for the failed years, but if you think of me at all, try to remember the last few weeks as well. You too, Józska. I am about to tell you why.

They are taking me somewhere worse. There was a sadistic sergeant with us who seemed to have special orders to do away with me, so I beat him up and they brought me here, to Szentkirályszabadja. I have been attached to a punishment unit that will shortly be dispatched to Bor, in Serbia, where we will be working in a coppermine under German command. My letter will reach you through one of the guards, Private Homola. Don't be frightened! No matter where they send me, I shall return. From the depths of Hell if need be. I won't die, not even in a four-poster bed, until Hitler and his cadaverous stench have been blown away by the wind. Be brave and circumspect. Look after your mother; I know she will continue to look after you. Avoid crowds. When the time comes, don't go into the ghetto. Escape, go into hiding! A good sailor runs before the storm. I shall come back, but I must know that you will be waiting for me when I do. I have heavy debts to pay, and you can guess that I am not talking about money. Forgetting that kind of debt is as good as paying it. I owe a great deal to literature, to people and, most of all, to you. I will try to be a better father. I sound a bit sentimental. But a man is kept alive BY WHOM HE LOVES. Every drop of my blood burns with love for you. Affectionate regards to your mother. I embrace you and I bless you, Abraham ben Jacob, your Father.

Private Homola spoke of Father with respect.
'A tough man. Made of steel. But his heart's like butter.' This probably meant that the soldier had been well paid for becoming a postman. He told us that the punishment unit had been cutting down a forest. Our father's section were carrying away the timber, three men to a tree – one at each end and Father in the middle. Suddenly Sergeant Zala, 'a tough man too, but hard as nails all the way through', ordered the two men at the ends to drop the tree. They did. Father managed to tilt the tree far enough to jump out from underneath it as it fell. He went up to the Sergeant, who reached for his revolver, but before Zala could fire Father flattened him with a single blow. Then he picked him up off the ground with one hand and began punching him systematically with the other until six soldiers ran up and overpowered him. None of them actually hit Father. By that time the sergeant's head was a ball of blood. 'It'd be a miracle if he had a single tooth left.' They took him to hospital in a lorry. He couldn't even sit up.

The news that Father had fallen into German hands would have stopped my heart if the war hadn't been going so well. The English and Americans were fighting their way through Italy, and one breakthrough would bring them to the gates of Budapest in a matter of weeks.

The word *Blitzkrieg* had been forgotten. The Germans praised their own 'unshakeable defensive tenacity', and assured their countrymen – and the rest of the world – that when the Red Army reached the East Wall – the line of the Dnieper – they would splash against it like water on a stone.

321

I regarded this kind of propaganda as a guarantee of the Germans' imminent collapse, although they had rescued Mussolini from the Americans. I decided that there was a secret agreement between the leaders of the various mortal enemies not to harm each other personally.

My father had arranged things with the Jewish grammar school while he was still in Budapest, but the good news might as well have been bad for all I cared. The teaching year started late because the school buildings had been confiscated and they had had to move the classes to the primary school. The little prestige that I had attached to grammar school evaporated with the move back to Berger-land.

The first day, I realised that most of the other boys in my class were well-off, and proud of it. I spent a long time scrutinising their faces, but I wasn't in a generous mood and found most of them extremely unattractive. When asked about their parents' occupation, several of them said: 'My father is away on labour service and my mother has "private means".' I didn't discover what 'private means' were until I got home, but I crossed swords with the son of one as soon as we'd finished filling in forms. It was during our first Latin lesson.

'Sir, sir, when will we learn about ablative absolutes?' asked a weedy, pretty-faced 'private means' kid.

The teacher acknowledged the new pupil's enthusiasm with a self-satisfied smile, while I made donkey's ears at the little creep and completed his question for him: 'Miaow, miaow, may I be the teacher's pet?'

'Is anything the matter?' the roundish, white-haired teacher enquired in a dignified tone.

'I didn't know that this class took girls,' I replied and, quite uninhibited by the teacher's presence, stuck my tongue out at my blushing classmate.

'You are not at nursery school any more!' said the teacher to put me in my place. The others made noises against me, but I drowned them out by laughing.

'So I see. I'm in a convent. Why can't we all wear skirts?'

'Don't play the fool and don't be cheeky. Otherwise you can pack your home and go back to your bags.'

With this astounding witticism, the teacher managed to steal my laughs. The class was enormously impressed by my cheekiness, but several of the self-assured, well-kempt weeds humbly helped the teacher to tell me off.

'Don't be cheeky! Stop playing the fool!'

'We want to learn some Latin!' chirped the 'private means' cissy.

At this moment, the *pedellus*, 'the school servant', shuffled into the classroom. Whenever the Head wanted to say anything to the rest of the school, he wrote it down in an enormous book which everyone treated with the respect due to holy scriptures. The *pedellus* then had to cart it around from classroom to classroom, where the messages were read out.

The teacher coughed meaningfully, and then read out the Head's latest revelation. The pupils of the two new first-year classes 'A' and 'B' were advised not to buy the school cap and badge, and the more senior pupils were asked not to wear them until further notice. In 'today's climate', such 'insignia' might lead to 'provocations' and 'incidents' in the streets.

So I was deprived of my grammar-school cap, the only sign of my new status. Even before this Mother had pestered me, asking why I looked 'so sad' and whether I was ill. I simply felt that I was suffering the same old boredom in a slightly different desk. Mother decided, repeatedly, to have me thoroughly examined by a doctor.

The next lesson was Hebrew. It was the Jewish primary school all over again: I was the class dunce.

In the middle of the lesson I suddenly understood why I hadn't yet seen a single interesting person in the whole class, because the door opened and Aaron Kohn walked in.

The teacher was sitting at his desk. He was the only teacher in the school who wore a *kapel*, the rest went bare-headed. Aaron Kohn had started speaking in Hungarian, but assessing the situation in a single glance, he switched to Hebrew in mid-sentence. The only word I understood was the ancient biblical term 'puncture', and I guessed that the Kohns had had a breakdown on the way back from their summer holidays.

The teacher's face lit up, and he chatted with Aaron Kohn in Hebrew for the next five minutes. Sometimes it was hard not to loathe Kohn, he hadn't even stepped inside the classroom and one teacher had already fallen on his knees. But as Kohn looked for somewhere to sit, he saw me and his eyes lit up. He waved at me cheerfully, surprised. There was no room where I was sitting. He

323

sat elsewhere, and within hours everyone was vying for his company, and the teachers behaved as if he were the source of all the light in the room.

I just shrugged. It all seemed completely natural to me. I wasn't angry with Aaron. I was angry with myself, and God.

My new classmates were a bunch of swots. They could only talk about pâtisseries and ablative absolutes; when it came to important things like the Germans being chased out of Smolensk and the Russian advance on the Dnieper they echoed the teachers' warnings. 'Let's not talk politics,' they said, and then changed the subject by saying that the English would be the ones to occupy Hungary. They seemed to think that armies had to RSVP before invading.

The teachers were very strict about our homework. Boys caught in cinemas without their form-teacher's written permission were severely reprimanded. Friday *shul* was compulsory. Although the school had been stuffed into a building that was far too small everyone behaved as if it were a whole world. They were all convinced that I was stupid. I was equally convinced that they were mad.

Dóra wrote to us. Virgula was back in Oszu on leave. He hadn't been to see her, he hadn't even dropped by for a minute or two, which Dóra regarded as a bad sign. Mother wrote back to say that Virgula would certainly have popped in to say hello if there were any bad news. The longer he stayed away the better. Dóra didn't dare approach him or his parents; she was a foreigner as far as the village was concerned. For her part, Mother didn't dare trust Dóra with the job of bribing the Virgulas to have Elek declared dead and Samuel demobilised. She had to persuade Dóra to use the money from the legacy, but Dóra was tight-fisted with money, like most people who are used to having it.

Her baby was now five months old. She had called him Imre, after the ill-fated Prince Imre, Saint Stephen's son. I had never heard of any Jew being called that, but Dóra's family were Hungarian peasants: it was a complete accident that they were also orthodox Jews. The only person Dóra ever saw – apart from the baby – was my grandfather's widow, old Iron-Nose. I pitied Imre in advance, and decided that as soon as he was big enough I would give him a peashooter with which to defend himself.

Harvest-time was approaching, and Virgula was in Oszu. Mother decided to take ten days' holiday to be there too. She intended to take me with her, as I was looking a little pale and I was sure that my school

324

could manage without me; Dávid was left with Gyula, whose visits were now mercifully rare. Our strategy was to buy Virgula through his parents first, and put Dóra in the picture later.

Baby Imre could sit up, turn round in his cot, and yell. His interest in the outside world was limited to his hands and his feet.

Dóra was a surprisingly firm and efficient manager. Elek had left detailed instructions for her, giving her approximate times for each stage of the wine-making process and the number of hands required, and even Borsodi the vintner didn't try too hard to con her. He knew that Elek would be grateful if he remained loyal while Dóra was on her own.

We needed a barrel of wine as an advance on the coming bribe. Dóra wasn't to know its real purpose for the time being, and Mother had to tell her that it was our duty to do something for those of Elek's comrades who weren't yet dead or missing. Dóra argued that their families ought to pay something towards the barrel, even if only at cost price, but eventually she gave in.

We hired a cart to deliver the wine, which was risky. We didn't want to find Sergeant Virgula at home before Mother had talked to his parents. But we were in luck: he wasn't there. Mother and I had agreed that I would go outside to play when she stroked her hair twice in succession; she wanted me to come along though.

'Even a Jew's child is a child,' said Mother. 'Especially when he looks like a *goy* angel.'

The house was freshly whitewashed. Inside, I hardly recognised it. Multi-coloured wallpaper had replaced the white paint, while Jesus Christ and his cross had doubled in size since the year before. Then, only the parlour had had floorboards, but now every room had them – and not even ordinary floorboards. It was parquet flooring, like the Konráds', covered with Persian rugs. The new furniture shone. The parlour had been rechristened: it was now called 'the Lounge'. One-third of it was taken up by a grand piano. I wondered who had learnt to play the thing so fast. What difference would a few hectolitres of wine make to people like this?

Very little, it seemed. Mother soon called me in from the courtyard where I was 'playing'; we only stayed long enough for it not to look as if they were throwing us out. They didn't give us back our barrel; they took it as a sign of our 'respect'.

'If he loots, then maybe he doesn't kill,' Mother said sadly as we reached the street. I didn't reply. Why should a sergeant be any

325

better than the lieutenant general who had extorted fifty thousand from Father before sending him off to a punishment unit with the intention of silencing him for good?

We bumped into Virgula a couple of days later. He was holding another of his one-man parades in the sunny High Street. He was now a sergeant major, the highest non-commissioned rank; there was a third medal hanging from his chest, and his fingers, which had been bare the year before, were adorned with three gold signet rings.

Sadly, almost humbly, Mother stopped and greeted him.

'Good day to you, Sergeant.' Virgula almost choked at the demotion.

'Good day, Sergeant Major,' I said in a jolly, military voice.

'That's better,' remarked Virgula, standing up straighter. He didn't return our greeting.

Sergeant Major Virgula was a grotesque sight. His brand-new dress uniform, the medals on his chest and the rings on his fingers all suggested that he'd taken Moscow yesterday, single-handedly, while in reality he was no more than a piece of rubble, a brightly coloured stone left over from the shattered, 'strategically neutralised' Hungarian Second Army of the Don. Unwounded, he was a big, strong man, his cheeks ruddy from the Russian wind; while Mother stood before him broken, almost mourning. The front, where the German army continued its headlong flight, was as far away as a fairy tale. The famous East Wall along the line of the Dnieper had already crumbled. The Red Army had treated the prepared, impregnable fortifications with the utmost contempt, knocking them out as they went along, without even bothering to regroup.

The passers-by had slowed down. Some didn't even bother to hide their curiosity, stopping only three steps away to see where this strange encounter between the Stone-Thrower and the fragile Jewish woman might lead. Everyone greeted Virgula; the few who greeted Mother spoke very quietly. I didn't say hello to anyone who hadn't greeted us first, even though I was only a child. Mother looked round warily.

'Have you any news of my brother, Elek, Mr Sergeant Major, sir?' she drawled with the faint whine of a beggar-woman.

Virgula also glanced about him, but his was a look of great pride; his eyes said, 'Watch me give them what they deserve!' and he spoke more to the onlookers than to Mother: 'Am I a shepherd? Do I have to account for every lousy yid who gets lost?'

Loud laughter rose all around us. A few people called for quiet, not wanting to miss any of the fun. Mother's eyes were ice. It wasn't anger or humiliation that froze them: it was hatred, yet her reply was spontaneous: 'Shame on you, Béni Virgula! Here you are, parading through the High Street like a carnival-horse while Elek lies dead! Is that how you talk of men who die like heroes for the Fatherland?'

Virgula's face turned red as a poppy. He lost his head.

'Dead?' he bawled. 'That son of a Jewish bitch fled to the Russians! A traitor – like all the filthy Jews! The Russian attack had hardly begun when your hero of a brother ran off to join them! I nearly got him with my sub-machine gun!'

Mother laughed happily. Virgula stiffened as if he'd got cramp. He realised that my mother had tricked him into telling her the one thing she wanted to know. Five barrels of wine wouldn't have bought the information he'd just given away as a present, but he'd done it now, and all he could do was rage.

'. . . I'll find him yet – if it's the last thing I ever do!'

Mother didn't usually have a sense of humour, but joy inspired her: 'And what will you do when you find him? Throw an anvil at him?' The onlookers roared with laughter. 'The Big Jew' who could lift a hundred-and-twenty-kilo anvil by its ring was a village legend.

'I'll shoot the bastard!' foamed Virgula.

I refrained from pointing out that he probably wouldn't have time to aim, and that finding Elek certainly would be the last thing Virgula would ever do. Instead, I flattered him with awe: 'Please, Mr Sergeant Major, sir, what did you get your third medal for?'

Virgula nodded meaningfully, not to answer my question but to silence the laughter around us.

'For the Don campaign!' he announced.

I widened my eyes and looked even more awestruck. 'For sprinting or for long distance?' I asked.

And I was running away, my feet scarcely touching the ground. I needed to get a good start on him; his legs were longer than mine and there were a few teenage Christian thugs among the audience. A stone whistled past my nose. The next thudded into my head. I stopped and put my hand to where it had hit. My fingers came away wet. I turned to face my pursuers; there were three of them. Three years before, gangs of ten would fight on the way back from *heder*, but in those days hits were rare and the thrower always ran away. These thugs didn't stop. I picked up a stone and hurled it at them, but only managed to hit a

327

shoulder. They slowed down, and then the grown-ups stopped them. They went off cursing.

The doctor came and shaved a circle the size of a five-pengö piece on the side of my head. He stuck gauze on it, and when it came off I looked like a lopsided monk. I had to swallow bitter pills for the next few days, together with endless moanings and warnings from Mother. But both of us were over the moon; Dóra too. It was suddenly a hundred times more likely that Elek was alive. Dóra made me repeat, over and over again, Elek's last words to me: 'The Russian front is a big place. Maybe I'll find a gun there too.'

Back in Budapest I played the wounded soldier, bragging of my exploits as if I'd broken Virgula's skull – at least!

Absences from school had to be explained on special cards. 'Visiting relatives' wasn't considered good enough, and I was hauled over the coals by my form-mistress, who taught maths and had a squint.

An absence of such inordinate duration was inexcusable, particularly where the offender was myself, whose already far from satisfactory performance would surely be further inhibited by even an hour of the most legitimate and necessary absence, given that my observable lack of diligence not only gave cause for worry in itself, but brought into question the ultimately inescapable issue of my intelligence, and whether the aforementioned faculty could continue to be presumed adequate to the demands shortly to be made upon it, discounting, if that were possible, the almost complete lack of any apparent motivation, which . . .

The sentence went on and on. She was reluctant to draw her obvious conclusion, but while she searched for a full stop I classified her as a pompous idiot and decided not to bother telling her how important the visit to Oszu was. She put this down to stupidity, and softened a little, 'dispensing with the reprimand stipulated in the regulations, as the disciplinable offence occurred with parental consent if not instigation . . .'

Every day my mother told me off for making 'irresponsible remarks'. She backed each accusation with a list of my crimes.

'It's not on to ask an Arrow Cross man like Kovács whether Hitler was praying for victory when Cologne Cathedral was bombed. You're endangering all three of us. You can't stand on the balcony shouting about the Russians beating the hell out of the Krauts at Kursk—'

'Why not? Isn't it true? The Krauts admitted it themselves in the end.'

'And don't call them Krauts. Look at what happened when you

asked Virgula what he'd won his medal for! They nearly cracked your head open!'

'Cheap at the price,' I laughed.

'Well these come cheap too!' yelled Mother, smacking me in the face. I went on laughing.

One of our acquaintances was a woman doctor whom Mother had met through her work at the Jewish foundation. I had already been to her place once; she was an ugly, kind, fat old lady called Dr Sarolta Schultz. We were meant to be going to see her again but for some odd reason Mother kept postponing the visit. When we finally set off, Dávid came too although even Mother hadn't been able to find anything wrong with him. Mother seemed almost humble when she asked me to listen to what Aunty Sarolta had to say; maybe her words would actually get through my thick skull and make me realise that what was going on around us wasn't a game.

We sat in a large waiting room; there was no one there but the three of us. At last, Aunty Sarolta emerged from her surgery, but instead of calling me in she shut the door behind her – hardly a good start to a medical examination. Mother had been moaning so much about my colour, my apathy, my appetite and my bump on the head that I expected to be tied down and bled.

'Is there anything wrong with you?' she asked me lightly.

'No.'

She opened the door of her surgery. Soaking the dressing on my head with wet cotton wool, she removed it and put on a new one.

'It's not deep. You were lucky.' She led me back to the waiting room. 'Do you eat enough?'

'Enough for me. Not enough for Mother.'

'What do you want to be when you grow up?'

'A footballer.'

'Footballers have to eat. Do many of the kids at your school play football?'

'Only a few. And they're hopeless. I go to the Jewish grammar school. Have you ever noticed how useless Jews are at football? The rich ones anyway. They're all rich at my school, and soft as butter.'

'Do you think that antisemitism is the fault of rich Jews?' asked Aunty Sarolta.

'No,' I replied. 'That's what the antisemites say.'

'Then who does cause it?' she asked severely.

'The Christians.' That made her smile. She asked me to open

329

my mouth and had a look inside, then examined my eyes with a pocket torch.

'Slightly anaemic,' she remarked to Mother. 'He must eat well. Otherwise he's fine.'

This was too much for Mother.

'He never opens his books!' she wailed.

'Bored with school?' asked Aunty Sarolta calmly.

'Bored stiff.'

'He's got plenty of time to become a good pupil,' she said soothingly to my scandalised mother.

'But he'll fail! He's cheeky to the teachers!' Mother accused, calling upon this half-stranger to be my judge.

Aunty Sarolta turned to me. 'Are you frightened of your teachers?'

'No way!'

'So why do you have to be cheeky?'

'I'm not. It's just that they take school far too seriously.' The doctor managed not to laugh, but asked me conspiratorially whether I was going to fail.

'Not if you pay me to!' I replied. 'Do the whole year all over again? It's boring enough the first time round!'

She asked me to sit down.

'Your mother is worried about your big mouth. Did you know that even Christians get gaoled for making anti-German remarks and for defaming the army?'

'They can't gaol children!' I announced triumphantly.

'They can gaol their mothers!' interrupted mine. I wanted to reply but Aunty Sarolta got there first.

'That's quite true: they can – and have – put the parents in gaol. Doesn't your mother have enough to worry about already? Just for her sake, shut up. Only speak your mind among friends. Don't let her worry herself to death.' The doctor looked at me. She didn't seem to want to extract a promise from me; she wished to see whether I had been listening.

Then, addressing Dávid as well as me, she said, 'What you are about to hear now, you will tell no one. Not even your best friend.' But instead of coming close to us and whispering some grand secret, she looked us over one last time as if wondering whether she could trust us. I nodded to her. I would be silent as the grave. She nodded too, then gestured to us to wait a minute, turned round, and left the room. She obviously intended to show us something rather than tell us.

330

She returned with a grey, emaciated man in a dressing-gown, who stopped uncertainly in the doorway. He glanced at us, alarmed, then looked at Aunty Sarolta who said something to him in German. The man stepped forward.

'Good day,' he said with a strong accent.

'This gentleman is Polish,' explained Aunty Sarolta. 'He is a refugee. Jewish. He is staying with me because he is in need of constant care. You mustn't mention even this much to anyone, as his papers are not in order. If they find him, he will be deported from Hungary and killed.'

I had never been so honoured. Completely alert, not just in my head, but in my whole body. I felt as if my life depended on saving a penalty shot that would cannon towards me in the next few seconds.

The man took another step forward. He was pale, his few movements uncertain, his eyes hollow. Under the cheap, thin dressing-gown he wore pyjamas. When he spoke at last, Aunty Sarolta translated quietly, colourlessly, as if interpreting the man's voice as well as his words.

'The Polish Jews have been exterminated . . . First they put us into ghettos . . . Outside the towns . . . The SS machine-gunned them in groups . . . Then . . . the railway trucks . . . Lemberg . . . Krakow . . . they lied . . . work, hard labour . . . the sick, the old people from rest-homes . . . children from orphanages . . . In trucks . . . Treblinka . . . he said that they . . . machine guns, starving to death . . . Warsaw rising . . . the ghetto, rubble . . . machine guns . . . trucks . . . Treblinka . . . Lemberg . . . Krakow . . . Vilna . . . Nobody ever came back . . . An SS major . . . I gave him twenty thousand dollars . . .'

It was as if the man were a vision, his words a hallucination.

'. . . Trust no one . . . Don't trust the Jewish officials – not for a minute . . . Trust very few of the other Jews . . . Don't even trust God too much . . .'

He looked at Aunty Sarolta, who nodded. The Pole bowed his head. After a few seconds I looked suspiciously at my mother. Had she heard too? She was standing there, pale and frozen, as if she were still listening. Dávid's forehead was bunched up, his eyes almost shut, as though he were trying to work out some impossibly difficult mathematical puzzle.

20: The Delights of History

Like caterwauling in the night, Latin words cut through the grey air of the classroom. *Non scolae sed vitae discimus* – 'we are studying not for exams, but for life'. These were the first words of wisdom that we had to learn by heart. The next gem was 'History delights', and then the class went into action against the fortresses of the ablatives and genitives. Test followed test; the zeroes flew around us like the artillery shells on the Eastern Front, where the Russians had already taken Kiev and were threatening to cut off the remaining German forces in the Crimea. Ever since I could remember, I had dreamt of the magic cloak in *A Thousand and One Nights*, the cloak that made its wearer invisible. But now, even more, I wanted a cloak of my own magic, a cloak that would protect me from shell and rocket, bomb and bullet, a cloak that no one could even approach without knowing the password. Plenty of the zeroes were aimed at me, but for once my magic cloak was real, and the innumerable noughts ricocheted off my body without leaving a scratch. I looked pityingly at the teacher as my stupidity drove him into deeper and deeper despair. Of course no teacher on earth could have grasped the truth. To me, any foreign language, whether Latin or Hebrew, was really German. Every strange word was a murderer bragging in the dark, and the sound of each syllable was a prophet of death, like the noise of the air-raid sirens or the flesh-tearing scream of a falling bomb.

In all my dreams, the sick, pale Polish man watched me from the corner of a doorless, windowless room. He watched me as I went through the day. Sometimes the room would be in ruins, and the pale man would lean against the half-blasted classroom wall while

332

indiscernible human shapes lay strewn amongst the rubble. They were Polish Jews. When the Pole caught my eye in class, the teacher's moving lips would suddenly be dumb and all the images around me flickered and blurred like old, faded films. Soon I could make this happen by clenching my teeth. Suddenly I would be deaf, caught in a silent movie. Sometimes I would watch another boy until the colour of his face or clothes became bright or pale. That told me whether he would be alive in a year's time. I shivered. My teeth chattered. But in the meantime I was master of life and death.

Many of the pavements in Pest were edged with narrow strips of concrete. They were about two and a half metres long, just less than three of my normal steps. When I was little I carefully used to avoid treading on any of the joins; sometimes I stepped on them deliberately, reversing the rules. But now the game was resurrected in an uncontrollable form. I had no power over it. I had to take four paces between each join: one for Mother, one for Dávid, one for myself, and one either for Father or for Elek. When I divided the distance into five steps my walk became a deformed shuffle, and Dávid noticed. I began walking normally again, terrified that the dark powers would punish me. My private demon's strictest law was that I mustn't tell anyone what I was doing. I made pacts with the shadows that flew about my head, bargaining for lives. But the power of these shadows declined with each life under their protection; twenty were only half as well guarded as ten.

Our history teacher was a small, broad-shouldered, slow-moving man of forty with a wide face and a flat nose. Before joining the school he had been in either Hell, the SS, or a mental asylum. The other teachers were cunning; they praised everyone – except me, of course – and told us that we were the best first year for a long time. They took off their ties, sat on our desks. When they wanted us to be quiet they were cheerful and friendly, but the history teacher was another story. He would stop suddenly, puff out his chest and turn a deep red. Then he'd pick on a child before deciding what his victim was supposed to have done wrong. He spoke slowly, dragging out each syllable: 'Sooo . . . you arre not iiintereeested in whaaat I am saaaaaying.' Even his insults took him a while: 'Aaanimaal, piiig, blockkk-heead, raat-eyyyed . . .' His favourite game was catching the daydreamers or, rather, their ears: 'Arre you haard of heeeearing? I shaall cuure you,' he would say, scrumpling up the child's ear and twisting it while he carried on with the lesson. When the child screamed the teacher would tell him off: 'First of aaall he doesn't liiisten, and now he won't let me speeak.' Most of the other kids would laugh at the joke, hoping that their complicity would protect them.

There were probably only two people in the whole class who were never touched: Aaron Kohn and myself. He watched me more often than anyone else, and for longer periods, and no one spent more time daydreaming than I did, but when I felt his gaze upon me my heart beat fast and overcame my fear. I carried on gaping at the empty air, knowing that if he touched me I would tear his spectacles off his nose and break them. In the end he always picked on someone else. For him, History was just a pile of dates and facts, none of which had ever been important. Everything had happened a long time ago – if it had happened at all. My old teacher, Torma, had made me believe that King Mátyás had died only yesterday. This man, who had done labour service on the Eastern Front, hardly seemed real himself. I kept my answers as short as possible, but something made him uneasy and he always made me sit down as quickly as he could.

The building was too small for the whole school, so the odd and even years took it in turns to have lessons in the afternoon rather than the morning. The timetable changed each week. Luckily Dávid and I walked to and from school together, as the first and third years had classes at the same time.

One lunchtime my serious, sensible brother made a sudden announcement: 'After the war we'll hang all the Christians.'

'But most of the English are Christians,' I objected, playing devil's advocate for once. Dávid didn't seem to think this a problem.

'When they see what the Christians have been doing in Germany, Poland and Slovakia, they'll convert. So will the Americans. The Russians don't believe in God either way, so they'll hang the Christians for being Hitlerites.'

'Torma isn't a Hitlerite!' I protested.

'Well then, he can convert too,' said Dávid impartially.

We never mentioned the pale Polish man, even between ourselves. Dávid only broke the rule once.

'Why did he tell us not to trust many of the Jews?' he asked.

'He was telling us not to trust the rich ones,' I guessed.

'But he was rich himself,' argued Dávid. 'He gave the SS officer twenty thousand dollars to save his life. I've never even heard of anyone who had that kind of money.'

Ours was not the only timetable to change from week to week.

Mother's workload increased steadily, and she spent less and less time at home. Dávid usually made us lunch. He learnt how to cook potato soup, with sausage in it if we were lucky; he made caraway-seed soup and minestrone, omelettes and potato pancakes. His speciality was French toast. He was very strict about how much I ate.

'You can't be full yet!' he said when I had finished eating what he'd given me. Producing something else, he'd make me eat half of it, 'just to be fair'.

Mother was more direct. 'Eat while you can,' she urged me.

Since our visit to Doctor Sarolta, Dávid hadn't hit me once. Not that it made much difference. He kept on trying to persuade me to do my homework with him. It was mainly Latin, but first-year Latin was child's play to a third-year. Dávid hardly looked at his own books any more, and he started getting 'B' minuses and even 'C's in maths, which used to be his best subject.

We still didn't have a *Chanukah* candelabrum. We lit two 'Friday candles' on each evening of *Chanukah*, since we had only two candlesticks and were too broke to burn more than two candles at once. We also lit a couple on Christmas Eve, but that was the extent of our celebrations. There were no presents, but it was better that way. When I looked into the flames I thought of Aunty Felice.

Gyula, who was living with 'some whore', popped in for a few minutes. The fact that he didn't stay for the rest of the evening was my only Christmas present.

One day I waited for Mik Lang outside the Jewish secondary modern. It was the second time I had seen him since my father's call-up. I boasted about my father beating up the guard and being sent to the top punishment camp under the supervision of the Death's Head SS. Mik was impressed but after a moment's thought he frowned.

'So do we have to pay you back the five hundred pengös?'

'Don't be silly. It wasn't his money in the first place: he milked a few rich Jews for it.'

Mik was helping out in a poultry shop. He had to go there straight from school. The owner was a fat, nasty-looking man who eyed me suspiciously and seemed to be counting his geese and chickens every five minutes in case one of them flew away.

We chatted while Mik put hundreds of eggs into boxes. The boss served a few early-afternoon customers, most of whom had ration tickets. At one point he withdrew into a corner to talk to a customer. He looked worried, but we soon discovered that he was talking big business – three black geese. While they were talking Mik smuggled four eggs into my pockets one by one. From then on I had to move as if I were fragile as an egg myself. Promising to come back soon, I sneaked out of the shop.

A foul, muddy March made the spring seem like autumn. Heading for school one lunchtime, I found that my only pair of shoes were soaked before we'd got halfway. Dávid and I agreed that we couldn't go to the cinema instead, as we were bunking off together rather too often, and sooner or later some bright teacher was going to notice that our tummy-, ear-, tooth- and head-aches always occurred at the same time, as if we were Siamese twins. We needed a better excuse than usual.

'I know! Let's go to school!' I exclaimed triumphantly.

Dávid looked at me, irritated. He hadn't grasped the full brilliance of my idea. 'After the first or second lesson,' I explained, 'I shall be taken very ill.'

Dávid looked sour. 'What's in it for me?'

'I'll be so ill, and I mean ILL,' I boasted, 'that you'll have to take me home. I'll have stomach cramps. Or worse.'

The classroom lights had to be switched on because of the foggy weather. There were no shutters or blinds on the windows, and one of the hairbrush brigade claimed that the mixture of daylight and electric light would damage our eyes. Our form-mistress switched the lights off. This proved that there wasn't any daylight anyway, so she switched them on again. The two lightbulbs pierced the air with ragged holes. The obscurity outside the window filled the room with damp. For days I hadn't had to clench my teeth to make myself deaf: the classroom had become a silent movie. The blackboard melted into its own shadow; the lightbulbs dangled from twisted wires. I was in such a bad mood that I scarcely had to lie. I stood up.

'I feel awful,' I said, sitting down again as the teacher turned away from the blackboard and faced the class. I slumped at my desk and she came towards me. At first, when she asked me what was wrong I just shook my head as if speaking were an effort.

'My stomach . . . cramps . . .' I mumbled at last. My faking was subtly natural; everyone could see that I was being terribly brave.

My imaginary illness worked in the same way as my superstitions: the air was filled with wicked devils wrapped in the same damp obscurity. They would soon descend mercilessly on the contented smiles around me, but by tiptoeing along the edge of the pavement

336

to avoid the joins, by touching the doorposts as I entered a room, I appeased the demons by making my fear into something real. My pretence of pain created real pain in my stomach, and within seconds I had completely forgotten that I was acting.

They took my temperature in the waiting room outside the Head's office. As every truant knows, the mercury moves up .2° with each flick delivered to the end of the thermometer. Unfortunately the teacher appointed as my nurse decided to double-check, and took my temperature a second time.

I wasn't worried about being found out. They could do what they liked. What was at stake was the belief that I could control my secret, interior demons. The teacher wouldn't take his eyes off me, so I couldn't touch the thermometer. The room grew dark. My forehead burned.

The thermometer read 38.5° C. I thanked God.

Dávid was called out of class. He put on a very serious, anxious expression, but he couldn't keep it up for long and I had to groan to attract their attention. Dávid was a lousy actor. Bent double, I went off down the corridor beside him, but didn't straighten up again, even when we'd reached the street.

'OK, you can stop now,' Dávid said after about fifty metres. I wasn't sure that I could stop. Perhaps I didn't want to. I walked on, still stooping and clutching my stomach.

Mother called Aunty Sarolta. I told her about the cramps, which were perfectly real by that stage, but I couldn't work out precisely what my symptoms ought to be because I hadn't yet decided on a specific illness. I answered Aunty Sarolta's questions, but made my replies as confusing as possible as I didn't want a doctor to give the correct diagnosis. They took my temperature again, and although I could have flicked the end of it quite easily I didn't bother. The illness had already done its job; I just hoped that Aunty Sarolta wouldn't ask much money for coming out on call.

This time my temperature was 40.2°.

'The thermometer's bust,' I assured them.

'How do you know?' asked Aunty Sarolta suspiciously.

'I don't feel as bad as that! It's 37.5° at the most.' Aunty Sarolta took another thermometer out of her bag: 40.2°.

'He'll have to be examined in hospital. It might be typhoid. Give him light food to eat – stewed apples, sponge biscuits – and I'll organise a hospital bed for him.'

The next day I was taken into the children's ward at the Jewish Hospital. The food was terrible, and I was strongly tempted to make a speedy recovery. At the same time I was rather proud of being able to fool all the doctors and nurses who were buzzing around me. I didn't even have to touch the thermometer. In the end I began to suspect that I might actually be ill. I felt no real pain. My skin was hot and my head buzzed a little, but that was because I'd been working at it so hard.

The social life in the ward was great. We played marbles and chess, and some of the kids knew how to play cards, but the best conversations took place in the evenings when the doctors, nurses, cleaning ladies and visitors had stopped bothering us. That was the time for stories and jokes.

The night nurse was a gigantic blonde; we couldn't have had better luck as she clearly suffered from sleeping sickness. Before turning off the lights, she would always emphasize the importance of a good night's sleep and ask us not to be noisy. A few minutes' silence would follow her departure, but it was an expectant silence. The first person to break it carried a great responsibility, and two of us competed for the honour every night. Having tested several gambits, we established a ritual after a few days. I would always open the proceedings with a deep, black, long-drawn-out wail: 'Whe-e-ere is my wo-o-oden leg?' The whole ward would explode with laughter, and only I knew that my great line was not my own invention.

My rival's opening went deeper. No one laughed at it, so the effect was harder to gauge, but it was undeniably more mysterious than mine. The boy himself was sixteen, and a little unhinged. Sometimes he talked nonsense; his father had been beaten to death by his guards in the Ukraine. His contribution was to tell part of an unknown, unfathomable story, a single sentence repeated over and over again: 'Then sir, the sergeant – that animal – hit the horse so hard that it bolted . . .'

Fear gripped us, and ghosts began to walk. One or other of us would wrap himself up in a sheet and roam among the beds, doubling the effect of the stories. One of the spookiest was the tale of the Ghost Army:

'A long time ago – more than two years – the Germans broke through and marched on Moscow. One of the regiments in the vanguard of the army took up position in front of Moscow. There was nothing to stop them: the way to the Kremlin was clear and the attack was planned

338

for the following morning. The German soldiers went to sleep.

'At dawn, the attack failed to materialise. The German HQ were worried; they called the regiment by field telephone and by radio but couldn't raise a reply. Reconnaissance planes were sent out, but there was no movement. Contact had been completely lost. They sent out a platoon. Three, five, eight hours passed, but the German HQ heard nothing. It was as if the earth had swallowed up both regiment and platoon.

'Meanwhile, the Russians deployed their reserves. They waited and waited for the German attack, but as it never came, they charged. Not a shot was fired against them. They slowed down, fearing an ambush, and moved cautiously forward until they reached the German positions. Two thousand three hundred German soldiers lay dead in the snow. Their throats had been cut . . .

'The Russians themselves didn't understand what had happened. But three nights later the mystery was solved. The night before the great Russian offensive, thousands upon thousands of German soldiers had the same dream.

'Soldiers with swords and muskets appeared before them in ancient uniforms. They were Napoleon's Imperial Guard. They had fallen in Russia, and had wandered as ghosts for a century and a half. Having invaded the lands of a peaceful foreign people, their souls would never be freed until they had paid for their crime. It was they who had cut the throats of the sleeping German soldiers.

'The rest of the German army panicked of course, just at the moment when the Russian attack fell upon them like a flood. As they ran through the din of shells and machine gun fire, they could hear behind them the rattle of bones. The skeletons of the Imperial Guard could only return to France in the footsteps of the German army.'

One morning, nobody woke us. This was a blessing because the boredom usually began at six o'clock sharp, but breakfast was late too, and the doctors whipped through their ward round in two minutes flat. We assumed it was Sunday-morning idleness, and thought nothing of it.

Then my mother dashed into the ward, followed closely by Gyula. Visiting time was hours away, and Mother was carrying my outdoor clothes and my shoes. She threw them at me.

'Get dressed!' she ordered. 'You're coming home!'

At first, I thought that they must have discovered I was faking,

and that Gyula had come along because I was so 'impossible'. But
I had been running a temperature the evening before, so I made up
my mind to deny any accusations firmly and calmly.

Mother urged me to hurry up. She didn't say why.

'I'll tell you later,' she whispered. 'I promised not to frighten
anyone here.'

'Is the hospital on fire?' I asked good-temperedly, but I didn't
hurry. I wasn't going to be jerked around on strings like a puppet.

The other kids had gathered around my bed.

'Are you going home?' They tried to cash in on my sympathy
for their extended sentences by offering bad swaps of marbles and
buttons. Once I was dressed, Mother rushed out of the ward so fast
I could hardly keep up with her.

Taxis were lining up outside the hospital; we jumped into the
nearest one.

'The Germans invaded Hungary last night,' said Mother, and
immediately I understood. The rounding-up of the Jews could easily
have started at the hospital. She had brought Gyula with her because
a retired sergeant major in the military police might just be able to do
something in case of trouble.

Mother was already on the run. She opened the door before the
taxi had stopped, banging the pavement. Gyula gave the driver an
extra twenty pengős and we pounded upstairs to the flat. Hurriedly,
Mother made my bed.

'Get in. I'll call Aunty Sarolta.'

'Don't. I'm not ill,' I told her. She must have been beside
herself because she didn't insist.

It started to rain, then stopped. The sun came out at intervals.
I hadn't spotted a single German soldier on the way back from the
hospital. The wireless didn't mention the invasion at all; the whole
thing might just be a scare. Apparently the information had come
from the BBC, which sounded even more ridiculous: if I couldn't
see any Germans in the street, then how could London? I announced
that I'd go and have a look round the town. Mother was speechless.
In the end Gyula went off to 'look around' on his own. Mother tried
a few more times to make me go to bed, then gave up. Unconvinced,
I peeped out over the balcony occasionally, but it was a waste of time.
There were no helmeted soldiers running around the courtyard, pulling
the Jews out of their flats. I went over to Pali's place to listen to the
radio but all we could hear was a load of military music. Pali cried

because his father wanted him to go and live with his gypsy mother in some bed-sit in the suburbs: there wouldn't be enough room for all his toys. Soon I was sent home. 'At times like this, a child's place is with his family . . .'

Mother was standing on the balcony looking down at the courtyard. She was waiting to see who would arrive first: Gyula or the German soldiers. She glared at me, as if I were responsible for Gyula's late return: if I hadn't chased him away he would have treated us as his family and saved our lives.

I was wondering whether the Germans would shoot us straight away, in the courtyard, or take us off to some central killing-ground first. I didn't believe a word of what I was thinking; it was the quietest Sunday in the world.

There were three staircases in the building but only one exit. Dávid said reassuringly that this problem wasn't worth worrying about as the Germans were perfectly capable of blocking off two exits. We watched each other, wondering whether it was worth taking the whole thing seriously. Dávid and I agreed that there was probably a big troop transport heading for the southern section of the Russian front and that the grown-ups were just panicking as usual. But it wasn't only Gyula and Mother who believed the rumours: the taxi-driver and Pali's family were convinced that the Germans had occupied the country. Purely out of a sense of duty I went to reconnoitre the coal-cellars in case the Germans invaded the building and we had to find an escape route. But as soon as I reached the balcony I heard words of command echo up from the courtyard.

The *goy* kids were playing soldiers. They were marching up and down under the command of Pista Rácz.

'Left-Right-Left-Right!' he was shouting, obviously confused as to which was which. And then my heart stopped as I realised that Pista was wearing a swastika armband. The Germans really had invaded Hungary.

I would have to pass the 'parade' to reach Laci Mester's flat. Laci was the person most likely to know which coal-cellars opened on to the street. But Pista Rácz wasn't going to let me go by without making some kind of comment, and in the event of a confrontation he'd be bound to call a real German soldier in off the street. I would have to wait until they left the courtyard.

The bells of the Basilica began to ring. On Sundays they used to ring for ages and you had to be a vicar to know what they meant. But now

341

they seemed to be saying: 'Self-de-fence . . . White-arm-bands . . . Self-de-fence . . . White-arm-bands . . .' Perhaps it was Pista's swastika that had put this into my head, and I remembered how Cardinal Justinian Serédi, the Catholic Primate, had urged the authorities to allow converted Jewish labour men to wear white armbands instead of yellow ones. It reminded me too of an old speech of his:

'Everyone agrees that the legitimate self-defence of our nation requires the limitation of Jewish activity in all areas of public and economic life.'

The Protestant bishop, László Ravasz, had made a similar remark: 'I cannot reject the Jewish laws on principle.'

I suddenly realised that Mother was standing beside me.

'Don't be scared,' she said. 'We only have to find somewhere to hide; we've enough money to last us several weeks.' I knew this was a reassuring white lie. It was the nineteenth of the month and by the thirtieth Mother usually had to turn her handbag inside out to find enough change for a bottle of milk. I gave her an irritated glance, but she nodded. 'Jewellery: my ring and my earrings.'

Mother looked enviously across the courtyard at the opera-singer's mother, whose moonlike hairdo had just appeared above the balcony railings. Laci Mester had told us that according to her Domicile Registration Form she was a Catholic. At Christmas she had kept the carol-singers in front of her door for a quarter of an hour, but even Pöci and Kaci knew the joke about her. We called her the Roman Israelite. That afternoon she had a prayer book in her hand and her maid was following her with a bulging shopping bag. They went down to the caretaker's flat, but when they reached the door the woman took the shopping bag from the maid and went in to see the caretaker alone.

On the second-floor balcony the girl known throughout the building as 'the whore' lounged against the railings in her dressing-gown. Men visited her regularly, but she was clearly on the lookout for a German officer. Perhaps a sergeant might do.

The silver-haired lady re-emerged from the caretaker's flat, her shopping bag empty.

The children were still marching up and down the courtyard, and when seven-year-old Kaci tried to walk normally instead of goose-stepping he was threatened with a kick up the bum from Rácz for high treason.

The whore gave up and went inside. Hardly had she disappeared when the retired army captain emerged from the next door along, wearing twenty medals instead of his usual two. The sound of orders issuing from the courtyard made him turn his head sharply, and he leant over the railings.

'Squad – HALT!' he shouted. 'Atten . . . SHUN!' The children stopped, alarmed, and looked up. 'Section Commander, report immediately,' continued the captain, and Pista Rácz charged upstairs. It would have been a good moment for me to run down another staircase and go and see the Mesters about the coal-cellars, but I stayed put, curious to see what the retired officer wanted from Rácz.

Pista stopped in front of the old soldier and saluted him smartly.

'You little shit!' shouted the captain. He tore the swastika from Rácz's arm and threw it into the courtyard. Then he smacked him across the face. 'Get out of my sight!' he bellowed. 'Can't you hear? *Abtreten!*'

Rácz ran off, whimpering. The kids in the courtyard laughed. When he reached the bottom of the staircase where the old captain couldn't see him, he shook his fist. Then he went over to where his armband lay on the ground. Glancing up at the balcony he saw the old soldier still watching him, so he stuffed the armband in his pocket and shambled back to his flat, avoiding the eyes of his disbanded army.

Around four in the afternoon we suddenly realised that we had forgotten to have lunch. Mother didn't feel like cooking, even though it was Sunday; she made a pot of tea and put some cheese on the table. Every five minutes we peeped over the balcony to see if Gyula had come back. The shadow of the rooftop moved slowly up the courtyard wall, cutting off the light like a knife.

An unexpected visitor emerged suddenly from the staircase, a man from Oszu who had moved to Budapest just before I went to live with my grandfather. Around thirty-five years old, he had only visited us once before, probably out of courtesy. He had originally been a teacher, but had then become a journalist and had written a book about peasant poverty. His name was János Varga.

'I was passing by,' he explained. 'I thought I'd drop in and say hello. I do hope I'm not disturbing you.'

Mother showed him into the big room.

'Are you sure I'm not in your way?' he asked apologetically. His careful politeness betrayed his peasant origins. His education had been paid for by the Church.

343

'I was watching from the balcony to see if our German visitors had arrived,' said Mother, trying to smile.

'Not yet, not here,' replied our guest. He smiled sourly. 'They've a few personal calls to make first. I saw a few of the Gestapo's yellow "Pol" cars . . .'

He fell silent. Mother waited patiently.

'I've no right to be here!' he said, standing up suddenly. 'They've already taken two of the other writers on the newspaper – I'm on the run from them myself. They took over the building while I was out, but the doorman's daughter sneaked out for a breath of fresh air and managed to warn me. Really – I was just passing – I don't have your address written down anywhere – they won't look for me here.'

Mother turned pale, then nodded. 'Please stay.'

Gyula arrived. His face was as taut as the skin of a drum.

'Without firing a single shot!' he hissed furiously. 'They have occupied the entire country without firing a shot! The famous nation of Rákóczy!'

'I know of one man who waited for them with a revolver in his hand,' János Varga said quietly. 'Hardly enough to save our national honour, but he had spoken out against the war and the Jewish laws from the start. It was Bajcsy-Zsilinszky. The Gestapo came round to his place at dawn. He fired at them; no one knows if he's still alive.'

'He would have been Prime Minister if he'd survived the war,' Gyula sighed.

'This nation of cowards won't be needing a Prime Minister,' murmured Varga. 'There won't be a Hungary after the war. "Cowards have no country," as Hungarians used to say.'

Gyula had been all round the centre of the town. There were German tanks in the streets near the Castle and German soldiers at the railway stations. Helped by Hungarian policemen, they were asking for people's documents and rounding up any travellers who looked Jewish.

Varga stood up.

'You've enough worries without me,' he began, but Mother made him sit down.

'Stay here. At least until it's dark.'

Gyula's head fell forward. He was thinking. Then he started digging in his pockets and one by one produced his documents. János Varga's face froze.

'You were in the military police . . .'

344

'Better than being a peasant all my life!' laughed Gyula. Varga relaxed.

'That's why I became a teacher and then a journalist,' he replied. They both laughed. 'A pro-Zsilinszky policeman! Who'd have thought it?'

Jealously, Varga examined Gyula's papers.

'These are worth more than a hundred thousand pengös.'

'I could lose them for a couple of days if you like,' offered Gyula. 'But we don't look at all alike. You'll have to make do with these.' Gyula handed over a couple of documents that didn't carry photographs, and Varga took a stamped, blank season ticket out of his pocket. He had bought it in a hurry earlier in the day. To avoid having his handwriting recognised, he asked Mother to fill in the form. Gyula offered to put him up for a night or two, and Varga accepted gratefully. They left separately in case they were stopped in the street.

The next morning, Mother woke me with some good news. 'You're not going to school,' she announced.

'What about me?' asked Dávid enviously.

'You're not going either.'

Dávid looked worried. He had recently failed in both Latin and German, while I had only failed in Latin, as German wasn't taught in the first year.

'Why aren't we going to school?' he demanded. Missing lessons made him feel guilty. Mother explained that a few hundred ready-assembled Jewish kids presented too tempting a target for the Germans. Her sudden firmness and clear, calm tone were a complete contrast to her nervous, hesitant nature.

'So we won't go tomorrow either?' said Dávid suspiciously.

'No.'

'When will we go, then?' It seemed too good to be true.

'When the war's over. Doctor Sarolta will certify that you're both ill.'

'Missing school is OK for Józska,' muttered Dávid, then fell silent. He was struggling with his conscience.

Soon afterwards Aunty Sarolta came round and gave me a long examination. 'I don't know what was wrong with this boy,' she stated, 'but there's nothing wrong with him now.'

I was filled with the clear spring air. The blue sky descended and the trees seemed light as trees in a picture. I stalked about more like a tiger on the prowl than a hunted beast. How many times had I run along the street, leaving my goal as I dribbled the length of the field to score the winner for Hungary against the Rest of the World? And now, all those imaginary games were paying off. The big match was about to begin, and I was ready for it, alert and calm.

A new government was formed. Most newspapers, political parties and other organisations were banned, although few of these had uttered an independent thought in several years. Thousands of people were taken into custody. Jews were arrested at railway stations by the Gestapo and by Hungarian policemen. The tram-stop by the Jewish cemetery on Kerepesi Avenue was raided regularly, and those visiting the graves were rounded up and taken in lorries to the internment camps. The *numerus clausus*, a restriction on the number of Jewish lawyers, journalists and doctors in any given organisation, was replaced by the *numerus nullus*. This required the sacking of those who had even one Jewish grandparent. Ten days after the German invasion it was decreed that 'All Jewish persons over and above six years of age, irrespective of sex, shall henceforth outside their domicile be bound to wear on the left breast of the exterior garment a canary-yellow six-pointed star of woven material ten centimetres in diameter . . . '. They allowed six days for people to make the stars, but two days before we had to start wearing them we received a heart-warming message of support from the United States, delivered in style by a thousand aeroplanes.

Mother was at work at the time. I was in the courtyard practising my headers with the smaller kids when the sirens began to scream. We had rather lost interest in air-raids, as the last ten had hardly dropped more than a hundred bombs between them. On this occasion Dávid didn't even bother to take our suitcase down to the cellar, he only brought the food-basket. Mrs Mester shouted at us to stay in the cellar but most of us kids escaped into the courtyard. Maybe this time we'd be lucky enough to see a couple of aeroplanes.

We heard the thumping of the ack-ack guns, then listened carefully to catch a far-away murmur, unsure whether our ears were humming or whether a fly was buzzing nearby. A few seconds later, aeroplanes began flying over the building in groups of three and five. They were smaller than the planes in the windows of toyshops, and little balls of white fluff exploded beneath them. We only knew they were American because someone had heard the warning on the radio, but I forced my eyes to see the markings on the wings.

'I can see the stars!' I lied. The others laughed at me.

346

We heard a huge explosion. This time it was the real thing. We all went down on our stomachs, and in the next five seconds another dozen explosions turned the air to thunder. I had been laughed at earlier: now I took credit for the explosions. Even Pista Rácz held me responsible. When I stood up proudly, invulnerable to American bombs, he whined fearfully: 'It's all because of the stinking yids!'

Dávid jumped up and pulled me down on to the flagstones before answering.

'Naturally. It was the Jews who declared war on the Americans in '41 . . .'

Like Rácz, the newspapers blamed this first big air-raid on American solidarity with the 'dirty Jews'. The next day, yellow stars became compulsory.

'Terrorist Bombers!' 'Gangsters of the Air!' screamed the newspapers. Their pages were filled with pictures of black American pilots with captions saying 'Gorilla Warfare' and 'Down from the Trees'.

So the five-branched star of America appeared in the newspapers on the same day as King David's star appeared on the Jews. That starry morning, Mother was unrecognisable. Normally happy to quarrel for a quarter of an hour over a broken cup, she pressed a ten-pengő note into my hand and told me to go and buy some cakes.

'Shall I spend the lot?' I asked greedily.

'Spend eight,' said Mother, economising out of habit. 'Off you go, don't be scared.'

Mother's morale had gone up over the last few days. She had decided that the fascist scum were a noisy but insignificant minority, and the Hungarians were a 'decent Christian nation' who would behave as the Danes had behaved. The Danish king, Christian X, had been the first onto the street wearing a yellow star, and every one of his countrymen had followed his example. In Denmark they would have spat on people who didn't wear the star. Mother thought there would be five times as many stars on the streets as there were Jews in Budapest.

I had hardly taken two steps into the street when a couple of strangers took me to task.

'How dare he walk in the same street as us!' shrilled an indignant, well-dressed lady.

'Clear off!' added a well-dressed gentleman. His chivalry impressed the lady, they looked at each other and nodded politely. I laughed in their faces, and for a second I envied Pöci, who could have spat in their eyes with perfect accuracy. But I suddenly remembered old Mr

347

Berkovics, who had pulled up his caftan and walked around the spitting Christian child as if the boy had been a pile of excrement.

I found the owner of the small pâtisserie deep in conversation with the lame army captain from the second floor. When I walked in they both fell silent. The woman in the white apron gave me a look of pity. The captain looked astonished.

'You?' he asked, pointing to my yellow star. 'How many of your grandparents are Jewish?' Without waiting for an answer he turned back to the woman.

'You see? Exactly what I was saying!' He shook his head, non-plussed.

I wondered what to say. If I told him that only one or two of my grandparents were Jewish I'd be able to count on the captain's help if the Germans invaded the building. His remark betrayed the fact that, like Cardinal Serédi, he only had sympathy for the Roman Israelites.

'Four,' I said.

'Four?' replied the captain, speechless.

'Where is your cellar, sir?' I demanded.

'Why do you want to know that?' he asked uncomprehendingly.

'I wondered, sir, if you might lend me the key so that I can hide there with my mother and brother if the Germans arrive. We'd be able to escape into the street or the sewers if necessary.'

'Don't you need my pickaxe too?' said the captain, trying hard not to take my request seriously.

'That would be really kind of you, sir,' I told him. He sighed. Then, slowly, he nodded, shivering.

'Sad times,' he said at last. 'Sad times.'

The pâtisserie owner gave me two extra cream cakes.

At the beginning of April teaching stopped in all Hungarian schools because the front was approaching Rumania. On the day the yellow stars were introduced, Eastern Hungary was declared a 'war zone'.

'It took them two years to exterminate the Polish Jews,' said Dávid during one of his morale-boosting drives. 'In two years' time there won't be any Germans left in Germany.'

'Where will they be?'

'Pushing up the daisies, mostly. The lucky ones'll be in Siberia.'

'Not the kids?' I asked, chilled.

Dávid thought for a moment. 'No, not the kids.'

'What about Pista Rácz?'

'Remand school. Eventually, anyway. I'm going to break all his bones first. After the war I mean.'

'What are we going to do with the Hungarians?'

'I already told you! We'll hang the baddies and let the goodies convert.'

Mother had become very quiet, as if her pulse had almost stopped. But occasionally she still exploded, usually over nothing. When the ban on public assemblies that had followed the German occupation was lifted – for Christians at any rate – I asked Mother for money to go to a football match. Without my star, of course. She turned bright red.

'When they're rounding up Jews in the street?'

'But you're always telling me I've got a *goy* face,' I protested.

'Don't tempt God!'

'There's nothing in the *Torah* about not going to football matches,' I argued, but all I received was smacks.

The three of us were rather ashamed that several weeks after the German invasion we still hadn't gone into hiding. We had no money for Christian documents, and although thousands of Jews had already converted we laughed at them. They were wasting their time. Cardinal Serédi was fighting to give converts the right to wear a white cross beside the yellow star. In fact they were perfectly entitled to do so anyway, just as long as the yellow star was visible. They could wear donkey-heads if they felt it would help . . .

Jews were no longer allowed to travel, so it was inadvisable for Mother to go to Oszu where everyone knew her. Gyula set off instead. The plan was to sell off all the wine and then bring Dóra back to Budapest; a metropolis, as every criminal knows, is a much safer hiding place than any forest. But Gyula returned empty-handed. Dóra thought that Mother was panicking; she only agreed to give her half our share of the wine on condition that Mother sent a written request counter-signed by a solicitor. Mother stared into the distance with empty eyes as she listened to the news. Uttering a couple of incoherent syllables, she disappeared into the kitchen so that Dávid and I wouldn't see the despair on her face.

21: D-Day

One of Gyula's friends was head waiter at a posh hotel on Lake Balaton. Every year the hotel took on extra staff for the summer, and the plan was that Mother would be a cleaning lady, Dávid a lift boy, and I would start a new career in catering as a *piccolo* – an apprentice waiter. Of course this plan depended heavily on the progress of the war. The Russians were approaching the foothills of the Carpathians. If they maintained their present rate of advance or if the Anglo-Americans were to break through in Italy, people would have better things to do than to take summer breaks on Lake Balaton and there would be no need for the hotel to call up reservist *piccolos*. On the other hand, the Germans and their Hungarian friends would have bigger problems than the Jews. It had taken the Nazis two years to wipe out Polish Jewry, and the Red Army was now only a hundred and sixty kilometres from our historical frontiers. We didn't have too much to worry about.

I had never been to Lake Balaton. You had to be rich to go there on holiday, but thanks to Hitler it now looked as if my chance had come. I would eat the same food and lie on the same beach as the paying guests. Somehow I'd wangle myself a sailing boat. I saw a book with a boy and a boat on the cover in the window of a bookshop. It was by an American writer called Mark Twain, and as it was second-hand I got it for half price.

Dávid and I played 'Restaurants'. I was the waiter and Dávid was the rather rude customer. I dashed up and down the flat with a tray balanced on one hand, doing sharper and sharper turns until eventually the tray went flying, together with five glasses and three mugs. Mother contemplated the damage with the special calm she reserved for major catastrophes. It was only minor disasters that resulted in instant smacks.

'Can't you practise without glasses?' she enquired.

'If I don't practise here I'll break the hotel's glasses and we'll all get the sack!' Surprisingly Mother agreed. She bought new glasses.

There were two sorts of policemen: the Police proper and the Constabulary. Mother began to hear some nasty stories about the Constabulary at her office, from supposedly reliable sources in the Synagogue and from 'patronesses' with 'connections' who worked there. But even a deaf man could tell that these stories were the inventions of terror: they told of provincial towns where the Jews were rounded up in isolated fields and factories; of a constable who pinned flags in the ground to mark out a line that the Jews weren't allowed to cross. A little boy of four had crossed one of these lines and his mother had rushed after him; both were shot dead by the constable. How was I to convince my mates that the Jews weren't cowards when this kind of drivel emerged from the Synagogue itself? Where did they think we were? Poland? The old constable at Erzsébet Square had trouble holding on to his stick when he shook it at us. I could hardly imagine him machine-gunning Jews who walked on the lawn!

The 'patronesses' were a wealthy bunch. Not only did they work for free; they also gave loads of money to charity, so their scaremongering was understandable. Terrified of losing all their cash, they were full of stories about rich Jews being clubbed with rifle butts and burnt with cigarettes or live wires to make them tell the constables where their treasures were hidden.

But maybe it wasn't all talk. The Virgulas had done up their house . . .

'Dirty yid – where's your gold buried?'

'I don't have any gold – No! NO! Please!'

'No? Perhaps you've forgotten.' *Thud!* 'Now then, where's your gold buried?' Even if a rich Jew were to give them all his money, how could he prove that he didn't have five times as much again?

Dávid and I also practised being *goys*. We learned a few *goy* prayers, went to a few Masses and Protestant services with Mother, not knowing whether we would need Catholic or Calvinist camouflage. With this in mind, I went on '*goy* walkabouts', wandering the streets without the star. Even Dávid thought this a 'silly risk' and told tales to Mother. Mother wasn't exactly keen, but she had to work. I'd peep out of the doorway to check that no one was watching – especially Pista Rácz – and then, in a single step, I'd baptise all my ancestors and make them Aryans. Walking the streets was a new experience, a pleasure I had never known till then. I only had to spot and avoid people from the flats or kids from my old school who lived in the area. When I left our district and began to be bored, I asked policemen for directions, never mentioning a Jewish district. I even made them repeat themselves to show off what a pure-bred Christian I was.

We intended to use our share of the wine to buy ourselves some Christian documents. Mother reckoned that prices would go up as demand for false papers rose, so we needed the money quite badly, but she didn't want to go into hiding until danger made it absolutely necessary, as we would certainly be interned if we were caught. In the meantime she earmarked a few people who would be happy to accept a little money in exchange for 'losing' easily replaceable documents.

She had a letter duly counter-signed by a solicitor and sent it off to Dóra. Before her letter could have arrived a reply was brought to us by a mustachioed old peasant. I knew him well by sight. He lived near the football pitch in Oszu.

Dóra had written her letter on the inside of a torn-off prayer-book cover. She must have been out of her mind: she spent half of the page wondering whether God would forgive her for tearing up a holy book. Then she wrote:

'*The constables have driven us all into the shul;* one of them struck me with the butt of his rifle, but luckily he only hit my shoulder and not the baby in my arms. No one knows where we will be taken; some say Tokaj, some Patak, some Kisvarda.' The message ended: '*God is sending us into the wilderness.*'

We didn't notice when the old peasant left us, and never discovered whether he had brought the letter for money or out of pity. The black prayer-book cover lay on the table; I saw Dóra at a lectern, writing. The silence felt like snow. I shivered. I was bitterly cold. My eyes were suddenly filled with the image of Jewish labourers freezing in the Russian snows. Until then I had only imagined fear.

'Whoever lies down will freeze to death,' whispered the breeze as it slid over a snowy landscape that was black with people . . .

'Into the wilderness,' stammered Mother. Dávid and I stared at her, mesmerised. We expected her to perform a miracle. Her lips quivered several times before I heard the fragmented syllables of the *Sh'ma Yisroel*. Light returned to her face, and in it I could see the power of prayer. What I wasn't so sure about was whether the prayer had any power over God.

One of the newspapers bragged of how the Minister for Jewish

352

Affairs had taken an unguarded stroll through a ghetto containing some thirty thousand people. Rumour had it that the Minister had shouted to the Jews: 'Why doesn't your famous Jewish God do something to help you now?'

Within a matter of days, the Jews of Munkács, Beregszász, Ungvár, Kassa, Nyíregyháza, Nagyvárad, Miskolc, Nagykanizsa and Pécs had all been locked up in ghettos and factories. Some were given three days in which to leave their homes, some only ten minutes. Some were only allowed to take with them the few possessions that they could carry; some were generously permitted to take more and were charged four or five hundred pengös a trip for cart and coach hire before being robbed on arrival by the constables. Trains, roads and stations were raided constantly by the police.

We wept for poor Grandmother. She was in her sixtieth year, and news had arrived that the people in her ghetto were living twenty to a room. There were richer Jews in her town than Grandmother; we hoped the constabulary wouldn't beat her to death for her money.

And then one beautiful morning the door opened and Grandmother walked into the flat. Luci was with her, neither of them was wearing a star, and Grandmother's sheer calm forced me to rethink all my ideas about courage. While we were still staring at her as if she were some kind of heavenly apparition she remarked that both Dávid and I could do with a hair-cut, then gently reminded Mother that she liked her tea strong and her toast cut thin.

The great story-teller began her own tale by saying that there was nothing to tell. She had just done what the old miracle-Rabbi of Keresztúr had done, and began to tell his story instead.

'Three Jews were boasting about their Rabbis.

' "Mine is the greatest," said the first Jew. "When our village was being devoured by flames he simply went to his window and said: 'Fire be gone!' Within seconds the fire was a pile of ashes!"

' "That's nothing," scoffed the second Jew. "When the Tisza flooded and our village was about to be swept away, our Rabbi just remarked, 'Water be gone!' and the water ebbed away."

'But the third Jew wasn't impressed. He was from Keresztúr, and his Rabbi was famous for his healing powers. One Saturday he was called to the side of a very sick man who lived in Nyíregyháza, forty-five kilometres away. So the Rabbi went down to the station, said, "Sabbath be gone!" and took the train.'

Grandmother had done the same, but I couldn't have been more

353

excited if she had passed herself off as Horthy's wife. I listened happily to her clean, warm voice, proud to know that the eldest member of our family still had so much zest for life. After all, it wasn't our brave blood that ran in poor Dóra's veins. I completely forgot that I didn't even like Grandmother.

While she was doing the shopping, she had heard that the Jews were being rounded up. She went home, changed her clothes, packed a small suitcase and went straight to the railway station. In the streets, constables were herding several hundred Jews carrying bundles and cases towards the ghetto, hustling them along, pushing them, beating them. Grandmother didn't even stop, nor did she deign to notice the checkpoints where the constabulary were examining travellers' papers. Marching up to the ticket office, she bought a second-class single to Budapest. She was too well dressed for third class and she considered first a waste of money.

'In any case,' she added, 'the guards always want to meet people who are grand enough to travel first class.' On arrival no one asked for her papers, and here she was.

Grandmother enjoyed our admiration but was unimpressed by her own courage.

'I'm glad you're pleased to see me, but you're all behaving as if I've done something heroic – like getting into an aeroplane!'

Luci wouldn't shut up. She went on and on and on about what a brave magnificent woman her mother was. Dávid had turned pale. His face twitched. We were struggling under the weight of the news, our eyes filled with images of Jews being driven through the streets, but Luci resigned herself to their fate with half a sentence of pity. Her chirping and wailing whipped the air.

Several hundred Jews had stumbled into the room with Grandmother. I felt like an uninvited guest in our tiny flat. Soon, the constables would arrive to throw us out. The window frames became prison bars. I expected the door to open and a skeleton or a helmeted German soldier to walk in.

At last Grandmother noticed the terror in Dávid's eyes and interrupted her daughter's torrent of words.

'I don't know what happened to your little Jutka. Maybe they managed to . . .' She reached over to stroke Dávid's head, but drew back her hand sadly.

'Why didn't you bring her with you?' demanded Dávid in a voice dry with fever.

'How can you possibly expect . . .?' began Luci. 'When my mother herself . . . Going to the station in the middle of the round-up and the police raids is itself such a singular act of courage . . .' She was blocking her ears with her own words. After a moment she tried to soften her reaction, remembering how she had gushed at every opportunity about Dávid and Jutka's 'beautiful childhood love'. 'They're bound to find a way out! They're not gypsies, they're highly educated, well situated, exemplary citizens. The Constabulary will undoubtedly give them special treatment.'

As they were leaving she tried to make us promise not to come and visit her with our stars on – or preferably not at all.

'I'll come to you,' she said, and praised her own great foresight in establishing herself and her ancestors as Christians in the eyes of her neighbours. Within days she would obtain any documents she didn't already possess to prove this fact. It wasn't hard to guess that the real reason she had come to see us was to tell us not to visit her.

Grandmother forgot to tell us what was in her little suitcase. I quickly forgot how we had wept over her possible fate, and I detested her more than ever.

'When he was dying Grandfather told them not to abandon Dávid!' I said indignantly after they had left.

'Your grandmother is a miser,' replied Mother resignedly. 'Your grandpa gambled; she sometimes had to sit at her sewing machine in her beautiful house to be able to feed her children. Don't worry: we won't sit here idly waiting for them to come and take us away! God will help us.'

Dávid lay on the divan for hours on end, his eyes fixed blankly on the ceiling. After two days we called Aunty Sarolta. She couldn't identify any definite illness.

'So it's just depression,' said Mother as she apologised for calling the doctor out, particularly as we paid only a nominal fee. Aunty Sarolta nodded morosely.

From the ghettos and the brick factories, the trains began to roll. The industrial rail network serviced the brick factories. That was why the Jews were put there in the first place. Where were the trains going? Abroad? Somewhere in the country? The news from Mother's office was contradictory.

We hardly saw Gyula once in every ten days. I flirted more and more dangerously with the idea of stealing Pöci's family's papers. He and his little brother were much younger than us, but the documents could be altered a little. The temptation was removed while I was playing with Kaci and he asked me if it was true that I was going to die. I was furious.

'You're the one that's going to die,' I told him. 'An American bomb's going to land right on top of you – SPLAT!' Kaci ran home crying and his mother came out with her broomstick. From then on they weren't allowed to play with us. I realised that if I stole their documents I'd be the Number One suspect.

Mother went to visit the fortune-teller one afternoon and dragged me along too.

'She has very good connections – she must know where we can buy false papers.' Mother didn't tell me where we'd find the money for even the cheapest papers, but we set off anyway. The fortune-teller had moved; she was now living in a villa near the City Park. It was owned by one of her bewitched fans, the wife of a textile-factory owner.

The living room could easily have passed for a posh dentist's waiting room. Our arrival was clearly unforetold; there were already six people waiting their turn, all women. Behind a pink desk sat a secretary. She wore no make-up and was exhausted to the point of rudeness. An old lady dressed in black sat glaring among the clear and colourful summer dresses. Her face was like parchment. I noticed with surprise that one of the customers was our neighbour, the silver-haired lady whose daughter was a famous opera-singer. She wore a rust-coloured costume decorated with bright geometrical patterns – one of which happened to be a yellow star ten centimetres in diameter. Some dressmaker had obviously knocked this up in a hurry to meet the demands of the new fashion. From her neck hung a cross of white bone, or perhaps ivory. It would have done justice to a chapel wall. Her daughter, the famous singer, was sitting beside her in a pale yellow dress that failed to hide her chubby figure. She wore no star.

A beautiful woman of twenty-two or twenty-three was sitting on one of the sofas. Her hair was blonder than a wheatsheaf. She fidgeted as if her skin were an uncomfortable new dress, and she smoked non-stop.

Old Mrs Parchment Face had a headscarf tied over her wig: she was an orthodox Jewess.

A real, peacetime maid with a white apron and a top-knot served tea all round. It was against the law for maids to stay on in Jewish households. She was deliberately sloppy and wore a contemptuous expression, but she was still a maid as far as the women waiting were concerned; they talked straight through her.

'The stink alone would be the death of me,' sniffed Silver Hair. This was her response to the news that eighty or ninety people were being squashed into each freight wagon. The constables provided three loaves of bread and two buckets: one full of water, one empty: the journey was said to last several days. The trucks were labelled 'Workers for Germany' but some people said the real destination was Poland.

'They've been rounding them up at hospitals and old people's homes. To work? Hardly likely! Cripples are being thrown into the wagons without their wheelchairs . . .'

The words conjured up red, deformed dream-images which hid their meaning behind a curtain of fire and smoke.

'. . . they chased them – quick march – whips, truncheons, gun-butts . . .'

'They took all the Jews out of the lunatic asylum . . .' said a bespectacled woman. She was almost screaming, but suddenly she burst out laughing. 'It was at Csap station . . . they stopped the Munkács train, dragged the mad ones out of the trucks and shot them on the spot.'

'How do you know all this, my dear?' asked the silver-haired lady.

'I heard it from an acquaintance who knows a railwayman in the area.'

'An acquaintance!' said the other, turning up her nose to reassure herself, if no one else. But the bespectacled woman refused to give in. She went into the exact details of the massacre.

'One of the madmen thought he was Hitler. He tried to order the constables around. They laughed and then shot him.'

A quiet woman of forty-five, dressed in grey, lifted her head.

'A mad Jew who thought he was Hitler? Must be a rare case.'

'Are you by any chance a psychiatrist?' asked the young blonde. The woman in grey shook her head and the blonde sighed dreamily. 'In the Middle Ages one simply converted and that was that.'

'The director of the foundlings' home at Kassa lined up all the children. Most of them were abandoned – illegitimate. The ones he thought were Jewish were taken away and put on the freight trains.'

The old woman in the wig had a photo album on her lap.

'The Rabbi . . .' she mumbled. '. . . Aren't you scared . . .?' It wasn't clear what she meant. She seemed to be addressing the blonde, who started looking through the old woman's album.

357

'What beautiful children!' she exclaimed.

The others talked about the Synagogue. The members of the Jewish Council were exempted from all the Jewish laws. Sarcastically, the woman in grey read out one of their statements in the *Hungarian Jewish Journal*.

'Those who carry out to the letter all decrees and orders will come to no harm and suffer no offence.

The Central Council cannot allow our received orders to fail as a result of the disobedience of a few individuals. Such disobedience may bring down unprecedented misfortunes upon the whole community. The life of both the individual and the community depends on our obedience to the orders . . .'

'It will be the people who disobey who will stay alive,' commented the woman in grey.

The blonde girl found out that the old woman was scared of the Rabbi's curse for consulting a fortune-teller – 'a sorceress'. The blonde saw me peeping at the photos that she was only looking at out of kindness. She showed them to me: kids with long plaits and toddlers wearing *kapels*. She said that her name was Éva Stein and that she wanted to be an actress.

The door that the secretary was defending opened. A bony woman of about forty backed out.

'Thank you, Borbála, thank you,' she said rapturously. 'If I do receive a letter I won't know how to thank you.' As she spoke she handed the secretary a banknote. I wondered whether one had to pay for bad predictions too.

'Don't let anyone in for five minutes!' shouted the fortune-teller from behind the door, but barely two minutes later she emerged. She hadn't changed a bit. In spite of the May weather she was wearing a heavy woollen cardigan. Her skirt was crumpled and covered in food-stains. Her hair was uncombed and full of knots; it hadn't been washed for months. It was as if a beggar woman had just walked into the posh waiting room.

'I prayed badly,' she complained. 'No inner piety.' She made it sound like a bad lunch. As she spoke she collapsed on to a sofa already occupied by two of the women. 'I'm really exhausted today.'

'Many of us seek hope through you in these difficult times,' said Silver Hair. 'But above all we seek hope through Christ,' she added, hinting at the fortune-teller's five-year-old Catholicism, in the hope of jumping the queue. But the fortune-teller merely looked confused, tugging nervously at her greasy locks.

'I can't give everyone hope . . . but even if I were infallible, what right would I have to take hope away from someone? It's hard to find twenty people a day. They might be anywhere in Europe. Especially when I've never seen them. Most people don't even bring photos . . .'

The orthodox woman lifted her head and her eyes flickered over the fortune-teller's cross. With the help of her stick she staggered to her feet and shuffled out, mumbling confusedly.

After a short breather the fortune-teller addressed the whole congregation. Her special gift allowed her to know that the Budapest Jews would shortly be put into a ghetto. This news was corroborated by her sources in the Synagogue.

'Those with money must buy Christian papers. Those without must convert and get a Certificate of Baptism.'

Éva Stein laughed scornfully. 'A Jew can stuff one of those up—'

'You're quite wrong,' interrupted Silver Hair. 'The Church looks after her own. In many places converts are transported separately.'

'And the pretty women go by sleeper!' laughed the blonde.

'You'd better not *befriend* German officers!' warned the fortune-teller. 'You'll come to a bad end if you do!'

Éva Stein winced: the remark was clearly indiscreet.

'I'll read their palms instead. Unless you have a better idea . . .?'

The fortune-teller wasn't prepared to continue the argument.

'. . . The Primate has intervened . . .' she intoned, 'as has Bishop Ravasz . . . but don't sit idly by, awaiting your fate . . .'

To give her words more mystical force she pointed at me. 'Not a hair of that child's head shall be harmed,' she remarked impressively. The others seemed to take this as something of a revelation; I was less easily fooled. I had a *goy* face after all, and she had to tell the occasional fortune to keep her reputation going. Even so, I stuck my chest out proudly as the silver-haired lady walked over and touched my shoulder. For a second I was a real live relic.

Unfortunately this state of grace was shattered all too quickly.

'It was my turn actually,' said the woman in grey. 'I should like to obtain information about the Jewish Council's rescue operation.'

'Which one?' asked the fortune-teller with some hostility.

The woman in grey looked furtively around the room but it was too late; everyone was watching her. 'The hundred thousand pengö operation. The train that goes to Switzerland.'

This time it was the fortune-teller's turn to look around suspiciously. She had to choose whether to tell the truth, or to go into the other room, thereby admitting that she was hiding something from her fans and customers. But she found a way out.

'Tittle-tattle,' she declared. 'All I know is that it costs more than one hundred thousand pengös per head. Unless you have some kind of arrangement with the Synagogue.'

'A hundred thousand per head?' gasped Silver Hair, leaning on her daughter for support.

'A businessman from Nagyvárad with a wife and three kids gave the Germans a million. They deported him anyway . . .'

'It only costs twenty thousand to get to Rumania, and once you're there the Russians are only just across the eastern border!' said the woman in grey.

The fortune-teller began spouting nonsense to cover up the obvious truth: even in Hell there was one law for the rich and another for the poor. Mother couldn't bear it.

'It's immoral!' she shouted. 'Why should my sons be punished for being poor? Every starving mother should pick up a brick and go to wherever these leaders are! A thousand mothers hurling bricks will make them pay attention!' My cheeks were on fire, but eventually Mother ran out of breath.

'My dear,' said the woman in grey kindly, 'the only bricks the Jewish Council are interested in are gold bricks.'

'Julia! Pull yourself together!' ordered the fortune-teller. 'Don't cause a scene in my waiting room and don't talk rubbish. Follow your youngest around like a shadow. He is protected by a magic circle. I'm sorry. I'm too tired.'

She left us to cover her retreat. They all stared at me like some famous football player in the ration queue or a saint on the tram. A few days later Mother went back to find out more, but all she could discover was what we already knew: that the rich Jews were negotiating some secret agreement with the Germans.

In order to organise the ghetto, the authorities began to draw up a list of Jews and where they lived. It was rumoured that Jews would be put into various different houses around the city rather than into a single district, as this would safeguard the Christian population against Allied reprisals.

June arrived. We waited for news of the expected Russian offensive. The summer holidays were on their way, but Gyula didn't come once in two weeks. With my father's help, I had succeeded in chasing him away, and although I didn't regret it I occasionally caught myself peeping over the balcony to check that he wasn't coming anyway, bringing false documents and news of work at the Lake Balaton hotel. Gyula stayed away.

'I'm scared to go out into the street without my star,' I confessed to Dávid late one afternoon. I hadn't broken the law for several days.

'You're right,' he told me. 'Don't.' I didn't. I even stopped visiting the safe darkness of the cinema.

Mother often spent hours at home when she was meant to be working. The general misery had increased so much that the Jewish charities could no longer help and their workload had actually diminished.

One morning she sent me out to the shop. The hunchback news-vendor, who two or three years earlier had trumpeted his news like a victorious general, was running along the street so fast that I could hardly catch up with him. I thought the police were after him. He was shouting and screaming at the top of his voice, 'The invasion has begun!'

I felt dizzy. By the time I opened my eyes the news-vendor was well ahead of me. I laughed. How on earth did he expect to sell his papers when he kept running away from his customers? In the end the passers-by blocked his way and grabbed the papers from under his arm.

Glancing at my star, he pulled his hand away. 'I bet you're enjoying this, you shitty little yid! Don't worry, we'll push your lot back into the sea!'

'You will? Then how come it's you who's getting wet?' I retorted, snatching a paper from his hand. He tried to catch me, so I threw the ten fillérs on to the tarmac as if he were a beggar without a hat.

The black letters were luminous.

THE INVASION HAS BEGUN
Allied troops land in Normandy
The German Army stands ready

The street was thronged with shadows. Only the sky was alive. It poured gold. I lost my head and went crazy for a second or two. I ran and shouted for joy as the hunchback had run and shouted in his pain.

'The invasion has begun! The *Wehrmacht* is on the run!' I yelled, and charged down the street.

The speed brought me to my senses. Realising that the *Wehrmacht* probably wouldn't be completely routed for another ten hours at least, I stopped shouting and ran even faster to escape any real or imaginary pursuers.

That day I went out without the star. Dávid came too.

The deportation trains kept on rolling.

22: Empty Boxes

In the six weeks since the beginning of May the majority of the provincial Jews had been deported. Only in some of the more populous towns, such as Debrecen, Szeged and Pécs, were there Jews still living in their homes. In Kispest and Ujpest, no more than an hour's tram-ride away, the Jews had been 'concentrated' but not yet deported. In Budapest we expected the concentration order every hour.

People stopped talking about 'Deportation Trains'. They were 'Death Trains' now. We heard of the crammed freight trucks where people were tortured by thirst, hunger, and lack of air. Corpses remained standing because there was no room to fall. Where there was, the living sat on the dead.

We had to escape or go into hiding during the period of concentration at the very latest. Gyula looked in on us, but the Balaton plan had fallen through. Mother started quarrelling with him. He left.

Grandmother and Luci had already gone into hiding. In their case this simply meant staying in Luci's two rented rooms, as they had managed to acquire false documents.

More despairing than the accounts of deportation and torture were the crazy hopes – rumours that the neutrals would intercede or that the Church had protested. All that the clerical protest achieved was to give converted Jews access to their priests for purposes of 'spiritual consolation.' At most camps even this was forbidden.

From his pulpit in Dohány Street, Chief Rabbi Hevesi had given the Primate and other Christian priests some religious instruction. We heard this second-hand, and wondered whether it would reach the bishops.

'All the churches should consider it their duty to command their followers to wear the yellow star in protest against the isolation of

363

the Jews. Such an action would make the annihilation of the Jews impossible. The yellow star will disappear from our chests; but those who condone it will bear the mark of shame upon their foreheads for ever.' He also told his congregation that the trains' destination was Death. The Jewish Council had appealed for 'absolute obedience to the decrees'. He warned everyone that 'if the leaders of Jewry speak of promises, do not believe them. Trust God, not Man, and be sure that your actions serve your safety and that of your families.' Finally, he brought down biblical curses upon all those in power. 'Very soon, the clay-footed colossus of Nebuchadnezzar's dreams will collapse and turn to dust. The words of the prophet to the arrogant tyrant, the usurper of the world, will come true: "Though you mount as high as the eagle, even to the stars, I shall cast you down saith the LORD." '

A decree appeared in the newspapers a few days later: all Jews in Budapest were ordered into designated accommodation. In other cities they had created ghettos in specific areas; in Budapest the ghetto was spread all over the city. There were two thousand six hundred and eighty houses for more than two hundred thousand people. Each door had to be marked with a yellow star thirty-one centimetres in diameter. Our enemies wished us to share the Allied bombs with our Christian brothers.

On the page opposite the decree was an article that explored the connection between Jewish corruption and American barbarism.

The Americans [it observed] *have never produced a single great painter, writer, sculptor, philosopher or inventor, with the sole exception of Edison. And now they want to liberate us! From what? From whom?*

The pure-bred Americans, those whose ancestors sailed aboard the Mayflower, *are unlikely to support Roosevelt. It is the Jews who are behind him, the Zionist Imperialists. Having finally enslaved the Fatherland of Freedom, they now seek to insulate their own world from a superior social order formed in Europe. The nation of the Talmud has decided that our European superiority, our developed socialism and higher culture should be destroyed, bombed out of existence. The poor American soldiers flee before the more efficient German arms, while behind them grins the satanic face of Achasverus, the Jews' five-thousand-year-old hatred for the rest of the world; behind them, too, bolshevism marches to conquer the planet.*

At school we had been plagued with tiny details of events that had long ago fallen into dust. Dávid had had as much trouble with Hannibal's elephants as had Hannibal. It seemed incredible to me that within a few days the newspaper lying in front of me would forget all that it said today in favour of new versions of events.

'According to American reports, Carentan has been re-taken by the Germans.' We hadn't even heard that the Americans had taken Carentan in the first place! Another article ranted about the evil terror-bombers who had attacked Budapest two days previously; meanwhile, triumphant headlines boasted that 'The Retaliation against England Has Begun', and that 'The New German Weapons Have Attacked London'.

The prominence given to the 'retaliation' and the huge exaggeration of Allied losses underlined the real impact of the invasion. Enough fragments of Radio Moscow and the BBC had reached us for there to be no doubt that hundreds of thousands of troops had by now created an impregnable beachhead on the Normandy coast. The best opportunity for the Germans to repulse the invasion had already passed. So although this battle was being fought two thousand kilometres away, and was for us a distant and hopeless victory, it was victory nevertheless: ours.

Despite this, the newspaper managed to offer more concrete presents to its ideological brothers in a feature entitled 'How Christians Can Obtain the Leases on Vacated Jewish Property'.

We had nowhere to go. Not only did we not have enough money for false documents, we couldn't even find a place in 'Starred Accommodation'. Well-off Jews who had lost their homes paid colossal sums for sections of flats in the better areas. No one wanted to move into the district around Dob Street and Wesselényi Street, where a voluntary ghetto had been established for a hundred years. The starred houses stood side by side there, and it was there that the deportation would find its first and richest prey. But eventually Mother resigned herself to visiting some distant relatives in Dob Street. By then there was no room.

We had to be careful. If we failed to find accommodation in the six days left to us, the authorities would take us straight to a concentration camp.

'Why look for a place in the ghetto?' I demanded angrily. 'Why not just reserve us some standing room in a cattle truck? You promised me that we'd escape! Into hiding!'

Mother turned white and sat down. '. . . Poor Dóra . . . If she hadn't been so mean we could've sold the wine . . . We'd be rich by now . . . It will all have been stolen . . . The Germans and the Arrow Cross will drink it . . . Poor Dóra . . .'

'I'm not going out with the star on!' I shouted to stop her whining. 'Never again!'

'Where can we go?' she asked imploringly. My strength left me. Mother wasn't trying to prove the futility of my anger and my bullying by asking an empty question: she wanted advice, a decision.

'If only I were fifteen,' I thought. I was eleven and a half.

'You see,' said Dávid sadly and calmly to prove Mother's point. But his sadness was sober, whereas Mother's was confused by pain and mine by anger. I knew I had to say something to stop them giving up.

'Let's take the train . . .' I stammered, '. . . head for the Russians . . . escape over the border into Rumanian Transylvania . . . Rich Jews pay twenty thousand to do that – the Russians will break through the Carpathians within a week . . .'

'We've no money. We haven't even got enough for the fare, let alone a bribe.' Mother was beginning to recover.

'Sell the furniture.'

'We haven't paid for it yet.' Mother looked at me severely. Then she remembered that the man she had bought it from had moved to the country: he had already been deported. 'Clever boy!' she exclaimed. 'We will sell it! Let's see – a three-door mahogany cupboard must be worth a bit – especially with a full-length mirror in it . . .'

While Mother praised the furniture as if she was trying to sell it to me, I remembered seeing an advertisement in an old paper that we hadn't yet thrown out. I found it.

'Three-door cupboard, divan, table, two armchairs: two thousand nine hundred and eighty pengös.' A fortune. Mother flushed with joy.

'We can't sell the divan – we need something to sleep on.'

'On the train?' I asked, but she wasn't listening.

'You're right, we'll get more for the complete set. We'll buy a cheap bed instead. It's a good price – they'd ask much more for it in a posh flat . . .'

'Are we going to travel or aren't we?' I demanded, banging the table.

'Without papers?'

'I thought you were going to sell your jewellery?'

'My jewellery!' Mother smiled for the first time since she'd come home from room-hunting. 'My wedding ring and my earrings. Enough to make Rothschild jealous.'

'Diamonds! They might be worth a thousand pengös.'

'I doubt it. Anyway, rich people pay that much for one Certificate of Baptism. We need . . . two and four make six . . . so twelve as far as me and your father . . . that's sixteen altogether. Sixteen certificates.'

I burst out laughing. She must have gone crazy.

'Twelve? How come? Why for Father?' But Dávid understood straight away.

'Everyone needs four Christian grandparents,' he explained. 'So we need Father's too – it's safer. So all in all we need sixteen Certificates of Baptism.'

'Fine,' I laughed. 'Let's just imagine we're on the train. They ask for our papers and we produce sixteen Certificates of Baptism. The stupidest Arrow Cross constable in Hungary would know we were Jewish.'

Mother smiled again.

'We can't afford to look suspicious.' She paled. 'You're boys! Why did I listen to my stupid bigot of a father? They'll kill you for it! In Western Europe plenty of non-Jews are circumcised, but here . . .'

The next day, at noon, when we had four and a half days left in which to move, Mother arrived home like a sleepwalker. She greeted us and then wandered onwards into the big room. Suddenly she stopped, picked up the alarm clock, and laid it face down on the table. Then she put on her headscarf, searched for her prayer book and, finding it, brought the low stool from the other room and sat down on it. Dávid and I stood aghast, our blood running cold. She was in mourning. We waited for her to speak but she opened her prayer book randomly and stared at it as if she were blind.

'Who's dead?' asked Dávid almost brutally. Mother shook her head.

'Everyone. Oswiecim.'

'Who's that?' I asked, suddenly reassured. At least it wasn't anyone I knew.

'A town . . . Death . . .' Mother replied. 'Gas-chamber . . . crematorium . . . straight from the train . . . Everybody died . . . not even died . . . worse.'

She was staring at a dark, far-away picture, her words crawling tiredly over her tongue and rolling from her lips half dead.

367

The death trains were taking most or all of the Jews to a Polish place that was now called Auschwitz, although its real name was Oswiecim. The old, the sick, the children were driven straight away to a gas-chamber disguised as a shower room. Nobody ever came out alive.

'Then how do you know about it?' asked Dávid.

'They found out. Two men did escape.'

Mother had heard all this at her office. She didn't go to work any longer, but she still went in for news and contacts.

'The Synagogue has received documents. Proof.'

'Have you seen them?' objected Dávid.

'No.' She stood up, gripping her prayer book tightly. 'I shouldn't have told you this. It might not be true.'

The moment she said this I knew that it was true. Until then I had been sure that her news was just a terrifying nightmare. But now I believed it all.

'It can't be true,' I told her soothingly. She gazed at me for a long time; but after a while I knew that she could no longer see me.

That evening when I went to bed I smelt gas in the flat. I kept quiet about it. I knew that I must be hallucinating.

In the morning I went round half a dozen furniture shops with Mother. It was now four days until the deadline. We invited the shopkeepers round to our flat to make us an offer, but they just laughed. We were thrown out of one place – so as not to spoil the air!

'Jews are moving out of six-bedroom houses into two-room flats – they'll ruin all the honest Christian furniture businesses . . .' Even the itinerant rag-and-bone man scratched his head when we called him up from the courtyard where he was offering his wares.

'Not really my line . . . what with the transport and storage and that. Too much worry and expense . . .' Eventually, out of the kindness of his heart, he offered us a tiny sum saying that 'at least you'll get something for it – it's no use to you anyway'.

'It's a bit early for robbing corpses,' remarked Mother, and the kind-hearted rag-and-bone man went off swearing at the yids. Mother didn't want to sell her jewellery yet. I couldn't work out what she wanted.

She racked her brains for someone who might lend us some money – 'at least until the end of the war'. She went off to Aunty Felice's old villa without me, not wanting to evoke wounding memories, but

368

the villa had new tenants. It was 'sequestrated Jewish property' and had been taken over by some government minister. According to the caretaker Aunty Felice's husband had gone to the country, which made us hope that he had managed to escape into hiding. He had enough money to buy himself a thousand Aryan ancestors and live incognito for two thousand years. He could even have a nose-job to make it the correct Hitlerian shape, a perfect right-angled triangle.

The silver-haired lady beckoned me over to her balcony.

'How long have you known Boriska the fortune-teller?' she asked.

'Years,' I replied shortly. She began making tactful enquiries to find out where we had got the money to pay for palmistry, so I told her that my mother had worked for the fortune-teller some years previously because she hadn't been able to find a better job. But in Silver Hair's eyes we had definitely moved up the social ladder.

'You and your brother both go to grammar school,' she said admiringly. 'I must give you some toys.'

She kept me waiting outside her door, eventually re-emerging with several cardboard boxes. I understood now: she was about to move into a starred house.

'Thank you,' I said, regretting it a few minutes later. I was still carrying the first box-load of presents towards our door when three kids materialised beside me: Pöci, his brother Kaci, and Sanyi Dara from the second floor. At first they followed me curiously, but soon they were carrying my boxes like servants.

The five big cardboard boxes contained four pairs of shoe-trees, three cookery books (of which two were in German), a still-usable handbag, and an infinite number of empty boxes of various shapes and sizes.

'She gave you all that?' asked Sanyi Dara indignantly. 'Jews only give to Jews.'

'What good is it to you when they're just about to deport you?' said Pöci pityingly. I pushed my palm under his nose.

'See that line?' I said, realising that my visits to the fortune-teller hadn't been a waste of time after all. 'That means I'm going to live till I'm eighty-five.' Without lowering my hand I grabbed his. 'Poor you,' I went on. 'If I were you I'd move my bed down to the air-raid shelter.'

But the little vultures refused to budge.

There was a large round box that I at first took to be some sort of posh stool. It was made out of a thin sheet of wood, and one had to be careful sitting down. On one side it had a ribbon handle, and to my surprise I also found a small metal catch. Inside, the box was heavily filled with a cardboard hump covered in silk. I'd never seen anything like it. You couldn't even keep anything in it. I took it in to show Mother.

'A hat box,' she said, showing off.

There was a tin box that was meant for a bottle of eau-de-Cologne. It too was lined with silk, so I kept it for my buttons. I decided that at some later date I would fit it with wings so that my buttons could travel to their away matches by aeroplane.

The three kids were still watching me with hungry eyes. With one magnanimous gesture I gave all the rest of the presents to them.

'Well, there are *some* nice Jews,' remarked Sanyi – his way of thanking me for my generosity.

'Ádám's mother will have to help us,' Mother decided, and we set off to visit Grandmother at Luci's place. Luci was still renting her two rooms where the neighbours waited with bated breath for the news of my uncle Józska's long-deserved promotion to first lieutenant. Grandmother had long ago changed her name from Jakobovics to Sondor, and had now bestowed upon her late husband the rank of Captain, together with the Silver Medal for Bravery – First Class – won in action during the Great War. Luci was doubtless disappointed by this, in spite of the documents and the medal. She would have preferred a colonel.

'What are you doing here?' she demanded when she opened the door, even though we weren't wearing stars. 'Come in!' she urged, hurrying us through the door. For the next ten minutes she refused to shut up about the danger to which we were exposing her, not that she minded, she was quite ready to sacrifice herself, but her poor ageing mother had to watch her heart . . .

The only thing Grandmother watched was her purse. Echoed by Luci, she broke my heart with tales of terrifying sums charged by profiteering *goys* for perfectly forged documents, which were only forgeries even so, and now she hadn't anything left in all the world and couldn't even be sure of lasting until the end of the war, after which her only hope could be her dear, good son, as long as God blessed him and kept him safe. Naturally she was referring to my uncle Józska and not my 'good for nothing' father.

I began to understand why Berger and Torma always gave separate marks for content and style. Grandmother's voice was so warm and velvety and compassionate that if one had listened to her voice alone one would have believed her ready to give her last scrap of bread to her grandchildren.

She already knew in her heart of hearts that she'd have to rely on her trusty sewing machine for support in her old age, but unfortunately that wouldn't do at the present moment as they had purchased too high a social position and work of that kind would inevitably arouse suspicion. Piano lessons might constitute a socially acceptable means of support, and in these difficult times Luci would be prepared to overlook her real vocation as a concert pianist, were it not for the fact that she was unable to advertise her services. She was living under her own name, and some former admirer might recognise her . . .

Grandmother accompanied all this with tea and biscuits. Dávid didn't touch a morsel: he was frozen to his chair. I ate everything out of sheer fury. In the end, with an affable expression, Grandmother offered my mother a hundred pengös. Mother didn't accept it immediately.

'If you're already worrying about your financial position after the war, I can give you security. There are still the two houses in Oszu and the vineyards, even if the wine disappears.'

But Grandmother knew perfectly well how honest and decent Mother was: her inability to lend us anything had nothing to do with the lack of security, and she would cheerfully *give* her grandchildren as much as she could if there were anything to give. With her hand on her heart she vowed that one hundred pengös was all that she could afford.

I looked away when Mother took the money.

'Please don't come here again,' said Luci coldly as she showed us out. Her voice was dry and hoarse. She looked like a horse too. We didn't answer. 'You wouldn't want to drive us out of here, would you, Julia?' she went on, using Mother's Christian name rather than her Jewish one.

'Grandfather is spinning in his grave,' I stated loudly.

'This child is completely unfeeling. I hope he doesn't try to endanger us!'

'Now why would he do a thing like that?' asked Mother with a look of hatred. We left.

'Why did you accept the money?' asked Dávid, tears rolling down his frozen face.

'It was half a month's salary.'

The next day we received a present from the government. The deadline for moving into starred accommodation was extended by two days. Instead of having only three days left we now had five.

Mother's contacts at work didn't help. She left her office with no more than a handful of half-promises.

'There'll be something left over . . . We'll place everyone by force if need be . . . We won't allow anyone to be deported for lack of a room to live in . . .'

Mother sat immobile for minutes on end. Then she swept the flat for the third time and washed up some dishes that were already clean.

'Let's get on a train,' I advised again and again. Dávid warned me just as often that he'd beat me up if I said it once more.

The following morning Mother made me put on my best clothes.

'A thousand Jewish children are being given safe passage into neutral countries,' she explained.

'Shouldn't I dress up too?' asked Dávid, his teeth chattering.

'They prefer children under ten. Under five if possible.' Mother's voice was quiet and terrified. 'But they like rich kids best of all, money . . . money . . . poor Dóra . . . ' she mumbled. Then she pulled herself together. 'Józska is thinner, too,' she argued. I could see that she was already living half in a dream. Her words were like knives at my throat; maybe at hers too.

'If Dávid isn't going, I won't go!'

'Go,' said Dávid resignedly. 'I'll be fourteen next birthday.'

'Let's get on a train!' I shouted.

Dávid hit me. I hit him back. Mother screamed, sat down, cried, then stood up.

'Come on, Józska,' she urged, then turned to Dávid: 'If they take Józska, you and I will escape the same day. It's easier for two to go into hiding than three.'

I was in a half-dream too as I walked beside Mother. I imagined a lady very much like Aunty Felice. After ten minutes I would come to the point and tell her that Dávid must come too . . . and Mother . . .

We went to a building in the Lipót district. Mother avoided the lift and headed for the thickly carpeted stairs, but I hesitated, wondering whether to ring the bell for the liftman. Then I realised that she wanted to save the tip and I followed her on foot. A maid in a starched apron met us at the door and showed us into a huge room.

We were finished. Sprawled on a golden sofa at the far end of the room was a fat, platinum-blonde, life-size doll. She didn't get up, nor did she offer Mother a seat. Anticipating Mother's preamble, she told her that she fully understood Mother's worries as she had two children of her own. Unfortunately Mother didn't ask whether these children were going to Switzerland. The fine lady sent me off to a heap of toys piled up in a far corner of the room: mechanical cars, fire-engines, lorries, an electric train, clockwork dolls, and several dozen Imperial Austro-Hungarian lead soldiers.

Mother began speaking where she stood, then sat down on the sofa beside the blonde woman. As they talked, Mother looked away from the blonde more and more often, towards me, into nothingness. She spoke less and less, while from time to time the woman uttered an occasional lazy word. I eavesdropped in vain. Only a few stray syllables reached me. 'Everybody . . .' 'God . . .' A louder half-sentence from Mother: 'Such a beautiful child – to Auschwitz . . .?' I started towards her when she got up to go; I took her hand.

Mother didn't let go of my hand on the tram. Her breathing was erratic; I was worried that she might scream or faint. When we arrived home she fell into a chair without a word. Dávid gave me a frightened look.

'Blonde tart,' I said. 'She's selling the places on the train to Switzerland.' My usual advice about the train was on the tip of my tongue but I restrained myself and struck a more cheerful note: 'In the Cherbourg peninsula the Germans are giving themselves up by the thousand.' I had picked this news up the day before, and had already announced it, but I thought it might help. Dávid just threw me a sad glance. For a second I felt a complete idiot. 'At least we're going to be together,' I told him.

I went out on to the balcony to escape the others' gloom. Hardly had I stepped outside the door when I saw the bony old spinster from the second floor beckoning to me. I was surprised: I had scarcely noticed her or her mother over the years. They usually stayed in their flat, even during air-raids, and were chiefly known for their huge number of cats.

I went over, but couldn't begin to think what she might want. Maybe they hadn't the heart to throw out some old saucepan with a hole in it. If we had it mended we might be able to make ten fillérs at the flea-market – good money for the poor . . .

She scrutinised me for nearly half a minute, wondering whether I deserved her great gift.

'Kindly come this way,' she said in the end, rather stiffly, and opened the door slightly. I had to squeeze in sideways. The old spinster probably hadn't talked to a child in her life, but she tried hard for the right tone: 'We have known you for a very long time. You are a good little boy. Not noisy.'

She was obviously confusing me with Dávid. An old woman shuffled out of one of the inner rooms: the mother. Her back was five times more bent than her daughter's, and as she was only half as tall she couldn't raise her head enough to see me properly.

'Who is it? Who is it?' she demanded loudly. She must have been hard of hearing.

'The child from over the way – the smaller one.'

'I can see it's a child . . . yes, him, him, a good child, quiet.'

I could hardly see. In the entrance hall a sweetish smell mingled with the stuffiness of old furniture, lace and mothballs. I wrinkled up my nose so much that my eyes became narrow slits. They led me into the sitting room, and as I stumbled through the reeking obscurity I tried to count the cats. It was impossible; the exact figure was somewhere between eight and two hundred and eighty. They offered me a seat, but the armchair was already occupied by an incredibly fat old cat which must have weighed at least ten kilos.

'Mulu, Mulu,' they miaowed at it. 'Let the little boy sit down . . .'

The walls were covered with old paintings and photographs whose frames almost touched one another. Three cats sat on the mantelpiece: two china, one live. The smell of mothballs turned my laughter into sneezes. When I came to, I found myself being closely examined by two expressionless old women and an equally expressionless cat. They were clearly awaiting some life-or-death decision.

'At least he didn't say no,' remarked the old spinster. To what? I couldn't guess. She seemed to be trying to calm some fear of her mother's.

'He'll have to ask his mamma!' bawled the old woman, but I hadn't the faintest idea what I was supposed to ask.

'We'll give them a pengö a day as well,' said the spinster.

'Explain to the boy,' urged the mother, 'explain that a litre of milk

374

is seventy fillérs and that three decilitres is enough for two and one of them doesn't even like milk, it can have water . . .'

'A cat who doesn't like milk?' I asked suspiciously. I must have said something funny: they both started hooting with laughter and clapping their hands, insisting over and over again that yes, it was true, a miracle, a real miracle, a cat who didn't like milk . . .

So they want to dump a couple of cats on me. I could make a profit. Is it one pengö per day or one pengö per cat per day . . .?

They watched me anxiously. I didn't dare insult them by asking them to repeat their offer.

'They won't take us anywhere with eleven cats,' said the old spinster, heartbroken. She couldn't have announced her mother's death more sadly.

'My poor wanderers . . . my poor outlawed wanderers . . .' mumbled the old woman in tears. I was scared that they might kneel in front of me, but instead the old woman gave me a piece of cake, which was worse: it was tasteless, thick, and very dry. I had a brilliant idea.

'Make the cats convert!'

'This child is wicked!' cried the old woman. Actually my idea wasn't bad, it was just that I'd put it too brutally because of the cake.

'If you pay well – let's say two fifty a day for two cats – you could get the Christian kids to take them in.'

I was thinking of the long queues outside the presbyteries, where hundreds of Jews waited to convert. Many of them wore plaits and still had their *tzitzits* hanging out under their shirts. I didn't regard conversion as a crime, and was sure that God didn't either; my only objection to the idea was that it was pointless. The Christians' thirst for blood wasn't going to be satisfied by a few drops of holy water. I had heard that in some Portuguese town in the Middle Ages, the Christians had watched the Jews' chimneys every Saturday. As long as there was smoke rising they didn't burn the occupants at the stake. They tolerated conversion in those days. I could never understand why anyone chose the stake – the Jews could always have got some *shabbes-goy* to light the fire for them.

'Will they only do it for a profit?' quavered the old woman, her voice wet with tears. 'How will they treat cats that have belonged to Jews?'

Nevertheless the daughter entrusted me with the investigation of this possibility, and I went off round the building to find accommodation for the cats. Our next-door neighbours took one in for free, out of pure Christian charity – to cats. Pista Rácz sent a message: he would be prepared to take in four cats at six pengős a day, payable in advance as the owners would shortly be deported. Pöci and family took one. Mrs Csolnoki, the pretty woman who lived next door, made me take her to visit the old women so as to choose her cat. My reward was another piece of the cake.

Mother was out while I was engineering the salvation of the cats. When she returned she sat down at the table and remained there for an hour, motionless. She didn't move when darkness fell; nor did she flinch when I switched on the light. When she finally came out of the trance she berated herself for not having fought the miserly Dóra, and promised that she would threaten Luci and her stingy, egotistical mother with denunciation if they refused to help. Then she told us that she had visited a decent couple from Oszu who weren't antisemites; she had offered them a quarter of a hectare of vineyard after the war in exchange for their documents. She was prepared to put it in writing, but the decent Christians wanted cash, preferably gold.

I tried to cheer Mother up by telling her about the cats. She didn't hear a word.

'You're a child,' said Dávid, but I let it pass. He often made ten years difference out of two.

'When you grow up you'll understand . . .' Lying in bed in the blackness of the small room, I tried to see what it was that I didn't understand. The darkness whirled around me like iron filings . . .

Unexpectedly, I began to worry about my father. I worried so much that my muscles ached. Was he still alive? There were terrifying rumours going round about the copper mines of Bor where he had been taken to be punished. They'd talked about them at the fortune-teller's the other day, and at school six months ago, and both times I'd shouted 'My father's there!' and the people's voices had stiffened. Perhaps that was what I had wanted them to do. I didn't dare think about Father's possible fate. I didn't dare think about mine.

There, lying in bed, I confessed to myself that I was a coward for refusing to allow my fears into my thoughts. The chances were that in ten or twenty days they would take me off to Auschwitz with Dávid and Mother and ninety other people in the same truck, and we'd have to walk along a corridor, and at the end there'd be a sign saying 'Showers'. Flames burned my body. I wanted to get up and go out into the night, walk through ditches and hedges to the front, and then through fire like Elek to reach the Russians. But I knew that this fever was cowardice too: Elek had bided his time, walking among mines, freezing, hungry and in rags; he had waited for a good opportunity to escape to the other side. Father had beaten up a guard . . . I'd beat one up too if I were a grown-up and didn't have to worry about Mother and Dávid . . .

My anguish exhausted me, and I grew calmer. Father's letter came into my mind, the one he'd sent us via the soldier almost a year ago. A goodbye letter, I thought, and began to panic again, but the blackness of the word 'goodbye' evoked the clear message of the letter:

'I shall come back, but I must know that you will be waiting for me, and if you are, don't think for one second that I shan't return.' There was something else in the letter that he must have written in a hurry: 'A man is kept alive BY WHOM HE LOVES.' I had never understood that; it was the people who loved you who kept you alive, like the old women's cats. Mother just smiled when I asked her what Father meant, she told me that I'd only understand in time, when I had children of my own. That wasn't an answer. Dávid hadn't understood either; he'd said that Father liked sounding wise. But it couldn't have been a mistake, because Father had printed those four words when all the rest of the letter was in his ordinary handwriting. It was as if he had known in advance that we might not understand. So why hadn't he written it in a way that would make sense to us?

The door creaked, and Mother came in on tiptoe to make sure that we were asleep. Dávid was; I pretended to be. Mother went out into the kitchen.

It was the hour of prayer. I closed my eyes. But the darkness failed to lift, and instead of a prayer I heard my father's words about the First Commandment. The Christian says, 'Love God with all your heart . . .' but the Jew hears only: 'I am the Lord your God, who brought you out of Egypt, out of the house of bondage.' The Christian accepts his fate because, for him, God is everything and he is nothing. God will make up for men's injustice in the next world. How did Father put it? 'What kind of God is it whose justice is no better than men's injustice . . .?' Something about free will . . . and God needing Israel as much as Israel needs God. Without Israel God would only have slaves to play with, toy soldiers.

I refused to pray.

'You let the people I love go to their deaths,' I told God. 'Your own people, and Torma. I'm a slave condemned to death, and if I'm a slave, then you're not God and I won't pray to you because that'd be cowardice. As far as you're concerned I'm no longer a Jew, because you've broken the First Commandment. From now on I'm only a Jew to fight the Germans and the Hungarians and the other murderers. Choose yourself a new people from among that lot. I'm only a child, but you could at least put a gun in my hand like the one you gave to Elek. Don't forget: you gave guns to the Warsaw kids.'

The darkness around me lifted a little. The great hall of the Oszu *shul* appeared before my eyes, its earthen walls lit with gold. I fell asleep with a light heart.

23: Hungarian Song

We had two days left. After that we had to move out whether or not we had anywhere to go. Mother came and went like someone half-paralysed. If she knocked a glass off the table she'd be woken up by the sound of it breaking. Three seconds later she'd start lamenting and shouting as if she'd broken some Greek vase worth millions.

That day she returned from room-hunting with nothing more than a leaflet. It was a rhetorical appeal to 'Christian Hungarian Society'. It contained no news. It reported that half a million Hungarian Jews had already been sent to their deaths on the deportation trains.

'If the beloved Hungarian people must condemn us to death, we beg to be buried in the soil of our dear Fatherland,' it said, affirming that the 'chivalrous Hungarian people' clearly didn't realise what was being done to a tenth of the population.

The fact was that the only people who didn't know were those who chose not to – and even they knew enough to make that choice. Maybe it was the decent ones who least believed what they heard and saw, because it was incompatible with their own decency. Otherwise the jubilation of the rest would have alerted them. They sang songs about the deportation:

'Through famed Vereczke's Pass came the sneaking Jew so sly,
Sidling like a thief along our tribal fathers' road,
A bundle on his twisted back, a whistle on his lips,
He mutters and he whispers, "I will sell to you and buy . . ."

The combat that is coming will return to us our homes,
The money from the usurer, the hamlets to the poor,
And through the high Carpathians we'll send him on his way
The lord of this our land shall be the Wandering Jew once more!

379

So there upon the summits he'll cast back a final glance,
Throwing curses full of hatred at the folk who make him flee
Yet his fury makes us joyful, fills our hearts with holy pride,
And his curse shall be our blessing: for the Fatherland is free!'

'We'll move in with Luci,' decided Dávid with all the authority of the head of the family. 'Grandmother will be forced to give us the money for false papers.'

Mother was dressing to go out.

'Where are you going?' asked Dávid, terrified.

'I don't know. I can't sit here waiting for a miracle to happen.' But we refused to let her go out alone, and went with her. None of us wore a star in case we decided to go and stay at Grandmother's.

We walked quickly and aimlessly through the streets for several minutes, and then Mother exclaimed nervously, 'Let's go and visit Boriska! The old gypsy can predict where we'll be the day after tomorrow!' She sounded almost crazed, but that was where we went.

The receptionist was hesitant. Business was nearly at an end. The famous fortune-teller was exhausted, almost asleep on the job. God alone knew how many lives and deaths she had distributed that afternoon. Mother set upon her as soon as we came through the door.

'Right. Tell me what's going to happen! What's going to happen to us tomorrow? We've no money for false papers and no place to go. We can't even find a cupboard in a starred house. They'll deport us. Come on: tell me to my face!'

Mother fell into a chair. Turning her head away, she began to cry.

'One must never give up hope!' said the fortune-teller. 'God looks after those who . . .' She tried to put energy into her voice, raise it from the banal to the sublime, but she was too tired. The congregation had all been preparing to leave when we had arrived. Now they were frozen in their seats. But Éva Stein, young and beautiful despite her make-up and her bleached white hair, had no respect for mourning or for tragedy. She ran across to Mother and pushed a handkerchief into her hand.

'Stop crying! Blow your nose and wake up. Come and live at my place.'

Mother looked at her as if she thought she might be hallucinating. Me too.

'Don't look at me like that or I'll start crying too,' laughed Éva Stein. 'I'm not a saint. I'm not even a nun. Far from it. I tried hard but I dropped out at fifteen.' One of the other visitors made an ugly noise. Éva ignored it. 'You'll get me out of a pickle,' she went on. 'It'll be a real blessing if you move in with me. I've got this two-bedroom flat in Király Street – all mod cons – and to stop the authorities dumping some family on me I had to pretend that my parents were moving in. I need privacy. And then yesterday my dad came round, all moral, and started moaning about my "licentious lifestyle". Can you imagine? He called me a whore! Me! As if I hung around on street corners! I put up with it of course. He's always been good to me; worked his guts out – and he's a socialist. But saving the world isn't good enough for him: he has to keep bothering me as well. I'm not going to spend my life lying flat on my back under other people's cars! I'll sit in my own – behind my chauffeur! Meanwhile, my mum wouldn't stop weeping until suddenly, right in the middle of all the gloom and doom, she slapped me round the face as if I were some knicker-wetting teenager late home from the cinema. But that was the least of it! The crunch came when they announced that they were moving in. To look after my virtue! So I told them that the authorities had already billeted a family on me and that it was against the law for me to throw them out. Please don't let them find out what a liar I am. Save me. Move in. I've plenty of money, so I won't charge much in the way of rent. What are you paying now?'

'Sixty pengős,' said Mother, and burst into tears again.

Éva Stein misunderstood. 'Is that too much?'

'Of course not!' hiccuped Mother. 'The rent was fixed years ago.'

'Then that'll be fine,' said Éva reassuringly.

'You're saving my sons!' cried Mother, grabbing her hand. The blonde gently disentangled herself.

'They're good-looking. Are they bright? And wicked?'

'The younger one's mischievous. He's not stupid either, although he failed his Latin exams at the Jewish grammar school.' Mother rambled on deliriously. My Latin seemed to be the only problem she had left.

'Dávid failed in German too!' I said defensively. 'He has to stay down a year. I only have to re-sit the exam when there's time.'

'The Jewish grammar school failed you?' asked Éva Stein. She burst out laughing. 'When did you get your results?'

'At the beginning of May,' answered Dávid. The blonde thought for a moment then shook her head slowly.

'The deportation trains were already on their way to Auschwitz. Boriska! Could you have predicted that? See where all this morality leads people? The Synagogue's grammar school won't give up its principles, won't compromise its standards. But try offering them anything less than a hundred thousand pengös for a place on a train to Switzerland – they'll laugh in your face.'

We decided to move the following morning, just in case Éva Stein took pity on someone else. We packed in a feverish dream. Although she hadn't said anything specific, Éva had given us the impression that she'd rather we left our furniture behind, otherwise she'd have to put her own into storage. This didn't bother us as we were already planning our next move: we had to escape from the yellow-starred building before the deportation began. In any case, the price we had been quoted for the furniture was less than the cost of moving it. The whole city was filled with carts, lorries and wheelbarrows. More than a hundred thousand people were on the move. We passed an army officer who was standing on a street corner swearing at all the dirty Jews because he couldn't find a taxi. All we had was two suitcases and a sack, so we took the tram.

We were given a pretty room overlooking a courtyard. Éva kept the smaller room, and stipulated that the sitting room was communal but more hers than ours. At the same time she assured us that she was hardly ever at home, as she had better things to do than sit around waiting to be deported. Most of the starred buildings were crammed; in others, there were only two to a room.

Our block faced south, overlooking the courtyard of a two-storey building below us. We were on the fifth floor, halfway up to the sky. I put my suitcase down and studied the building from the corner of the balcony. Many of the inhabitants were sunning themselves on the balconies, reading and chatting. I noticed with horror that most of them were over sixty. The staircase was in the middle of the courtyard, and divided the building into two wings. Looking down, I soon spotted a familiar curly black head on the balcony beneath ours.

'Pianist!' I shouted. He didn't budge. Either he was deaf or he didn't know that I called him that. He was too big: he must have been András the Pianist's elder brother.

But it was András himself. He had grown.

'Raindrop!' he screamed. I had almost forgotten my totem name, but the sound of it jogged my memory and I remembered his.

'Calm Bear! Hurrah!' I yelled, and we ran towards each other, almost knocking one another off the staircase.

'It's good to see you here!' he said, hugging me as if he'd

waited several years for me to arrive. 'It's a real stroke of luck!'

'Don't you have enough money to escape either?' I asked. He put his finger to his lips.

'There are still some Christians in the building,' he hissed. 'They refuse to move unless they can have bigger flats for half the rent.' I nodded, and he began speaking normally again. 'What about your brother, Quick Lizard? What's his real name? It's great you're here – this is an old folk's home.'

He told me that his family had always lived there. Éva Stein used to be a society whore, but now she'd sunk so low that she'd even gone to bed with German officers. Five of the families who used to live in the building had gone into hiding; taking a total of seven children with them. Of these, two had been his friends, three had been too small, and the last two so vile that it was good riddance. A boy called Pista Bognár had stayed – he was very fat and brainy, and it was madness to play chess with him . . .

András talked so fast that I scarcely had a chance to put in a few good words for Éva Stein. Before I knew it he had dragged me off to visit this Pista Bognár.

'Look what I've found!' he exclaimed as he exploded into their flat. 'He's got a brother as well – what's Quick Lizard's name again? Dávid, yes? We met at cubs – great blokes! We won't be alone any more!'

'The only time András stops talking is when he's playing the piano,' laughed Pista Bognár. 'I hope you're good at interrupting him.' Pista was indeed fat, and moved as slowly as a fat grown-up. He was actually a year and a half older than me, and six months older than András, but he looked like a good-tempered kid in spite of his specs.

András took the floor again.

'For days the only people arriving have been grown-ups and grandmothers and women with babies. Our new neighbours have got two babies – the mother wants to ban me from practising and I want to ban them from crying. Veronika on the second floor is beautiful, but she's already thirteen and boys have to be older than girls. We'll have to change all that.'

'Boys have to be thinner too,' remarked Pista morosely.

'That's no problem,' said András, obviously thinking that this was directed at him. 'The real obstacle is the mother. She won't let Veronika make friends with boys.'

'Poor András,' teased Pista, 'they've been here a week and she still hasn't proposed to you.'

I realised straight away that I was third in the queue for the beautiful Veronika. Two already-established suitors posed a problem – especially if Dávid . . . My philandering mood faded. Dávid was still waiting for his Jutka to come home from Auschwitz . . .

'Do you play chess?' asked Pista tactfully, like a judge putting a delicate question to the accused.

'No, he doesn't!' interrupted András. 'No one plays chess except you. Play on your own! I play the piano on my own!' But Pista didn't deign to listen to this objection. Fixing his specs on me severely, he waited for my reply. I shrugged and nodded but this didn't satisfy him.

'Do you play *well*?' he insisted.

'Rottenly!' pleaded András as counsel for the defence. 'Disastrously! Pista, haven't you noticed that everyone except you is useless at chess?' He turned to me with a big grin. 'I drew against him twice in three hundred games. Don't play with him,' laughed András. 'He even beats grown-ups to a pulp.'

Pista Bognár put a map in front of us. He had drawn it himself.

'The Americans have reached the outskirts of Cherbourg,' he told us. The newspapers were still standing firm on the subject of the German defence lines, but Pista laughed at them. He had access to foreign news. He didn't say how. All Jews had been forced to hand in their wireless sets months ago. He took out another map; this one was printed. 'The Russians have broken through somewhere around here,' he announced, pointing to a section of the front. 'They've crossed the Dvina. It may just be a tactical move, or it may . . .'

'Isn't that a bit too far west?' asked Dávid, who had come to drag me off on another luggage trip.

The next day further restrictions came into force. Jews were only allowed on the streets between two and five in the afternoon. They had to travel in the second coach on the trams and were banned from parks and playgrounds.

In fact it took several more days to fetch all our belongings, and we were still picking up some bits and pieces two days after the expiration of the deadline. When we arrived, four policemen were standing outside the second-floor flat where the old spinster lived with her mother and their cats. The rest of the inhabitants of the building had turned out to watch. Apparently the two old women had barricaded themselves in for the last three days, but no one had noticed until Mrs Mester had gone to put the flat in order before it was sealed up by the authorities. She probably wanted to ease the state's burden by removing a few pieces of furniture. When she found the door bolted she called the police.

Some people were concerned. More were indignant at the way these Jews refused to listen to reason. Most, including the four policemen, merely laughed. When one of them put his shoulder to the door the old spinster finally appeared at the window and asked them to help her move the cupboard that was barricading the door. Two policemen clambered obligingly through the window and a minute later the door opened. The old mother, seventy-five or eighty years old, emerged on to the balcony with her hands in the air.

In the meantime, several of the cats had escaped, first by the open window and then by the door. The old spinster had managed to pick one of them up and was holding it in her arms; the rest were being chased by various children, either for fun or in an attempt to catch them. Frightened by the crowd and the chaos, most of the cats eventually took refuge in their old home.

We had to hurry to get back to Király Street before the curfew at five. The last I saw was Mrs Mester adopting the cat that the old woman was cradling, resisting further entreaties with a shake of her head.

Playing chess with Pista Bognár proved to be a waste of time. When I looked around the board after four or five moves I realised that I was already losing. In our first game I lost a rook after four moves. Pista explained that the 'Maróczi System' allowed me to capture his rook in return but at the cost of my queen, thanks to the something or other gambit. Chess wasn't a game for him: it was a real war. But his maps made up for everything.

One evening I found him in front of his maps, both excited and irritated. He was measuring distances on the large-scale map he had drawn by hand from a printed original. The front lines were represented by red and blue crayons and tiny flags.

'I don't understand! I don't understand!' he complained, but he sounded delighted. He wasn't the only one who was confused. When I looked at the map I could guess how the German generals must be feeling.

'There's something in the newspaper about intensified defensive activity in the central section of the front,' I said helpfully. Being a quiet kid he didn't give me a kick up the bum; he laughed.

'The Russians have occupied Orsa and reached Bobruisk. They've taken Mogilev on the Dnieper and three days ago they recaptured

Vitebsk. Now they're striking north-west towards Polotsk.'

'So what don't you understand?' I asked even more helpfully; fortunately Pista had nerves of steel.

'I can't draw the front lines. I know where to put the arrows but I can't work out how many directions the Russians are attacking from . . . As far as I can make out from the news, the Red Army has launched an offensive on this section of the front, but it's four hundred and fifty kilometres wide! I can only guess where the breakthroughs and the encirclements are.' Then he showed me his secret: an innocent-looking cupboard in the living-room which contained a hidden drawer. In it was a battery wireless tuned to London.

So until the military situation became mappable we were forced to play a little more chess. Pista was irritated by my continual refusal to resign in the face of overwhelming odds. Like the Germans, I never gave up hope that he might blunder and lose his queen. One day, I was struggling to avoid checkmate when my mother flew into the Bognárs' flat with the news that there was someone waiting upstairs to see me. She wouldn't tell me who it was; she just gave me a cheerful and mysterious look.

Aaron Kohn was leaning on the balcony outside our door.

'You're moving in here!' I shouted, jumping for joy. He shook his head.

'I came to say goodbye,' he replied calmly, almost formally.

'Are you going into hiding?' I asked, puzzled. His chocolate-coloured shirt carried the yellow star.

'Please don't try to guess,' said Kohn, his voice heavy with anxiety. 'I can't tell you any more. My father didn't even want me to come and see you.'

I pointed an accusing finger at him: 'The child rescue plan! One thousand rich kids!'

Aaron looked as if he wanted to cry, but instead he laughed. 'That hasn't worked out. The Germans called it off. Look, my telling you where I'm going won't help you; but if they find out that I've told you I won't be allowed to go.'

I felt dizzy. I couldn't tell whether I was searching my memory or my imagination.

'Are you going to Palestine with the Synagogue?'

Aaron Kohn reddened.

'Who told you about that?'

'A fortune-teller.'

'Don't be silly. Who told you?'

'No one,' I laughed, confused. 'Rumours.'

'Someone's let the cat out of the bag,' he remarked stupidly. Then, after taking a deep breath, he lowered his voice and went on: 'It's true. But it wasn't me who told you! Now that people know about it the whole thing might fall through.'

I had never heard such a fairy tale as Aaron Kohn now told me, not even from Uncle Samuel or from my wicked grandmother. The Jewish Council and the Gestapo had agreed that in exchange for some fabulous sum of money, a few thousand very rich and important Jews were to be allowed to leave for Palestine, via Switzerland. Any of the bosses of the Synagogue and the Zionist Alliance who weren't rich enough to pay were to be subsidised by their richer fellow-travellers. The first group, about two thousand people, were due to leave within days, maybe hours. They had been given separate accommodation and were forbidden any contact with ordinary Jews so as not to create panic. They would go by train. A gold train!

The Synagogue, with the exception of Chief Rabbi Hevesi and one or two others, was indistinguishable from the Jewish Council. They had promised safety in exchange for obedience ever since the Germans had overrun the country, and now, with half a million people already deported, the Synagogue was still requesting obedience. They were less certain now about their side of the bargain, but still managed to argue that obedience was better than resistance. This had to be a lie. The Synagogue's messengers delivered the German and Hungarian authorities' 'individual' internment orders so as to give the victims four or five hours' 'grace'. They begged such victims not to attempt escape in case they brought down a bloody revenge upon themselves, their families, and the whole of Jewry.

There was a story going around about a Jew who gets woken up in the middle of the night by a hammering on his door.

'Who is it?' shouts the Jew.

'Gestapo!'

'Thank God for that!' sighs the Jew. 'I thought it was the Jewish Council.'

'Blood-money,' I hissed. Aaron's teeth chattered. He stood petrified, like a statue. You can't strangle a statue. Instead, my hatred was strangling me, sucking the blood from my veins. I couldn't lift my hand. He stood before me, his golden locks a condensation of the June sunlight. Here we were, the two of us, but he was going to

387

Palestine where the sunshine is even brighter, and I was to stay behind, freezing in the summer heat as I waited for them to come and take me away to the gas-chambers. It was as if the Gold Train had already left, with Aaron and the other two thousand privileged Jews, the Chosen People of the Gestapo and the Jewish Council. I was standing on a platform, but the station was empty. The night had come down, and outside the terminus there was nowhere to go.

Terror burned in Aaron's eyes like the reflection of an SS machine gun.

'You came here . . .' I heard myself say, 'to tell me this? Why did you come?'

'I . . . had to say goodbye. My father didn't want me to. He wouldn't let me. He was wrong. You don't understand.'

'It's you who don't . . . ' I stammered, but he wasn't thinking what he was saying either. Words were just dust raised by some departing car.

Aaron's eyes turned cold, and suddenly it was no longer his statue standing there, but his shadow. He must have gone mad then, though his voice was calm.

'Take my place on the train. Nobody will know that you are Józska Sondor and not Aaron Kohn. There's no photo on the list, just a name. We'll swap papers.'

Nobody would know . . . That was absurd. What about his parents? But Kohn was now no more than a shadow; his life had already left him. He had given it to me.

We fell on to each other's neck, our legs too weak to hold us. We sobbed like toddlers, and then, as if coming out of a deep sleep, we smiled.

Hesitant and ashamed, he tried to cheer me up and I began to hate him again. He came out with a rumour that the deportations were about to stop.

'Has the Jewish Council run out of lies too?' I laughed. That carcass had been picked dry weeks ago. But Aaron assured me that his information came not from the Council, but from some junior minister of state his father had known for a long time.

Aaron told me another fairy tale. Apparently President Roosevelt had sent a message to Horthy via neutral Switzerland, threatening that if the Budapest Jews were deported, the Americans would bomb Budapest to dust, like Hamburg and Cologne; and after the war Horthy would be tried for genocide and hanged.

388

The tale was partly believable, partly not. Horthy had already given his blessing to the deportation and murder of half a million Jews. He would be hanged anyway: how could the fate of the Budapest Jews alter that?

'Are the Americans going to double-cross Horthy?' I asked hopefully.

'Possibly,' answered Kohn, 'but you know what a dirty business politics is. If they reckon that they can save two hundred thousand lives by sparing his, they might not hang him after all.'

'Why didn't they do the same for all the Polish and Slovak Jews?'

'I suppose because they couldn't even bomb Germany effectively in those days.'

'OK, but what about the provincial Jews?'

'Maybe they didn't know what was going on.' This time Kohn sounded less certain.

'And why can't they just bomb the Auschwitz gas-chambers? And the railway lines that take people there?'

'I don't know,' he admitted sadly, as if my last question had destroyed everything he had said.

We parted as if we'd be seeing each other again at school the next morning. I felt dizzy again after he had gone. The following day, he and seventeen hundred other chosen Jews left Hungary by the Gold Train.

When I told Dávid that Roosevelt had ordered Horthy to stop the deportations, he examined my face carefully to see whether I was ill or had gone mad. Mother, András and Pista Bognár were all astounded by the news; neighbours came round to call; even people from the first floor. The old, the women, the children all pumped me for information, but all I could tell them was that a friend's father had heard the news from a highly placed source in the government. Some people shook their heads, some hummed thoughtfully, some nodded; only the shoe merchant from the second floor was openly sceptical. He claimed to be in possession of contrary information from an equally highly placed source, a former customer of his whom he had met in the street during 'permitted hours'. This ex-customer was a colonel, and had told the shoe merchant that the deportation of the Jews of Budapest would begin in three days' time, at midnight on Saturday, the second of July.

The shoe merchant had more convincing evidence on his side than I did. Over the previous three days the number of constables in the streets had increased dramatically. The official reason for this presence in the capital was that there was some flag dedication taking place. This wasn't exactly a cast-iron alibi. Furthermore, the shoe merchant claimed that among the units in question were the Constabulary's Galanta and Nagyvárad divisions – both of which had seen extensive active service during the provincial deportations. At this, the various inhabitants of the house panicked, and competed for the distinction of having seen more constables in the streets than anyone else. Meanwhile Altmann, the little shoe merchant, joined his hands over his belly and cross-examined me delightedly as if rubbishing my news were bringing him immeasurable profit: 'And what did Horthy say to Roosevelt, eh? You see!'

Everyone was packing. The tenants stood on the balconies even after dark, watching out for constables. Some tried to predict the night's events from the behaviour of the two fat detectives installed in the two-storey building opposite. Mother packed a special sort of spirit for the journey; it was supposed to be better than brandy if you were taken sick in the packed freight wagons. I tested it and liked it; tasted it again and felt gently dizzy. Soon all my doubts about Roosevelt's warning were happily dissolved.

Sunday morning arrived uneventfully, but Altmann the shoe merchant remained quite unperturbed.

'So they put it off a few hours? So what? It's a big job, organising a deportation!'

The Christians' radios announced an 'aerial incursion' near the frontier. This became 'Air Danger' and then 'Air Alarm'. 'A large American formation' was approaching. The little shoe merchant stood in the doorway, wearing his greatcoat despite the heat. At his feet was a knapsack, probably full of treasure. As if his life and honour depended on it, he argued that the deportation would begin that very day.

'Air-raid? Don't make me laugh! They announced air-raids at Munkács and at Nyíregyháza too – it's the best way to drive the Jews off to the railway station without any witnesses. Go back to your flats and have a decent meal at least. It'll be the last chance you'll have. I had a hearty breakfast myself – my belly's still hurting from it!'

'They won't deport us on a Sunday!' shrieked a deaf old woman. 'The Hungarians are a Christian nation!'

Someone gave the caretaker twenty pengős to see if there were any constables round the back of the building. He said not, but he might have been lying.

'Air Danger Budapest,' announced the radio, and then, almost interrupting itself, 'Air Alarm Budapest!' Everybody swarmed down to the cellar, but instead of the usual suitcase and basket, everyone carried all their movable belongings with them.

Pista Bognár's mother, Aunty Sári, who was as calm, fat and bespectacled as her son, discussed the radio announcer's voice with Altmann. Had the announcer sounded frightened of the bombers? Or was he quite unshaken – and therefore lying?

'They are simply providing a reason to keep everyone indoors as long as possible. The bigger the raid, the longer they can spend on the deportation.' Altmann's arguments seemed inexhaustible.

The rest of the tenants called for silence so that we could listen. The deaf old lady heard the noise of aeroplanes. Altmann heard lorries.

'What make of lorry?' teased Aunty Sári, but Altmann put his fingers to his lips and stood on tiptoe to hear better.

No audience had ever awaited the world's finest orchestra in such silence. And then, far away, two drum-beats sounded.

An enormous explosion shook the cellar. The ceiling buckled like some gigantic bubble, but by some miracle it didn't cave in. After their initial fright everyone jumped to their feet. Many applauded and Pista Bognár hugged me. Outside, it was raining bombs.

'It looks as if Roosevelt isn't too happy with Horthy's reply,' the little shoe merchant proclaimed after half an hour. He seemed to have forgotten how he had scoffed at my news for days.

The bombing went on for several hours. Afterwards, as scores of ambulances and fire engines hurtled through the town, Altmann must have felt some remorse towards me. He contemplated my feet for a while and then remarked, 'It's a pity that I've never dealt in children's shoes. Send your mother down and I'll choose her a pair of beautiful crocodile skin shoes. They cost twenty-five pengös before the war.'

Mother asked me to thank him for her, but to tell him that she wouldn't be going to the Opera for another few weeks.

The air-raid far surpassed all previous attacks on Budapest. They estimated the number of bombers at around seven to eight hundred, and the fascists were shell-shocked for days. The people who had rubbed their hands with glee at the thought of the recent 'retaliation' against London were now throwing up their hands in horror.

'It was a lovely sunny Sunday morning . . . people were on their way to church when the barbarian bombers . . .' For a change, the newspapers' compassion extended across religious frontiers: 'Enormous destruction also occurred in Jewish districts, where unfortunate

391

babies and little children were caught out in the open air. Boys and girls were strafed by machine-gun fire as they played innocently in the playgrounds . . .' The writer of this particular tear-jerker had obviously forgotten that Jews weren't allowed out of doors before two, and were completely banned from playgrounds in any case. More to the point, no civilian was supposed to be outside after an air alarm had been given.

On the next page this pious voice gave way to righteous indignation.

World opinion was yesterday scandalised by the news that Rome's new Chief of Police, a Polish-American Colonel, has sent a telegram to the Chief Rabbi of Rome congratulating him on the re-opening of the synagogues. What of the ruined churches? The ancient monuments? What of Christianity?

Underneath this, however, were a few consoling lines about the Pope.

In his letter to Count Preysing, Bishop of Berlin, the Holy Father expressed his admiration for the courage shown by the long-suffering people of Berlin in the face of heavy air-raids. Pius XII also stated that, of all the towns of Germany, Berlin was closest to his heart. Count Preysing brought the Pope's message to the attention of the public in a pastoral letter addressed to the Catholics of Berlin.

By contrast, there was still no sign of the long-awaited pastoral letter from the Christian Churches protesting against the extermination of the Jews.

All over the town, people shook their fists and shouted insults at the Jews, who were forced to clear away the rubble. In the meantime, the tenants in our block whispered that it wasn't only the neutral embassies that had raised their voices against the deportations: the Pope himself had intervened. They seemed to forget the photos in magazines a few years before, where the Pope had been shown blessing Mussolini's troops. As for King Gustav the Bad of Sweden, it was he who had allowed Hitler's troops across Sweden to stab Norway in the back!

My victory over Altmann was rewarded, though not with a pair of shoes. The shoe merchant was often prepared to chat affably to me outside his door, and since his neighbour was the beautiful Veronika, this gave me the opportunity to wander along their balcony without betraying my true feelings. By watching from our top floor I could see when the princess of the ghetto was about to emerge, and on one occasion I found the courage to intercept her. Taking the steps two at a time and jumping the last five of each flight I managed by pure chance to meet her face to face.

'Hello,' I said with an air of bored politeness. 'I'm looking for my friend Mr Altmann, the shoe merchant.'

'I haven't seen him,' said beautiful Veronika, looking at me awkwardly and wondering why I was so out of breath if all I wanted to do was talk to Altmann.

Hardly a week had passed since American bombs had destroyed the possibility of immediate deportation, when the sirens ordered us back into the cellar. The more cowardly among the Jews moaned that Horthy would get the message anyway and hoped that fewer bombs would be dropped this time.

No sound reached us. For hours on end. The grown-ups shouted at us for whispering, as if it might lead the constables and the SS to us.

The shoe merchant was praying: 'Please God, just one bomb, just one little bomb . . .' After three hours, even we children began to get scared. The air alarm was called off.

Two hours later we discovered the truth. The town had been occupied at strategic points by Hungarian tanks brought in from Esztergom and infantry units that could be relied upon to obey Hungarian rather than German orders. The three thousand constables had been ordered out of Budapest under cover of the air alarm. This proved that a combination of Roosevelt's ultimatum and the German defeats had created a rift in the government, which was now divided into pro- and anti-deportation factions. The army's protection only extended over the capital, however. Eight days later, twenty-five thousand suburban Jews were concentrated in the brick factories of Monor and Budakeszi and subsequently deported.

Altmann somehow got hold of a copy of the Primate's pastoral letter, which was to be read out in all the Catholic churches by the following Sunday at the very latest:

Over the two thousand years that our Church has endured, the Successors to the Apostles have raised their voices in defence of those who have suffered condemnation without trial and without having offended against the laws of God or Man . . .

The letter protested against 'the State's encroachment on its citizens' birthrights, the right to life, human dignity and freedom of

393

worship, the right to earn one's living and to own property'.

But the Primate apologised for this protest as soon as he had made it:

We do not doubt that certain sections of the Jewish community have in the past exercised a criminally disintegrating influence over all aspects of Hungarian social, moral and economic life. It is also true to say that the more responsible among them failed in this respect to take proper action against their co-religionists. We entirely agree that the Jewish question must be tackled, but it must be tackled in a legal and just manner. We do not dispute this, indeed we judge it desirable.

So the Church believed in a 'just' Jewish question; it merely desired a more peaceful solution. It considered the extermination of half a million people to be a rather over-enthusiastic response to a basically good cause. Nevertheless, we awaited the reading of the letter in the Churches week after week in vain. Pontius Pilate washed his hands in better faith. In the end, instead of the pastoral letter, the priests read out a 'message' from the Primate:

Justinian Serédi, Cardinal Archbishop and Primate of Hungary, together with their excellencies the members of the episcopal bench, to the Catholic Faithful.

With respect to the decrees concerning the Jews, and especially to those concerning the Converted Jews, the Hungarian Church has made repeated representations to the Royal Hungarian Government and will continue its negotiations on the issue.

The Protestants followed suit.

Mother had frequented Protestant circles, discussion groups and lectures for ten years. At one time she had nearly converted, and had only held back for fear of driving Grandfather into an early grave. Now she gave up the very idea of conversion. They had been weighed and had been found wanting.

She had expected them to put on 'Jesus's yellow star' like the Danish King, Christian X.

24: Elek to the Rescue!

The American bombers had chased the Constabulary out of Budapest. The exterminators were divided amongst themselves, and were quarrelling with the Germans almost publicly. Our 'permitted hours' were extended, and the two chief hangmen in charge of the deportations were dismissed. But the grown-ups still spent at least one day a week in a state of panic, to make up for the other six days of hope. Within five minutes of someone on the first floor receiving 'reliable information' about an 'immediate deportation', we'd find ourselves packing to leave. The worst time was the day a Christian widower, the shoe merchant's neighbour, saw hundreds of German soldiers, some of them SS, marching along one of the main avenues of the city. It was a blue and gold day; most of the world was made of light and reality was only a noonday shadow. But the grown-ups stood about with sinister expressions or rushed about breathlessly as if they'd just run in from the rain. The optimists believed that the SS wouldn't come in force to deport the Jews; the march-past was just a warning to the anti-deportation lobby. The pessimists, on the other hand, predicted that one rank would peel off from the rest of the column at each starred house. They used the Christians' telephones to ring around all the railway stations – preparations for the deportation of two hundred thousand people would paralyse the rail network. But all the trains were running according to schedule, so the optimists were winning the argument when Aunty Sári came in from the balcony to order me and Pista to stay indoors. This wasn't like her: she was normally calm and cynical about the rumours. We were playing chess at the time, and hadn't intended to go out until that moment.

The balconies were swarming with spectators. On the first floor, two policemen and two ambulance men in white shirts were standing in front of the deaf old lady's flat. She was the one who had heard aeroplanes when they were nowhere near us, and then, when the bomb fell next door, had asked her neighbour if he'd said anything. The anxiety had proved too much for her; she had poisoned herself. They brought her out on a stretcher, her face covered by a sheet. The sheet shimmered in the light; it was difficult to believe that it concealed a corpse.

Altmann was cheerful. He was always cheerful, he couldn't help it, it was the result of chatting up his customers for forty years.

'Wise woman: eighty-three and chose to die in her bed. But me! I'm not even sixty-five! My heart's as sound as a bell: if I survive Hitler I'll live till I'm a hundred!'

The suicide put a stop to the panic.

By that stage I was the only person prepared to play chess with Pista Bognár, even in the cellar during the long air alarms. In general, losing didn't bother me, because I was learning his tricks. On one occasion, though, when he was thrashing me as usual, I caught András's pitying glance. I began to suspect that his reason for refusing to play against Pista was a superstitious one. Defeat might attract demons, eventually destroying the loser's chances of survival.

I decided that I had to win at something, no matter what. Playing football in the courtyard was out of the question: neither the strict caretaker nor the grouchy old tenants would have put up with it. Pista, Dávid and András showed no more than a theoretical interest in football, and didn't want to bring trouble upon their own heads.

These superstitious fears brought real ones. I was getting out of practice. The war would soon be over for Hungary. Once the Red Army arrived, the Jews would be allowed back into the playgrounds and, what's more, we'd be able to play in the First Division. I wanted to get into the Ferencváros cubs, but the fact that I was unable to train meant that the Christian competition would still have the advantage when the Russians arrived. From time to time this thought made me shiver, which was crazy.

My suspicion about the demons of defeat was reinforced when I played button-football with Pista and András. I set to with great confidence, and announced that I'd never been beaten. I was surprised to see that Pista and András used two buttons per player, sticking them together with tar and filing one-third of the edges with sandpaper to give the 'ball' the right degree of lift. I lost 8:1. As a consolation prize,

András and Pista gave me some tar and sandpaper so that I could bring my team up to scratch.

When we tired of games, we read. For years, whenever I had whined about my prickly shirt or our staple diet of bread with dripping or marmalade, Mother had called me 'Little Lord Fauntleroy'. I had taken this partly as a compliment: after all, she was comparing me to an English child. Then I discovered a book on András's shelves that bore this very title, and unearthed a major German propaganda coup. The book was the most revolting piece of nonsense I had ever read. The twisted way of talking, the pompous speeches and polite chit-chat gave me a headache. Not even a German child could have been so pathetic, and even the German aristocracy weren't as degenerate as this little lord. The whole thing was evidently a hoax. The book had been written by the Germans to make people despise the English and laugh at the monarchy. Mother could say what she liked; I knew what I knew. András, who owned the book, agreed with me, so we burnt it like the Germans and the Hungarians burnt the works of Jewish writers.

The Americans had saved us from immediate annihilation, but they couldn't have been too satisfied with Horthy's reaction to Roosevelt's note. The bombs continued to fall.

The good news conflicted with the bad, although it was usually the bad news that turned out to be true. Most of the cheerful rumours could be dismissed at first hearing; they were spawned by nothing more than hope: Jewish food rations were to be raised to parity with the Christians; the English were allowing unlimited immigration into Palestine; the railway line to Auschwitz had been bombed; the Swiss were taking in all the Jewish children; and so on. Mr Altmann delighted in bad news and collected it fervently via his neighbour's telephone. One day he reported excitedly that the deportations had by no means stopped: in the largest of the internment camps the SS had put fifteen hundred people on a train to Auschwitz.

Everyone in the building started packing again. All afternoon and evening they listened avidly to Altmann's fragmented conversations on his neighbour's telephone, but no news reached us until the following day. Then we heard that, acting on orders from the government, Hungarian railway officials had stopped the train and redirected it to Kistarcsa internment camp. A week later, the Germans descended on the camp and this time succeeded in deporting the fifteen hundred.

The frightened Horthyites were trying to save their skins at the last moment, while the rest of the fascists remained completely rabid. The Jews of Budapest were two hundred thousand footballs being kicked between the two camps. It was lucky for us that not all the fascists were attacking the same goal. American bombs had restored the Horthyites' sanity and improved our lot, but our ultimate survival depended on further feats of arms.

Accordingly, our main occupation became the production of strategic maps. Pista drew, while the rest of us made measurements with compasses and monitored the news in each of our allocated sectors of the front. Mother listened more and more closely to my bulletins and I showed her the blown-up maps increasingly often.

'Look! Elek's marching to our rescue!' I told her.

Elek was wearing seven-league boots. In the twenty-five days since the crossing of the Dvina, some divisions of the Red Army had advanced nearly four hundred kilometres on a front that extended from the Baltic to Byelorussia.

The unprecedented victories on the northern and particularly central fronts filled me with pride but the Russian armies in the south, by whom we expected to be liberated, had hardly moved. Pista tried to encourage me, but rational arguments failed to convince me. I was being ground in the jaws of a terrible suspicion. Where was Zhukov? The BBC talked of no one but Rokossovsky in the north and Malinovsky in the south. Yet Zhukov had to be commanding the Byelorussian offensive. The Germans must have known it too . . . he had clobbered them so often: at Moscow, Stalingrad, Leningrad and Kursk.

On the balcony, I discussed the issue with Altmann the shoe merchant.

'I hope my uncle isn't unlucky enough to be fighting for Malinovsky,' I said. Altmann gave me a hard stare, and I told him that Elek had escaped to the Russians. At first he smiled, but eventually he believed me and would have raised his hat had he been wearing one.

'It'd be better for Elek if he were fighting for Zhukov.'

'Why for Zhukov?' asked the shoe merchant, slow to understand.

'Because for every step that Malinovsky advances, Zhukov advances a kilometre. Also, great generals are better at promoting people: Murat was a sergeant under Napoleon, and he ended up as a Marshal of France.' I had read this when I was little, in a book about a drummerboy given to me by Aunty Felice.

'But what are you trying to say?' laughed Mr Altmann. 'Everyone's fighting for Zhukov. He's the Commander in Chief.'

My heart missed a beat.

'Commander in Chief . . .? I thought Stalin . . .'

'Stalin's only the official CIC, and Zhukov's his lieutenant. It's the same as Kutuzov and the Tsar – tsarism is much bigger in Russia now than it was before—'

'Zhukov . . . Commander in Chief . . .' I said in amazement. Then I shouted so that all the world could hear: 'Zhukov's the Commander in Chief! You've had it, Hitler!'

A day later we discovered that the German generals agreed. They had killed Hitler. With a bomb.

It was a bizarre story, and the Germans never came clean about it. They pretended that he had survived. But from that day on he disappeared from the stage. We heard his voice for the last time immediately after the assassination. As in Hungary, the crazy chief fascists were quarrelling with the scared chief fascists, and the scared ones had blown Hitler up so as to be able to blame him for their own filthy crimes. But the madder lot had come out on top, and they avenged themselves by capturing and executing the executioners. They then pretended that Hitler was still in one piece by installing another buffoon in his place. One had to admit that the new clown did a brilliant imitation of Hitler on the night of the assassination. It was almost as good as mine, especially as the actor spoke German. The fellow obviously took his orders from Himmler, and had probably undergone cosmetic surgery in advance. In any case he rarely showed his face, even in photographs.

All the stupid Jews in the building swallowed the story whole. I imitated Hitler better than the radio could, but in vain. When the first news of the coup came in they kissed and hugged each other on the balconies, but after the impressionist had done his bit on the wireless they started packing again. I couldn't understand why they ever bothered to unpack.

'They'll take it out on the Jews!' they whispered. 'They'll deport us all! Tonight!'

The only grown-up who believed me was Mother, although her reasons weren't the same as mine. Boriska the fortune-teller had predicted numerous events, usually contradicting herself several times so as to hedge her bets. Maybe she just forgot her bad guesses and used hindsight to recall her better ones. It wasn't that she cheated: she just had a rotten memory and a marvellous imagination. Nevertheless, I had seen with my own eyes a newspaper cutting from 1918 in which

Boriska had said that in the 1940s European Jewry would be taken away in wagons and destroyed by fire. In the same interview she had predicted that a 'typhoon' would sweep through the world in the mid-'30s, and that the Japanese would become temporary masters of the globe. She had just survived the fifth date of her own death, and was looking forward to a sixth, but one hoped that God would bless her with another mistake. To my own knowledge she had been prophesying Hitler's assassination for the last three years, but on this matter she had been quite adamant about the date: the twenty-first of July, 1944. I remembered the consternation and incredulity of her fans when they heard that Hitler still had so long to live. The attempt had actually taken place on the twentieth, but it was possible that the beast hadn't died of its wounds until after midnight. This was one prediction that was absolutely spot-on, and I had to accept the fact without any hope of explanation.

Even Hitler's death couldn't help the Germans any longer. Their defeats continued. The Russians stormed onwards towards the Vereczke Pass, where Árpád and his Hungarians had reached the Carpathian Basin one thousand years before. They also took Przemysl, where the Hungarian army had been so heroically defeated in the last war, but the patriotic old lion at Margit Bridge took no notice. Spread out on his belly, he chewed lazily at his old stone laurels.

In forty days the Red Army had advanced from the Dvina to the gates of Warsaw.

'They've gone halfway since the twenty-fifth of June,' remarked Pista Bognár as he drew his maps.

'Halfway?'

'To Berlin.' Pista's manner remained calm, a little shy, just as it did when he said 'Checkmate'. But his cheeks turned pink with excitement.

The caretaker, as the powerful representative of the state, always wore a suit. The Jews paid him to keep the gate open or shut, depending on what the reigning fear happened to be. Whenever the panic began to dwindle, he went from door to door to try and stir it up again.

'Exactly how many people are living here?' he asked, as if he didn't already know.

'Infuriating! Exasperating!' he said at all the flats where he wasn't given a tip for asking who was living there. For a larger tip he let on that he was meant to be listing the Christians so that he could put up a sign outside their doors saying 'Christian

Dwelling'. This was to stop them being deported accidentally when the time came.

The shoe merchant stood in front of his door, ready to receive his marching orders as usual.

'We pay this man to frighten, us!' he complained.

'Why be frightened, then?' I asked him.

'Because being brave won't help us.' He didn't say what good being scared would do.

'Aren't you going into hiding?' I asked him. This was a sensitive area. The whole building knew that Altmann provided short-term loans at a high rate of interest. 'You've got enough cash to buy false papers!'

'I haven't, of course I haven't . . . and in any case, what good would they do? People like me don't need the yellow star. I couldn't get as far as the next street corner with my face, not even if I were wearing an SS officer's uniform.'

Carefully, I brought the conversation round to business. I tried to persuade him to lend us money until the end of the war against the security of half a hectare or maybe a hectare of vineyard. It was the perfect way for him to protect his wealth, and we would have our false papers. He hummed; bit his lip; tasted my proposition. He didn't like it.

'Not a very mobile form of capital,' he said heavily. Out here on the balcony with his bag at his feet he remained the dyed-in-the-wool businessman he must have been in his shop. But I hadn't been born yesterday either.

'Quite right, it's hard to move land. The Germans can't take it away with them.' He had his answer ready.

'Not the Germans,' he laughed. 'House, land, it'd be lovely. It's the Russians who'll take it all away.'

'Take it away? To Russia?'

At that point Mother arrived. I had hoped that the caretaker's scaremongering hadn't reached the fifth floor, but no such luck.

'I've been looking for you everywhere!' she screamed. 'Go and get ready! Straight away!'

Being ready involved sharing out our food supplies between three string shopping bags. I had to put on two pairs of pants and two shirts in the boiling heat, and Mother distributed her money amongst us. This meant fifty pengös at the beginning of the month or twenty towards the end – at most. It was lucky we wouldn't have to pay for our train ticket.

401

'Hurry up!' yelled Mother.

'Why? Are we going to miss the train?' I asked, but my wit only gained me a smack. 'Why can't you get some documents instead of smacking me!' I shouted. Mother calmed down.

'Please come,' she sighed. When we reached the flat I explained that she had interrupted my negotiations with the shoe merchant at the worst possible moment, and for no reason, as the alert was just a hoax by the caretaker. By way of compensation for the smack I was given a fistful of sugarlumps from our one-kilo emergency reserve. I had to share this with Dávid even though he hadn't been smacked.

Jewish ration tickets provided little more than a taste of sugar and meat. Only babies got milk, and very little at that. Black-market prices were beyond our means. Mother knew someone at the flea-market who dealt in ration tickets; she bartered her spare clothes, and those that we had outgrown, for Christian ration tickets. These were cheaper than the Jewish ones, and in any case shopkeepers gave you two or three times as much food at the same official price if you used the Christian tickets. Mother went into shops without her star and exchanged them. The best shops to use were the ones that had signs in their windows saying: 'We do not serve Jews.'

The outgrown clothes soon ran out. Poor András and Pista offered us buttered ham rolls at least once a week, but they slowly grew resigned to eating nothing but bread and marmalade at our place.

The Red Army established three bridgeheads on the Vistula. The Hermann Goering Panzer division 'advanced irresistibly', but was soon reduced to scrap iron. To consolidate their conquests, the Russians took up defensive positions in the centre and switched their attacks to the south. Meanwhile, the British and the Americans broke out of their bridgeheads, encircling the Germans at Falaise and taking fifty thousand prisoners. Next, the Allies landed in the South of France.

During this period of colossal actions, unprecedented in the whole of military history, the Germans and Hungarians succeeded in establishing a record of their own on the home front. In Poland, where the extermination of the Jews had enjoyed similar popular support, it had taken two years to complete the operation. In Hungary the annihilation of the provincial Jews, from stigmatisation to cremation, was achieved in only three months.

In this battle between Heaven and Hell, the Church took up its position with little or no hesitation. The much-trumpeted pastoral letter, denouncing the Jews' 'criminally disintegrating influence' as well as their unlawful murder, went on circulating clandestinely but was not read out in the churches.

Meanwhile, the Church maintained its august defence of the purity of the Faith: *'The prescribed term of religious instruction should be extended until the priest responsible for the baptism is fully satisfied with the candidate's serious intent towards the Church of Christ.'* Vicarage doors bore a new message: 'Conversions suspended until further notice.'

We pitied and despised the converts, but in spite of this Mother brought catechisms and prayer books home by the bagful. Dávid and I crammed both Catholic and Protestant prayers into our heads, just in case the Grace of God provided us with Christian papers without the assistance of the Churches. My Latin teacher would have stroked his tummy with delight if he had heard how beautifully I spouted the *Pater Noster* and the *Ave Maria* in my sleep.

I was helping Pista with the maps one morning when Mother called me outside. Daisy was standing on the balcony, Father's rich friend Daisy. She wasn't wearing a star.

She had received a letter from Father via one of the Death's Head SS. She hadn't brought it with her, for fear that they might search her on the way, but she told us exactly what was in it. Father was working in the Bor copper mines. His was a labour camp rather than a death camp, and fewer than one in ten of the inmates was murdered outright. They were guarded by SS and Hungarian soldiers. He had lost weight, but was in good health. 'He would return!' He had asked Daisy to pay the SS postman at the blackest of black-market rates: twelve salamis, twenty kilos of bacon, and three thousand cigarettes, which he had already received from the SS on credit. The other thing – if she hadn't already done it – was to get us three Christian birth certificates. Daisy gave them to us and left.

Mother showed us the documents: three stamped, blank birth certificates. If the worst came to the worst, we could escape.

'You can yellow them over a flame,' said Dávid, worried by the obvious newness of the documents. Mother asked him to practise on cheaper paper.

One hot Sunday morning in August, when most of the tenants were out on their balconies having a holiday, another unexpected visitor turned up. He was a small, stocky corporal whom we had met by chance a few weeks before; it had never occurred to us that we might see him again. I hadn't even discovered his name.

He had been walking down the street when the air-raid siren went off, and he had sought refuge in our cellar. Most of the tenants didn't deign to notice him. Had he been a lieutenant they would have gone into his connections and assessed his possible uses, but a corporal . . . a peasant nobody? At least he wasn't an Arrow Cross and didn't start shouting abuse at the yids – but couldn't he find himself a Christian air-raid shelter? For his part, the corporal leaned against a column and kept out of everyone's way.

It was lunchtime, and after about an hour, people began to get hungry. Discreetly, they opened their lunchboxes. Eggs, ham and butter appeared, as if the whole cellar were a depot for the black-marketeers. The corporal was forgotten; he had melted into the grey column. But Mother remembered him.

'Have a seat, Corporal,' she said, offering him a place on my bench. The corporal took a couple of steps forward.

'I don't mean to intrude,' he said shyly. Mother was making tea; she gave him a cup.

'How many sugars?'

'I prefer it without,' he replied quickly.

'Rubbish!' laughed Mother. 'How many?'

'One,' nodded the soldier, smiling. 'How did you know?'

'You weren't very convincing.'

'Sugar is hard to come by,' explained the soldier, then blushed as if he had drawn attention to our poverty. Mother gave him a reasonably thick slice of bread and some marmalade, but that was all he would accept.

So we were surprised when he appeared at our door that Sunday.

'I'm on leave. I just dropped in to say hello. I don't know a soul in this town. My regiment's stationed at Pestszentimre, but I'm not stupid enough to stay in the barracks when I'm given some leave.' He opened a small case and put a big tin on the table: two kilos of liver pâté.

'I don't have that kind of money,' protested Mother.

'It's a present,' he stammered. Mother looked irritated.

'Don't insult me,' she said, then laughed so as not to sound too rude. In the end they agreed that the soldier would sell us the tin at the official price of eight pengös per kilo instead of the real black-market price of twenty-two pengös.

'It comes our way from time to time,' he explained, so that we wouldn't think he'd lost out.

'It's not exactly Sunday lunch, Corporal, but can I invite you to enjoy some of your own pâté . . .?'

The following Sunday he came again, but apologised for coming. He had only dared to do so because he might not be able to for a couple of weeks. He was going home on leave for a few days to visit his family in Hódmezövásárhely.

Ten days later he paid us another visit. He asked us whether we were in good health, and whether we had come to any harm since he had last seen us, and then, without sitting down, he pulled a bundle of yellowing pieces of paper out of his pocket. They were his family's documents. They went back one hundred and six years, his great-great-grandparents' birth certificates: the lot. He had only left a few at home for his wife and children, they had been living there a long time, and in any case could always ask for duplicates at the Town Hall.

The corporal could quite easily have sold the complete, unforged set of documents for two hundred thousand pengös, and bought himself a villa on Rose Hill. Yet he gave the papers to Mother as if his gesture meant no more than a tin of liver pâté.

In civilian life he was a cobbler. His name was Ferenc Jáger, and although he must have been of German origin he didn't speak one word of the language. It was the best name a Jew could possibly have had. We could put it on our blank birth certificates, one of which was spare, as Mother could use the one belonging to Jáger's wife, Rozália Dragomér. The paper was already brittle and yellow with age, and had to be treated carefully.

This time it was I who started to pack. Mother and the corporal stopped me, laughing. It would be enough to leave the building an hour or two before the deportation.

I remembered how I had damned God in my prayer and, in order to avoid breaking the spell, I looked up at His dump in the sky and refused point-blank to thank Him.

25: Stars of Day

At our strategic councils, attended by Pista, Dávid, András the Pianist and myself, András proposed a British occupation of Hungary. He feared the confiscation of his piano under a Russian occupation, and so the Allies were to invade from the Adriatic near Fiume and strike directly at Hungary, thereby preventing the Russians from laying their hands on our country.

Dávid only just tolerated these debates, regarding them as childish, but our hopes seemed to wake him from his sombre daydreams. He warned András that if he had any sense he'd look after his life before his piano, but András wanted to hang on to both. Indirectly, the newspapers took the view that the Russians would be the first to arrive; they praised the indomitable resistance of the German Army Group South. Put into plain Hungarian by the BBC, this meant that the Germans' resistance was cracking.

To listen to the news, we usually had to draw the curtains and kneel in front of Pista's murmuring radio, but the next major event was broadcast to us live while we were sunbathing on András's balcony. This balcony was a privilege; we had heard that in the provincial ghettos, windows overlooking the street had to be boarded up. A news vendor was selling copies of *Hungary*:

'Read all about it! Read *Hungary* for the latest news!

> 'Buy *Hungary* from your vendor
> For the Rumanian Surrender!'

Proudly, he repeated his poem over and over again although his customers would have snatched the paper from a deaf-mute for news of a Rumanian collapse.

The Jewish curfew was in force at the time, so I tore my starred shirt off and ran into the street half naked. A minute later I was back in the building, being chased up the stairs by a good twenty of the tenants. Altmann offered me first fifty fillérs and then a pengö for the fourteen-fillér paper. I scarcely heard him.

Over the next few days the Rumanian armies withdrew from the front line. Soon afterwards, the Russians encircled and then annihilated twelve German divisions, while the rest ran as fast as they could to form a new line further to the north-west.

The Red Army crossed our historical boundaries. We all expected Hungary to take advantage of the confusion caused by the German collapse, and to follow the Rumanian example by laying down her arms. We also expected the Germans and their remaining Hungarian chums to vent their fury on the Jews. There'd be no more mucking about, no deportations or gas-chambers. They'd march into the starred houses and machine gun us all on the spot. I urged Mother to go into hiding but she told me to be patient and wait for the storm to begin.

As it turned out, neither prediction came true. Horthy sacked his Hitlerite Prime Minister and installed a general. The inaugural address was a beauty.

'Our solution to the Jewish question will be in the true tradition of Hungarian chivalry.' Presumably this meant 'legal and just', as the Primate had suggested.

Not one line arrived from Samuel. Generosity towards the Jews didn't extend to letting him send a postcard. My father had found a way to use the SS as a postal service, but Samuel had neither Father's bravado nor Elek's quiet courage. He was a good man, nothing more. The thought made me tremble.

We played chess, button-football and cards in the air-raid shelter. We read. We lay around waiting for news of the approaching Russians. Pista Bognár invented a new version of chess. Whenever my position became hopeless he would turn the board around. When my new position had deteriorated enough, he'd turn it round again. This system allowed me a few victorious draws and even a couple of wins. My button-football improved more rapidly, as the reason for my 8:1 defeat was a technical one that had since been remedied. Having learned all the ins and outs of filing down the buttons, I was soon nearly as good as András.

Since messing up my courtship of Veronika, I had been reduced to the position of a movie goer, watching and sighing from a distance of three storeys. I plotted to sit near her in the air-raid shelter so as

407

not to miss any opportunity of dragging her to safety when the roof collapsed. András, who was a year my senior in any case, abused his status as an indigenous inhabitant of the building by visiting another native, an insignificant girl from the first floor who happened to be Veronika's playmate. His stratagem won him an invitation to tea.

'What did you talk about?' I asked him indifferently afterwards.

'This and that,' he shrugged. 'School, music, the Palatinus Baths where I used to go swimming before they kicked the Jews out, that kind of thing.'

Music was all right. András's years of study deserved some reward. But swimming pools? Only a base opportunist would discuss such inanities with a girl like Veronika. But András went to see her several times, undaunted by the de-briefing that followed each visit. Finally he let me know his verdict.

'I'm through. We played duets. Her hands are only good for washing up.'

What was I to do? Carry on chasing her? She wasn't good enough for the Pianist . . . I suddenly understood why Father had looked so shocked at our second-hand clothes. I hummed a few bars, then half a line, and then sang the whole verse, loudly, like a marching song:

> 'White is the acacia, white is its flower,
> Forgotten is the lover and the love gone sour,
> She is only beautiful, whose heart is still untried.'

I sang it everywhere, self-pityingly, proudly, over and over again. I fell in love with song. It removed the need for courtship. My voice wasn't too beautiful, but on one occasion the warm clear voice of Éva Stein answered mine from the other room. She wasn't mocking me; she had caught my mood and wanted to sing. Her song went to the same tune as 'John Brown's Body':

> 'We're not exactly posh and we are often rather broke,
> We never get enough to eat like well-respected folk,
> We're building up a better world than hunger, dust and smoke,
> And our work is beautiful.
> Glory harder than a knife is,
> Glory deeper than our grief is,
> Glory is to live for others
> And our work is beautiful.'

She was expecting her parents. Maybe she wanted her father to hear her singing this song. They had come looking for her several times, but she was never in and we never told them that she had been away for a week or ten days. It was reasonable for her to be out during 'permitted hours', and they couldn't visit her during the curfew anyway. Nevertheless, the parents weren't fooled. They would walk into Éva's room. The father, a broad-shouldered, heavy man of fifty, wore an immaculate brown woollen suit in the middle of summer. His back was rigid, his gestures angular and uneasy. Already tense with pain, he would listen embarrassed to his equally heavy wife's investigation of the clues left by their daughter.

'The bed's made. Even the cover's on. Not a single fag-end in the ashtray. Not one unwashed cup or plate. Where are the dresses and stockings on the floor? Where's the dirty linen, the sweet-wrappers? Come on, Lajos! Defend your daughter! Where did the little tart suddenly learn to be tidy? Her sponge is dry as paper, hard as stone. Your daughter's turned into a whore; honest workers like us weren't good enough for her because all you ever cared about was the union! Never gave a damn for your family!'

'Didn't I give her everything I could?'

'Everything! And more! That's what did it! Singing lessons! Acting! Posh clothes!'

The parents' visits always followed the same pattern, whether Éva was there or not. The mother delivered an uninterrupted monologue. If Éva had any talent for the stage, she must have inherited it from her mother, who could maintain her verbal barrages indefinitely. In the end, Éva would slam the door in their faces, whereupon the mother would continue to shout on the balcony for another five minutes before storming away, her husband's slow steps echoing her retreat. They had to be back for the curfew.

Our strategic council agreed that the threat of deportation diminished with every step the Russians took. The grown-ups viewed the future more darkly because they played no chess or button-football, didn't read, didn't draw maps, and consequently had no occupation but fear. It was difficult to distinguish information from hallucination. Pista Bognár's mother had the self-control to smile while sifting through illiterate fascist newspapers to discover the gist of their lies, but even she could hardly hide her anxiety in that climate of all-pervading fear.

The new government stuck to traditions of Hungarian chivalry by promising that, in future, Jews would not be deported to destinations

409

outside Hungary. In this way they hoped to please the Germans, the Russians, the Americans, the Christians and the Jews all at once.

'The destinations inside Hungary will be transit camps for Auschwitz,' predicted Altmann. He had stopped shaving his upper lip. Moustaches were in: they were the fashion among the military.

'What about a beard and plaits to go with it?' I asked, but he looked so taken aback that I felt sorry for him. 'You look like a real Aryan,' I assured him.

'I'm too small for a Swede, but it's worth a try,' he confided, and after making me promise not to tell anyone he revealed that the Swedes were distributing passports to the Jews, and money didn't matter. As soon as you had a passport you could go straight to Sweden, but there was only a limited supply. I didn't expect to hear good news from Altmann, and only reported it to Pista and András and Mother as an example of human credulity. But all three of them had heard the rumour. Mother hadn't mentioned it to us because she hadn't wanted to raise false hopes, but secretly she had gone to some external office of the Swedish Embassy. The queue for application forms was so long that she could see no prospect of reaching the front before the curfew. Jews had arranged for Christian friends to start queueing at dawn. Even the Synagogue seemed to regard the scheme as genuine. The King of Sweden had sent a special envoy to Budapest, and the envoy had more than a hundred Jews working for him. They gave out passports by the thousand, and anyone lucky enough to get hold of one could tear off the yellow star and head for Sweden.

Mother and I sometimes went outside without our stars. It wasn't bravado. I was bored with that now and impatient to go into hiding for real. But Mother needed to do some shopping, and a butcher near our old flat still gave us good meat, either because he didn't know we were Jewish or because he felt sorry for us. Mother always took a random selection of Christian papers with us, although they wouldn't have been much use if we'd met an old acquaintance.

One afternoon, strolling along beside the Basilica, we passed a man brushing the last dollop of watery glue on to a new poster. It was big, in full colour, and showed the Hungarian coat of arms. Above the seven hills and the double cross were great red letters: 'The Fatherland in Danger!'

Tears of joy filled my eyes. Liberation seemed to punch a hole in the grey wall. But Mother's face was pained. She was shaken, and sublimely, almost ridiculously, Hungarian. We were right beside the door of my old school, where Torma had taught me about the Hunyadis and the Black Army and Saint Stephen, founder of Hungary. For me, Torma was Hungary, the country he had tried to defend and which had sent him to that murderous front. My tears continued to flow, but I was no longer sure that I was crying for joy.

Suddenly I came to my senses.

'I must be crazy to cry!' I laughed hoarsely. A moment later I noticed the other people standing in front of the poster with frozen faces and open mouths, their eyes hypnotised and huge. A stocky, mustachioed peasant turned to us immediately.

'What?' he demanded brutally.

Mother kept her head. 'He's ashamed of crying,' she explained.

'No shame in that,' replied the stocky man, his face softening. 'I feel like crying myself.' His eyes darted back to me but he was too late by then. He nodded. We had been saved by my *goy* face and Mother's quick wits.

Mother's eyes remained foggy. She loved poetry, and as we wandered along she hummed a nostalgic, patriotic verse. But Torma's Hungary was gone. It was too late even to say goodbye.

One sunny Indian-summer morning, we sat drawing maps at the Bognárs' flat. The Allies were converging on Aachen from three directions. The Russians were at the gates of Riga. But all these events were suddenly dwarfed by an announcement from Radio Budapest.

'Hungarian troops, assisted by our German allies, are heroically beating off the Soviet forces, and their Rumanian auxiliaries are flooding into our country in the vicinity of Arad.'

'Stinking bloody Rumanians!' exclaimed András, our political expert. It galled him to think that only one month after their capitulation the Rumanians were fighting on Transylvanian soil. It made my blood boil too, but my reason prevailed.

'It's Rumanian Transylvania anyway.'

'There's no such thing as Rumanian Transylvania!' raved András. His years among the Chocolate Wolves clearly hadn't been wasted.

'The Jews weren't deported from Rumanian Transylvania,' I reminded him. 'They were deported from Hungarian Transylvania. All my grandmother's relatives have been taken off to Auschwitz. As far as I'm concerned, the whole of Transylvania can be Rumanian. They can keep it for ever. That way the Hungarians might learn a bit about justice.'

They were all against me, even Dávid, but I refused to budge.

411

Losing Transylvania would make the Hungarians understand, make them remember how they cast the Jews of Hungary aside, sent them off to be slaughtered. Transylvania would be the murderer's amputated arm.

Mother arrived and told me to hurry up and eat lunch: my Latin re-take was scheduled for two o'clock that afternoon.

'My what? Oh, right . . .' She had been nagging me about my Latin for the last three months. I didn't even know where my books were. Desperately, Mother turned out all the drawers, but I calmed her down.

'Don't bother looking for them. I know where they are now. I last saw them the day I . . . felt funny. Just before I went into hospital. I must have left them on my desk. If they're not there, they'll be in our old flat. They're no good to me here.'

'But you'll fail!'

'I can't. I've failed already. The worst that can happen is that I won't pass the re-sit.'

'I'm coming with you.'

'I'm not a baby!'

'A Jewish child, all alone in the street!' she panicked. All her other fears had got mixed up in her stage-fright over my exam.

'Calm down,' I told her. 'I won't take the book and I won't wear a star. And I'll bet you anything that Bonkers Benke will have both.' Benke was the Latin teacher.

Standing in front of the Jewish grammar school, which was still temporarily housed in my Jewish primary school, I thought of Berger and our battles of old. Poor old Berger. In the battle that awaited me now, Éva Stein was my inner ally. Éva had laughed when she heard that Jewish teachers had failed children who were awaiting deportation.

'They must have got an Iron Cross for it,' she had smiled.

There were only a few dozen pupils loitering in the building. The re-sit crop was poor that year. The school servant directed me towards the slaughter-house door, where I waited for a minute. A shiny-faced second-year emerged after a while: he had passed with flying colours. I went in. The desk had been taken off the dais, it stood facing the door with a chair in front of it for the victim. Behind it, Bonkers Benke sat in judgment. He obviously didn't dare confront me alone: he had arranged for a minder to be present – my form-teacher, the bespectacled mathematician who had trouble finishing her sentences.

'Are you . . . exempted . . .?' she asked, gazing dreamily at my starless jacket with the respect due to war heroes, munitions experts, members of the Jewish Council, their families, and incredibly rich Jews capable of paying for the privilege of going without stars. I knew that I only had to say yes and I would pass with a distinction and no questions asked.

'I've given up stars for Lent,' I explained cheerfully, observing the dilemma on Benke's face as he wondered whether to frown on a cheeky pupil or admire a hero of Warsaw.

'You haven't brought a Latin book!' he informed me, deciding on the first course of action. I thought of telling him that I had lost the books six months ago and hadn't noticed until half an hour before the exam. It would have given him a heart attack. 'I lost it,' I said, spreading my arms diplomatically. 'I hoped you might have one on you, sir.'

'I have!' he replied wittily, rubbing his hands in the traditional manner to show that he'd made a joke. If he didn't, his toadies wouldn't know when to laugh.

There was a book lying on the table. He opened it at random and pushed it towards me. I read out the designated passage and then, without making any attempt to translate it, pushed the book back to him.

'Well?' asked the patient and benevolent Bonkers. A few seconds later, distinctly less benevolently, he tried 'Ergo?' I just looked at him curiously. 'Come on, come on!' he insisted, beginning to threaten me.

'I wonder if you could tell me something, sir,' I said casually. There was no reproach in my voice, only a scientific curiosity. 'Why did you fail me? Me and the others?'

'Are you telling me that you did not deserve to fail?' he intoned, pointing solemnly at the book.

'We're not talking about merit.'

'What are we talking about, then?'

'Well, sir,' I explained patiently, 'it's just that in May, you can't possibly have thought that Latin was important—'

'And you still don't!' he interrupted, sitting up straight while his bodyguard opened her eyes so wide that I thought they might swallow her glasses. She was warning me not to gamble away the Latin master's good will. I smiled.

'I see you're still trying to make me believe—'

413

'What?' yelled Bonkers, blowing his top. 'What am I trying to make you believe? Why would I teach Latin if I didn't think it was important? Explain yourself, boy!'

I knew that his stupidity wasn't for real. It wasn't humanly possible. After all, he must have read a fair number of books to have become a Latin teacher in the first place. I genuinely didn't understand why he had failed me, although I did have a vague theory about it.

'Why should I want to make you *believe* that it's important? It *is*!' he insisted, swooping down on my silence as if it were retreat. Until then I had been sure that he was acting, and had left him a way out.

'I imagined, sir, but please tell me if I'm wrong, that your reason for failing me in May was to take my mind off other worries. Am I wrong?'

The teacher groaned; he must have had a heavy lunch. He belched. His eyes met his bodyguard's lenses. Not very briefly. Amorously? Bonkers turned to me. He looked solemn.

'I'll pass you. But two months after the beginning of the next school year I shall test you on the entire first-year syllabus. Understood?'

'No, sir. You haven't yet told me why you failed me. If you can pass me now, why couldn't you pass me first time?'

He sighed and turned to his colleague. 'Sad times,' he remarked wisely. 'Moral standards have been completely eroded.'

'Is Latin a moral standard?' I asked, mystified.

'Go to Hell! I've passed you. Don't forget: two months after the next school year begins I shall examine you on the whole first-year syllabus. *Punctum*. Do you hear me? Now show me your certificate so that I can sign it and then get out!'

'I don't have one.'

'You don't WHAT?' he raged. 'You haven't lost that too?'

'I'm not wearing a star,' I explained. 'If they stop me in the street, I hardly want to be found carrying a certificate from the Jewish grammar. Don't worry, sir, if you say I've passed I'm sure I can take your word for it . . .'

'You have! You have!' he shouted. 'But two months after—'

'Yes, sir, two months after. Oh, and sir . . .' I said innocently, fixing him with my big blue eyes.

'What now?' he snarled.

'When does the next school year begin?'

He hissed. My form-mistress's eyes closed behind her triple-glazed spectacles. But their noble principles wouldn't allow them to fail a Jewish kid twice in these difficult times.

I didn't bother Mother with the details. I just told her that I'd passed. 'Then they must have failed you unfairly last time!' she concluded immediately. 'You haven't opened your books once since March! You can't have got better at Latin since then!'

'They were a bit more lenient this time,' I said in the teachers' defence. 'They must have felt ashamed of themselves.'

'What about Dávid? They failed him in two subjects: he'll have to stay down a year!'

'Maybe they can only compromise their principles on one subject at a time . . .'

Dávid had failed in both Latin and German. German would cost him a year of his life whether we survived the war or not. German! What would happen to the German language after the war? Would people still speak it? And what about the orthodox Jews with their Yiddish? Hitler's words, Nazi words, German words, dripping with blood. What would happen? Would German be banned?

I told Dávid and my friends the full story of the re-sit. Pista's reaction was very odd: he shoved one of his maps under my nose.

'The Russians will take Makó and Szeged in a matter of days! They'll be on the great Hungarian plain!'

'Well done,' I replied. 'That's exactly what I said last week.'

'You don't understand,' Pista went on calmly. 'No mountains, no natural obstacles, nothing between them and Budapest.' This was a bit much. I began to lose patience.

'So what's new?'

'You'll have to learn some Latin!' said András. I could only laugh.

'What's Latin got to do with it?' I asked. Pista took a deep breath and, like a mother talking to a very stupid child, he began to explain.

'In three weeks' time the Red Army will arrive in Budapest. There's a good chance that four weeks from today, we'll all be back at school. Do you want to celebrate victory by sweating over your Latin?' My heart missed a beat. For a second, the arrival of the Red Army seemed a very frightening prospect.

From then on we counted the days to the Red Army's arrival. Hungarian place names sparkled like lamps in the obscurity of the BBC broadcasts: Nagybánya, Beszterce, Szászrégen. Horthy gathered his remaining forces together and joined the Germans in a counter-attack. The French had liberated Paris; the Belgians had marched into Brussels; even Bucharest had 'fallen' to Rumanian troops, although the battles had all been fought by American, British and Russian forces. The Poles had risen when the Red Army had reached the Vistula. Would we Hungarians be Hitler's only faithful dogs? The last servants of a dead and decomposing master?

One evening, personal news arrived from London. Pista's mother understood English a little, and listened to the BBC news as if it were a concert. The Russians had occupied the second-largest copper-producing area in Europe: Bor, in Serbia, where my father was a slave, guarded by Hungarian and SS guards. Until then I had imagined the mines to be black, like coal mines, because of the black SS uniforms. Suddenly I saw sparkling gold mines.

'He'll have escaped before the Russians got there,' nodded Mother wisely. 'Devils don't die in Hell. Yet Boriska said that he wouldn't come back . . .'

In Mother's words I recognised my own games, the bargains struck with demons. Boriska had also predicted that we would survive, and Mother's faith was shaken by the unexpected good news. Maybe she had been ready to pay for our lives with Father's. My rejoicing was in any case short-lived. Altmann had heard that the Germans had behaved at Bor as they had done at other labour and death camps, herding away the prisoners ahead of the approaching Russians.

Gyula came to visit us. I was friendly to him.

'You've got thinner since I last saw you. How do you manage to age so fast?'

'Józska!' shouted Mother, but then she laughed because she thought I was teasing Gyula, not commiserating with him. She answered my question for him: 'It's true love that does it.' I didn't understand, but Gyula did. He laughed politely and with bad grace. Then, a little reluctantly and guiltily, he asked about us. Mother added to his sense of guilt by telling him that we had finally got some Christian papers, when the Russians were practically on the doorstep. Gyula's face lit up. He thumped me on the shoulder.

'That's great! You may need them yet!'

'They've already taken Makó!' I told him, challenging his lack of faith. Gyula smiled, nodded, and deflated me.

'They've come to a standstill on the Vistula.'

'So what? They're regrouping.'

Apart from questions of strategy, I had no quarrel left with

Gyula, and hardly even bore him a grudge. He had done what I had wanted: he had gone away. I went off to play so that he and Mother could have a row.

Instead of squabbling, Mother sent him off to the Jewish affairs section of the Swedish Embassy. He returned the next day empty-handed. He had been unable to get even an application form. The hundred Jewish aides were so overworked that they couldn't find time to replace the printed forms with typed ones. Gyula had insisted until a furious official had pushed his own, typewritten 'orders' into his hand. These stated with absolute clarity that only two categories of persons were eligible for provisional passports: those who had close blood relations in Sweden or, alternatively, long-standing and substantial trade relations. The document stipulating these conditions was signed by the Swedish King's special envoy, Raoul Wallenberg. Mother laughed bitterly at the news.

'They've made plenty of noise over these few passports, but they were remarkably quiet when their Gustav let the German troops cross his territory to stab Norway in the back!'

There was no longer any question about it: only arms could save us.

'Tank-battles south of Nagyvárad end in Soviet defeat!' bellowed one headline. Only Aunty Sári and I remained capable of reading the fascist press. Five days later the same paper announced the strategic withdrawal of the all-out offensive to relieve Kolozsvár. We stopped drawing maps of Hungary. It was too time-consuming when every village was a milestone. The tank-battle for Hungary was now raging near Debrecen. Kolozsvár, Nagyvárad and Szeged had fallen. The great Hungarian plain had been reached at several points. The Red Army had opened the way to Budapest.

Like water bursting through a dam, refugees flooded into Budapest from all directions. Schools were opened up to accommodate them; special trains were laid on. Official propaganda competed with ear-witnesses to tell the most gruesome tales. Drunken Russian hordes were raping young girls and grandmothers, beating the gold teeth out of people's heads, driving away the poor man's cow and eating his lame horse. At the same time, 'panic-raisers' and 'scaremongers' were threatened with martial law. There were appeals for 'heroic calm' and 'orderly flight'. A new poster appeared beside the 'Fatherland in Danger'. Dávid and I took a good look. It was square, divided into sixteen sections, each of which contained a picture and a caption. I found the whole thing funny, but Dávid examined each section

417

with a poker-face. He drew my attention to a few in particular: a scarfed peasant woman with a rope round her neck, a skinned hand, and a skinned foot. The captions read: 'Stalinist tie; Stalinist glove; Stalinist sock.'

'What do you reckon?' asked Dávid calmly. I made a face to signal that I had no comment. Dávid insisted. I gave in.

'If that isn't scaremongering, what is?'

'Admitting the German defeats. Reality. Nothing else,' said Dávid.

There had been no air-raid warnings for several days. Factories and offices carried on working normally, and the Indian summer persisted so long that only the calendar and the newspaper told us how close we were to winter and the front.

One Sunday the three of us were having lunch when we heard a huge commotion on the balconies. We stiffened, the food halfway to our mouths. Had we stayed to become sitting ducks for the SS and the Constabulary? Or had the shoe merchant managed to start another panic? Then András's voice cut through the noise.

'HUNGARY HAS LAID DOWN HER ARMS!'

Within five seconds I had reached the centre of the commotion outside Pista Bognár's door, where the battery-powered radio, which had previously been carefully secreted in a drawer, stood in the entrance. Sixty or seventy people were standing around it, crying, kissing and hugging each other into silence.

'Horthy!' whispered Altmann, pointing at the radio. 'Capitulation!' But he too was told to be quiet. Everyone wanted to hear what Horthy had to say.

Our leader was washing his hands. Hungary had not entered the war to rob corpses, but as a result of German blackmail. A year and a half late, and in a modest way, the wireless quoted Torma. It brought tears to my eyes. I wondered whether he was listening.

'By now, every sober-minded person realises that the German Reich has lost this war. As the great German statesman Bismarck said: "No people should sacrifice itself in the name of an alliance." We cannot reduce our ancestral homeland to ruins fighting a series of rearguard actions on another country's behalf. Under the cloak of German occupation, the Gestapo has applied well-known and inhumane methods to resolve the Jewish question, just as it has elsewhere. I have therefore communicated to the representative of the German Reich our intention to establish a preliminary

truce with our erstwhile opponents, and to cease all hostilities against them forthwith. Trusting to their sense of justice, I wish to safeguard the continuity of the nation and to realise our peaceful aims in accordance with theirs. I appeal to all right-thinking Hungarians to follow me along the stony path to save our nation.'

Veronika was sobbing on her mother's breast. The small, smart mother rested her forehead on her daughter's hair; she was crying too. During the speech, Dávid, András and I had begun to unpick the stars from our shirts with our fingernails. Pista attacked his star with scissors, which other people then borrowed. Altmann had grabbed the balcony railing and was swaying to and fro in a prayer of thanksgiving. Pista's mother threw back her dyed blonde hair and whistled, deep in thought. She was an intriguing woman, with her mocking smile as she read the Nazi newspapers, her half-conscious understanding of English, her lazy, calm way of reasoning, the discipline which hid her fear during air-raids, and the detached good humour which was so like her son's. She was completely approachable and at the same time the inhabitant of a strange, better, clearer and more colourful world. Pista sat smiling happily, as if he'd just swallowed a whole kilo of chocolate in one go. Veronika's mother wiped the tears from her daughter's face, forgetting her own.

'Go and wash your face,' she ordered quietly, 'and put on your pretty pink dress. The Russians will be here any minute.'

The two corpulent detectives in the building opposite ours could have passed for twins. They stood on their balcony and gazed openly at us. I gave them the new, two-fingered Hitlerian salute. One of them shook his fist, the other didn't even have the strength to do that.

I hadn't noticed that Altmann had disappeared, but he suddenly popped up again without his moustache, armed with three bottles. Aunty Sári provided some glasses, and the old usurer filled them up with wine.

Mother stood beside me with her hand on Dávid's shoulder. Her eyes and face were luminous. The shoe merchant lifted his glass high, and in a ringing voice like the Rabbi's, he sang the few words of Hebrew that I had ever really known, the blessing of the wine. His voice was silver. The wine glittered.

'Mr Altmann!' interrupted Aunty Sári ruthlessly. 'Surely you don't wish to celebrate with German wine?'

'It's Moselle 1939,' protested Altmann, then laughed and turned his glass upside down, urging the rest of us to do the same. I paddled happily in the German wine. But Pista's mother showed Altmann no mercy.

'You've shaved off your beautiful moustache, so why not take the star off your jacket?'

Altmann didn't reply for a moment, then said very slowly: 'I shall not take that off for as long as I live.'

Aunty Sári shook her head. Altmann smiled triumphantly, then went away and returned with two bottles of Tokaj. He had just cleared his throat for a new blessing of the wine when András began to play the *Hatikva* on his violin. It was all the same to Altmann as long as he was allowed to sing:

> *'Still within the heart,*
> *A Jewish soul breathes . . .'*

This was too much for the two detectives. They started towards their staircase.

'Are they coming here?' asked a cowardly Jew.

'They're hardly going to feel like joining in the celebrations,' said Dávid patronisingly.

> *'We have not yet lost our hope,*
> *The hope that has lasted for two thousand years:*
> *To be a free people in our own land*
> *The land of Zion and Jerusalem.'*

At the end of the song Mother spoke for the first time. 'Come on. I'll heat lunch up again.'

Afterwards, when we were getting up from the table to go back to the Bognárs' radio, an unexpected visitor arrived. It was Éva, our hostess.

'No chocolates, I'm afraid! This was all I could find.' She put a bottle on the table. 'Champagne. I'm sorry there's no ice in the ice-box: we'll have to drink it warm.'

'Isn't it German?' I asked nervously.

Éva gave me a ladylike, haughty look. She was play-acting.

'German champagne? What an insult! It's the real thing – French.' She turned to Mother proudly. 'I've sacked two of my German fiancés.'

'Then where did you get the champagne?' asked Mother suspiciously.

'I bought it off a third German. For a lot of money.' She lifted her chin. 'Yes, I bought it. I told him that he'd never need champagne again.'

Éva was the only person who drank any of the wine. The rest of us just gilded the bottom of our glasses. After three glasses she began to sing her song about building a new world. After four she made a resolution.

'I shall go to bed with the first Russky I find this evening. For love, if he's good-looking—'

'Not in front of the children!' warned Mother.

'If only they weren't children!' laughed Éva. She took Mother's hands in hers. 'Judit, I promise you that from tomorrow on I'll be a good girl.' I couldn't tell whether she was serious or just having fun. 'And from the day after tomorrow . . .' But Mother didn't want to know.

'This will end badly, Éva.'

'It's already ended well!' Éva laughed.

We went back to the radio, but it was only playing music.

'Come with me,' said Dávid, and set off down the staircase. András and I followed. We went to the main gate and took down the huge yellow star. It was totally unlike Dávid to have thought of this: I knew that I would never forgive him for having had the idea first.

'Give it to me,' said András. 'I want it as a souvenir.' Not content with being both a pianist and a violinist, he now revealed his flair as an art collector. Dávid refused.

'Haven't you seen enough of it?' he asked. So we burnt it. Then, slapping each other on the back, we returned to the throng of grown-ups around the radio. It was still playing music.

'This is a German military march,' remarked Aunty Sári. 'Bad omen.'

'You're a pessimist,' accused Veronika's mother. She was scared. Veronika stood beside her in a pink dress, a pink ribbon in her black hair.

'Yes, I am a pessimist,' nodded Aunty Sári. 'I've been preparing for good news for so long that now . . . What was it Horthy said?' She frowned for a moment and then quoted from memory: ' "I have therefore communicated to the representative of the German Reich our intention to establish a preliminary truce." Good God! We're in trouble.'

The radio urgently summoned a well-known Arrow Cross general to Budapest. The army was ordered to continue the fight to the sound of German and Hungarian military marches.

'Bad omen,' people repeated. Altmann, who for some unknown reason always liked to be first with the bad news, made up for his delay by repeating Aunty Sári's suspicions at full volume.

'Horthy warned the Germans in advance so that they could take action. He was just trying to wriggle out of the blame from both sides. He dares to blame the deportations on the Gestapo! Hitler was still a little corporal sucking blood at his mother's breast when Horthy launched his first pogrom at Siófok in 1919.'

This time, however, Altmann really was first with the bad news. He borrowed his Christian neighbour's telephone and rang his former customer, the colonel.

'They're arming the Arrow Crosses at their headquarters in Pasarét! The Germans control the bridges! Panzers in the streets!' Altmann began to cry. 'I shaved off my moustache, shaved it all off . . . How could I have trusted that animal Horthy . . . ?''

It was getting dark. The radio had been silent for several minutes; I thought someone must have switched it off. Suddenly it burst into life: 'The National Socialist Party and the Hungarist Movement have taken power under the leadership of Ferenc Szálasi. Fight on! Long live Szálasi!'

Szálasi was the Hungarian Hitler.

Mother ordered us home. We thought Éva was in her room, but she must have gone out. After a few minutes she came in from the street, still tipsy.

'I got scared on the Boulevard. Armed Arrow Crosses everywhere. They've seized power. They're shouting, handing out leaflets. Most of them are drunk. They thought I'd been celebrating their victory.'

'Éva,' said Mother abruptly. 'Can you lend me a hundred pengös?'

'I can lend you two hundred.' She opened her handbag and turned it out, then struck her forehead in annoyance. 'The champagne! I gave all two hundred to that sodding German. It's normally only a hundred.' Éva offered us the fifty pengös she had left, but Mother turned it down; she had exactly that much herself. 'You can use everything in the flat. You can sell anything.' Éva sat down, exhausted. 'And I . . . I had to go and split up with two of my fiancés today. Two out of four.'

Two seconds after flopping down on the sofa, Éva sprang up again, fresh, laughing, almost sober.

'Who cares? Two's enough!' She ran down to a Christian's telephone and ordered one of her fiancés to come and pick her up in his car. Ten minutes later we heard hooting from the street.

'She's a good girl all the same,' said Mother after Éva had left. 'A very good girl. Let's pray that God helps her.'

We were now alone in the comfortable three-roomed flat. Mother sat quietly in the living room. She looked so anguished that I couldn't bear it.

'What's for supper?' I asked, both to distract her and because I was hungry.

'I'll cook something in a minute,' Mother replied, although she hadn't heard me. 'Have some bread and marmalade for now.'

'Again!' I protested.

'Be glad we've got that much! You might find yourself longing for it tomorrow!'

'Great! After the war I shan't eat marmalade for at least ten years. Anyway, what's the matter with you?'

'I'm thinking.'

'Have we really only got fifty pengös?'

'Really and truly.'

'But it's only the fifteenth of the month! How can we have spent a hundred and fifty in two weeks?'

'I was planning to sell some clothes tomorrow. Go and find your brother.'

Dávid was at the Bognárs', where thirty people were standing huddled around the radio. It had been hidden in the drawer again, although the two detectives had already seen it.

'They'll come straight here and shoot the lot of us! Everyone! We'll all be punished for one person's crime!'

'What crime?' I whispered to Dávid and András.

'The star flew off into the sky,' giggled Dávid.

'Some Arrow Cross nicked it,' suggested András. 'He thought it was made of gold.' I laughed out loud, breaking the icy fear in the room and attracting everyone's attention.

'You think it's funny! So it was you!' accused Altmann, but I could see by the fury in his eyes that he was looking for a scapegoat and had no inkling that what he said was true.

'Me?' I laughed. 'Why would I want a bigger star than the one I've got already?'

'He stole it for the family coat of arms!' joked Dávid.

'Then who did steal it? Who stole the star? They'll come here

423

and shoot everyone! We can't all be punished for this one crime!'

'Mr Altmann,' said Aunty Sári firmly. 'The Arrow Crosses won't come here. But they would come if there were a star on the gate. Whoever took it down was extremely wise.'

'It was you!' shouted Altmann. 'You took it down. Well, you were NOT wise! Those two spies opposite will have already notified the Arrow Crosses. They're on their way!'

'Stop prophesying doom, Mr Altmann. I would certainly have taken the star down if someone hadn't beaten me to it, because our lives depend on the toss of a coin, and I'm calling heads.'

'Don't flip coins for my head!'

'Your head?' smiled Aunty Sári. 'Have you got one?'

'Have I got a head? Me? Do you know how much money I had when I started my business? You're the one who has no head! If they find out that we're defying them we'll be their first victims!'

'Quite right, Mr Altmann,' parried Aunty Sári. 'But if they don't find out we won't be their victims at all. And if you don't shout about it, the two detectives won't hear you. Those two are so used to it being there that they won't look to see if it's gone. Surely a clever Jew like you can see that much?'

The compliment calmed the shoe merchant.

'You are a wise woman, Mrs Bognár,' he said, but it seemed that he was unable to live without fear, because five minutes later he started to sigh and groan about his beautiful moustache.

'Put a false one on,' I suggested. 'Twice the size of the old one.'

'It won't be the same . . .'

'Who'll notice the difference?'

'*They* will. When they pull it it'll fall off . . .'

'If they get to the stage of pulling your moustache you're done for anyway. At least a false one won't hurt when they give it a tug.'

'Done for . . . done for anyway, no, not at all the same . . .' mumbled Altmann. He was drunk with fear.

The caretaker arrived, attracted by the raised voices. He raised his finger significantly, and a respectful silence ensued. Aunty Sári tapped him on the shoulder and whispered something in his ear.

He nodded, then raised his index finger once more. 'If I don't see it up again by tomorrow morning at the very latest, I shall have to report it!' he announced.

Aunty Sári turned to Pista. 'Paint one this evening,' she ordered. 'We can't convert the building permanently.'

424

Mother was packing when we returned to our room.

'There you are at last. Go to bed.'

'No supper?' I whined.

'Eat some bread and marmalade.' I didn't protest any further: the fact that Mother was packing was a lot more interesting than supper.

The doorbell rang. Ferenc Jáger was standing outside in a military coat.

'I couldn't come any sooner. I was worried that you'd already gone into hiding.'

'We'll be leaving tomorrow morning.'

'That's what I hoped. Drunken Arrow Crosses are firing guns in the streets tonight.'

It was at that moment that I noticed the gun on his belt. I couldn't resist it. 'Why are you doing this for us?' I asked.

Mother glanced at me in alarm. Dávid stared angrily. Jáger's head jolted upright. He hadn't expected the question. Had he never asked it himself? He frowned slightly, as if he resented my posing a question that he couldn't answer.

'Why not?' he said after a while. 'If I hadn't walked into your air-raid shelter, the papers would still be yellowing in a drawer.'

'You could have bought a villa on Rose Hill.'

His face darkened.

'Don't make me angry. Money for lives? That would be blood money. God doesn't bless that.'

He sighed. His words tired him. He realised that he didn't understand himself either.

'Go to sleep,' said Mother. 'We'll have a long day tomorrow, if we live to see the sun.' She went out on to the balcony. Jáger followed. They leaned over the railing, keeping watch.

26: The Three Miracles

When I opened my eyes the next morning, Mother was standing in front of the window taking a few things out of a suitcase that was lying on a chair. I sat up in bed.

'Are you unpacking?' I asked, frightened that she had changed her mind during the night.

'I'm wondering what to take.'

'Why haven't we left yet?' I demanded.

'We're waiting until there's a bit more traffic on the streets. Get up. Dávid's already dressed.' My brother was making breakfast in the kitchen. Jáger was leaning against the wall.

We had two suitcases. Mother didn't want us to take anything that wouldn't fit into these two cases. She was unhappy about them anyway.

'This one's too posh for a cobbler's family. It's all leather. Your father gave it to me. The other's made of waxed cardboard. It looks good but it'll melt if it gets wet.'

She selected the clothes she needed. The best things were presents from Aunty Felice. She must have been the only woman in Hungary with a gold-embroidered cardigan and no money. We told her so, but she knew already and refused to take it off.

'I'll lie if necessary,' she laughed. 'I'll tell them I stole it. I'll wear my shabby clothes on top; I'm already wearing three layers – that's why I'm so fat.'

We had coffee and toast. Mother nagged us, she wanted us to eat several eggs because she didn't know when we'd get another chance, but it isn't possible to eat meals in advance. She put ten hard-boiled eggs, a loaf of bread, and two jars of marmalade into a string bag. The bag and the suitcases were our only luggage. We were ready to leave.

Mother had filled in our forged birth certificates, modelling them on our real ones, and put the third, which was spare, into an envelope. Mother had Jáger's wife's birth certificate for herself. Jáger was to leave the spare one with our old neighbours in case Samuel turned up. Then she crumpled our new documents and smoothed them out again.

'From now on, Dávid, your name is Endre Jáger. There are Christians called Dávid, but they tend to be from Transylvania, and the Arrow Crosses consider every Dávid to be a Jewish king. I've made you a year younger to the day, so that you're not eligible for junior military service. Józska Jáger, your birthday is the same as Józska Sondor's was, but don't forget that your brother is only one year older than you. You both went to a secondary modern. You were born in Hódmezövásárhely, and we fled from there to escape the Russians. We're scared to death of them. My maiden name was Rozália Dragomér, my birthday is on the tenth of April and I am three years older than I am. That can't be helped because my papers are real. Your father is a shoemaker. He has a workshop in our home. He works by himself and he was born in 1900. That's easy to remember, and his birthday is the first of December, which is easy to remember too.'

The exam followed immediately.

'I forgot the most important thing!' exclaimed Mother suddenly. 'We are Protestants – Calvinists. Quick, the Lord's Prayer, both at once.' We spouted obligingly. 'All right. And now forget the *Credo* and the *Ave Maria*.'

'Done,' I reported. 'What a waste of good Latin.'

'Stop fooling around!' snapped Dávid, frightened.

Mother gave us one minute to say goodbye to András the Pianist and Pista Bognár. András was still in his pyjamas.

'You're lucky. You're pure-bred Aryans,' he said enviously.

'What about you?'

'Swiss protection. Even that cost six thousand pengös. A full Christian pedigree is worth anything between twenty and a hundred thousand.'

The Bognárs were packing.

'Have you got papers?' I asked.

'Yes, thanks. Catholic.' Pista held out his hand to introduce himself. I shook it.

'Protestant,' I laughed. 'Do you know your *Ave Maria*?'

'. . . *Gratia plena*,' answered Pista.

427

Mother had already locked the door of the flat.

'Where's your overcoat?' she demanded severely.

'I'm boiling,' I complained. Dávid was wearing his coat.

'Put it on now,' ordered Mother, re-opening the door. I decided to be bloody-minded.

'I won't. Not for just three days.'

'You will. What three days?'

'The Russians are attacking Szolnok, which is one hundred kilometres away. Within a day, two days at the most, Malinovsky will attack Budapest from the east and from the north-east. Tolbukhin . . .'

Mother didn't give me time to present my analysis of what Marshal Tolbukhin would do after he had encircled Belgrade. She was red with the effort of trying not to shout.

'Put on your coat or I'll smack your face.'

'Put on your coat,' repeated Jáger. He spoke quickly, so that I couldn't accuse him of playing father. I pushed the door open with the sigh of a martyr, and went to fetch my coat.

A new yellow star was hanging on the gate. A few people loitered near the tram stop, and I started towards them to ask them whether the trams were running. Jáger stopped me.

'On foot,' he ordered curtly. He had a point. The danger of meeting someone who knew us or had seen us wearing the star was ten times higher at the stop nearest the flat. Denunciations had been pouring in to the Gestapo by the thousand. We used the side streets. Suddenly I surprised myself by laughing. I had no idea where we were going.

'We'll try to get to Pestszentimre. Your "father" is stationed there,' said Mother in a broad country accent. 'This is overdoing it,' she added before I could imitate her. 'We'd better just speak simply.'

I remembered that there was another reason for trying Pestszentimre. Mother knew a Protestant pastor called Reverend Eliás. He had given her the address of some people who helped converts escape into hiding by finding addresses where they weren't known. These people lived in Pestszentimre.

The soldier walked at the head of his family, his wife and children following him in single file. You couldn't have found a more beautiful family in an Arrow Cross newspaper. The father carried one suitcase, the elder boy carried the other, and the mother had the string shopping bag. I stayed obediently in line.

'Put your coat on,' said Jáger, turning to me without stopping. I had been carrying it over my arm, but I realised that he was right. Only posh people carried their coats, especially in the country.

We reached Népszinház Street. Jáger asked a lance-corporal whether the trams were in service.

'Only tanks, Corporal.'

Jáger thanked him, and the other waved at his superior rather than saluting him. Uniformed discipline was becoming a little threadbare.

Dávid walked behind our soldier. I walked behind Mother, my head down. If I saw nothing I wouldn't be seen. We had been on the streets for a good hour. Suddenly, a rattle of small-arms fire sounded from our left. I lifted my head. There was a tank standing only thirty-five or forty metres away. I had been walking so blindly that I had hardly recognised the square where Mother and I had exchanged clothes for Christian ration tickets. Armed men, some of them in uniform, stood around the tank. They were watching a star house. The morning sun had just reached its façade. It shone like copper. A huge, gaping hole had been blasted out of the second-floor wall. Behind the tank, a hundred or a hundred and fifty people were lined up like supporters at a football match.

'Make it bigger!' shouted a bass voice from the crowd.

'Bigger!' repeated several other people.

Some shouted witticisms: 'Don't feel sorry for her, she's not your mother!'

'Don't worry, they're not virgins!'

'Aim for his head, don't cripple him!'

Jáger put his suitcase down for a second.

'Let's go,' urged Mother. We went on. The square was full of stalls. A few of these were open for business, selling odd bits of merchandise: a pair of trousers, a paraffin lamp. This was the Teleki Square flea-market. Business was brisker at the far end, away from the tank.

'Judit,' boomed a male voice. We were done for; I couldn't understand why I felt no fear. Dávid's eyes narrowed in pain.

'Zoltán!' Mother exclaimed with apparent delight. I began to pay attention. A huge, broad-shouldered soldier was bearing down on us. He was wearing army trousers and a jacket with stars on the lapels. He was a sergeant major. A shopping basket dangled from his fore-arm. In Mother's place I would have refused to recognise him.

429

'Where are you going?' asked the soldier called Zoltán. 'Have you got somewhere?'

'We won't know until we arrive,' laughed Mother. 'Our friend Ferenc Jáger is stationed at Pestszentimre, so that's where we're heading.'

'On shanks' mare? Isn't that a bit far for today? I'm Zoltán Jankó,' he added, turning to us.

'Józska,' I said cautiously. Poor Dávid had to choose between his false name and his real one.

'Endre,' he said.

'I thought you were Dávid,' said Jankó. 'I must have remembered it wrong.'

'No . . . ' stammered Dávid, 'you didn't . . . only it's Endre now. Have we met before?'

The Jankós were neighbours of ours from Oszu. Zoltán had left before I had arrived, but he was still a 'distant neighbour', as he put it. We all laughed. Mother leaned towards him.

'Are you deserting?' she asked.

'Me?' laughed the sergeant major. 'Shall I show you my written orders?'

'Only if you want to see my Certificate of Baptism,' laughed Mother. Jankó's voice dropped to a whisper.

'You've got one?' he said admiringly. Mother nodded. 'I could use a few of those for some friends of mine.'

A civilian with a gun and an Arrow Cross armband passed us for the second time. Mother and Jankó stopped their whispering. The man looked at us. Jankó noticed him.

'What's that man gaping at us for? I'll ask him.'

'Don't! Please!' hissed Mother.

'Always seem confident,' he advised her. The civilian was a greying, fattish man of about forty. Without his gun and his conceited expression he'd have passed for a jovial barber. He was coming straight towards us: we were about to face our first test.

'Can I help you?' asked Jankó, taking the initiative.

'Help me? You can salute me! Both you and the corporal.'

Jankó laughed in his face. 'Hasn't anyone ever told you to stay off the drink in the mornings?' he asked pleasantly.

'I object to your tone,' said Fatty pompously. 'Just this once, I will refrain from retaliation, as I can see that you are not aware of the new regulations announced on the radio.'

430

'On the radio?' grinned Jankó. 'That changes everything. Soldiers are supposed to salute civilians now, are they? I'd never have guessed! Thanks so much for telling me!'

'Not every civilian,' said the man, trying to explain.

'Oh, I see,' interrupted Jankó. 'Just you.'

'Everyone up to the rank of captain must salute all members of the Arrow Cross wearing the Árpád armband. For the higher ranks it's a matter of politeness.'

'Super!' grinned Jankó. 'But I'll be happy to wait until I hear it with my own ears.' Suddenly, the sergeant major raised his voice to parade-ground pitch: 'Joking apart, mate, how many years did you do on the Russian front? How many times have you been wounded?'

The fat man's head jolted like a dog's when it hears the whistle. He forced his face to look as weather-beaten as his sagging jowls would permit.

'My apologies, Sergeant Major. On this occasion, allow me to be the first to salute.' He did. Jankó and Jáger saluted back. The fat man moved off.

'Listen to the radio! I can assure you that you'll hear about the salute with your own ears, Sergeant Major.'

'Then I shan't believe them!'

'Wouldn't it have been simpler if you'd just saluted him in the first place?' chided Mother after the man had gone.

'He'd never have left us alone if I had.'

'How many years did you spend on the Russian front?' she asked compassionately.

'Not one minute, thank God,' Zoltán smiled. 'Pestszentimre is a long way on foot. Come and stay at my place for a day or two. I only live just around the corner in Örömvölgy Street. My wife is with the children in Oszu. They're staying at my father's.'

He lived in a narrow, winding, shabby street.

'Come on up,' he urged. 'You can always come down again if you get scared.'

'You really will frighten me if you go on like that,' said Mother irritably. We followed Jankó, who opened a door on the first floor but didn't show us in.

'It's me,' he said in a hushed voice, entering first. 'I've brought a few guests.'

The curtain was drawn. There were four men in the room, two of them sitting on a cheap carpet on the floor. They didn't get up when

Mother came in. None of the men wore shoes, although there were boots scattered all over the room. The smallest of the men was wearing a jacket that came down to his knees; only his fingertips peeped out of the sleeves. We all had to take our shoes off so as not to make a noise on the wooden floor. Jáger had cloths wrapped around his feet like a peasant; he unwound them, embarrassed. Jankó lent him a pair of socks.

The sergeant major then issued us with our standing orders for living in the flat. Walking was to be kept to a minimum. He recommended lying down and doing minor exercises to avoid cramp. Only Dávid and I were allowed into the kitchen. If the neighbours noticed signs of life they would assume that Jankó's children had come to visit. Putting a blanket over the window would look suspicious. The lavatory wasn't to be flushed more than once an hour. If someone attempted to force an entry they were to be deterred by means of the sub-machine gun, which was entrusted to Jáger during Jankó's absence.

After the briefing, we proceeded to introductions. The others were labour men. The one in the out-sized jacket was a Dr Hönig. He had to roll up his sleeves to shake hands. The two men on the floor rose briefly, nodded, then sat down again. They had ashes in their hair: they were in *shivah*, mourning.

'Did you bring any food, Sergeant?' asked Dr Hönig.

'Only friends,' laughed Jankó. 'I'll go back to the market in a minute.'

'It's a bit early for eating friends,' answered Hönig seriously.

Mother distributed the ten hard-boiled eggs and the bread. The mourners wouldn't eat. I was given permission to switch the radio on, but had to keep the volume down to a murmur. The set could only receive Hungarian stations.

'By the authority vested in me by the State, I hereby discharge you of all further duties with immediate effect. Ferenc Szálasi.' This communication was addressed to the general commanding the Hungarian First Army. The order was repeated for the chief of staff and about ten other high-ranking officers.

'They must have refused to salute,' remarked Jankó. 'But where are their units? If they'd changed sides, the Russians would have been here by now.'

Yet another officer was sacked. Jankó hissed.

'That's fucked up our written orders! His adjutant signed them in

432

his name. We'll have to fill in the next lot of blank forms ourselves. Whose name shall we use?'

'The National Socialist Party and the Hungarist Movement have taken power under the leadership of Ferenc Szálasi. Fight on! Long live Szálasi!' shouted the radio for the benefit of those who hadn't already noticed. A newly promoted minister promised, in his own name and in the name of the Hungarian people, to 'wash the filth of Jewish plutocracy from our boots!' At first, no one would explain to me what plutocracy was. Finally Dr Hönig did so in order to shut me up.

We heard another kind of news. The doors of all starred buildings were to remain locked night and day. Jews were not allowed into the streets under any circumstances. They were forbidden to receive Christian visitors, and it was an offence for a Christian to visit a Jew. We had got out just in time.

The next order summoned all those who had left their posts back to their units. They were to return by Friday on pain of death.

'Good God,' sighed one of the mourners. 'Do they expect to stay in power another five days?'

'If we're back by Friday they'll forgive us for not letting them shoot us this morning,' commented Dr Hönig from the folds of his gigantic jacket.

I soon realised that all four labour men were doctors. Sergeant Jankó had saved them from a mass-execution. He and Jáger were discussing how they could get us all to safety.

'Two NCOs guarding four Jews – no one could object to that,' argued Jankó. 'I've got at least twenty-five blank written-orders forms and a stamp from divisional HQ! They're doctors, they've been ordered to the military hospital at Szolnok. With any luck the Russians will come to meet us.'

'I'll think about it,' answered Jáger. 'But my first duty is to the family.'

'We'll come with you!' interrupted Mother. 'You've endangered yourselves now because of us.'

Sergeant Major Jankó went off to do some shopping. Dr Hönig put his jacket on his lap and tried to thread a needle. After half a minute of unsuccessful attempts he turned to his mate.

'You do it. You're the tailor,' he said, but Mother took the needle and thread out of his hands.

'Unfortunately I'm only a psychoanalyst,' laughed Hönig. 'I have

433

no practical skills whatsoever. For the last three years the whole of Europe has been struggling to provide work for Grünwald here, who is a surgeon. Ever since these madmen have been in power the number of curable psychiatric cases has dropped like a stone.'

'Ever since yesterday?' asked Mother hesitantly.

'Yesterday, my dear? All that happened yesterday was that the padded-cell brigade took over from the ministers and generals of the basket and plot-weaving ward. In the last two or three years all the straightforward cases have cured themselves, without the slightest psycho-therapeutic intervention. War, my dear lady, is magic. I had begun to suffer from unbearable anxiety over my future, and if the demented fascists had not invited me to enjoy free board and lodging in the Jewish labour service, I would probably have starved to death long ago.'

'Please, Hönig, don't joke!' said one of the mourners, looking up from his companion's prayer book. 'Or at least joke more quietly.'

'Everyone mourns as best he can,' answered Hönig. 'Do I sound too jolly? I suppose I am trying to boost my *joie de vivre*. Am I so weak as to want to stay alive despite all my experience of human behaviour? That surprises me. I hadn't realised that I was thinking aloud, but if you can pray in silence, then I can . . .'

But he went on aloud: 'At least I won't die of starvation, I thought happily when I received my invitation from the state. How could I have known that the uniformed champions of tradition, hierarchy and the family would throw me straight to their cannibal subordinates, the NCOs of the labour service?'

'I've asked you to stop your joking once already,' said the mourner.

'And I've already told you that I'm not joking any more than you are with your prayers. For instance, when I say "cannibal", that is precisely what I mean. In my own language they are "cannibal-sadists" – or *dementia praecox* if you must know the Hebrew name for the disease. If you prefer more recent terminology, try "paranoid schizophrenia". A frustration in the infant that separates the mother into good and bad breasts, and then turns this destructive instinct upon the world, dividing it into irreconcilable good and evil. This disease is particularly prevalent among NCOs, while the traditional melancholic form of insanity is restricted to the officers and politicians. My research is aimed at identifying the connection between the two, since it seems curious that two distinct types of irrational behaviour can serve the same ends so effectively, as in the army for example.

434

What, indeed, is the distinction? Do the officers manifest some kind of cultural sublimation? Under different circumstances, would they exhibit the same symptoms as their subordinates? What do you think, Grünwald?'

'Let me pray, for God's sake!' interrupted one of the mourners. 'How can you generalise about cannibalistic NCOs in Sergeant Major Jankó's flat? If there'd been ten men like him in Sodom, God would have spared the whole city.'

'Firstly, God is probably more generous than I am. Secondly, Strausz, do you seriously believe that God could find ten Sergeant Jankós in Budapest when he couldn't find them in a mildly bohemian city like Sodom?'

'There's one more in this room alone,' said Mother, glancing across to where Jäger was chatting to Dávid. 'A true Christian.'

Hönig sighed.

'Precisely the point, my dear. Christianity is the alternative manifestation of cannibalism. I am sure that Dr Strausz will bear me out in saying that Jews don't eat their God for breakfast. Christianity . . . paranoid schizophrenia . . . hmmmm. What can we call our Christian patients? Christomaniacs? Their main symptom: manic self-denial.'

'You keep talking about the sick, irreconcilable division of good and evil, but you don't seem to be able to distinguish the two,' objected the handsome Grünwald.

'Excellent, Grünwald. Coming from a surgeon, a layman, that is a truly astute observation. But I have kept some notion of goodness, and you are right: Sergeant Jankó is some kind of psychological miracle. After the war, if thanks to him I survive, I shall cure him at a reduced fee.'

Dr Hönig seemed very bright, but I couldn't understand a quarter of what he was saying.

'Who am I to talk about lunatics?' he asked finally, confusing me even further. Luckily Mother asked Grünwald to tell us the story of their escape, which was easier to follow.

There had been around two hundred labour men serving in their company, almost all of them doctors. Their commanding officer was a decent Hungarian, who occasionally swore at having to make doctors do navvies' work when soldiers at the front and peasants in poor districts were dying for lack of medical attention. He treated his men well. He never allowed them to be cheated out of their rations; he ensured that letters arrived, gave plenty of breaks and sent men home on leave whenever he could. Compared to other labour men, they led the life of Riley. One by one, the crueller guards were replaced, all except Sergeant Szajkó, whose turn had not yet come. Szajkó had served as a guard in Russia, and the humane treatment of the labour men in this company drove him up the wall. 'Just wait till I get my hands on you!' he had said, but the doctors had laughed. They felt safe under the commander's wing. Everything had been fine – until yesterday. At the news of the capitulation, the company commander had provided wine for all the company, guards and labour men, two or three glasses each. They sang and hugged each other openly, expecting the Russians to arrive at any moment.

They were stationed in a Transdanubian village, inhabited for the most part by naturalised Germans, who gathered around the labour men and ground their toothless gums until the company commander chased them away. Later, during the afternoon, the news came: Szálasi . . .

Either the villagers or Szajkó must have alerted the local SS company stationed at Székesfehérvár. At dawn, Jankó realised that the SS had encircled the farm buildings where the labour company was billeted. Quietly, he woke one of the Jews and told him to wake the others without making any noise. Stumbling around, the Jew had only succeeded in waking three of his companions when Sergeant Jankó pointed a sub-machine gun at them and marched them out of the camp under the noses of the SS. At first they had thought that they were dreaming. They had always known Sergeant Jankó as a kind man who was well disposed towards the Jews, and now he seemed to want to kill them. He led them to a peasant's house and ordered them into the loft, telling them not even to peep out until his return.

Jankó then went back to the company to save some more people, and was almost caught. By this time the company commander and his guards had all been arrested and disarmed, with the single exception of Szajkó. The SS were holding the doctors at gunpoint; Szajkó was lounging around in front of them holding a pistol.

'Yesterday you thought you'd see me swing, you filthy yids! It would have been lovely, wouldn't it? Well, you won't now! Not even if they do hang me in the end! Capitulation? Are the Russians coming? Are these gentlemen Russians? Have they laid down their arms? Come on, show a bit of courage, take a good look down those gun barrels!'

Suddenly he had a splendid idea.

'Hey, you!' he shouted, picking on a father of two called Klein.

436

'Tell me, yid, how many eyes does a man have? Even a yid doctor should be able to tell me that!'

Still listening, I sneaked into an alcove beside the kitchen door so that Mother wouldn't send me further away.

'Two? Do you think I need a doctor to tell me that? But tell me how many eyes a Jew has, you little yid, tell me that. Two, you reckon? Wrong, yid, wrong.' With that, Szajkó walked up to Dr Klein and shot out one of his eyes.

The SS disarmed Szajkó on the spot, and mercifully shot the wounded Jew dead. Within minutes, Germanic order was restored: the Jewish company could have passed muster at a parade. In a short speech, the SS commandant let them know that he and his officers constituted a court martial, that the charge was mutiny, the verdict guilty, and the sentence death. The executions began immediately. In groups of twenty, the doctors were driven in lorries to a quarry two kilometres away. There they were shot.

Jankó hadn't been able to discover whether the company commander had been shot as well or whether the SS had simply taken him into custody. Jankó himself escaped to divisional HQ on a motorbike, where his news was received with powerless consternation. An officer gave him a wad of blank written orders, a stamp, an inking pad, and a lorry, and Jankó had driven the four labour men to Budapest.

I couldn't tell how long I stayed in the alcove by the kitchen door after Grünwald had finished his story. For some time after I had crept away, I couldn't hear or see anything around me. When I came to, I found myself howling like a whipped dog.

'Be quiet for God's sake!' hissed Mother, dashing across the room.

'Hang them all!' I screamed.

'Don't shout for goodness' sake! You'll get us all killed!'

I carried on screaming.

'Atten-SHUN!' barked a bass voice. I looked up. I hadn't noticed that Sergeant Jankó was back. 'What's the matter, Józska?' he asked gently.

'I don't know.'

'The last twenty-four hours haven't been easy for him, either,' said Mother apologetically.

'That's true,' said Dr Hönig, sitting down beside me. 'But, Józska, we can't be sure that the next twenty-four hours will be any easier. Or even the next twenty-four days. And who knows what will happen after that?'

437

I was amazed that this genius could come up with such a silly remark.

'Twenty-four days for Malinovsky to get from Szolnok to Budapest? A man who takes his orders from Zhukov?'

'All right,' smiled Hönig, but so cynically that it was hard to tell whether he was giving in to my arguments or diagnosing my mental state.

His jacket was now too tight. Jankó had bought him a new one at the flea-market. Jankó must have been to the black market too: there was a feast on the table. Sausage, bread, butter and two bottles of wine. The mourners decided it was time to break their fast, and after muttering a few prayers in Hebrew, set about demolishing the pork sausages.

Having satisfied their immediate hunger, Jankó and the four doctors counted up their money. Dr Hönig had fled in his shirt, and didn't have a bean, but the rest had six thousand pengős between them. Enough, as they said, to live comfortably until the Russians arrived; but they had greater ambitions than the consumption of black-market food.

Grünwald was walking on diamonds: they were hidden in the heels of his shabby boots. They were worth a fortune, but unless Jáger could find the tools to turn the safes back into boots Grünwald would have to go barefoot. Sergeant Jankó had been a printer in civilian life, but all the worthwhile printing presses were under strict official control. An improvised press would be primitive at best, and only good enough for leaflets. Mother asked whether they intended to print Certificates of Baptism.

Jankó laughed. 'They're not worth much more than leaflets. A man with a nose like Hönig's isn't going to convince a policeman by showing him a Certificate of Baptism.'

'Stop Jew-baiting, Sergeant,' laughed Hönig. 'I've got your birth certificate in my pocket – I'll write "Jewish" on it.' The four doctors were sharing Jankó's birth certificate in case one of them had to go down into the street. Jankó didn't need it as he had his military log book, which was worth a thousand times more. Without the log book, the blank written orders were useless. He and the doctors were thinking of forging military log books by the dozen, but to make sure that they'd be a bit better equipped until then, Mother gave them our blank birth certificate. In exchange, they promised to leave a log book for Samuel with our old neighbours, the Csolnokis. Mother gave Samuel's photo to Jankó. Jáger was also given a blank set of written orders.

That night, we piled up the furniture to make room for nine

sleepers. In the darkness, images of the slaughter of the doctors flashed in front of my eyes; but the silence was so heavy that I didn't dare cry.

It was noon when I awoke. The food on the table was as plentiful as the day before.

Dr Hönig was holding forth: 'That devil Horthy can't have wanted to capitulate. He may be an amateur, but he couldn't have bungled things that badly without doing it deliberately. It was his wife who got him his titles and his job in the first place. He'd have screwed it all up if she hadn't screwed the top brass of Vienna as soon as they got back from their honeymoon. The capitulation was a fake, just an attempt to save his neck after the war. He's never seen further than his own personal gain. He's never looked.'

Jankó's plan for the afternoon was to find a safer hide-out than his own flat. After a quick bite to eat, the mourners sat down on their carpet again.

We were given half a salami, four pairs of sausages, and half a loaf of bread to take with us. We had already survived one day and had more food than when we had left the starred block. Anxiously, Jankó saw us on our way.

'I'd like to be able to tell you to come round if you need anything, Judit. But I don't know where we'll be. I'll drop in here from time to time, but that's the best I can promise you. Until then, take this,' he added, counting five hundred pengös onto the table.

'No, please. Take it back,' said Mother. 'There are five of you and within a few hours you won't even have a roof over your heads. You don't have documents, all you have are diamonds. I've got a pair of diamond earrings myself,' she admitted, trying to shake off temptation.

'Take it anyway,' urged Jankó.

'I won't.'

'Regard it as an advance on two hectolitres of wine.'

'Don't be an idiot, Zoltán. Who's going to drink that wine?'

'Us,' replied Sergeant Jankó. 'So that's settled. I'm ripping you off on the wine, by the way.'

'Go on, take it, take it,' chorused the four doctors. Mother took a hundred-pengö note from the pile.

'I hope you won't need this as much as I do.'

We walked. Occasionally we waited for trams that didn't come, and walked again. Then we took a bus to Pestszentimre. Then we walked again, searching for the address that Reverend Eliás had given to Mother, looking at little houses along a dusty, village street until we found the right one. Only two of its windows overlooked the street, it was tiny. The fence only came up to my chin. We couldn't see anyone, so we opened the gate. A woman in her early thirties came towards us from a vegetable garden. She wore a headscarf tied at the back of her neck.

'Piroska Daniellik?' asked Mother. The woman nodded. 'Reverend József Eliás sent us.'

'Welcome, my sister. Come inside.'

'Don't you even want to know our names?' said Mother, surprised.

'For me, everyone he sends is Eliás,' smiled our welcomer, and Mother smiled too although I didn't see the joke at first. Then I remembered how Grandpa had given a pengö to the beggar at Passover in case the beggar was Elishah. Even then I didn't see the joke. Elishah was our prophet, and when he comes again he will come as our Messiah. Didn't this Christian woman know anything about religion? She looked a bit simple: her face was red from the wind, her jaw large, her carroty hair was dull and her hands rough with hard work. She led us apologetically into the house.

'I'm afraid I'm running a little late, but I'll soon have a room for you.' How could she be running late when she hadn't even known that we were coming?

She showed us into the living room. A door opened and a broad-shouldered, tall, white-haired man joined us.

'Gábor Daniellik,' he introduced himself. I was confused, not knowing which of my surnames to use.

'Julia,' said Mother, using the invention she had always kept for Aryan occasions.

'Dvvnndre,' stammered Dávid. Luckily Jáger had no problem, and I could stick to my own 'Christian' name.

'Do sit down,' said the old gentleman. 'I only came in to welcome you. God has sent you to us.'

He went straight back to his room, and his daughter brought us milk, bread and cheese on a tray.

'Tea will be ready in a minute. Are you very tired?' Mother shook her head, but she did look tired.

A pretty and expensively dressed woman breezed into the room, a crocodile-skin handbag on her arm. She was younger than Mother.

'So sorry to disturb you. Piroska, would you be a darling and tell me how one gets hold of a taxi in this charming little village of yours?'

'I don't know,' answered Piroska Daniellik. 'I never need one. The first time a car ever stopped outside this house was the day you arrived, my sister. Two cars in succession . . . I would be grateful if you could renounce the taxi this time. It would attract attention.'

'But, Piroska! How can we possibly, *possibly* take all our luggage with us on foot? Make an exception, please, just this once . . .'

'An exception?' smiled our hostess. 'You do as you wish. I only ask for your understanding. Come back for your luggage, twice if need be.'

The posh woman turned to Jáger.

'Sergeant, could you get me a taxi and wait for me a little way up the street? I would be most grateful.' Discreetly, she touched her handbag with her free hand, but Piroska's eyes were on her and she took it away. She soon found a witty solution to her problem. 'I shan't remain in your debt,' she said meaningfully.

'Indeed you won't, madam,' replied Jáger stiffly, 'as I cannot do what you ask.'

'By bus? From here to Kispest or wherever it is!' whined the woman despairingly, obviously trying to make Piroska and Jáger take pity on her. They didn't. 'Eight suitcases and two children on a bus!' she went on, her despair becoming real.

Hearing their mother's panic, two well-dressed kids ran into the room. The boy was ten, and looked as if he'd come straight from the Chocolate Wolves in Daddy's car. He might have been Half Wit's twin: all he needed were the gold-rimmed specs. The little girl was about six, and only slightly less lifelike than a wax doll.

'I don't even know where it is, not even the name of the street . . . Where did I put the bit of paper . . . ?'

'I honestly couldn't tell you,' answered our hostess. 'I deliberately ask for the addresses to be given to me in sealed envelopes.'

The elegant lady turned her handbag inside out.

'Don't you have a copy? Well, what happens now?' she demanded, as if Piroska Daniellik had been her servant.

'There's no great harm done,' answered our hostess. 'You can stay here another day or two while I get someone to send the address again.'

Glancing worriedly at us, the lady ran out of the room, followed closely by her children. Five minutes later, with the children still in tow, she ran back into the room waving a piece of paper.

441

'I've found it! I've found it! What buses go there from here?'
Our hostess gave her a plan of the bus system, but in her impatience
the woman started looking at the wrong side of the map. Eventually
Piroska went to her rescue and sorted out the mysteries of public
transport.

'As I understand it, the first month's rent at the place I'm going to
has already been paid on my behalf by Reverend Eliás's organisation.
I pay them back via you, don't I?' said the lady, her voice suddenly
becoming hard and businesslike. At least she'd be able to work as
a cashier in a fashion house if fate were unkind to her. 'Here we
are: four hundred pengős. Four hundred for one month? Daylight
robbery!'

'You did ask for three rooms,' answered our hostess. 'I have heard
that rents have gone through the roof. It's because of all the refugees
from the Russians. But someone else will take the rooms if you don't
want them. The deposit won't be lost. We have other addresses where
they charge less: there's three for less than two hundred and one place
where they only charge fifty pengős.'

'Fifty pengős?' This time the lady really panicked. 'That must be
a single room without hot water! With rats! Where is it? The Virgin
Mary shanty town?'

'It is only one room,' agreed Piroska.

'It's called the Mary-Valeria Estate,' corrected Mother.

'Thank you so much,' said the lady. 'I'm not familiar with that area.'

'I am,' said Mother curtly, without explaining that she only went
there as a relief social worker. I was worried: anyone might think we
lived there . . .

'I suppose that's rather an advantage, these days,' smirked the lady
contemptuously, looking straight through Jáger. Yet to my surprise her
voice became friendly again. 'Is the sergeant major your husband?'

'Yes,' replied Mother. 'My name is Mrs Ferenc Jáger. This is
Endre, this is Józska.'

'Aaaah, I see,' said the posh woman. 'You must be Piroska's
neighbours. My name is Mrs István Kovács. This is Árpád, and this
is my daughter, Mária – Molly,' she added, translating the name into
the language of simple country folk like us. The little girl immediately
began to scream and wail. 'Don't cry, Mary, don't cry. Nice soldier
won't hurt you.'

I almost burst out laughing. Where had she been living for the
last three months? I had heard rumours that certain influential Jews

442

had been allowed to stay in their own villas. All they had to do was to hang a star on their gate. I was pleased that she had immediately taken us for Christians. Ferenc's presence must have set the seal on our irreproachable Aryan pedigree.

She brought two small suitcases into the room and counted out four hundred pengős to pay Piroska back for the rent on her new lodgings. Still holding a wad of notes, she displayed her extraordinary tact once again.

'Won't you accept a little something for the poor box?' she asked our hostess. But, however simple Piroska Daniellik seemed, she wasn't fooled.

'There's a poor box in every church, my sister, if you really wish to give to the poor.' Puzzled, the woman returned the banknotes to her bag. On her way out she stupefied me by pushing a piece of paper into Mother's hand.

'If you happen to hear of a good, clean daily who works hard and doesn't steal, send her to me at this address. I pay well.'

'I'll keep a lookout,' promised Mother.

Her ladyship made her children thank the Danielliks for their hospitality, then thanked them herself. Lifting her suitcases, she called over her shoulder, 'I shall send for the rest of the luggage tomorrow. I'm sure I'll be able to find someone. We can't take any more with us today.'

'Don't send for it, please! I have asked you once and I am asking you again, do not send for your luggage. Come yourself. Twice, if necessary. Think for a moment, my sister.'

'*You* think, Piroska! How can you expect me to do the round trip three times with two children? The other suitcases are even heavier. They hold everything we have left . . .' She was almost crying.

Jáger took pity on her. 'I'll come with you. There'll be less to take tomorrow.'

He fetched the two heaviest suitcases from the other room. Árpád, a proud child, was carrying a small suitcase, and was already outside reassuring his mother: 'It's not really that heavy, Mummy.'

'You are a very strong boy . . . Árpád,' she said, hesitating slightly over the name.

'I'm glad Ferenc went with them,' remarked Mother after they had left. 'That woman couldn't cross the street on her own. With him there they'll be taken for the family of an officer who's sent his batman to help them with the luggage. Mind you, that'd look better if they took a taxi.'

'I'm sure they will,' commented our protectress. It was the first time I had heard her laugh. 'I didn't want there to be anything unusual around the house. Even the innocence of the rich shines like gold,' she sighed. Perhaps she wasn't so simple after all.

'Doesn't it frighten you to think that her ladyship knows your address?' asked Mother.

'I would be more frightened if I knew hers. She gave it to you: throw it away, my sister.'

'I've already looked at it,' Mother laughed, embarrassed.

'Then forget it. I make very sure that the chain stops here, with me. I don't know the name or the address of whoever sends me the envelopes, nor of the person who delivers them, nor whether the two people are the same.'

'Are you scared that you might talk if you were caught?' asked Mother.

'Of course I am. We have returned to the catacombs, my sister, but the apostles aren't here to help us.'

'Only their successors!' interrupted Piroska's father from the doorway.

'I shouldn't have said anything. My father is very angry with the prelates. Please, Father, remember your heart trouble.' Turning back to us she went on: 'Not even our eventual martyrdom would bring us any glory now. It would only ease our burden of sin. You see, my sister, even in this darkness I seek reward.'

'Is there a better reward than life?' asked Mother.

'Which life are you talking about? This one or the next?'

'This one,' answered Mother roughly.

Sadly, our protectress nodded. 'You can, I hope, save both at the same time. We are only expiating.'

Mother looked at her, shocked.

The father began to speak: 'Some of our prelates – most of them, unfortunately – consider the Jews' fate to be more or less deserved. They carefully refrain from throwing their theological arguments at the Jews from behind the cover of Hitler's firing squads, but they compete with one another in condemning the Jews' evil influence on Hungarian society. While hundreds of thousands of Hungarian Jews were being transported to the gas-chambers, the bishops were nobly insisting upon a more humane settlement to the Jewish question, as if the Jewish question could ever be humane. Pontius Pilate tried much harder to do something for Jesus than our ecclesiastical superiors have done for the Jews – and yet he didn't consider himself to be Jesus's vicar on earth. Our Pharisee Cardinal and hypocritical bishops have chosen not to provoke the Nazis' wrath, saying that it would damage both their own cause and that of the Jews. Serédi and Ravasz and the others have whispered and plotted amongst themselves: "For God's sake let's not cause a public scandal, let's shout 'Barabbas' . . ." If only that were all they shouted. But they cried: "Crucify him! Crucify him! But do it gently!" '

Piroska was holding her breath, looking for some means of calming the old gentleman's outburst. With a hopeless gesture, she pushed a cup of tea closer to his hand. Without even touching it, he pushed it aside.

'In the hour of the triumph of Evil, the hour of trial and crucifixion, the Italian, Polish, German and Hungarian Churches have thrown away the shepherd's crook. They have joined the murderers, they have counted Israel's bones and thrown dice for his tunic. How can they absolve themselves of the crime? How can my bishop say that he "cannot condemn the Jewish laws on principle"? What the hell can he do? Out of crass stupidity, or grotesque hypocrisy, they behave as if they were forced to make some choice between the Hungarians and the Jews. Like tragic heroes, they have chosen the lesser evil. Barabbas. "Let's face it," they said to themselves, "a little crucifixion will teach these Jews a lesson, and we won't have to upset our beloved Hungarian people's deep-seated feelings towards the Jews." They have tacitly accepted that the Jews are not Hungarian, and when the Jews therefore began to feel less and less Hungarian, the bishops pointed to their alienation as proof that they were actually aliens. And it isn't just the blood of the Jews that soaks their cassocks. They have tolerated the war against Russia without a word, they have actively recruited for it. Our soldiers were sent off to war with the holy zeal of the Crusades. The bishops have invented prayers and even put the church bells at the disposal of the High Command. I have tried to be glad that all I taught was Latin, that my daughter only taught geography . . . Our heroes were risking their lives, protected by the bishops' prayers. As early as 1941 I read a newspaper article that said, "We have given God back to the Russians." Our soldiers had reopened a church in an occupied Ukrainian village. The Ukrainians were celebrating our arrival, ours and God's. They dragged the Bolsheviks out of their hiding places – Jews almost to a man, of course – and even our humane soldiers were unable to defend them from the people's righteous indignation. Then

445

God's soldiers – yes, I've heard stories about our soldiers that would make your blood freeze – God's soldiers joined Hitler's, burning tens of thousands of villages, thousands of towns, looting and murdering the population by the million, raping wives and daughters. In the prisoner of war camps, the Russians are eating their dead. We gave God back to the Russians. We brought Him into their homes. We even went to the trouble of carrying Him all the way to Moscow. And what does this ungrateful race of subhumans do? They don't want our God. They're bringing Him back to us. And by tomorrow they will arrive. All the priests and politicians, journalists and generals are crying out: "Here comes the Tartar! *Hannibal ante portas!*" They throw their arms up to the heavens: "Here come the Asian hordes! Pagans! Bolsheviks!" We tremble; and how could we do otherwise? Having done what we have done, how could we believe in God and think to escape punishment?'

With a deep sigh, the old gentleman stopped. He wasn't ill, his breathing was deep and slow, but as soon as he was able to continue, his daughter beat him to it. Without seeming to interrupt, she began to sing:

> *'Nothing in my hand I bring,*
> *Simply to thy Cross I cling . . .'*

Mother, Mr Daniellik, and then Dávid joined in. I knew the song, but kept quiet. I was too moved to lie.

'We are clinging to your Cross, Lord,' sighed Mr Daniellik. 'Without its weight we could not hold up our heads. We would wilt from the unquenchable thirst of despair.' With that he said goodnight.

' "He that findeth his life shall lose it, and he that loseth his life for my sake shall find it," ' said our hostess, although I didn't know what she was quoting. Then she turned to Mother: 'Sister, they want to kill you for your body and for your soul, because of your blood and because of the faith of your father. From my faith they demand the complicity of indifference, and the little I can do in His name must be kept hidden from my own people.'

'I know how that feels,' answered Mother. 'I had to keep my own conversion secret. For years from my father . . .' I knew for a fact that she hadn't converted and that thanks to the Churches' behaviour during the previous few months she had abandoned the idea of conversion for good. She was trying out our cover story.

446

I was troubled by the thought that by pretending to be converts we were cheating this good man and woman, betraying their self-sacrifice, their courage. At the same time, I suspected that they were only helping us because we were converts, and that if they knew the truth, they would withdraw their help. They wouldn't betray us, of course not, but they would no longer consider us their own, or worthy of their sacrifice.

'I am Jewish!' I announced.

That was that. On the first day, at the first opportunity, I had betrayed myself. I had betrayed Mother. I had betrayed Dávid too: he was gasping as if he were being strangled. And I had done it on purpose, out of anger and indiscipline and pride, despite knowing that I had to be as tolerant as a saint. I knew perfectly well that our protectress wouldn't run to the Gestapo, and probably wouldn't even throw us out into the street at dead of night; but nevertheless I hadn't been able to keep my mouth shut. In a way, I had betrayed Piroska: I had deprived her of the fruit of her sacrifice, her reward for risking her life. She had believed that she was saving us for the sake of some kind of 'true' Christianity. Now she must be thinking: 'The Jews have deceived me!' But she pretended she hadn't heard me. She ignored my outburst. It was very kind of her . . .

'I haven't asked you who you are,' she said, turning to me. 'I know who sent you. You knocked and I, in the name of the Lord, opened the door for you. I should give you what you ask without hope of reward but, all the same, I do secretly expect something in return . . .'

What could I give her? Mother should have accepted the five hundred pengös . . .

'You cannot give me what I ask now, but one day my hope may bear fruit, and you may live to know that no Christian has Jewish blood on his hands. That hope eases the burden of my cross.'

'How could we ever believe that?' exclaimed Dávid, emboldened by the realisation that we were still safe. 'All our persecutors are Christians – from Hitler down to the caretaker.'

Our protectress nodded slowly, then lifted her head.

'But not all Christians are your persecutors.'

'And those who are, are not true Christians?' said Dávid, politely hiding the irony in his words. Mother blushed. Piroska too.

'God forgive them,' our protectress sighed. 'Because His people have forgotten Jesus, do these priests in their purple somehow imagine

447

that they can make Jesus forget His people? Our Church was built upon rock, but the rock has split. We will find no refuge in our thoughts, and only as much peace in our hearts as we have courage, the courage that burns there now. Our temple is caving in, and whether our faith will be buried in its ruins depends on us alone. We can only hold up our heads and look to the sky: whoever bows his head now will never raise it again.'

She was silent for a minute.

'Will you say . . .? That there were some among them who did what they could . . . that they didn't all betray God . . . and the Son of Man, and men? You, who crossed the deserts of thousands of years bringing nothing with you but a book, the Book that brought you across those deserts, those years . . . Can our cross bring us through this sea of blood? Two thousand years after Moses, Jesus repeated "Thou shalt not kill" in front of all the world. How can killing be justified in His name? How can mass murders be concealed by silence? How can evil go unopposed when all we have to fear is death?'

A wise Rabbi could convert her right now, I thought. Of course, we don't convert . . .

'The same old reason,' I said despite Mother's hiss. 'Because we crucified Him.'

Piroska looked at me, wondering whether to speak to me as a child, then saw that I was listening and answered me seriously.

'We believe that Jesus is part of the indissoluble, indivisible One. Why should we imagine that He would deny all His teaching by seeking revenge, or that He would use us as the tools of such vengeance, treading all his commandments, laws and words into a mire of blood?'

'But it's His fault we're being murdered, He allows it to happen!'

Our protectress stared at me fearfully.

'He doesn't allow . . .! God's fault . . .!' For a while she stammered about God-given freedom, retreating from the fight, from Jacob's struggle with the Man. But slowly she regained her self-possession. She said that Judaism and Christianity were in essence one religion; I didn't understand what she considered to be the essence . . . I suspected her of trying to convert us. I suspected some deep corruption, something I couldn't see through quite yet. But her smile was clear, not cunning.

'Evil is attacking you,' she went on quietly. 'Through God's people, Satan is attacking God, and our souls. In his devious way, he sets his snares for the Christians too. But we know as well as you

448

do that, however great the triumph of Evil in this hour, Satan will fail again. Don't worry. Would I dare to try to convert Jews when Jesus and His Apostles could persuade so few of their own people? Luther failed in his attempt to convert them and his Germanic fury nourishes Hitler's hatred. In a different way, I am more frightened for us, for the Christians, than I am for you. The Jews have been bled white, reduced to almost nothing, but passing through torment, misery and mourning, they will emerge victorious as ever from this battle with Evil, from this living Hell. God promised to keep Israel until the end of time. Some explain this by seeing the cross as an extension of Israel, but that isn't enough. The millions and millions of Jewish dead will be a light for as many years, a light that will make the *Torah* still more splendid. Thirty or forty generations will not replace the spilt blood.'

We sat there silently. Then Piroska said, 'I pray with all my strength and all my faith that the day will never come when they raise a memorial column beside the Auschwitz crematorium saying:

Here Ended
After Two Thousand Years
The Faith Called
Christianity'

27: Winter Winds

We spent two nights at the Danielliks'. By the second, two more families had arrived. Jáger slept at the barracks and Piroska moved into her father's room to make space. She was expecting more guests on the third day, and we realised that we would have to move on. Jáger went off to have a look at the address Piroska gave us, where the rent was only fifty pengös.

'It's worse than I expected, but it might do until the frost begins,' he told us when he returned. He hadn't taken the room, but had asked the landlady not to rent it until his wife had seen it. Our protectress saw us on our way.

'Come back straight away if it's unbearable, my sister and little brothers. We'll manage somehow. Can I offer you some money, Julia? Don't be proud, I know you haven't got much.' But Mother was proud.

'I've got *two* diamond earrings!' she boasted, as if two were more than a pair.

We walked through dusty streets. I didn't know where we were or where we were going. Jáger walked ahead with sure, steady strides. Some way in front of us we could see a row of proper houses, the real Pestszentimre, one of the outer suburbs of Budapest. But immediately ahead of us lay a region of weed-covered fields and empty allotments, where low, crumbling buildings faced in all directions. This area formed a dent in the side of Pestszentimre, a hole on the edge of a sub-suburb. Only people who had nowhere else to go lived here.

We turned towards a group of small, decaying, L-shaped houses that faced each other in twos across narrow courtyards. We stopped at the first. Jáger knocked.

Piroska had found this place herself. She had seen an advertisement

450

pinned to a tree and had written it down, knowing that it might be better than nothing. We were the first people even to take a look at it.

Jáger pushed open the door and we walked into a kitchen where an old woman was sitting on a bed with a cooking-pot between her knees, eating squares of pasta with her fingers. The bed was covered with a sack-coloured blanket. Her skin was stretched tightly over her bones, and her dirty white hair, gathered up in a bun, was stiff as a wig. Her clothes looked as old as she did.

She didn't get up when we entered; she just looked up from the pot, scrutinising us suspiciously, as if she didn't want to let the room to just anybody.

'So, this is your family,' she said to Jáger by way of greeting. We must have made a good first impression because she stood up and came towards us. 'Right, I'll let you have a look at it,' she said, taking a key off a nail in the wall. To my surprise, she walked straight out of the door. Outside, five metres from the house, was a tiny makeshift square shack. I hadn't even noticed it before. She stopped beside it, unlocking the door with some difficulty.

It was a one-room shack, with a floor of luxuriously beaten earth. There was a bed, a camp bed, a weather-beaten table, two chairs, a stove, and a sink with a tap above it. There was no blanket on the bed, one could see the loose springs under the clean, damp sheet. On the table were a few plates and glasses, some cutlery and a saucepan.

'There you are,' said the old woman. 'Come inside and think it over in the warm.'

If anything, it was colder inside the shack. The walls had once been white. They were probably made of thin boards daubed with mud, and if anyone had driven a nail into them he could have hung up his coat outdoors. The place might once have served as a shed, although the sink suggested that it had recently been a washroom. A window had been cut into the wall opposite the door, narrow as an arrow slit. It was just under the roof, and was opened and shut by means of a frayed string.

'The WC?' asked Mother. The old woman pointed to another, smaller and shabbier shed that lay exactly on the halfway line between the two buildings.

'Communal,' she remarked.

We returned to the warmth of her kitchen and introduced ourselves. The old woman was called Mrs Szaniszló. I was worried that Mother might be rude about the shack so as to knock down the price, and would lose the good will of the landlady. On the other hand, it would look suspicious if she didn't haggle. I couldn't help; I was modelling my behaviour on peasant families, and peasant kids didn't speak unless they were asked a direct question at least three times.

'I didn't see any blankets,' said Mother.

'Blankets! Blankets!' exclaimed the old woman, raising her arms in a bad imitation of my ginger Rabbi. 'Where am I going to find blankets? I need one myself! I give mine to my grandson when he comes to visit me – he's here now, I don't know where he's got to . . . ' Suddenly her voice oozed syrup: 'That's a lovely suitcase you've got there, Mrs Jáger.'

'If only it weren't so old,' Mother sighed dreamily. 'In those days my man wasn't a soldier . . . but even then I could only afford to buy it second-hand. It must have been a real gentleman's case once—'

'It is! It is!' interrupted the old woman. 'What does the sergeant do when he's not in uniform?'

'Shoemaker,' answered Jáger.

'Great trade! Always have to have shoes, rain or shine. My poor husband, God rest his soul, was on the railways. I'd be ashamed to tell you how much they give me now he's gone. My daughter's man is away at the war. It's bad being old, bad being old, believe me.'

The woman was as old as the hills. Her eyes were dim, yet her stare had darted out and almost physically grabbed Mother's suitcase. She catalogued her troubles almost indifferently, like a good gambler throwing down the cards. She announced her conclusions, in an effort to frighten Mother into submission.

'It's not much for that room, seventy pengös these days, not much at all.' The emphasis was on 'these days', and not the seventy pengös. We had one hundred and fifty in all.

Mother answered her immediately: 'You asked fifty on the advertisement – and I thought that was too much. I also expected some blankets. They're always included in furnished accommodation.' The woman couldn't have been a very experienced landlady; she ducked the argument over the meaning of 'furnished' and went for another angle.

'The advertisement! How long ago did I stick that up! It was still summer! Where were the Russians then?'

'And there was such a rush for the room that you had to put up the price!' smiled Mother.

'They would have rushed, but I didn't let them! There are so

452

many refugees these days – not that you need telling. They pay anything just to have a roof over their heads!'

'Not quite anything,' said Mother, still smiling despite her anxiety.

'I changed my mind! That's why they didn't rush, because I thought my grandson would come more often if he had a room to himself. He won't let me move out of my room, Bandi won't, he always sleeps on this dog-bed here in the kitchen when he comes. He's a good boy, that one, even if he is a bit flighty. He didn't come so much then, so I thought I'd give him a room to himself. But now they've gone and called the poor lad up, so I said to myself . . .'

She rattled on, but even her lies were banal. Her imagination couldn't take her further than her own door.

'People kept on coming, crowds of them, but I told them straight: my grandson comes first with me . . .' She was going round in circles.

'I'll give you fifty,' said Mother severely. 'I'll have to buy blankets – think how much that'll cost.'

'But the sheets, I'm giving you two! And four pillows! I didn't include the wood – there's enough there for a whole day, or even more! You'd never get that for seventy anywhere else!'

'Fifty,' corrected Mother.

'Fifty! Fifty!' Suddenly the old woman was mortally insulted. 'When the shopkeepers have rationed potatoes so that they can put the price up! It's not what the poor hoped for, not at all, we thought prices would go down when they took the Jews away, but did they go down? They went up! Twelve pengős for one kilo of the best apples! I saw it with my own eyes! It's enough to take your appetite away just thinking about it! Come to town if you don't believe me, Mrs Jáger, I'll show you! Maybe they're golden apples,' she went on, her imagination growing by a hair's breadth. 'It's the war that eats up all the money and makes food and everything so dear. They ought to lock all those Hitlers and Churchills and Stalins and Roosevelts and Horthys in a room, and give them each a big stick, and the one who comes out alive can have the world, only they should leave the poor in peace.'

I must have heard this view expressed a thousand times over the years, but the fact that Mrs Szaniszló was diluting her argument with her political wisdom was a sure sign of weakness. Mother pounced. She offered fifty-five, the old woman asked sixty-five – including Bandi's blanket when he left in three days' time – and they immediately split the difference. We had to pay a month in advance. Being a soldier, Jáger was faster on the draw than Mother and paid for us. He even

453

told Mother off for trying to pay. So our original fortune of one hundred and fifty pengös remained intact: the price of twelve kilos of first-class apples or seven kilos of black-market meat. After all, Jáger was supported by the army and even received a small amount of pay. Mrs Szaniszló decided that if we couldn't drink to the bargain we should eat. She picked up the pot of pasta and offered it to me.

'This child is thin. You must be hungry.' I couldn't say that I wasn't: it wouldn't be in character. Luckily Mother came to the rescue.

'Can I give the bigger one a bite to eat as well? And could I ask for a couple of plates, so they won't fight over it?'

In the last half hour, I had seen my mother display more cunning than in all the past twelve years put together. Despite Mrs Szaniszló's encouragement, she doled out very little of the pasta. While we were choking it down, the eighteen-year-old grandson arrived. His name was Bandi – which is short for Endre, like Dávid's. They celebrated the discovery happily, and I could stop eating without being noticed.

'Do you do gym too?' asked Bandi. He wanted to show off, so while Jáger returned to his unit, we went into the other room. It was clean but cold, and everything except a cupboard was piled on one side of the room to make space for Bandi's gymnastics. From among the religious pictures on the walls, a martial railwayman gazed severely into the middle distance. There was nothing else in the room but a crucifix.

'I can only do floor exercises here,' the grandson announced, but Mrs Szaniszló made a virtue of necessity.

'They're the nicest! The most difficult!' she cried on behalf of the whole audience. 'You watch the way Bandi flies through the air!'

Bandi's idea of flying was doing forward and backward somersaults.

'Now you do something!' he said. Dávid looked so shy that I could have guessed he was Jewish.

Every word, every movement, every facial expression was a test of our Christianity. I decided to open my big mouth:

'Come and play head-ball with me! You're a great gymnast, but that doesn't mean you're a good goalie!'

'I've never been that mad about football,' said the grandson, so the match ended in a draw.

We went into the shack. Mother and Dávid looked sour. I felt cocky.

'Szálasi himself wouldn't look for Jewish plutocrats here!' Beside the stove was our store of firewood, enough for a whole day or even longer according to the old woman. Perhaps the miracle of *Chanukah* would be repeated and our fire would keep burning until the Russians arrived, like the oil in the Holy of Holies. We wanted to light the stove but had no matches.

'This is one way to make it last,' said Mother, and laughed so hard that I thought she would burst into tears. I offered to get some matches from Mrs Szaniszló, but Mother decided that it wasn't that cold and told me not to bother.

Taking out a pen and paper, she began to do some sums.

'A cobbler's wife doesn't carry a fountain pen in her bag,' warned Dávid.

'Einstein himself couldn't balance our accounts,' laughed Mother. 'I'm trying to work out which is the cheapest way of keeping warm: firewood or blankets.'

Apparently a really good blanket cost a hundred pengös, and even a thin one was at least fifty. There was no question of borrowing from Piroska; she had only been able to give one blanket to each person the night before. Mother decided to go to the Teleki Square flea-market the next day; she could buy them there for as little as fifteen apiece.

'As long as they're warm and aren't full of bed-bugs . . . ' said Mother. For a moment she was worried that someone might recognise her at the market; she had been there recently to sell clothes and buy Christian ration tickets. Then she remembered that she had never worn her star, and her face lit up. I felt very proud of having invented the practice of going out without the star. The training was paying off.

Jáger arrived with a worried, stiff expression. Taking off his coat, he unrolled a blanket that had been fastened around his waist with a safety pin.

'I borrowed it,' he said. He wasn't joking. It was an army blanket.

'I don't suppose the Russian quartermaster will claim it,' said Mother, throwing it over the divan straight away.

'All the same,' said Jáger irritably, 'I didn't dare take two.'

Mother seemed to get annoyed. 'The crime wouldn't have been any worse,' she said.

'I'd have been too fat,' answered Jáger, but there was still no trace of humour in his voice. 'We've been given our marching orders – to Transdanubia, so the rumour goes. The attack has already started there. We leave today.'

Mother stood motionless for nearly a minute.

'Desert, and we'll head towards the front! Now!' But Jáger didn't want to go. 'Our papers are in order,' argued Mother. 'You've got your blank written orders, we can write what we like on them.'

'It's more dangerous together,' decided Jáger.

'So it's more dangerous, so what?' shrugged Mother, but her certainty had left her. Jáger shook his head. Mother stopped arguing and took out her money. She offered a hundred pengös to Jáger. 'You need it more,' she told him. 'For trains, shelter, food. You won't be able to cook, and cooked food costs more.'

'Fifty will be enough,' replied Jáger. 'I still have some left over.' When Mother wasn't looking he tried to give the money back, first to Dávid and then to me. Then he shook hands with us and left.

We had one blanket between the three of us. Mother overcame her scruples and went back to the Danielliks, but there were still three families there. She only dared ask for one blanket, and arranged to return it as soon as Mrs Szaniszló gave us the blanket included in the rent. We borrowed some matches and lit the fire just before going to bed. The stove didn't draw well, and we warmed ourselves by blowing into it. Dávid and I were to share the divan; we put the camp bed beside it for Mother, but the divan was too high and the blankets too narrow to cover both. The few clothes we had went on top, but I was so cold in the middle of the night that I slipped under the sheet, where it was slightly warmer and a lot less comfortable. Dávid woke up, and we quarrelled. He wanted me to lie on top of the sheet and I wanted him to join me underneath. Eventually we got up, managed somehow to relight the fire, and eventually fell asleep.

Mother worked out that we were going to have to spend considerably more on blankets and firewood than the difference in rent between our shack and a decent room.

'Misers always pay twice,' said Mother. 'What am I keeping my diamonds for? My wedding?' Instead of her planned visit to the flea-market, she spent the day hunting unsuccessfully for rooms. All the cheaper addresses known to the Danielliks were already gone, whilst elsewhere even the most expensive were taken.

'Now I know why all these people are so scared of the Russians,' said Mother in annoyance. 'They're all millionaires.'

On the way to buy firewood, Mother popped into a jeweller to see if she could sell the earrings. She came out of the shop in a fury.

'The crook offered me five hundred for them! Suburban trinket merchant. I won't part with them for less than fifteen hundred. They belonged to my mother! I'll go to Váci Street.'

That night, Mother prodded and blew the fire until we fell asleep. In the morning, she had to put off her expedition to Váci Street. We needed ration tickets, but you couldn't get them without a Domicile Registration Form, which could only be obtained from the local police on presentation of a Domicile Departure Certificate, which was in turn supposed to have been provided by the police at your previous address. Alternatively, you had to have papers proving refugee status. These were the only documents we didn't yet possess, but they were considered to be as effective as birth certificates in the event of a police raid, and were therefore expensive.

Mother got our landlady to sign the form and went off to the police station. Alone. She was scared to take us with her: it was too easy to establish whether boys were Jewish. We waited in the shack, dashing out into the street every minute to see if she was back. As the day dragged on, Dávid kept up my courage by inventing reasons why Mother might have been delayed. Then he told me off for being such a mummy's boy. And then we simply waited, letting the fire go out, shivering.

It was well after noon when Mother returned. Her string shopping bag was full.

'I bought this with ration tickets!' she shouted triumphantly, pulling a chicken out of her bag. She had also bought sugar, bread and 'Hungarian tea'.

The police had asked her for proof that she had really left her former address. She had a few documents in her bag that referred to the Jágers' home, but she didn't want the plain-clothes policeman to taste blood. Show a bureaucrat a form and he'll want it in triplicate.

'You want me to show you a Domicile Departure Certificate, Inspector,' she said. 'Well, I'm sure the Russians would have given us one if we'd waited for them.'

'Why didn't you apply for one in good time? Surely you could have got refugee papers?'

'The Russian hordes don't stick to timetables, Inspector. And anyway,' she added slyly, 'the police in our town were the first to leave.'

'They must have been going to the front,' said the policeman defensively, quickly stamping Mother's form.

'I'm sure you're right,' said Mother by way of thanks.

457

Her next stop was the ration office at the Town Hall. She filled in a form and handed it in at the window, keeping her new Domicile Registration Form in reserve. They asked for her control book so that they could stamp it. Christian control books were different from Jewish ones, naturally enough.

'I left it at home,' said Mother.

'Well, go home and get it, then!' ordered the official.

'Fine, I'm on my way. To Hódmezövásárhely. Can I borrow a couple of Panzer divisions in case the Russians try and stop me?'

'So how am I going to issue you with ration tickets? What have you got?'

'Two hungry children,' said Mother, still not bothering to mention the Domicile Registration. 'And a husband who was posted to the front from here, yesterday.' Without another word, the official filled in a new control book and got his boss to countersign it. Then he made a note in a bigger book and handed Mother the ration tickets.

We felt slightly ashamed at not having done all this before. After a feast, we spent what was left of the afternoon room-hunting. On the way, we invested in a paraffin cooker so that we wouldn't have to blow our lungs out every time we wanted a cup of tea.

'Always useful to have an emergency cooker,' we agreed, trying hard to justify our extravagance. It did come in handy though. When we woke up shivering in the middle of the night we didn't have to take it in turns to battle with the stove. The little cooker even dried the air in the room a little and, up to a point, took the edge off the cold. We could rub our numbed hands at the flame and boil water on it.

The next morning we were woken by the sound of bells. It was Sunday. Mrs Szaniszló appeared in the courtyard in her best clothes; her scarf was almost new.

'Don't Calvinists go to church?' she asked Mother. Until then we had seen no point in attracting public attention by our religious zeal. Once again, Mother found a way out, and I began to wonder whether she'd done a university degree in underground living.

'I can't go like this,' she complained. 'The suitcase with our good clothes in it got lost on the way.'

The fact was that Mother hadn't packed any of the decent clothes left over from our father's fit of generosity. She now regretted it, as we could have sold them at the flea-market. She cheered up Mrs Szaniszló by telling her that church wasn't the only place where God could be found, but the old woman must have made an early start because she hung around for a little theological chit-chat.

'Are there many Calvinists at that Hódmesövásárhely?' she asked, trying not to let her voice betray her competitive feelings.

'Not all that many, not like in Transylvania,' replied Mother. 'But there are enough of us.'

'No harm in that,' said the old woman, relieved, trying to please God with a noble attempt at religious tolerance. 'We're all people underneath, aren't we?'

In safe situations we had taken to giving each other lessons in Christian Behaviour. This soon became a game with its own rules, called the 'Lying Game'. We didn't consider our shack to be safe. Like heat, sound drifted through the walls as if they weren't there. We agreed on signs for 'shut up' and 'let me talk', and touching the left ear with the right hand signalled a need for immediate confidential communication.

That Sunday we were given Bandi's blanket, but we didn't have to give the other back to the Danielliks until Monday. We would lose out on the exchange, but for that night, at least, Dávid and I could sleep under two blankets while Mother piled our coats on top of hers.

Monday was an important day. Mother went into the smart part of town to sell her earrings and buy some more essentials. Blankets were no longer on her list, since we had decided to move at the first opportunity.

Before leaving, she told us to clean out the stove pipe, as it might still take days to find a decent room even when we had the money. We finished the job quite quickly, and when we lit the fire, the wood burned like tinder. By chance, Mother had packed our chess set. Dávid was an average player, but in the absence of Pista Bognár I was the world champion. Having lost two games already, poor Dávid was struggling against checkmate when he scratched his left ear with his right hand to signify that he wanted to say something confidential.

'What football team do you support?' he asked.

'As if you didn't know,' I shrugged, not letting him break my concentration.

'Of course I know, idiot!' he replied after glancing at the board to check I hadn't blundered. 'But what about in public?'

'Forward, Fradi,' I sang aloud, as I didn't consider it a secret and felt that Dávid was abusing our system.

'Ten penalty points!' he flared in consternation.

'Move!' I said, showing that I understood his tactics.

'How can you support Ferencváros when you're from Hód-mezövásárhely?' he demanded in triumph. He still hadn't moved.

'The same way you support Szolnok when you're from Budapest, that's how!'

'OK, I'll take one point off the ten,' he said kindly. 'All the same, you can't support the Fradi. Provincials always hate Budapest people.' He had diverted his remaining intelligence to the argument: it would have been wasted on the game.

'Give it up,' I advised affably, referring to both games. Dávid was suddenly seized with fury.

'If Jesus had had a little brother, do you know what they'd have called him? Satan!' With that he swept all the pieces off the board.

'I accept your resignation,' I told him. 'Everyone has his own way of losing.'

'Resignation, my foot! I was bored! Give me one simple reason why a country boy would support the Fradi. One!'

'To drive his big brother up the wall for a start. Reason Two: the Fradi brought honour to the beloved Fatherland by beating Uruguay, because "Green is the corn, Kati . . ." ' I sang.

'Almost acceptable. I'll let you off another two penalty points.'

For lunch we ate our remaining sausages to celebrate our approaching wealth. For the first time ever it was too hot in our shack. We went out into the courtyard and had hardly begun to cool down when Mother came round the corner. We could see from a distance that the news was bad: she was carrying a folded blanket over her arm. That meant we were staying in the shack.

The earrings had been worth two thousand, and we'd been determined not to part with them for less than twelve hundred. Mother had seen several jewellers and the best offer had been eight hundred. She had only sold one earring, for which she was given three hundred and twenty-five pengös after a long argument. The good news was that she had picked up a real bargain on Teleki Square. She had bought two good blankets for forty pengös; they must have been stolen.

'Who cares?' laughed Mother. 'They'll hide the army one.'

We had to admit that we had been counting our chickens well before they were hatched. Of our original hundred and fifty pengös, we now had fifty-six. But how could Mother have had the strength to refuse to buy the chicken when the butcher had given her an extra half kilo at ration price? We had needed the paraffin cooker, too, and it wouldn't have been much use without the paraffin. How could we have known how thoroughly the jewellers would take advantage of our need?

Altogether, we now had three hundred and forty-one pengös. It was hard to tell whether Mother had been right to sell only one of the earrings. She had lost seventy-five pengös in the process, and her bargaining position when she went to sell the other would be very weak. Her reasons were fairly feeble too: 'The diamonds belonged to my mother – and, anyway, jewellery is better than money in a situation like this.'

Dávid's solution to both the military and financial positions was surprisingly pithy and imaginative.

'If they can't get here on foot, the Russians had better occupy Pestszentimre with airborne units,' he whispered after scratching his left earlobe.

With four blankets, we no longer had to fear the nights until it got really cold. Our stove awaited the frost like an anti-tank gun awaiting the Panzers. Coal was good ammunition. Our ration tickets bought five times as much sugar and three times as much meat as the Jewish ones had done, but we only bought bones for stewing, as they were a third of the price of chicken. We spent a lot on coal. Mother reckoned that heat was cheaper than medicine.

What I missed most was a ball. I applied to Mother for money to buy one. To my surprise, she agreed.

'It'll keep you warm. You'll be hungrier, but potatoes are cheaper than coal. You can have a pengö for a tennis ball.'

'A tennis ball? Where am I going to get a tennis ball? Shall I open a sports shop in Pestszentimre?'

I made a rag ball. Dávid threw it at me for goal practice but he soon got bored. We started a game of chess, but as soon as his rook was in danger Dávid scratched his earlobe.

'What's your maths teacher's name?'

'Szabó,' I answered, taking the rook.

'Hungarian?'

'Kovács.'

'Latin?'

'Isaac Kohn,' I laughed. 'A chief Rabbi in civilian life.'

But Dávid hauled me over the coals for joking, and even for giving the teachers the most common Hungarian names. So we settled down to invent plausible names for the vicar, the mayor, the doctor,

461

and soon populated a whole village. This pedantry bored me. I had a better idea: 'Let's get ourselves an Iron Cross. Then no one will ask us questions.'

'They will. They'll ask us who won it and where.'

'Our grandfather did. On the Russian front. He was a general.'

'Why not an admiral?' scoffed Dávid. 'What was his name?'

'Who cares? I know the names of twenty generals. I'll teach them to you.'

'How many are called Jáger? Why is his son a corporal?'

'He's Mother's father.'

'General Dragomér,' Dávid laughed. 'Little lies go further. Big ones need proof. If you want to pretend you're an eagle, you have to be able to fly,' he added poetically.

'Then we'd better say that you're a donkey. We won't have to lie,' I retorted.

Mother bought a ball for two pengös, but Dávid was an academic kid at heart, and preferred to stay indoors reading Mrs Szaniszló's old 'treasure calendars'. We were burning up our coal alarmingly fast. According to the newspapers, the Germans had retaken Nyíregyháza and Hungarian soldiers were advancing on the Russian bridgeheads south of Szolnok, one hundred and twenty kilometres away. Meanwhile, Mother toured the shops, searching for news of a better room; but every day she returned after an hour or two, her face withered, having run out of places to look. Then, on the first of November, seventeen days after we had gone into hiding, Mother came back with a bag of potatoes and a huge smile. 'We're moving,' she announced.

I had never known Mother to be as calm and controlled as she had been over the past few days. It was as if she hadn't a care in the world.

In one of the shops where she had become known, they had informed her that a solitary gentleman was looking for some kind of caretaker. Mother went straight to the address they gave her, and discovered that the post involved no work at all. The gentleman was a white-collar worker in a factory, and because of the rising numbers of burglaries he wanted someone trustworthy to come and live in, so that the house wouldn't be empty in the daytime. There was no money in the job, only accommodation, and that was the reason why he had failed to find someone locally. He was glad to see Mother at first, but when she told him about us he grumbled that he wasn't used to children. Mother boasted that we were the quietest children on earth,

462

but he refused to argue and said that the job would depend on what impression we made on him.

The responsibility for the whole family lay on my shoulders alone. Dávid had always made a good impression on everyone, but I hadn't the first idea where to begin. My best strategy was to pretend to be deaf and dumb . . .

Mother was particularly pleased that our new abode had a deep bunker in the back garden. This didn't interest me in the least. The Russian planes flying to bomb Budapest and the airport at Ferihegy, three kilometres away, wouldn't give a damn about Pestszentimre. A bomb once fell on the area by mistake; Mrs Szaniszló wouldn't stop jabbering about it for days. She spent hours of each day in the cellar of the house that backed on to our estate, as the air-raid sirens went off at least five times a day and we had no bomb shelter. This cellar was full without us, and Mrs Szaniszló told us 'with all due respect' that the 'regulars' were squashed enough as it was.

We were to sit our good-behaviour exam the following morning, since for some reason the solitary gentleman wasn't going to work. He lived at the opposite edge of the little town. Scrubbed and combed, in the smartest of our shabby clothes, we set off for his house; but the rain was coming down in buckets and we arrived soaked.

The house was a bungalow. There was a vegetable garden with a few fruit trees and a tiny vineyard. The owner was a tall, wiry man of about fifty; his face was expressionless but not stupid. He offered us chairs, and watched like a lynx to see whether Dávid and I would sit down before he did.

'Do you like school?' he asked me, going straight for the family's weakest spot.

'He loves it!' answered Mother like a shot.

'Not that much,' I said, playing down Mother's enthusiasm to add a bit of realism. The man laughed briefly, but I couldn't tell whether he was being sarcastic or sympathetic.

'What's your favourite subject?' he asked.

'I don't really have one,' I replied diplomatically. I couldn't exactly say football. Mother came to my rescue.

'He's good at all of them,' she said, then diverted attention away from me by adding: 'The elder one is a real mathematician.'

The lean man turned to Dávid and made him do some simple sums. After three minutes he became indignant: 'How can you send this boy to a secondary modern? He's cut out to be an engineer!'

463

The man, whose name was Péter Demeter, told us we could move in straight away. He showed us our room, which was big and well lit with good furniture and carpets. The iron stove in the corner was bigger than I was, and the fuel went with the room. All we had to buy was our food. We had hit the jackpot. We went out and used up all our ration tickets, spending thirty-two pengös on food. Back at our shack we lit the fire and dried our clothes and shoes. Outside, it drizzled for a while and then started to pour again. We could feel winter in the wind. We all needed a pair of good boots, but the subject was taboo. Half the streets of Pestszentimre were unsurfaced; three days of wet weather would finish off the only shoes we had, putting us under house-arrest. It was obvious that the weather wasn't going to improve: from beyond the horizon came continuous, muffled thunder. Mother cooked us a real, peacetime meal. We planned to move to our new place the following day so as not to seem too desperate. As we ate, the thunder became louder and louder, seeming to come from all around us.

We went out into the courtyard and listened to the storm. Steady thunder sounded from the south, the south-east and the south-west, but there was no lightning, near or far. We looked at each other warily, none of us wanting to be the first to believe our hope. For minutes I stood there, motionless and dizzy, not daring to utter my thoughts for fear of committing sacrilege.

It wasn't thunder. It was artillery fire.

Dávid and I went for a stroll during a lull. Mother ran after us with our coats and told us not to go too far in case the rain started again. We solemnly promised not to catch cold, and Mother shrugged her consent.

We had hardly gone a hundred metres along the road when, turning a corner, we almost bumped into a field gun that hadn't been there at noon. Four soldiers, including an ensign, were grouped around it. A gypsy-faced private was stirring a pile of embers at the foot of a wall. The end of the street was closed off by a solid column of lorries and tanks moving at a snail's pace towards the main Budapest highway. In the grey early-afternoon light, it slowly became clear that there were in fact two columns moving in opposite directions and wrestling for possession of the badly cobbled road. Among the vehicles, infantrymen were pushing their way forward in groups of a hundred or so. Occasional civilians were wedged amongst them, some pulling hand-carts. A bedraggled woman trudged past pushing a pram. Beside her, an elderly man was carrying a screaming child.

464

Aircraft buzzed overhead, and dogfights were in progress above the nearby airport. I stretched my arms out like wings and imagined being an aeroplane. Only my feet remained rooted to the ground.

Through a gap in the traffic, I saw a man lying just beyond the shallow ditch at the side of the road. I threaded my way through the crowd. The man was wearing civilian clothes and a yellow armband. His head was a mass of blood. A few metres away lay the corpse of another Jew. I couldn't tell how long they had been lying there in the mud, or who had shot them, or why. Maybe they had tried to escape, or maybe they had been too tired to keep up with their unit. Dávid pulled me away as I stared at them in horror.

The lorries and tanks heading in the direction of Üllöi Avenue were black with mud; those going in the opposite direction were cleaner. There were ten times as many infantry in the muddy column, many of them wounded. Some were being helped along by their comrades. The civilians were travelling in the same direction as the wounded; their hand-carts were mainly pulled by women and pushed by children. The officers in each column ordered their men to keep to the right, shouting at the civilians from time to time in an effort to chase them out of the way. Eventually both columns stopped dead. An officer arrived on a motorbike and yelled his head off at the lorry drivers and infantry officers.

'Avoid Üllöi Avenue! It's even worse there!' he shouted over the din of men and engines.

The column hardly moved at all. A train of horse-drawn carts creaked into view, forcing the traffic to a standstill again. The carts were piled high with wounded men, boxes and weapons. A convoy of lorries appeared from the other direction, hooting loudly and frightening the horses. An SS jumped down from a lorry, yelling in German. Grabbing the shaft of one of the carts, he pushed the horses towards the ditch.

All this time the air-raid sirens had remained silent.

Three soldiers broke away from one of the infantry groups. One of them was wounded. He sat down at the side of the road and waved the other two on, but they refused to leave him. Dávid and I went towards them, arriving at the same time as the second lieutenant commanding the next group.

'Keep moving!' he bawled.

'That's what I keep telling them myself, sir,' said the wounded man. 'Go on, Béla . . .'

A first lieutenant from their own company came running back to

465

them: 'What's going on here? Are you tired? You won't ever have to get up if the Russians catch you!'

'He's got a piece of shrapnel in his knee,' argued one of the unwounded soldiers.

'We all know that dodge! One gets wounded and three hop it. Let's see your knee.' The officer bent over the wounded soldier, who pulled his coat off his leg. The officer pulled a notebook out of his map case and, writing as he spoke, he told the unwounded men to stop the first medic's wagon – or any other vehicle. 'Then the two of you had better catch up with the unit and report to me. If you lose track of us, head for the regimental HQ at Kispest – or wherever you find it. This order expires at six tomorrow morning; from then on you'll be deserters! Understood? And you, Lieutenant,' he added to the officer from the other unit, 'had better go and look after your own men.' Without waiting for a reply, he ran back along the road.

'Where have you come from?' asked an onlooker, an old man with a white moustache.

'We were at Örkény yesterday,' answered one of the soldiers.

'How many kilometres is that?' I asked.

'About a thousand on foot,' grinned the soldier. 'The Germans took all the lorries. Fair enough,' he added, 'they've got much further to go!'

'What's happened?' asked the old man.

'Can't you see?' snapped the wounded soldier. 'The Russians broke through our lines.'

'Örkény,' mused the old man. 'That's about thirty kilometres. But you're inside the Attila Fortress now. They'll never break in here!'

The soldiers didn't bother to listen to these inspiring words, so the old man decided to inspire me instead. I learnt that our little town lay in the exterior section of the Attila Fortress, which was the code name for the defensive cordon around Budapest. He also told me that the thunder was caused by Hungarian guns.

'You must have a very good ear!' I said admiringly.

'We've stayed out too long!' exclaimed Dávid, elbowing me hard in the ribs and dragging me away before the old man could interpret my compliment as an unpatriotic remark.

As we charged triumphantly into the shack, Mother changed her anxious expression into a severe one to hide her relief.

466

'The Russians have broken through!' I shouted, not giving her time to tell us off. 'The fascists are on the run!'

'The run? They're running so fast the highway's jammed!' Dávid reported. He explained about the Attila Fortress, and managed to convince Mother that the fight would be a long one. 'They'll hold Ferihegy to the last,' he told her. 'It's the biggest airport in the country.'

'Lucky the bunker at our new house is so strong,' said Mother, trying to calm us down. But we couldn't go there, the rain was beating on our door and on the narrow window, almost drowning out the guns. The patter was suddenly replaced by the rattle of machine-gun fire: a dogfight was going on above our heads. We huddled pointlessly against walls that would hardly have stopped hail, let alone bullets. The rattling came to an end, but the patter of the rain went on for a good hour. The thunder, too, continued, though whether it was the storm or the guns, God alone knew.

Given a choice between fire and water, Mother decided to get drenched.

'We can't stay here,' she announced, throwing clothes and potatoes randomly into our elegant leather suitcase. Ten seconds later she closed it, threw the blankets over our shoulders, and rushed out of the door with us following. Then she dashed back to pick up the key that was lying on the table and ran over to Mrs Szaniszló's door.

'We're going to a bunker!' she yelled to the trembling old woman. 'We'll come back for our belongings tomorrow.'

'Don't go, for God's sake!' cried Mrs Szaniszló. 'Not into the blind night!'

But we went. It was dark outside, the streets completely empty and the houses blacked out. All around us we could hear the clatter of machine guns and other small-arms fire. The fighting could have been a hundred metres away or a thousand; I was no expert. We reached the centre of the little town within minutes. Suddenly, through the gloom, we saw soldiers standing along the side of the street in groups of fifty or a hundred, accompanied by three tanks and a couple of guns.

We walked out on to a small cobbled square roughly the size of the courtyard at our old block of flats. It was surrounded by single-storey houses. Beams of weak blue light cut moving stripes across the cobbles. A tank stood beside one of the houses, and in front of the tank, ten helmeted German soldiers were listening to their NCO, who was giving them orders quietly and quickly. A couple of dozen Hungarian soldiers

467

waited nearby. They had five helmets between them. We hadn't come across a single civilian since we had left our shack.

The exact centre of the square was occupied by a machine gun. A small number of soldiers were grouped around it, and the weapon itself was lit from above by a white light. After about ten seconds one of the soldiers clipped a blue filter over the bulb. The machine-gunner sat on a low, three-legged stool. If he had been standing up he would have been two metres tall, and his shoulders were even broader than Elek's. He wore no camouflage: his jacket was clean and bright as at a parade. He was a sergeant, and there were the ribbons of at least ten medals on his chest. The tank beside him seemed like an inert block, a rock of iron.

I thought of Gyurka Sternberg, and how we had collected scrap metal together. Old Grossman would have given twenty pengös for that tank – twenty pre-war pengös, worth fifty now . . .

In the blue light, the cobbles flashed like steel. The soldier's jacket and face were like steel too. I couldn't take my eyes off him. His face was open, calm, brave. Anywhere else, I would have wanted to chat to him. But now it was as if he were preparing to wrestle with Elek, and for a second I felt scared: what if he were the stronger?

He looked at me. His eyes were not angry, but hard, as if I were an enemy who didn't scare him. He spoke, keeping his eyes on me.

'Don't cross the road in front of me. Here they come. I'm about to open fire.'

The barrel of the machine gun pointed in the direction from which we had just come. In the last ten or fifteen minutes, stumbling through the darkness, we had crossed no man's land twice.

I turned cold. My skin jarred like a tin plate struck by a knife. Until that second I hadn't known what fear was. I had experienced sudden fright, like when a bomb had brought down a six-storey block only fifty metres from ours, but this was different. Until now I had watched the war from the stalls.

We wandered on through the blackness. The rain had slackened to a drizzle. We only knew vaguely where we were going; when we had come this way at noon, it hadn't mattered whether we had taken the occasional wrong turning. It upset me to think that the Russians might already have liberated our shack, and I was ashamed of my fear in the hour of victory.

'Tonight!' I whispered to give myself courage. The sergeant at

468

the machine gun was made of steel, but the Russians had fought their way here from Moscow through fire and steel. Three days ago the newspaper had said that our troops were advancing on the Soviet bridgeheads south of Szolnok, a hundred and twenty kilometres away. Now I had to be careful that a Russian tank didn't run me over in the dark. I could have drawn a map of the Siegfried Line with my eyes shut, but I had only a vague idea of my present surroundings. The darkness had thinned a little. Trees blundered into my path as I looked for the blacker blocks of the houses. Guns flashed in the distance. We had reached the edge of the little town again, maybe the edge we wanted.

Suddenly I saw a familiar-looking garden gate. The house was twenty metres from the street, its door closed. Between two trees I could just make out a black heap about the height of a man. That was the bunker. I had already admired it earlier: a direct hit would hardly dent it. Climbing down the ladder, I saw only one pair of eyes, but heard the breathing of several people. Politely, I wished the darkness good evening.

Someone lit a blue torch. There were two people sitting on the earthen bench to the right of the entrance, a tall man and a woman. Opposite them sat Péter Demeter.

'This is my side,' he said politely when Dávid sat down beside him. Once we were settled, the group resumed the conversation that our arrival had interrupted. The calm of their voices and the stupidity of what they were saying surprised me almost equally. Our host expected Hitler to make peace with the English so that they could unite together against bolshevism.

'Let's face it, we're all European Christians,' he reasoned. The tall man, who was a neighbour, was appalled by Demeter's defeatism and guaranteed a final victory on all fronts. Judging by the explosions that interrupted the conversation every half minute, the Russians were already less than a kilometre away, if not in the garden itself.

I couldn't keep my eyes open. I dreamt of explosions and machine-gun fire. Every so often I would be startled awake by the thought that the Russians might arrive while I was asleep.

I woke up in a bed the next morning, not knowing how I had got there. Mother and Dávid were up already. There was silence all around.

'Are the Russians here?' I asked anxiously. They were not. They had been either stopped or pushed back. The image of the machine-gunner surfaced in my memory, but this time in a menacing, metallic light.

We could keep ourselves as warm as we liked: our host had enough fuel for two winters. Mother offered her services as a cook, but Demeter politely declined this cunning plan, saying that he never left such important matters in the hands of others, avoiding even the most famous restaurants. He was a professional bachelor. We had found him in the garden, digging among large mounds of earth in his oldest clothes. He stopped to chat with me and Dávid, telling us what marvellous luck it was that the Russians hadn't arrived during the night. I was ready to turn a deaf ear to a continuation of last night's line of reasoning, which had assumed that the imminent loss of Pestszentimre would precipitate an alliance between Roosevelt, Churchill and Hitler; but the reason for Demeter's relief was simpler and more personal.

'They can go and get drunk somewhere else,' he said as he worked to make the roof of his wine-cellar collapse. He didn't want the Russians to commandeer the wine and ransack his house. He was ready to take a few days of his annual holiday in order to prevent this, but his bosses at the factory wouldn't let him, as they were trying to move the whole factory to Germany. Nevertheless, they turned a blind eye to absences of a day or so, and he had the excuse of last night's battle. The trams weren't running and it was still too dangerous to go by bicycle. I was non-plussed by this ridiculous sense of duty, and asked him how far the Russians had been pushed back.

'Maybe as much as three or four kilometres,' he said confidently.

We decided to take advantage of this brilliant fascist victory by salvaging our other suitcase, which still contained more than half our possessions.

Wheatsheaf Lane, Mayfly Road, Boundary Way. The little town had been a village not long ago. We walked along an unsurfaced road that was bordered by small cottages and gardens on one side, and open fields on the other. Ahead of us, two streets led off to the left, the far one forming the corner of the town. On the right was a field of maize.

Suddenly, two Hungarian soldiers dashed out of the maize towards us. Neither was wearing a cape or a coat; one wore a jacket, the other a shirt. Both were unarmed. Almost simultaneously, an ensign in a cape appeared from round the corner.

'Get back!' he shouted, drawing his pistol on them.

'Sir! Please don't shoot!' implored the one in the shirt. 'We haven't got any guns!'

470

'There are Russians in the field!' begged the other.

My world turned white around me . . . Russians . . we could run into the field . . . but they might not understand that we were civilians . . .

'Mr Ensign!' Mother protested. 'You can't shoot them! They are our men! In the name of Christ!'

The ensign walked slowly to the corner of the street. Thirty metres away, the deserters began to run. The ensign lifted his pistol and took aim. Then he glanced towards the maize and lowered his arm.

'You would do better to take your children inside,' he said, and started back the way he had come.

'God will bless you for this, Mr Ensign,' Mother said to his back. The ensign didn't answer.

28: The Goat

Unbelievable order prevailed in the town. Two hundred metres from the maize field, we passed a barber's shop. It was open. The little barber, in his white coat, was trimming a man's moustache with a pair of scissors. A lieutenant sat patiently reading the newspaper, waiting his turn. We passed dozens of tanks and guns, hundreds of soldiers, but every third or fourth shop was open for business as usual.

'The rationed potatoes are all gone,' said the pudgy, dirty green-grocer, a satisfied smirk on her face. 'The rest are four pengös.'

'Four?' stammered Mother. 'I don't want a ton!'

'Four per kilo,' said the shopkeeper, gaining another kilo of self-importance.

'Carrots?' asked Mother shyly.

'Two – and cheap at the price,' replied the puffy-faced woman with her nose in the air. Mother bought two kilos of carrots and two of potatoes, hardly a very optimistic gesture as we still had five kilos of potatoes in the shack, bought with ration tickets at thirty-five fillérs per kilo. Altogether this was enough food for a week. Mother must have reckoned it would take that long for the Russians to walk from the maize field to the shack. The fat shopkeeper, who lived even nearer to the front than we did, obviously intended to sell enough potatoes in that time to build herself a house on the Grand Boulevard.

The butcher had sold out of rationed meat.

'What about the other sort?' asked Mother in a daydream.

'Thirty-five pengös a kilo,' answered the butcher. Six times the official price. Mother bought 'bone meat' at five pengös a kilo – bones with a few scraps on them.

'They'll do for soup,' she said to justify her extravagance. She had spent seventeen pengös in ten minutes, and obviously considered

Pestszentimre's defences to be impregnable. Our host would doubtless be pleased by this, but I wasn't.

There was a long queue outside the baker's. We joined it.

'Why have they left those Jews here to stink us all out?' asked an indignant woman of fifty. Her waved, dyed hair withstood the wind like a wig made of glued horse hair. Fifty Jewish labour men had been sent to dig trenches in the area. They had been quartered in a local school. During the night, their guards had led them out into the road and shot them. The local residents had stumbled upon the half-buried corpses at dawn. The two dead Jews whom I had seen at dusk the day before must have come from elsewhere. Dávid had stopped me from seeing one of their faces. It couldn't have been my father . . . he was seven hundred leagues away, and free, unless Altmann the shoe merchant was right and Father had been whipped back to Hungary by the SS and their Hungarian bloodhounds . . . The corpse couldn't have been Samuel, either. Was it Elek waiting in the maize field . . . gun at the ready . . .? Maybe a machine gun!

The woman in the wig rattled on. A diamond brooch glittered on her coat. It was glass, false, like everything else about her. She was furious that dead Jews had been left to rot alongside decent people's homes. We didn't dare walk away.

We bought the bread at the official price. Mother offered her ration tickets, but the baker waved her down. He wouldn't sell more than a kilo to each customer, saying that others needed bread too. He could have charged five times more than he did.

As we went away, I wondered aloud what made some people murderers when others were brave and generous. How could one tell them apart before they showed themselves for what they were? But Mother didn't answer me.

The Russians hadn't occupied our shack during the night. Perhaps they were still waiting in some nearby maize field. Over the next few days, silence reigned for hours at a time, as if the front were leagues away. Then, suddenly, both sides' artillery would open up for anything between ten minutes and several hours. There was a festive disorder, a macabre air of carnival about all this. Fifty shells would land on the town in the space of ten minutes and the sirens would remain silent. Then a few hours later they would start wailing when there was nothing happening at all. We used to run towards the bunker through deafening gunfire, only to cower for half an hour surrounded by complete silence. When the house next door was hit by a shell, we were in the bunker.

473

The neighbours were not . . . Demeter rang the army medics first, and then, since three of his windows had been smashed by the blast, he went off to find a glazier. The glazier arrived before the military ambulance. Demeter got Dávid to help him dig around his wine-cellar, and once a shell exploded in the middle of the vegetable garden while they were both there. Mother dashed out of the house to find them still working, arguing heatedly over how close the shell had landed. Proudly, Dávid showed her a fragment of still-hot metal.

Back indoors, Mother pulled her left earlobe. 'You can't afford to get wounded, Dávid. If they have to strip you to stitch you up, we're all finished.'

The field gun that had been near our shack took up a new position close to Demeter's house. I recognised it by the bespectacled officer, and the gypsy private who had lit another fire and was blowing on the embers. It was from them that I now obtained my strategic intelligence.

'How far away is your target, Lieutenant?'

'A long way. Five kilometres. There are thirty-four divisions around Budapest, but we'll eat them away bit by bit,' he assured me. This was the most precise piece of information I had received. The Soviet forces were attempting to encircle the capital with three hundred thousand men.

One day the lieutenant wasn't there. He had been killed by a Russian plane. His replacement was reluctant to reveal this military secret; he stared at me distrustfully and wouldn't let me talk to his men. The next to disappear was the gypsy private.

'Where's "Black Józska"?' I asked. 'Did he get hit?' The officer looked sour. He had never liked the way I had fraternised with my namesake.

'He did a runner, the scabby little gypsy.' A few days later I found a bomb crater where the gun had been.

Many of the shops continued to open every day, if only for a few hours. People bought up everything they could; we had to queue at the pharmacy to buy soap. Potatoes went down to three pengős a kilo, but at the butcher's the bloodstained walls and shelves were bare.

'No meat's come in for ages,' the butcher apologised. 'Not even on the quiet. What little salami and sausage I have left I'm keeping for the family.' So why was he still open?

'How much would you charge me to share a little salami with your family?' asked Mother.

'Sixty.' Nine times the official price. Wisely, Mother beat a hasty retreat. Our entire worldly wealth was worth three and a half kilos of sausage.

Péter Demeter had always reserved one of the two earthen benches in his bunker for himself, no matter how many other people were there. He kept the house meticulously tidy, and when Mother cleaned the living room, he pretended not to notice. He went to work every morning, bicycling to the factory along dangerous roads, since apparently his bosses couldn't do without his organisational and administrative skills during their move to Germany. He was geared to solitude. His wireless set was like a small cupboard. Several hundred records lined his shelves, carefully arranged by composer and title. He was partly self-sufficient as far as food was concerned: in a good year he could harvest three hectolitres of wine, though he preferred French red and German white. He kept a goat, using the milk primarily for making the finest cheese in Hungary. He kept chickens, too, for eggs and poultry. Yet this gourmet was lean and wiry; and this champion of solitude was a good talker when he decided to talk.

In exchange for roping Dávid into the digging, Demeter provided Dávid's food: enough flour, cheese and dripping to keep all three of us from starving. Cleaning the living room wasn't in our contract either, and every day he gave us two or three eggs and two or three decilitres of milk.

'They'd just go off otherwise,' he'd explain. Perhaps he needed to apologise to his meaner side.

Demeter brought the news that soldiers had been bursting into people's houses. Before stealing money, jewellery, food, or anything, they ransacked the cupboards for men's clothing. Demeter put a ladder up to the loft and opened the doors of his treasure rooms, and to our surprise we glimpsed carpets covering the floorboards, with pretty vases and lamps everywhere. We weren't allowed into the loft, but we had to pass his suits up to him. He had twenty, all of them impeccable. What good were they to him?

While we helped we chatted. He sounded us out about the English, who were not entirely taboo under the rules of the 'Lying Game', although we had to speak about the Bolsheviks with aversion at the very least. We wouldn't have been very convincing if we'd pretended to loathe the English, but Demeter chided us indulgently.

'Boys, I'm afraid it's time to give up hoping that the German occupation will be replaced by a British one. We won't gain anything by losing the war.'

He had something like a hundred books, many of which were foreign but not German. I could recognise German.

'Do you speak English, Mr Demeter?' I asked, though with no more respect than was due to any foreign language. 'I saw your books.'

'Those aren't English, they're French,' he smiled. 'For twelve years,' he announced with enormous pride, 'I was a waiter in Paris! Pierre Demétairr! Oh, là là!' he cried, throwing one arm into the air and almost falling off the ladder.

One evening he started talking about the Jews. I couldn't tell whether or not he was probing; all three of us had enough sense not to look at one another.

'Jesus's people,' said Mother, as Demeter carefully avoided showing his colours. 'They shouldn't be treated like this.'

'It is a bit much,' agreed Demeter. 'But even the French don't like the Jews.' He glanced at us. His suspicions had to be calmed before he became aware of them.

'I can't stand the Jews,' I yawned. Demeter turned to me, a little too interested.

'No? Why not?'

'Their noses are too big,' I replied. He laughed.

'And what about Jesus?'

'His nose is too big as well.'

Demeter laughed again, a belly laugh this time. If he had ever felt a shadow of doubt, he now forgot it for good. He even defended me from Mother.

'Every good Hungarian is taught to hate priests at his christening. God Himself can't change that!'

He gave up on us being Jews. He still found something odd about us, but I didn't know what it was and so I couldn't throw dust in his eyes. Occasionally I felt that he was a deadly enemy. He asked lots of questions, he nosed into every corner of our lives.

My thinness and pallor proved to be a blessing in disguise. Whenever I went shopping, people did me favours. Once I was given five kilos of potatoes on ration tickets, and on another occasion the shopkeeper produced half a kilo of sugar from under the counter, again at the official price. Then the butcher gave me thirty decas of salami for two pengös fifty. A week later I went back to see if I could push my luck, but the butcher was fed up with being kind. Every day I searched the town for bargains.

Walking down one of the side roads, I saw a group of fifty people standing on a small rise. I went to see what they were staring at.

Jews were being driven along the road. The head of the column trudged past in well-ordered rows, but the rest trailed behind, mainly limping women and elderly men. Most of them had torn shoes and carried bags on their backs or suitcases in their hands. At least half of them had blankets on their shoulders. My first thought was that they had been wiser than us; they had known that blankets were the most important thing to have. But, like us, most of them had failed to realise the importance of shoes or a good pair of boots. Their clothes hung loosely on them. They were dirty and muddy. On every face I saw the frozen lethargy of the dead. From the conversations going on around me, I realised that this was an everyday spectacle.

'They're paying for it now,' said the elderly peasant woman next to me. There was some compassion in her voice.

The Jews were accompanied by Arrow Crosses. They walked up and down the column, or stood in one place hurrying the stragglers along.

A woman of about twenty-five stepped out of the column. She was carrying a baby in her arms. Her hair was dishevelled. She had slipped her coat back over her shoulder and undone the top of her dress. Her breasts were showing. She sat down on a large stone by the side of the road. A large Arrow Cross guard wearing an armband strode over to her shouting: 'Move!' But the woman might as well have been deaf. Cradling it with one arm and protecting its head with the other, she began to breast-feed her baby.

The Arrow Cross hit her on the hip with the butt of his gun. The woman stumbled forward, then lurched back into her former position. She didn't utter a sound. The Arrow Cross stood in front of her for five seconds, powerless. The woman went on feeding her baby. Then the man said something. The mother still didn't move. The Arrow Cross raised his gun and pointed it at her.

Slowly, the woman nodded. She went on suckling the baby for another four or five seconds, then stood up and walked calmly back to the road.

'Call yourself a man? Arrow Cross!' shouted the peasant woman beside me. It was the first time since the Arrow Cross takeover that

477

I had heard their name thrown in their faces as an insult. The large man turned to the spectators.

'Who was that?' he bawled. The peasant woman raised her head but said nothing. The Arrow Cross's gaze met hers, but she held his stare and his eyes moved on to someone else. Then he turned round and went on his way.

Suddenly my heart stopped. Ten metres away from me, on the edge of the road, was Laci Mester, the goalie. There was a gun on his shoulder and an Arrow Cross band round his arm. He was certain to notice me, even more so if I moved. I didn't, but he saw me anyway. His eyes lit up. He came towards me. Then, after a few steps, he veered back towards the road. He passed me. Then he stopped, turned round, and waved at me.

I can't wave back . . . However stupid it sounds, I'll tell him he's got me mixed up with someone else . . .

Laci Mester shook his hand in the air as if restoring the circulation, then joined his hands together above his head. He turned and went on with slow steps. Soon, the whole column had passed.

Two years before, Laci had dreamed of marching down Moscow High Street. He'd walked the Captain's dog in the hope of getting into the army.

Maybe one kilometre away from us, maybe three, the front froze while the Red Army caught up with itself. In the north-east, near Oszu, and in the south, the Russians were moving faster. I heard all this from the neighbours in the bunker and in the shops, as I no longer bothered with the radio or the papers.

Demeter hardly left the house any more. His factory was ready to move to Germany but he wasn't.

'My patriotism stops at the Hungarian border,' he said. He and Dávid had now completed their preparations for making the cellar roof cave in, and only a few temporary pillars now needed to be removed. Demeter was putting this off, just in case the Russians met their Stalingrad at Pestszentimre. Their two-week halt at the edge of the town raised his hopes. With the digging finished, we were no longer entitled to any food from him. We didn't eat much, and what we did, we ate slowly. Potatoes had become our staple diet, four or five a day. Mother didn't eat that many, claiming that she had already had most of her share when we weren't looking. We had one hundred and seven pengös left. Mother was hoping that the depreciation of money would raise the value of our earring.

478

In the evenings, Demeter invited Mother in for tea. I used to stay with them in the living room for as long as possible, and even Dávid would hang around for a while. We read, but couldn't really talk between ourselves: it was too much of a performance. Our room led off the living room, and after going to bed I'd eavesdrop for the next hour. Occasionally I'd get up and press my ear to the door, but Dávid ordered me back to bed. I obeyed, but only because I was afraid that his voice might attract attention. I always waited up until Mother came to bed, by which time Dávid had usually fallen asleep. Sometimes I pretended to be asleep myself. Occasionally I sat up in bed and told Mother off for being so late.

'I almost came to grief,' Mother said one night. Demeter had asked her why she was so well read, and why her speech, for all its simplicity, was so polished, when she was only the wife of a simple cobbler. Mother just couldn't feign illiteracy for hours on end. 'I told him', she recalled, 'that I'd had a secret friend for years, a judge.' Demeter had swallowed it, but my mother's cleverness infuriated me. She had deprived herself of her best defence against Demeter's advances: her fidelity to her soldier husband. She had already allowed Demeter a little way into our lives.

However tiresome I found it, I was trying my best to live on potatoes and to accept nothing from Demeter. It was often very difficult, as our main meal was soup made of potatoes, egg, vegetables and beef cubes. Mother had always been a slow eater, but now her half plateful lasted longer than our full ones.

'I shan't force-feed myself like a goose when I'm not even hungry,' she'd say, and I'd gobble up what she transferred to my plate. It was only after I had finished that I started to feel ashamed of myself.

One late afternoon, a continuous rumble began in the south, much further away than the usual artillery noise. I listened anxiously in the garden, worried that the Germans and Hungarians might have launched a counter-attack. But after a while the local guns started too. They had become something of a joke: one gun would go off by mistake and then all the rest would join in. Soon they fell silent, but the distant rumbling went on through the night and the following morning. Demeter left the house and returned in a bad and nervous mood. He paced up and down the garden and the house, holding a council of war with himself.

'They're coming from the north too. Short of a miracle, they'll encircle Budapest.' So that was why they had stopped here. They were regrouping while the rest of their troops completed the encirclement.

Péter Demeter's worry was this: we were on the edge of the Attila Fortress, in the outer defence zone. If he risked his life to stay with his treasures, he couldn't be sure that he'd save any more of them than if he took the best stuff to his brother's house in Kispest. He started packing, getting ready to withdraw from the outer to the intermediate defence zone.

'We'll stay here and look after the rest,' suggested Mother. 'We've run far enough from the Russians already. If they catch up, they catch up,' she added in a resigned tone. Demeter nodded reluctantly, and that day he rented a horse and cart to begin the move to Kispest.

'Dirty peasant!' he cursed quietly and furiously. 'Five hundred pengös for one day. It's like paying for all my belongings twice over!'

The next day, fighting broke out around us. The artillery kept up an incessant barrage, and planes roared overhead every few minutes. The sirens were silent: it was up to us to choose between the safety of the bunker and the comfort of the house.

Demeter knew a few officers, and went out on reconnaissance. He came back in the evening with bad news: the authorities had ordered the evacuation of Pestszentimre. At the far end of the town, German soldiers were forcing people out of their houses at gunpoint. They had shot several civilians.

Our host immediately assured us that he had reserved us a room in his brother's house at Kispest. The rent was to be fifty pengös a month, which was now hardly worth twenty fillérs according to Demeter. He was very enthusiastic about the house, and about his hard-working brother who ran a pub near Üllöi Avenue. Apparently the pub was doing well: all the Arrow Crosses from the surrounding streets congregated there. We had always dreamt of living in a place like that.

I wanted to stay put at all costs. Of the three of us, I was the scatterbrained hothead. I felt like screaming and shouting, I wanted to jump into the Danube and swim to Rumania.

Mother decided that we couldn't afford to expose ourselves to the additional danger of resisting the evacuation order. Moreover, all our documents suggested that we would run headlong from the Russians if we could: it would be difficult to explain our change of heart if we stayed. Demeter would be unlikely to let us live in his house without him, and we couldn't go to the Danielliks for fear of endangering them.

The next morning it poured with rain. There was thunder in the sky, accompanying the guns as it had two weeks before, when the Russian offensive had come to a halt in the maize field. I was sure that this time they would overrun us in a few hours, and told Mother that potatoes would be twenty a kilo in Kispest within a week. We had no money left.

But the guns grew quieter, and Demeter arrived in the garden with a horse and cart. We had to load all the precious sacks on to it, and weren't allowed to stop until each bag we put on knocked another two off. There was no room for the goat, let alone us, so it was decided that Mother and I would walk the goat and Demeter made space for Dávid on the driver's seat so that he could keep an eye on the luggage and help with the unloading. Like an idiot, Dávid agreed to this. I whispered to him that he was just a hostage for the goat, but he ignored my arguments and reminded me that we had already decided to go. Mother came down on his side, and that was that.

Our host took one of our suitcases in exchange for Dávid's help, and offered to take the other on condition that Mother carried a set of fine porcelain that would have got broken on the cart. Wrapped up in bedclothes, the bundle was three times heavier than our suitcase. Demeter consoled himself with the thought that he could come back for a few things, then locked the house behind us and left.

Mother hoisted the bundle on to her back, and I took hold of the string that was tied around the goat's neck. We were ready to go. My hair was soaked, and even my skull felt soggy from the rain. We hadn't brought caps with us when we had left Éva Stein's flat: caps looked too Jewish.

The goat refused to budge. She dug in her hooves. I had to turn and face her before I could win the tug-of-war, and as soon as I turned my back she pulled sharply on the already weakening rope. Her beard was as white as the rest of her, but she was a young goat in her prime and she had eaten more than one potato and one carrot for breakfast. I had to drag her.

Although I had once been a village kid, it was Mother, after a quarter of an hour, who thought of breaking a stick off a bush. Not that it helped much, the goat simply pulled sideways instead of backwards. I still had to drag rather than drive her, which required

481

almost as much strength. We waded through puddles and tripped over stones while the wind threw the rain in our faces. My feet would have been drier without my shoes, one of which had come unstitched: it was alternately sucking up the mud and spitting it out. We reached a big road. Black waves of people churned through the mud: women stooped under bundles as big as Mother's, young children and men over military age pulled hand-carts, people wearing knapsacks pushed bicycles with luggage attached to their frames. Here and there we could see the loaded carts of the rich. Both sides of the Budapest road were choked with refugees. We couldn't see a single soldier.

The goat took fright in all the commotion. This time she didn't dig in her hooves: she jumped about, shook her head, tried to free herself. I attempted to pull her back on to the right course, and was lucky not to fall over. Then I let her pull me, but a passing horse almost kicked her and she leapt aside, knocking me into the mud. I staggered to my feet and gave her a good kick. That made her even more savage. Taking the knot of her bundle in one hand, Mother helped hold the goat's rope with the other.

Our ancestors must have stooped like these refugees when they hauled stones for the pyramids. The carts of the rich reminded me of the chariots of the Pharaohs. But at least the Pharaohs hadn't murdered our ancestors. The Jews must have had enough to eat or they wouldn't have wanted to go back to the 'flesh-pots of Egypt'.

In my pain, I decided that Demeter had invented the stories about the German soldiers shooting civilians who refused to leave. He just wanted us to take the goat so that there would be more room on the cart.

'I'll let the goat go,' I groaned, my vision grey and blurred with hatred.

'Then we'll have nowhere to go,' answered Mother. 'Give me the rope.'

I let her take the rope from me, too tired to protest. A minute later she had to put down her bundle. The goat was tired too, she was pleased to take a break. Then the crowd swept us on, and we stopped again a couple of steps from the edge of the highway.

Two aeroplanes swooped out of the clouds and roared along the line of the road. They were Russian. One of the wingtips almost shaved my head, and I saw the pilot as clearly as if he were in the same room. The noise of the engines sent the goat mad. I nearly had to strangle her with the rope to keep her in one place. She wrestled with me, rearing up, pulling on the rope and throttling herself. I sat on her back. It occurred to me that I should laugh. I was riding a goat. I burst into tears.

Around me, a thousand people lay on the ground. When the Poles and the Russians had fled before the advancing Germans, Stukas had strafed and bombed the roads. These Russians didn't even drop leaflets. They were just checking that the road was covered with civilians and not soldiers. Scarcely had the crowd got to its feet when the two planes made another pass over our heads. Everyone hurled themselves into the mud, leaving their carts and hand-carts standing in the road. One plane flew so low that I nearly grabbed its wing to escape the goat. The Russians didn't open fire this time either, but my goat panicked again and I had to sit on her. When I dismounted, she started to run round in circles like a mad thing.

Four more planes were approaching. The crowd hit the mud, not noticing that the aircraft were Hungarian. Neither did my goat. She went completely crazy.

A hand-cart passed us. One person was pulling, another pushed.

'We'll try,' nodded Mother hopelessly. She had already begged room for her bundle on two carts, promising that we would help push, but we had been refused for lack of space. It would have taken a lot of good will to make room for the bundle; Mother was swaying under the load. The goat knew that we were weakening. Ever since the first aeroplane had deafened her, she had stopped pretending. She was in a real rage now. I clung on to her alone for about half a minute, and then her rope slipped out of my hand. Mother caught it, but the two of us could hardly hold her. We were managing about ten steps a minute. Another hand-cart passed us. To show willing, I put my shoulder to it before Mother begged for space. Since my efforts were directed elsewhere, the goat decided to follow me, and I got a good two minutes' rest. When I straightened up, Mother was nowhere to be seen.

The crowd swirled like the sky. Black and grey clouds, rain, dirty yellow faces. I didn't know where we were going. Fog rose in my chest, my muscles loosened and dissolved in the thickening mist. Then, like a drowning man whose head breaks surface, I began to breathe again and my limbs regained their strength. My eyes pierced the obscurity of rain and fog as if they were searchlights, as though I were standing metres above the road. But Mother was nowhere. I sank into the fog. The goat dragged me backwards. My thoughts burned down to ashes, but a last weak flame of intelligence told me that I should stay in one place. Mother would look for me.

Women with bundles came and went. None of the bundles was white, most were ominously dark. I turned again and drifted along with the crowd. The goat pulled and I followed, zigzagging across the road. Reaching the edge, I turned her around by twisting her horns, and was amazed how easily she obeyed me. 'Take the bull by the horns,' I remembered, proud of my resourcefulness and annoyed that I hadn't thought of this earlier. I shortened the rope, and at last the goat was walking beside me, not me beside her. She was weakening. I knew that I was boss, and she knew it too. But I only touched her horns when I had to, wary of rousing her to a last desperate effort.

I couldn't go to the police and say I was lost.

My head cleared. I was being an idiot. I knew the address – Demeter's pub, Kispest. If that wasn't an address, what was? I almost despised myself for my former panic. Of course Mother wouldn't think of looking for me at the police station, she wouldn't even be all that worried. She knew I wasn't stupid. It didn't matter that I had no documents; it would only look fishy if I did. There were no signs of a police raid – after all, this was a patriotic rout. At worst they would check the crowd for deserters or labour men. Who the hell would think that a child with a goat was a Jew? All the provincial Jews were long dead, and how many Budapest plutocrats kept goats in their villas? The goat was in fact the perfect document, worth eight Christian great-grandparents. It proved that I was a peasant boy.

After an hour of being obedient as a lamb, the goat was well rested and had begun to fidget again. A few twists of the horns and sharp tugs on the rope taught her a lesson, and my self-confidence and strength were renewed.

The fog darkened. I hadn't covered more than seven or eight kilometres since the morning, five forwards and two backwards. It felt like a thousand. Kispest was still one and a half kilometres away, and the town was itself three kilometres long. I couldn't remember the exact name of the pub, but I knew for sure that it was the place where the Arrow Crosses met and that it wasn't far from Üllöi Avenue.

I had the splendid idea of going into a phone box to look Demeter up in the book. There were at least fifty Demeters. If I'd had a map I could have worked out which was the most likely address, but then I wouldn't have known where I was on the map anyway. If I'd had enough money I could have rung all the numbers, but I didn't have

484

a bean. All the same, I wasn't too worried. I was proud of being in such a difficult situation, and imagined myself boasting to Mother and Dávid about how clever I had been. After the war I could boast to Mik and Pista and all my friends as well. Mind you, the story so far wasn't wildly impressive. 'I got lost and then found out where I was . . . ' I decided that I'd better have some more exciting adventures before finding my mother. These were luxury worries. I realised that I was dizzy with hunger, and not with fatigue as I had at first thought. I also noticed that the rain had almost stopped now that I was totally soaked.

The goat had accepted me as her master. We wandered along for about a kilometre until I saw a man wearing an Arrow Cross armband. I went up to him, respectfully took the goat's rope in my left hand and gave the Hitler salute with the right.

'Fight on!' I exclaimed.

The Arrow Cross gave my goat rather an odd look, but he returned the salute. She looked even less Jewish than I did.

'Long live Szálasi!' barked the Arrow Cross.

'Do you happen to know Demeter's pub, sir? It's on a corner.' He sent me to a pub on the corner but it wasn't the right one.

I didn't strike lucky until my fourth Arrow Cross.

'Demeter?' he mused, staring at my goat as if he were going to ask for her Baptism Certificate. But he started to joke instead: 'You know there's a ban on alcohol, young lad?'

'If you're thirsty, sir, I can squeeze you a glass of milk,' I returned.

'It doesn't quench the thirst,' he laughed.

'Where can I find something that does?' I asked in a good country accent. 'Demeter's is a patriotic pub.'

'I think I know the one you're talking about; it's owned by my mate Villi's dad. That's a real pub, Hungarian wine, Hungarian hearts. And they don't baptise you with water either! Turn round, my little mate, and take the third on the right.'

I was cheered by the thought that all I needed was a saucepan and I could chase away my hunger by milking my goat. But first I wanted to check out Villi's dad's pub. There was no more than an hour of daylight left, and I didn't have time to visit every pub frequented by the Arrow Crosses, who were all complete drunkards. My chances of finding the right place diminished with every step I took away from Üllöi Avenue, and I would look even odder walking a goat in the dark. Where could I stop for the night . . .?

'JÓZSKA!' I turned to see Mother, thirty metres behind me. Her shout betrayed a far greater anxiety than I had felt; her features sagged with exhaustion, and only her eyes sparkled. It surprised me that I didn't explode with joy. Even my heartbeat remained steady. But the fog melted from my eyes and the air suddenly became warm.

'Did you go to the police?' asked Mother, imagining that I had bearded the lion in his den.

'Of course not,' I replied, raising myself even higher in her estimation.

'You didn't know the address!' she cried, scandalised by the thought of her unnecessary anguish.

'Of course not! It wasn't exactly difficult to find the Arrow Crosses' favourite pub when I knew the landlord's name.' I could see that Mother had decided that I was a genius, and I didn't want to disillusion her. 'I just asked four Arrow Crosses where they got pissed last night.'

'You didn't!' cried Mother, horrified.

'Not in so many words,' I assured her, restoring her faith in my sanity.

Dávid was waiting in the pub courtyard. He was wet and shivering, his face drooped, and even when he saw us, he went on shaking. Only his voice managed to escape the icy cavern of his fear.

'Where the hell have you been?' he demanded, turning red with fury. I felt nothing but contempt for the way he had run away on his cart, and refused even to insult him. Abuse was too good for him.

'Mother got lost,' I told him condescendingly.

Demeter told us off when we went into the house.

'At last!' he said. Mother was furious.

'Soulless old bachelor! You've got a heart of wood – and even that's got dry rot! I'm not surprised no one married you!'

'Your goat is a complete idiot,' I told him. 'And by the way, I let it go.'

'No, he didn't!' shouted Mother like a coward. Demeter actually resembled a dried-up old goat. Mother had been quite complimentary about his heart.

'I was beginning to think you really might have lost her,' he said, letting the insults pass. 'Where is my dear Denise?' Denise was the goat's name.

'In the courtyard,' Mother said meekly.

'Grazing on the cobbles,' I added.

'This child is cheeky. Did you leave the gate open?' Demeter ran off to clasp his long-lost goat in his arms.

'Mother,' sighed Dávid, 'it wasn't wise of you to insult Uncle Péter.'

'Wise?' I sneered in Mother's defence. 'You little creep!'

Mother told him that we had lost each other. Dávid hadn't taken this in until then, and immediately forgave us for his anguish and my insults.

'Oh well, it's good you've arrived.' Suddenly he looked frightened. 'Did you really get lost?'

'Mother got lost, I've already told you.'

'How could you possibly get lost, Józska?' he said indignantly. 'You're an idiot.'

Our window overlooked the courtyard. The room only contained one bed, but there was a bare mattress on the floor and we would be able to use the bedclothes in Mother's bundle. There was also a chest of drawers, a table, a stove, and an empty coal bucket shaped like a big jar. If two of us moved at once we had to be careful not to bump into each other. It was a good room, and a gift at fifty pengős a month. The house was big, although there was only one floor. A third of the building was taken up by the pub, but there were six rooms leading off the central corridor and another two or three leading off from these. The entire Demeter family could live there easily.

There were two branches of the family living there apart from Péter. His cousin, who was a railwayman, had moved in, together with his wife and sons, one of whom was fourteen and the other fifteen. The publican and his wife also had a son, Villi, who was condescendingly friendly with me from the start. He was nineteen or twenty, a real barber's shop heart-throb. His hair was unnaturally curly, his voice too warm, his manner suffocatingly agreeable. I knew straight away that we had to watch him. He was of military age, but wandered around in civilian clothes. Either he had exceptionally flat feet, or a particularly important post in the Party. But I never saw him wearing an armband.

A small, separate flat opened off the courtyard. It was occupied by a German called Hutter, who spoke about twenty words of Hungarian and boasted of working for the Gestapo. People said that he was a minor clerk of some sort. His wife trembled when anyone so much as looked at her, and although her Hungarian was faultless, it was difficult to understand her because she spoke so quietly.

The public bar was open for only a few hours a day because

of the alcohol ban, so its function was largely taken over by the enormous living room behind it. All day there was a steady stream of regulars, among them soldiers and Arrow Crosses. The landlord, Péter Demeter's brother, was preparing to move to Germany. He and his small, kind, open-faced wife were going to 'München', as he already called it, to open a pub there. He reckoned it was better to be hanged for a sheep than for a lamb. He'd be travelling in his own car, but there was no hurry. In his opinion the Russians would never reach the Györ–Vienna road.

'We'll be in Moscow well before the Russians get to Budapest,' he predicted. So why the hell was he preparing to go to Munich? Himmler had just announced the latest 'wonder weapon'.

'They can hit Moscow from here!' said a wine-swilling Arrow Cross. They couldn't get Moscow out of their heads. His companion said that the secret of the wonder weapon was not its long range, but its ability to explode into a million fragments, wiping out an entire infantry division in one go. A third Arrow Cross claimed that the weapon was a ten-ton bomb, and that the plane to carry it was almost ready. They didn't argue about it though, they clinked glasses to the Final Victory.

For me, the wonder weapon wasn't new at all. It had existed in poor Laci Mester's jokes since at least 1940. The Hungarian had always been able to piss on Moscow from Budapest. I was worried about Laci. Should I shoot him after the war or should I let him off as he had let me off when he'd seen me on the road? Dávid wanted all murderers to be hanged, but Dávid hadn't experienced my meeting with Laci, nor was he a goalkeeper.

Having learnt from past mistakes, Mother didn't wait for the price of potatoes to go up any further. She bought as much food as she could on ration tickets and then went out again and bought even more at black-market prices, which were still low. Altogether she had thirty kilos of potatoes and ten of dried beans, enough for a month if we were careful. There were just twenty days left until the New Year, and only Mother thought that the Russians might not reach us in that time. They needed to cover the same distance as I had covered in seven and a half hours – and they didn't have to lead a goat! In the meantime, we ate twelve potatoes and a third of a kilo of beans between the three of us every day.

One evening the publican's wife came in while we were eating our second course, the potatoes.

'Mrs Jáger, I'm so sorry I haven't had a chance to chat to you yet. We're off to Germany and I don't know whether I'm coming or going. Neither does my old man, taking fifty pengős a month in rent when your husband's at the front!' She gave the money back. It represented half our wealth. She left the room and returned with some lard and a fist-sized piece of bacon.

'It makes it slip down better,' she said, then blushed and left.

Incomprehensibly, Christmas lunch became Mother's chief worry. As if we had any cause to celebrate! I laughed when I discovered that the stupid, flat-faced Gestapo clerk's worries revolved around the same theme. After a few glasses of wine in the living room, his world became rosy.

'At Christmas we'll eat our supper on the Carpathians.' The fact that he didn't mention breakfast was a step in the right direction, compared with the other customers, who spent their time singing the praises of the wonder weapon that was due to be launched within hours and was improving by the minute. Among the secret drinkers avoiding the alcohol ban in the living room, wine began to taste like blood. Through the rose-tinted sights of the wonder weapon, they saw a happy future full of whores, unrationed meat, and dead Jews.

'At Gyálpuszta the dirty little fuckers were already dancing and crying for joy,' remarked a huge Arrow Cross with a Hitler haircut. He was talking of the day that the road had been jammed, the day the Russians had broken through. Jewish labour men had been digging the trenches for the outer line of the impregnable Attila Fortress, and the Russians were approaching. 'The lousy Bolsheviks weren't a kilometre away, and the filthy Jews were snogging and whispering and waving their arms around, right under our noses. They thought their yid Messiah was going to arrive in the next ten minutes and turn them all into guards while we became their prisoners! There were shells landing all around us, and their saviour's guns managed to splatter a few of them too, but they were too bloody happy to care. I felt like diving for cover, it was a bit cooler down on the ground, but you know me . . . Anyway, this grinning little shit in pigtails starts pulling off his yellow armband, right in front of me. So I gave him a short burst from my Schmeisser. That stopped the dancing all right, though they didn't even blink at the Russian shells. So I shouted, "Line up, the party's over!" and within one minute they were all in order. We dealt out a few knocks with gun butts, finished off one or two straight away, gave the rest a few well-aimed kicks, and they all lined up with long respectful faces, the way they should. Then we started to chase

489

them away from their Bolshevik friends, and anyone who didn't keep up: bang! We weren't going to let them hang around. We shot one or two at the front of the column so that they wouldn't slow down and show a bad example to the ones at the back. We had a bit of fun, I can tell you. Their faces were so black and blue you didn't have to see their armbands to know they were yids! They hurried all right. The next day you could have made a carpet of Jewish skins from Gyálpuszta to Kispest . . .'

Hutter, the flat-faced Gestapo clerk, expressed the view that all of them should have been finished off at Gyálpuszta, but conceded that they could still dig the inner fortifications and be shot when the Russians were within grenade range. I saw the wounded faces of the Jewish labour men and thought of what my father had said about Cain branding the foreheads of his victims. When these conversations were in progress, I stayed frozen where I was. At least I had the sense not to leave the room, and to try to look bored, as if I were listening to the weather forecast. Sometimes, Dávid didn't manage to escape to our room in time, and would stare rigidly in front of him with eyes of stone. I almost had to tear my ear off or elbow him in the ribs to make him stop. Afterwards, although he hadn't listened to a quarter of what was said, I would find him huddled in a chair, his thoughts graven clearly on his face . . . Judit, burnt at Auschwitz. It was impossible to talk to him and I wasn't fool enough to try and console him. I said the occasional word to break the ice of his pain, but he would be deaf for minutes on end, or would answer me like a sleeptalker.

I was encased in cold, impenetrable, unbreakable steel. I was a born soldier, tense as the hammer of a weapon that was ready to fire. This was my secret self, a self that I knew only by the orders it gave me. Since June, when I had refused to pray and God had turned my desperate words into sky-lifting magic, infinite power had risen in me again and again. It was part of me, but it could also turn against me. I was not allowed to speak of it, nor did I want to, not just because I would have been ridiculed but because my power was connected with religion in some strange and secret way. This was not the ceremonial religion with its well-fed routine, its alternation between boredom and ecstasy. Nor was it madness: the first commandment was the use of common sense. This power knew the hatred in my heart but condemned it to servitude.

Everybody had left the living room. I was alone. The weak, dirty electric lights constricted me. I turned them off and half opened the shutters. The darkness outside was not the darkness of prison. Black iron shadows rose from the greyness. The sky was empty of stars. I stared unblinking at the shadows, trying to check their imperceptible advance towards the window. I knew that only light could stop them, but I didn't know what kind of light. I would happily have defied the blackout, but a torch or even a searchlight could only scratch the iron darkness. The shadows were closing in.

Lightly, shadow drawn on shadow, Ágnes's face emerged from the soot of her hair like smoke against black clouds. I could feel, almost see her eyes upon me.

At the corner of my vision, Uncle Samuel appeared, glassy eyes of fixed horror rigid in his moon-white, dead-white face. He was laid out like the dead.

I was not hallucinating. I was calm, and knew that I was imagining these shades, not seeing them. I didn't hear voices, but somewhere inside my head, in letters of gold and flame, were the words: 'Ágnes? Or Samuel?'

I knew that I shouldn't answer. My lips moved to say 'I will not'. But my gaze returned to Ágnes. I protested, but my eyes were stronger than my thoughts.

The demons returned to the shadows of the courtyard. Outside the window lay indifferent night. But something had happened, something fatal, something wrong. I had committed a crime.

29: 'I Will Awaken the Dawn'

'Christmas is coming, the shops are closing down,' said Mother after a morning's shopping. Stocks had been running low for several days. We had wandered in circles, cheerfully trying to find in one shop what we had failed to find in all the others. When we hadn't succeeded, we had congratulated ourselves on the money we had saved. But now all the shops were shut, as if they'd been locked by a single key. Some incurable optimists had formed a queue thirty metres long outside a closed baker's shop on Üllöi Avenue. I couldn't understand why the shopkeepers in Pestszentimre had tried to cash in as much as possible while the ones here in Kispest, eight or ten kilometres further away from the front, had closed down.

The only place that was still open was a little shop nearby. We scarcely wasted a glance on it. For the past ten days it had stocked nothing but paprika, salt, aprons, shoelaces, and paper for covering shelves. A small, plain woman in a faded dress stood there on her husband's orders. I knew him well from the makeshift bar in the Demeters' living room. He strutted around the neighbouring streets like a farmer surveying his fertile fields. He wore a fancy armband with the 'Árpád' stripes, which apparently indicated some high rank. The other Arrow Crosses at the pub whispered that he wasn't really entitled to it, and that he only got it because his brother Kapor was a big shot at headquarters.

Those who wasted their time listening to the radio and reading the papers learnt nothing. I kept my ear to the ground, but the only news I heard was the gossip in the living room in the evenings. This had to be deciphered, as it was all in the language of wonder weapons, but the gist of it was that the Russians had repulsed the German and Hungarian counter-attacks and were fighting to broaden their front. In the Budapest ghetto, people were paying a hundred pengős for a kilo of bread and a gold watch for a chicken, although the Arrow Crosses usually kept the chicken.

'I bet they'd eat pork now,' said the witty, flat-faced Gestapo clerk.

'They even cheat each other in the ghetto,' said the 'Árpád' Arrow Cross, his serious tones reflecting the importance of the issue. 'But we can't provide any freight trucks for them, we need the transport elsewhere. They're dying on us by the thousand,' he sighed. 'They'll bring the plague down on us next.'

Just as it was possible to drink in the back room despite the prohibition of alcohol, many of the shops could have done good business through the back door. But to take advantage of this we'd have needed to know the area better and, above all, we'd have needed money. Mother was convinced that you could always buy anything if you had enough money, but she was equally sure that within two weeks our hundred pengős would buy little more than a clove of garlic. Nevertheless, she didn't try to stock up on potatoes because she didn't want to leave us completely bankrupt.

To whom could we turn? Piroska would have shared her last crumb with us; but if she weren't already homeless she was either in the firing line or had been overrun by the Russians. Mother decided to try the posh Jewish woman we had met at the Danielliks', the one who modestly called herself Mrs Kovács, the commonest name in Hungary. They were in the same boat as us, even if they were rich.

Mother considered my thinness to be a major family asset, and took me with her. We left Dávid behind; starvation seemed to have had no effect on him. I was worried that the Kovácses' money might have given them away, and that we were walking into a trap, but Mother dismissed my fear with an apathetic wave of her hand.

'If we're stopped, I'll say I came about the cleaning job she promised me.'

The trams were running. We had hardly more than a kilometre to go, but we both wanted to jump aboard just to remember what everyday life was like. The conductor was sitting with his feet up on a seat, taking no notice of the passengers.

'Are you going to the front?' asked an elderly man. The conductor laughed.

'We're sure to cross it by chance one of these days, but any Russian

493

without a season ticket will have to walk. I don't take fare-dodgers.' Mother offered to buy a ticket. 'Only if you pay for it with brandy,' the conductor joked.

The Kovács family lived in a good two-storey house in a quiet street in Pestszentlőrinc. The woman opened the door. She and her kids were in the middle of lunch. They were eating soup, but there was pâté and cheese on the table. And butter! I gaped at the food.

'We came to ask you a favour . . .' Mother began.

'Aren't you . . .? Piroska's next-door neighbour . . .?' asked the woman. I couldn't believe that she hadn't guessed the truth, but her frightened face was proof.

'We are like you . . . ' said Mother reassuringly. This was a shame. If Mrs Kovács had thought that we'd come round for a spot of gentle blackmail, she'd have given us anything. It was too late now.

'Astonishing!' she cried, clapping her hands. 'I'm so jealous! It doesn't show at all!' Suddenly her face became wary. 'What about the corporal?'

Like a fool, Mother explained about Ferenc. We could still have saved the situation by saying that we were Christians, but that we had lied to make her confess she was Jewish. 'Five thousand, please, Mrs Kovács.' But the psychological moment passed, and her ladyship dug in her heels.

'Difficult times,' she sighed almost sincerely.

'At Piroska's you offered to give to the poor,' said Mother. 'I'm only asking for a loan.'

'I have already given what I could. In church, as Piroska suggested. Without witnesses, to avoid the sin of pride. Marika!' she exclaimed, conveniently switching her attention to her little girl. 'You haven't eaten your soup! You shan't have any chocolate.' The girl began to snivel and the mother's heart softened. 'It'll make you strong, Marika. Just one spoonful . . .'

'I'm not Marika!' the kid answered angrily.

'You are now!' hissed her brother, who had finished his soup and was trying to call her to order.

'I'm not! And you're not Árpika – you're Robika! Give me chocolate, Mamma!'

Mrs Kovács looked at us, begging for pity. Mother looked at her, pityingly. Even I had to admit that they had far bigger problems than we did. If we ate two potatoes and fifty beans a day we could survive twenty days, and liquids alone would keep us going for another twenty.

494

That made forty in all, and by that time the Russians would have taken Vienna as well as Budapest. This whining china doll could get them all killed in one second flat.

'You promised to be Marika in front of strangers!' said Mrs Kovács with some vigour.

'Only if bad men come. The lady isn't a man and the skinny one is just a boy. And I won't eat my soup if I'm Marika.'

'One spoonful, Marika,' entreated the mother, but the little girl knew that she was winning.

'No! And no Marika! Gisella is nice, Marika is nasty. It sounds like that maid, Mariska, the one who broke the vase. I didn't break it!'

I felt as if I was in a circus. Mother and I sat shamefacedly through their lunch. I was worried that Mrs Kovács might think we were hoping for scraps, but Mother didn't want it to seem as if we had been thrown out like beggars. Mrs Kovács seemed to understand this; she certainly didn't offer us anything to eat. The little girl ate a mouthful of pâté, but she was still given two spoonfuls of cocoa powder, just like her big brother, who was a good boy and ate all his soup and didn't mind being called Árpika.

The following day we went to Zoltán Jankó's flat, which made me realise just how worried Mother was. I couldn't imagine the Russians letting me starve to death when all they had to do was walk eight kilometres to save me. Jankó wasn't at home. A neighbour told us that he only looked in once a week.

When we went back down to the street I noticed a familiar-looking kid coming towards me, a classmate from the Jewish grammar school. He was alone. He glanced at me, but we didn't greet each other. What could we say that could not be told at a glance? He wore a good coat and good shoes. His head was bare. There was a spring in his step and his face was round. He had enough to eat.

The centre of Pest was not yet within range of the Russian artillery, and most of the shops were still open. The bombing had been heavy, however, and many of the houses had been completely destroyed or had lost their upper storeys. Windows had expanded to five times their original size, and looked on to the everyday life of the streets like grotesque, blind eyes. We took the tram to Teréz Boulevard on our way to see an enormously fat lady who had liked me when I was a toddler. Mother had probably thought of her because of her weight problem.

'She's bound to give us some food even if she doesn't give us any money,' explained Mother, and although I couldn't see the logic of this I didn't want to argue.

'Don't be scared, we'll go round it,' said Mother before I had a chance to see whatever it was that was supposed to scare me. 'Come on,' she urged, prodding me. We were thirty metres away from my school. It was just around the corner. Mother grabbed me by my coat as I looked down the street.

It was closed off by a plain wooden fence, three and a half metres high. The ghetto. In front of the planks stood a man clothed in black velvet and surrounded by four or five armed Arrow Crosses. A single burst from a sub-machine gun would have wiped out the lot of them. Twenty men could have finished them off with stones and knives. That was why the decrees had stated that only children and the old and sick could live in the ghetto. Even most women under forty had been driven out.

'We'll go somewhere else,' Mother said in a controlled voice. She didn't even want to chance the Christian end of the ghetto street, and decided to go and visit the old dairy-shop owner who had laughed so much when I had asked her about her cardboard cheeses.

We took the tube for two stops. Mother emerged with brisk, steady steps, but when I looked round I became rooted to the spot. Seventy metres away, another wooden barrier closed off the street. We had already reached the far side of the ghetto. It was tiny. I almost laughed, but Mother went on rapidly without acknowledging that I had stopped. I had to follow. We reached Gisella Milky's flat, and stood for two or three minutes on a bleak staircase of brown stone before she opened the door. She was wearing a cotton dressing-gown pulled hastily over a nightshirt. She had always been old, but now she looked like her own mother. I could hardly hear her speak, and each word was succeeded by a long pause. Gisella Milky was ill. Alone. Her neighbours looked in on her once or twice a day. They fed her too. Mother changed the old woman's bedclothes, remade the bed and swept out the flat.

We headed straight for the Basilica where we had lived for so many years. I felt we were defying fate, and Mother was white as a sheet, speechless and hurried. I said nothing. A Protestant charity called 'The Good Shepherd' had an office nearby. Reverend József Eliás worked there, the priest who had given Mother the Danielliks' address a few weeks before.

Mother made me wait outside in the street. She didn't want the people in the office to realise that a child knew about them. Their activities defied both law and death. But her worries were unfounded. She came out empty-handed. The charity had ceased to defy anything. Eliás himself had gone into hiding, and in his absence his office could only offer spiritual consolation as they hadn't enough food for their own organisation. For safety's sake, we hurried away.

We didn't go far. We turned down the side street where our old butcher had his shop. We had been going there for years; he had served us as Christians when we were living at Éva Stein's and it was unlikely that he knew we were Jewish. Five or six people were trying to have a quiet word with him. Among them was an old classmate from my primary school called Gergely.

I looked straight through him. He scrutinised me carefully. He knew that I was Jewish. My only hope was that he wouldn't recognise me. No chance: we'd sat in the same classroom for two years. I hadn't changed much more than he had in the intervening one and a half years. I decided that if Mother said anything to me I would answer her in sign language. My voice would give me away completely. Mother took out her ration tickets. The butcher sighed. Gergely's lips trembled. My face twitched. Gergely must have noticed. He turned away and looked out of the shop. He didn't want to frighten me by winking. The butcher gave us nothing, not a single gram of meat. Having risked our lives for nothing, we returned to Kispest.

From then on we lived on one potato and one bean soup a day. Every second or third day, after hours of queueing, we got half a loaf of bread.

We were jolted awake one morning by a storm of gunfire. It sounded as if the pub had been hit by five shells inside two minutes, but we already knew that our eyes were more accurate than our ears in assessing damage. One of our windowpanes fell into the room, but we could hardly hear it break above the infernal din. We dashed down to the cellar. Usually, since Vilmos Demeter's parents had left for Munich, there were thirteen of us in the cellar. This time we were spared the unlucky number: at least ten of the neighbours squashed in too, most of them without luggage.

After an hour and a half, there was silence. Vilmos, Péter Demeter and Hutter's wife were trying to cheer up poor Hutter, whose fellow workers in the Gestapo had left Budapest by aeroplane. He swore that the Russians would never take him alive. He had been pouring Dutch courage down his throat all morning.

'Heads up! Christmas we supper on the Carpathians!' he slurred loudly in his execrable Hungarian.

'Isn't it the twenty-third of December today?' I asked with a poker-face, knowing that he could hardly see past the end of his own nose, let alone mine.

'It is!' Hutter shouted proudly. He decided that the Führer had already deployed the wonder weapon, only we didn't know it yet. It wasn't worth asking how he knew; but three seconds later he went crazy anyway: 'You not believe?' he screamed in my direction. I realised that if I suddenly said I believed him, his Gestapo instinct might tell him I was lying. If I didn't he might decide I was Jewish. Only a Jew would refuse to believe in the wonder weapon.

'I don't suppose we'll have any supper at all at Christmas,' I laughed. 'We've only got fifteen potatoes left. And a kilo and a half of beans.'

Hutter started to sob: 'Heroic Hungarian child!'

'Children without a cake at Christmas!' exclaimed Mrs Hutter, who was skin and bone herself. She stood up and left the cellar. Two minutes later she returned with two paper bags and a small jar of sugar. 'For the cake,' she said. There was flour in one of the bags and poppy-seeds in the other. Then she went and fetched a big slice of bread and two sausages, and lard for the cake. By way of thanks, I took a big bite of sausage, then forced myself to stop eating so as to save the rest. The Gestapo sausage tasted good.

The next morning I took the poppy-seeds down to the Arrow Cross's shop to be ground. When I walked out of the gate I saw that a deep ditch had been dug across the road. A tank trap. Twenty metres away, men in civilian clothes were digging another. They wore yellow armbands. I had to pass them. They were guarded by soldiers and Arrow Crosses loitering on the edge of the ditch, and I would only draw attention to myself if I suddenly turned around. I swung the paper bag casually but my feet would hardly move. I couldn't take my eyes off one of the Jews. He was wearing a short coat, the kind Elek had always worn in the fields. The man was small and weak, not in the least like Elek, whose guns I could hear two kilometres away.

An Arrow Cross stepped in front of me. Was it my imagination, or had he done it on purpose? I was sure that he meant to bar my way. I could have gone round him, but it might have been risky. I took a deep breath, and handed matters over to my double.

'Fight on!' I said, saluting.

'Long live Szálasi!' replied the Arrow Cross, returning my salute.

The Jew stopped digging. His eyes filled with pain, as if I had scratched them with a knife. For him, I was the barefoot, dirty little kid who had mocked us in Oszu as we returned from *shul*, the kid whom Elek had nearly thrown over the rooftops. Quickly, I turned my head away and moved on. But his gaze accompanied me in my mind. I went mad.

'Fight on!' I exclaimed in a strident voice to the next Arrow Cross I passed. He smiled at me as if I were a kind of mascot. 'Tank trap, brother?' I asked him conversationally. Two thin, broken Jews slowed down their digging.

'That's right,' answered the Arrow Cross.

'Why?' I laughed. 'They'll never get this far.'

'Are you sure, little brother?' he asked proudly.

'On New Year's Eve we'll have supper on the Carpathians!' I shouted. 'We'll deploy the wonder weapon!'

The Arrow Cross believed my every word. There was someone else using my body, a Christian kid, a good little patriot who looked to the Arrow Crosses to protect him from the danger all around. The lie was sweet in my mouth. It made me drunk. My skin burned. I was stronger than ever. If I had wanted to, I could have flown. The two Jews went on digging.

The plain little woman was alone in the shop. She was bored. There was nothing to sell but courage. I was still intoxicated by my triumphant lies.

'Fight on!' I said as I walked into the shop. It was a mistake. The woman probably hated her husband.

I started to grind the poppy-seeds.

'You're not local, are you?' said the woman.

I should have given her a brief, vague answer, but my earlier success made me over-confident. 'No,' I said loudly. 'We're running away from the Russians. From Hódmezővásárhely.'

'Really? That's where I come from.'

I sobered up in a second. Had the Jewish labour man put a curse on me? Could a curse begin to work so fast? I had broken the first rule of the 'Lying Game': I had answered more than the question. I turned round, as if my right arm had got tired of working the grinder and I wanted to use my left instead. I now had my back to the woman.

499

'Do you know where Zrinyi Street is?' she demanded. This was straight interrogation.

'Everyone does,' I said, talking as fast as I could. 'But I was only four when we moved away—'

'So you're not really from Hódmezővásárhely,' she interrupted as if she had caught me lying.

'Of course I am. But we were only passing through this time, we stayed three nights at my grandmother's house in Árviz Street.'

'Where's Árviz Street?' she asked. She seemed genuinely unsure whether or not she had heard of it.

'Out on the edge of town. That's why we had to move when I came along, my dad's workshop couldn't get enough business and he had to go and work for someone else for four years – trying to support all four of us, just imagine . . .'

'What is your father?' She had only half followed my torrential explanations and was still a little suspicious. I knew that my answer would decide our fate.

'Only a corporal,' I said shyly. 'But he hasn't been on the front until now. They just sent him there from Pestszentimre. He's very brave, it won't be long before they make him a sergeant.' Casually, I sauntered out of the shop.

Three days later, in the living-room bar, I heard that the Russians had occupied Esztergom, closing the ring around Budapest. The tank trap in front of the house had been covered up with planks, then earth and pebbles had been thrown on top.

I had to get some proper information about the front. I waited until after lunch the following day, when the living room was deserted and the house was completely quiet. I went over to the gigantic wireless, glued my ear to it and switched it on.

'This is London speaking!' it bellowed. Someone must have forgotten to change the station after listening to the BBC.

A policeman appeared instantly in the courtyard. He was leading an Alsatian. I couldn't afford to hesitate. I twiddled the tuning knob. God must have had his hand on mine, because the wireless immediately roared: 'Germany Will Win!' The bass voice seemed to come from some vast, empty, echoing hall. I just had time to read the tuning dial to see what station it was when the wireless itself helped out: 'This is Radio Danube speaking . . .'

The policeman walked in from the terrace with his dog.

'You're coming with me!' he said immediately. My luck with the tuning dial didn't seem to have done me any good at all. At that point Vilmos Demeter walked into the room. He must have heard the policeman.

'Maybe,' I said. 'If you tell me why.'

'You know why,' answered the small, well-fed policeman. Then he turned to Vilmos. 'I am taking the radio and the boy,' he said officiously. 'He was listening to London.'

'The hell I was,' I said calmly, sounding very slightly irritated by the misunderstanding. 'That's what came out when I switched it on. I was listening to Danube. Look, it's just next to London on the dial. I didn't put it there.'

'I am taking . . . ' the man said again, but he was already hesitant.

'Sit down, Uncle Pista,' urged Vilmos Demeter calmly. 'Have a glass of wine.' He started to pour one.

'I'm taking them all the same,' said the policeman and sat down.

Vilmos Demeter became both affable and severe at the same time. 'You're not taking anyone or anything, Uncle Pista. While you're strolling around here, this kid's father is fighting at the front. And the radio is ours.'

Vilmos sat down beside the policeman. Mother turned up, but seeing that everything was all right she went back to our room. She didn't add to the man's suspicions by calling me out of the living room. I had to make it clear that I had no cause to run away. Uncle Pista drank so much that when he tottered to his feet an hour later, to be led away by his dog, he could hardly remember why he was there.

'So you listen to London, do you?' asked Vilmos. He sounded only a little reproachful. I shrugged, neither denying nor admitting anything. I didn't want to detract from his achievement in having sent away the policeman. 'I do too, sometimes,' Vilmos laughed. 'But I found out more from Uncle Pista than we would have heard on the radio. The Russians are only two kilometres away.' He sighed deeply. I didn't dare risk a sigh.

We ate one slice of cake a day. We had finished our sausage the day it was given to us. We only seemed to feel our starvation when we had food. All three of us slept a lot. Sometimes I would fall asleep in the house and wake up in the cellar.

Once I dreamt that the house was falling down around me. I woke to find the ceiling still in place, the walls too. But the air shook with the noise. Dávid and I started arguing over where

501

the shells were coming from. Mother shouted at us to go down to the cellar.

'It's no better there,' said Dávid. 'The safest thing to do would be to put cotton wool in our ears.'

I felt neither courage nor fear. Perhaps I went a little deaf. A whimpering, whistling noise rose again and again into multiple screeches, ending in a series of explosions that tore up the air. It was the sound of the *Katiusha*, the twenty-four-barrelled Russian rocket-launcher. The impact sometimes sounded more distant than the firing. The launcher couldn't have been more than a hundred metres away.

In fact it was a hundred and fifty metres from the pub, just behind the Lajosmizse railway line which closed off the far end of the street. We learnt this in the cellar. Hutter, the Gestapo clerk who had been so treacherously abandoned by his office, had got the information from a German soldier. Within minutes, the cellar had turned into a kind of doss-house. It was thought to be the safest shelter in the neighbourhood. We brought two camp beds and a couch down from the house. Mother lay on my right, on the couch. A girl of twenty-three called Erzsébet had the place to my left, and beside her lay her greying mother. The cellar was lit by about twenty candles and a few 'air-raid lamps', which were a kind of modified miner's lamp. The electricity had been cut off by then. Dávid's bed was the closest to the entrance.

A terrifying, monstrous clock marked out our nights and days. Long, unmeasured tracts of time were filled only by the monotonous ticking of distant machine guns and the far-away click of self-loading artillery. Then suddenly ten, twenty, or even fifty huge explosions would strike the hours. Sometimes, the hour would seem to be our last, and we would be happy just to hear the next explosion and know that we were still alive. The most frightening moments were when the candles went out. One or two always managed to stay alight, but my courage flickered, only flaring up, like the candle flames, at the last possible moment before extinction. I measured the noise in terms of weight. Sometimes, when the rumbling diminished to as little as half a ton, I would be filled with a blaze of jubilant light. It was no longer the din, but the power of the guns that overwhelmed me, the amazed awareness that their titanic strength was tearing down my prison, Józska Sondor's, Mother's, Dávid's, blasting the walls of the ghetto into powder.

When my exhilaration flagged, I would glance across at the table with the lamps, where Hutter sat with a friend. I wanted to squeeze new joy from his hopeless terror, a malicious joy, the pleasure of triumphant hatred. But I never could. Beyond their barricade of bottles, the two men gazed with open mouths and blinking eyes at a shadow. I'd have given quite a bit to see Hitler forced to listen to the victorious Russian guns for a few hours, here in the cellar, at the gate of Hell. But his madness would probably have been able to cloud his brain with some alcohol of unconsciousness.

We had to bring water from a pump about a hundred metres down the road, in the street that ran parallel with the railway. It was Mother who fetched the water. If Dávid or I were wounded it could mean the end for all of us. We cooked soup over our spirit burner during the breaks in the firing, and boiled our daily ration of potatoes – one each. Once, when everything had fallen silent for an hour, I ventured out to the bakery in Üllöi Avenue. Two or three hundred people were queueing outside, and after a long wait my initiative was rewarded with half a loaf of bread. Mother was too pale to be pleased with the bread when I returned. She didn't even have the strength to tell me off for going out alone. A couple of days later I persuaded her to let me go again. This time there was no queue, but the boarded-up window carried a sign saying that the bakery no longer existed.

The earth and sky would quake for a couple of hours at a time, then a longer period of silence would follow before the rocket-launchers resumed their whining and shrieking. It was like listening to the cries of the damned. Occasionally Dávid and I would go up to the courtyard for a breath of fresh air. The Russian planes would almost brush the roof, and the ground was often littered with black, twisted, empty machine-gun belts.

'If you aren't scared to be outside, go and fetch the water!' shouted Mother one morning, then set off herself, bucket in hand. Since everything had just gone quiet, I decided to show off my courage by snatching the bucket away from her.

I strolled nonchalantly along the street beside the railway. I could have walked into most of the houses through the huge holes in the walls. Now and then I heard the crackle of small-arms fire. I passed a side street to my left. To my right stood a tall wooden fence. Suddenly it began to make a loud knocking sound, and I looked up curiously. A neat row of holes was appearing just above my head. I watched them in amazement: the bullets would have hit

503

Mother in the head. A few moments later, my legs started to shake with fear.

Returning from the pump I had to pass the fence again. Whoever had been shooting at me must have realised that I was a kid because they didn't open fire. I looked up at the fence. The holes were definitely there.

When I got home I gave the story the treatment it deserved, magnifying the bangs by a factor of ten. Mother became convinced that I was guarded by a supernatural power, but Dávid was jealous. He cross-examined me with a grim, bitter face, and was openly sceptical about the number of holes in the fence.

Territorial boundaries were established in the cellar, unmarked but unquestioned. No one sat down in another family's chair without being invited, and you greeted the inhabitants of each part of the cellar whenever you crossed their patch. Addressing a member of another family while they were in the middle of a meal was the equivalent of begging, unless you yourself were eating. Even cousins shared their food very rarely.

Vilmos Demeter's bed was protected by an arch. His table was unfairly large, considering that he was the only person using it. He also had a chair and an armchair, which no one ever touched, although Vilmos was absent from the cellar more often than not. I suspected him of having walled off part of the house, hiding the door with a wardrobe. After all, he was some kind of deserter, protected from conscription by a medical certificate or a job in the Party, or perhaps only by his Arrow Cross chums. He would need a hiding place after the Russians arrived. Péter Demeter remained in his room, risking his life to guard his treasures. His railwayman cousin, the other Demeter, had been taken prisoner by the Russians during the Great War and had picked up a certain amount of pidgin Russian. This confession brought him numerous cigarettes, and Hutter never stopped offering him drinks, but everyone hung on to their food. Hutter sat with his friend, a fattish man with a soft white face. He must have been in his late thirties but his degeneracy had aged him prematurely. He drank constantly, consuming even more than Hutter did. Despite his civilian clothes, he didn't bother to hide the fact that he was a deserter. Hutter was already practising the part he would play to the Russians: '*Ja civile, ja civile,*' he kept saying. I wasn't particularly bothered by this. 'Gestapo' must mean something in Russian too. The two of them drank in silence or muttered to one another, and only the deserter's occasional shouts carried the length of the cellar.

Vilmos Demeter lent me a patriotic book. I read three and a half pages, sang its praises, and was allowed to choose another book from his collection. He came up to the house with me, so I didn't discover his hiding place. Not that I'd have had any use for it. He was only trying to save his skin, no harm in that. After all, he had saved mine from the policeman, even if his main priority had been the wireless set.

Searching the shelves, I came across a thin volume. I picked it out and examined it hesitantly. The title suggested that it might be another piece of camouflaged German propaganda, like *Little Lord Fauntleroy*. This was more than likely in the Demeter household. The book was called *The Prince and the Pauper*, and claimed to be by the American author who had written the wonderful book with the boats on the cover. I was determined not to be taken in, but I could see immediately that it wasn't about some degenerate German imbecile dressed in English clothes.

Gunfire sounded outside. I had to make a snap decision whether or not to take the book down to the cellar. I decided I would. Vilmos Demeter came with me this time, although he was more frightened of becoming a prisoner of war than of the Russian shells. He had heard somewhere that the Russians were rounding up civilians of military age, which was hardly surprising since every soldier carried civilian clothes with him, just in case.

We didn't have any candles. We had to borrow other people's light. I edged my way towards the far end of the cellar, where the railwayman's family were encamped and where Hutter and his friend sat and drank in the light of the two lamps, their table crowded with bottles and glasses.

At first, I couldn't understand why on earth a prince would want to put on the yellow star of poverty. And once he'd decided to try it out, why would he immediately start whining that he was a pure-bred Aryan prince? Then I remembered how I had got cold feet when the Arrow Cross had barred my way to the Jewish labour men and I had pretended to be a good little fascist. Anyone can be a prince, but not everyone can be a pauper. Aaron Kohn's smile wouldn't be so bright on one potato a day. Aaron must have been eating figs in Palestine for months, assuming the English hadn't minded upsetting the Arabs and had let him in. Would he still have changed places with me? Edward

505

Tudor was lucky to come across Miles Hendon so soon. Hendon was a kind of Christian Elek.

I felt sorry for Edward, and couldn't understand why a pauper's misfortunes seemed so much worse when they happened to a prince. But my hands could hardly turn the pages for fear that Tom Canty, who was in far greater danger, might be unmasked.

I had to read the bit about London Bridge twice to get an idea of how big it had to be to support a whole village where people could live out their lives without ever visiting either bank. The book said 'one fifth of a mile', but I didn't know how long a mile was. I had to find out. Carefully. If the people around me discovered that I had nothing better to worry about than the length of an English mile, they might get suspicious. For me, a mile was like a league, an unknown quantity that belonged in the realm of fables.

All that Mother and Dávid knew was that a mile was longer than a kilometre. This left me none the wiser. The railwayman's two sons were one and two years older than Dávid. The younger of the two looked brighter, so I tried him. He didn't know how long a mile was, but he did get suspicious. I went up to the house to go to the loo, but on my way back I found him waiting for me in the courtyard.

'Do you know this song?' he asked, trying to sound casual.

'In the Fortress of Lipót,
Listen to the whistling Jew,
He'll buy everything you've got,
Then he'll sell it back to you.'

'I've never heard it before,' I replied. 'Where's the Fortress of Lipót? I've heard of Sziget Fortress, and Drégely, and Nádorfehér Fortress. I once read a book about the Fortress of Eger – we really taught the Turks a lesson there!'

'It isn't that sort of fortress,' explained the dark-haired Mátyás, who wasn't as bright as he looked. I had side-tracked him completely. 'Lipót Fortress is a joke name for part of Pest.'

'Near the Royal Fortress?'

'No, stupid, the Royal Fortress is in Buda! Lipót is nothing but shops and yids. The fortress bit is just a joke – do you get it? Of course, you're from the country . . .'

'The provinces!' I said defensively, producing yet another red herring for this amateur Arrow Cross.

'OK, then, the provinces. But even you should know where the Royal Fortress is!'

I still didn't know how long a mile was. Suddenly I remembered that Péter Demeter was a well-travelled man: he had been a waiter in Paris for twelve years. I went to see him in his treasury.

'One thousand, six hundred and fifty metres,' he told me proudly. I was disappointed. That made the Thames only three hundred and thirty metres wide, which sounded like German propaganda. Yet the book was good – it couldn't be German . . . London Bridge was no bigger than a duckboard compared to the two-mile bridge being built at Margit Island. I had to give up trying to visualise the village on London Bridge. Maybe it was a fifth of a mile *wide* . . .

It was difficult to take sides. Edward wasn't a nasty kid, even if he was a weed, bragging about his title like a Chocolate Wolf with a new watch. Tom Canty, as pretender to the throne, did more good in three days than Henry VIII had managed to do in his whole life. Yet Tom was in far greater danger than the prince. I couldn't understand why I was so anxious that the prince should get his crown back.

By now, Hutter was shouting in concert with his pasty-faced friend, Béla. One moment they would be hailing the final victory, the next would find them weeping over the conquered Fatherland. It was impossible to tell whether they meant Germany or Hungary. They sang and swore bravely, while outside shells fell thirty or forty metres away. My book absorbed my fear like a sponge; I found it easy to imagine the stink of booze in the thieves' and beggars' den. Once, a bomb fell nearby. In the morning we discovered that it had actually landed eight houses away, but it sounded as if it were right on top of us. I jumped up, glanced at the roof, then returned to my book, my heart racing at the thought of the two heroes' plight.

Béla's stories frightened me like the voice of the dead, though he chuckled as he spoke.

'The shitty little Ukrainians hid their vodka better than their women. Don't worry, we found both!' Sometimes he told how the greasy Jews and Commies tried to lead everyone up the garden path by daubing yellow and red patches on all the neighbouring houses as well as their own. But they couldn't outwit the good Hungarian and German soldiers, who massacred the lot to be on the safe side. If they didn't get enough denunciations, they rounded up the whole village in the marketplace.

'They were very shy at first,' said Béla, hooting with laughter.

'But when we took out about thirty as a sample run, they started giving up their own fathers! On their knees, the gutless turds. We'll be back! Just you wait!' he cried, raising his bottle to Hutter. They had long ago given up using glasses.

The vilest stories were those about women. Béla drooled as he told them.

'There's me, shafting away, pistol at her head, and she won't stop blubbering! "What are you sobbing about, slut?" I said. "Trying to hide how much you love it! You never felt such a nice one up you!" But the stupid tart went on screaming like the Virgin at the foot of the cross.'

When a 'dirty Russian whore' had her baby with her, Béla would hold a pistol to its head, drop his trousers, and explain in sign language how she could get her child back. When they were bored, he and his friends used to throw toddlers in the air and use them for target practice.

It was Mrs Demeter, the railwayman's wife, who most often told him off.

'How can you talk like this in front of women and children!'

'I hope you'll be virtuous when the Russians come, missus,' laughed the drunken Béla, and went on with his stories. Mother dragged me away.

Contrary to my expectations, my hunger didn't increase with the passing days. If anything, it became dulled. The pain and dizziness of the first week became a vague light-headedness. Sometimes hunger stabbed at my stomach, ten to twenty times in quick or slow succession. Sometimes it just held a knife to my belly for minutes on end without actually stabbing. I tried to work out whether it hurt more during the Russian bombardments, since all three of us had promised ourselves that the Russians would arrive before we died of starvation. The firing signalled their approach: did it therefore inflame my appetite by promising a feast in the near future? Or did the expectation of food, accompanied by my underlying fear of the shelling, actually appease my hunger? Then again, perhaps the silent periods were worse because I had less to distract me . . .

In the end I was unable to discover a consistent system. Dávid suffered more than I did because he refused to philosophise about it, stating humourlessly that the only cure for hunger was food. This wasn't true, of course. I was always hungrier after I had eaten.

In the evenings, or whenever most people went to bed, my

508

neighbour Erzsébet would touch my bed with her hand and put a finger to her lips. A few seconds later I would find three or four lumps of sugar under my blanket, or a couple of cold, boiled potatoes. Once there was even a hard-boiled egg. I passed two-thirds of the gift to Mother, who always returned some of it to me. Nevertheless, we ate our one soup of the day in the evenings, as we agreed that going to sleep hungry was the worst.

It was quiet. Hutter lifted his friend off the floor and put him on his bed. I slept. I woke to the sound of bombs: at least three of them exploded above my head at once. In the light of a single lamp I saw the ceiling sink and begin to smoke. It was dust. The ceiling dipped again, but then bounced back like rubber.

'A rolling barrage,' I thought. The Russians were advancing behind a screen of falling shells. The continuous explosions became the only measure of time, but slowly, after several hundred deafening bangs, the shells seemed to move away from us, first ten, then twenty, then a hundred paces. Beside me, Erzsébet was sitting up in bed, praying. There was dust in my mouth. I spat it out. My face was as rough as a man's, and I wondered whether my hair had turned grey with fright.

Béla was standing unsteadily in the middle of the cellar, gesticulating wildly with a pistol in his hand.

'They're about to charge!' he shouted. 'Hold your fire!' Hutter's wife pleaded with him to give her the pistol. Péter Demeter and the railwayman surrounded him too. 'Only to Hutter! Never to the enemy!' he yelled, pointing the gun at Péter Demeter, who slowly and calmly put up his hands. Mrs Hutter started shaking her sleeping husband while the screaming of the *Katiushas* and the explosions of their rockets tore the air to shreds. Hutter struggled to his feet. It was obvious that he hadn't the slightest idea where he was. Béla lowered his pistol and turned towards his friend, to whom Mrs Hutter was explaining something. Hutter stumbled over to the table and poured a drink for Béla.

'They find pistol – they shoot us!' mumbled the Gestapo clerk, pulling himself together. He thought the Russians had already arrived. 'They shoot everyone.' Then, handing the drink to Béla, he took charge of the pistol.

The firing went on for at least another hour. Then, suddenly, it stopped. There was total silence for a quarter of an hour. Half an hour. Cautiously, I opened the cellar door. I couldn't even hear rifle fire in the distance. Béla had been wrong. Yet again, the Russians hadn't charged.

509

Things went from bad to worse. Miles Hendon had been disowned by his deceitful brother the night before, but what surprised me was that his beloved Edith had also betrayed him. Edward narrowly avoided a whipping. In the end he escaped, but poor Miles Hendon didn't. Meanwhile, it looked as if Edward would be late for his own coronation. The procession was already passing through the great arch towards a huge stage. Above it was a white rose with a portrait of an ancient queen in the middle, and a red rose bearing a portrait of a king.

Vilmos Demeter walked past me. I asked him where Hutter and Béla had disappeared to, and whether they had hidden the pistol. He didn't know. Those who had food were sitting down to breakfast, but Mother didn't want to start on our three potatoes yet. Erzsébet pushed a hard-boiled egg into my hand under her mother's nose. Mother cut it into three. The cellar door was opened wide to let in some fresh air. Erzsébet's mother changed her sheets, while Mrs Demeter sprinkled the earth floor with water to get rid of the dust. Her husband had gone to the other end of the cellar to tell everyone there about their eldest son, who had passed his matriculation with a special mention and was going to be an engineer once he came home from the front. The families around him had already heard the story several times. Meanwhile, the bigger of the two Demeter boys was carving a shepherd's crook out of a stick. He had been doing it for days and now only a few ornamental patches of bark remained. There hadn't been such silence around us for weeks. All we could hear were the everyday noises of people eating and chatting.

It was an unusually mild day for January. I took a chair out in front of the cellar door. At last I could read comfortably, by daylight. A Russian plane flew over the house but didn't open fire. There was no doubt about it. The Russians had been pushed back at dawn . . .

I peeped out into the street. No soldiers; no civilians. Not a soul.

Apparently there is no way of undoing a coronation. If Edward arrived late the Wars of the Roses would begin all over again. The book was quite definite about this although it didn't explain why. Then, finally, he turned up, although the silly idiot couldn't remember where he'd put the Great Seal, so no one believed it was him and they all thought Tom had gone mad again.

An old peasant woman in a long pleated skirt ran into the courtyard. She didn't even close the gate behind her. She gesticulated

510

to me and gurgled wordlessly before dashing down to the cellar. I got up to see what was wrong with her. I had never seen an old woman run so fast.

'They're coming!' she gasped, panting so much that she almost choked. 'They're here! I need a chair! The Russians! At the Zámoris! They raped his wife! And Mrs Veres and Annika Veres! Mrs Pálinkás too!'

A crowd surrounded her.

'You were lucky not to get raped yourself,' laughed Mother.

'Laugh! Laugh if you like! I saw it with my own eyes!'

'All four?' asked Mother. The others burst out laughing too, but the old woman didn't give in.

'They dragged Mari Zámori out of the cellar before they'd even got through the door!'

'If they hadn't even got through the door they must have dragged her out with a rope,' teased Erzsébet. 'It wasn't very nice of Mrs Zámori to hang on to the rope.'

'You'd do better to hide yourself,' retorted the old woman. 'A beautiful young girl like you! There'll be twenty of them on top of you!' I could have sworn that the old bag was Béla's mother. 'They're here! I'm off to tell the rest of the neighbours! God protect you! Hide yourselves!'

Off she ran, without giving me time to ask her how she had managed to break through enemy lines without the help of a tank. Everyone knows that spies always disguise themselves as old women . . .

Everyone went crazy. They believed her. Several people started praying. I looked questioningly at Mother. She nodded, and I went back up to the courtyard. I peeped excitedly out into the street, not noticing that Vilmos Demeter was standing nearby, watching me.

'You're glad the Russians are here, are you, you little shit?' He spat, and smacked me in the face. I hadn't even answered. A second later he turned on his heel and went into the house to hide in his secret room. Mother came over, having seen what had happened from the cellar door.

'It's good you said nothing,' she said. She wanted me to go back down to the cellar, but I reminded her that we hadn't heard any shooting for hours. The street was as empty as on a Sunday lunchtime. I promised Mother that I would run downstairs at the slightest noise. She still refused to believe that the Russians were about to arrive, and headed back to the cellar. I opened the gate again.

A short distance away, on the far side of the road, walked a young soldier in Russian uniform. I stepped outside the gate and watched him. He looked at me, but turned his eyes away immediately. He drew level, then passed me. He was about seventeen years old. A half-smoked cigarette was lodged in the corner of his mouth. There was a sub-machine gun in his left hand, bigger and thicker than the German ones. His right arm swung free, and he wore a cap instead of a helmet.

'*Tovarish!*' I shouted, remembering the word for 'comrade'. My ears rang. The boy looked back, then turned round as he walked, smiled, and waved at me, glad to know that he was welcome. Then he went on, but after another three steps he spun round again. Stamping heavily with his right foot, he gestured abruptly at our gate, ordering me to make myself scarce.

I decided he was joking. Mother was looking over my shoulder. I didn't know how long she had been there. Dávid was standing in the middle of the courtyard, dazed. Suddenly he woke up and dashed over to the gate, looking curiously first at us, then at the street. Mother's face was smooth and bright, like someone who is having a beautiful dream.

One by one, Russian soldiers appeared at intervals of fifteen or twenty metres. After a while, they came in twos, then in small groups. Three soldiers broke off from one of these groups and headed towards our gate. They went into the courtyard, and I followed them. Mother and Dávid followed me.

'Gun? Soldier?' one of them asked, a big-eyed man with broad shoulders. Like the others, he wore a padded jacket rather than a military cape. I was only wearing a jacket myself, and even I didn't feel the cold. His rank was shown by stripes on his shoulder instead of the stars on the collar worn by Hungarian soldiers. I shook my head. Two of them went down into the cellar, while the big-eyed man stood beside me at the doorway with his sub-machine gun trained on the stairs. I must have looked at him as if he were from outer space, because he made a silly face at me and laughed. His two comrades were already coming up the stairs. One of them gave me a big pat on the shoulder as they left.

'Fifteen women in two minutes! That's quick work!' I remarked to Dávid. He laughed. Mother told us off for bad taste, but smiled. We laughed even more.

No one else had come up from the cellar since the first Russian had walked past the gate. I went back down. The lamps and candles were burning as usual. Everyone was sitting or lying on their beds, immobile. A few were whispering or talking in half-tones, but nobody uttered any normal sound. Vilmos Demeter wasn't in the cellar. Nor was his uncle Péter, who was probably with his treasures. He was well over fifty; no one was going to make him a prisoner of war unless they took him for a deserting general. The grey-haired railwayman was the only person who wasn't in his usual place: he was sitting on Dávid's bed near the entrance so as to act as an interpreter for the Russians. People seemed to be awaiting their fate like condemned criminals.

'Don't worry, Erzsébet,' I told my neighbour.

'I'm not all that scared, Józska. Come and sit beside me.' I sat with her for a minute or so, but there didn't seem to be much to defend her against, so I went outside. I couldn't allow events to develop without me.

A small group of soldiers were standing around in the courtyard. Mother was chatting to a man who had four five-pointed stars on his shoulder. An officer. I went over to them. They were talking in German or Yiddish, but as I couldn't understand a word of either, this didn't help me much.

'Józska,' said Mother, introducing me. 'This is Captain Nikolai. He's Jewish.' Mother went on talking and I heard her mention Elek's name. Nikolai looked thoughtful.

'Alexei Salamon?' he mused. Then he laughed, spreading his arms. He obviously couldn't know everyone in the Red Army.

I nagged at Mother to interpret. Nikolai just tousled my hair when I asked him whether he had met Zhukov. He had only seen pictures.

'I told Captain Nikolai who we were,' Mother said. 'He and his men are searching for weapons, soldiers and fascists.' But my insistence on constant translation ruined their conversation, and Nikolai left. 'He'll be back in a minute,' Mother told me.

'Soldiers and fascists . . . Didn't you tell him about Vilmos? He smacked me round the face for being happy five minutes before the Russians arrived!'

'Would you have informed on him?' asked Mother gently. 'For the sake of a smack?'

'I don't know!' I retorted angrily. 'Why not? He only saved me so as to save his precious radio! Why didn't you tell them about him?'

'Józska!' shouted Mother. 'You are not to tell Nikolai about Vilmos!' Then she went on more quietly: 'His mother gave us bacon and dripping when we hadn't any to eat with our potatoes.'

'Hutter's wife gave us poppy-seeds and flour for our Christmas cake,' I replied. 'Does that mean that we wouldn't tell anyone about Hutter and his friend Béla if they were here?' Mother didn't even answer. She just looked at me with an air of surprised curiosity, as if she wondered whether I was really as stupid as I seemed. I shrugged.

Nikolai returned, bringing a large rectangular loaf of bread which he gave to Mother. We thanked him. Mother spoke in German, which seemed absurd. Nikolai must have thought so too because he wagged his finger at me like a teacher.

'*Spasibo!*' he said. I guessed that it meant 'thank you'.

'*Spasibo, tovarish,*' I replied, showing off my Russian.

Nikolai only stayed for a short while, but he assured us that we were in a safe place as the area was very unlikely to change hands. After a bit of prodding from me, he explained that the Germans and Hungarians had withdrawn without firing a shot after the dawn barrage. They were now almost completely encircled. He promised to come back as soon as he could, especially if they were forced to retreat after all. I warned him about the tank traps in our street.

'*Spasibo,*' he laughed.

The crackle of small-arms fire began again two or three hundred metres away. Out of habit, we returned to the cellar and set about demolishing the bread. Everyone looked at us. Maybe they found the shape of the loaf peculiar. They had food, and we had never watched them eating, even when we had had nothing. They whispered amongst themselves. When I caught someone at it he smiled at me. We finished off the bread in one go.

Mátyás, the thick little amateur Arrow Cross, took me aside for an intimate chat.

'Aren't you frightened of the Russians?' he asked.

'Did they bite you?' I returned.

'Why aren't you frightened?' he insisted. He was thick as planks. I couldn't tell we were Jewish in case Nikolai had been mistaken about the military position, so I said nothing. 'Lick an elephant's arse and he won't sit on you,' he remarked, quoting a popular proverb.

'Then you'd better lick mine,' I replied. He shut up.

While I was in the cellar a new group of soldiers arrived. They were wearing capes and the stars on their collars looked like the Hungarian ones. They occupied the pub and set up a mortar and a small stove outside the door. Some cooked, some lazily fired the mortar. I could see from where they were aiming that there was something wrong with my calculations. The Germans and Hungarians were where I had supposed the Russians to be. So we couldn't pick up our two suitcases and stroll away from the front: the opposing lines were a zigzag. Captain Nikolai had been right to tell us to stay put.

I was also surprised to see one of the mortar crew shaking with the cold. Whenever there wasn't a shell in his hands he breathed on them to keep them warm. Rain had been falling for the last half hour, but there was no reason for a Hungarian to feel cold, let alone a Russian.

'Russky brrrr?' I asked in signs and grimaces.

I was answered in broken Hungarian: 'Not Russky – Rumanian.'

'Ah,' I said and slipped away as soon as I could do so without showing my contempt for Rumanians. People in the cellar panicked when they heard the news, but the soldiers soon moved off without hurting anyone and a Russian unit took their place. The inhabitants of the cellar weren't reassured.

Evening fell. Two women slept on the floor, under their beds. The rest of us laughed at them. The following day passed without incident. We were hungry, but Nikolai didn't come back. Two Russians came into the cellar in the evening, and with the railwayman acting as an interpreter they collected everyone's wristwatch. The collection couldn't have passed off more peacefully in a church. Later, three more Russians came in and there was a row when they didn't find much loot. One of them had wristwatches up to his elbow.

I was jolted awake by a gunshot in the middle of the night. To my left I saw a Russian soldier. He had fired at the ceiling. Another Russian was standing on the stairs to my right, a powerful torch in his hand. He started walking along the corridor between the two rows of beds. He lurched a bit. He was drunk. There were two or three other Russians in the cellar. One of them was yelling and swearing. The man with the big torch had a sub-machine gun in his other hand. He flashed the torch at Dávid's bed. Dávid pretended to be asleep. So did Mother, she had the blanket over her head. Erzsébet peeped from under her bedclothes with frightened eyes. My stomach tightened. I half sat up,

515

then stiffened as the beam fell on me. The soldier was completely plastered: he could hardly keep the light on me. With Mother and Erzsébet on each side of me, I was in the least danger of the three of us. Slowly, so as not to alarm the soldier, I sat up completely and let the blanket fall off my chest to show that I was a boy. I tried to look into his eyes, but his head was swaying and only the barrel of his gun met my gaze. Then his glassy eyes fell on me and a couple of seconds later he stumbled on.

'*Chsy! Chsy!*' shouted another. '*Davai chsy!*' *Davai* was new to me but I already knew that *chsy* meant 'watch'. From time to time the drunkard flashed his torch at a bed. Another Russian punched the railwayman in the face. The drunk fired a burst from his sub-machine gun, perhaps by mistake. I couldn't tell whether he had hit anyone. The barrel wasn't pointing in our direction.

If they had been the SS, I wouldn't have been so frightened. I would have been able to breathe. Perhaps not. But the air would not have turned bitter in my mouth.

A blonde girl, whom I knew only by sight, was standing between two Russians. One of them grabbed her by the shoulder. She fell. Horror piled on horror. At least two other women were begging the soldiers to let go of her, while she sobbed at the other end of the cellar. The interpreter stammered uselessly in Hungarian: 'Please . . . no . . . we are civilians . . . not enemies . . .'

I hadn't seen the two officers arrive. One was standing by Dávid's bed, wearing a flat, peaked cap. He had a pistol in one hand and a torch in the other. His companion passed in front of my bed. He too carried a pistol. He marched down to the far end of the cellar, shouting orders, but he wasn't in the least frantic. With his free hand, he disarmed one of the soldiers. Within a minute, four Russian soldiers were filing past my bed without their weapons. Two of them had their hands up. The officer shoved one of them in the back to hurry him along, and they left. The cellar was filled with the sound of sobbing and men's curses.

When I awoke, I felt as if I had dreamt the terror of the night. The air was clear, crisp, cold, dead.

Step by step, the front was moving away from us. We were now a good kilometre behind Russian lines. The German and Hungarian artillery concentrated on the front line, and only the occasional stray shell fell anywhere near us. All the same, almost everyone stayed in the cellar. Some feared a counter-attack, while others thought that

516

there was safety in numbers against pillaging Russians. Periodically, the neighbours dashed back to their homes to cook or to keep an eye on their belongings, but never for more than half an hour.

One day at noon, Erzsébet's mother returned to the cellar like a sleepwalker. She stopped in front of Erzsébet's bed. When she spoke, her voice was aghast and tearless.

'They've killed her.' It was almost a question. Her words were fluent, unbelievably clear, and seemed to come from somewhere deep and far away. 'He looked round the room and pointed at Erzébet's hand, at the ring on her finger. Erzsébet just drew back her hand, like this. The Russian shot her. He was a Cossack. He had a red cap on. Drunk. Erzsébet would have given it to him. She didn't hide her hand behind her back. She just drew it towards her. Like this.'

The mother's eyes were frozen. She couldn't see or move. A group surrounded her dumbly.

'Didn't he rape her?' asked a weak voice after a while. The mother shook her head. Perhaps she didn't even know where she was.

'He wanted the ring,' she said finally, amazed. 'She would have given it to him. What's a ring . . .? A Cossack.'

All thought, all feeling ebbed out of me. I had told Erzsébet not to be scared of the Russians. I staggered away. Dávid's eyes were alight with terror. He stared at me demanding an answer. Maybe I looked at him in the same way.

A Russian soldier brought us a letter from Nikolai, inviting us to move to his billet, where we would be more secure in the event of a counter-attack. We set off. The streets were surprisingly crowded. People looked at us in pity and incomprehension, not knowing that the Russian soldier was our bodyguard.

Ten young women were standing at a crossroads chatting and giggling. One of them lifted her skirt over her knees to tease their Russian guard. A plump girl shouted at Mother: 'Come with us! We'll be given meat as well! You don't have to have more than one if you don't want to!' Mother laughed and we walked on.

We went about a kilometre, away from the sounds of gunfire, towards Pestszentlörinc. Soon we found ourselves in a boiling-hot room. A good dozen Russian soldiers were cooking and eating. One was cleaning his sub-machine gun, another was polishing his boots. Nikolai turned up, and managed to guess which of us was Józska and which was Dávid. He told Mother that they would be very grateful if she cooked for them, as neither he nor the others had had a decent civilian meal for at least a month. When Mother asked him about numbers, he told her to cook for as many as possible. Enough meat, potatoes, flour, eggs, dripping and vegetables for fifty were brought into the room and dumped around the improvised stove and on the three-metre-long table. Mother began to cook. The stove was soon covered with pots and pans. She pushed a knife and a potato into my hand and told me to do some peeling. Two Russian soldiers were also conscripted as potato peelers, but two minutes later she told us all off for peeling too much potato off with the skin. She sounded so fierce that one of the Russians saluted her from his chair, while the other almost fell on the floor laughing.

After I had finished doing the potatoes I went into a corner to watch the Russians. They came and went, cutting bread for themselves and bringing in wood for the stove. I stared too long at a man who was eating.

'*Kushai!*' he shouted. He didn't like me watching him eat: it was bad manners. But I was hungry, and furious. Mother was cooking for them and they hadn't even offered her anything. I turned my head away, but the soldier shouted '*Kushai!*' again. I decided that he must have been a teacher in civilian life. No one else would go on about a mistake like that. Remembering Berger, I shrugged as cheekily as I could. Of course this didn't please the Russian, who headed towards me. I was about to scream for Nikolai, but the Russian suddenly turned towards the table and cut a huge slab of sausage and a hunk of bread. Then he came up to me and pushed them into my hands. This time he didn't shout. '*Kushai!*' he laughed. At last I had discovered what it meant. I went straight to the door.

'*Kushai!*' I bellowed at Dávid, who was loitering outside in the garden. The Russians roared with laughter. Mother told us to leave room for lunch, but we told her not to worry and went on stuffing ourselves.

I settled down beside the soldier who was cleaning his sub-machine gun. He showed me all the bits, then reassembled them without the magazine and put the weapon in my hand. My eyes filled with tears as I thought of Elek, who was holding the same kind of gun in his hands. The stocky Russian thought that I was crying for someone killed by a Russian bullet. He put his hand on my shoulder, saying '*voina, voina*' and shaking his head slowly to show that he shared my grief.

Another Russian laughed out loud when he went to the stove with his mess tin and Mother put his food on a plate and gave him a knife and fork. Soon Nikolai came back with a couple of other officers, and we all gathered around the table. Wine appeared, then an accordion. They sang and sang. One of the soldiers drank a little too much and the others had to hide him from the officers. They had stronger heads than their comrade, but their officers reprimanded them all the same.

We were given a small room. In the middle of the second night I woke up. Mother wasn't there. I waited. I hadn't the strength to get up and search the house. Dávid was asleep. The snow-covered garden was clearer than the sky. I looked and looked, hoping to see Mother and Nikolai sitting on a bench, talking. How many stories had I read where the girl falls in love with her liberator? But Mother wasn't a girl . . . and why should Nikolai stay in this evil, fascist country when he could live at home among decent people . . .?

I couldn't see Mother in the garden. Dávid was still asleep. I hated him for it, but I didn't wake him. A smell of putrefaction oozed from the dark corners of the room. Grown-ups are ashamed in front of children, I thought. They have to hide something that's no better than hunger. Love must be a childish toy that kids outgrow . . .

My skin stuck to my bones as if it had been glued on with tar. I got up and staggered along the corridor like my own ghost. I found Mother and Nikolai sitting over a bottle of wine at a table in the big room.

'What are you doing here?' Mother scolded.

'What are *you* doing here?' I exploded. She accompanied me back to our room and stayed there.

Two days later we went back to the pub for our belongings. The neighbours had all gone home by then, and only a few of the Demeters' relations were still around. Péter complained at great length about how impossible it was to hire a cart. In any case he didn't dare risk his treasures on the road with the Russians pillaging and looting everywhere. He had already lost his second-best watch to them. He now intended to leave his valuables in the care of his nephew Vilmos, who was still hiding in the pub. Péter himself would return to Pestszentimre to guard his house.

By the time we had returned to the Russians' billet, Nikolai and the others had been posted elsewhere. We hadn't counted on that. We were left standing in the street in the snow and the cold without a bite to eat. Some friends of Gyula lived nearby, but we found their house abandoned, the door wide open. There were no signs of looting, but there wasn't a scrap of food in the whole place. We lit the fire and went to sleep.

The following morning we set off again. This time we headed for Budapest, partly out of instinct, good or bad, and partly because there was no civilian transport within a hundred kilometres. We trudged through snow and slush. I must have looked fairly gloomy because Dávid had to remind me of our situation ten days before. That cheered me up completely.

We suddenly started worrying about our identity papers. What if a policeman stopped us? Then we realised that there weren't any policemen, and in any case, who'd want to stop a woman with two kids? The only papers we had were the false ones. The thought made us laugh.

The sky was low and grey, the earth white. Military lorries and cars drove past in both directions. Soldiers on foot too, hundreds of them, their faces dull, tired, expressionless voids, the faces of men who had carried their burdens a thousand kilometres and had a thousand more still to go. Most of them looked straight through us, though one or two seemed surprised to see civilians. We asked for bread when we saw anyone eating. Most of them gave us some.

The number of corpses by the sides of the road increased as we approached the city. We passed burnt-out tanks and disabled artillery pieces, and heard, more and more often, the rattle of nearby rifles and machine guns. The Russian soldiers began to move faster, and once they ordered us off the road.

We came to a ruined house. Huge black letters, both Russian and Hungarian, covered its only remaining wall.

'Death to the German occupiers!' said the Hungarian letters. The Russian words must have meant the same. We looked at the wall, then at each other. Our eyes filled with tears. We asked a passing Russian soldier to read out the Cyrillic letters.

'*Smert Nemetskir Occupanten,*' he said, not understanding why we were crying. I was afraid he might think that we were mourning for the Germans. He didn't.

We reached Budapest. There were heaps of rubble ten or twenty metres high and rows of blackened walls. Nothing was undamaged. In some places we saw scattered corpses; elsewhere, the ground was thick with the dead. The silence all around us was broken every couple of hundred metres by sudden bursts of machine-gun fire or the occasional rifle shot. When we reached the Danube end of the

József Avenue, Mother decided to stop. We went to find a family from Oszu called the Báránys. A few months previously we had tried to buy their documents in exchange for land, but they wouldn't take anything but hard cash.

They lived in an old block of workers' flats. Everyone there was still camping in the cellar. We listened to dozens of horror stories of the vile deeds that the Russians had committed during the two-day occupation. From our cellar they had taken two girls away 'to peel potatoes' and rounded up several of the men.

The Báránys had plenty of dried peas, but nothing else. They gave us some. Mortars and guns went off nearby. A couple of shells exploded metres away.

At one point someone dashed into the cellar shouting, 'A horse! Second corner on the left!' Dozens of men and women rushed out armed with knives and pans. Mrs Bárány, a wiry, energetic little woman, soon returned with half a kilo of meat. The next morning we heard that the local food depot was being looted. Mother tried to hold me back by saying that dried peas were enough for us, but I disagreed and ran off.

There was a pawnbroker's shop beside the food depot. People were swarming in and out, carrying clothes and boxes. Three Russian soldiers were trying to hold the looters back. One man was ordered to stop. He didn't, and the Russian hit him on the shoulder with the butt of his gun. The man dropped his load on the pavement. A small metal box burst open in front of me: rings and jewellery rolled out of it. A small diamond ring landed near my foot and, making sure that no one was watching me, I bent down to pick it up. Then I changed my mind. Unaccountably, I had suddenly remembered my teacher, Torma.

'You came here to steal food, not jewellery!' I told myself sternly, and went down into the depot.

It was huge, maybe twenty or thirty metres wide. In the gloom, I saw men and women pushing and trampling one another. Boxes stood in towering stacks or lay scattered on the floor. Near me stood a Russian soldier with his hand on a gun. He seemed indifferent to the chaos. I picked up a box filled with tins of pâté, but a man snatched it from me. The soldier noticed: he fired a shot into the ceiling but failed to come to my rescue. Nobody even glanced at him, and he didn't bother to shoot again. My next piece of booty was a small box containing tins of tomatoes. It wasn't until I had reached the street that

521

a man grabbed it from me. All I managed to snatch back from him were two quarter-kilo tins. I was ashamed to return to the cellar with so little loot, but Mother was very pleased to see me and the tomatoes were a bonus. I was glad I hadn't stolen the ring. Mother would have smacked me and called me a thief for the rest of my days.

Mrs Bárány was in tears. While I'd been out, the Russians had raided the cellar and taken her little brother away as a prisoner of war. He was seventeen. She was out of her mind.

'He's never been a soldier,' she sobbed. 'Is it his fault that he looks older than he is? I'm going to their headquarters!' She went, but it did no good. The Russians were systematically rounding up everyone of military age, because most soldiers had put on civilian clothes as soon as the Red Army had arrived.

We moved on. The streets were quiet. We found Grandmother and Luci at their old address, only half a kilometre from the ghetto. They had survived the months of mass-murder. They were over the moon, though not at the sight of us. A few hours earlier they had received news of my Uncle Józska. He was alive. In her usual ecstatic fashion, Luci announced that Józska had become a partisan leader. I gaped. Anyone who knew him from Luci's reports alone would have imagined my Uncle Józska to be a spineless and opportunistic piece of filth. In fact he was a gentle, quiet, kind man. Uncharacteristically, Dávid asked Luci whether Józska had become a partisan because the dirty fascists hadn't promoted him to first lieutenant and hadn't even given him a lousy silver medal for bravery against the Russians. Luci looked a little sour and told Dávid that the question was in very bad taste, but explained that her former enthusiasm for Uncle Józska's military activities had been no more than a ruse to protect her from the neighbours' suspicions. In the meantime, Grandmother put a feast in front of us: ham, salami and cakes. We were allowed to eat as much as we liked.

We listened. There was silence. Maybe the road to our old flat was clear by now. We went back down to the street. After five minutes of walking along Erzsébet Avenue we were stopped by the sound of firing nearby. There were still pockets of German and Hungarian resistance. Russian soldiers were standing by the walls, weapons at the ready. Occasionally they raked the streets with sub-machine-gun fire.

We were standing between Király Street and the Royal Hotel, former headquarters of the SS. A few metres away lay two Arrow

Cross corpses. I had lost count of the corpses I'd seen over the last few days, but one of these two frightened me. He had worn an 'Árpád' armband. He was huge. His pistol lay beside him. A few minutes before, looking for a brave death, he had tried a last, audacious break-out. Something about him wasn't quite dead, his face hadn't hardened and his hair still shone from the light snow. I looked for concrete proof that he had only just died. He was wearing an expensive white sweater – good camouflage in the snow. Well-cut trousers. A good pair of boots! That was the proof. His was the first well-shod corpse I had seen. People always took the boots first . . .

We turned back, looking for a quieter route than the ring road. A few of the boards that had closed off the ghetto lay broken by the roadside. A woman of forty or so was trying to break a piece off one of them as a souvenir. Corpses lay along the walls, covered by sacking and newspapers. A grey-haired, unshaven ghost with staring eyes passed us pulling a cart. There was only one suitcase on it. In Klauzál Square, dozens of people were coming and going, stepping over graves hastily dug in the earth of the square. There was a fresh grave every couple of metres. The brownish snow was piled up in hillocks, some taller than me. Heaps of corpses peered out of the shops, a bearded face, a man in a *shabbes* suit. Bodies stacked on top of one another. The living searched among them for friends and loved ones.

I passed a classmate from my grammar school, then another from my primary school. I saw a familiar-looking man approaching, but his face was a frozen skull and his eyes protruded from their sockets. On his back he carried a dead child. Passers-by went up to him to try to make him put the body down, but he walked on, slow, deaf and blind. It was Berger, who had once been my teacher.

A *bocher*, an apprentice rabbi, scuttled by with a bucket. An old woman passed us dragging a sack of wood. Two bearded Jews met and gazed at one another, wondering if they were really still alive. Set back from the pavement, I saw a child's corpse lying among broken bricks and fallen plaster at the foot of a wall. The head was covered by a sack. There were gym shoes on its feet. I pulled the sack away.

Mik Lang. There was a narrow slit and a spot of clotted blood on his forehead. He had been killed by a bullet. His eyes were open, staring suspiciously at death. Mother shouted for a doctor. It was too late for Mik Lang, but she thought I had lost consciousness. Together, she and Dávid lifted me to my feet.

523

'God is wicked,' I said.

'What did you say?' asked Dávid, his teeth chattering. I repeated it, but I could see that he couldn't hear my voice.

'God is mad,' I heard myself say a few seconds later.

I wasn't sure that I hadn't dreamed the last few minutes. Why didn't my head ache? Why did I feel no pain? Seeing the pallid robots trudging past the corpses that gazed at them from the shop windows, I realised calmly that I was in the land of the dead. I was dead myself.

Mother told Dávid that I had to lie down for an hour. We were in the middle of the ghetto, in Dob Street. Mother led us to a dark stinking staircase, the home of some distant relations called the Mendelssohns. There was rubbish everywhere. A rat ran across our feet. The corridors were packed with grown-ups and small children. A woman of about eighty opened the door, her face dried up and wrinkled. She said nothing. She put out her hands as if to the candles on a Friday evening, then raised them in blessing.

We were given tea without sugar. There was nothing else in the house. Mother and the old woman hardly talked. They mentioned a few names, answering each other's questions with a nod or a shake of the head. Mother was the first to find words.

'Israel has been thrown into mourning,' she said. The old woman was silent for a while, then began to tell us a story. She spoke with a Yiddish accent, but her Hungarian was good.

Three days before the arrival of the Russians, that is four days ago, the great *tzadic*, a famous Rabbi from the provinces, had been sitting in the cellar shelter. Despite the crush, everyone made room for his table and his books. At times he would look up and fix his burning eyes upon the disheartened or the dying, silently moving his lips and exhorting them to pray, as he had been doing for days.

Two Catholic priests arrived. They were frequent visitors. They began to preach, trying to convert people. The *tzadic* continued to pray silently. The two priests soon felt that all their promises of salvation and all their lies about the treatment of converts were no match for the rabbi's silence. So they tried to provoke him into speaking.

'You persist in your obstinacy,' they told their audience. 'You still listen to your old Rabbis and shut out Christ's message. That is why you are exterminated every five hundred years. It is your Rabbis who are to blame!'

524

'Are you sure of this?' asked the *tzadic*.

'Sure? The obstinacy of the Rabbis . . .'

'Not about the obstinacy of the Rabbis. We can agree on that. Are you sure about the five hundred years? Does it happen as rarely as that? Do you have any certificates to prove it? Where shall I sign?'

The two priests were dumbfounded. The Rabbi raised his voice: 'You are worse than body-snatchers. You snatch souls!' He turned to his congregation. 'Remember the Psalm: "I will sing praises unto my God while I have any being. Put not your trust in princes, nor in the son of man, in whom there is no help." And again: "Yea, the darkness hideth not from thee, but the night shineth as the day." Would you lose your faith now? Listen!'

Outside, shells and bombs were exploding. The old men, the women and children in the cellar didn't know what they were supposed to be listening to.

'Don't you hear? The wind blows from the north in the dead of the night, the wind of Evil that awakens Dávid's lyre. Its five strings are the five books of the *Torah*. Only our sacred language can express this truth: *Shahor*, darkness, contains *Shachar*, the dawn that rises from it. Do you hear the screaming of the rockets in the depth of the north wind, the night wind, the wind of Evil? It groans, it is dying, for Dávid's lyre has stirred from its sleep: "Awake my glory; awake the lyre and the harp: I will awaken the dawn".'

'*Shachar!*' echoed the congregation, and the Rabbi taught the condemned and the sick all through the night, while several among them died.

But I heard nothing, nor did I sense the stirring of any lyre. I closed my eyes and opened them. The darkness was heavy as iron and the light dead as stone. Outside, in the street, people were stepping helplessly over the dead, loaded down with luggage, wandering mournfully out of the ghetto as if unsure whether they themselves were alive or dead. There was no joy or relief for any man, woman or child. The Temple lay in ruins. Israel's children were broken bricks scattered on the dead ground.

A few days later, while the battle for Buda continued, famine and epidemics ravaged Pest. Putting our few belongings into a washtub that served as a makeshift sledge, we headed for Oszu. András the Pianist had survived. I hadn't been able to find out about Pista Bognár and his mother. Mr Altmann the shoe merchant had been shot into the Danube by the Arrow Crosses along with thousands of other Jews.

Grandmother and Luci decided to come with us. We helped them leave their ten sacks of food with their neighbours, whom they trusted because the neighbours had even more food than they did. We weren't allowed any of the ham, flour, sugar, coffee or salami. A few hours later, on the road, we encountered more and more people coming in the opposite direction who had been turned back by the Russians. A sanitary cordon had been established fifteen kilometres outside Budapest to isolate the outbreaks of typhoid and dysentery. Grandmother and Luci turned back. We went on through the snowstorm. The cold was hard and white. We dragged the washtub along behind us, but we didn't have a scrap of food. We reached the 'railway' Demeters' house, where we were allowed to stay the night. They didn't offer us any food, though. Not even a cup of tea. They had three pigs in their backyard, two of them fat enough for slaughter. We abused the Demeters' hospitality and helped ourselves to some of the pigs' bran.

We were turned back by the Russians five times. We tried crossing several snow-covered fields to get away from the main traffic, but there was a Russian soldier posted on the little cart-track and he turned us back yet again. Then I asked him for some bread. He didn't have any. He put his hand on my shoulder and stepped past me. Then he walked past Mother and Dávid and began to contemplate the clouds. We were through.

We waited two days for a train at Vecsés station, but managed to buy some bread and sausage in exchange for clothing. We travelled on a simple freight truck with no sides to it. The train took fourteen hours to cover the seventy kilometres to Szolnok, so that the passengers wouldn't fall off or freeze to death in the minus-fifteen temperatures. We went on from Szolnok to Püspökladány in a closed cattle-truck. One of our travelling companions was a freed labour man, all skin and bone, who had been dragged to a railway station a few weeks before to be deported, despite his Swedish 'certificate of protection'. Some of these certificates had proved worthless. The Swedes had issued a total of four hundred valid temporary passports and several thousand completely useless pieces of paper. Our companion had been queueing up for the deportation train when he and four hundred and ten other labour men had been rescued by a daring bluff on the part of Raoul Wallenberg. Nevertheless, many of those rescued were later deported anyway. Wallenberg had moved heaven and earth in his effort to be a plank across the abyss, but the Swedish government had refused point-blank to take in more than four hundred Hungarian Jews on passports and had issued several thousand spurious bits of paper.

'If they'd issued a few thousand more passports,' sighed the ex-labour man, 'a few thousand more Jews would be alive today. Three thousand Jews were saved by three thousand Spanish passports issued by an Italian, Giorgio Perlasca, who did not expect thanks and will never get a statue. They turned out to be forgeries, but they were perfect ones.' He laughed.

We asked him where he was bound. He shrugged.

'First thing I'm going to do is have a proper meal. Then I'll see if any of my family are still alive. After that: Palestine. Maybe the British will let in more Jews now that there are so few of us left. And with Rommel out of the way they might be a bit less frightened of their Arab masters.' He was a sour man.

From Püspökladány we travelled in a normal second-class carriage to Debrecen, where we heard that a group of four thousand labour men who had been driven from Bor in Serbia, had been murdered to the last man by their SS and Hungarian guards. I shook for days. I didn't pray. That was how I mourned my father.

At last we arrived in Oszu. Grandfather's house had been stripped bare by the people of the village, like all the other Jewish houses. Even the window frames were gone.

Three days after our arrival, a car pulled up outside our gate and Father got out. He was as thin as my finger, but it was him.

There had been only three thousand six hundred labour men in the group brought from Bor. Not all of them had been murdered either. Fifty-three had survived. Father had done so by escaping twice. The first time had been in Serbia, where a small group of them had slipped away. They were tracked down by the SS. Father had seen one of the SS men approaching the hut where he was hiding. Finding a rusty bayonet, he had concealed himself behind the door and stabbed the man as he entered the hut. Then, deciding that the pursuit was too hot, Father had rejoined the column. Later, in Hungary, he had escaped a second time. A pretty woman had hidden him for six weeks.

He laughed when I told him how thin he was. His weight had dropped from eighty to thirty-eight kilos in the camp, since when he had put on fourteen. He had a thousand stories to tell us. At Tservenka, more than five hundred of them had been shot in a single night. Dávid asked him whether that had been the most frightening

527

moment. He smiled. He had plenty of moments to choose from. I asked him what his bravest moment was.

'The most frightening,' he replied.

Two stories captured my imagination more than the rest. They were both bizarre. At one point several hundred men had been made to lie on the ground while the guards galloped over them on horseback. Father's one wish was to put his mess tin over the back of his neck, but he didn't do it because he knew that if he did, he would definitely be trampled. Another time, a half-drunk SS guard had lifted his sub-machine gun and had started shooting at them, lazily and absentmindedly, a cigarette hanging from his lips. Father realised that if he didn't do something fairly soon, he would be shot. He had a cigarette butt in his pocket, so he took it out and went up to the guard. Nonchalantly, he asked for a light in German. The SS man shook himself, and politely gave Father a light from his cigarette. Father then thanked him civilly, and the SS told him that it was a pleasure. He stopped shooting. He had been jolted back into normal life. I asked Father whether he was going to write all these stories down.

'Oh yes,' he laughed. 'But I'll get rich first.'

We talked non-stop for three days and nights.

'What will become of us, the Jews?' I asked him.

'We will continue,' he said.

'And the Hungarians? What will their punishment be?'

'Their punishment?' he laughed. 'Being forced to celebrate their defeat should be quite a punishment. But we've been a nation of well-trained slaves for a good five hundred years. We'll learn to love our Russian masters soon.'

'What will happen to the Germans? How will they be punished?'

'How should I know?' he shrugged. 'Their country will be divided for a thousand years.'

'Won't they be punished?' I asked, appalled.

'Certainly. People are always punished, after a fashion. Occasionally it's the guilty who receive the punishment. The division of their country won't be much fun for them, but it's only a precaution. All I can promise you is that they will not repent. I know them. "History is written by the winning side. We knew nothing," they will say, and later: "There was nothing to know." Everyone talks about "collective responsibility" these days, but it would be too German to punish an entire nation.'

528

'Is that true?'

'Possibly. After all, even I wouldn't smack Hitler round the face for something he *hadn't* done. So collective responsibility is probably a myth. Collective *irresponsibility*, on the other hand, certainly does exist. So what will happen? What should happen?'

Father stopped talking and bowed his head. A deep shadow fell across his face. He sat silently for minutes on end. I couldn't know what horror filled his mind. I didn't want to disturb him. I had to let him forget my question. But then, slowly, he lifted his head.

'In the last resort, I still try to believe that Mankind is moral. If that is true, then over the last few years the Germans have created something more lasting than the Thousand Year Reich they so badly wanted. Because in two or three hundred years' time what will people remember when they think of England? Shakespeare, Parliament, the Empire, Elizabeth and Richard the Third, Jack the Ripper, the fairest judicial system in the world . . . Keats, Shelley – they have so many poets . . . Churchill standing alone to face the beast that dominated Europe. The brave nation in its finest hour and Europe's darkest, saving the soul of Europe. The sixth of June, 1944, with a bit of help from the Americans . . . And if they think of Italy? Rome, Leonardo, Mussolini and his blood-soaked Commedia del'Arte . . . The French? Napoleon and the Revolution, Versailles and Danton, Molière, Racine . . . The shame of the Second World War, their self-betrayal, their Renaissance to come. Russia? Peter the Great, Kutuzov, Dostoevsky, Communism: a great and obscure movement. The October Revolution, Lenin, Trotsky, the Counter Revolution and Stalin. The Hermitage in Leningrad, Zhukov and Stalingrad. The heroic people who saved Europe from destruction. Give them fifty or a hundred years and they'll catch up with their armies, turn into Europeans. Until then I'd rather keep my distance, but Europe owes its existence to the Russians and they can expect some reward.'

'And Germany?' I demanded.

'That's what I'm talking about,' Father replied gloomily. 'When people think of Germany in four hundred years, they'll think of Auschwitz, the SS, Buchenwald, *Blitzkrieg*. A thousand burning towns, a million burning libraries. Cannibals in Stukas. The eternal thirst for revenge. Hitler. Dachau.' He paused. 'And what of Goethe, Beethoven, Heine, Marx, Einstein, Thomas Mann?' Father thought for a moment before answering his own question. 'They will be remembered, like the Jews, as the German victims of Auschwitz.'

Father couldn't stay. He had to rush. He wanted to get rich quick. Reaching into his trouser pocket, he took out a handful of coins. He dropped half of them into my hand, half into Dávid's.

'Give them to your mother. She'd belittle anything that came from me.' I was shocked. Coins were worth nothing: they had all but gone out of circulation. Father looked at my face and laughed. 'Gold Napoleons,' he explained, and drove off.

Gazing after him, I noticed a dust cloud that wasn't made by his car. A few minutes later, Russian soldiers appeared on the road. They were driving horses. It would have been impossible to count the number of horses. The procession filed past our gate for over an hour. Peasants stood and watched from their gates with pinched faces and stony eyes. Perhaps they were looking out for their own beasts. I tried not to feel bitter. If the Russians stripped the whole country bare, they would not make up one tenth of the damage our soldiers had caused in Russia. Defeat has its price.

One of the neighbours brought back three of our chairs of his own accord. He had just borrowed them for safe-keeping, he said. Others denounced each other. The Sarkánys had taken the big sideboard, said the Kovácses. The Kovácses had taken the table, replied the Sarkánys. We went into everyone's house uninvited. We were looking for our furniture. Very few people took offence, none of the honest ones anyway. They understood.

I turned off the High Street several times to go and visit the *shul*, along the badly cobbled road that I had taken so reluctantly when Grandfather had condemned me to *heder*. Now I was twelve and a half but, however often I entered the narrow street where I had once jumped from stone to uneven stone, I turned back.

Eventually I forced myself. I walked into the dim hallway where the *heder* had taken place. It stank. Inside were the huge double doors leading to the *shul*. I remembered how they had closed behind me when we left the *shul* during the '*Kaddish* for the dead'. When I opened these great oak doors, I found that the main hall of the *shul* had almost caved in. Soaking wet plaster hung from the walls. Floorboards had been ripped up and the ground was covered with rotting straw and manure. The stink made me retch. The Germans had used the ground floor as a stable. They themselves had slept upstairs on the balcony, where Ágnes had once sat with the women.

Mother went down to the Village Hall and demanded that they

530

lock up the building until it could be restored, instead of leaving it open to the shame of the whole village. They locked it up and gave us the key. We were the only Jews left. Dávid and I took a couple of pitchforks and began clearing the manure out of the *shul*.

Elek really had gone over to the Russians at Voronezh in January 1943. He met his death as a soldier of the Red Army. On German soil. Fifteen members of his labour company remained alive, four of whom had fought for the Czech Legion. Béni Virgula was one of the few mass-murderers actually hanged after the war. Imre Torma, my primary-school teacher, whose heart would not have allowed him to fire on his own countrymen, died *pro patria*. So did Ferenc Jáger. Mother set about helping his family as soon as we heard the news. The Danielliks were spared martyrdom. They were still alive, as was Reverend Eliás. Gyula, too, survived.

Dávid and I worked hard to shift the manure, even on Sabbaths. Mother hired a cart to remove it from the courtyard.

My Uncle Samuel died of starvation in Gunzkirchen, near Mauthausen. My cousins, Ágnes and Jutka, were murdered, as were Kica, and Dávid's Jutka. Dóra and her baby, and her sister Kata perished too. So did Iron-Nose. Out of all the *heder* kids and all the seventy-three children at Mr Dévai's school, I was the only one to survive. Not one returned from Auschwitz. Laci Fried, Gyurka Sternberg, Ignác Schwartz . . . They murdered our teacher, Mr Dévai, as well. Of the eight hundred Jews in the village, thirty-five remained alive. When about twenty of them had returned, a joke went around the village.

'Ten went away, and twenty came back,' they said.

In the *shul*, two broken prayer lecterns lay beside an enormous iron stove. All the others must have been burnt: not one still stood by the wall where the men had once bowed and swayed. Our temple was dead and decaying, it didn't even have the dignity of a gravestone. It was a lion's carcass left to rot by vultures.

No gravestone . . .? The two tablets, inscribed with the ten commandments, still stood unscathed above the tumbledown arch. A shadow in the shape of a bird clung immobile to a broken windowpane. Then a ray of sunshine filtered through above, wrapping the crumbling walls in gold.

I looked at the stone tablets of the law in the empty temple. The dead are dumb, I thought. They cannot call God to account. I hesitated, wondering whether to yield to the anxiety, the fear, the hope that I still cherished for those I loved. Was it cowardice now? Could I accept the sparing of my life as a bribe, and believe in God?

Through the cracks in the walls, through the damp smell of putrefaction, mould and stale manure, I heard a sound. At first it was no more than a rumour, like smoke in the night, but slowly it grew into an impenetrable murmur, led by the quiet voice of my teacher Dévai, singing . . . The voices of dead men, from deep within the walls . . .

> '*Let my right hand forget her cunning,*
> *Let my tongue be stilled for ever*
> *If I forget thee, O Jerusalem.*'

Notes

p. 5 'I had carved up Countries myself . . . '
The Treaty of Trianon (following World War I), 4 June 1920, reduced the territory of historical Hungary from 282,870 km² to 92,963 km², that is, by more than two-thirds. Instead of there being about five million Rumanians, Slovaks, Serbs, etc, living within Hungary, there were now approximately 3 million Hungarians living in the neighbouring countries.

p. 20 '*Laï lüni*'
Yiddish corruption of the Hebrew *lo aleinu*, meaning 'not on us!', a spell to avert evil. There is no Satan in Judaism. (That would be the beginning of polytheism. Maimonides explains that even in The Book of Job the Devil is only a symbol.)

p. 21 '*Numerus clausus*'
Statute No. XXV./1920. Restriction on the number of Jews at universities and in the professions. The effects of this law were greatly reduced under the premiership of István Bethlen (1921–1931). He was among the few who spoke out against the anti-Jewish laws: 'Can you not see that if we resort to such means, our country's economic and financial order will collapse?' ' . . . We will not be Germany's friends but her serfs.'

p. 50 ' . . . they persecute us . . . with laws . . . '
Statute No. XV./1938 took effect on 29 May 1938: 'First Jewish laws.' Statute No. IV./1939: 'Second set of Jewish laws', took effect on 5 May 1939. The title of the latter was: 'The Restriction of the Expansion of Jews in Economics and Public Life.' These anti-Jewish laws were commonly called 'Jewish laws'. Both sets of laws were approved by an overwhelming majority in both the Upper and the Lower Houses of the Hungarian Parliament; the legislation covered everything from the entitlement to land-ownership, to the number of Jewish lawyers, judges, teachers, doctors, traders, craftsmen, etc., that were to be tolerated. All the Christian Churches voted in favour. In the Upper House the Primate of the Catholic Church, Cardinal Justinian Serédi, while asking for the exemption of Jews converted before the fall of the Hungarian Commune (31 July 1919), argued as follows:

'*I want to say first of all that in the cause of legitimate self-defence of the Nation, the proportional repression of Jewry in public, economic and other fields is judged necessary by everyone who, like me, has viewed with concern the fact that ever since their emancipation, a section of the country's Jewry (helped by non-Jewish liberals and with the tacit approval of the rest, and in the face of constant Catholic protests) has in the press and in literature (under the pretext of art), in poetry, in the theatre, cinema, music and painting, challenged or discredited everything that is sacred to Christianity: Religion, Church, Marriage, Family, Fatherland, etc. In agriculture, industry, commerce, finance, briefly, in the whole of our economic life, furthermore in our private and public life, the Jews have been trying to destroy Christian morality . . . *'

Later in this speech the Primate also asked the Upper House *'to include under the Jewish laws converted and unconverted agnostic Jews.'*
(Taken from the daily paper: *Magyar Nemzet* 16/4/39.)
The following is taken from a speech made in the Upper House by Bishop László Ravasz, leader of the second most important church in Hungary, the Calvinist Church (in Hungary Calvinists have bishops):
'If the position of a group could be judged harmful to the balance and health of my nation, there is no principle of justice on earth that could make me tolerate it through respect or duty . . . I cannot condemn the Jewish laws on principle . . . Generally speaking, the Jewish soul, in spite of all its qualities, its dazzling, superb intelligence, remains uprooted, earthless, decadent. This once holy people has turned away from the spirit of holiness . . . '
(Taken from the daily paper: *Magyarorszag* 18/4/39.)
Neither prelate ever had to face trial.
p. 103 'Let the Song of *Purim* rise . . . '
Festival in commemoration of Esther and Mordecai who saved Jewry from extermination in Persia, in the middle of the 5th century BC.
p. 105 '*Chanukah*'
'Dedication'. Festival of rededicating the Temple when Judah the Maccabean temporarily liberated Jerusalem from Syrian-Greek rule in the 2nd century BC.
p. 196 'Mátyás . . . invited the Jews into Hungary.'
Not strictly true. They came. Mátyás founded a Jewish Prefecture, with a Jew at its head, and while elsewhere in Europe Jews had to wear identifying patches and hats, in Hungary their officials were even allowed to carry weapons. But when Mátyás took Vienna he sought to gain favour with the Austrians by accusing certain Jews of forging money; he then gave their fortunes to the towns from which he drove them.
p. 230 'Elishah has been walking among us . . . '
Tradition holds him to be the herald of the Messiah.
p. 349 'Cardinal Serédi was fighting to give converts the right to wear a white cross beside the yellow star.'
The Primate's Circular Letter to the Bench of Bishops, dated 17/5/44, gives an account of his requests to the Prime Minister of Hungary:
'Exemption from wearing the yellow star should be given to all Catholic priests, monks and nuns and to certain categories of Christians of Jewish origin. Other Christians of Jewish origin should be given the opportunity to wear a cross on their clothes alongside the yellow star.'
OL Kum Be (National Archives, Budapest), Kum Be Dept.

11/2/27/(41/A).

p. 358/a '*Those who carry out to the letter all decrees . . . '*
Magyar Zsidok Lapja (Hungarian Jewish Journal), 27/4/44.
p. 358/b '*The Central Council cannot allow . . . '*
Magyar Zsidok Lapja, 6/4/44.
p. 389 '. . . chosen Jews left Hungary by the Gold Train'
1,684 passengers left Budapest on 30 June 1944, first for Bergen-Belsen, where, fenced off from the death-camp, they lived in 'privileged' conditions, and then in August 1944 318 people were allowed to reach Switzerland. After the war an Israeli journalist of Hungarian origin, M. Grünwald, wrote a series of articles in an Israeli newspaper about one of the organisers of this rescue operation: R. Kasztner, accusing him of corruption and collaboration with the Nazis. In 1957

Kasztner brought a libel action against the journalist but lost the case, leaving himself wide open to public or private prosecution. As he was walking out of the court, a young Polish man, whose parents' places on the train had been taken up by richer people (with the result that they had subsequently died), shot Kasztner dead.

pp. 393–94 'Over the two thousand years that our Church has endured, the Successors to the Apostles . . . '

The date on the Primate's Pastoral Letter (which he signed in the name of the Catholic Bishops) is 29 June 1944. A copy of it, attached to a letter written by the Primate, Justinian Serédi, dated 8 July 1944, to Lutheran Bishop S. Raffay, can be traced [Ev. OL. Banyaker. Ev. Ppki. Hiv. (Lutheran National Archives. Banyaker. Lutheran Episcopal Office.) 1944–774]. This reference is taken from '*Vádirat a Nácizmus Ellen*' ('Indictment Against Nazism'), Vol. III, p. 112. According to this collection of documents, Jenö Lévai (in 'Jewish Fate') quoted the text of the Pastoral Letter from the above source.

p. 394 ' . . . "message" from the Primate . . . '

OL (National Archives, Budapest), Film-depot E.PR. L. 3230
Box 103 Title 78f.

p. 403 ' . . . The prescribed term of religious instruction . . . '

Magyar Kurir (semi-official Catholic paper), 24/7/44.

p. 417 ' . . . signed by . . . Raoul Wallenberg.'

Raoul Wallenberg: His Romantic Life, Heroic Struggles, and the Secret of His Mysterious Disappearance, Jenö Lévai (Magyar Teka, 1948).

'*On the 18th August, 1944, Wallenberg issued his directives . . . '* These were summed up on 3 September as follows:

'The procedure to follow for the issue of passports: Because of the changed circumstances, from today onwards the following directives are in force: These applications may be responded to positively:

A. Family relations of Swedish citizens, possessing proof in the form of private correspondence or other means.

B. Business connections are accepted where:

(i) they have existed over a long period of time

(ii) they have existed until recent years

(iii) the applicant was prominent in the afore-mentioned business

(iv) deals with Sweden represented an important part of the business's turnover.

Satisfactory evidence as to the existence of these business connections must be produced. If only one of the above requirements cannot be met, the applicant can still be admitted but he can only bring his immediate relatives.

C. Theatrical agents, patent agents, supervising committee members, artists and other people in cultural fields can only be accepted if they can prove that they have accomplished something outstanding for Sweden. Eminent people in the field of culture must be placed in a separate group (with a KL (Kultur Leiter) sign, and the letters KL must appear on their application forms).

p. 437 ' . . . the verdict guilty and the sentence death.' From Béla Vihar's *Sárga Konyv* ('Yellow Book'), published by Magyar Teka:

'An account given by one of the surviving doctors, which was partly based on Sergeant-Major Laszló Jakab's eye-witness description, tells how at Pusztavám, in Pannonia (Transdanubia), a Jewish Company, formed mainly of doctors and

chemists, originally numbering 168 men, was massacred at dawn on the 16th of October, 1944, by the SS. A few men managed to escape.'

The name of the Sergeant Major in question was actually Zoltán Jakab, whom the author himself met late on the morning of 16 October in the company of some of the few survivors of the massacre.

p. 527/a ' . . . issued several thousand spurious bits of paper.'

J. Lévai, *'The History of the Schutz Pass'*:

'With the [Hungarian] Foreign Office . . . Ambassador Danielsson negotiated on behalf of only 300–400 protégés . . . But a formula was to be found that would allow Sweden to protect Hungarian citizens without taking on excessive or impractical commitments.' Lévai goes on: *'Then at the Swedish Embassy, under the chairmanship of Wallenberg, H.W., V.F., and Dr. B.F. discussed such a formula. The new document had to look like individual passports but without giving their holders the right to travel . . . '*

The Germans were not fooled:

'The German Embassy gave a note to the Hungarian Government, made by S.S. Haupsturmführer Legationrat dr. Grell.' J. Lévai, *Zsido Sors* ('Jewish Fate'), Magyar Teka, 1948. The note read:

'The agreed measures are as follows:

1. Hungarian exit and German entry visas are being made possible for 400 Hungarian Jews.' (19 Oct. 1944, S.S. Haupsturmführer . . . dr. Grell.)

Four hundred was about the number of real Swedish passports issued. Three days later Wallenberg sent a report by messenger to the Swedish Foreign Office:

'Results: The [Hungarian] Foreign Secretary has let me know that 4,500 protected Jews can freely leave the country. The German Embassy has let me know that there is no obstacle to the transit [via Germany] of four to five hundred people. Concerning the other four thousand Jews, the German Embassy has no knowledge of any negotiations taking place with the Swedish Embassy in Berlin . . .

Budapest 22nd Oct. 1944 (Signed) *Raoul Wallenberg'*

J. Lévai, *Raoul Wallenberg*

In December 1944 and January 1945 thousands of Jews from houses under Swedish (and other) protection were taken to the 'unprotected' ghetto without ceremony and hundreds more were shot into the Danube. Most of the 'Swedish houses' were alongside the Danube, while the 'unprotected' ghetto was a good 2 km away . . . The author has read generous accounts which, if one believed them, would confirm that out of the 150–160,000 Jews in Budapest on 15 October 1944, at least 600,000 survived thanks to the rescue operations of Sweden, Switzerland, the Vatican, etc, just as after the Liberation of France it turned out that 120% of French people had joined the Resistance.

p. 527/b ' . . . three thousand Spanish passports . . . '

An unsung hero, Giorgio Perlasca was an Italian antifascist who had lived in Hungary for years. In December 1944, at the approach of the Red Army, all foreign Embassies were evacuated. Only Danielsson, the Swedish Ambassador, stayed behind, trying to create an official background to Wallenberg's daring personal interventions, which was denied to him by the Swedish State.

Perlasca – the perfect con-man – set up office in the abandoned premises of the Spanish Embassy, promoted himself to the post of Spanish *'chargé d'affaires'*, and issued 3,000 authentic Spanish passports, which the Germans and Arrow Crosses, great admirers of General Franco, enthusiastically accepted. This was the most daring and successful rescue operation. Few people remember his name.

536